SISTERS OF TOMORROW

publication of this book is funded by the

BEATRICE FOX AUERBACH FOUNDATION FUND

at the Hartford Foundation for Public Giving

SISTERS OF TOMORROW

THE FIRST WOMEN OF SCIENCE FICTION

Edited by LISA YASZEK and PATRICK B. SHARP

With a Conclusion by KATHLEEN ANN GOONAN

WESLEYAN UNIVERSITY PRESS Middletown, Connecticut

Wesleyan University Press
Middletown CT 06459
www.wesleyan.edu/wespress
© 2016 Wesleyan University Press
All rights reserved
Manufactured in the United States of America
Designed by Richard Hendel
Typeset in Chaparral, Gill Sans, and Typeface Six by Tseng Information Systems, Inc.

publication of this book is funded by the
BEATRICE FOX AUERBACH FOUNDATION FUND
at the Hartford Foundation for Public Giving

Published in part thanks to a special grant from the
Ivan College of Liberal Arts at the Georgia Institute of Technology.

Library of Congress Cataloging-in-Publication Data
Names: Yaszek, Lisa, 1969– editor. | Sharp, Patrick B., 1967– editor. | Goonan, Kathleen Ann.
Title: Sisters of tomorrow: the first women of science fiction / edited by Lisa Yaszek and Patrick B.
    Sharp; with a conclusion by Kathleen Ann Goonan.
Description: Middletown, Connecticut: Wesleyan University Press, 2016. | Includes bibliographical
    references and index.
Identifiers: LCCN 2015034455| ISBN 9780819576231 (cloth: alk. paper) | ISBN 9780819576248
    (pbk.: alk. paper) | ISBN 9780819576255 (ebook)
Subjects: LCSH: Science fiction, American—History and criticism. | Science fiction—Women
    authors—History and criticism. | Fantasy literature—Women authors—History and criticism. |
    Women and literature—United States. | Women journalists—United States.
Classification: LCC PS374.S35 S57 2016 | DDC 813/.08762099287—dc23
LC record available at http://lccn.loc.gov/2015034455

5 4 3 2

Lisa dedicates this book to her grandmothers, Betty Repko and Wanda Yaszek, for showing their children that women can succeed everywhere from the kitchen to the shop floor, and to her mother, Gloria Yaszek, for introducing her to science fiction and teaching her that girls can do everything boys can do — plus they get to wear both pants and skirts.

Patrick dedicates this book to his grandmother, Delpha Sharp, a riveter in the Los Angeles shipyards during World War II, and his mother, Savonia Sharp, for her unwavering support of his science fiction fandom from the beginning.

CONTENTS

....

List of Plates *xi*
Acknowledgments *xiii*

Introduction: New Work for New Women *xv*

1. AUTHORS *1*
Clare Winger Harris *8*
  "The Evolutionary Monstrosity" (1929) *9*
Leslie F. Stone *26*
  "Out of the Void" (1929) *27*
Lilith Lorraine *106*
  "Into the 28th Century" (1930) *108*
L. Taylor Hansen *142*
  "The Man from Space" (1930) *144*
C. L. Moore *164*
  "Shambleau" (1933) *166*
Dorothy Gertrude Quick *191*
  "Strange Orchids" (1937) *192*
Amelia Reynolds Long *212*
  "Reverse Phylogeny" (1937) *213*
Leslie Perri *223*
  "Space Episode" (1941) *224*
Dorothy Louise Les Tina *230*
  "When You Think That . . . Smile!" (1943) *231*

2. POETS *237*
Julia Boynton Green *242*
  "The Night Express" (1931) *243*
  "Evolution" (1931) *244*
  "Radio Revelations" (1932) *244*
Virginia Kidd *247*
  "Untitled" (1933) *248*

Leah Bodine Drake *249*
  "They Run Again" (1939) *250*
  "The Wood-Wife" (1942) *251*
  "Sea-Shell" (1943) *252*
Tigrina *253*
  "Defiance" (1945) *254*
  "Affinity" (1945) *255*
Lilith Lorraine *256*
  "Earthlight on the Moon" (1941) *257*
  "The Acolytes" (1946) *257*
  "Men Keep Strange Trysts" (1946) *258*

3. JOURNALISTS *259*
Ellen Reed, Fran Miles, Henrietta Brown,
Lynn Standish, and Laura Moore Wright *265*
  Ellen Reed, "Natural Ink" (1942) *267*
  Fran Miles, "Oil for Bombing" (1944) *267*
  Henrietta Brown, "Marine Engineering in the Insect World" (1945) *268*
  Lynn Standish, "The Battle of the Sexes" (1943) *269*
  Lynn Standish, "Scientific Oddities" (1945) *271*
  Laura Moore Wright, "Sunlight" (1946) *273*
L. Taylor Hansen *275*
  "Scientific Mysteries: The White Race — Does It Exist?" (1942) *278*
  "Scientific Mysteries: Footprints of the Dragon" (1944) *282*
  H. Malamud, I. Berkman, and H. Rogovin, "A Protest" (1943) *286*
  L. Taylor Hansen, "L. Taylor Hansen Defends Himself" (1943) *288*

4. EDITORS *290*
Mary Gnaedinger *301*
  "Editorial Note" (1939) *302*
  "The Editor's Page" (1940) *303*
  "The Editor's Page" (1943) *304*
Dorothy Stevens McIlwraith *306*
  "The Eyrie" (1940) *308*
  "The Eyrie" (1940) *308*
  "The Eyrie" (1941) *312*

Lilith Lorraine 314
   "Cracks—Wise and Otherwise" (1943) 315
   "Training for World Citizenship" (1946) 315
   "The Story of *Different*" (1950) 320

5. ARTISTS *331*
Olivette Bourgeois 336
Lucille Webster Holling 337
Margaret Johnson Brundage 338
Dorothy Louise Les Tina 341
Dolly Rackley Donnell 342

Conclusion: Challenging the Narrative,
Or, Women Take Back Science Fiction 343
   Kathleen Ann Goonan

Notes 363
Bibliography 371
Index 383

Color plates follow page 334

PLATES

5.1. Cover of the *Black Cat* by Olivette Bourgeois for the January 1917 issue

5.2. Cover of *Oriental Stories* by Lucille Webster Holling for the Autumn 1931 issue

5.3. Cover of *Weird Tales* by Margaret Brundage for the October 1934 issue

5.4. Cover of *Weird Tales* by Margaret Brundage for the April 1935 issue

5.5. Cover of *Weird Tales* by Margaret Brundage for the March 1937 issue

5.6. Interior art by Margaret Brundage for the April 1945 issue of *Fantastic Adventures*

5.7. Interior art by Dorothy Les Tina for the December 1942 issue of *Future Fantasy and Science Fiction* depicting a scene from "The Leapers," by Carol Grey (pseudonym of Robert A. W. Lowndes)

5.8. Interior art by Dorothy Les Tina for the December 1942 issue of *Future Fantasy and Science Fiction* depicting a scene from the John B. Michel story "Claggett's Folly"

5.9. Interior art by Dolly Donnell for the Summer 1944 issue of *Thrilling Wonder Stories*

ACKNOWLEDGMENTS

....

First and foremost, Lisa Yaszek wants to thank Doug and Case Davis for their love, support, and sharp editorial eyes—you guys are the best! As a close second, Lisa thanks her colleagues at Georgia Tech for every kind of support possible. She is particularly grateful to Nihad Farooq, Narin Hassan, Carol Senf, Jay Telotte, and Kathy Goonan for provocative conversations about science fiction (SF) across media and in relation to other generic forms; Adam Le Doux, Matt Guzdial, and everyone else at the Sci Fi Lab on 91.1 FM WREK radio for providing airtime to discuss this project; Shawn Sorenson, Paul Zaitsev, Keith Johnson, and Lorin Young for tracking down amazing stories and weird tales about the women featured in this anthology; Whitney Rusedale and Amelia Shackleford for heroic typesetting and database compilation efforts; and, as always, Katharine Calhoun, Shirley Dixon, and all the people of Georgia Tech's Interlibrary Loan Program for service above and beyond the call of duty. Lisa also thanks the Center for the Study of Women, Science, and Technology and the Ivan Allen College for funds to support both her own and her students' research. The women of early SF believed that educated men and women could work together to build better futures; you all are collective proof that this is happening today, in our own present.

Patrick wants to thank Sharon Sharp for her love and support and for her invaluable insights on art history and SF in visual culture. He certainly owes her those future trips to Ireland and Italy. Patrick also thanks his colleagues at California State University, Los Angeles (CSULA)—particularly the faculty of the Liberal Studies Department and the program in Women, Gender, and Sexuality Studies—for their support and encouragement of SF in the curriculum and on campus. Patrick appreciates the financial support of Dean Peter McAllister and the American Communities Program at CSULA during the various stages of this project. Patrick is thankful for the students, staff, and community members at EagleCon for their enthusiasm and support for this anthology. Patrick would like to acknowledge the CSULA librarian Romelia Salinas for her assistance with chasing down images used in this volume, as well as Romelia's colleagues Brian Miller at Ohio State University and Tim Edward Noakes at Stanford University. Patrick also thanks Sara Stilley in Special Collections at the library of the University of California, Riverside for her assistance in getting high-quality reproductions from the holdings of the Eaton Collection. Special thanks go to CSULA alumnus Gerrymi Bernardo for his work in preparing the images for publication. For their assistance with research and typesetting, Patrick would like to thank Michelle Blackwell, Marissa Elliott-Baptiste, Jeffery Anderson, and Joe Aragon.

Lisa and Patrick also want to recognize the support they have received from the greater SF community. Lisa is particularly grateful to Bob Weinberg of Argosy Communications, Vaughne Hansen of the Virginia Kidd Literary Agency, and Cristina Concepcion of Don Congdon Associates, Inc. for reprint permissions and to Ron Unz of Unz.org, Patrick Belk and Nathan Madison of the Pulp Magazines Project, Bud Webster of the Science Fiction and Fantasy Writers of America's estates project, and Johnny Pez of Johnnypez9.blogspot .com for generously sharing their time and expertise regarding early SF copyright. Both Lisa and Patrick thank Melissa Conway, Rob Latham, and Sherryl Vint at the University of California, Riverside and Andy Sawyer and David Seed at Liverpool University for ensuring that their research trips to these two institutions were both fun and productive. Lisa and Patrick also thank the Science Fiction Research Association for providing seed funds to begin this project, as well as conference and print venues in which to share ideas about women's work in SF, the SF archive, and the digital turn in SF studies with others.

Finally, Lisa and Patrick thank the entire editing and production staff associated with Wesleyan University Press. We are particularly grateful to Parker Smathers for guiding us through the writing and production process; Suzanna Tamminen for feedback on the book title and cover image; and Susan Abel and Mary Becker for their sharp (and impassioned!) editorial eyes. Lisa and Patrick are also grateful to Joanne Sprott of Afterwords Editorial Services for her indexing services. We hope that our readers enjoy this book as much as we've enjoyed working with you to make it happen.

INTRODUCTION

NEW WORK FOR NEW WOMEN

In a 1974 speech delivered to the Baltimore Science Fiction Society, Leslie Frances Silberberg—better known to science fiction (SF) fans by her pen name, Leslie F. Stone—cheerfully noted that "while I cannot claim myself as the pioneer SF woman, since Mary Wollstonecraft Shelley beat me to it in 1818 with *Frankenstein* . . . I do happen to be one of the first woman writers in the fantasy pulps" (Stone, "Day" 100). As an author in the "fresh and new" genre magazine community of the early twentieth century, Stone was able to accomplish a number of firsts, including the creation of the first woman astronaut, the first black hero, and the first alien civilization to win a war against human characters (100). These innovations did not go unnoticed. Fans debated the merits of Stone's action-packed but socially provocative stories in the letters pages of the early SF magazines, and at least one such fan— a young man named Isaac Asimov—was so inspired by her 1936 story "The Human Pets of Mars" that he "decided to try, for the very first time, [writing] science fiction" (Asimov, *Before* 773).

While Stone was one of the first women in "the fantasy pulps," she most certainly was not alone. More than 450 known women published SF in professional and amateur venues between 1926, when Hugo Gernsback created the first dedicated SF magazine, and 1945, when the end of World War II ushered in a new constellation of practitioners and periodicals. As such, they made up approximately 16 percent of the SF community in the first two decades of its formal existence.[1] Most of these women (like their male counterparts) were fiction writers. However, they took on work as SF artists, poets, journalists, and editors as well.[2] In doing so, they helped shape their chosen genre at a critical moment when its meaning and value were hotly debated throughout the nascent SF community. *Sisters of Tomorrow: The First Women of Science Fiction* is an introduction to their collective accomplishments.

So who were these women? Most were born and raised at the turn of the century, when progressive political ideals—including first-wave feminism— were opening new doors for women as social, economic, and even sexual subjects. In many ways they were exemplars of the "New Woman." As the U.S. public intellectual Randolph Bourne put it in a 1915 letter, such women "are all social workers, or magazine writers. . . . They have an amazing combination of wisdom and youthfulness, of humor and ability, and innocence and self-reliance, which absolutely belies everything you will read in the storybooks or any other description of womankind. They are of course all self-supporting and independent, and they enjoy the adventure of life; the full, reliant, audacious way in which they go about makes you wonder if the new woman isn't to be a very splendid sort of person" (qtd. in Stansell, 231). This was certainly true of the two dozen women featured in this anthology, who embraced their work as writers, artists, and editors. The author L. Taylor Hansen, the poet Leah Bodine Drake, and the editors Mary Gnaedinger and Dorothy McIlwraith spent decades in the SF community, while the author/poets-turned-editors Lilith Lorraine and Virginia Kidd dedicated their entire lives to their chosen genre. Clare Winger Harris and C. L. Moore received awards for writing excellence from their peers in SF and fantasy, while Drake and Lorraine earned numerous poetry prizes and the fan poet Tigrina (the pen name of journalist and folk singer Edith Eyde) was inducted into the Lesbian Hall of Fame for her pioneering work in gay news reporting.

The first women of SF were New Women in other ways as well. Most were middle class and white, with the notable exceptions of Lorraine and Hansen, who proudly claimed Indigenous American ancestry. Many achieved independence through education: more than half the women featured in this anthology attended art school or college, and Hansen and Long pursued graduate work as well. Still others, including Hansen, Harris, the author/illustrator Dorothy Les Tina, and the poet Julia Boynton Green, pursued "the adventure of life" through extensive travel across North America, Mexico, Europe, Greece, and Egypt. The adventure continued for some in second careers outside the SF community: Gnaedinger and Tigrina worked as journalists; Les Tina wrote domestic and children's fiction; Moore taught creative writing and produced television scripts; the writer Leslie F. Stone was a prize-winning gardener and ceramicist who also worked at the National Institutes for Health; and the author Amelia Reynolds Long served as curator for Harrisburg's William Penn Museum.

A number of these women were also social activists who connected their art to their politics. The artist Margaret Brundage participated in the Chicago African American arts movement, the author-turned-journalist L. Taylor Hansen encouraged *Amazing* editor Ray Palmer's interest in Indigenous civil rights activism, Tigrina modeled the first U.S. lesbian newsletter on the SF fanzines published by her friend Forrest J Ackerman, and Lorraine was the first—and, as far as we can tell, only—person to have an FBI file opened for the dissemination of seditious speculative poetry. Taken together, these achievements suggest that women working in the formative years of genre fiction imagined brave new worlds in their art precisely because they were forging such worlds in their own lives.

So where did these women work in the SF community? Our survey of the forty-three specialist, multi-genre, and amateur magazines that featured SF in the 1920s, 1930s, and 1940s indicates that while women published in almost every one of these magazines, their work appeared most prominently in three key venues. Authors who specialized in scientific extrapolation gravitated toward magazines founded by Hugo Gernsback, including *Amazing Stories*, *Amazing Stories Quarterly*, and *Wonder Stories*. In 1927, just one year after he founded *Amazing*, Gernsback regretfully noted that women rarely made good SF authors, because their science education was all too often "limited" by social convention ("Headnote to 'The Fate'" 245). Yet he was quick to publish those women who did write SF, and by 1931 his successor, T. O'Conor Sloane, could claim women such as Leslie F. Stone as "staff writers" without undue comment.[3] In many ways, women's rapid assimilation into the *Amazing* fold was inevitable. Gernsback featured women writers in the scientific magazines he published prior to the founding of *Amazing Stories* and continued this practice in his genre magazines. Moreover, he encouraged authors to draw on literary traditions that had long been popular with women writers, including utopian and Gothic fiction, and women easily adapted his conception of SF as a vehicle for scientific inspiration in order to explore how the genre might also serve as a vehicle for social change.[4] Gernsback's successors at *Amazing*, Sloane and Ray Palmer, expanded the mandate of their magazine to include the work of women poets such as the critically acclaimed Julia Boynton Green and science journalists such as the provocative L. Taylor Hansen, who used her monthly column to challenge scientific racism. Meanwhile, the managing editor of *Wonder Stories*, David Lasser, cultivated the progressive political visions of women writers, including Stone and Lilith Lorraine.[5]

Women were also significant contributors to the multi-genre magazine *Weird Tales*. In direct contrast to their counterparts at *Amazing*, the editors Edwin Baird, Farnsworth Wright, and Dorothy McIlwraith never directly commented upon this trend. Indeed, the relatively high proportion of women contributors might not have seemed significant to them because the first generation of pulp magazines that appeared in the 1890s, including *All-Story Weekly* and the *Black Cat*, were also multi-genre magazines targeting and featuring women writers.[6] Moreover, Wright and his fellow editors were even more committed than Gernsback to showcasing speculative fiction written in literary traditions forged by earlier generations of women writers, including Gothic romances and fantastic poetry as well as newer ones in which women were just beginning to make their mark, such as the laboratory monster and bizarre SF adventure tale. Indeed, Harris—an early woman writer of care-fully extrapolated SF usually associated with *Amazing Stories*—was actually a *Weird Tales* discovery (Ashley, *History* 28). Additionally, *Weird Tales* was home to Margaret Brundage, whose sexually and racially charged cover illustrations made her one of the most-talked-about artists in the early SF community, re-gardless of race or gender. It was also home to the editor Dorothy McIlwraith, who was tied with Mary Gnaedinger of *Famous Fantastic Mysteries* for the honor of being named the first female lead editor in SF and who successfully oversaw her magazine's transition from pulp magazine to midcentury slick.

Amateur and semi-pro publications offered many women a third way to engage their chosen genre. Lilith Lorraine was a true pioneer in this respect, appearing in the May 1930 debut issue of SF's first recognized fanzine, the *Comet*, and contributing regularly to the Hugo-nominated fantasy fanzine the *Acolyte*. Between 1943 and her death in 1967 Lorraine founded more than half a dozen of her own amateur press publications, including *Challenge*, the first magazine dedicated to SF poetry. While Lorraine moved from commercial SF to semi-pro publishing to better enact her own vision of SF, other women launched professional careers based on their involvement with fanzine cul-ture. Virginia Kidd, an active member of fandom, published her first poem in the *Fantasy Fan* in 1933, when she was just twelve years old. Kidd cofounded the Vanguard Amateur Press Association in 1945 and published many of her own fanzines, including *Heeling Error*, *Snarl*, and *Quarterly*, through that or-ganization before trying her hand at professional writing and establishing herself as a literary agent. In a fascinating variation on the same theme, Ti-grina wrote weird poetry for the *Acolyte*, served as an associate editor for the Detroit-based fanzine the *Mutant*, and edited *Hymn to Satan*, the first SF and fantasy music publication. Inspired by her positive experiences with genre fandom, in 1946 Tigrina launched *Vice Versa*, the first publication in the world devoted to lesbian issues, and embarked on what would become a decades-long career in gay journalism.

So what exactly attracted women to SF? The women featured in this an-thology addressed this subject in a wide range of interviews, guest lectures, and essays, offering four main reasons for their interest in this genre. First and perhaps foremost, women were drawn to SF because they had an af-finity for science. Clare Winger Harris connected her lifelong love of SF to the "love of science" that she developed at Smith College, a single-sex insti-tution that was the first of its kind to create a dedicated science building for its students (Harris, *Away* 11). The SF author and science journalist L. Tay-lor Hansen claimed that the impetus for her work was the desire "to capture something of the thrill" of scientific discovery while overcoming the limitations of traditional scientific perspectives: "Most laymen who live within the limited horizon of a daily job can never experience the personal thrill of a scientific discovery which is the near look of science; while by the same token many scientists . . . through lack of multidimensional concept, [have] lost contact with the advanced horizon which is, in essence, scientific far vision" (*Ancient Atlantic* 7). Hansen's stated desire to re-create the thrill of science for laypeople and encourage a "scientific far vision" was very much in line with Gernsback's influential definition of SF as a "charming romance intermingled with scientific fact and prophetic vision," and so it is perhaps no surprise that she published most of her early work in *Amazing Stories* (Gernsback, "New" 3). SF also offered women a way to engage science when there seemed to be no other option. As Batya Weinbaum's interviews with the author's family reveal, Leslie F. Stone turned to genre writing in large part because while she was interested in science, her family saw it as "a male pursuit" and so did not provide her with "any encouragement" to study it (35). In an era when increasing opportunities for women in education and the professions competed with patriarchal assumptions about the proper sphere of women's work and the masculinization of science, SF provided women with opportunities to engage science in both critical and creative ways.

Women also chose careers in SF because they loved the genre. Clare Winger Harris "grew up reading the stories of Jules Verne and H. G. Wells" (Harris, *Away* 11). Leslie F. Stone grew up loving the John Carter stories of Edgar Rice Burroughs and said that she wrote SF as "a creative outlet for my rather vivid imagination" and "for the sheer pleasure of it" ("Day" 101–102). C. L. Moore, too, said that she was "weaned on the *Mars* books" of Burroughs and loved the fun of reading SF, which "was a grand, glorious experience, a new way of looking at the world and sharing in exciting new adventures" (qtd. in Elliot 46). Moore recounted the moment she rediscovered SF: it was "at a local newsstand across the street from the bank where I was working at the time. On my way to lunch one day, I spied this copy of *Amazing*, which stood out like a sore thumb. . . . I just loved the stories, the fact that they took me out of myself and my narrow little world" (qtd. in Elliot 45–46). As a thirteen-year-old, the future SF poet and literary agent Virginia Kidd related a similar story in the readers' forum of *Wonder Stories*: "Many years ago, I saw a magazine . . . on the drug store mag-racks, and investigated its presence . . . one of stories was Part One . . . of Taine's *The Time Stream*. I've been reading [SF] ever since" ("From" 628). Whether they grew up reading the classics of Wells and Burroughs or the new pulp magazines, girls fell in love with SF just like their boy counterparts and were inspired to contribute to the ongoing development of this new genre on their own terms.

For some women, SF was an ideal way to contribute to the creation of new and better political sensibilities as well. The most direct advocate of SF as a form of political expression was Lilith Lorraine, who argued that genre fiction was "not an escape literature," but a powerful mode of storytelling that "holds out a challenge" for humanity through its propensity for "constructive dreaming" and "by cutting the imaginative patterns for better social conditions, more mature systems of government, more advanced biological research . . . and more daring encroachments upon the secret of life itself" ("Not" 13–14). Even "prophet of doom" SF had a progressive political function for Lorraine because it could be used to show readers "the picture of a world charred and atomized," thereby prompting them to "wonder what we can do to prevent it" (13–14). Although she was less direct in her discussion of it, Leslie F. Stone appreciated the political possibilities of her chosen genre, too. As she rather gleefully recalled, even when "women's Lib was just a gleam in feminine eyes," she was able to provoke controversy among readers with stories about adventurous women, skilled African Americans, and less-than-all-powerful white men ("Day" 101). For authors such as Lorraine and Stone, the future-forward orientation of SF provided an ideal way to explore widespread cultural hopes and fears regarding the politics of nations and the politics of everyday life.

Finally, women were attracted to SF because it offered the opportunity for meaningful paid labor in a relatively egalitarian environment. Margaret Brundage sought employment at *Weird Tales* because she was "trying to break away from fashion" illustration to better support her family during the Great Depression and the magazine paid her a handsome "$90 a cover" (Everts 28, 31). Authors generally received less monetary compensation than artists such as Brundage—Leslie F. Stone calculated that she received a "not-so-very-grand total of $1872" for the twenty stories she published over the course of her career—but appreciated that for the most part they were welcomed as equal partners in the creation of a new popular genre ("Day" 103). As Stone put it, "On his discovery of my gender, Hugo Gernsback accepted it quite amiably. In fact, I'm sure he liked the idea of a woman invading the field he had opened. Nor did T. O'Conor Sloane . . . have any qualms about women writers" (101). Amelia Reynolds Long had similarly fond memories of her time in the early SF magazine community, noting that "being a woman [did not hold] me back with any of the science fiction magazines" (qtd. in Williamson). Similarly, C. L. Moore recalled that "I've never felt the least bit downed because I was a woman" (qtd. in Elliott 47). For women such as Stone, Long, and Moore, the opportunity to be treated as equals in the workplace seems to have been even more important than the fact of a paycheck itself.

Sisters of Tomorrow is part of the ongoing project to recover the history of women's contributions to SF in all their forms. For the past four decades, feminist scholars have successfully challenged the notion that early SF was simply about "boys and their toys," pointing to the work of SF luminaries such as Leigh Brackett and C. L. Moore as well as more recently rediscovered authors such as Clare Winger Harris and Leslie F. Stone as evidence of women's long-standing interest in SF. In a related vein, feminist anthologies of SF — beginning with Pamela Sargent's groundbreaking *Women of Wonder* (1974) and extending through Justine Larbalestier's more recent *Daughters of Earth* (2006) — provide readers with direct access to stories written by these authors.

Sisters of Tomorrow weaves these traditions together and extends them in two ways. Previous scholars and anthologists have focused primarily on the fiction that women published with professional, SF specialist magazines of the type inaugurated by Hugo Gernsback with *Amazing Stories*. By way of contrast, this collection presents women's contributions to SF in the genre's formative years across specialist, multi-genre, and amateur press publications. Additionally, *Sisters of Tomorrow* features not just stories written by women in the early SF community, but also the poems, editorials, science columns, and artwork they published in professional and amateur magazines alike. By considering the ecology of SF across publishing venues and across the various features included in genre magazines, we demonstrate how women shaped historic understandings of science, society, and SF in different arenas of SF production.[7]

Apropos of our goal to explore the ecology of women's work in all kinds of SF, we devote each chapter to a different aspect of genre magazine production. Chapter 1, "Authors," examines the largest group of female contributors to the early-twentieth-century SF community: fiction writers. While Clare Winger Harris, Leslie F. Stone, Lilith Lorraine, and L. Taylor Hansen all wrote action-packed, dramatic tales designed to educate readers and even inspire scientific and social change, C. L. Moore and Dorothy Quick crafted spine-chilling tales that disrupt readers' most cherished beliefs about human dominion over the universe. In a related vein, Amelia Reynolds Long, Leslie Perri, and Dorothy Les Tina drew upon the social sciences to tell tales about the hopes and fears of modern technocultural people. Even as these authors produced fiction that embodied the different visions of SF offered by different magazine editors, many drew inspiration from women's traditions of utopian, Gothic, and domestic fiction to critically assess the patriarchal impulses of science and to imagine how new and more egalitarian technocultural arrangements might produce new spaces for female adventure and new men to accompany women on their adventures.

Chapter 2, "Poets," explores the types of verse that women wrote for genre magazines. Women who wrote such verse drew from well-established traditions of nineteenth-century fantastic poetry by women that make the private sphere a gateway to fantastic worlds populated by female heroes. This is particularly evident in the weird poems of Leah Bodine Drake and Tigrina, which revolve around the adventures of women who gladly exchange the restrictive world of human men for the more exhilarating company of demons. It also informs the light verse of Julia Boynton Green, who used domestic settings to introduce scientific ideas and feminine sensibility as a way of confirming scientific theory. Meanwhile, Cosmic poet Lilith Lorraine employed both light and weird verse on a grand, galaxy-spanning scale to celebrate the possibility of human expansion throughout space and to warn readers of the elemental forces that, if left unchecked, might destroy all of humanity. Taken together, these women created a body of speculative verse that connected the themes and techniques of their nineteenth-century predecessors to the issues of gendered perspective and gendered authority that are still central to feminist SF poetry.

In chapter 3, "Journalists," we examine the science journalism that women wrote for SF magazines. Most of the women who worked as science journalists in the SF community, including Henrietta Brown, Ellen Reed, Fran Miles, and Laura Moore Wright, wrote in the new journalistic style developed at E. W. Scripps's Science Service in the 1920s, using eye-catching headings and the drama of human discovery to interest readers in what might otherwise seem to be dry factual material. But Moore, Lynn Standish, and L. Taylor Hansen also strategically redefined science journalism to better suit the needs of a boisterous fan community confident of its intellectual abilities. Standish and Hansen were particularly adept at producing science columns that scrambled the hierarchical model of reporting made fashionable by Scripps, questioning the authority of the professional scientific community, celebrating the insights of laypeople, and inviting readers to challenge the relations of fact and fiction as they inform science writing as a whole.

Chapter 4, "Editors," connects the work of women as SF editors with the practices of their counterparts in commercial and noncommercial magazine production. Like the pioneering female editors of the wildly popular and profitable women's magazines that flourished throughout the late nineteenth and early twentieth centuries, Mary Gnaedinger of *Famous Fantastic Mysteries* and Dorothy McIlwraith of *Weird Tales* were seasoned professionals brought in from outside their respective magazines' communities to enact preestablished publishing agendas. To ensure the success of their publications, Gnaedinger and McIlwraith adopted the persona of the editor as facilitator, using written editorial comments to assure readers that the creation of genre fiction was a joint endeavor by the editor and her audience, while quietly shaping those audiences' ideas about good SF through story selection and layout design. By way of contrast, Lilith Lorraine, the editor and publisher of half a dozen semiprofessional SF magazines, including *Different*, followed the example of women editors associated with the modernist "little-magazine" movement. As such, she took on the role of the editor as impresario, using her publications to speak directly about the relations of aesthetics and politics. While they were a true minority in their own time, Gnaedinger, McIlwraith, and Lorraine paved the way for the scores of award-winning female editors who are active in speculative fiction today.

Our fifth chapter, "Artists," considers the critical role that visual art by women played in the economic and aesthetic success of early-twentieth-century genre magazines. Like much SF fiction and poetry, SF art tended toward either technophilic celebrations of science and technology or Gothic depictions of a terrifying universe that directly challenged the Enlightenment dream of human dominion over nature. While artists such as Dolly Donnell and Dorothy Les Tina worked primarily in the technophilic vein, others—most notably Margaret Brundage of *Weird Tales*—perfected its Gothic counterpart. Whichever mode they adopted, women working as visual artists for the genre magazines of this period used their training in commercial art to quite literally paint women into the story of SF. By making the figure of the modern, active young woman (complete with bobbed hair and fashionably sporty or seductive clothing) central to the fantastic landscapes of SF art, Donnell, Les Tina, and Brundage established a legacy that still resonates in the work of contemporary female SF artists.

In her concluding essay, the award-winning SF author Kathleen Ann Goonan considers some of the factors that have led to the erasure of women from SF history and the efforts of female scholars and artists alike to take back their chosen genre. After briefly reviewing the factors that encouraged American women to try their hand at SF in the early twentieth century, Goonan considers both how men continue to question women's ability to produce SF today and the reactions of contemporary female authors, editors, and artists who must "prove" their worthiness to join the SF club time and time again. For Goonan, the problem of women's invisibility in SF is linked to larger cultural attitudes about women in science and other highly visible social and political endeavors. But, as her concluding case study of recent sex- and gender-based controversies in the Science Fiction and Fantasy Writers of America and in the Hugo award voting process suggests, such attitudes might well hold the seeds of their own demise, as women (and sympathetic men) claim their rightful place in SF and are publicly awarded for doing so.

1 AUTHORS

In 1926 the Luxembourgian American inventor and publisher Hugo Gernsback released the inaugural issue of *Amazing Stories*, the first magazine dedicated exclusively to a new mode of storytelling: the "charming romance intermingled with scientific fact and prophetic vision" ("New" 3). In doing so, he set off a decades-long debate about the meaning and value of what would quickly become known as "science fiction" (SF). While editors made direct pronouncements on this subject, authors indirectly dramatized and refined such pronouncements through the creation of SF stories themselves. But even as the scores of women writers who joined the genre magazine community in its formative years enacted contemporary editorial visions of good SF, they invoked the representational strategies developed by earlier generations of popular women writers to critically assess the patriarchal impulses in modern science and imagine other, more egalitarian technocultural arrangements. In particular, they drew inspiration from women's work in Gothic, utopian, and domestic fiction to introduce into SF the new spaces and modes of interpersonal relations that, they insisted, would foster truly new and better futures for all. In doing so, they anticipated many of the themes and techniques that would be central to later traditions of postwar women's SF and contemporary feminist SF.

The women associated with Gernsback's publications were particularly adept at generating stories in line with his editorial vision. As his pronouncement in the first issue of *Amazing Stories* suggests, Gernsback believed that authors should infuse older genres of popular fiction writing—including the scientific romance, the utopia, the satire, the travel narrative, and even the Gothic—with "detailed explanations of current scientific knowledge and discoveries" as they might be applied in the future (Westfahl, *Mechanics* 39). This would enable authors to entertain a general reading audience, educate young people, and inspire scientists.[1] Indeed, Gernsback directly cited Clare Winger Harris's Gothic-tinged "The Evolutionary Monstrosity" as an exemplar of SF that could educate young people and inspire scientists, reprinting alongside the tale the newspaper article about bacteria-based evolution that provoked Harris to write her story. Leslie F. Stone's "Out of the Void" and Lilith Lorraine's "Into the 28th Century" provided audiences with two other takes on the classic "charming romance intermingled with scientific fact and prophetic vision." While Stone wrote the kind of action-packed interplanetary adventure that readers loved, Lorraine depicted a high-tech utopian future much like the one imagined by Gernsback in his own 1911 serial novel, *Ralph 124C 41+*. These tales offered readers plenty of action and, for those who were interested, a dash of romance. But even as their protagonists grappled with domestic and alien threats (including their feelings for one another), they did so in ways meant to inspire scientists and social activists alike.

Even stories published by women in *Amazing* after Gernsback's departure from that magazine continued to reference his vision for the genre. Gernsback's successor, the retired natural history professor T. O'Conor Sloane, remained firmly committed to printing stories "founded on, or embodying always some touch of natural science" (qtd. in Westfahl, *Mechanics* 164). But he was more interested in established science than prophetic vision and downplayed the value of SF as an inspiration to scientists and engineers. Accordingly, in "The Man from Space," L. Taylor Hansen carefully avoids all reference to manned space flight (which Sloane believed was impossible), using the classic dream vision to move her characters from their earthbound science classroom to the depths of outer space. At the same time, she preserves the Gernsbackian belief in SF as science education by using her protagonists' adventures among the stars to make astronomy come alive for readers in ways that are both prompted by and in excess of the scientific lecture that inspires the narrator's dream.

Women also contributed to the development of SF in the multi-genre horror and fantasy magazine *Weird Tales*. Although neither Farnsworth Wright (who edited the magazine from 1924 to 1940) nor his successor, Dorothy McIlwraith, were particularly interested in SF per se, they recognized their audience's enthusiasm for it and so promised to print "the cream of weird-scientific fiction that is written today," especially as authors used the cosmic horror story, the laboratory monster tale, and the bizarre SF adventure to tell "tales of the spaces between the worlds, surgical stories, and stories that scan the future with the eye of prophecy" (qtd. in Weinberg, *"Weird"* 120).[2] C. L. Moore's "Shambleau"—one of the most celebrated stories in SF history—blends elements of cosmic horror and the bizarre SF adventure to warn readers that the universe is large and complex and, as such, may not always be amenable to scientific scrutiny or technological control. In a related vein, Dorothy Quick's weird-scientific surgical story "Strange Orchids" demonstrates the potentially horrifying aspects of technoscientific intervention into the natural world. While Moore and Quick explore two very different aspects of the utopian engineering paradigm gone awry, both seek to unsettle readers with the lush descriptions of physical space and detailed depictions of characters' psychological reactions to untenable scientific truths that Wright attributed to "the cream of weird-scientific fiction."

Like their counterparts elsewhere in genre magazine fiction, women writing for *Astounding Stories* and the dozens of new magazines that sprung up in the 1940s embraced the editorial principles of their chosen literary homes. In the mid-1930s, F. Orlin Tremaine distinguished *Astounding* from its competitors with the introduction of the thought-variant story, whose "driving force was a speculative idea, rather than a gadget or a sequence of cliff-hangers" (James 49).[3] While other SF editors, including Gernsback and Sloane, emphasized the natural sciences and engineering in their publications, Tremaine encouraged authors to draw from the social sciences to develop complex characters and detailed alien cultures. For example, Amelia Reynolds Long's 1937 *Astounding* publication "Reverse Phylogeny" extrapolates from ideas in anthropology and archaeology to flesh out descriptions of ancient human cultures that turn out to be just as strange as those that other SF authors imagine on alien worlds. In a similar vein, Leslie Perri's "Space Episode" and Dorothy Les Tina's "When You Think That . . . Smile!"—both of which originally appeared in Robert A. W. Lowndes's *Future Fiction*—mobilize insights from psychology and sociology to dramatize characters' reactions to surprising new technocultural situations in outer space and the home, respectively. Taken together, Long, Perri, and Les Tina update some of the oldest tropes of speculative fiction—mesmerism, space flight, and telepathy—for modern audiences through the strategic use of this new story form and its associated writing techniques.

Women also contributed to the development of SF as a unique literary genre by drawing on the themes and techniques of popular women writers who came before them. In particular, many borrowed from their feminist predecessors in Gothic fiction to explore the inequities of patriarchal scientific practice. As Donna Heiland explains, "The stories of Gothic novels are always stories of transgression. The transgressive acts at the heart of Gothic fiction generally focus on corruption in, or resistance to, the patriarchal structures that [shape a] country's political life and its family life" (5). Much like Mary Shelley's Gothic SF tale *Frankenstein*, Harris's "The Evolutionary Monstrosity" and Quick's "Strange Orchids" demonstrate the danger of male scientists who tamper with natural "powers of reproduction" (Roberts 25). Meanwhile, C. L. Moore's "Shambleau" pays homage to the female Gothic as pioneered by Anne Radcliffe, who used her characters' encounters with the sublime as "an aesthetic that multiplies differences, and that therefore empowers rather than effaces women" (Heiland 5). As Moore's hypermasculine protagonist encounters a seemingly feminized Martian sublime, he—and, by extension, Moore's readers—are confronted with a set of differences that erode the patriarchal assumptions guiding some of early-twentieth-century America's most dearly held scientific and social beliefs.

Elsewhere, SF authors used the themes of feminist utopian writing to imagine better futures for all. Such authors were particularly indebted to works including Mary E. Bradley Lane's *Mizora: A Prophecy* (1881) and Charlotte Perkins Gilman's *Herland* (1915), in which women use advanced sciences and technologies to create "collective or mechanical alternatives" to traditional patterns of housework and childcare (Pfaelzer 50). This is evident in the human future of Lorraine's "Into the 28th Century" and the alien society of Stone's "Out of the Void," both of which show how new domestic technologies such as the production of chemically synthesized foods might free women to pursue "further education and . . . public responsibilities" (Donawerth, "Science Fiction" 142). Additionally, Stone depicts her male and female humans as equitably sharing the domestic chores associated with shipboard life. Although they are faint, traces of the feminist utopian sensibility also inform Les Tina's "When You Think That . . . Smile!" In this case, the scientific (or magical; Les Tina does not provide much detail) transformation of a masculine domestic ritual—pipe smoking—undermines masculine assumptions about marriage as an institution. In contrast to those utopian writers who made women's technoscientific discoveries central to their narratives, early SF authors such as Lorraine, Stone, and Les Tina usually displaced such discoveries into the deep past, focusing their prophetic vision instead on the potential benefits of such discoveries to both women as a specific group and humanity as a whole.

Whether they worked in Gothic or utopian variants of SF, women writing for the early genre magazine community insisted that the home could be just as exciting a space of technoscientific action as the laboratory or the alien frontier.[4] Indeed, many authors followed the example of their literary predecessors by insisting that the private and public spheres are always interconnected. Harris and Quick, for example, underscore the connection between bad science and bad marriages by locating the laboratories of their mad scientists in isolated homes. Conversely, Lorraine and Stone link utopian change to the public transformation of private rituals such as mating and marriage. Although their stories seem radically different on first reading, both Moore and Les Tina insist that the incorporation of alien people and new technologies in the traditional home necessarily upsets conventional ideas about natural gender relations. In a similar vein, Perri and Stone explore how the new domestic spaces created by space flight might yield newly egalitarian social and sexual relations. Taken together, such authors used the experiences of women as technocultural subjects to expand the scope of what makes for good SF.

Women also contributed to the ongoing development of their chosen genre with the introduction of new voices. As Jane Donawerth explains, many women writing SF in this period followed the example of their male counterparts, using male narrators to appeal to what was then presumed to be a primarily male audience. At the same time, they used a variety of techniques to "subvert masculine dominance" in SF storytelling (*Frankenstein's Daughters* xxvii).[5] Authors like Stone and Lorraine followed the tradition established by Shelley's *Frankenstein* of employing male narrators while introducing female points of view through letters, recordings, and other documents. While Stone's story uses a male narrator reading a female explorer's journal to convey her points about utopian social reform, Lorraine offers readers a more novel—and dizzying—experience by relating one woman's account of a future utopia founded by women through the letter that another woman publishes on behalf of her male nephew. SF authors also borrowed the technique pioneered by Charlotte Perkins Gilman of using male narrators to show how men might be converted to feminine and even feminist points of view as they encounter women from other times and places. This conversion story is central to Lorraine's "Into the 28th Century," prompting the male narrator to wonder how he might introduce utopian ideals in his own time, and to Les Tina's "When You Think That . . . Smile!" in which the male narrator comes to a new appreciation of his marriage and his wife's role within it.

Women employed other techniques to convey their perspectives on science and society as well. For instance, in "Reverse Phylogeny," Long seizes on the emergent SF cliché of the humorously "absent-minded" and "benignly scatty or dotty scientist" to gently mock male scientific pride, especially as it fueled early-twentieth-century fascination with pseudoscience (Langford, "Mad"). While Long makes feminist arguments about science without employing a single female character, other authors did indeed use female narrators to make these arguments. Such stories appeared with some frequency in *Weird Tales*, where authors drew upon the rich history of the female Gothic to expose the failings of patriarchy through "the central figure [of] a young woman who is simultaneously persecuted victim and courageous heroine" (Moers 91). Dorothy Quick's "Strange Orchids" embodies this tradition while updating it for twentieth-century audiences, using the female narrator's encounter with a mad scientist to critique the masculine appropriation of a feminized nature. These stories also appear, albeit less frequently, in SF specialist magazine tales such as Leslie Perri's "Space Episode," in which the female narrator realizes that true heroism entails breaking free of sex and gender stereotypes.

Finally, early women SF authors borrowed from a third tradition of nineteenth-century popular women's writing called domestic fiction to nuance science fictional representations of masculinity. As the literary critic Nina Baym explains, domestic tales such as Susan Warner's *The Wide, Wide World* (the 1851 novel that engendered the notion of the best seller) revolve around the adventures of an intelligent young woman who seeks agency in both the workplace and the home. Along the way, she earns the love of a man who is "solid, ethical, generous, frank, hardworking, energetic, an admirer and respecter of women who likes the heroine as much or more than he lusts for her" (Baym 41). Variations of this domestic hero appear frequently in early magazine SF. For example, both the gentleman soldier of Lorraine's "Into the 28th Century" and the flannel-suited businessman of Les Tina's "When You Think That . . . Smile!" are hardworking but somewhat directionless men who find new political and domestic purpose in their encounters with intelligent, strong-willed women. In a related vein, Stone's "Out of the Void," Quick's "Strange Orchids," and to a lesser extent Harris's "The Evolutionary Monstrosity" relate the tale of dynamic women who fall in love, respectively, with a socially compassionate engineer, a confident government agent, and a mild-mannered biology professor, all of whom recognize women as extraordinary people involved in extraordinary adventures. Indeed, even the scheming aliens and mad scientists of these stories evince traces of domestic heroism in that they value these authors' heroines as much for their bravery and intelligence as for their beauty. As such, these stories demonstrate how women shaped the political and literary agendas of SF as a distinct popular genre.

Even as women helped create modern science fiction in its formative years by combining old story forms with new ones and updating earlier modes of women's popular fiction for the twentieth century, they identified themes and developed techniques that would remain central to later SF as well. The postwar era saw an influx of new women writers, including Judith Merril, Alice Eleanor Jones, and Anne McCaffrey, whose interest in the impact of science and technology on women as homemakers and caretakers fostered the development of women's SF. Like the first generation of women writing magazine SF, midcentury authors working in this new subgenre insisted that the home could be an exciting space of technoscientific action and that men could be domestic heroes who respected women's intellectual authority. Additionally, postwar women writers capitalized on an emergent trend seen in the work of their predecessors Dorothy Quick and Leslie Perri by narrating their stories from the perspective of women as both scientific and domestic subjects.

Since the late 1960s, the revival of feminism and the advent of an overtly feminist SF have encouraged authors such as Joanna Russ, Marge Piercy, and Octavia E. Butler to look back to the Gothic and utopian fictions of early women SF authors and to explore, in their own work, both the masculinist impulses in modern technoscience and the new domestic (especially reproductive) technologies that might enable more equitable power relations among men and women. Meanwhile, authors such as James Tiptree, Jr. (the pen name of Alice Sheldon), Marge Piercy, and Rebecca Ore have continued the practice of using male narrators to explore why men do not recognize the impact of science and technology on sex and gender relations and how they might be converted to more expansive points of view. Finally, as the themes and techniques pioneered by women in the early SF community have become a standard part of the genre's repertoire, male authors have increasingly employed them as well. John Varley, Bruce Sterling, and Geoff Ryman have all written family dramas to assess the technocultural arrangements of their own era and imagine alternatives. Meanwhile, Trent Hergenrader, Albert E. Cowdry, and Kim Stanley Robinson use updated versions of the domestic hero to explore how men might reform both science and society from their perspective as fathers, husbands, and lovers. Taken together, such authors demonstrate how women's work as fiction writers in the early SF magazine community continues to structure our thinking—and our art—at the beginning of the new millennium.

CLARE WINGER HARRIS (1891–1968) was a pioneering SF author who published more than a dozen genre stories in the late 1920s and early 1930s. She was the first woman to publish stories under her own name in SF specialist magazines and is remembered for providing SF with some of its first strong female characters. Born Clare Winger in Freeport, Illinois, she grew up reading the work of Jules Verne and H. G. Wells. Winger attended Smith College in Massachusetts, a school known for educating women in the sciences.[6] After college Winger "made two trips to Europe and one to Egypt and Greece" (Harris, *Away* 11). She married the industrial engineer Frank C. Harris in Chicago in 1912. By 1920 Harris had three sons and lived in Fairfield, Iowa; on the back cover of her 1947 short story collection entitled *Away from the Here and Now*, she proudly proclaimed that all three of her sons had "inherited their mother's love of science" and had grown up to become scientists and engineers (Harris, *Away* 11).

Harris considered herself primarily a housewife and even listed her occupation as "none" with the census. However, she enjoyed a successful writing career throughout the 1920s. Her first novel, *Persephone of Eleusis: A Romance of Ancient Greece*, appeared in 1923 and her first SF story, "A Runaway World," appeared in the July 1926 issue of *Weird Tales*. Dramatizing an apocalyptic future in which Mars and Earth leave their orbits and humans must use an atomic heater to stay alive until their planet settles around a new sun, "A Runaway World" demonstrates Harris's ability to write action-packed, scientifically inspired tales. Given her optimism about the possibilities of science and technology, it was inevitable that Harris would publish most extensively in Hugo Gernsback's new SF specialist magazines. The first story she published with him, "The Fate of the *Poseidonia*," was written for a contest and appeared in the June 1927 issue of *Amazing Stories*.[7] In introducing this story, Gernsback made his often-quoted comment about women in the genre: "That the third prize winner should prove to be a woman was one of the surprises of the contest, for, as a rule, women do not make good scientifiction writers, because their education and general tendencies on scientific matters are usually limited" ("Headnote to 'The Fate of the *Poseidonia*'" 245). Harris went on to sell ten more stories to the *Amazing* franchise, and by 1929 Gernsback no longer expressed amazement at her writing but simply referred to her as "our well-known author, Mrs. Harris" ("Headnote to 'The Evolutionary Monstrosity'" 70).

Harris's careful attention to science and technology is evident in "The Evolutionary Monstrosity," which appeared in the Winter 1929 issue of *Amazing Stories Quarterly* and was accompanied by the newspaper article about bacterial evolution that inspired it. "The Evolutionary Monstrosity" is written in the tradition of Gothic science fiction and includes elements similar to those found in Mary Shelley's *Frankenstein* (1818) and H. G. Wells's *The Island of Dr. Moreau*

(1896)—among them, most notably, the character of the mad scientist who refuses to accept the shared standards of his community, preferring instead to pursue questionable lines of inquiry from the privacy of his isolated laboratory. Much like other women writing Gothic SF for genre magazines (such as Dorothy Quick, whose "Strange Orchids" is featured in this anthology), Harris uses her story to critically assess patriarchal scientific practices in a manner reminiscent of Shelley, whose novels can be "read as a warning about the dangers of female exclusion from science as well as about the powers of reproduction" (Roberts 25). However, Harris departs from Shelley in two key respects. First, she uses the character Dorothy Staley to show how even the most radical scientific practices might be beneficial if applied in moderation. Second, she draws on another popular nineteenth-century literary tradition, domestic fiction, to show how the home can become a space of scientific adventure and to imagine a new kind of compassionate hero who is the ideal partner for the modern woman.

Like other women featured in this volume, Harris achieved a number of firsts within her chosen genre. In addition to being the first woman to publish in the SF specialist magazines under her own name, Harris may also have been the first author of either sex to create a taxonomy of SF themes: in a letter published in the August 1931 issue of *Wonder Stories*, Harris lists sixteen such themes, including some that were particularly relevant to her own historical moment, such as "ray and vibration stories" and "gigantic man-eating plants" as well as those that continue to engage readers today, including "the creation of synthetic life" and "natural cataclysms; extraterrestrial or confined to the Earth" ("Possible" 426–27). In 1947, she republished all her stories in "one of the earliest collections" by an SF writer from the Gernsback years (Bleiler and Bleiler 172). That collection, *Away from the Here and Now*, earned Harris an award from the Los Angeles Manuscripters. Today, feminist scholars credit Harris as one of the first authors to recognize SF's potential for both scientific and social extrapolation, especially as it pertains to issues of sex and gender, and her stories appear in anthologies including Justine Larbalestier's *Daughters of Earth* and Mike Ashley's *The Dreaming Sex*.

....

"The Evolutionary Monstrosity"

Amazing Stories Quarterly, Winter 1929

I

I believe you three fellows are going to startle the world yet," Professor Lewis of the biology department of our college remarked when we three students, who had termed ourselves the triumvirate, gathered in the laboratory at the close of class. "Marston, what was that theory of evolution you hinted at just before the bell rang? It sounded interesting."

Ted Marston laughed in a slightly embarrassed manner, though modesty was not ordinarily an outstanding attribute of Ted's character. His environment, judging from the little information we were able to glean from time to time, had been one of poverty and squalor. He was working his way through college and had proved a credit to that institution.

"Oh, it's a little far-fetched, professor, and I'm afraid my two highbrow pals here will think I'm cuckoo," and he tapped his head significantly, "but the idea's been grinding away in my brain for several days now."

"Out with it, Ted," said Irwin Staley jocosely. "Remember this triumvirate holds no secrets from itself. All thoughts are shared."

Irwin was the son of a wealthy New York broker and had been raised with every luxury that the modern age was capable of producing. His was a brilliant mind, too, but it somehow lacked the initiative that necessity had instilled into the being of Theodore Marston.

"Well, if you insist," replied Ted more seriously. "It's something like this. I wonder if evolution isn't the result of a certain bacterial growth which slowly and continuously changes the cellular structure of living organisms, causing the formation of new tissue and organs and breaking down the old."

"Poppycock and fiddlesticks!" ejaculated Professor Lewis. "Environment must also play a part in evolutionary change, for evolution is adaptability to environment, and Darwin was right in his theory of the survival of the fittest."

I'll admit I was dumbfounded by Marston's assertion, but not so Irwin Staley.

"Ted," he cried with enthusiasm, "you've got the right dope. It sounds so reasonable. But can you prove it?"

"I sure will," he answered, "if only for the satisfaction of convincing those doubting Thomases," indicating the professor and myself, who looked our incredulity.

"The only way you can prove it," I said, "is to develop specimens more rapidly than environment could possibly change them."

"That is precisely what I intend to do," he said.

II

I, Frank Caldwell, could boast of no extremes either in environment or hereditary. My people were middle class, my father being a factory owner in a small town in Iowa. My collegiate rank was slightly above the average, though I showed a decided preference for biology, in which study my two friends excelled.

Following graduation I became Professor Lewis's assistant, after the position had been refused by Marston. It seems the enthusiasm that Ted Marston felt had been shared, as I feared, by Irwin Staley, who placed at his chum's disposal ample funds for the purpose of developing his theory of evolution. Thus the "triumvirate" dwindled temporarily to two, while I, troubled with no new, fanciful ideas, taught my classes with no inkling of what was to come.

One warm day in June at the close of the school year, I received a letter from Ted and Irwin, who were at the latter's specially equipped laboratory, endeavoring to carry out Ted's great scheme for proving to the world the primary causes of evolutionary changes in mankind.

The letter ran as follows:

> Dear Frank,
> A meeting of the triumvirate is called for the first possible moment you can get here. We want you in on this. We are in a position to convince you whether you will or no! You can be of real assistance to us in the carrying out of our plans. Don't delay.
> Ted and Irwin

I had vaguely planned a European trip for the summer, but abandoned the rather hazy idea upon receipt of my friends' letter. My curiosity was unquestionably aroused. Had the two succeeded in isolating the "evolution germ" and in putting their theory to a test? It seemed incredible and yet stranger things have happened.

Wonderingly, and not wholly without excitement, I presented myself at the Staley mansion, which stood secluded in the center of a twenty-acre estate. I was surprised to have the door opened, not by a servant, but by Mrs. Staley herself, and I could tell at once by her manner that something was the matter.

Irwin had always been proud of his mother, and justifiably so, for she was a woman of keen intellect and young in appearance for her years. She was obviously nervous when she bade me be seated for a moment, before going out to the laboratory on the rear of the estate. We exchanged a few pleasantries, but I felt that she wanted to approach me upon what was a vital subject to her, but that she lacked the courage to do so. I finally decided to "break the ice" myself.

"How are Irwin and Ted getting along with their experiments?" I asked. I knew the subject had to be broached, painful though it was.

She looked away with a quick, nervous movement that had something of fear in it, then she seemed to gain control of herself.

"Frank," she said earnestly, "can't you stop them? It is my opinion they are guilty of great desecration. One cannot so distort God's laws without evil results."

At once my old habit of defending my friends came to the front.

"But is it distortion?" I countered. "They are breaking no natural laws. They are merely speeding them up. Where would we be today, Mrs. Staley, had we failed to speed up and control the use of electricity? Left to its natural manifestations, it would not turn the wheels of our machinery nor send our voices to remote parts of the world."

"Well, I do not know," she said miserably, "but I cannot feel that it is right."

Suddenly she stiffened and gave vent to a muffled scream. "It is coming. I can feel it near!"

Before I had time to question her meaning, I felt rather than saw a malign presence in the room. I turned from the woman, who was now frightened into speechlessness, to gaze down into a pair of evil eyes a few inches above the floor.

"My God, what is it?" I cried, sharing her terror in spite of myself.

My fright seemed to cause her to find voice, and she replied, scarcely above a whisper. "It was once my beautiful tabby cat, Cutey."

"Cutey!" I gasped. "What a name for *that!*"

I have always been very fond of cats, and at one time was nicknamed "old maid" because of the fondness I showed for the species. But this unnamable horror! It stood upright on two clumsily padded feet. Furless, its flesh the color of a decaying corpse, it seemed to me a miniature ghoul. The lidless eyes stared up into mine with an implacable hatred. But it was what I presume had once been whiskers that held my half-reluctant, half-fascinated attention. They bristled separately as though imbued with individual volition.

Suddenly a shrill whining voice spoke and I forced my eyes whence it came. It issued from the tiny, malformed object on the rug—from the travesty of feline beauty as we know it.

"You are wanted in the laboratory. Come at once."

Yes, that hairless, furless object, no bigger than a mouse, that stood on two feet and gazed at me with deep malevolence, had issued a command, and I could do naught but obey!

I turned to Mrs. Staley, but she was sitting with her head buried in her arms, so I silently left her and followed "Cutey" from the room.

As I entered the reception hall I heard the approach of a light footfall. I must have jumped unknowingly for my nerves were a-jangle after the experience of the last few minutes, and a peal of merry laughter tore my eyes from Cutey.

A girl was standing at the foot of the stairs regarding me with a quizzical smile. My first impression of her was that she was beautifully and expensively clothed, and I am not a man who ordinarily observes clothes before people. In this particular instance, however, the clothes really possessed more personality than their wearer. The girl was pretty in an insipid, baby-doll way. I knew at once that she was Irwin's sister for she was a feminine counterpart to her brother, minus Irwin's rather attractive personality.

"Isn't Cutey a dear?" she asked with a giggle.

"I don't quite agree with you—er—Miss Staley?" I asked stepping toward her.

"Yes, I'm Irwin's kid sister and I suppose you're Frank Caldwell. Irwin's mentioned you so often. But I don't see why you don't like Cutey. She's quite intelligent, you know."

"Ye—es, I don't dispute that Miss Staley, but she seems to lack some necessary qualities to make her attractive," I said, and to myself I thought, "and so does a certain young lady!"

"Your mother seems genuinely distressed over this evolution business, Miss Staley, and well she may be. I think it has gone too far," I continued.

"Gone too far!" she echoed. "Why it's only just begun, and by the way, call me Dot and I'll call you Frank. It's easier."

"Why what else have Irwin and Ted done along this line?" I asked, ignoring her remark.

"It isn't Irwin," she corrected. "It's Ted," and at the mention of the latter's name she smiled simperingly, I suppose to give me the impression that there was an understanding between them.

"Well, he's welcome to her," I thought. Aloud I said, "It seems to me your mother's feelings should be considered in this matter and I know she disapproves."

"Oh, mother's so fussy," she replied as she tripped to the full-length mirror and surveyed herself critically but with very evident ultimate approval. "Ted is really doing something wonderful for humanity, you know. At least that's what he says, and I like to believe him."

Suddenly I looked at Cutey, my gaze drawn in that direction involuntarily. The round, blinkless eyes of the cat (if I can call it such) were regarding me with impelling magnetism, and all the long whiskers were pointed toward me. With a brief "good-bye" to Dorothy Staley, I opened the door and followed the feline horror into the open. As I shut the door behind me, I heard Mrs. Staley call her daughter to her.

III

"If I could but kill it!" I thought as I followed the thing along the flower-bordered path. "Is it a representation of the future? God forbid the development of such life upon this globe! It would seem that the evolutionary processes minus the modification of environmental influences point toward retrogression instead of progress. Man dare not tamper with God's plan of a general, slow uplift for all humanity."

At length the laboratory appeared ahead of me and I hurried toward it, with something of joy at the prospect of meeting my old chums once more. Forgotten for the moment was the diminutive horror that had once been a cat, as I eagerly grasped the hands of Ted and Irwin, who drew me into the building with many expressions of cordiality.

"Quite some workshop, eh?" queried Ted with an air of pardonable pride.

"Indeed it is," I replied fervently. "I wish the college had half the equipment you've got here."

Irwin's brow puckered into a little frown. "I have neglected dear old Alma Mater. They would appreciate some more paraphernalia there, wouldn't they, Frank?"

"Indeed they would," I echoed heartily. "The department's running down, and poor Professor Lewis is about at his rope's end."

It was now Marston whose brow clouded, but not with remorse.

"Lay off the sentimental Alma Mater stuff, Irwin," he said. "They've got enough equipment there to educate the mediocre college boy. Your money and energy can do more good here."

I was not a little shocked at Ted's depreciative words—he who had always been such a loyal alumnus of the university! It displeased me to find none of the former joviality and loyalty that had characterized him in college days.

It was on the tip of my tongue to voice a protest against the preferable equipage of a private laboratory over that of a public institution, but on Irwin's account I stayed the impulse.

"Well," I said finally, in well-controlled tones, "how are the evolution bugs 'evoluting'?"

Ted and Irwin exchanged hasty glances, and I looked at Ted, for it was evident he was the spokesman and mastermind.

"What did you think of Cutey, if I may answer your question with another?" Ted Marston asked with a half smile.

Immediately my indignation was aroused. I had presented one side of the argument to console Mrs. Staley, but it was the other side that I proposed to give to Marston.

"If you want my honest opinion," I said frigidly, "I think that what you are doing is the most hellish practice since the days of necromancy."

"And *that* from a member of the triumvirate, if you please!" said Ted smiling unpleasantly at Irwin.

Irwin Staley was obviously embarrassed and ill at ease. I had a feeling that he was "in deep" with Ted and couldn't get out, though why was a little hard to explain. The laboratory equipment was all his, and legally he could have kicked Ted out anytime he chose, but morally he lacked the courage to do so. Ted and Irwin were living examples of mind over matter.

"Yes," I said, "and I am here to fight you to the finish if need be! Professor Lewis was right. Without the modifying and mollifying influence of a changing environment, evolution is a tool in the hands of the devil."

"I thought you never believed in his Satanic majesty," said Marston sarcastically.

"Nor do I now," I replied heatedly. "I have always maintained that evil was not a positive force, merely negative good; a misdirection, so to speak, of the same forces that can result in good. Just so is evolution a force for good if used as the Creator intended, but woe befall humanity if its laws are tampered with. Electricity is an example of a force that can benefit us or kill us, according as we obey or disobey its laws."

"Very well, Parson Caldwell," said Ted sneeringly, "granted there is some force to your argument, what are you going to do about it?"

"Be reasonable, Ted," I pleaded. "If you—"

"*Reasonable!*" he mocked. "What does the world know about reason? Since the days of Plato, Aristotle, Socrates, and Anaxagoras have we advanced one iota in mentality? Answer me that! True, we have invented machines, have increased our luxuries, but have we any purer logic or do we come any nearer to knowing the Why of God than some of the philosophers of 500 BC? Let us hope, my friend, that a rapid evolution will increase the reason in most of us!"

"But look at that—that—cat!" I finally found voice to say. "Isn't that thing a warning to you, Ted?"

"That cat, so far removed from your present state of evolution, is a shock to you merely because it is unfamiliar," he said quietly. "Had you progressed parallel to it, you would look upon it as a delightful pet."

"Pet be hanged!" I blurted forth. "If that object could ever be a pet, I'm going home to get a rattlesnake for company!"

"A very good idea! It would prove an excellent partnership," with which cutting words he arose and disappeared into an adjoining room.

"This situation is awful," I said to Irwin after the door had closed behind Marston. "Do you share his views, may I ask?"

Irwin Staley cleared his throat and glanced nervously toward the ante-room, which closeted his companion.

"To tell the truth, Frank," he said huskily, "I think Ted is going too far. It was all immensely interesting for a while. I didn't even mind Cutey as you seem to, but when he began introducing evolutionary bacteria into his own system to change the tissues and organs through the many stages of bacterial infection, I confess I began to feel that he had carried the matter to an extreme. He has seemed different ever since he commenced it."

"Good heavens!" I exclaimed. "How long ago was that?"

"Only a couple of weeks," came the reassuring reply, "and in very moderate doses, but just this morning he intimated a desire to speed up the process, as he is becoming impatient."

"Irwin, if I were you I'd clear out and let him alone, even though it might mean considerable financial loss," I admonished. "He is dangerous."

"I can't, Frank, that's the trouble. He wants me in his experiment."

I looked at him in exasperation. "You can't? Has the man any power over your will?"

"I believe he must have," Irwin mumbled pitifully, "for it seems I have to do his bidding."

I turned away in disgust.

"Count me out," I said harshly. "I believe I'll take my trip to Europe after all."

I walked down the path and he followed me, a forlorn, unhappy man. His courage seemed to return as he left the vicinity of the laboratory.

"I rather wish I could get out of this whole business," he said sheepishly. "I'd love to go to Europe with you."

"Come on, old boy," I said delightedly, "can you be ready by Thursday? The boat actually sails Friday."

His eyes were wistful and he seemed almost persuaded when Ted Marston's voice called from the region of the laboratory, "Where on Earth are you, Irwin? Come here. I need you for an experiment."

Instantly all the joy faded from Staley's countenance.

"Sorry, Frank, but I'll have to give up that trip. Some other time maybe," he muttered vaguely.

I stared mutely after him till he vanished behind the shrubbery at the turn of the path.

IV

As luck would have it I learned upon my return that I had been granted a sabbatical year, and so instead of returning to my teaching that fall, it was not until a year from that autumn that I came back to the States and plunged immediately into college work. In the interim I had heard no word from Ted and Irwin. The following summer I planned to visit them, but the death of Professor Lewis shortly before the close of the school year necessitated my remaining and working at the college, for I had been appointed head of the department of biology to take Professor Lewis's place. I missed the kindly old man and hoped I would prove a worthy successor. Thus it was three years before I returned to the laboratory that stood upon the beautiful Staley estate.

I had read about the death of Mrs. Staley two years before, so I did not stop at the house as I had upon the previous occasion but started immediately in the direction of the laboratory. As I approached, a strange sensation took possession of me. I had an irresistible desire to flee, and yet it was not exactly fear that possessed me. Imagine my amazement when I realized that *contrary to my will* I had turned my back upon the laboratory and was walking away with the intention of returning home!

I had reached a turn in the path when I was startled by a hoarse, inhuman cry. I turned to see a decrepit figure hurrying toward me in obvious distress. There was a vague familiarity in the uncouth stranger and I stood puzzled on the verge of discovering the elusive identity.

"Who are you?" I demanded in fearsome apprehension.

Before he could reply, he turned inexplicably about and retraced his steps toward the laboratory, and I, discovering my movement now unhampered, followed him with quickening pace. To the very threshold I followed, but the door closed with a loud bang between us, and again I felt powerless to enter. Whatever the force that controlled me now as it had a few moments before, it had ceased to act while the degenerate was returning to the building. I was confident that the control was from a source within the laboratory and that, mighty though it was, it was limited in its power of concentration to one subject at a time.

Surely here was a state of affairs that needed investigation and yet I seemed powerless to act! I returned to college and pondered the situation. Should I return with an armed force or should I try it again alone?

Several days after this inexplicable occurrence I was the recipient of a letter from Dorothy Staley:

> Dear Mr. Caldwell:
> I heard recently that you are again in the States, and if it would not be too much trouble I should appreciate your coming here at once. Things have been going from bad to worse, and I am in serious trouble. May I count on your help?
> Dorothy Staley

I confess I was puzzled. The letter did not seem like the product of the pen of the addle-pated girl I had met three years before. Could three years, even of trouble, so tone down and change the frivolous maid whom I recalled with a feeling almost of disgust? Or was the author of the note someone who was trying to trick me by the use of the girl's name?

It was late afternoon as I approached the estate. The long line of poplars like sturdy sentinels seemed to guard the mansion from external danger, but what was symbolic of its protection against an encroaching menace within? As I mounted the veranda steps, the door opened—and Dorothy stood framed in the entryway. For a moment I discontinued my ascent of the steps and gazed speechlessly at her, for it seemed I had never seen this girl before—yet I knew it was Dorothy. What refining process had altered her nature and appearance so intrinsically? Trouble is the refiner's fire necessary for some natures, yet somehow this change in Dorothy was not so much one of degree as one of actual difference of quality.

"Mr. Caldwell," she said with a quiet, sad smile, "I sent for you, because I believed you could help me as no one else in the world can."

"I am flattered, I assure you," I murmured as I followed her into the large gloomy interior and passed the long mirror, where, three years ago, she had primped herself so vainly.

When we were seated in the luxurious living room, whose windows opened on a fountain outside, she began the explanation of her worry. Her beautiful face with its serious sincerity held my enraptured gaze as she talked.

"Things have advanced to a terrible state between Ted and Irwin, and even I . . ."—she paused and glanced about her apprehensively—"am fearful of what the future has in store for us all. Ted has—" Here she broke down completely and was unable to continue.

"Just what has Ted done?" I asked partly to relieve the embarrassing and distressing silence.

"I have not seen Ted in the last year," she replied, sitting up straight in her chair and making a renewed effort to control herself, "but I have heard of his progress through my brother, who is his helpless tool—and it is my understanding," she lowered her voice to a whisper, "that Ted has progressed (if one can call it progression) beyond any semblance to humanity as we know it!"

"Horrible!" I ejaculated, mentally recalling a certain example of feline evolution.

"I thought I loved him once," continued Dorothy, "but now I do not even respect him."

"No, I should think not," I replied dryly. "And it seems to me he should be made to relinquish his hold on Irwin. Maybe what he does to himself is his own business, but he should not be allowed to involve others."

"'Be allowed' is a strange term to be used in regard to Ted Marston," said the girl bitterly. "He is his own master. For some reason or other he will not allow me to see him but sends Irwin to me with his messages. A week ago Irwin came to the house looking so wretched and miserable. I pleaded with him to force Ted to go away, but all I could get from him was, 'I can't, Sis. I know it is unbelievable but I've got to do what he says. He really is wonderful. If you knew him as I do, you would think so too.'

"I was sitting in this very chair, Fra—er, Mr. Caldwell, a week ago," the sweet voice went on, "during this conversation with my brother Irwin. He looked so unhappy, even while he praised Ted, that I knew his tongue belied his real feelings in the matter. Suddenly he told me very earnestly that Ted still loved me, but that he knew that two beings so far apart in evolutionary development would not be suited to one another, so he intended inoculating me with the germs in order to advance me to his stage of development. Then we two, he told me through Irwin, would rule the world! I was so terrified I found myself unable to move, and as I sat there stunned, Irwin quietly advanced and without the slightest warning of what was to follow, plunged a hypodermic needle into my arm. I must have fainted, for the next I knew I was in bed and Cora, our maid, was moving about in my room. Strange to say I felt no ill effects; in fact, if there was any difference, I felt better, not physically so much as mentally. I seemed to understand things in a quiet, impersonal sort of way, and was, so to speak, above petty emotions and passions that had swayed me constantly prior to this experience. If this was evolution, I thought, it was very much to be desired and I wondered at Irwin's very apparent fear of Ted. Then that night Irwin came again, but this time he seemed different."

Two tears rolled down Dorothy's fair rounded cheeks, but she continued with obvious effort.

"He told me that Ted was asleep, and that upon such rare occasions as he slept, he, Irwin, seemed free to follow the dictates of his own will. Previously he had found himself locked in, but upon this occasion he had escaped through an open window and a torn screen. He warned me earnestly not to allow him to inflict me again with the germs of evolution.

"'This dose, which was very light for the initial treatment, would have very little effect on the body tissues,' he told me, 'but each subsequent injection would cause such obvious change that in time one would be, as Ted is, unrecognizable as a human being!'

"I begged him to tell me what Ted looked like, but he only shuddered and turned away and his last words were a repetition of his first, 'Don't let me administer to you any more germs of evolution.'

"That was a week ago and I have not seen him since—my own brother—yet I dare not seek him under these awful circumstances. I want to see that he is well, but I dread his approach for what it will mean to me. Can you help?"

Her last words expressed such utter anguish, I longed to put my arms about her and comfort her, but instead I merely said, "Dorothy, if I may be allowed to stay here until this danger that threatens you is put out of the way, I shall count it a very great privilege."

For answer she smiled a grateful acquiescence.

V

"You may have the southwest bedroom during your stay here," Dorothy informed me. "Its windows overlook the laboratory, though the latter is so completely surrounded by trees and bushes that only its approximate locality can be detected."

A few minutes later I stood at a window of the beautiful room assigned to me and looked out across a veritable Eden: winding gravel paths, a splashing fountain, tall trees, and clumps of bushes. And suddenly, with something like a shock, I knew that the large mass of vegetation at the far end of the estate hid from view the laboratory that housed my former friends.

"Former!" Was it true that I could no longer think of them as such?

"Such is the effect upon normal man of gross distortions of God's laws," I thought.

It was dusk by this time, and as I turned from my survey of the grounds below me to put on the light, I detected a movement in the shrubbery near the spot where the laboratory was hidden from view, and then much to my surprise, a figure emerged from the surrounding shadows. As it walked with a slouching posture and shuffling gait toward the house along the flower-bordered path, I recognized with a disheartening shock Irwin Staley—no longer the aristocratic-appearing youth I had left three years go, but a disheveled hobo with apparently one vague but persistent idea obsessing his mind.

I rushed to the door of my room, opened it and peered down the dimly lighted hallway. There was no one in sight, but I heard Dorothy moving about in the lower hall.

"Are you going to lock the house for the night?" I called to her from the top of the stairs.

"Yes," her sweet voice floated up to me. "I am on my way to the front door now."

Leaning over the broad banisters, I glimpsed her as she approached the door, but before she reached it, it was thrust open from the outside and Irwin staggered in. Her face white with terror, Dorothy turned beseeching eyes in my direction and I lost no time in descending the stairs. Irwin looked at me with apparently no recognition. If his had been a one-track mind in college days, it was now even a narrow-gauge one-track mind, for it seemed that no other idea entered his brain other than his mission in regard to his sister.

"Hey, Sis," he said, ignoring me as if I were nonexistent, and for ought I know, I may have been so to him, "Ted wants you to come out to the laboratory. He wants me to give you the evolutionary bacteria treatment in his presence. He claims he can advance you to his state in a remarkably short time."

As Dorothy shrank from Irwin, he continued. "It's no use opposing him, Dorothy. He is determined. And really you don't know what an honor it is to be chosen as mate and co-ruler with one who is in a position to rule the world. You and he would be so far in advance of the rest of the human kind that the establishment of your recognized authority would be immediate. Your progeny, the royal family would—why, Dorothy!"

Dorothy swayed unsteadily. I thought she was going to faint, but she rallied and turned to me. I stepped up to Irwin and seized his shoulder in a firm grip.

"Irwin Staley," I said harshly, "whether you know it or not, I am your old friend, Frank Caldwell, and though you and Ted are apparently not the same fellows I knew in college days, I am unchanged, and I propose to bring you two to your senses. Of all the crazy 'goings on' I ever heard of, this caps the climax!"

During my outburst, Irwin regarded me sullenly and with a suspicion of defiance, but the latter quality was not outstanding in his demeanor. To me it was apparent that he was a coward doing another's will.

Suddenly he put a hand in his pocket and quickly drew forth a small hypodermic syringe, at the same time roughly laying hold of Dorothy's arm. In another second I had caught him in the chin with my fist and sent him sprawling on the floor. He staggered to his feet whimpering and I grabbed him by his coat collar.

This scene must have been very distressing to Dorothy, but I could spare no one's feelings if I was to cope with the will of this monster of the future.

Turning to the girl, whom I knew now I loved dearly, I said, "Wait for me, dear. Irwin and I are going to see Ted and we'll be back again."

"Oh, Frank," she cried, her voice trembling, "I am afraid for you! Brave and fearless as you are, what can you do against the accumulated knowledge of centuries?"

"But it isn't that, sweetheart," I exclaimed joyfully. "Don't you see, it couldn't be! Environment *must* play a part in the future development of the race, and Ted has no greater environmental experience than we've had. His physical body may have changed but not exactly as ours will, for the mollifying influence of man's changing surroundings would tend to soften and temper any radical tendencies of development. We are all subject to the inexorable law of cause and effect, which will develop everything proportionately. Ted is an anachronism, and as such he has no place in his condition in our world, now or in the future."

"I believe you are right," she said smiling through her tears.

As I opened the door with one hand and clutched Irwin firmly with the other, a disquieting thought came to me, and I said to Dorothy, "If I succeed, as I hope I can, in returning Ted to his former state, so that he is really the Ted Marston of old, am I liable to lose you to him, Dorothy?"

She came close to me and laid a hand on my arm. "Don't worry on that score, Frank. I believe I'm changed myself, for I could never again love Ted." Coming close to my side and putting her lips to my ear, she whispered, "And do you know I don't believe I've been quite the same since I had that light injection of evolutionary germs. Could it—do you think—?"

"I *know* it," I laughed. "Probably the very first dose improved Ted too, but he did not know enough to quit when he passed beyond the range of present possible environmental influence. He became drunk with the lust for power which he mistakenly thinks is his."

"I'd hardly say 'mistakenly,'" said Irwin, who had been a silent listener. "His power is a fearful thing."

Stooping, I kissed Dorothy as she stood close by my side, and in another moment Irwin and I were outside in the darkness.

VI

I kept a firm grip on Staley's arm, for I did not want him to escape and apprise Ted of my coming. No words passed between us as we proceeded in the direction of the secluded laboratory.

What an ideal place it had been, from their point of view, in which to develop their nefarious scheme. Completely hidden by tall trees and dense shrubbery, it seemed as completely isolated as a desert isle.

Knowing that Ted expected Irwin's return with his sister, I permitted Irwin to enter first and watched him through the open door as he slunk abjectly into the large room that was brilliantly lighted and occupied the front portion of the building. Beyond this, its door in a line with the entrance at which I stood, was a smaller dark room where could be glimpsed the faint reflections from bottles, test tubes, and various chemical paraphernalia. It was apparent in his every move and his self-conscious mien that Irwin hoped to reach the other door before it became necessary to reveal to Ted the fact that Dorothy was not with him. In thinking it over, I presume that Ted's eagerness to see the girl enter, and his firm belief that she was with her brother, allowed Irwin to reach the other door unmolested, and just as he entered the darkened interior, I stepped boldly into the first large and well-illuminated room.

I say I entered boldly. I did, but with that act my boldness ceased for I was rendered craven by what I beheld. Upon a cushion at the far end of the room reposed what looked to me like a phosphorescent tarantula. As I gazed with widened eyes and gaping mouth, I realized that it was not of the spider family at all. The circular, central part was not a body, but rather a head, for from its center glowed two unblinking eyes, and beneath them was the rudiment of a mouth. The appendages, which had upon first appearance resembled the legs of the spider, I perceived were fine hair-like tentacles that were continually in motion as if a soft breeze played through them.

When I realized that the thing was regarding me with those staring expressionless eyes I tried to summon forth what little dignity I could muster, for instinctively I sensed that the repulsive form housed an exceptional intelligence. But I had never undertaken a more difficult task, and I was thankful for the moment that I was not standing in front of my biology class at the university.

"Well, what do you think of the bacteria theory of evolution now?"

Had the thought flashed through my brain, or had a thin, piping, gasping voice put the question to me through the medium of sound? Evidently sound had played some part, for as I looked at the cushioned monstrosity, I saw that the aperture beneath the eyes was moving.

"Don't you recognize your old friend Ted Marston?" came the derisive query in thin, wheezing tones. "Is the gap too great for your feeble consciousness to cross?"

"God in heaven," I fairly screamed. "You—Ted Marston!"

"The same," continued the voice, which though faint, carried with it a quality of undying persistency. "Do you realize that as you stand before me you are perfectly powerless to do other than my will? Do you know that it was I who prevented your entering the laboratory a few days ago? When my mind is concentrated upon you, you have no volition of your own?"

I realized that what he said was indeed true. He controlled me as completely as a master mechanic controls a machine.

He continued, satisfied with the demonstration of his power.

"You have evidently prevented Dorothy's appearance, but I can attend to that later. For the present I will astonish your feeble mind with a few facts. The rapid growth of evolution bacteria has reduced my body to an efficient minimum. The tentacles that surround my body take the place of all the old five senses except that of sight, and in addition to the five senses known to man in your stage of evolution, I have added seven more, and I verily believe more will evolve in time. These tentacles are more sensitive than the radio antennas of your era, and they pick up thought waves with little or no difficulty."

At this moment Irwin was visible on the threshold of the farther door, a decrepit being completely robbed of his personality. I questioned Marston in regard to him. The inhuman monstrosity gave a mirthless laugh. "Here we are, the triumvirate," and again the sardonic laughter wheezed on the air. "I found Irwin easier to manage with decreased mental ability, and I find all I rule must be like him, before Dorothy and I can control the world."

"Your scheme," I cried in horror, "is to impair men's minds and then to rule mentally as a god?"

"You are really very intelligent for so low a creature," he mocked. "I would do well to begin with you. Irwin," he called, "I need your assistance."

As he called to Irwin, I felt his mental hold upon me relax, and I moved a step toward him while Irwin looked at me in surprise. An invisible barrier stopped me almost instantly. He continued to hold his attention upon me, while the man in the adjoining room was moving about apparently carrying out his command for a mind-enfeebling treatment upon me.

"You know, it was one of your theories in the old days, Frank," the thing that was Ted continued, "that God accomplishes His purpose through the agency of man. Well, that is exactly the manner in which I shall accomplish my purpose: through mankind. But unfortunately I have yet to take humanity back mentally, for I am not God—yet!"

"*Yet*—you vile blasphemer!" I screamed, and then I saw it! I knew that the only thing to do was to forget what I saw in the adjoining room and occupy all of the monster Marston's attention, *all* of it! I cursed him, threatened and even attempted violence, and all the while, a being that stood mentally at the dawn of humanity approached from the anteroom bearing in his arms a great crowbar.

Could I keep from betraying by so much as a batting eyelash the approach of the man with the clouded brain?

"I will defy you, Marston," I screamed, "and I will do it alone, I—I—I. Do you understand? It is I, Frank Caldwell, who will oppose your rule."

A gathering mist blurred my vision, but as if viewed through a breeze-wafted veil, I saw the spidery product of evolution rise apparently without support and float in the air toward me like a bloated octopus in the water. Another second that seemed an eternity and the bar descended with all the force of brute man behind it, and I knew that the quivering mass of flesh could exert no more evil influence upon humanity. A few more blows and the thing that had been Ted Marston was no more.

LESLIE F. STONE (1905–91) was the pen name of the Philadelphia-born science fiction writer Leslie Francis Silberberg (née Rubenstein). She began writing stories at the age of nine and made her first professional sale, a series of original children's fairy tales, to a local newspaper when she was fifteen. At nineteen she discovered the adventure magazine *Argosy* and Edgar Rice Burroughs's Mars stories, which inspired her to try out SF writing. Stone recalls that "back then, women's lib was but a gleam in feminine eyes," and so when a friend cautioned that the nascent SF community might not be friendly to women authors, she decided to send out stories under the androgynous pseudonym Leslie F. Stone ("Day" 101). Hugo Gernsback bought her first batch of stories in six weeks, and Stone quickly learned that the editor "liked the idea of women invading the field he had opened" ("Day" 101). Accordingly, she retained her pseudonym but, like most other women associated with early magazine SF, allowed Gernsback and other editors to publish her portrait and to refer to her as a woman in editorial comments.

Between 1929 and 1940 Stone published twenty stories, mostly with *Amazing*, *Wonder Stories*, and *Weird Tales*. However, between her "sexist experiences" with new editors who entered the field in the late 1930s and the "horrifying use" of nuclear weapons in World War II—which seemed to herald the beginning of a future far different from those she crafted in her fiction—Stone decided to retire from SF in 1945 ("Day" 102). She spent the next two and a half decades caring for her labor journalist husband and their two sons while launching a second career as "a prize-winning ceramicist and gardener" (Davin, *Partners* 410). In the 1960s Stone started a third career at the National Institutes of Health in Bethesda, Maryland. At that time she also reaffirmed her commitment to SF by revising her 1929 novella "Out of the Void" (reprinted in this anthology) for publication in book form. Her stories have been featured in anthologies such as Groff Conklin's *The Best of SF*, Isaac Asimov's *Before the Golden Age*, and Arthur B. Evans et al.'s *The Wesleyan Anthology of Science Fiction*.

If Stone was welcomed into the early SF magazine community on her own terms as a woman, it is likely because, regardless of her sex or gender, she produced fiction that was clearly in line with Gernsback's vision for the genre. As an interplanetary romance that follows the adventures of two humans who lead a slave revolt on the distant planet Abrui, "Out of the Void" provides plenty of thrills for a general reading audience. Meanwhile, Stone's detailed description of rocket propulsion—dropped into the middle of the story textbook style, complete with italics in case readers miss it—and the shorter lectures on subjects ranging from the benefits of vegetarianism to the possibility of satellite suns introduce young people to basic scientific and technological principles. But Stone also goes beyond the current state of technoscientific knowledge in her depiction of interstellar travel and communication, irradiated houses, and pre-made foods, all of which seem designed to inspire scientists and engineers. As such, "Out of the Void" delivers the entertainment, instruction, and prophetic vision that Gernsback insisted would make SF a truly distinct popular genre.[8]

Furthermore, while Stone downplayed the impact of first-wave feminism and the suffrage movement on her life as an SF author, issues of sex and gender are central to her storytelling practices. Like many other women writing fiction for the early SF magazine community, in "Out of the Void" Stone employs a male narrator to appeal to what many assumed was a predominantly young male audience, but then introduces her female lead's voice indirectly through letters (for other examples of this very common practice, see Lilith Lorraine's "Into the 28th Century" and Clare Winger Harris's "The Evolutionary Monstrosity," both featured in this anthology). She also uses elements drawn from popular forms of women's writing to speculate about the future of sex and gender relations. For example, Stone invokes the turn-of-the-century feminist utopian belief that new sciences and technologies would liberate women from domestic labor to imagine a future where women and men participate equally in home-making, education, and statecraft. She also draws on the gender ideals central to nineteenth-century domestic fiction to cast her male human lead as "an admirer and respecter of women who likes the heroine as much [as] or more than he lusts for her" (Baym 41). Significantly, in an era when authors often treated the alien other as a Darwinian competitor for scarce resources (including women), Stone extends the characteristics of the domestic hero to her alien antagonist as well, using the alien's encounter with her brave, intelligent female lead as the means by which he is transformed from ruthless competitor to partner in progress and exploration. Thus "Out of the Void" emerges as a complex piece of feminist SF that weaves together the literary techniques of the past and the technoscientific issues of Stone's present to imagine how men and women might build better futures together.

....

"Out of the Void"

Amazing Stories, August–September 1929

THE NARRATOR STARTS ON A FISHING TRIP

The possibility that life is sustained upon a number of our sister planets has changed to probability, but we on Earth have as yet had no conclusive proof that such life is to be found on other orbs. There has been talk of sending a man to the moon by a rocket, and we hear much about radio telegraphing to Mars. Yet, up to the time of these events of which I am writing, none of our scientists had taken seriously the possibility of a visitor reaching Earth from another planet.

Neither had I!

I am not a scientific man. In fact, I am not even a radio fan. To me, the moon is an appendage—an interesting appendage, to be sure—of this good old world, and the stars are there to relieve the monotony of the night sky. It doesn't matter to me whether the Earth is round, whether it moves around the sun, or whether there is life on our sister planets or not. I offer these introductory remarks because I want it understood that this is being told from a layman's viewpoint—from a disinterested layman's viewpoint. I have no theory or explanations. I have only cold, bare facts.

I am one of those beings usually designated as the T.B.M. I go to the shows whose patronage depends largely on that class of man. And like a great many brethren, I am a devotee of the art of fishing. This is not a fish story, however, though it has its beginnings in a fishing trip!

It was on one of those rare occasions when I slipped away from the turmoil of Wall Street to my own particular fishing lodge, a ramshackle little hut on the bank of one of the finest trout streams in the east, bar none, that I had my adventure.

That afternoon I had telephoned the wife that I would not be home for dinner for three or four nights. Catching the last train out, I was soon disembarking at my wayside station. I carried nothing but a small grip containing my necessities and my beautiful fishing rod. Walking briskly I left the confines of the tiny New Jersey village, and plunged into the dense woods that hedged in my shack.

It was already night, and I hurried, for I had the city man's fear of the dark. I met no one, though once or twice I had the sensation that the woods were full of spying men. Once through the trees I saw the gleam of what appeared to be the eyes of a cat, or a wolf, but I laughed that off, realizing it could be no more than two fireflies.

I hurried on my way whistling. Then my furtive eye caught the gleam of glass. Ah, thought I, a new neighbor! I resolved that I would pay him a visit the next day. The shack was reached at last, and with hands trembling with joyful excitement, I pushed open the door. I lit the oil lamp, filling it from a tin I kept for that purpose. The night was warm and I needed no fire. I busied myself in making the place habitable.

It was about five minutes later that I discovered the theft, and the jewel. I had always kept an old suit of clothing hanging on a nail against an emergency such as a wetting, for instance, although I always brought an extra suit of khaki with me. Now the suit was gone! The suit wasn't worth anything; an old-clothes man wouldn't have given me a cent for it, but I did not like the idea of a thief around my hut. What could anyone have wanted with that suit? Then I saw the jewel!

There, on a small shelf, where I usually kept my toothbrush, hairbrush, razor, et cetera, quite close to the rack on which I had hung the old suit, was the most perfect ruby I have ever seen. At least I thought it was a ruby. It flashed and glowed like a thing alive. For several moments I stood there, too enraptured to touch it. I knew immediately that the jewel had been left in lieu of payment for the old suit! But what sort of person would do such a thing? To whom could that suit have been worth a ruby? A thief, an escaped convict? No. A thief or an escaped convict would hardly have considered payment at all.

I went to sleep with that ruby under my pillow. And for the first time the door and windows were locked. The next morning I was up early with a tingle in my blood. Just outside my window I could hear the song of the stream as it bubbled and swirled among its rocks and pools. Dressing, I stopped only for a cup of coffee.

All morning I fished, completely oblivious of any mystery. It was not until after three o'clock in the afternoon, when I finally went to the shack for some food, that I recalled the ruby. That jolt knocked all spirit out of me. I lost every desire to resume my sport. I sat brooding over the jewel. It was too strange. I recalled the curses that some notorious jewels had cast over their possessors. This might be such a gem. Or again, what if the thief had not intentionally left it and should return?

Hurriedly I left the hut. I needed air, but the stream and its trout did not lure me. The gleam of glass that I had seen the night before appeared again. The owner of that glass might know something about this mystery. Anyway, I needed to talk to someone.

Half running, I quickly came to the spot where I had glimpsed the glass. There was no mistaking it—right there was a converging of two paths. At first I saw nothing; the trees and vegetation hid it, until looking upward, I saw the gleam again. I thought it was the roof of a greenhouse. Wondering who in the world would build such a structure in this part of the country, I walked toward it.

A STRANGE VISITOR

The country was clearing, and I came to the edge of a large natural open glade, where I stopped short. Astonishment halted me in my tracks. There in the center, or rather almost taking up the entire clearing from one side to the other, reposed a giant construction. It was cylindrical in section, and of the same general design as a torpedo, except that it had two conical ends. It was fully a thousand feet long and perhaps fifty feet in diameter.

I did not stop to conjecture about the whys and wherefores of this strange thing. After my first surprise I walked up to examine it. It was glossy white, and seemed to have a glasslike finish, and it was opaque. I discovered later that it was constructed of glass, but I would not have believed it then. I walked all around trying to fathom its secret, its purpose. There was not a single opening anywhere. It seemed to have been made of some highly polished stone, and picking up a sharp pebble, I tried to scratch the smooth surface. I pressed with all my might, but the white surface withstood me. I could make no mark upon it and the stone's tip was blunted. It was then that I perceived that the thing was of a clear transparent material, and the whiteness behind it might be a blind drawn over it!

Since a stone could not scratch it, I tried the edge of the diamond in my finger ring. It made not the slightest impression. Determined to discover some way of breaking it, I backed away several yards, and picking up a stone, hurled it with all my strength. The stone bounced off like a rubber ball.

For all of an hour I dallied around the cylinder, trying to discover what it might be, or its purpose in that spot. Half a dozen times I encircled it, running my hands over it as low as possible and as high as I could reach, endeavoring to find some weak place on its wide expanse. With much difficulty, for I was not as slender then as I was once, nor as spry, I climbed to the top of a young tree to see what lay atop. There was nothing but a smooth, unbroken surface. My curiosity was now very much aroused, but I could find no plausible explanation. At last I decided to inquire about it in the village.

With the chagrin of a baffled man I picked up a rather large rock as I turned to go and flung it with all my strength against the thing, exactly as a peeved boy might have done. I was startled to hear a deep hollow boom. At least the thing was hollow. But the stone left no blemish. In disgust I headed for the village. And then I was frightened by the most inhuman shriek.

It was beginning to get dark. It was that time of evening when the dusk is settling and nothing seems real in the half-light. This is particularly true of the woods. It came bearing down upon me, a thing of white that in the twilight appeared to tower over me many feet. A ghost! I had no time to think. I saw that it was clothed in flowing draperies that streamed behind it. And in those flying things I saw a face—if it could be called that. It seemed more like a mask of many colors and distorted features. I saw all this, as it descended upon me, screaming. And in the growing darkness I saw a pair of eyes that gleamed like the eyes of a cat!

It closed down upon me—flesh and blood, strong and wiry! I could get no hold on it. Something fell on my unprotected head, and there came a painful blackness. I recall a hazy awareness of other beings and I was being borne off toward the white cylinder, and through the walls!

When I regained my senses I was comfortably spread out upon a wide soft couch. A blinding light filled my eyes, and I quickly closed them again. I lay there, wondering what had happened to me. Then like a flood the memory of it all returned! The stolen suit, the strange ruby, the white cylinder, the attack—it all came back to me.

I opened my eyes again; this time the light did not bother me. I saw that I was in a room—the strangest room I had ever seen. Close at hand, just below my couch, lay a pool filled with water, that lapped gently at the sides. Strange flowers, of forms and colors I had never seen before, grew in pots around the pool. The flooring was of tiles, and the ceiling was of glass. A light seemed to flow from the entire surface of the ceiling, and lit the room with a diffused glow that was like sunlight. The walls of the chamber held my attention.

They were of mosaic tiling, depicting a pretty piece of scenery. It was as if I were lying in a valley surrounded on all sides by low tree-covered hills with a bit of sky above. On one wall was a meandering river with a pretty water-fall, and above it was the sun, only it was shown as being relatively about as large as an apple and half-covered by clouds. Another wall showed a city of tiny white houses built on a terraced hill. The other walls carried out the hill scene. It was above the city that there was one bit of incongruity that spoiled the entire landscape. It appeared like a second sun, yet almost three times as large as a sun should be, and its color was a pinkish lavender, that contrasted strangely with the greens, browns, blues, and whites of the scene.

After looking about me, I sat up, and was immediately overcome with a dizziness and a shoulder that pained. I now looked wildly about for a doorway, but nothing seemed to break the continuity of the tiled walls. I tried to get to my feet. Finally I succeeded in standing up. I swayed and reeled; fell into a dead faint a second time.

————

When I regained consciousness I was back on the couch. A man was bending over me. Beyond him I saw that a section of the wall had opened, sliding into grooves on either side of the opening.

"Do not attempt to rise," I heard him say. "Your collar bone has been frac-tured, so you must move about as little as possible."

I think I cursed, for the blood rushed to my head. A pretty predicament I was in.

The speaker continued. "I regret exceedingly that you have been put to this discomfort, sir; my servant was overzealous in performing his duty!"

"His duty!" I exploded. "Do you think it was his duty to attack an innocent . . ." Here I fumbled for a word.

"Meddler?" supplied my host.

I bristled at that and was about to say something caustic, but the surprise I experienced on looking up at my host — or captor — made me forget my anger.

He was a large fellow, standing a good six inches over six feet, with a body perfectly proportioned. I thought of the statue I had seen in the Vatican of the Apollo Belvedere. His feet were small and his hands were almost as fine as a woman's. His clothing was cut to show the body to advantage, fitting the legs as tightly as a glove, with a smock cut close to the shoulders and low at the neck, and girdled tightly at the waist.

Still it was not his form that struck me so forcibly. It was his skin! Picture a statue of fine well-polished silver — silver generations old — radiating an inner luster. The man was truly a *silver man*. Face, arms, hands, and even hair, fine as silk falling to his shoulders, were silvery. Only the inner flush that glowed under the skin gave proof of red blood behind that strange complexion. And he had lavender eyes!

I was speechless! My eyes strayed about the strange room, to the man's stranger garments, and back to those peculiar eyes. At last my tongue came free. "My God!" I cried. "What kind of man are you?" A hundred questions raced through my mind.

"We come," said the strange man, "from a most distant planet, of which you on Earth are not aware, a planet quite on the edge of your solar system. We have no name for it but Abrui, which translated means 'Home.' However, we are concerned chiefly about the present, and must consider this untoward situation."

His words left me oddly chilly. A cold sweat broke all over me. I could not think, but somewhere something was repeating over and over again, "Men from another planet, men from another planet!" I closed my eyes to arrange my thoughts once more. I knew that I was not dreaming, and that this was reality. There was a pain in my shoulder. I turned once more to the man. "But I don't understand. How did you come here? How?"

I saw him shrug his shoulders slightly, and I realized he considered me a nincompoop. He answered, "You are aboard an interplanetary vehicle. We call it the *Yodverl*, which in your language means 'the Ship of the Void.'"

"How is it then you speak my language?" I demanded.

"That, my friend, is because I am not the first to have traveled through space. He who went before was from this, your native planet."

I tried to comprehend what he had said, but it was difficult. Having been penned in by a routine of business all my life, it was difficult for me to conceive such possibilities or to follow such a train of thought as this man's words had opened up for me! I saw he was waiting for me to continue questioning him. "And now that you are here, what are your intentions?" I thought of what a reception New York City would give this man. Lindbergh and Dr. Eckener (who had but recently crossed the Atlantic from Germany in a dirigible) would find their noses out of joint.

THE SECRET MISSION

He was smiling at my question, and I had a feeling that he had read my thoughts. "My mission here is a secret one. I am concerned with nothing of this world except one man, to whom I bear a message. We arrived on this planet two nights since, and I hope that by tomorrow night we may be in a position to make our departure — that is, after we have returned you safely to this spot." He sighed, but not I. I wanted to know what he meant by his last words.

"You, sir," he explained, "are luckily the only trespasser who has had the misfortune to discover our retreat here. We landed at night and slipped into this quiet glade without discovery. On reaching your planet we picked out a spot near one of your large cities. We needed some equipment as well as a map, by which we might find our destination. Fortune led us to New York, which we found by means of its great lights. Thence we traveled this far. I went foraging and discovered the old suit in the cabin, which I take to be yours, and I hoped that its owner would not return before we were on our way.

"When you came to find us it meant but one thing. We had to capture you before you carried your story to the village and brought intruders here. Hence you find yourself within our vehicle. And though we regret it, we must act so as to insure the keeping of our secret during our stay on Earth. You may rest assured, however, that you will be returned to this spot safe and well."

I glanced ruefully at my shoulder. "It will be six weeks before that can heal."

"On the contrary. We have with us a salve, which has healing power that your medical men would, no doubt, consider miraculous. Your collarbone will be completely well within a week's time. Allow me to bandage it again and rub it with this salve."

As he worked on my shoulder with his cooling unguent, another man entered the chamber. He was like the first, silvery and handsome, but somewhat younger. His knowledge of English was no equal to that of the older man, nor did I take to him as readily as I had to his companion. He addressed my host as Sa Dak, while the younger fellow answered to the name of Tor.

Later, as I began to notice Sa Dak more particularly, I saw that his face was one of power, while in the eyes was an expression that bespoke some great sorrow. There was no way to determine his age from his features, and one could not see gray hairs among the silver. I judged him as a man in his prime, probably in the late thirties or forties. The other had no fine marks of character in his youthful face, and his lavender eyes expressed no emotions. He seemed to be no more than twenty-five years old.

After rubbing my shoulder well, Sa Dak asked if it still pained. There was only the discomfort of the tight bandage and an ache that was no more than a slight toothache. I admitted as much, and felt better about the prospect of my imprisonment. Suddenly I remembered that I had told my wife I would stay away several days, and she should not expect me until I showed up. Somehow it never entered my mind to doubt Sa Dak's word, and I was looking forward with childish curiosity to this strange adventure.

Just then another creature entered the room. He was bearing a tray on which there were three glasses filled with liquid, and several dishes filled with food. The servant was somewhat smaller than his master, just as finely built, and had an extremely intelligent face; but his skin was different. Whereas his masters looked silvery, he looked golden! Hair, skin, and lips were like virgin gold polished, and glistening with the blood flowing under the skin. And his eyes were red! As red as vermilion, and they looked quite natural in that golden face!

My host, on perceiving his entrance, said, "Ah, here is the culprit!" and rapidly he spoke to the fellow in a strange tongue. The servant cringed; his tray trembled as he looked in my direction. He managed to distribute his burden among us and waited nearby while we ate and drank. What the liquid was I did not know; the food was also strange but was vegetable-like and very delectable.

After taking the dishes, the servant waited patiently, just beyond my couch, with fear in his strange eyes. His master paid him no attention, but continued speaking to me.

"When you appeared in our vicinity, we knew immediately that it would be necessary to make you our captive. My companion and I enjoyed watching your attempt to discover what we were, and when you started away with the thought in your mind of making inquiries, and possibly to arouse the authorities, we sent this poor fellow out to capture you. It was his overzealousness in the duty of capturing you that caused him to wound you. Hence he is now at your mercy. Punish him as you will." And with a movement of his arm he brought the trembling slave into our circle.

I was greatly embarrassed. Had my captors suggested earlier that I punish my tormentor, I would gladly have taken an eye for an eye, giving him the same that he had given me, but the situation had taken a different turn. I, who had thought these interplanetary visitors the intruders, was convinced that I was the intruder. I managed somehow to smile, though I was feeling like a bully who was beaten by a smaller fellow. I waved the slave away.

"You are to be complimented upon possessing a servant who performs his duties so fully," I said, and I smiled smugly to myself as I thought what a good example of my countrymen I was setting myself up as in so magnanimously forgiving the man who had injured me.

The silver man turned to the golden one and spoke in their soft language. The slave looked at me with his odd eyes, and in the manner in which all mankind expresses gratitude, he threw himself at my feet and taking my hand in his, he kissed it. More embarrassed than ever, I looked to Sa Dak for relief. He spoke and the slave slowly backed out of the room. It is needless to say that during the rest of the time I spent on the *Yodverl* he followed me about like a faithful dog, fulfilling my desires before I had time to express them.

It was now quite dark outside and Sa Dak observed that within a short time we should be moving. I was rather inquisitive as to where our destination lay, but at a motion from Sa Dak the other followed him and they both hurried away through the doorway.

CURIOSITY UPPERMOST AGAIN

Cautiously I rose to my feet. This time I knew no dizziness, and I found that my shoulder pained not at all. Walking to the door I peered through and saw that a small chamber lay beyond. At its far side was a second doorway, and I surmised that the two silver men had proceeded through it to their pilot room.

I glanced about the room. It was furnished very simply, with furniture made from a strange light metal. There was a broad desk in the center, sitting on a square rug of gray, woven from some rough material like camel's hair. Several chairs were set about, three-legged chairs with seat and back built to conform to the lines of the body. All about the room were set square cases three feet in height. I surmised that they contained books, although the shelves were concealed behind metal. I noted that the walls of the room were like the ceiling and the light came from all sides. There was nothing to relieve the whiteness of the glass.

The desk held my attention. On it was a tall slender metal vase with one of those strange exotic flowers that I had seen growing in the other room. Beside the vase were several strange oblong boxes of metal about ten inches in length and only one inch in width. Curious, I picked one up. On one side was a small metal tab, which I immediately pulled. One side of the box drew out and to it were attached about two dozen thin sheets of metal, each one as thin as a sheet of writing paper, and on them was a strange form of writing. The letters were oddly shaped, and on examining them closely, I found that instead of having been printed or written, they had been photographed on the sheet. I took this to be a book.

Besides the several "books" that were on the desk was a square box of metal. Of course, I had no right to be prying but I was curious. I wanted to know all there was to know about these people. It would be something to remember all my days. So without any scruples I opened the box and let a cry of wonder escape me, for there on the same sort of metal sheets was a manuscript, written not in Abruian, but in English!

> To Professor Ezra Rollins:
> Data concerning the results gathered on the arrival of the Rollins rocket upon an unknown planet called by its peoples "Abrui."
> With greetings and best wishes to the Professor.
> Dana Gleason

I looked no further. I closed the box, my mind now in a whirl. *Dana Gleason*, Dana Gleason. Where had I heard that name? Then it came to me. Years ago, when I was no more than a boy, I had heard the story of Dana Gleason, one of the wealthiest men in the world, of fine aristocratic stock, dating back to the early settlement of the country.

Dana Gleason had been one of the young society men whose very name brought envy to youthful hearts. Tales of his exploits, his polo ponies, his yachts, his globetrotting were read avidly by the curious public. His marriage into another house of equal rank and fortune appeared on the front pages of the newspapers. Then for two years, at which time his baby was born, Dana Gleason was completely forgotten. Almost immediately upon the arrival of the baby, both father and child disappeared completely. Later it was discovered that the father had spirited the baby away on his yacht. Several weeks later there came a sensational story when young Mrs. Gleason was killed at a railroad crossing in an automobile.

For months no more news was to be had, but an inquisitive reporter learned that the father had planned, with the aid of nurses and tutors, to bring up his boy with a hatred of women. Five years later the last woman left the yacht, but she had been paid not to give interviews. Next we heard of the yacht (which was almost as large as a small steamship) from various corners of the world—from the north, east, west, and south. Dana Gleason, Jr., was having the finest education that man could acquire. The greatest teachers from every nation were taken aboard the yacht, and one heard of the famous men of the day being invited for cruises. The yacht was said to have a swimming pool, a gymnasium, a chemical laboratory, and an astronomical observatory. It carried its own wireless, and motion pictures of historical events were screened especially for the benefit of the heir. The accounts of his life aboard the yacht read like fairy stories.

The child grew up, and his father and he were heard of in every conceivable place on the globe. They were exploring the arctic regions; they had their fingers in some political pie in Latin America. They were skiing at Biarritz; they were shooting tigers in India, lions in Africa. They were at the Kentucky Derby; they were taking in the nightlife of New York. They were with an archaeologist on the Nile; they were studying conditions in Manchuria. They were presented at the Russian Court; they were abducted by Arabs. They had attempted to climb Mount Everest. But why should I write all this? You, too, have read these accounts and reveled in them and envied.

You, too, can recall when the Gleasons joined the British forces to fight Germany. And you read the account of Gleason Senior's death in the third year of the War, and of the record the son made in the Air Force. And that was the last you ever heard! The name of Gleason was forgotten with the rising of new stars of front-page brilliancy. What happened to the son after the leadership of the father was gone? Was this manuscript perhaps the answer? Had Dana Gleason, Jr., accomplished the last possible thing left for him to do?

I turned again to the sheets of metal lying before me, but as I started to read further, suddenly the light about me began to fade, and I was in darkness! In wonder I looked about. Overhead, as through a very thick glass, I could see the stars, and close at hand I could make out the shapes of trees in the darkness. Then as I gazed in wonder, I saw that we were rising above the trees. Soon they were far below, and I could see nothing but the twinkling stars in the distance.

There was no pulsation or vibration to suggest motors; it was only a gentle rising and a feeling of being suspended in space. Then through the darkness of the room I saw something that startled me. Two glowing orbs had appeared in the doorway. It was my host. He spoke.

"In traveling through the atmosphere of a planet, we shut off our lights. Our light does not travel far; that is why we allowed it to shine in the clearing, but it is enough to be seen from below. I trust its absence does not inconvenience you."

I made some inane remark that passed. I enjoyed watching our progress. I added that I regretted I did not have the power to see in the dark as he had.

"Dana Gleason could never become quite accustomed to the fact that we on

Abrui could see in the dark as well as in daylight," he observed, and I realized that he knew that I had found the manuscript.

"Yes," he continued, "we are on the way to deliver that report to Professor Rollins, who invented the first interplanetary vehicle. We are bound for Africa. Come, join us in the pilot room."

LOOKING OVER THE WORKS

I followed him into the nose of the machine. Here the pilot, Tor, sat at some controls. All about us was clear glass; below we could see the woods we were leaving. A small light glowed here, a small round globe that contained a light in its center, although I could see no connecting wires fastened to it. A shade trained its light down upon a map of the two hemispheres, so that the light could be perceived nowhere else. I could see faintly two vertical rods rising from floor to ceiling, upon which were various levers and meters, and with these the young man was working.

On the map was drawn a line from the point which he had left, down through the center of the Atlantic Ocean, along the equator to Africa. At a point approximately three hundred miles above Johannesburg and about one hundred miles in from the coastline, our destination was marked by a small cross.

A chair was given me and I sat down where I had a good view of everything around us. Below we saw the lights of scattered communities, but these quickly dwindled to single lights of squatters and fishermen along the Jersey salt marshes. Then the dunes slid by and the rough waters of the Atlantic billowed. "How long do you judge this trip will take?" I questioned the youth at the controls. Sa Dak had left us for several minutes.

"Not more than three ro, which equals about four and a half of your Earthly hours," he declared.

I was incredulous, but the estimate proved almost correct, for we were there in exactly four hours! What would Lindbergh say to that?

Sa Dak returned from an examination of the motors. These engines were located in the far end of the ship. All I gathered from the details that he gave me was that the power of these motors was derived from that element very rare on Earth—radium.

Fifteen minutes or so passed. We saw a ship with its lights all aglow steaming on to New York. It was a pretty sight. I wondered what its passengers would say if they could see us. My host suggested that I lie down for a while, for my shoulder was still sore and he thought it best for me to rest as much as possible. He himself led me back to my couch so that I should not stumble in the darkness. I was tired and the bone was beginning to ache from weariness.

The golden servant soon appeared, with a glass of liquid that was strangely refreshing. After I had sipped it, the stranger insisted that he must dress my shoulder. He rubbed a salve in with his cool deft fingers, then with a salaam he was gone, and I fell asleep.

Two hours later I awoke and returned to the pilot room. The two men were still at the controls. Water lay below us. We saw another ship bound, we supposed, for Cape Town. We quickly passed it by. In another half hour the servant appeared again with food, a sort of cooked fruit. I might note here that all the dishes with which we had been served, including those containing liquids, which later I have called glasses, were really of metal, like almost everything else the Abruians used.

At last we saw the shoreline of Africa, and after skirting it for some distance we turned inland and the wide unvarying veld, with its low hills, and occasional groves of tropical trees, was below us. The moon had risen very late and now it was shedding its silvery glow upon everything. The skin of the two strange men caught its light and reflected it.

Lights now shone out in two or three directions: here the lone camp fire of some traveler or hunter; there the house lights of an isolated farmhouse. Then we came suddenly to a halt, hung suspended for several minutes in the air, and like a rocket we shot down toward a group of three lights that were shining from a low bungalow and its accompanying outhouses.

It was now one o'clock in the morning and the country lay still. Quietly, for all its bulk, the *Yodverl* made a landing, sinking down on the smooth grass several hundred yards from the darkened house. The bungalow was not completely dark, for lights shone from two of its windows. A single light burned in the Negroes' quarters beyond.

"We have arrived," stated my host. "It is rather late to be calling, but I believe we will be welcome." Then, turning to his companion, he made a remark in their own tongue and disappeared through the doorway.

"That was some voyage," I remarked to the youth.

He smiled. "It was necessary for us to travel at so low a speed," he said, quietly putting me in my place. "Out in space we travel many times faster than this."

I had noted from the start that this fellow spoke English with more difficulty than did Sa Dak. His was an English that had been learned book-wise and he spoke haltingly as he carefully picked each word. Sa Dak's mastery of the language was different. With perfect ease he used our idioms and slang expressions, and never seemed at a loss for a word.

Sa Dak reappeared shortly. He had changed his clothing and was dressed in a suit of white linen. The Earthly clothing could not hide the beauty of his superb body with its easy natural grace. Instead it made him look taller, more massive, and more outstanding.

"The suit I took from your cabin was too small, unfortunately," he said, "but it had to do until I reached a store where they could fit me properly. This is the only suit they had that fitted me without alteration."

I wondered how he had managed to walk around the streets of New York without attracting a crowd, but then New York was accustomed to all sorts of strange people on its streets.

"Yes," remarked the man, "I did cause a stir. Of course, I had painted my skin to a semblance of white, and in the first pawnshop I came to, I sold several jewels to obtain money with which I purchased a pair of dark glasses to hide my eyes. But my size continued to attract attention, and several people made remarks about the circus in town." He laughed at the memory.

I could not quite accustom myself to the fact that this man could read my thoughts. From the first I had noticed that he had been aware of what passed through my mind. It was unnecessary for me to as much as ask a question; he answered before I voiced my question. Even now he was explaining:

"Reading another's mind is merely a science, my good sir. Your world is coming to it. The difficulty in my world is in keeping the other fellow from reading your mind. My friend here," and he pointed to Tor, "as well as my servant, have no trouble in reading what passes through your brain. I have had much pleasure in learning your reactions to us, but let me explain that human nature is much the same the Universe over, and any man of Abrui would react exactly as you have done under similar conditions."

His words made me rather uncomfortable, but the look in the smiling lavender eyes comforted me.

THE OLD SCIENTIST

And now, sir," he went on, "would you care to accompany me on my little visit? I feel that I owe you some recompense for detaining you as my prisoner. Perhaps you will be interested in what is to come. The person we are visiting is Professor Ezra Rollins, a scientist that should hold the highest place amongst your great men, but he prefers to end his days in this deserted spot. Shall we go?"

I gladly accompanied him, my broken bone now completely forgotten.

My idea of how we had entered this craft was that we had come in through its glass walls. My kindly host now pressed a small lever that was fitted on his desktop. To my surprise a doorway opened where there had been naught visible but a blank wall. The door was simply a large square section, which slid outward and now rested on the grass outside. "There are forty layers of glass here," explained Sa Dak. "Our glass, unlike Earthly glass, is almost unbreakable, yet I do not like to take a chance on the possibility of a crack; hence the thickness, made up of plates set in layers, one over the other to several of your feet."

"No wonder I could not throw a stone through it," I laughed.

He grinned. "You gave us quite a bit of merriment in your attempts."

We walked over to the compound of the bungalow. Dogs were howling from their kennels, but none came to stay our progress to the front door. A cool night breeze was stirring. Somewhere off in the distance we heard a lion roar. Sa Dak knocked on the house door.

We heard the shuffle of feet. "What is it?" asked a querulous old voice.

"One who comes with a message."

"Then kindly come in."

The door was opened and I followed the silver man into a cozy little room, a much-lived-in room. A lighted lamp was on the table; the Professor had been reading. He was a little old man with the high smooth forehead of the savant, but his eyes were burned-out lights.

"It is a late hour to be calling, sir," said Sa Dak. "We saw your light and concluded you were awake."

The old man shrugged his shoulders. "I cannot sleep. I can only wait."

"For a message?"

The old eyes brightened, then saddened again. "A message that can never come. I was once a scientist; but I committed the crime of sending two men to their death. That deed awakes the dormant man within me, and awake now, I can never sleep again . . ."

"Yet a message would change all that!"

"No message has come."

"I bring such a message, Professor Ezra Rollins."

"You mean . . . why, who are you? I . . . I . . ."

"I come from those two, sir, from Dana Gleason and Richard Dorr . . ."

I have never seen a face and body change as did the wrinkled, weary face and stooping body before us. He was suddenly taller, younger. In a half a dozen steps he was across the room at a door through which we could see a flight of steps. "Elsie, Elsie," he cried. "They are safe! D'y'understand? They landed on Mars!!"

———

There was movement in the room above our heads. The Professor turned to us again. For the first time he seemed to note the strange appearance of his nocturnal guest. "Did you, too, come from Mars?" he questioned almost fearfully.

The Abruian shook his head. "No, Professor, not from Mars, but from . . ."

He didn't finish his sentence, for the old man had fainted away before the sentence was completed.

The big man was on his knees by the Professor's side. He picked him up as easily as if he were a child and laid him tenderly on a divan close at hand. Then we were aware of a slender girlish form that had entered the room and rushed to the old man. "What have you done? What have you done?" she moaned. "You have killed my uncle!"

"He has only fainted. His heart is weak, and I erred in not speaking more carefully. Water, please!"

His calm voice reassured her and she hurried for a glass of water, but the Professor was already recovering. Tears commenced to flow down his cheeks. The other hastened to speak. "I am sorry, sir. I broached my subject poorly. Dana Gleason and Richard Dorr live, but the planet they reached was a more distant one than the planet you call Mars. They are both well and happy, and asked that I come to you with their message."

The tears halted. "I should have realized, naturally . . . you spoke of a message. I . . . I . . . cannot stand too much excitement. Ah . . . the message . . . you have it?"

The manuscript was brought forth. Quickly Rollins was scanning the pages. "Ah, Dana's handwriting. Thank God, they are safe!"

He fumbled for his glasses and, putting them on his nose, began to read. The girl, with the glass of water still in her hand, stood beyond the table. She was holding her dressing gown at her throat. I saw then that she was not so young as I at first imagined. Obviously, she had already passed her twenties; the bloom of her youth was gone, given without thought of self to the service of the old scientist. She was Elsie Rollins, niece of the Professor. It is to her I owe the story of all that had gone before this date. When years had passed, she came to me in New York to help me in this work, and so together we compiled this record, giving facts and descriptions as we remembered them.

Professor Ezra Rollins had been a world-famous figure not so many years before. When he let it be known that he was working on a vehicle that could carry a man to the moon or, better still, to our sister planet, Mars, he had been ridiculed until, in disgust, he left the college where he had held the scientific research chair, and had come to Africa to work unmolested by reporters, who had interviewed him only to laugh at him.

With him had come his several disciples, who believed fervently in his theory. A mechanical engineer and a world-renowned astronomer had joined him in his retreat, and for almost twenty years they had worked together over the plans, until at last the gigantic rocket that they were to shoot to Mars was ready. All that was needed was the man who would undertake the journey. It required a man of great daring and courage, a man who would be willing to sacrifice everything, even his life, in the hazardous feat. It needed a young man, a man of learning, an extraordinary man.

For two years Rollins had roamed through the cities looking for his subject, as he may be called, and at last he found him, a youth whose life's training seemed to have fitted him for this very deed. Dana Gleason, Jr., had finished in the War with great honor, but now he was at loose ends, bereaved of his father, with no friend, and a family of which he knew no member. He had done everything that man could do on the planet Earth, and he had become undeniably bored with life thereon.

Gleason did not jump at the chance to go to Mars. At first he thought the scientist was crazy. When he realized that he was in an extremely sane state of mind, that all plans had been developed, and that the rocket was there and ready, he agreed to consider the suggestion, and he considered it as soberly as such a proposition could be considered. He accepted the Professor's invitation. He waited only long enough to make a will and straighten up all his Earthly affairs; thenceforth he was in Rollins's keeping.

GETTING READY FOR THE TRIP

It was seven months before the rocket was to be shot into space, for then Mars would be in perfect conjunction with Earth for the experiment. In that time Rollins taught the brave youngster of twenty-six years all he would have to know on landing on the red planet. Once there, he was to set to work to build a gigantic radio, a replica of the one that was stored in the attic of the Rollins bungalow, and broadcast his find to Earth. Then if he discovered intelligent beings on the planet, which was a probability, he was, with their aid, to get himself shot back to Earth!

Miss Rollins described Dana Gleason as being a slender young chap about five feet seven inches in height, with dark chestnut hair, brown eyes that were almost black, and a fair complexion, regular features that were almost girlish except for a masculinity developed by the full life of a globetrotter. He was a quiet person, little given to talking, with a throaty but well-trained voice. Only in anger would he become eloquent, and then his tones were rich, though not very deep. He seemed rather temperamental, given to moods that were affected by the elements — rain made him dreamy; storms excited him, bringing color to his cheeks; but the sun left him a quiet and serious person. When he spoke of his proposed journey in the rocket his eyes sparkled and glowed. On horseback he would roam for hours on the veld, and though he enjoyed the chase he seldom bagged any game. He was witty, with a somewhat satirical turn to his humor.

He spent much of his time reading the heavy volumes that the Professor gave him, and he had a lively interest in the mechanics of the rocket. He made friends readily with the workers and scientists, asking questions, learning facts. His thirst for knowledge of all things was extraordinary. He would go on long walks with one of his new friends, or sit relating to them some of his own experiences, though he was never one to brag. And he never spoke of his wealth. His bearing with servants was such that he was greatly beloved by them. However, he never made any overtures of friendship to Elsie Rollins, preferring rather the society of men. He showed that he appreciated the fact that the girl had set him on a pedestal and admired him, and his attitude to her was one of consideration, but during the seven months of his sojourn on the veld, she was never one of his intimates. He had great respect for Professor Rollins and they became as true friends as the disparity in age would permit. He had one friend to whom he appeared to be drawn on sight. That one was Richard Dorr.

Richard Dorr was practically the only neighbor that the Rollinses had, aside from the inhabitants of the few native villages here and there. He was by profession a mining engineer, and somewhere in the hills was his gold mine, but on his word it was a poor sort, and he did not seem to spend much time there. With him had come the rumor of an *affaire de cœur* that had not gone well, and one could wonder, having seen him, how any woman could give him up.

He was tall above the average, broad of shoulder and graceful of limb, strong and powerful, with the face of a Viking. His blue eyes were accustomed to looking over great distances. His hair was the color of old copper and crinkled and shone in the sun. His skin had been tanned nearly to the shade of his hair, so that he looked almost as if he had been cast out of reddish metal. He was a great humanitarian, and it was known that he was doing a lot to help the natives of Africa find themselves. All the servants within the Rollins's compound adored him. Out in the world he might have become a great leader of men.

At first he paid little attention to young Gleason. He noticed him no more than he noticed the other men around him. He and Professor Rollins were staunch friends and could sit for hours discussing the rocket around which the latter's life revolved. Dorr had given many valuable suggestions for it, and had been at hand to help during the casting of parts that could not be obtained in any market. He had known and played with Elsie since she came to the veld at the age of ten when both her father and mother died. She had seen the friendship grow up between Gleason and Dorr, and noted the many hours they were together.

Many evenings were spent in the little sitting room of the bungalow, with the three men reading and talking, while the girl sat in her corner mending and embroidering. Secretly she was initialing all of Gleason's handkerchiefs and shirts. Often the four sat down to a game of bridge. One night she was surprised to see an expression she could not fathom on the face of Dorr as he sat studying the absorbed face of Dana Gleason sitting there reading one of the Professor's heavy tomes. It was an expression that she could not interpret and it puzzled her for many a day.

Then Dorr's visits became less and less frequent and days passed before they would hear the beat of his horse's hoofs across the veld. His absences were noted. Once the Professor intervened and a boy was sent to learn if he was sick. He returned with the answer that he was merely busy. And when he came, there was an evident surliness.

The time drew near for the departure. One evening Rollins faced Gleason. "In just six days, my boy, you shall go!" he told him, and Rollins's eyes shone brightly. There was no change of expression on the youth's face; there was only a new glitter in his eyes.

A messenger was dispatched to Dorr to apprise him of the fact. He came that night, and a quiet evening was spent. Not until he was ready to leave did he speak directly to Gleason. The Professor had gone into the kitchen for a glass of water; Miss Rollins was seated in the shadows, unnoticed.

"So you are going through with this?" Dorr had suddenly demanded of Gleason.

The other looked up in surprise. Then he straightened and got to his feet. "And what reason have you to believe that I should not?" he asked coldly.

"I had, or rather thought I had, a reason, Dana Gleason, but I see now that I was wrong." And without another word he had gone out of the door. Rollins returned surprised that he had gone without a word of farewell.

This is an opportune moment to speak of the great vehicle that was to carry the youth on his way. Miss Rollins has described it to me and tried to make me understand the principle by which it worked. As I said before, I am a layman and have little knowledge of machinery.

THE GREAT INVENTION

The machine was a great cylindrical thing eight hundred feet long and about fifty feet in diameter. Its walls were very thick and its nose was pierced through with great springs. It was of smooth steel and the only things to break its surface were four great windows, many inches in thickness, set in its girdle.

Within was a space hermetically sealed, in which were the living quarters for the traveler. These were slung on springs, which were set in slides in such a manner as to keep the chambers within on an even keel no matter how the shell might twist and turn. From the living quarters a passage led to the great windows, where small cells were provided for the observer. The living room was no larger than an ordinary chamber, fifteen feet by ten, and only seven feet high. The reason for the low ceiling was that once outside of Earth's power, there would be no gravity, and the inmate of the room would find himself without weight, perhaps floating about the room. By pushing against the ceiling he could draw and push himself about. For the same reason rails were set around the room at convenient heights, and the floor, walls, and ceiling were heavily padded. Chairs, table, and cupboards were all fastened to the floor, and a low padded seat the width of a bed ran around the entire chamber. Here the voyager would sleep. Pillows and coverlets were stored in the cupboards beneath the seat.

Beyond the living room was a small kitchen wherein was installed an electric stove, an iceless refrigerator, a cupboard for dishes, and a small sink. Food, in a concentrated form, and water were provided to last for almost a year's time. There was also a goodly supply of fresh foods. The rocket carried its own dynamo with sufficient battery to keep it running for several months. For the purification of the air, the same device that is used in submarines, which renews the air by absorbing the carbon dioxide by soda lime and purifying the air chemically, was used. There were also tanks of fresh oxygen provided and by opening a valve this could be let into the room. Oxygen masks and portable cylinders were also stored to be used if the traveler found he could not breath the air of the alien planet. Adjoining the living quarters was the bathroom with all its necessary fixtures; the medicine chest was stored with innumerable tubes of toothpaste, powders, soaps, et cetera, together with medicines for first aid. Nothing, Miss Rollins said, was missing. Below was stored a small dismounted airplane to be put together for use in an emergency.

The machinery that was to keep the rocket moving was set in the stern. Once released, powder was to be shot off automatically, causing explosions that furnished its source of power.*

* Because of his lack of technical knowledge, the writer has failed to explain the fundamental processes by which the rocket, when once out of the atmosphere of Earth, could hold and increase its speed as it flew through space.

First, one must take into consideration Newton's Third Law of Motion, i.e., "to every action there is an equal and opposite reaction"; that to push anything forward there must be a backward motion, just as a man in walking pushes with one foot backwards as he propels his body forward. In Professor Rollins's rocket, this push is given by means of a "kick" from an explosive powder. This powder is confined in a strong steel chamber capable of resisting the pressure of the explosion, and the gases thereof are ejected through, or driven out of, the base of the cartridge

The hour came. For the two preceding days the house, laboratory, and compound seethed with activity, and last-minute preparations were made. Everyone was too excited to think, but Elsie Rollins continued to wonder why Richard Dorr had not made his appearance since the night he had spoken to Gleason so strangely.

The rocket had been slung long since on the giant catapult that would shoot it off, and there was much climbing of the ladder and last inspection. Only newspaper reporters were missing. Then there was supper, when all the mechanics, helpers, engineers, and scientists gathered together for the last time to pay homage to the valiant youth who was putting his life into the care of the God of the Void. Toasts were drunk to success, to the Professor, to one and all. It was a very quiet meal, though the Professor was in high spirits and there was a slight flush on the cheek of Dana Gleason.

The meal came to an end and Gleason retired to his sleeping room to gather his last personal effects. Miss Rollins had seen to it that his linen, his socks, and his handkerchiefs were all ready. He was also taking several suits of khaki. The last thing he did before leaving the bungalow was to stuff his pockets full of chocolate and cigarettes, though several large cases were stored in the rocket. A number of cases of whiskey for stimulant and medicinal purposes were also provided.

It was just about time to start. The rocket was to be shot at exactly twenty-two and a half minutes after eight o'clock. How long the trip would take was not certain. Professor Rollins judged it would take about seven weeks. Of course, he had experimented with miniature rockets in a vacuum, but how fast the giant rocket would travel was conjectural.

There were the farewells, the last bits of advice were being given, the last

---

through an expanding nozzle, a nozzle that resembles that of a steam turbine, and is designed to give the highest possible velocity to the gas. In this manner a great rate of speed can be obtained, each explosion adding acceleration to the speeding body.

At the "shooting" of each cartridge of powder the chamber is thrown off, so that those kept are full ones. This gives the rocket less weight, and consequently greater velocity. So with each ejection of the gas the speed of the rocket has a twofold increase, and though the machine can start at a comparatively slow rate, the nearer it is to its destination the faster it is traveling. On sighting its destination the traveler will then shut off all power, so that the rocket will arrive in the atmosphere of the planet traveling only on the acquired momentum, and an easy landing can be made.

On the rocket, weight, as it may be termed, would be greatly increased by the rapid acceleration at the start, but this was all calculated in advance and allowed for; the acceleration would also be under perfect control, being maintained by means of a time clock at just as great a degree as the passenger could stand.

round of handshaking was going on. Gleason leaned over and kissed Elsie Rollins's cheek gently and then he was climbing the ladder with the Professor, who had one more word to say. And so Dana Gleason, Jr., disappeared from the sight of men into the aerial vehicle. Rollins went in but reappeared in a few minutes and started his way down the ladder.

Then came the unexpected. All were too engrossed with the leave-taking to hear the beat of horses' hoofs and none was aware of Richard Dorr's arrival, until he had his hands on the ladder. In his hurry and excitement, he almost threw Rollins off his balance. Already Gleason was drawing to the great door, fitting in its socket like the breach block of a cannon, when Dorr slipped within.

For another minute the door stood open, then slowly and ponderously it closed—just at the moment that Professor Rollins placed his hand on the release lever. It is doubtful whether, in the high tension of that moment, he realized that a second passenger was on his way to Mars!

There was a deafening explosion, the force of which sent large pieces of machinery flying through the air, killing two mechanics, wounding several others, and all but killing the Professor. He was knocked unconscious and did not recover for many minutes, so that he was not an eyewitness to that awful departure.

———

Professor Rollins now looked up from his study of the manuscript the silver man had brought him. His face was screwed up into a grimace such as a child would make, his mouth trembling. "But . . . but this contains nothing but facts about this unknown planet," he muttered.

"Yes," said Sa Dak, "Dana Gleason has made a worthy survey of the planet. I find it complete."

"That is all right for the universities, but that isn't what I want, man. I want Dana's own story. What happened? What happened?"

The other smiled gently. "That is all there is, sir."

Tears came to the eyes of the old man. "And I want more. I want facts. I must know just what occurred, everything that took place, the story, the story . . ." He looked up helplessly. "You say they are well and happy. How did they find this happiness and contentment?"

"It is a long story, sir."

"You know it then? You will tell me? You were an eyewitness?"

"Yes, I was an eyewitness. And since you insist, sir, I shall do my best. In my desk I have the diary of Dana Gleason; that may interest you. Will you accompany me to my machine, sir, or shall I bring it here?"

"We will go with you, only let's hurry!" cried the old man in his excitement.

"And you, Miss Rollins?" inquired Sa Dak.

She nodded, then remembering that she was not dressed for outdoors, asked that we wait a moment. She returned very soon, with a light coat on. We went to the *Yodverl*, whose glass surface was aglow with its inner lights.

My host and the Professor walked ahead. Miss Rollins and I followed. Sa Dak was trying to direct the eye of the scientist to the construction of the great vehicle modeled after the Professor's invention, but the old man paid no attention; he was intent on hearing the story. I told Miss Rollins something of my abduction, and she told me a little more of what had preceded that astounding departure. Soon we entered the vehicle.

Tor was there to greet us. Sa Dak explained why we were there, and then he turned to us. "Now," he said, "if you will accompany me through the vehicle I can demonstrate to you some of the devices which Dana Gleason and Richard Dorr found in use on Abrui. That will make the telling of the story easier for me."

THE HOUSE OF A "NEIGHBOR"

I was beginning to feel a little weak on account of my shoulder, but, forcing it from my mind, I followed the little party. We went into the room in which I first found myself. "This," said our host, "is called the 'atol' or main living room of the Abruian home. Here is where the family gathers to eat their meals and discuss the day's events. Here they greet their friends, here they start the day with their morning swim. The lowliest home possesses its swimming pool, its potted flowers, its scenic walls. The scene you see depicted here is typical of Abruian scenery.

"In arranging the rooms in my rocket, I have tried to reproduce exactly my home in Abrui," he continued as he led us to the next room, which proved to be a small reproduction of the first room, with a smaller pool, and fewer flowers. There were four small doorways, two in either wall, leading to bedrooms. The scene on the walls was that of a garden. A group of two or three women were seated on low stone benches under the shade of some low trees, and a short distance away, two men were practicing some knife play, each holding a short dagger in either hand with which he attempted to break through the other's guard. On another wall several children were seated in a circle, with the markers of some strange game in their hands. A golden slave girl stood nearby with a silver baby in her arms. A game of tag, played by youths of about fifteen or sixteen, was in progress among some shrubberies. Another slave was working in a flowerbed. It was a happy lifelike scene and the reproductions of the people of Abrui were very fine. I noticed that the costume worn by the women was exactly like that worn by Tor, while the children wore suits of the same style, somewhat abbreviated. One of the women wore a long flowing cape that fastened to the shoulder and reached to the ground. The colors used were of every shade and hue and some were unknown to us. The light that shone over everything was rosy and seemed to come from the overlarge pinkish globe that I had seen painted in the atol, and had objected to. It was in truth the second sun of Abrui!

"This room," said Sa Dak, "is called the 'cof,' and is the inner room of the house. Here is one of the bedrooms," and he brushed aside the curtains of one of the small doorways, revealing a small cell-like chamber furnished simply with a wide couch, a chair, a chest of drawers, and a long mirror. "In these rooms the family sleep, but this chamber is sacred to the women of the house. Here they come when not disposed to mingle with their friends, and only the family is allowed entrance. Here the mistress of the house carries on her affairs and directs the welfare of her house."

The next room, we were informed, was the kitchen, though at first glance it was no more than a small chamber with the walls of opaque glass. However, by touching a small lever close to the doorway, it was transformed. The glass covering opened out, revealing shelf after shelf containing various dishes. On one side was a glass-enclosed refrigerator and we could see the array of food placed within. All around the room projected a piece of smooth glass about two feet into the room. This could be utilized for the table. I saw neither stove nor any other means for cooking.

We were enlightened, however. Removing a small dish made of glass from one of the shelves, our host took from the refrigerator (which I call by that name, although there was no visible means for the preservation of food) a strange vegetable about the size of a grapefruit. This he dropped into the glass dish he held in his hand. Immediately before our eyes a change took place. The food began to cook! We saw it soften, its juices run, and a delicious odor filled the room. In less than five minutes the vegetable was entirely cooked. Taking three small metal plates from another cupboard, our host then served the vegetable on the plates, cutting it with a knife of glass. Tor went for three spoonlike articles that had tiny prongs on their tips somewhat like our ice cream forks at home. The vegetable was quite good.

———

Taking another glass dish, the man poured into it some milk from a metal container and, dropping into it several small pellets, he stirred it well, while we watched the process that was taking place. The milk had begun to freeze! When we ate it we found it was somewhat like ice cream, flavored with something that tasted like sweetened cinnamon.

We all marveled over these utensils, and our host went on to explain that the "cooking dishes" were treated with a solution derived from radium, which caused the food placed within to cook immediately. It was the same for the "freezing dishes." Only the inside of the dishes were treated, so that it was possible to hold them in one's hand while the change was taking place. The inside of the "refrigerator" had been treated in a similar way, but to a lesser degree than the dishes, so that foods could be kept indefinitely and still be edible. How my wife, who is quite a cook, would have envied such cooking methods!

"I shall now show you our 'stable,'" went on Sa Dak, and led us to a small chamber. Like the others, it was scrupulously clean. A low manger was arranged in one wall, and there were four of the prettiest little creatures I have ever seen. They were somewhat smaller than our cows, standing no more than three feet high, and looked somewhat like deer, with soft liquid eyes and faces that were doglike. One was a "bull" while two had the large, developed udders of a cow. The fourth creature was no more than a calf.

"These are called muti. The little one there was born since leaving Abrui!"

The little creatures had looked up at our entrance, and in their eyes was an expression of intelligence that is never seen in the eyes of earthly cattle. Their master made some soft sounds in his throat, and there was response from the bull, which made a like sound. For a minute or two they continued and it almost seemed as if they were actually talking. "Yes," went on the man, "we have discovered the language of our beasts and make it a practice to converse with them!"

We showed our astonishment.

"And why not?" he continued. "Why should animals be denied the right of speech? Naturally, their intelligence is not equal to the thinking mind of man, but it is far better that they understand what is expected of them."

"How can you kill them then? It seems horrible to me to think of eating their flesh," observed Elsie Rollins.

The man smiled. "We do not eat their flesh, Miss Rollins! That is, civilized man does not. We know that fruits and vegetables are quite as strength giving as meat. No, our muti are raised only for the milk they give. And when that supply is gone the animal is simply done away with in a manner that gives no pain. They know this, and understand that we treat them no differently than we treat ourselves!"

"You mean that when age comes you kill the old?"

"Is not that the better way? The aged are only a burden to themselves as well as to others. Their value to the state is nil. Only we do not kill! We go to sleep. We have discovered a ray that destroys animal life, dissolving the compounds that make up our bodies. This ray turned upon us does away with the body completely, the chemical compounds returning to their former state. There is no pain, no suffering. Only a last sweet sleep."

"And the soul?"

"Goes to its appointed place. Of that we do not pretend to know anything."

I could not but think how pleasant such an end would be. No suffering, no funeral, no grave, no tombstone.

"I would like to die that way," sighed the Professor. I saw that Elsie Rollins was trying to break the spell that these thoughts had wrapped about us. Our host was quick to see this, and he now suggested that we return to the atol, where we could comfortably discuss life on Abrui.

"You will notice," he said, "that the ceilings of the rooms we have passed through are all of glass. It is so on Abrui. Every house is but one floor in height. The light from the two suns of the planet shines upon these roofs, giving daylight to the rooms. Again we use radium, which, being a phosphorescent element, takes into itself the sunlight thus distributed, responds to it, and at night re-dispenses it, so that at all times we have an even glow of light. We find that people living under this light are greatly benefited. Disease is therefore completely done away with. It took many years to discover this use of radium, for radium in its raw state, as you must know, does bodily harm to anyone exposed to it. We also have the means of shutting this light off at will."

We had now returned to the "living room." The golden slave appeared, and was arranging several couches into a small circle, and we were invited to take our places there. Tor, the youth, had thrown himself on the floor on a pile of cushions, while our host drew up a chair that was standing near. My shoulder pained again and I appreciated the relief of repose.

At a word from his master the slave left the room and shortly returned, carrying a small black leather-bound book. Miss Rollins exclaimed, "The diary of Dana Gleason!" It was handed to her.

"Perhaps you will read a few of its entries for us; they may prove of interest," said Sa Dak. She was already skimming the pages.

"Why, here," she said, "is the date on which Uncle Ezra first approached Dana with the proposition of his taking the trip to Mars!"

"Read it," said the Professor. Since entering the *Yodverl*, Rollins seemed a different man. He had gotten a new interest. He seemed younger and brighter. He was happy, perhaps for the first time since that fateful night.

The young woman acquiesced and commenced to read in a clear voice.

THE DIARY

"Today fate came to me in the guise of Science. At first, when Professor Ezra Rollins spoke of a trip to Mars, I thought him crazed yet as he talked, his face alight with the fire of his passion, I realized how earnest and intense he was. He left me with my mind in a whirl. Shall I take this one chance in a million? Can I do it? Would Dad have done it? Had the Professor only known me for what I am, he would never have come to me, but haven't I proved myself equal to any man? Why can't I do this?

"I am sure Dad would have done it and he would have expected me to do it. To remain here on Earth can mean but one thing for me—exposure. Howard Courtland will keep his promise, even though I put the world between us, and I, born of woman though I am, cannot and will not give up the heritage my father has given me. No man shall force me to admit that I am a woman-thing even though I was born with the body of one . . ."

Miss Rollins looked up in wonder. Her face had gone white as she read and a low groan from the Professor showed that he understood. "Dana Gleason, a woman!" the three of us exclaimed in one breath, and turned to our host.

He smiled somewhat sadly and there was sorrow in his eyes. "True, I had forgotten that you believed Dana Gleason a man. I am not certain, but I believe her father hated women and was resolved to raise his daughter as a son. This Courtland of whom she speaks had discovered the truth and would have disclosed her secret, thinking he could make her his wife. Dana Gleason is an attractive woman."

"A woman," mused Miss Rollins. "Then," and her eyes brightened, "that explains many things I could never understand. Did . . . did Dick . . . Richard Dorr accompany her . . . knowing?"

"Yes, he knew."

"Read, Elsie, read what happened aboard the rocket," said the Professor impatiently.

"I do not feel quite right about reading this," she said.

The silver man shrugged his shoulders. "Dana wrote the story of her own experiences, and I fear I could not do the tale justice. I am certain she would have no objection to your reading it."

None of us thought to ask how he had obtained the little book.

Throwing aside her qualms, Miss Rollins hastily turned the page.

"Aboard the Rocket," it read.

"Mars is due ahead and Earth is behind us. For the first time, Man has stepped into the great, unexplored vacuity—space. It takes time for one to collect one's thoughts out here. Already forty-eight hours have passed and I can only now bring myself to write. Writing in this diary has become such a fixed habit with me, that to neglect it is like neglecting a dear friend.

"When I climbed the ladder for the last time I hardly expected what next took place, although I had looked for Richard Dorr among the friends that bade me good-bye. Six days before he had addressed me in an odd manner, believing that I, who had given my word, would back out before the moment of departure. I could not imagine what had made him think such a thing, knowing me as he did.

"The day had passed and at last I was ready to leave, forgetting Dorr entirely in my concern for the rocket. After a few more words and a warm handclasp the Professor backed out, and I was ready to swing the great door that would seal me within, when suddenly Richard Dorr appeared at the aperture. In surprise I cried out for him to go back, for only a few minutes would elapse before I should be hurled on my way. Instead of obeying, he came toward me. 'For God's sake,' I cried, 'go, the minutes are precious.' He still came on with a smile on his face. Then he had his hand on the door and made ready to push it to. 'What are you doing?' I demanded.

"'I am going with you!' he said quietly.

"I must have lost my head then, for I was commanding him to leave, even while I was fastening the bolts and pulling and adjusting the levers into place.

"'What? Would you have me killed by the moving machinery?' he questioned and there was a twinkle in his eyes.

"I could say nothing, and then all conversation was cut short. Rollins had pulled the lever, without taking into consideration the fact that his friend was within. The shock of the explosion was terrific and we were both thrown off our feet. I had been thrown to the floor in a corner and a great pressure seemed pushing down upon me, so that I felt I should be crushed. It was almost impossible to take a breath, so tightly were my lungs compressed, and my ribs seemed strained to a breaking point—then a darkness swept over me. It was several minutes before I came to, feeling bruised and sore in all my body. Painfully I tried to sit up. I had known that something of this sort would happen, caused by the great shock of shooting the rocket, but I had not been prepared for anything as bad as this.

———

"Looking about I saw Dorr quite close to me. He was coming out of his stupor. I managed to sit up and he did likewise. Later he admitted that he had believed all the oxygen in the chamber had been forced out, leaving us without air to breathe. Everything was working smoothly, however.

"As we left Earth we had both slipped to the rear of the chamber as Earth's gravity tried to retain its hold upon us. That, too, passed, and we knew that strange sense of having practically no weight. We both started to our feet, and were unprepared for what followed. We were suddenly plunging toward the ceiling as easily as feathers. By putting out a hand against the ceiling we pushed ourselves downward to the floor and so gained our feet. Grasping one of the handrails, we managed to keep there. Then by planting our feet firmly and using a swaying motion we were able to walk upright. I could foresee funny experiences to come.

"'Well,' I observed quite superfluously, 'we are on our way, out of Earth's orbit.'

"Dorr shrugged his broad shoulders, and going into the bathroom, returned with a bottle of iodine and quietly painted a slight scratch on his hand.

"'How did you fare?' he questioned, holding out the bottle.

"Impatiently I brushed it aside. 'Now tell me, why have you come?' I demanded.

"'And if my reason does not suit, will you open the door and ask me to step "out?"' he queried with a grin.

"I could not help but laugh at such an idea, but I waited for my answer.

"'Oh, I merely figured that two heads'll be better than one, Dana Gleason,' he answered.

"'And the true reason? Surely had Professor Rollins known of your aspiration, he would not have had to seek me out. Kindly explain!'

"He lifted his eyes to mine. They were hard-looking eyes. 'Less than six days ago I had no thought of this. I was heartily contented with my corner of the world. I did not then, nor do I now, approve of you or anyone else making this hazardous trip. One can die much more easily at home. However, that is neither here nor there. Professor Rollins is a friend of mine, one of the finest men, with one of the finest brains in this world. I admire his courage just as I admire your courage, and it is in the interest of Rollins that I decided at the last moment to accompany you!'

"I was still not satisfied, for I knew that Dorr was not speaking the truth, and I could not be content until I was sure of his real purpose. 'Had Professor Rollins felt that it would take two men to make this trip, we would have recruited another,' I stated.

"He answered in a resigned tone. 'I have told you why, but since you require more . . . let us suppose that you do reach Mars. You are certain to find strange conditions there, perhaps wild beasts, wild men or . . . a dead world of nothing! True, you have considered all that, prepared for it, but you have forgotten one thing in your enthusiasm, Dana Gleason . . . are you able to cope with these adversities? Are you . . . are you . . . ?'

"'Man enough?' I put in.

"'That's just it . . . are you man enough, Dana Gleason?'

"It dawned upon me what Dorr was driving at. Somehow he, like Howard Courtland, had learned the truth. He knew me to be a woman! He nodded as he saw that realization in my eyes. 'Just that. Oh, yes, I know your records

. . . I know all your courageous deeds, your researches, your science, your war experiences, your bravery. Yes, I know all that, but with it all . . . you *are* a woman. You are brave, strong, great-willed, yet you *are* at a disadvantage, and you are attempting a tremendous thing. How stupendous neither of us can guess. So I came, you see, with no ulterior motive. I simply came in the interest of my friend, Professor Rollins . . .'

"I couldn't speak for several moments, and when I did it was in a trembling voice. 'And knowing this . . . you didn't go to the Professor and tell him the truth? He would not have let me go, then . . .'

"'And break his heart? No, I saw that you were really going through with his plans and were the person for it. Henceforth, you may look upon me as your bodyguard!'

"'How heroic,' I said with a curl of my lip.

"'No, rather like a fool, I should say.' I liked his easy manner.

"'Then, you count us both fools?'

"A smile came to his bronzed face. Impulsively I held out my hand and we gave a hearty handclasp. Together we would see our foolishness through.

"The room was quiet but for the hum of the electric motors and our voices. We are in a perfectly sealed chamber, where no sound can penetrate. We hear nothing of the timed explosions that are now taking place according to schedule, shooting us onward across space. I examined the various meters that showed our rate of velocity and our mileage. The oxygen gauge, the water gauge, and the electrical instruments showed everything to be working in proper order."

VIEWING THE VOID

"I was now prepared to visit the lookouts, and invited Dorr to accompany me. We crept down the short passage and faced the windows. At first we could see nothing. We were in an inky blackness, for since there is nothing to reflect the rays of the sun, they travel onward to more distant bodies. Then far off we began to distinguish the things we call stars. Their brilliancy was almost blinding, for here there is nothing to affect their rays. Overhead the Milky Way glistened, and we saw the light of more stars than we had ever seen upon Earth. Directly behind us lay the sun, a great flaming ball that was blinding. A little to the left, appearing as large though not as bright as old Sol, was Mother Earth. Near her hovered the good old moon, now only a darker blot against the dark side of the planet. In several directions, above and below, we could see the brilliant stars. They did not twinkle, but looked clearly back at us.

"After about an hour of this we returned to our quarters and I proceeded to take Dorr on a tour of inspection of our quarters. Then finding we were hungry we sought food. There were enough fresh foods to last perhaps three weeks—if the refrigeration held out. And there was a quantity of perishable foods that would hold without refrigeration for a while. We dined on a young fried broiler that I knew thoughtful little Elsie Rollins had prepared for me. I found a number of jars of jam just as thoughtfully placed there for me. What wonder would be reflected in her brown eyes if she knew that the 'hero' she has been worshipping all these months was of her own sex. Had I been of different stuff I would have confided in her all my hopes and desires, my joys and disappointments, but I am not womanish or mannish enough either to indulge in such a pastime. Never having had a confidant, I should not know how to confide. Only this little book knows me for what I am. How the devotees of the daily papers would revel if they could read this volume! How anxiously they used to seek 'copy' from Dad and me. I only trust that Mars knows nothing of yellow journalism."

So ended that entry. The next was made three days later.

"Seventy-two hours have passed. I can't count by days, for day and night are all one to us. Even in our lookout there is no change in that darkness about us. We eat, sleep, and awake by the clock. Several meteorites passed a few hours ago—great masses falling, ever falling. Do they ever reach 'bottom'? In the lookout I feel as if I were trespassing upon the domain of the One who controls this great illimitable sameness.

"Dick and I share alike in all the chores aboard our 'ship.' We have arranged to take turns at arranging meals, each vying to make his or her meal the most appetizing, and at the same time conserving the fresh foods. Of dishwashing we make a great ado, jealously attempting to prove our individual superiority in the feat. We are both reading the heavy books with which Professor Rollins so thoroughly stocked the cupboards—books that teach us even more about what we are to expect on Mars. When the hour grows late and we are weary, the pillows and coverlets are brought from their places. We lie down after first removing our boots and loosing our belts and collars. We sleep thus fully clothed, for as Dick says, 'One can never tell what pranks the Void might play upon us, and we want at least to be dressed and ready.' Then, smoking our last cigarettes, we toss a coin to see who is to turn out the light. We leave only a small light burning in a shaded reading lamp for an emergency.

"How thankful I am that Richard Dorr elected to join me. How dreary the hours would have been alone. And it is surprising how much fun can be had in our tight quarters. How surprised our friends, with whom we have gained reputations for being staid and serious, would be. Yet it is through the means of play that we forget the vastness outside and the meagerness of our chance to live!

"Our instruments show that we are now traveling at the rate of fifty thousand miles per hour! We are already seven million and two hundred thousand miles from Earth. In another twenty-four hours we shall be traveling several thousand miles faster, for as each magazine of powder is shot and its gas ejected we gain velocity. Sitting down with a paper and pencil I calculated that we should average sixty thousand miles per hour throughout the entire trip of thirty-four million miles, which is the present distance of Mars from Earth. It will, therefore, take us exactly twenty-three days thirteen hours and a fraction to reach the red planet. Professor Rollins had computed that it would take us at least thirty-five days, but of course he was not able to judge just how swiftly the rocket could travel!"

The next entry was made ten days later.

————

"In approximately nine days more we shall land upon Mars, if we do land. Never have we allowed ourselves to forget that word 'if.' These days have been pleasant in the company of Richard Dorr. He has proven himself a perfect companion. He is a well-versed man with a fine working knowledge of people. His love for his work helping the natives of Africa was sincere. What a pity that it is all over and that such a man is lost to Earth. I, who have led such a worthless indolent life, seeking only my own pleasure, pitting my own strength and mind against that of man, proving to myself that nothing is impossible to me, am a poor sort of a person beside this man, who has always given himself in behalf of his fellow men. I see now that I have shirked my duty as a woman in the guise of a hater of that sex. And what crude stuff I am made of compared to this man who gave up his life work in the interest of a friend.

"One has much time out here in the Void to think of the past. God! Are we to live? Shall we ever see grass and trees again? Shall we ever see sun on the water? Shall we ever know the glory of a storm again? Shall I be allowed to begin a new life? I can only feel the appalling minuteness of man who tries to place himself on the level of a God who can create this bigness. How scornful He must be of us! Have I been right in hating my mother as my father taught me to do? Is it not possible that he was at fault also? Are they somewhere watching?

"Now we see due ahead the red eye of Mars. In size he has become as large as the sun appears to us from Earth and glows with a copperish light that is strange and awesome out here in the blackness. Hourly Earth has dwindled, a dark brownish globe (we see only its dark side) with its one moon. Beyond lies the sun, red and fiery, with never a setting. Far below and above, all about us are the lights of distant constellations, some appearing blue to us, others green, and so for all the colors of the spectrum. One star glows with a beautiful violet light! How strange it must be to have a green sun lighting one's world! We passed a number of meteorites today, and we feared that one particularly large one would surely hit us. We passed by ere it reached our path.

"What God, what Mind could have conceived this terrible greatness? Is He laughing at us here in our tiny atom traversing this God-place? Does He pity us in our fall? Does He look with wonder and amazement at His creatures that so boldly dare? Or did He plan this, eons ago, and is He merely watching intently now as we go our fated way?

"Dick and I were discussing this, but he knows no answer. His belief in a God, a true God who sees the sparrow fall, cannot be shaken, and I, who have been taught to laugh at men's belief in God-things, am shaken. Can one look on these vastnesses, these great worlds, and doubt?

"We are now traveling much faster than I ever believed possible. At every well-timed explosion we gain velocity, and with each discharge of the magazine and the lightening of ton after ton, the rocket shoots ahead—like a hound from hell (Dick said that). At this rate we shall reach Mars earlier than my schedule. Even as I write the red planet comes closer. It lies above us, or so it seems, but I am sure we head directly for it."

————

Twenty-four hours later:

"Earth is behind while before us Mars looms hugely. Its strange spots and markings are very clearly defined. The lines that are believed to be canals pass black and wide across its face. We wait breathlessly as we draw near, leaving the lookout chambers only long enough to eat. Today we ate the last piece of meat, rashers of bacon."

————

Sixty hours later:

"God has answered! We are passing Mars! For many breathless hours we were uncertain, but now Mars lies not in our path, but away thousands of miles to our left. I cannot think. I cannot talk. Only by putting down these little black words can I remain calm. Dick has nothing to say. He sits with me here before the window smoking his pipe. This is the end. We have shot our bow and failed. Could there still be a possibility that Mars will reach out and draw us into his orbit? Therein lies our hope. Still, he is senile; his strength has left him.

"For hours we watched Mars draw closer until we thought we saw grass and trees. We put everything in readiness. One pull of the lever and the gauge that controls the powder charges would have closed. Proudly we would have swung in line with the great planet. We inspected everything; saw that nothing was forgotten from rifles to pickaxes. I gathered together all my data, the blue prints for the giant radio set and for the loading of our rocket. We stuffed our pockets with chocolate and cigarettes. But Mars disdains us. There is no welcoming pull of gravity; the instruments show no change. Is there still a chance that we might land on Mars? Perhaps a slim bare chance.

——

Two days later:

"It is true we have completely passed Mars. He lies there slowly swinging in space. How long we can travel we do not know, perhaps a year, or even two. It will be all the same, ever falling, falling. We will be caught like rats in a trap. There was but one chance in a thousand, a million, and that chance failed us. Yet there remains one last hope. Another planet may accept us. But what will be our fate?

"Jupiter? He is yet too young. Saturn is older, but could he sustain us? Neptune? He is so poorly warmed by the sun. And there is distant Uranus. Beyond that, what?

"Still, why should I complain? Did I, in losing a world, not gain something else, something more precious? Who could have said that Dana Gleason should be happy in discovering her womanhood? Oh, the irony of it! On Earth I was not ready to recognize the chance. Now . . ."

AN AWAKENING

"When we knew at last that Mars was not for us, that the hoary old fellow was laughing at us, something seemed to break within me. I experienced a dizziness, a faintness, a blackness, and a desire to cry. I, Dana Gleason! I reeled and would have fallen if Dick, dear Dick, had not caught me and carried me back to our living quarters and laid me gently on the couch. For what seemed hours he cradled me in his arms. Was ever a man kinder, gentler? And then . . . he kissed me, Dana Gleason, who had never been kissed!

"'Dana,' he was whispering, 'we have lost, it is true, but did we not undertake to leave Earth behind? A little less time to live, but a longer time to learn the meaning of eternity. You have been brave, wonderfully brave. Is this the time to forget your courage?' He said more and more that I scarcely heard. Something new was creeping into me, a strange warmness that I had never known. What was it? Was it this newly realized womanhood that was grasping me?

"A new life was flowing into my body. 'Dana, Dana,' he whispered, as if anyone else could hear, 'how I love you. I loved you before I knew you were a woman, and I have adored you more each day. True, I have suffered every day that I was so near you and could not tell you. Always I forced myself to act the role of a friend. I did not dream that it would come this way . . . I thought that on this other world we should find love together, in the need for each other, work together, live for each other. Instead, God is giving us death . . .'

"Tears stood in his eyes, and now it was I who must give comfort. Was there not at least a year? Our provisions safely guarded would last even longer. At least we had each other. Each other, how sweet that sounds. For hours we did not move, scarcely talking, sitting there, delighting in each other. We fell asleep there with arms intertwined, and the majesty of Mars passed us by.

"Dick was the first to awaken, and I opened to the sound of his whistle from the bathroom as he bathed and shaved. I had heard him do the same thing every morning aboard the rocket, but this morning it all sounded so different. It made me indescribably happy. Then he came forth, fresh and glowing, and took me in his arms again.

"As I performed my ablutions I heard him in the kitchen with the coffee percolator, and I hurried to help him prepare breakfast. There were two oranges left and some eggs in a wax jacket. We made bread from our supplies, and for the rest we were now eating chemically compounded pellets that are as nourishing as meats, vegetables, and fruits, except that they do not satisfy the taste. There is still a whole case of chocolates and the wherewithal to make other sweets when that supply gives out.

"Never have I eaten a happier meal than that breakfast. It was as if I had never eaten before, and there would be at least 365 more of such breakfasts. Beyond that we do not try to think. We have begun to live, why think of dying? Imagine happiness aboard a rocket traveling farther and farther into the space where time is an unreckoned quantity, and age is ageless. Was there ever a like honeymoon?

"We climbed again to the lookout. There was Mars, immense, serene, and out of our reach. We turned away with little concern. I hate to think of what might have been had not Dick climbed into the rocket at the very last moment. We laugh to think that I tried to put him out.

"'I'll admit that I lied to you in saying I came in the interests of Professor Rollins. No man could be that great. I feared I would lose you irrevocably if I told you the truth.'

"'I can't imagine how you learned that I was a woman. I was so careful. Dad taught me that, even to lathering my face each morning and running a bladeless razor over my face!'

"How he laughed at that. 'Well, do you recall the little pool set in a circlet of trees about four miles from the bungalow where you so often went for a swim? Incidentally, that was a favorite nook of mine. You startled me one day from a reverie when you came, thinking there was no one within several miles of you. Before I could announce myself you had undressed and were swimming in the pool. I crept away without your knowing I was there at all!'

"'I was astonished, but then I felt I had always known. I could not guess why you were masquerading this way. Of course, I knew your reputation and knew that you had always lived as a boy. At first I thought you were intentionally duping the Professor for some ulterior motive, or perhaps in the interest of others. I hated you then, and I dreaded the moment you would disclose the truth to him. Then when I knew that you really were going through with this I was at my wits' end. I could not break the Professor's heart by telling him, nor could I let you go alone. So, in part, I was truthful in saying that it was for Rollins's interest. That is all, Dana . . .'"

BREAKING THE SPEED LAWS!

"Many, many hours, days, and nights, as we figure time on Earth, have passed and faster and faster we are making our way across the Void. We have passed Jupiter and his bright glow is intense. Far ahead and thousands upon thousands of miles to the right we can see Saturn with his numerous satellites and rings. Old Sol grows more distant, less brilliant. The blackness appears blacker. Yet we care naught for any of this. Science has succumbed to Love and we, mites in a cheese box, are living hour for hour, a whole lifetime to be lived in a day!

"We do not count time. Everything now is in the present. We do not rewind the clock. It is too cruel a reminder. We eat, sleep and live only according to desire."

Later:

"We have passed the distant planet Uranus. Our Universe lies behind. Before us stretches the inconceivable waste that lies between the solar system and its nearest neighbor millions upon millions of miles away. It is black, inconceivably black. There is only a glow of the great world across this sea of nothingness, and of worlds and universes that are more immense than that which we leave behind. Looking at the meters for the first time in many days, we discover that we are now traveling at an incredible rate of speed, nearly as fast now as light itself. And science tells us that it takes many years for light to travel from the nearest stars! And we have only a year to live!"

Later:

"We are wrong! Life is not for us. The God of the Immensity has declared himself. After realizing that we were out of the universe we did not return to the lookout for over twenty-four hours. We found then that the glass was becoming smoky, so smoky that we could not even see the stars. That can mean only one thing. The smooth shell of our rocket is burning. Friction in a vacuum! It seems impossible, but what else could it be? Friction is wearing away the steel of our smooth coat. How long ere it will burn through? Can the shell of our sealed living chambers withstand that? No, we are not even to have the sanctuary of a coffin. We are to be belched out into space to fall forever with sightless eyes before the awful grandeur. God is revengeful!

"After our discovery Dick and I sat staring at each other with hands interclasped for long hours. 'It is the end,' we whispered together. 'How happy we have been!'

"'How long can we last?'

"'Only God knows that.'

"'Must we wait?' I hated to picture what the end would be. 'Can't we go together with arms around each other?'

"What to do?

"In answer I pulled out the small automatic that I had carried with me since childhood. I saw the glow come into Dick's blue eyes. He caught me by the shoulders and looked into my eyes. 'You are brave, Dana Gleason.'

"'Only a coward,' I answered. 'We will wait until we see that all is lost. A few hours still remain to us.'"

Elsie Rollins looked up from the diary. "That is all, the book ends here." She turned to the last page of the book and sat staring at it lying in her hands.

LANDING ON ABRUI

The Professor had been drinking in every word. "And, what happened? It must have taken a miracle to save them!"

Our host, who had been listening with half-closed eyes, looked up. "What happened, the two lovers could not guess, trapped as they were in the rocket. It was a miracle that saved them. For beyond Uranus there lies Abrui, a small planet that has never been discovered by Earthly astronomers and follows somewhat the path taken by Uranus. It was this planet that reached out and drew the rocket into its orbit.

"They thought that space had set their vehicle on fire, but nothing burns out there. In truth they were circling our planet. Their belief that they were traveling as fast as light was probably incorrect. The meters lied; due perhaps to the attraction of the planet, their velocity had decreased rather than increased.

"Abrui's gravity was slowly drawing the rocket within a narrowing circle until men of the planet saw it in their sky. Every hour brought it closer, and the whole world stared in wonder. Astronomers watched and surmised. Heretofore, meteorites had fallen without number on our globe, but never had a meteor acted in such a fashion. By day it shimmered and at night it glowed, for it had, of course, become red hot as soon as it entered our atmosphere, driving at such high speed.

"Lower and lower it came, and then it was evident that in another day it would fall. It was Moura-weit who was the first to realize that this was no stray skyrocket, but in truth a manmade thing, born of some other world. The conjectures were many. However, it was Moura-weit and Ubca-tor, his companion, who followed the course of the rocket in their flyer, to arrive at its landing. Moura-weit was the only one who conceived the thought that men were riding in that red-hot thing.

"So these two men came to see the landing. Fate steered toward a wild section of the globe, an arid, infertile place inhabited only by barbarians. It fell with a horrible cacophony of sound, exploding in midair and burying half its length in the unprofitable soil of the plain.

"Moura-weit had wisely kept his plane at a good distance from the rocket, and he and Ubca-tor exclaimed at the beauty and horror of that tremendous fall. They saw debris flying off in every direction; for after the first explosion there came another and another until like a giant firecracker it was popping and cracking wildly. It was Ubca who saw the thing that looked like a body, limp and lifeless, coming toward them.

"In the great fall of the rocket both of them marveled at the majesty of the breaking up. It could be seen that in falling every piece of debris settled slowly, the larger pieces dropping more rapidly, the smaller following with more deliberation, as a stone that is thrown in a pool of thick mud slowly sinks out of sight, the thick liquid buoying it up until by its own weight it sinks. Abrui being somewhat smaller than Earth has not as great a power of gravity, and consequently the Earth-things were of less weight.

"And since the body of Dana Gleason was lighter in comparison to those great pieces of steel, her fall was even slower and more gentle. She fell to the ground like a bit of fluff, scarcely sustaining a jar.

"As soon as the two men descried the human body they were after it and Ubca jumped from the flyer before it touched the ground. Carefully he lifted the lifeless body and returned with it to his companion. Sharply the plane arose, for there was still falling debris; the explosions of the twisted racked structure had not ceased.

"They laid the body on a couch in the enclosed cabin and Ubca took control of the flyer so that Moura, who was acquainted with the art of medicine, might examine her to see if life still remained. He felt the faint beat of the heart, and taking a phial from his pocket, forced a drop of its contents between her lips. That action was greeted with convulsions at first, then the patient commenced to take deep breaths, and from the moaning it was apparent that she suffered at every gasp. Moura had already discovered that the rocket's passenger was a woman.

"From her lips there came a sound. 'Dick!' the lips formed. Immediately Moura-weit turned to his companion. 'Quick, circle about. There was a second passenger!'

"By this time the air was practically clear of falling debris, except for a few lighter objects that sank slowly to the ground circling and twirling. The great mass of iron and steel lay on the ground glowing and smoking. Ubca directed the plane close to the ground. He was suddenly aware of shapes taking form some hundred yards away. They were the barbarians that had been encamped not far away. Recovering from their fright they were now slowly approaching the ruin to puzzle out what had fallen. Ubca saw a second body lying on the ground. The nearest barbarian was five or six hundred yards away. The plane touched the ground while Moura took control. Kneeling beside the unconscious man, Ubca turned him over. In the red glare from the wreck he saw the face and with an exclamation of disgust he rose to his feet and scurried back.

"'It's naught but a Goran,'* he declared.

"Circling about another few minutes they could discover nothing else. By this time the barbarians were coming in full force. Their eyes turned to the flyer and their weapons were unslung. They found the man Ubca had disdained.

"Moura-weit was confident now that if there was another passenger in the rocket with the woman, he had died in the flames. He did not know that Ubca had mistaken the reddish hair and tanned skin of Richard Dorr for one of the barbarians, whose skin is likewise bronze. Turning the plane about, they headed for Carajama, the capital of their own country.

"So came Dana Gleason and Richard Dorr to Abrui, my friends." Our host smiled down upon us. During this narration he had been pacing back and forth before us.

* *The race of Gora, considered barbarians, whose skin and hair are bronze-like.*

"Surely, you are going to tell us more?" demanded the Professor.

"It grows late, sir. Already the sky is becoming light!" he protested.

"What does that matter? I insist that you tell us all."

THE STORY OF SA DAK

The other shrugged his shoulders. "It will delay our departure, but since you wish it, sir . . . First, however, I should suggest a swim in the pool to refresh us, and a bit to eat and drink."

Rollins said he did not swim, but the bath would be welcome. Miss Rollins was delighted. I was declared unfit for swimming because of my shoulder, yet I would be allowed to take a dip. The golden slave appeared without a summons and escorted us to the various bedrooms. Swimming suits were brought. These consisted of one-piece affairs of a strange white material that was silky to the touch and as heavy as jersey. The trunks reached halfway down the thigh, and the neck and armholes were cut low. The slave aided me in undressing, and insisted upon rubbing my shoulder again with his salve.

Neither the thin frame of the Professor, nor my own, already inclined to corpulency, cut a very fine figure, but the sight of the two silver men held the eye. Never have I seen two finer-looking men, both over six feet tall and with the smooth, flowing muscles of highly developed bodies. Both wore no more than short trunks. Miss Rollins looked pretty in her suit.

Rollins and I descended into the pool by way of a flight of steps, but the other three dived off the side of the pool into the deep water. They had a race. The stroke used by the silver men was strange. It mostly resembled the breaststroke, except that it was more "frog fashion," both propelled the body through the water by jerks, hands and feet moving in unison in one great effort, and each stroke carried the men almost twice their length through the water. Naturally enough, Miss Rollins, with her pretty sidestroke, was left a considerable distance behind.

They joined us, and as the two men stood beside us I saw that the water ran from their broad chests and shoulders without seeming to wet them. "That," said Sa Dak reading my thought, "is due to the oil with which we polish our bodies. It is a matter of pride to keep our bodies highly polished. The bronze man who neglects this vanity is not a pretty fellow with his dull ochre body. We have a saying that 'a well-oiled body gives evidence of a well-ordered mind.' And the poorest of men oils his body."

Our bath finished, we returned to the dressing rooms and were given great towels that were very absorbent. I noted how well I felt, how my body glowed, and how the spirit of well-being pervaded me. Later, we were informed that a small quantity of a solution of radium in the water produced these effects.

My shoulder seemed completely healed, so that I was never to feel more discomfort from it.

In the atol we found food awaiting us on small tables set beside our couches. There was a fresh fruit that had the taste of both apple and peach and looked like a melon, some sort of cooked meal, and a hot beverage that had the taste of many flowers. After eating, we settled ourselves on our couches once more to hear what remained to be told of the story of Dana Gleason and Richard Dorr.

"I am telling this in the third person," began our host, "to avoid any unnecessary personal references, and for easier sequence. Perhaps first I had better explain a little about the planet, its peoples, its geography, its history."

THE NARRATIVE

On Abrui there are three races. The Tabora, who hold in their grasp the single ocean of the planet, and esteem themselves the only civilized people of the planet, though once they were barbarians occupying the "backlands" into which they drove the Gora, the simple-minded. From the Moata, a more ancient race than themselves, they got their culture, their science and their social codes, subjugating these people to their will and enslaving them.

The Tabora is the silver man of Abrui, a fine upstanding man, taller in stature than men of the other races, with well-formed features and a quick, ready, clear-thinking mind. The Moata are golden, smaller than their masters, weaker, and with fear bred in their minds. The Gora is the barbarian, made so by circumstances. He is bronze-colored, bronze-skinned, bronze-haired, and brown-eyed. He is not quite so tall as the Tabora, but he has a stockier, more powerful body; is fearless, though superstitious; and his imagination peoples his country with hobgoblins and god-things. He has little science, since all his days are spent in forcing his barren plains and swamps and deserts to yield him a livelihood.

Moura-weit and Ubca-tor were of the Tabora. They were Doatans, and Doata is the most powerful of the three nations of Tabora. Of Tabora there are three countries, Doata, Zoada, and Loata, all bordering on the one ocean, Sehti. Sehti covers a little more than a third of the planet. Rich, fertile plains border the sea, and beyond the plains are the great mountains, Hopli, which almost entirely encircle the ocean and are the backbone of Tabora, separating one fertile plain from another. Deserts, swamps, wide rivers, all help to separate Gora from Tabora. Tabora has thousands of cities on the broad plains, in the rolling tablelands and foothills, and in the mountains themselves, which are not overly high but are great irregular chains.

In the ocean, Sehti, lies Ora, a large island, with a few smaller ones near it. Ora is the seat of all learning; it existed in the day of the Moata. Here any man or woman is welcome to study, to forward science, to teach. Ora belongs to no nation, having a government of its own. It is a place of refuge for the exile, the outcast. Once within its bounds, the malefactor is safe and can in no way be extradited.

To the south of the ocean lies Zoada, extending over a thousand miles from east to west and several thousand miles to the low-lying swamps that separate her from Gora. Beyond her boundaries is the ice cap of the southern magnetic pole. To the west of her lies Loata. Loata's west coast fronts all of the eastern shore of the ocean, and extends over a great part of the northern coast besides.

One might wonder how Abrui, which lies so far from the sun as to have a solar year of 365 Earthly years, can be inhabited. The answer is simple; for, whereas all her sister planets depend solely upon the common sun for their heat and light, Abrui is fortunate enough to have a sun of her own. Dana Gleason is certain that on Earth astronomers have never conceived the possibility of a planet possessing a sun of its own in the same manner as Abrui possesses one, although the phenomena of twin suns encircling each other, as well as triple suns, have been observed. Taboran astronomers have observed many planets with satellite suns exactly like Abrui's companion.

Still the satellite sun is no rival of Sol, so called by Earth people, but named Coe by Abruians. Tradr, the second sun, gives off a warm, rosy pink glow; unlike Sol it does not send out sharp rays but shines more like the glow from a lamp, so that it is possible to look directly at the satellite without discomfort. It is believed that once Tradr was nothing more than a moon shining only by reflected light. Then the planet must have been cold, unable to foster life in the poor warmth from the distant sun. However, something warmed the moon's core so that its center seethed as a furnace, and gradually the heat penetrated the whole shell, turning its solids into gases. Many theories have been brought forth from Ora concerning the reason of this strange occurrence of a sphere, once dead, coming to life. The most prevalent and the most generally believed theory is that on Tradr is a vast quantity of the element radium. They understand the power of this element, and it is certain that its presence accounts for the "catching afire" of the satellite.

Tradr, therefore, controls the day of Abrui, and it encircles the entire globe in a little less than thirty hours while the planet, which turns slowly on its axis, has a solar day of almost one hundred hours. Sol, therefore, is like unto a moon to Abrui in the nights when it still lingers in the heavens while the planet depends entirely upon its satellites for both heat and light.

Tradr never alters its course; it gives an even heat, day after day, with no change of climate year in and year out, a pleasant warmth and, except at the southern pole, extreme cold is unknown. It is toward the northern pole that Sol directs his rays, and the warmth is enough to keep that part of the globe from freezing.

The planetary year is naturally reckoned according to the phases of the satellite sun, counting ten phases to a year. A phase is of twenty-two days, while the length of each day is thirty hours.

A VISITOR FROM THE VOID

It was night when the Earth rocket dropped into the unfruitful land of the Gora. Sol had been hidden for many hours behind clouds, but now he was drawing himself out of the blanket. In size he looked not as large as an orange, and the light that came from him was silvery. All about him were myriads of stars that tried to rival his splendor, great brilliant stars that twinkled and winked and refused to be extinguished in the light that Sol shed about him.

Moura-weit and Ubca-tor had no time for the light of the sun. They were busy with their patient, trying to bring her to consciousness; yet she seemed to be fighting them. This bothered the two men. "She is seeking for the other one who accompanied her on her journey," observed Moura. "Were it not for those ropts (rodent-like creatures)* we could search for the remains of the other traveler; for, no doubt, he was caught within that debris. Were the Gors to find him they would only kill him, thinking him a demon or whatnot. Well, at least we have this one."

Ubca said nothing, his eyes fastened on the strange being in her queer clothing. He had come on this adventure because Moura-weit had so directed. He was no more than a boy, who had taken Moura-weit as his hero and who followed blindly wherever the other might lead. He was a younger son of the brother of Kirada Walti (king of Doata), as the suffix *tor* added to his name implied. And as Moura was merely of the Weitas, the lowest rank of Taboran nobility, it was surprising to find the boy in his train. However, Moura-weit was not a common man. He was ambitious.

Already it was whispered that Moura-weit had attained enviable power behind the throne of Doata. He was beloved of the masses for it, and hated by his superiors—the nobility. Abrui is not unlike Earth. It has its kings to rule, its common people to rave and rant and dictate, its slaves to suffer. And Moura-weit's ambition was to be a dictator not only to Doata but also to Zoada and Loata.

* *Gorans.*

Moura-weit's social rank can be compared to that of the English baronet. People declared that this Moura was not born of woman as are all men but of the Unkonatas, a group of scientists, who years before taught that the foundation of life was not flesh but mind. It was said that they had produced a child by means of thought with the aid of a woman. Their next step was to bring forth a child without women's help. The Wukonuals, a second group that were materialists, preached against the Unkonatas, calling them traitors to the state. Consequently the sect was sought out, many were killed and the rest dispersed. What happened to the child, if there was a child, was not known; but the masses liked to believe that the Unkonatas, on dying, had bequeathed to the child their brains, so that the child, should he grow to manhood, would possess their collective consciousness entire. And it was said that Moura-weit was that child!

Moura-weit liked to foster that thought. True, he had a great mind; none could best him in any line of endeavor. His oratory, his science, abstract and concrete thought, his knowledge of diverse things, his understanding of all that went on in the world marked him as a man apart. Nothing that he set himself to do was left undone, either in art, mechanics, science, or athletics. And it was always he who did it best.

————

On Abrui man has learned more about the brain than he has on Earth. He has solved the secret of thought transference from mind to mind. And in a world that finds it a common thing to know another's thought, Moura-weit surpassed them all. He not only read his fellow man's thoughts, his secrets, his desires, he followed the train of thought of the thinker and knew what his next move would be ere that man himself knew it. And no man could close his mind to his penetrating gaze. He could know what a man separated from him by a wall was thinking. Consequently, he was feared by those who hated him and while many would willingly have done away with this man of power, they dreaded his prying brain, knowing that Moura-weit would forestall any attempt made on his life.

And it was this man alone who knew that there was a living person in the rocket that came swimming into the atmospheric belt of Abrui. So it was he who was thereafter to have Dana Gleason in his keeping.

His attention was now focused on the woman. Her breath was still coming in gasps, due to a slight difference in the atmosphere of this planet from that of her own. Soon, however, her breathing became easier as her lungs adjusted themselves to the change. Moura-weit studied her strange covering, her coloring, her appearance, her strange mind.

Dana Gleason knew nothing of mental telepathy, though she had heard its theory expounded on Earth; she knew nothing of closing her brain, even had she been conscious of the fact that Moura-weit was searching out its nooks and corners. She was at that moment living over again all that had passed in the last two months. Many nightmarish dreams swept across and clouded out the actual memories from time to time, but the man knew how to differentiate between the two.

Recurring time and time again, he saw the figure of a man, a figure that at first had puzzled Moura, for the complexion of the figure seemed to Moura to be that of a bronze Gora. Then, as the figure became clearer to him, he realized that the tall, handsome man was not an inhabitant of Abrui, that he had neither the squatness of the Gora nor the broad face and features of the barbarians; his eyes, too, were the color of the sky, while Goran eyes were brown.

Covertly Moura flashed a look at Ubca. Had he seen anything of this? Did he read Moura-weit's mind? But no, his eyes were on the quiet figure on the couch, his thoughts were elsewhere. So Moura kept his own counsel. He might then have told Ubca that the man he had found and thought to be a Gora was in truth the companion traveler of Dana Gleason, but he said nothing of that. Had he told him, the train of events might have turned out differently.

Moura-weit had not as yet shaped his plans. He realized that he had indeed a find. Doata and Ora would do him honor when he brought the news of this voyage from Out of the Void. Science would be forwarded. And Moura would prosper.

Ubca-tor broke the line of his thoughts. "What planet could this creature have come from, Moura? They must have progressed far, to be able to send a vehicle through space. And to send a woman!"

"Yes, the planet must be far advanced. Yet it must be one of the four planets upon which our observatories have discovered life, one of the four planets that lie close to the Great Sun. The other four we know to be either too hot or too cold to sustain life. It was a long journey to make! And it is indeed lucky that we discovered this woman in time. If she had a companion, as I believe she had, he must surely have perished in the flames of the exploding machine. But it will be a great day for Ora when we take her thither!"

"Surely you will take her to Doata first?" said the boy.

"Naturally to Carajama first! Are we not Doatans?"

Moura had really been wondering which would be the best course—to take the woman first to Doata or to Ora. He knew that by presenting her to the Orans he would gain favor with the people of Zoada and Loata, who would appreciate the fact that he had not first given Doata the honor of greeting the space traveler. On the other hand, the advantage it would give him in Doata was to be considered. Yes, it would be better so. Zoada and Loata must wait.

The woman had not as yet regained consciousness. Moura continued to minister to her from time to time, and was rewarded to find that the heartbeat was becoming stronger. A glow was coming into the waxen skin; her lips, which seemed to have been drained of blood, were red now. They had only to wait until the brain was ready to resume the burden of consciousness once more. Slowly she opened her eyes and glanced about, breathing the name "Dick" once; then she slipped back into her unconscious state.

Moura was again looking into her mind. "Ah," he suddenly exclaimed, "she lives again on her own planet: I see a city, a ship, airplanes, a battle, strange engines. I see men, men very unlike us on Abrui. Ah, I see, I think, the machine by which they shot their rocket into space." Ubca sat staring uncomfortably at Moura. It is one thing to read the mind of the man to whom you are talking, but another thing to peer into the sleeping brain of an unconscious being from another world.

"She awakes!"

The voices had disturbed Dana Gleason, for suddenly she opened her eyes and was staring around the cabin wildly. "Dick, Dick, where are you? Why do you not come?"

Then, as her eyes focused upon Moura-weit's strange face and stranger eyes, a cry of surprise escaped her. "My God, where am I?" she asked. "Who are you, and what have you done with Richard Dorr? Oh God—the heat, the explosion, the fall . . ." Then she covered her face with her hands.

The Taborans could not understand her words, but they could read her agitation and understand her emotions. They knew hysteria, and Moura was not anxious to have a hysterical woman on his hands. He did not know that Dana Gleason was not given to hysteria. Had he the words, he could have spoken and reassured her; but not having these, he sat quietly by, and a force transferred itself from his mind to that of the woman. A calm came over her.

When she looked up again, she was rational. She wondered at this feeling that had crept through her. She knew that all was well. For the first time she saw the strange appearance of things about her. She saw she was no longer in the living quarters of the rocket. She was now in another room. Through the sensation of a gentle vibration she knew that she was in a machine that was moving. She saw that she was surrounded by a glass wall, and that below lay the darkness of a sleeping country. She saw that she had been made comfortable on a couch, and that she was being cared for by these two men of such strange appearance. She looked down upon her own person and saw where the khaki of her trousers and shirt had been scorched, where a sleeve had been torn, a boot partly burned. She looked more closely at the man seated opposite her on a low stool. She had a knowledge of men, and in this one she saw a leader.

Moura-weit, whose power of telepathy surpassed that of any of his fellow men, now had the opportunity to attempt a thing that neither he nor any other had tried before. Could he project his own thought-images into the mind of a being of another world? Could it be done at all? He knew already that the brain of this woman differed somewhat from those brains of his own race. The two main lobes were of different shape and thickness, and their convolutions took a different form.

Leaning forward, he reached for her hands, and by magnetism of his eyes forced her to look into his own. She did not remonstrate; caught by his stare, she looked back. Moura then attempted to fill her mind with his thought-images. He began with something she was familiar with, the rocket.

Dana Gleason knew no emotion when the silver man took her hands in his. She did recognize that some bond existed between them; for even in her wild dreams her subconscious mind had been aware of his searching eyes. She was without thought, unable to think, as if her mind had been literally washed clean. Then her thoughts became clouded. She began to recognize that this cloud was night with stars twinkling.

For a time she tried to fight against the cloud, but it was mastering her. When she at last gave in to it, she became aware of a darker spot in the cloud. Gradually the night passed, and she saw the dark spot taking shape. It was long and cylindrical, and it was black and ugly and fiery. It was smoking, it was burning. Now below the rocket appeared a landscape, an inhabitable land bathed in a reddish light. Three times night descended upon the rocket, and on the third night it was evident that the rocket was about to fall on the ground. She saw it fall; she saw its fiery course, the explosions, the flying debris, her own fall!

She saw Ubca-tor pick her up and carry her to the flyer. She saw the plane circling the wreck, searching; and she knew they were searching for another body. None was found! It showed her the heart of the burning rocket, flames leaping up fifty feet. Now she saw the approach of the Gora, and recognized them for barbarians. Then the retreat of the plane. With that the vision vanished. Moura dropped his hands, freed her eyes.

For several minutes she did not move. Her eyes said nothing. She was remembering the last minute on the rocket before that awful explosion that had torn her from Richard Dorr's arms. "We can at least die together," said Dick. "He can't take that away from us!" Only He had taken Dick's life and given her hers. Dick dead! Impossible. Something, a feeling, a voice, was telling her that he lived. Still, no man could live in that conflagration she had just seen. Had she really seen all that happened? Was it all? Could not Dick have been thrown out just as she had been? Those brown men, the barbarians—perhaps they found Dick? If only it were so.

She could not cry, tears would not come. A cold lump lay where her heart had been. She now remembered that this strange man with his stranger eyes had come into her mind and pictured to her all that had gone before. What manner of man was this? Where was she, then? When she and Dick thought they were about to die, they had already reached another planet that was waiting for them. If only they had known, and could have landed in their waiting plane.

That was over, however, all over. Happiness, it seemed, was not for her. What was there for her? Existence on a strange planet, a new life, new interests? What new interests could she have? Oh, she wanted to cry, to turn her face to a blank wall. And since she could not cry, since she could change nothing, there could be naught for her to do but to accept things as they came. She sighed deeply, then turned her interest again on the two men and the chamber in which she lay.

She saw that the walls of the cabin were of glass, and above her she could hear the beat of wings. A few yards from her was set an instrument board on which were a series of levers, dials, and strange instruments. A carpet covered the floor, and there were several low easy chairs and the couch upon which she was lying. Through the glass she could see the black shapes of mountains below and an occasional light shone out. Above was a moon, a moon that sent out rays of weak light. Myriad stars glowed brilliantly.

She turned now to Moura-weit. Her eyes asked a question, and, understanding, the man formed the word "Abrui." She repeated the word, and in turn pointed to herself and thence out into the dark sky. She pronounced the world "Earth."

She realized the necessity of learning the language of the people among whom she had descended. Pointing to herself again, she next said, "Dana Gleason." Moura said the name after her and, pointing to himself and then to Ubca, gave their respective names. The next half hour was spent in pointing to objects about them and calling them by name. Dana repeated each word. Taking a small notebook from a pocket, she jotted down each word, spelling it as it sounded to her ears. The little book and pencil interested Moura, and he asked to examine them. Taborans write on sheets of thin metal, and in writing use a brush and a thick paint. They have no printing presses. From the original hand-painted copy subsequent copies are photographed.

Feeling in her pockets, she now discovered that she had about a half-dozen packages of cigarettes left, also several cakes of chocolate. She offered a cake of the latter to the two men, and they enjoyed the taste. Next she extracted a cigarette, found that her patent cigarette lighter still contained some fuel, and lighted it. She extended the package of cigarettes to Moura and Ubca. They each took one.

At the flash of the lighter, both men drew back. They exclaimed aloud when they saw the woman put fire to her cigarette and breathe the smoke from her mouth, for on Abrui there is no fire! However, that statement is somewhat misleading; for instantaneous combustion is known and understood, and Taborans are familiar with the fact that the great bright stars are flaming; they themselves, however, have no use for fire. In a world that has radium for fuel, heat and light, it is unnecessary to produce fire for man's use.

Therefore it is easy to picture the wonder of the Taborans, to whom fire is merely an accident, at seeing Dana Gleason deliberately set fire to her little paper tube and breathe in the smoke. Their wonder was greater even than that of the first European who saw American Indians smoking their pipes.

Rather gingerly Moura accepted the lighter. Dana showed him how to light it, and he was careful that the flame did not reach him, for Abruians know how painful fire can be, even though they work with an element that can burn and hurt far more severely. He managed to light the cigarette, but one mouthful of smoke was enough, and the woman could only laugh at the ludicrous face he made. Ubca made no attempt to light his cigarette but returned it to the Earthling.

She smoked her cigarette with rare enjoyment, but seeing that the smoke of it distressed the two men, she quickly extinguished it. Moura had taken his cigarette apart, and he saw that it was made of some sort of dried leaf. He slipped it into the small pouch he carried hanging from his girdle. Later he would analyze it and see what it was. He was glad for the little incident, for he saw that the laugh had done the woman good, making her forget for the moment her past experiences and bringing color to her cheeks.

Ubca arose and went to a small cupboard, whence he brought out some pellets of highly condensed foodstuffs containing all the ingredients necessary to the body. A traveler always carries these instead of being bothered with more bulky supplies.

Dana's attention was now caught and held by something outside the plane. To the right of them she had suddenly become aware of a change taking place in the landscape. From beyond the irregular shapes of the mountains a grayness was pervading the sky. As she watched the grayness it turned to a watery pink, then to red. And over the edge of the mountains Tradr, the satellite sun, began to rise. At first a joy came into her being. The sun! The one familiar object that spelled "home" to her. She had left Earth without qualms, joyously, as a traveler leaves familiar scenes with the prospect of viewing new ones. And like the same traveler, she was knowing homesickness for those same homely familiar things.

Yet, as the sun rose higher, she became puzzled. Sol had never appeared so large and so brilliantly red from Earth! Then he turned a lavenderish pink. What had happened to him? Here she was many millions of miles more distant. It couldn't be possible that he . . . No that was not Sol. She stared in wonder, almost in fear. Her eyes sought Moura's.

He knew what was passing through her mind. Pointing, he showed her Sol high in the sky; it was the sun she had mistaken for a moon. Then she understood, and her wonder grew greater as she stared at the strange sun at which she could gaze directly without blinking.

They were now on the edge of the pretty country of rolling hills, large forests, wide estates, and serene meandering rivers. The second sun was not rising high in the sky. Dana Gleason saw all this with a disinterested eye. With the coming of the sun she had sunk into an apathy from which she could not arouse herself. The first excitement of the landing was gone; the strangeness of the things around her had lost their interest. Her heart was cold and her eyes dry. The landscape looked barren, the sun's bright light weak. She had won love on a gamble and lost it. She wanted to die, but was living. Life was giving her another chance, and she did not want it now.

Moura now suggested that she lie down and sleep. He did not like the look that had suddenly come into her eyes. He wanted her to be fresh for her interview with the king. By motions he expressed what he wanted, and without a word of protest and as docile as a child, the woman acquiesced. Moura recognized the fact that this woman was going to be as putty in his hands, and he smiled to himself as he thought of what would come.

Lucky that Ubca-tor could not read his thoughts, for the youth knew nothing of the brain of Moura-weit. He could only admire him, glad to shine in his reflected glory. Ubca-tor, the son of a minor prince, had no ambition. From childhood he had been taken by Moura-weit, and he was happy when that man accepted him as a companion, though he was never a confidant. He did not realize the fact that his hero accepted him only because of the advantage it would mean to be associated with a prince and in order to let the masses know that Moura-weit could pick his followers from the princely body. And had he known, it is possible that he would not have remonstrated. He feared, and at the same time loved, the one he fondly called master, and gladly he did what the other directed.

Now as he gazed on the youth, Moura-weit saw that he was staring with intent eyes upon the sleeping woman. He was attracted by her strange coloring, her red lips, her distant air. And in the boy's unguarded mind Moura read an awakening, a fascination for the stranger being. Moura chuckled to himself.

THE TABORANS

So came Dana Gleason to Doata. The capital lay on the bank of the Fierutl River that ran down to the ocean. The city was built, as all Taboran cities are built, on a promontory. One side was a gentle sloping hillside that rose a thousand feet, and the other side a sheer bluff rising straight up from the wide river.

On the cliff's crest, a space almost a mile and a half long and half as wide was given over to the palaces of the Kirada, the royal heir to the throne, together with the great Council Chambers, the government courts, and the barracks that housed the members of the Royal Guard.

Below its crest the hill had been cut by terraces, terraces that marked the ranking of the people who inhabited them. The first two terraces were given over to those of royal blood, the taiis (crown princes and crown princesses) and the tors (lesser princes). A wall, moss-grown and vine-covered, separated these terraces from the next below. Ten such terraces lay in order, all joined together by wide flights of stairways, the center one rising directly up to the palaces on the top.

The last terrace belonged to the rank of the Weitas, and here dwelt Moura-weit in the home of his fathers. A high, straight, unclothed wall divided this from the city below, where dwelt the commoners. Rarely did a commoner ever climb the steps that led over the wall separating the lower and upper cities.

Among the commoners were as many classes and castes as among the nobility, if not more, from the commonest laborers to the skilled artisans and the foremen and superintendents who directed their labors.

As for the houses of the Taborans, none was built taller than one story, and all were of uniform stone with glass roofs, and each had a bit of garden surrounding it. No house in the whole land rivaled that of the Kirada, nor did any other house rival those occupied by the taiis. The size and beauty of the home was entirely determined by the rank of the family to which it belonged. So were the furnishings that went into it, the food, the clothing, the fittings, the slaves.

One can liken the social system of Tabora to that of Peru, under the Incas, since all men work for the state and their worldly goods are meted to them according to their standing in the community. And no man is a slacker. Each is given the work that is best suited to his temperament; he is given the right to choose his vocation and is taught his profession in the state's universities.

Nor are the Taborans held by ironclad rules of class. Let a man prove himself worthy of a higher position in life and he is given it gladly. A laborer may become a superintendent, a mason, an architect, a miner, an engineer. Even princelings gain a place in the sun only by their own efforts.

Dana Gleason had awakened from her nap and saw the strange city stretching below. On the wide plain surrounding the sloping hill were thousands of small houses, each set in its own plot of ground with proper regard for the general symmetry of the city. The glass roofs shone brightly in the sunlight, glowing like thousands of jewels. The plane had been hovering over the city, and it could be seen that its presence was noticed by the people in the squares below.

It would be well here to describe the Taboran plane, built as it is along the lines of the one bird of Abrui, the oc, a waterbird that has no feathers and whose wings are batlike. The wings of the plane, like those of the bird, beat the air, and both wings and tail are controlled in a natural birdlike manner. By simply balancing the machine by a gentle motion of the wings, the plane can be held in one position, can rise straight up into the heavens or drop straight to the ground. Ubca had pulled a lever, and by tilting the wings they now were dropping gently.

It was the rest hour in the city, when all work is suspended for a fourth of a ro;* and people were stretching themselves and chatting together in the sunlight. Immediately on recognizing the blue of the plane with the emblem of two staring eyes on the underside of the wings that Moura-weit affected, a great halloo came up from the city to their favorite.

In answer to the salutation, Moura dropped on the heads of the populace a basketful of artificial flowers that Ubca had taken from a cupboard earlier, and in the midst of this shower the plane descended to the terrace upon which Moura-weit dwelt.

There is no need of describing all that took place in the next few hours—the visit that Moura-weit made to the palace to inform the Kirada in person of his find, the great reception that was given the Earthling in the palace, to

* One ro is equivalent to two hours and ten minutes of Earth time.

which the flower of all Tabora hurried on summons, or the garments into which Dana Gleason was put or the homage that was done to her by all.

A small throne had been placed for her beside that of the Kirada and Kiradaf (queen). The great throne room, whose walls were lined by solid slabs cut from semiprecious stones, was filled to overflowing. Rare tapestries, exquisite pieces of carving, wonderful plaques of rare metal hung on the jewel-encrusted walls that sparkled and glowed. Moura-weit had taken his place at the foot of the dais, and in a voice that held the attention of all and with well-chosen words, he described all that had taken place. At a sign from the Kirada, a tapestry high on the wall was drawn aside, revealing a large plain metal disc. The light was made low, and the weit was commanded to project the scene of Dana Gleason's descent upon Abrui for all to see.

THE MOVIE ON ABRUI

Facing the screen, Moura-weit proceeded to describe the scenes that had actually taken place, and before the assembly, the same events that Moura-weit had shown to Dana Gleason earlier were broadcast. At the same time every house in the land was given the same vision on the sensitive vision screens. Only a few men in the realm were able to do what Moura-weit was doing, and he was an acknowledged master of that art.

It is in this manner that most of the news of Tabora is broadcast over the land, and men are trained for this work alone. Sometimes it takes several men combining their efforts to project their thoughts, so that all can see. Strange as it may seem, Tabora does not broadcast the voice as we do on Earth. Instead, the actual scenes are thrown on the screen, and by way of explanation, words are also sent out in the same manner.

The reception ended after the Kirada had presented Dana Gleason with a mansion on the terrace of the taiis, the terrace that heretofore had been occupied only by the direct descendants of the royal family. To her were given all its privileges with jewels, fine clothing, and great riches. To Moura-weit was given the right as her guardian to dwell in the palace of Dana Gleason.

The Earthling gave thanks in her own tongue. Later it was arranged that a great teacher was to instruct her in the language of Tabora.

For many days thereafter Dana Gleason's reception room was filled with callers, men and women who had been absent from the great assembly in the court. The women were anxious to have a glimpse of a woman from another world; the men were fascinated by her strange coloring.

Several noblemen also sought the hours when Rieuta-Dak (Dak-master) was with her teaching her the Taboran tongue. This group of men elected to learn her language even as she learned theirs, so for every Taboran word she learned she gave its English equivalent. And by the time she showed some proficiency in Taboran, her pupils were almost as proficient in English. Moura-weit and Ubca-tor were often present during the lessons, but they did not take part in the little club these men decided to form. And they gave their club the name that meant Earth Club, Roata, for by this time they had discovered that Dana Gleason was from the planet that was third from the sun and was called Rui in their language. It was greatly due to this lighthearted little gathering that Dana Gleason got back her heart, enjoying it all as much as they rejoiced at speaking her mother tongue.

When she could speak the language well enough, she explained to a small gathering of astronomers the physical aspects of her planet. The Roata listened to the tales of her own world. They were anxious to learn its games, its pastimes, and not wishing to be outdone by their tutor, they learned to smoke her cigarettes. One Uila-jor, who had vast plantations, found a certain weed that had theretofore been considered worthless made a very fine smoking leaf. He set up drying rooms and put a number of slaves to work growing the leaf and making the cigarettes so that the Roata would not be without their smokes, for Dana's small supply was quickly depleted.

Now that her knowledge of the language was quite good, the time came for her to visit Ora. Several of its scientists had already called upon her and were anxiously awaiting the day when she could converse easily with them. The Roata insisted upon traveling with her. Moura-weit also accompanied her, and Ubca-tor, together with a brother of his, Tapor-tor.

On the island of Ora they were given a palace, yet there was none of the pomp that marked her welcome at the Kirada's court. Here everyone met on equal footing. In the great auditorium of the Hall of Knowledge Dana Gleason faced the assembly of great minds and told the facts of her journey through space. Questions were asked, and she quietly answered them. She told all she could about her home planet. Her early training under some of the greatest minds of Earth stood her well, and day after day she stood upon the rostrum telling of Earth, its peoples, its thinkers, its astronomers, its theories.

Women asked her of the social life there, of women's accomplishments, of child welfare. Soldiers questioned her concerning wars on Earth. Statesmen wanted to know about politics, about economics, about statecraft, diplomacy, and she had to answer numberless questions asked by members of all professions.

Then Dana Gleason commenced asking. She learned all there was to know about the Taboran understanding of mechanics; of airplanes, of radio, of astronomy, and other sciences; and something of the history of the country. She learned that man's development here was hardly more than upon Earth, and only because of his possession of that one element in plenty (which is upon Earth a rarity) has the Abruian progressed further than the Earthling.

The Orans were anxious to aid her in building a radio such as she described and which was unknown upon their planet at that time. Yet they doubted the possibility of electric vibrations carrying across the great Void. She was impatient to begin immediately; but Moura-weit wished her to continue her travels, for he had other plans.

Already Moura-weit had discovered that Dana Gleason was invaluable to him. Through her he had risen from the terrace of the Weitas to that of the Taiis, and already he was hearing himself addressed as Moura-tor and men were listening to his word quietly without recourse on his part to oratory.

A WORLD TOUR

With their escort of thirty planes, ten of which contained members of the Kirada's personal guard and ten the female guards that had been presented to Dana Gleason and whose planes now carried her insignia of a rocket emblazoned on the wings, the party was headed for Zoata. The trip across the ocean was one of interest. There were the long low ships that ply across the waters carrying heavy freight from country to country. These ships could be compared to the "whalebacks" of the American Great Lakes. They drew a hundred feet of water and lay low in the water, with their hatches covered. The crew lived in a small house at the bow. The ships were run by means of a simple radium motor and traveled at a speed of 62 cu, as Taborans figure speed, about 150 miles per hour.

Islands dotted the ocean, and great flocks of the single bird of Abrui, the oc, flew about or settled either on the water or on the islands. A large fleet of airships, shaped like balloons, and of great size, passed them on their way to Loata, bearing lighter freight than the ships on the water.

At Treij, capital of Zoata, Dana Gleason was received with the same splendor as in Carajama. At Oiugut, capital of Loata, it was the same. The entire tour took over five months or duits, for at each stop they lingered many days. At both capitals and at Ora Dana Gleason made it a point to meet women, to learn what she could about them, to understand them. She remembered her promise, made aboard the rocket, to accept her rightful heritage as a woman, and to do what she could to aid her sex. It was as if she had erased her past life from her mind. Both Zoata and Loata presented her with a mansion and placed slaves and wealth at her disposal.

In the meantime Moura-weit, now known as Moura-tor, was doing what he could to insinuate himself into the esteem of the people of both these nations. His name had gone abroad among the masses, and they acclaimed him everywhere. He had the chance to prove himself a great man, and the Kiradas of both Zoata and Loata granted him private audiences. Statesmen paid him homage, accepting his aid in weighty questions.

Back in Carajama, for they returned there with a great welcome, Dana Gleason settled down in her palace. The Kiradaf Moule was a kindly woman and sought her companionship, and the royal daughters were often in her atol. Dana Gleason found that the lot of the Taboran woman was not an unhappy one. Women, as well as men, did their part in the nation's work, and wives were as well acquainted with statecraft as were their husbands. Nor were they denied the right to do any manner of work they desired. To understand more of the social system of Tabora, it is best that something of it be explained.

Of amusements there are many varieties, men and women taking part in everything alike. There are singers, poets, and actors, and most of the arts are broadcast into every home. There are holidays on which games are played by both amateurs and professionals: contests of strength and swimming. Men have clubs wherein they may gather, and there are the same for women. The state thinks well of its people, and knows how to keep them content.

In her home Dana Gleason had a gymnasium set up, for she had no intention of allowing herself to grow weak and flabby. There she kept in trim, running, fencing, and boxing, not to mention the swims in her own pools. The Roata still courted her favor, and they practiced with her in her gymnasium, teaching her their games while she taught hers.

She visited about with the Roata. Uilajor and Yidvetor both invited her to their plantations, and she spent a great deal of time at them. The plantations were conducted with military discipline. There were superintendents, overseers, foremen, laborers, and slaves, not to mention the large company of herdsmen who watched the great flocks of muti.

Abrui has but a few animals. In the mountains are several species of wild animals, which the Taborans hunt, not for their flesh but for their beautiful hides. A beast of burden is unknown; the only domestic animal in addition to the muti is the ayop, a small, longhaired creature, somewhat like a cat, which the women favor. In the mountains traveling is difficult. Slaves are bred as carriers, and can bear twice their own weight on their broad shoulders. The overseers use these men to bear them rapidly from field to field, and on hunts these golden men carry the hunter over the rugged passes.

On returning from one of these jaunts into the country, Dana Gleason arrived at Carajama to find that Moura-tor was now a great man. Among the three nations of Tabora a dispute concerning a tax on imports and exports had been brewing for a long time, and the indications were that if the dispute were not settled war would surely take place. None other than Moura-tor himself had been sent as special envoy to straighten matters out. He was highly successful, and the three nations of Tabora were knitted more closely together than ever before. Moura-tor was acclaimed throughout the cities, and, whereas men had earlier whispered "Moura-Ur-tor" (over-prince), now they cried it aloud in the streets.

Next had come whispers from the borders of Tabora that Gora was arising out of the slough into which she had been cast centuries before. The raids of the Gora into the fertile plains, where were great flocks of muti, were becoming more daring, more defiant. Consequently Moura-tor went to Hierpowi, the capital of Kirada Yal, the strongest of all the chieftains of the Gor, who lived in large tribes.

Moura returned from Gora somewhat disquieted. The Kirada Yal had received him coldly. Gora was hostile, but Yal agreed to see what he could do about the raids of his people. Gora felt no love for Tabora, her despoiler. She hoped one day to win back her lands on the shores of Sehti. The men of Gora were numerous now, and one day they would swarm over Tabora. No, not now, but sometime later. Perhaps in centuries to come. So much had Yal spoken, but Moura-tor the wily had seen something else in the mind of the Goran king.

———

And what he saw greatly disconcerted him. Again he saw the strange image of the man from Earth, the same that he had seen a number of times pictured in the brain of Dana Gleason, the image of Richard Dorr. He knew him immediately, the man with hair and skin almost like that of the Gora, but whose shorter stature and blue eyes were different.

This knowledge had set him thinking. Gora then had a champion. Hence the reason for the new fearlessness, the new hatred. He knew then that Yal lied when he spoke of succor for his people in centuries to come. The plan was almost ripe!

Not allowing the man to know what he had seen in his brain, he went on to remind Yal how futile it would be for Gora to war upon Tabora. Gora knew little about radium, but Tabora knew. She knew how to disintegrate a man's body, how to dissolve any chemical body. Gora would have no chance. Instead for Gora there was the friendship of Tabora, a brotherhood of the two great races.

Yal listened, but had nothing to say. He kept his own counsel. He reflected that Gora had not had the friendship of Tabora for over a thousand years, nor did she want it now.

Moura returned to Tabora with little to say. He advised that a larger contingent of soldiers be sent to the border garrisons and that watch be kept upon Gora. However, he intimated that friendship with the Gorans would be a good policy. Tabora could gain much by trading with that nation, for it was known that Gora had five mines, where much metal and radium could be obtained in exchange for a few of the luxuries that Tabora possessed.

The Councils decided to take up the question, but even with Moura-tor's untiring efforts, it took quite a time to make any sort of decision. Moura made a number of secret trips to Gora, but nothing much came of them. Behind Yal he recognized the now hated figure of Richard Dorr, though that man was never present at any of the conferences.

Moura-tor had no doubt that Richard Dorr was unaware that Dana Gleason was still alive. Between the two races there was practically no intercourse, and the man evidently was left in ignorance of the fact that the woman he loved was but a few thousand miles away from him. Moura wondered of what value it would be to acquaint Dorr with the fact.

And yet Moura-tor had other plans for Dana Gleason. Moura-tor, although in his fortieth year, had never taken a mate. There were but few bachelors among the Yuika, to which class he belonged; but the issue had never been forced in his case, and he preferred a life of celibacy. However, it is needless to remark that Moura-tor was considering taking the Earthling to mate. She looked upon the man as a friend, and he allowed her to consider him as such. His own feeling toward her he did not trouble to define. He knew that it would be well for Moura-tor to wed the Earthling. The people would be overjoyed at such a match, and it would give him fame. So he was not anxious for Dana Gleason to learn that Richard Dorr still lived.

For many months now Dana Gleason had been living at Ora. With the aid of the Orans she had built her giant radio, but there had been innumerable failures. Earth could not hear her appeals. Life now lost all taste for her. All interest in her new existence was gone, as she realized that she was in truth separated for all time from Earth. Although she tried again and again, building new radios, changing and improving, it seemed an impossible task.

However, the Orans had made use of her knowledge, and now her name was to go down in history, not only as the space traveler, but as the inventor of the radio by which Tabora could now transmit the voice through the air. She was a sacred person to Tabora, and wherever she went people proclaimed her name; letters and gifts were showered upon her by a grateful people, and nothing that she could ask for was denied.

Men were now seeking her out, as they never had before. She could have married any man she wanted, but Dana Gleason had no thought for marriage. Her days were quite full, but her nights overflowed with the thought of Richard Dorr. For hours, before sleep claimed her, she lived over again the short life they had had upon the rocket, and waited only for the time when she might die and go seeking him wherever he might be. She had taken Moura-tor's word that he had died in the flames of the rocket. She would have made a pilgrimage to the ruins, but Moura explained that it would be impossible because of the antagonism of the Gora to the Tabora. Still it was hard to think the man dead, he who was so full of vitality, he who had been so richly endowed with the essence of life.

Moura-tor had been her only confidant. He had drawn from her the story of her love for Richard Dorr, and he falsely gave her comfort. Wisely he kept from her his plans regarding herself.

However, on the evening of his return from Gora he faced her. He had made a decision. First he would make her his wife. After that he would see that Richard Dorr learned that she was living. How easy, then, to trap the fellow and do away with him, and Dana Gleason never to know! Thereafter with Dorr dead, Gora would be his. Why should not the Ur-tor of Tabora also become the Ur-tor of Gora, which would mean Ur-tor of all Abrui?

He told Dana Gleason of his mission to Gora, also that he had made an attempt to learn if the body of Dorr had ever been found, but the Gora knew nothing of him, and therefore he was conclusively dead! He knew that to bring to life the memories of the man would hurt his cause, and yet it was better that the woman no longer possess any hopes.

Dana Gleason heard him in silence. True, her heart warmed to the man who had her interests at heart, he who had saved her from the savagery of the barbarians. To her, he was her only true friend. The Roata was no more, for each man of it in turn had asked her to become either his mate or, at least, his *amante*. To each she had given the same answer and her reason, and one by one the Roatans had drifted away. Only three remained, and they secretly were building for her a vehicle, which, they hoped, could make the trip to Earth and return. They were Uila-jor, Rexz-tor, and Heipa-tor.

Now Moura-tor approached Dana Gleason with the entreaty that she become his mate, to share his triumphs. She looked up wearily. "Even you, Moura?" she asked, and smiled.

Moura hurried to protest that he loved her; that he wanted to give her happiness. He wanted to be a substitute for the love she had lost.

She smiled sadly at that. "Can artificial light replace the sun, Moura; can an artificial flower replace the real?"

He smiled quizzically. "On Abrui we do substitute the sun so well that the substitute outshines it, and surely our artificial flowers are beautiful." And he touched an exquisite jewel she wore at her girdle that had been cut in the semblance of a flower.

"True enough; but take away the sun, and you could not light up your entire planet any more than you can give a scent to this jewel."

He laughed, realizing he was bested, but he was not done. "Dana Gleason," he said, "I offer you my love, but you disdain it. Enough! Yet we are not finished there. Doata demands that the Earthling take a mate! We have no monks or nuns, which you speak of having on Earth. All our people do their duty for the state!"

"I am not of Doata, Moura-tor. How can that rule have anything to do with me?"

"You are one of us now, Dana Gleason, and Tabora is anxious that the name of Dana Gleason continue on down into history! She wants one of your name always in her annals that she may venerate you even after you are no more!"

Dana shrugged her shoulders. "I regret that this is impossible. I am the last of my line either here or upon Earth, and it must continue so. No. Moura-tor, go to your Kirada and tell him that Dana Gleason does not like such an arrangement!"

The man laughed an ugly laugh now that brought surprise to the Earthling's eyes. "We shall see. I must go now, for I still have some matters on hand to attend to before I retire. I bid you good night." And he was gone.

A FRIEND IN NEED

For some moments Dana Gleason sat where he had left her. She became aware of a slender little golden-skinned slave girl who had crept to her side. She was Dure, Dana's personal slave, a girl to whom she had become attached. Dure was just her own height, and Dana Gleason often thought she saw in her features a resemblance to herself.

"My mistress, you are sad tonight?" she asked softly. "Sadder than you usually are when night falls."

Dana nodded. She had told Dure something of the love she had lost, for Dure knew of her sleepless nights. She told her now that she had learned that he was really dead.

"I heard much of what this Moura-weit (the slaves of Carajama had no love for Moura and never deigned to call him by his new title) had to say to you.

He is an ambitious man, my mistress, and he seems always to get what he desires. Beware of him!"

Dana Gleason had nothing to say. She cared not at all for the ambitions of the man. She was sadder now than ever before, with the news that her lover was truly dead. Dure, seeing that she was occupied with her own thoughts, turned away, and Dana got to her feet. She strolled out into the garden.

Night had settled now. The distant sun was lighting Gora, and in the sky only the brilliant stars were showing. A few glowing lights were evidence that some of her neighbors had not yet retired, but their lights did not penetrate into the thicket of shrubberies that surrounded her favorite nook and formed a bower over a stone bench.

Looking into the sky she tried to distinguish the planet Earth in the firmament, but she knew that Earth's gleam was not strong enough to give much light at this great distance. Only with strong telescopes could it be seen close to the sun. Nor were any of the constellations she had known from Earth visible here, although the distant stars shone more brightly because of the fact that Abrui is many millions of miles nearer them than is Earth.

Moura's words had caused her some disquietude, and she could not shake off the vague doubts and restlessness that had crept over her. She knew that some big issue was at hand, and she must be careful to see that she was not forced into something she did not wish.

Repelling these thoughts, she allowed her memories to dwell again on Richard Dorr. Strange that Moura's words had not seemed to ring true and Richard Dorr seemed very close tonight.

Suddenly she became aware that she was not alone. A tall slender figure was coming toward her. Could it be he? Could the dead come to claim her? But no, she quickly recognized the voice of Ubca-tor, who so often visited her and sat mooning on her chairs.

"Dana Gleason," he murmured, "I prayed that you would be here."

"And why should Ubca-tor pray for such a thing? Is it not strange for you to be calling at such a late hour?"

"Not strange, for I know it is your custom to come here always at this hour."

"Then you have been keeping me under surveillance?"

"Only the surveillance of love, Dana Gleason. Ah, how many hours I have spent watching you, always watching."

"You too, Ubca? Must every man in the Kirada's court offer me the same thing—love? Is it not answer enough that I refuse each one?"

"Ah, Dana Gleason, you mistake me, for though I do love you, I come not to ask for love in return. I come only to sit and bask in the warmth of your presence. Send me not away, for I would be a slave to you—anything, that I might be near you."

A low laugh escaped Dana Gleason's throat. Too many had asked her for the same thing of late, and now it was this callow youth. She was about to say something caustic to him when he spoke again.

"You sit and watch the stars each night. Do you then know an old legend that has been handed down from the days when our race believed in godlike beings?"

She admitted she did not.

"It is a pretty legend. It tells us that the stars are the eyes of lovers who have died and left their loved ones here on Abrui, and they, with a lover's ardent gaze, are seeking the one they left behind. When they find that one, they then turn their glowing eyes upon all who dare to love the one of their heart and pierce them through and through with the gleam from their eyes so that the presumptuous one becomes mad for evermore!

"Ah, Dana Gleason, were I only a star to make raving maniacs of all who would dare to love you."

"That is a pretty story, Ubca, but you forget in your ardor to ask if perhaps there is not one who has precedence over you. Perhaps it is one who loved and died, who looks to find me, only to stab you through and through so that you might become mad."

"You mean, then, that there is another? It is not Moura-tor to whom you propose to give yourself? Many nights I have lain in fear that this might be the truth! For though I realize how young and foolish I am to presume to love you, I should hate to see you favor Moura-tor, who seeks you only through his love of ambition.

"Many years I have loved Moura-tor, but of late I have grown to hate him. Did I know that he truly loved you, I should be satisfied, but now I know that Moura-tor loves no one but himself! Promise then that you will never mate with him, and if you ever need help, you can call on one who holds you in reverence!"

As he spoke, Dana Gleason's impression of the youth changed. She knew now that here was a true friend, and she respected him now in his attitude toward her. She told him of Richard Dorr, and promised him solemnly enough that she would never marry Moura-tor.

As she spoke, Ubca-tor was remembering something else. He remembered the night when they had discovered her limp form. And he also remembered the body of the man he took for a Gora. Excitedly he asked that she describe Richard Dorr for him. She did. Then, in a voice that shook, he told her what had transpired.

"The Gora found him. I know he was living. They must have taken him for their own, and possibly he is with them now!"

A great silence fell upon her. Then she was right! Richard Dorr lived! Quickly she repeated all that Moura-tor had told her. Ubca was convinced that Moura had lied. "Something is behind all this, Dana Gleason. It would be well to discover what we can! Wait . . . *I* will go to Gora. I know their language; I can disguise myself as one of them. I will seek and perhaps I shall find Richard Dorr for you!"

"Go then! And I will go with you. I too can disguise myself."

"No, no; your absence will arouse comment. Moura will know then. If I go alone he will not even miss me, nor care. I must not see him; for then he will read what goes on in my mind. And you must try to keep him from reading your thoughts, though few can stand against him."

"Hurry then, and may God be with you!"

"I like this God of yours, Dana Gleason. We of Tabora have no God; but if there is really such a spirit, let him look after you while I'm gone!"

And the boy left on his self-imposed mission. A new hope had come into Dana Gleason's heart. Did Dick but live! She was praying now to the God he had taught her to love. Now let Moura-tor attempt to win his case. He could never accomplish his purpose.

To make this more certain, Dana Gleason, with a company of her guardswomen and Dure, her slave girl, embarked for Ora, where she knew she would be safe from Moura-tor. Once before she had run away to escape a man, Howard Courtland.

Moura realized that his purpose was thwarted for the time being, and though he sought Dana out at Ora, she laughed at him, taking care to keep her mind a blank so that the man could not read what hopes were there. She succeeded, and Moura returned to Doata none the wiser. A duit passed before Ubca returned. He came to Ora.

"It is true, Dana Gleason. Richard Dorr lives!"

A cry escaped her lips, and she sank into a faint. Frantically Dure and Ubca hastened to restore her. She revived, feeling embarrassed at her weakness. She demanded more news from Ubca, her heart singing within her bosom.

Ubca's eyes were mirrored with pain. He had learned a lot in Gora, and he was worried. He had discovered that Gora intended to make war upon Tabora, and that Richard Dorr was behind the movement. Still he was certain that Gora could not win, but there would be bloodshed. And he had not seen Richard Dorr in Gora because at the present time he was in Tabora!

"I think," said Ubca slowly, "I can find him for you, Dana Gleason, but to do so and not turn him over to my people would be criminal; for, without his leadership, Gora would not consider war against the Uriem (the death ray) of Tabora."

Dana was exultant when she learned that Dick was in Tabora, closer than before. She decided to return to Carajama immediately. She was certain that Dick would hear her name and come seeking her. "It is well," she told Ubca, "that you do no more. Richard Dorr will come to me. Then I will persuade him to give up his attempt to bring the two races to war. Trust me, I will do all I can to avert it. Come, let us return to Carajama. But first we must let it be known throughout Tabora that Dana Gleason returns to Carajama, so that he will be sure to hear my name and know where to find me."

"I will attend to that," Ubca agreed.

In Carajama, Dana Gleason had a royal welcome. That night her palace was filled to overflowing with people of the court. She was happy, happier than she had been since her coming to Abrui. Her eyes glowed, and there was fresh color under her skin. Men did her homage that night, and the women were suddenly jealous. Moura-tor was absent, being out of the city for that evening.

THE GREAT PLAN

After the last guest had gone, Dana Gleason stood peering into the garden, anxious to make sure that her nook in the shrubberies had not been sought by anyone else. Dure came to her side. "My mistress," she whispered, "I have news of Him!"

"Him" meant but one person. She asked Dure for her news. "Your Richard Dorr is in the city now! He is here on a secret mission. His dealings are with the people of Moata alone. Mistress, he promises us freedom!"

"What do you mean?"

"It is a wonderful plan! A plan by which we are to rise against our master (her voice was very low now) and join ourselves with our ancient ally the Gora. This Richard Dorr is a great person, mistress. The golden people already love him, as they hate the Tabora. You have been kind to your slaves, and they are anxious to return your kindness.

"Tonight Richard Dorr will seek you out—in the bower!"

Dure's words had brought tears to Dana's eyes, and now, without a word, she hurried out into the garden. Richard was waiting for her in the bower and she rushed into his arms. It was Dick, but a Dick transformed. His skin and hair were now as silvery as any Taboran's, only his blue eyes were the same. For some time neither spoke, content only in each other's nearness. Then they told each other the story of their experiences since their arrival on Abrui.

Dorr had been picked up by the Gora more dead than alive. Thinking him one of their own, they revived him. On discovering that he had come out of the rocket, they would have killed him. But he had been taken to Kirada Yal for judgment. Yal saw in the Earthling the answer to a prophecy made centuries before—that there would come a stranger man, one who was like themselves yet unlike them, who would come wearing strange clothing, and with strange words on his lips, who would lead Gora back to the lands of which she had been deprived. So Richard Dorr was acclaimed to be the promised savior for whom they had been waiting.

"Their plight is pitiful, my dear. They eke a mere pittance from a barren soil; they are always hungry, and have little to cover themselves with, and the Tabora kill them when they come to the borders to steal enough to feed their babies. So I have sworn to free them from this awful bondage! Nor are they the barbarians the Tabora make them out to be. They were civilized centuries before the Tabora. But in their struggle for existence they have no time to give to science; hence they are fast deteriorating into savagery."

"But, Dick, you can never fight against the Tabora. They have superior weapons, better brains!"

"No, you are wrong, Dana Gleason! True, they have a better weapon, but I have discovered only today the secret that will make its power nil, and they have only this one weapon! They have not been at war for centuries, and I have just come out of a war. Remember I was an engineer during the war on Earth, and made it a point then to study artillery, too. No, Gora will win."

"Do you realize what you are doing, Dick, in bringing war to this planet? Have you and I not had enough war?"

"That is not the question now. If there is no war now, there will be one later. And not until there is bloodshed can Gora have the comfort and ease of which she has been despoiled.

"Oh, yes, there is a possibility of trade being established between the two races, but believe me, it will be Tabora who will get the best of the bargain. A diplomat by the name of Moura-tor came to Kirada Yal with promises. What are promises? Pieces of paper, treaties. Bah!

"Naturally, I have thought all this over carefully. I do not like the matter of throwing this planet into warfare, but only through war can justice be done. Gora wants her place in the sun, facing the Sehti ocean. She and Moata will have that before I am done!

"Surely you, Dana Gleason, cannot countenance one strong race lording it over another. True, Tabora has culture, a fine social order, great learning; but why must she have it alone? Why should not these other two races share and share alike? I have already been to Ora, where I was received kindly. The great minds there agree that I am right, that Tabora, Moata, and Gora should live peaceably side-by-side! Can you say differently?"

———

Her silence was her answer. Then she told him of what Ubca-tor had done, the danger that Richard Dorr now had to guard against in Carajama. He laughed aside her fears. "They will do nothing to me, and were they to capture me, Dana, I should not be a prisoner long. Moata will stand by me as one man!" He gathered her in his arms again.

"My work will be finished here in another day, and I shall return to Gora directly. Before I plunge Abrui into war, Tabora will be advised, but I am certain she will not agree to terms. Then it will be a war, a war that will not last more than a day or two! Then, my sweetheart, I will return for you."

"You will return for me . . . ? What do you mean, Dick Dorr? You don't think that you are going back to Gora without me?"

"How can I take you back with me, Dana? It's a hard road back, and Gora offers you none of the comfort you have here. No, you must wait!"

The woman stared in wonder. "You are talking that way to me, Richard Dorr?" she demanded. "What do you think I have degenerated into? Have you forgotten who I am? Do you think that Dana Gleason has become a weakling? Why do you talk to me of comfort, of fearing a hard journey?"

The man smiled. "I see you have not changed, Dana, but all the same I do not want you to suffer any more hardships—besides . . ."

"Besides what?"

"Well, my mission is a secret one, even though your Ubca-tor discovered me. Were I captured, I should be killed as a spy. And to take you back with me would most surely raise a hue and cry."

"And you think I cannot plan as well as you?" She laughed softly. "No, Dick, we were separated once. I won't allow it to happen again! I have a slave girl who is my height, resembles me somewhat, and it will be easy, I am sure, to disguise her as myself, announce that I am returning to Ora, and then let her take my place. Several days will then elapse before the deception is discovered, and by then they will not know where to look for me."

"Good, then. That is settled. How much easier my work will be with you by my side!"

The hours of night passed swiftly. Soft tendrils of light aroused them to the fact that Tradr was rising. They had one more caress. "We shall leave two nights hence! I will come again tomorrow night. Wait for me, my darling!" And he was gone. Slipping out of the garden, he appeared with the early risers as he descended to the lower city.

PLOTS AND COUNTERPLOTS

Dure was waiting for Dana. She had fallen asleep on the floor, but she awakened as she heard the light, happy steps of her mistress. She insisted that the woman lie down for several hours of sleep. She awoke later in a blithesome mood. With a smile she received Moura-tor, who had only just returned to Carajama.

"I have only just heard that you had come back from Ora, Dana Gleason. Am I to take your return to mean that you have accepted me? You will go to court to register today your decision to marry me?"

At his words, her happiness departed. She had forgotten Moura's plans for her in her own joy of finding Richard Dorr. She must somehow stall Moura along until she was ready to depart with Richard Dorr. She was thinking this when she realized that she allowed her thoughts to escape her. In terror she looked into Moura's eyes, and saw that he had indeed read what had passed through her mind. For the first time she saw the real man behind those cold glittering eyes. A short laugh escaped him.

"So you thought to defeat Moura-tor, eh?" He laughed again. "Yes, I know your lover Richard Dorr is in Carajama. I, myself, have just returned from Gora. Here," and he held forth a metal scroll, "is a treaty I have just drawn up with Kirada Yal.

"For providing Gora with foodstuffs, clothing, and whatever necessities and luxuries she will demand, Gora in turn will permit our miners to take out precious metals from her unused mines. Airships will henceforth fly between Tabora and Gora. Educators, architects, and various workers will go into Gora to aid her in building up her country. Agriculturalists will study conditions there and do what they can to revive her barren soil. Yes, a brotherhood shall be established. And all that, my dear Dana Gleason, is the work of the man you shall mate — Moura-Ur-tor!"

———————

He allowed her to gather the full import of his words, then he continued: "And as for Richard Dorr . . . I also have a note signed by the Kirada that the Earthling is a renegade, a man who ruthlessly induced the Kirada to consider warring upon Tabora, deluding him into thinking that he could beat Tabora. I already have men searching for this Richard Dorr, and he shall be killed as a conspirator!"

Dana Gleason from the first had doubted Moura's word, as she had learned from experience to doubt him; but she could not submit to hear the last, for she knew that Moura meant what he was saying.

"Moura," she cried, "you wouldn't dare to do that!"

He smiled. "Moura-Ur-tor," he said proudly, "dares whatever he wishes to dare, Dana Gleason. He knows not the word 'No'!"

"But, Moura, you have been my friend. Won't you be my friend again? Won't you save Richard Dorr for me? You have been my confidant. I have told you everything. Surely you would not be as cruel as to kill the man I love?"

"Perhaps I wouldn't, Dana Gleason—for a consideration."

She understood his implication as she muttered, "Are men the same the universe over?"

"Yes, I sadly fear that they are. Well, is it to be your lover's death or will you be my wife? Speak up, I cannot be kept waiting!"

A sob escaped her throat. "All right, Moura-Ur-tor . . . they are right . . . you always have your own way. Come, I shall go with you immediately."

"Good."

Without another word he led her out, up the stairway to the Corona of Carajama, and into a small office in one of the government buildings. Here, before a magistrate, Dana Gleason swore she was ready to take Moura-Ur-tor to mate.

"It shall be tomorrow night," was Moura's words when he left Dana Gleason. She sat in her atol with folded hands and downcast eye, while at Moura's command her slave women were busy getting materials ready to fit her into her wedding dress.

Her first visitor that day was Ubca-tor, who had already heard the news. She confessed to him all that had happened. "By your God, Dana Gleason, if I myself have to murder the man who so presumptuously calls himself Ur-tor, I will do so!

"Hear? The people are rejoicing over the news of the new treaty signed by Kirada Yal, and the news that you are to be wed to Moura. I won't have it! I won't!"

"Who says he won't?" the voice was that of Moura-Ur-tor. "Ah, it is you, my erstwhile friend." And reaching out he gave the tor a cuff that sent him reeling.

Dana Gleason was on her feet, her eyes blazing. "You beast," she muttered between closed teeth. "Be gone. I don't care to see you until tomorrow night, and then perhaps no more. For," she added turning to the youth who had slowly crawled to his feet, "I will declare myself the mate of this man, but henceforth he will have to seek me in Ora!" And again to Moura, "Go, now, go!"

Surprised by the ire he had aroused in the woman, he departed. He laughed to himself when he thought of her threat. She was not done with Moura-Ur-tor yet!

A LONELY TRYST

That night Richard Dorr waited hours in the bower for Dana Glea-son. He did not know that after Moura had left Dana Gleason fell into a dead swoon from which the slave women could not arouse her. She lay as if dead, and only by holding a glass over her face were the women able to see that she breathed. Ubca-tor had carried her to a couch, knowing that Moura was the cause of her condition. He had seen him practice the same thing upon slaves.

Dorr had heard the proclamations that day concerning the treaty with Gora, also the one that Moura-Ur-tor and Dana Gleason had avowed their betrothal that day. Of the treaty he had been aware, advising Kirada Yal, on leaving Gora, to accept any terms that the ambassador from Tabora might present to him; but he could not account for the second announcement. Nor for the intended ceremony the following night. Possibly Dana Gleason was wisely playing for time. Yet he could not understand why she did not appear at their trysting place.

Suddenly his heart quickened. Coming toward him was the slender form of Dana Gleason. Only it was not Dana. It was Dure, her slave girl. Breathlessly the girl hastened to tell him all that had happened. She had heard the words that Moura had spoken to Dana Gleason, heard him force her to mate him, else to have her lover die, and she told him what state she was in now.

Dorr swore under his breath. Then he recalled that Dana had spoken of a slave girl who resembled her. This then was the girl. He asked her if she thought she could disguise herself as Dana Gleason, and quickly outlined his plan, for he knew that all the slaves of Tabora were with him and anxious to do his bidding.

"Do you love your mistress enough," he asked, "to die for her, perhaps?"

"Yes, I love Dana Gleason and Richard Dorr enough. And in dying, I can be happy in knowing that you two are saving my people—and mayhap I shall not die"; and she laughed. "No, I do not fear to pit my wits against those of Moura-Ur-tor."

"Is anyone with her now?"

"Only the slave women and Ubca-tor, who swears that Moura-weit (curse his name) shall never have her. It was through his love for Dana Gleason that Ubca-tor went into Gora to discover if you lived."

"One can be brave for love; a pity that he loves one who is not for him. However, I should be afraid to trust him. I must not be captured."

"I will see if I can send the tor away. Wait here until I return . . ."

She was back shortly and motioned for the Earthling to approach the house. He found Dana supine upon the couch, her face white and drawn, eyes closed; she was scarcely breathing. He tried such methods as he knew early hypnotists to use, slapping her cheeks gently, snapping his fingers and breathing in her face, but to no avail. He could not arouse her.

No one else was about. Dure had sent the other slaves to their quarters, for as her mistress's favorite, she ruled them all. She hurried away to return with a box containing various paints. "We Boatans, as well as the Taborans, paint our bodies and faces when our color is sallow or spotted. Hence I already have the proper paint to make Dana Gleason as golden as I am." So with Dorr's help she applied the paintbrush on the face, arms, hands, and feet of the unconscious woman, though first she mixed other paints to the exact shade of the Earthling's complexion. At her direction, Dick rubbed in the oils that gave the right polish to Dana's disguised skin.

———

With that done, Dure proceeded to daub herself. She knew that on the following day they would come to dress her in new garments so that her entire body would need to be painted. She divested herself of the dress that marked her for a slave, and began covering herself with the paint. Abruians have no false modesty for the body, so that she thought nothing of appearing before the man without clothing. He was surprised when that was done to see how much she resembled Dana Gleason. She rouged her lips and applied a dye to her hair, and, but for her eyes of red, she was a twin sister of the Earthling.

Between them they changed Dana Gleason's clothing, dressing her in the slave's garments and redressing Dure in Dana's discarded suit. They were too busy to see that the day was already dawning when they at last completed their task. Then Dure ordered Dorr to carry Dana Gleason into another bedroom. He must leave her lying there until the night, when he could come for her and carry her to Gora. Dure did not doubt that Moura's spell would lose its hold in a few more hours. She now prevailed upon Richard Dorr to leave ere he was discovered there. She threw herself upon Dana Gleason's couch, closing her eyes and assuming the same deathlike pose.

Richard Dorr was about to leave as he had come, when suddenly retreat was cut off. Moura-Ur-tor had entered the room undetected. He smiled coolly when he recognized in this silver-skinned man the Earthling with his blue eyes.

"Ah, so the prey has come to the hunter, eh?" he remarked jovially. "And how do you like my handiwork, Richard Dorr? I suppose you have been trying to revive her?" he said with a wave of his hand toward the couch.

"Nice of you to come calling this way. It saves my men the work of searching the city for you. I have decided to allow you to be present at the ceremony that will make Dana Gleason and myself mates. And in Tabora, you know, there is no practice of divorce. Once wed, always wed! Nice custom, eh?"

Dorr had nothing to say. He knew that behind him lay the slave quarters and that he could escape out into the city through them. He had heard much of Moura-Ur-tor, and found he did not like him at all. He hoped that Dure could carry out her part of the contract.

"So Richard Dorr has nothing to tell me, I see," observed Moura with a smile still on his face. "Richard Dorr does not enjoy the prospect of seeing the woman he loves take another man to mate, nor the thought of prison and death!"

At his words, a low laugh now broke from Dorr's lips. "Quite a nice picture that, but believe me I have no idea of carrying out your plans, my villainous friend. And as for your schemes concerning Dana Gleason, I fear you have come into a ringer there." It chagrined Moura that he could not see behind Dorr's inscrutable eyes, for the Earthling had learned early on the planet to withhold his thoughts from another. "As to your marriage to this woman here, you are welcome to her. I have nothing to do with a lifeless thing!"

And he turned away as if contemplating some future course to take. His words, as Dorr expected, aroused a fear in Moura-Ur-tor's mind. Quickly he was at the side of the couch. Concentrating his thoughts upon the figure lying there, he ordered her to awaken. There was no response! And he was surprised to find a blank mind into which he could not delve facing him.

Reaching down he shook her, only to feel the lifeless, unresponsive body. He half drew her to a sitting position, and her head lolled back, her arms drooped. Dure had understood what was in Dorr's mind, and she reacted accordingly. She would have enjoyed the spectacle of seeing Moura's wroth. Now, in consternation, he faced Richard Dorr.

"What have you done to her?"

Dorr shrugged his shoulders. "I have done nothing. I found her that way. I believe she is dead."

"You lie, you inhuman beast. Can you stand there and look with such little concern upon the woman you have professed to love? Is that the temper of your Earthly heart? Can you stand there and laugh down upon the woman who has loved you these many months, even though she thought you dead?"

Dorr was staring in wonder at the other. He had hated Moura, but now when he saw the look of a broken man in his eyes and heard his voice trembling with emotion, he felt pity for the man instead of hatred.

"So do you love Dana Gleason, Moura-Ur-tor?" he asked softly.

Moura looked up in surprise. "I love Dana Gleason—I—don't know. I had not thought of her with love in my heart. I have never known love." Then the soft mood forsook him, and he realized his position. Straightening, he got to his feet. "Well, no matter. But you are wrong, Dana Gleason still lives, and you shall see her tonight as she becomes, as you say in your language, my bride!"

Putting a whistle to his lips, Moura blew a blast. At the same time Richard Dorr headed for the doorway to the rear and soon had reached the back entrance of the house. What slaves he met hurried out of his way. They knew who he was and would have protected him with their lives. They did make the attempt, too, when he discovered that the entire house was surrounded by the Ur-tor's guard.

The slaves gathered around him, but he commanded them to stand off, as he did not wish to implicate them in his capture. He was captured and when Dure got up from her couch to watch, she saw Moura leading the way to the palace above.

The slave women gathered about her and she told all that had happened. Then she hurried to the room in which Dana Gleason lay. She found her with her eyes open, staring about. Moura had attempted to awaken the slave girl who lay disguised as Dana on the couch. In the adjoining bedroom Dana Gleason had heard the summons and opened her eyes. She lay listening to the talk from the other room, and made out something of what was going on there. Wisely she lay still until she made sure that Moura had gone. She understood the fact that Richard Dorr had been apprehended, and tears stood in her eyes. Dure found her silently crying.

Glad to find that Dana had been aroused out of the coma into which Moura had flung her mind, Dure rapidly told her all that had happened. "Go, call Ubca-tor. I am sure he will do something to aid us," commanded Dana, and Dure hastened to summon the youth.

He came, surprised at the transformation of Dana Gleason. He avowed he could do nothing to free Richard Dorr, who was now a prisoner of the state, but when the three put their heads together, a plan was concocted.

The sunset was already painting the sky when Moura-Ur-tor came to the atol of Dana Gleason. He found Dure lying dressed in the magnificent costume that had been prepared for Dana Gleason. He now bent over her and carefully smoothed her brow, spoke to her and called her mind back to the brain chamber. Dure had carefully been practicing the part that she knew was to come. Slowly she moved her eyelids but took care not to open her eyes wide. She gave a single glance at Moura and turned away her head, as she knew Dana Gleason would have done in the same position.

"Come," said the man, "we shall be late!"

A slave woman standing by spoke for her. "My mistress had not a bite to eat all day, Ur-tor."

Impatiently the man waited until food was brought and eaten, then he slowly led the woman at his side up the broad stairs. The great square before the palace was filled with a thousand guardsmen. The setting sun bathed them in its rosy hues, tinting their flesh and metal accoutrements. The great jeweled door of the palace stood open, and they entered side by side. The Kirada himself joined their hands. The supposed Dana Gleason stood with eyes meekly downcast. Moura-Ur-tor proudly stared about him. His heart was full to overflowing. He was acknowledged Ur-tor of all Abrui. He had for wife the bravest woman in the land. He had for prisoner the man he hated most vehemently.

Hidden by tapestries that were arranged so that he might see all stood Richard Dorr among his guards. He was slouched against the wall, taking delight in the scene before him. There was nothing downcast in his manner. His guards eyed him warily; doubtful as to what he was, doubtful as to his intentions. Not that Dorr showed he was anxious to make an attempt to escape, but he did have the air of one who knew that he would not be detained overlong by his captors.

The ceremony was over, and Dorr's heart beat wildly when he realized that Dure, the slave girl, had played her part letter perfect. He was anxious to know how Dana fared. Had she been released from her coma? He feared the worst, and he waited impatiently until his guards were ready to lead him back to his prison. Only they did not lead him back immediately.

BEFORE THE KING

Moura-Ur-tor had one more trump to play. He was now facing Kirada Kalti, and he was telling him about a spy in their midst. Dorr lifted his eyebrows as he heard himself described as a most despicable character. When he was led before the Kirada, he held his head high and his eyes flashed, but he was able to control himself and told the Kirada he had nothing to give in answer to the accusations. He listened to the long speech Kalti made before sentencing the prisoner to death. He was standing within five feet of the dais where Dure sat on the throne chair especially designed for Dana Gleason. He caught the whispered words of the slave. She had been carefully drilled to say the few French words. Her message was, "She waits for you."

With a light heart he was led away to the cells below the palace floor. Moura took his bride by the arm and they embarked in his plane. Moura had planned a honeymoon such as Dana Gleason had described; such as all newly married couples took on Earth. Such a procedure was unknown to Abrui.

In the mountains was a small estate that he had inherited from his family. Here in its seclusion he had planned to bring Dana Gleason and break her to his will. In the privacy of the cof he took his wife in his arms and embraced her. She lay passive in his arms, and as he looked into her face she opened her eyes wide. They were the red eyes of Dure!

That night was rung the death knell of Tabora, yet Tabora was unaware. That night was to go down in history as a night of the greatest terror the Taboran world had ever known. It was henceforth to be called the Revolt of the Slaves. There was no bloodshed, only desertion.

At the proper hour all Tabora succumbed to sleep and its great cities lay quiet. Just what happened none was certain, but, at the hour that is midnight, every house gave up its allotment of slaves. Like wraiths they crept forth. Noiselessly every airplane was rolled forth from its hangar, every airship was released from its moorings. What guards there were to object were silenced, each one by a hand on the throat, a gag in the mouth; hands and feet were then bound together.

There was a rustle like wind in the trees when the planes lifted their wings; their motors were silent, they soared to the heights above the cities. Every metropolis, every city, every village, every hamlet, every plantation, every farmhouse was silently divested of its wings! The guards and soldiers were not even aroused from their games or their catnaps. People serenely slept and dreamed.

And not until morning did they know what had happened. But the few faithful slaves who remained behind would not speak. The slaves were gone, bag and baggage, with every flying machine in the land. And with them had gone Richard Dorr!

Of him his guards had nothing to say. They evinced surprise when they learned that he had disappeared. Had not Ubca-tor, nephew of the Kirada, come and claimed that his majesty wished an audience with the prisoner? True, guards escorted him as far as the anteroom of the palace, but beyond that—was he not in the keeping of the king? Ubca-tor was not to be found.

Evening found Moura-Ur-tor in Carajama. He arrived on the back of his one remaining slave, the only slave in Tabora who had a kind word for the master. It was a sorry story Moura had to tell. His bride had held him off with a devilish little weapon, the one Dana Gleason always carried with her. She had demonstrated its power to Moura, and Dure had shown him *she* knew how to use it. Then with the company of slaves who maintained his country house and estate she had arisen in the air in Moura's plane, and he had seen the plane head for Gora!

Tabora was in a state of fear, disorganized, fearful of what the next hour was to bring. They blamed Moura-Ur-tor and his treaty with Kirada Yal. Yal had been but stalling for time, waiting for the return of his champion, who had promised to bring the Tabora planes to him, for Gora had no planes. In the streets people shrilled the name of Moura-Ur-tor, whom they now disdainfully called Moura-weit. They hissed, they spat.

Moura called the three Taboran Kiradas together. From Ora had come word that she would have nothing to do with the dealings. She agreed with Richard Dorr that justice should be done. Give to the Gora the lands that had been wrested from them! Give Moata land to live in!

The Kiradas, with Moura backing them, cried *no*! As rapidly as it could be done, every city was prepared for siege, on every citadel was mounted the great death ray machines with which they were certain they could wipe out any fleet of planes that should come warring. Old obsolete planes were brought out of hiding. In the airship workshops thousands of men were put to work to build the new airships and complete half-finished ones. A great activity was apparent.

At noon a voice was heard on the new radio of Dana Gleason. It was the voice of Kirada Yal. He explained that Gora was ready to do battle, but first she was giving Tabora a chance to do the sporting thing. The demands of Gora were simple enough. She only wanted her own lands back, the lands occupied at the present by Doata! For Moata she demanded Loata. Gora would be magnanimous. She would not drive Tabora back to the wastelands from which she had come. Gora would give Zoata to Tabora for her own, that they might all live together in peace and brotherhood, that they might all have their place in the sun.

Tabora jeered at such terms. Gora dictating to Tabora! The ropt dictating to the sef (the Abruian lion). However, Tabora was wary enough to say she would consider the terms, and would give her answer two days hence!

Richard Dorr was with Kirada Yal. Everything was in readiness. He understood Tabora's strategy. He knew that Tabora would agree to no terms with Kirada Yal.

For months he had been quietly working for such an end. In Gora he had found the necessary ingredients for gunpowder—saltpeter, charcoal, and sulfur. Small hand grenades and bombs and shells had been manufactured, crude but efficient enough for their work. Men had been drilled in the practice of throwing them, and of shooting the tiny cannon that could be carried by planes. And these cannon were now distributed among the thousands of Taboran planes now in possession of the slaves. Then after these planes had been painted in the solution that Dorr had manufactured from a formula stolen from Carajama, they were sent throughout Gora to pick up the tribesmen who had already been trained to do their part.

The solution used was the only thing that could render man immune to the power of the disintegrating ray of Tabora. Once Doata had warred upon her sister nations, and because all three nations had possessed the same solution, the war had proved futile. Peace had come to Tabora, a peace that lasted many years until it was forgotten that the formula lay in the vaults of Carajama.

Now every piece of metal, every prop, every piece of fabric, every man was daubed with the solution, so that the entire fleet should be immune to the ray.

With every fleet of a hundred planes, an airship filled with the officers whom Richard Dorr had created and trained for the work was ready to lead them to battle. Under orders, a hundred of these fleets proceeded to the frontiers of Gora and lay in waiting for the command to descend upon Tabora from every direction. Every plane was provided with one of the new radios, and Dorr had evolved a system of signals by which orders could be dispatched without Tabora understanding.

By his side was Dana Gleason, still in her golden disguise, and with her was Dure. Dana was not happy over the thought of this war, but she was beside her lover, and that was all she asked for.

Two days later Tabora radioed her refusal of Kirada Yal's terms, which was the signal for the fleets of Richard Dorr to set out for Tabora. With Kirada Yal, Richard Dorr, Dana Gleason, and a great number of high-ranking officers and statesmen of Gora, in the largest airship that had been captured, set out for Carajama.

THE STRANGE WAR

There is no need to tell what took place on that fateful day. The battle lasted only a day and part of a night before Tabora knew she was beaten. Not an enemy plane fell to the power of the Ureim, while at a signal from the flagship thousands of missiles fell upon the unprotected cities and their environs. Parties landed from the planes, and the Taboran citizens tried to do battle with the Gorans, only to find that they were armed with small metal balls that exploded and caused havoc among the citizenry.

Still no very great damage was done, outside of the killing of thousands of Taborans. A few private dwellings fell, but they could easily be rebuilt. The farmlands were left unscathed. Bombs continued to fall, but they were dropped with no precision and without doing much harm.

At midnight of the same day, the Taborans cried for peace. At Ora, the three Kiradas gathered and Kirada Yal and Richard Dorr descended there. Only by his power over his armies had Richard Dorr held the Gorans from completely demolishing all the cities of Tabora, and it was because of his counsel that Gora did not claim all the rich lands of the planet.

He drew up the terms of the treaty, which gave to Gora her old country, to

Moata half of what she had once possessed, and to Tabora the remaining section sandwiched in between her erstwhile enemies and her erstwhile slaves. Had Dorr been another type of man, he might not have succeeded in gaining his point; but he had made warriors of the Gorans, and now he made civilized men of them. Ora approved all that he demanded.

Tabora was given time to evacuate her lands and move into the space allotted her. New cities had to be built to contain her people. Her three Kiradas were forced to divide the lands between them, and over them was placed a regent from Ora. It will take her wounds long to heal.

Moata elected a Kirada for herself, and old national lines were reestablished. The golden people are still wildly exuberant over their emancipation, and Gora is overjoyed in the new wealth that has come to her.

Dorr and Dana Gleason stayed at Ora, planning to seek some out-of-the-way plantation where they would henceforth dwell in peace; but Gora and Moata would not hear of it. With one accord they elected Richard Dorr as their Ur-Kirada to see that justice was carried on.

It will take many years, no doubt, to force the three races to live on friendly terms. It will take years for the raw sores to heal; but with a man like Richard Dorr at the head, peace and understanding will grow and mature in the hearts of the people.

————

And so our host wearily finished his tale. In his eyes we saw a great depth of feeling.

"But what became of Moura?" we all demanded.

He apologized for his omission. "With the defeat of Tabora, Moura disappeared. The Taborans sang a song of hate for him. They forgot what good works he had done and remembered only that he had failed. They remembered him for the ambitious, arrogant man he was. They searched for him, but he was not to be found.

"Only Ubca-tor knew where he had gone to hide with his single faithful servant. In his name Ubca sought out Richard Dorr, and asked for mercy for the man whom his people were seeking in revenge. For Ubca-tor still loved Moura, although he had deliberately set out to save Dana Gleason from the man.

"Dorr sought Moura out, and promised him his aid."

————

So the story ended. We were all surprised to discover how stiff and cramped we had become, and arose to our feet to stretch. The golden man appeared again with trays of food and drink, of which we partook with enjoyment. We were all silent as each reviewed in his mind the tale he had just heard. I could not but wonder what had happened to Moura-Ur-tor. Looking up, I saw the eyes of our host upon me.

The Professor broke the tension of the moment. "I wonder," said he softly, "if you would mind telling us your name, sir. Strange that last night none of us thought of introductions," and he smiled blandly upon us all. True none of us had been formally introduced. I did not even know my host's name after traveling half across the world with him. I knew him only as Sa Dak (good master), and his companion as Tor, which I knew meant prince. It occurred to me that the Taboran had deliberately avoided an introduction and an exchange of names. I saw his eyes travel to his companion as if seeking aid there; then he turned to Rollins. "I swore long ago, sir, that nothing that Professor Rollins should demand of me would I neglect to fulfill. And yet most of all I dread to disclose my name. But you ask it.

"The man who faces you, sir, is none other than one who has since learned that too much ambition is as bad for the soul as too little ambition. Ambition overshadows one's vision, so that he sees nothing but his aim before him and is willing to sacrifice his fellow man to forward that ambition. I, sir, am Moura-weit."

Somehow, I failed to be shocked at the disclosure, but Professor Rollins dropped the plate he was still holding. Elsie Rollins's eyes widened, and I cannot find words to describe the expression that crept into her face, an expression that was a combination of surprise, distrust, disbelief, disappointment, together with anger and something akin to pity. I could only feel pity.

"Yes," went on Moura-weit, "I am the man who did all in his power to break the will of Dana Gleason and to do away with Richard Dorr. I did not recognize the fact that I loved Dana Gleason. Can you forgive me?"

Professor Rollins slowly answered: "It is not for me to forgive you, for I had almost succeeded in murdering those two. I have lived in sorrow for the deed, but now that you have told me that all is well, I know I can die happy. Wherefore should I judge you? No; rather I am glad you have escaped the wrath of your people and can spend the remainder of your life happy in the thought that you did not accomplish your purpose."

Silently the two clasped hands.

Again a deep silence enveloped us, but I was still anxious for facts. "How did you manage to construct this machine and escape, since men were seeking for you?" I asked.

Moura-weit turned his strange eyes upon me. "That I owe to three people: Richard Dorr, Dana Gleason, and—Ubca-tor," and he held out his hand to his companion in exile. "I have spoken of the machine which the Roata (the Earth Club) commenced to build, hoping to gain favor in Dana Gleason's eyes.

It was abandoned at Ora when half-completed. Dorr gave me help to complete it. Then Ubca-tor and my faithful servant Urto elected to accompany me. Richard Dorr and Dana Gleason saw us depart and wished us Godspeed. On leaving, Dana Gleason, whom you would now call Mrs. Richard Dorr, presented me with the manuscript I brought to the Professor, and she also gave me the little diary as a memento; for she said she no longer needed it, since the past was past, and she thought it would aid me in convincing the Professor that she had truly sent me to him!"

There was much more said, but that is irrelevant to this story. Moura-weit conveyed me back to the spot where he had first captured me, but the Rollinses went back with Moura-weit, for the Professor was anxious to see the Void.

Professor Rollins died aboard the *Yodverl*, but what Elsie Rollins experienced aboard the interplanetary vehicle is another story. She returned only to straighten out the effects of the late Professor Ezra Rollins. She came to New York and stayed long enough to help me compile the above story, which will not be published until I am dead. Perhaps after I die, Moura-weit may return to Earth and so corroborate this exceptional history.

Doctors have examined my collarbone, but can find no proof that it was ever fractured. My wife refuses to believe a word of what I told her, declaring I must have hidden away a cache of whiskey in my fishing hut, and drunk too deeply. I have only the ruby that Moura-weit left in payment for my old suit. Gem experts declare it to be as perfect a ruby as ever was found and insist it is of terrestrial origin. I know differently. But—I cannot prove it.

LILITH LORRAINE (1894–1967) was the pen name used by the Texas-born author, editor, and publisher Mary Maude Wright (née Dunn). A self-styled Leonarda educated in "science, dancing, swimming, wild horses, psychology, philosophy and boy friends," Lorraine attended college in Arizona and California before taking on work as an educator, administrator, crime reporter, radio announcer, public lecturer, estate manager, poultry farmer, and housewife to support her literary endeavors (Lorraine, "Story" 2). Although her writing appeared in a variety of newspapers, literary journals, and genre magazines, SF was always her first love.

Throughout the 1930s Lorraine's short stories appeared frequently in *Amazing Stories* and other Gernsback publications, and she was described by fans as "one of sf's [top] three women writers" (qtd. in Sneyd, "Empress" 210). In the 1940s she built upon her already well-established reputation as an SF pro by branching out into poetry and editing as well (see the biographical entries on Lorraine in chapter 2, "Poets," and chapter 4, "Editors," of this anthology). Fans and fellow writers recall her as something of a character: she was a Christian socialist feminist partial to silk robes and turbans in bright colors who liked to use her double thumb as a test of people's character. Lorraine took the name Lilith because she saw herself as a troublemaker, and indeed, she seems to have lived up to that description—as the SF poet and historian Steve Sneyd notes, Lorraine's political convictions led the U.S. government to watch her closely, and to this day she is perhaps the only person whose FBI file includes speculative poetry as proof that she was an "advanced radical" (Sneyd, "Lilith Lorraine" 197).

While her career spanned decades and areas of SF production, Lorraine entered the genre community as a fiction writer. Her first sale was the 1929 novella "The Brain of the Planet," which appeared as issue 5 of Hugo Gernsback's Science Fiction Series. She sold four more stories to various Gernsback publications over the next six years. By the mid-1930s, Lorraine—like a number of other women writers who began publishing SF in the 1920s—found herself alienated from what she perceived to be the increasingly "stereotyped and standardized" state of commercial SF ("Cracks" n.p.). Accordingly, she turned her attention to the production of amateur and semi-pro magazines, including *Challenge*, the first magazine dedicated to SF poetry, and *Different*, which brought together mainstream and SF artists and provided Lorraine with a forum in which to write fiction that reflected her political and aesthetic convictions.

"Into the 28th Century" was Lorraine's second SF sale, appearing in the Winter 1930 issue of *Science Wonder Quarterly*. It was one of several stories with "feminist-socialist utopian" elements that the managing editor, David Lasser, solicited for that magazine, along with tales by Leslie F. Stone and Margaret F.

Rupert (Davin, *Pioneers* 189). Significantly, the headnote to Lorraine's story does not address its potentially radical political elements. Instead, it emphasizes the universal appeal of SF to all thinking writers, enthusiastically noting that "it speaks well of the times in which we are living, when women authors such as Lilith Lorraine have the vision to take science fiction seriously enough to make extended studies of it" (Gernsback, "Headnote to 'Into the 28th Century'" 251). And, indeed, telling as it does the tale of an early-twentieth-century man who travels to a future Earth where mechanical technologies have been replaced by their telepathically driven counterparts and where carefully planned inter-racial marriages have engendered a nearly immortal "super-race" of humans, Lorraine's novella is very much in line with the action-packed, scientifically in-spired and inspiring SF that Gernsback claimed was the best the genre had to offer (258).

Of course, Lorraine's story does rework at least two other popular modes of women's fiction to make strategic feminist points about the future of science and society. Like other turn-of-the-century feminist utopias such as Mary E. Bradley Lane's *Mizora* (1880) and Charlotte Perkins Gilman's *Herland* (1915), "Into the 28th Century" imagines a future where "women's domestic duties . . . [including] cooking, canning, preserving, cleaning up, and managing ser-vants" have been reduced or eliminated by the strategic application of new sciences and technologies, thereby liberating women to pursue higher educa-tion and participate in statecraft (Donawerth, "Science" 139). Lorraine's work also echoes that of her predecessors by attributing the creation of utopia to the work of women themselves. However, while Lane and Gilman suggest that utopia can emerge only when women act collectively to eliminate men from society, Lorraine more diplomatically proposes that women might build utopia by withholding sex until their male counterparts are willing to reform them-selves and the world.

Lorraine also updates the conventions of nineteenth-century domestic fic-tion to demonstrate what the reformed man might look like. As literary scholar Nina Baym explains, the heroine of the domestic novel who ventures out into the world to make a living and build a new life for herself is typically rewarded with the love of a sensible, well-educated man who stands somewhat apart from the daily operations of patriarchal capitalism and "who likes the heroine as much [as] or more than he lusts for her" (41). While the traditional domestic hero is often a man of the cloth, Lorraine suggests that his modern counter-part might just as well be a man of either the sword or science. Accordingly, she casts her narrator Anthony as a well-educated, scientifically inclined, and gentle-manly former soldier who longs for a world better than that of the early twen-tieth century into which he is born. Anthony finds that world in twenty-eighth-century Corpus Christi, where he falls in love with a woman whose ability to quote Shakespeare is every bit as desirable as her bright green hair. In this way, Lorraine synthesizes the emergent conventions of SF with the established ones of the feminist utopia and the domestic novel to create a future where economic and racial inequality have been obliterated and men and women of the new super-race live completely fulfilling lives.

....

"Into the 28th Century"
Science Wonder Quarterly, Winter 1930

CHAPTER 1

At the expiration of my four years' service in the navy in the early summer of 1932, I was convinced that I had had my fill of the sea. I soon discovered that I had merely had my fill of the navy. After all, a ship is no place for a young man with traditions and a fair education but with neither money nor influence. Minus the first two factors I might have been content with such fair advancement as can be wrested from life by unaided effort. These two factors become hindrances when an individual endowed with the culture of a fading aristocracy finds himself in a position where minds of coarser sensibilities can lord it over him. Eventually he has to choose between solitude and such companionship as can be found among those of his own rank. This is neither a plea for the vanishing aristocracy of the South that distilled its fragrance from the rank, black soil of slavery, nor is it a justification of my own attitude. It's only a statement of that attitude, of a state of mind inherited and hence unchangeable. It's only a passing regret that something of the graciousness which constitutes the soul of aristocracy cannot be woven into the fabric of democracy that *all* may share alike.

That the siren that sings in the winds and waves still sought to lure me over perilous seas was evident enough when, some three weeks after my discharge, I spent the bulk of my savings for an antiquated motorboat. I had gone to visit my grandfather at my childhood home in Corpus Christi, now a newly opened deep-water port on the coast of Texas. My father was long since dead, and my grandfather's only surviving child, my aunt, was somewhere in the Orient. She had always been a wanderer, writing when the mood swayed her. There was always a sort of unspoken understanding between us, and because of this, I have chosen her to give my story to the world. When it reaches her I shall be—elsewhere.

The glory of sunset and moonrise over Corpus Christi Bay remembered from of old, and the thrill of rushing through its phosphorescent waters leaving behind a trail of radiance like a comet's tail, might have been the subconscious allurement impelling me to purchase the motorboat. Dutifully, I decided to spend my mornings and afternoons pursuing an elusive job and my other hours cruising around the Bay and the nearer waters of the Gulf. Had I foreseen the unprecedented, inexplicable happenings that were to follow in the wake of my investment, I might have hesitated before paying that departing tourist the ridiculously low price he asked.

Still, I regret nothing, provided I can get back. If I succeed in that, which will involve my disappearance from the world, my aunt will give this document to the public. If I cannot get back, no one will ever know where I was for exactly forty-eight hours between the tenth and twelfth of May 1932. If I tell this tale at all it will be told at a safe distance. Even then my aunt will be instructed to label it "fiction" lest she be incarcerated in a madhouse or arrested in connection with my disappearance. Nevertheless, there is a small circle of her acquaintances that know the real facts underlying much of her "fiction" and these few will be interested in my adventure from a scientific standpoint. Others will regard it as the wildest imagining, but what does it matter? He who tells a man a truth that he is not ready to receive tells him a lie, but he who garbs the truth in the raiment of fiction sometimes teaches the soul a lesson.

The moon was just beginning to rise over the water as I put out to sea in the very early morning of the tenth of May. The old craft was humming along fine. I was lost in the beauty of the night and wrapped in the seductive mystery of the stars. My imagination was racing along like the phosphorous stream that cut a swath of radiance through the sea. Suddenly—without warning—the thing happened! I felt a checking of my speed, a sickening lurch, the boat shivered beneath me, reared and shot straight upward under the pressure of a shining column of water that carried me fifty feet nearer heaven than I ever expect to be again. Then slowly—ominously—the column of water subsided, carrying me down far more gently than I had ascended, and leaving me flopping around in the middle of the Bay. The boat was nowhere to be seen. It had simply vanished.

The next thing I noticed was the brilliance of the sun. All at once I remembered that the moon had been shining when I "went up." Thinking perhaps I had been momentarily stunned, and was merely suffering from the illusion of brightness, I began to take further stock of my surroundings. Imagine my consternation when I saw coming straight toward me a great craft resembling a warship. Yet its design was very strange. But I couldn't help wondering what a warship, probably of a foreign nation, was doing in Gulf waters. Even more uncanny than this was the fact that she flaunted a coat of shining gold paint for all the world like a 1930 Ford. Of course, it might have been the sun in my eyes, but even then by all the laws of Nature there shouldn't have been a sun to be seen at this time of night.

For the next fifteen minutes I was too busy getting rescued to think much about midnight suns, golden battleships, or anything else. Finally I was "hauled over" and dumped unceremoniously on the deck. I rubbed my eyes and looked about me. Then doubting my senses, I rubbed them again.

Crowding around me was a group of some fifty young men and women with hair of every color of the rainbow—red, green, yellow, purple, and intervening shades unknown to me. Both sexes had curls falling to their shoulders, but the boys, notwithstanding, did not convey the impression of effeminacy. They were perfectly formed, athletic, muscled, and gracefully lithe. The girls were a combination of Venus de Milo and Diana the Huntress. What I mean is that their forms were neither angular nor voluptuous but carried that dual appeal to both the senses and the soul that comes only from the blending of the most refined spirituality with the most perfect health. They were of those pleasing proportions that combine both softness and strength and suggest power expressing itself through delicacy. Both sexes were unusually tall, yet formed proportionately.

The girls' costumes—I couldn't think of their apparel as clothing—had the classical lines of the Ancient Greeks—simple—clinging—revealing—almost devoid of ornament. The boys were garbed in abbreviated tunics cut somewhat after the Roman fashion and made of a shining material that resembled scales of gold. A graceful cloak was thrown across the shoulders. Both sexes wore sandals of a silver or golden sheen evidently designed more for ornament than for use. Bracelets and even anklets were in evidence but not in profusion. Around the heads of the young men were plain gold bands set with a central jewel whose scintillating splendor I have never seen matched before. The headdresses of the girls were varied, consisting of gorgeous plumage rivaling the feathers of birds of paradise, wreaths of flowers so fresh and beautiful that at first I thought them natural, or long transparent veils of rainbow colors held in place by golden circlets.

My first illogical idea was that this might be a motion picture company in the costume of another age—but what age? These youthful godlike beings had robbed all the ages of their choicest secrets of adornment and had magically blended them into one harmonious galaxy of grace.

Any further dazed impressions that might have come to me were interrupted by the sound of voices—English voices. A green-haired damsel of bewildering beauty was executing a war dance right in front of me and crying out in a high extremely musical voice vibrant with excitement:

"Well! We've got it! Roped it in! Captured it! Style of the twentieth century! Pants! Shirt! Shoes! Everything!"

"Oh, do be quiet, Iris!" interrupted a well-modulated voice that I later discovered belonged to a young man named Therius. "He may be hurt—frightened."

This friendly evidence of civilized consideration loosed my paralyzed tongue but all that I could accomplish in the way of speech was the trite old formula, "Where am I?"

"You're just about where you were before, comrade," replied Therius, "so far as space is concerned. In regard to *time*, however, you are, if I place your epoch correctly, about 800 years in your future."

THE GOLDEN AGE

Reason rebelled against this preposterous joke that I thought was being played upon me.

"Impossible!" I retorted. "Why, this is a modern battleship."

"Of your age?" questioned Iris with the wide-eyed serious simplicity of a child.

I began to feel decidedly queer. At least these people were not joking, whatever else might be the matter with them.

"Certainly it might have been of his time," remarked a gorgeous purple-haired young princess. "This boat was used to carry on their wretched wars in about 1980 — to murder each other, you know, to appease the fetishes that they called patriotism and democracy and—" She faltered for lack of the right word.

"Hundred percent Americanism," tersely supplemented Therius.

At last I realized that there was something more to all this than a practical joke and that these young people had nothing in common with my day and age. Still slightly dazed, I staggered to my feet, assisted by the friendly hand of Therius. Another youth brought me an enormous velvet cushion and indicated that I was to be seated upon it. The other young people likewise appropriated numerous cushions that were lying around the deck in Oriental profusion. They grouped themselves gracefully around me gazing into my face with the eager, smiling expectancy of highly intelligent children.

"How did I get here?" I demanded, determined to satisfy my own curiosity first.

"You were accidentally captured," said Therius, who seemed to have elected himself spokesman. "You were literally snatched out of your dimension, out of your time, into ours. Our time flyer had been left open and at your period and was therefore receptive to anything which might have been in the neighborhood subject to its pull."

"This invention," I questioned excitedly, "is it a machine?"

"Certainly," replied Therius. "Why way back—shortly after your time— science and metaphysics declared a truce and united their forces. They realized at last that the wind power of the latter could operate only through the instruments of the former. By different routes the ancient rivals had arrived at the same truth, namely, that to operate through time, energies must be provided with material instruments through which to function. Science eventually had perfected machinery so delicately sensitive that the hitherto uncaptured elements of the time curve could be conducted through the centuries as electricity was captured and directed through wires. But science, having neglected the laws of mind, did not know how to so concentrate and focus this energy as to make it usable. So they turned to the metaphysicians, who through the centuries had been studying and perfecting the laws of mind and finding them as definite and invariable as the laws of chemistry. Thus ended the warfare between science and metaphysics through the mutual discovery that each school had what the other lacked.

"It was—just after radio—" he explained rather haltingly, "that the first thought transmitters were put into practical operation, and—just before Socialism, they began to run nearly all machinery by means of thought-vibration. During the final revolution known as the Revolt of Youth, the deadly disintegrating ray controlled by thought-power was invented by rebel scientists and turned the tide of victory in their favor.

"After Socialism, when the need for government save in its broader sense had practically vanished, the reintegrating ray was discovered and controlled by the same process. Finally, what we thought to be the summit of human achievement was attained in the so-called 'creation of matter' through the materialization of thought. *Now* we know that there is no end to the unfoldment of the divine potentialities within us, so long as we use them in the furtherance of the Undeviating Plan. You, yourself, are a living testimony that we have not only discovered and controlled the mighty energies of our own age, but have reached back through time and brought into the Golden Age a splendid representative of the age of gold."

With this graceful compliment Therius paused, but I still had many questions.

"This battleship," I asked him, mentally reaching out to it as to a tangible link that bound me to reality, "is it also navigated by thought-waves?"

"Of course. Everything is so operated. All our machinery, which is really quite simple, is nothing more or less in most cases than thought-focusing crystals and thought-projecting mirrors. In your day machinery was so alarmingly complicated that the scarcity of it in even our largest cities will, no doubt, astonish you. Of course, the great secret of our thought-machines lies in the composition of the crystals and the mirrors. They are made from a synthetic substance, the key to whose discovery was found by experimentation with the so-called 'magic' crystals of the Orient. We found that their peculiar properties lay in the fact that they facilitated the concentration and projection of thought."

CHAPTER 2
Ageless Race
"Why is this ship in such a remarkable state of preservation? And why," I asked him, "in such an obviously warless age, have you seen fit to retain its accoutrements of destruction?"

"The golden substance with which it is coated throughout is the secret of its preservation. This substance, and anything protected by it, is as indestructible as thought itself, for it is thought materialized. We have preserved this battleship and its war equipment along with several other gruesome relics of your time, for historical purposes."

"Good Lord," thought I, "if its old crew could only hear the ship called a gruesome relic."

"We are using it also," he continued, "as a sort of floating university. We have junked its clumsy machinery, of course, and turned that space into a gymnasium and a reading room. Our regular college curriculum requires a year of travel during which our students visit all the important centers of the World-State. Thus it has come about that this old battleship represents the University of Nirvania, of which institution I have the honor to be president."

"You! Its president!" I cried incredulously. "Why, you are only a boy yourself."

"I may seem so to you," he answered smilingly, "but I shall be ninety-six my next birthday. We have discovered the secret of rejuvenation; hence, you will never witness the crumbling specter of old age among us. Disease and death have retreated far back into the charnel houses of antiquity along with war, and poverty and greed."

"But 'death!'" I exclaimed incredulously. "How have you conquered it?"

"Well, generally, the process has become automatic." He seemed to be searching for words to convey to my complex mentality a truth divinely simple. "Why, it just doesn't *come*. When we discovered that mind is the creator, controller, and destroyer of matter, we began to study and apply the *laws* of mind. The whole secret is contained in a verse of a book you folks once set great store by but never proved its truth. This Bible of yours said, 'Be ye transformed by the renewing of your minds.'

"Humanlike, we didn't find the secret there. In those days we preferred to grope through the labyrinthine mazes of science rather than to take the straight and narrow path of revelation. That would have been too simple and we are out for complexity. The new school of psychoanalysis, after it had discarded quackery and settled down to serious investigation, satisfied all our yearnings for complexity. It delved down into the musty catacombs of our twisted brains and brought out the gibbering ghosts of dead desires that we had thrust back into the slime of the subconscious, afraid to face the facts of our own natures. Man finally began to live normally, and better than all, he no longer carried with him the burden of the *consciousness* of sin. 'We are not fallen gods,' we courageously asserted, 'we are risen beasts. As the water lily pushes upward from the ooze of the riverbed, so the soul of man has emerged from the primeval slime and has pushed upward to the sun.' This we have done because of that spark within us that has burned steadily in the darkness of savagery even as now it flames in laughter and in light. Thus we left behind us the clanking chains of impure thinking that had been fastened on us by the festering moralists. At last we realized that *all* of God's works are perfect, that to impute impurity to any of God's manifestations is to impute impurity to God Himself, to poison the stream of life at its sacred fountainhead."

I stared at him open-mouthed. Was this man mad? Were they all mad? He seemed to divine my thought. "Hear me out," he said.

"When our mentality changed, our institutions changed accordingly, though not so peaceably, as you shall presently learn. Our innumerable agencies of repression became channels of *expression*, glorified expression on higher planes.

"At last it happened that the physical ills that follow in the wake of mental repressions, in the wake of the consciousness of impurity, vanished along with the mental stagnation that had bred them. For we had learned that mental stagnation—crystallization—is death, and mental plasticity—eternal flux of mind—is youth eternal. Thus were we transformed by the renewing of our minds, by the eradication of the prejudices, intolerance, impurity, and bigotry that caused the soul of man to shatter its crystallized instrument in its struggle to expand.

"Long before this, science had eradicated the germs of contagious disease and had purified the bloodstream of hereditary contamination. The only ills remaining were imaginary ones and all that was needed to insure immortality was to purify the imagination. Scientists even in your day had boldly stated that there was no inherent necessity for death—our scientists proved that statement.

"Notwithstanding, even now we become a little emotionally twisted at times. I say *emotionally*, because we have purposely kept alive our emotions. We have deliberately intensified and refined them until we have attained a capacity to enjoy and suffer that would have spelled madness to those of your day, when there was so little to enjoy—so much to suffer. But when we get mentally twisted now-a-days we just go to a specialist and get taken apart and reassembled, the same as when we have an accident."

"Taken apart! Reassembled!" I gasped. "What do you mean?"

"We go and get our mental twists removed," he explained. "By a process of psychoanalysis, highly refined mental twists are straightened out just as any twisted thing is. It is nature's law that the parts of any given organism will continue to vibrate in perfect harmony with each other unless some foreign influence disturbs their relations. In the human organism, perfectly adjusted to its environment, this distortion, this disharmony that produces disease and death, can occur only through mental or emotional perversion. During the restorative process following the untwisting, our minds and emotions automatically resume their natural relations to each other, just as a spring would return to its normal state once pressure is removed. Our physical ills disappear, and the mind, aware of its errors and working consciously to rectify them, is in a position to make a fresh start. Ordinarily we can take ourselves in hand and iron out the kinks unaided, but if we let ourselves slip too far, we can always fall back on science."

"It's all too unbelievable!" I exclaimed.

"No, it's all too simple," amended Therius. "That's what held humanity back so long; expecting to find life's greatest truths most wrapped in mystery, in complexity. At last we had to learn that there is nothing complex in all God's universe except the twisted ideas of human minds."

A Twenty-Eighth-Century Diet
"You speak of God," I told him. "Why, we had almost discarded God in my age. Surely you don't believe in a personal deity."

"Of course not. That would be an absurdity. But there is the eternal spirit in all things, the flaming essence that throbs and pulses at the heart of life, that dances in the atom, thunders in the tempest, holds the stars to their courses, the mind to its aspirations, the soul to its mate. It is that spark within us, within all humanity, that has led upward through the long, dark eons of frustrations to the Splendor—and the Laughter—and the Light—"

His voice trailed off into ecstatic silence as his thoughts were lost in the inexpressible, and I knew that I was face-to-face with one who had seen—God. A reverent hush ensued for a moment as among those who are conscious of the benediction of an unseen Presence and the rush of mighty wings.

"You spoke of the change in human institutions," I asked him presently. "In what did this change consist and how was it effected?"

"That's a long story, and a sad story," he answered, "and I'm going to let Iris tell it to see how well she remembers her history lesson. The young lady's researches into the history of your time and the stormy period that followed it have earned her an enviable standing in her class. But first let us inhale, or as you would say, let's eat. Althus, bring our new comrade a flask."

A young man left the group and returned in a moment with a jewel-encrusted flask of glittering beauty that he uncorked and handed to me. Under the impression that I was being invited to imbibe something forbidden by the 18th Amendment, I raised the bottle to my lips.

"No! Don't drink it! Inhale it!" cried Therius. "It's the essence of food."

Embarrassed at my error, I raised the flask to my nostrils. Immediately my whole being was permeated by a delicious and seductive fragrance. In a few moments the pangs of hunger, which had been annoying me for the last thirty minutes, were miraculously assuaged. As I continued to inhale under the captivation of the delicate perfume, I began to experience a feeling of surfeit as one does who has overeaten. I noticed that my companions, who had likewise been inhaling, were replacing their flasks in cunningly concealed pockets in their garments.

"Does this constitute your entire diet?" I asked Therius. "Oh no," he replied. "Although it satisfies every dietetic requirement, we can't resist the temptation of biting into the luscious fruits that overburden our orchards and of partaking occasionally of the foamy concoctions and icy beverages that the ladies insist on serving at our social gatherings. It would be better—much better," he went on academically, "if we denied ourselves these pleasures. I have every reason to fear," he prophesied with the air of one predicting a cataclysmic disaster, "that if we continue these indulgences, somebody on this planet will someday be stricken with that ancient curse, the stomachache."

With much difficulty I restrained myself from bursting into hilarious laughter on observing from the serious expressions of these young people that a stomachache would be a matter of international concern.

"By the way, comrade," said Therius, "you have not yet told us your name. I am called Therius, as you may have already gathered. This young lady," pointing to the beauty with the sea-green hair, "is, as you have heard me call her, Iris. This young man," indicating a striking-looking youth, "is Heriod, and this lady," pointing out a purple-haired vision, "is Lyria. It is needless to present them all, for you would forget their names, but you will learn them all in time. We have, as you see, dropped the surname, and for purposes of distinction have made it compulsory to resort to a greater diversity of Christian names. And your name, comrade?" he asked again.

"My name," I replied, likewise omitting my surname, "is Anthony."

"Ah!" said Iris, gazing at me with a new light in her beautiful eyes. "It was Anthony who lost the world—for love."

"It is well lost—for love." I answered her—and what she saw in my eyes caused her to drop her own shyly while a faint blush suffused her cheeks. I was thrilled to the uttermost depths of my being that my green-haired sea goddess had been chosen to relate the changes leading up to the divine perfection which she so gloriously symbolized. Something, old as creation itself, had flashed between us in that first direct meeting of our eyes, defying time and leveling dimensions. In a low, vibrant voice that my soul drank in like music, she began:

CHAPTER 3

How It Happened

"You will naturally know more of the events immediately preceding and embracing your own time than we. Hence, I shall not take up the story until about the year 1950. Your day was called by later historians the Age of the Great Unrest. It is especially interesting to us because in that epoch were set in visible motion the hitherto hidden forces that were to rock society to its foundation. From the very dawn of history momentous forces had been working in the shadow, shaping not so much the material destiny of man as the warp and woof of human character. These silent forces were dual. We have called them simply, as did some of your religionists, the Powers of Light and the Powers of Darkness. But you must understand exactly what *we* wish to signify by the terms we have appropriated. By the Powers of Light we understand all the innumerable agencies, visible and invisible, that have impelled man to broader freedom, greater happiness, and more perfect unfoldment of the latent powers within him. By the Powers of Darkness we designate everything that impels the soul to limitation, the mind to intolerance, the heart to selfishness, and the body to imperfection. All that man has accomplished materially, the institutions he has molded, the battles he has fought, the creeds he has believed, the civilizations he has created and destroyed, all these are but the visible reflections of that higher conflict that has gone on in his own nature between the two forces I have mentioned. Yet out of this very conflict with spiritual darkness was generated the desire for its opposite, spiritual light. And with the desire for that light came the wisdom to recognize it, the courage to fight for it, the will to attain it.

"In your day the inner conflict had almost reached its climax as evidenced by the utter impossibility of remaining neutral. Like two opposing armies on the eve of a decisive battle, two mighty schools of thought lined up against each other. One school represented the soul-killing tendencies that had created standardization, competition, and inhibitory creeds and institutions, which the soul of man had long ago outgrown and repudiated. The other school espoused the cause of higher freedom, greater tolerance, and escape from standardization. Like a grim juggernaut crushing everything that stood in its path, the chariot of diabolical 'efficiency' rolled on and either converted all men into cogs in its machinery or crushed them to powder under its wheels. In your day the odds were decidedly in favor of the Powers of Darkness. The World-Trust was beginning to emerge from the wreck of private ownership: absorbing independent enterprises and preparing to absorb the functions of government.

"All this would have been very well had the right motive been behind it, had it been possible for the soul to emerge alive from the process. Surely the centralization of the means of production and distribution means the elimination of waste, the conservation of energy, and thereby the creation of leisure for the soul to expand. But it didn't work out that way. The same diabolical powers that had brought private ownership to its highest expressions, foreseeing its inevitable decline, began to retract their own gospel. They established a travesty of Socialism—dictatorial, merciless—with themselves as dictators. Instead of shortening the hours of labor they employed an army of experts to devise new tasks of increasing complexity. With the collapse of private enterprise the former middle classes and finally the upper strata of the social structure collapsed into the ranks of labor.

"To insure the continuance of their system, the dictators, after binding men's bodies to their giant machines, began to attack the hitherto impregnable fortresses of mind. Always before in the course of history, whenever human freedom had been seriously menaced, a leader had arisen. A thinker had always emerged, often from the very ranks of the oppressed, who, keeping his mind alert and his ideals uncontaminated, had inspired his comrades to revolt. 'But now—' so swore the Dictators in their secret councils, 'there shall be no more thinking on the part of the masses, save such thoughts as we, their masters, shall implant in the mass mind.' Controlling all employment, since the crumbling governments had long since disclaimed any responsibility in the matter of whether their subjects should work or starve, the Dictators finally issued what was later referred to as 'The Unspeakable Manifesto.'

"'We have created jobs for all,' they proclaimed grandiloquently, through the medium of the subsidized press. 'We have, therefore, suspended all agencies of charity supported by our capital, for where there is employment for all, and compensation for such as we find unfit to labor, there is no further need of charity. There is no longer an excuse for idleness, and he who will not work must starve.'"

The Unspeakable Manifesto
"Yes, there were jobs for all, but at what a price! Oh, my comrade, that I might mercifully veil from your eyes this stain on civilization! But you must understand if you are to comprehend what followed.

"At this time surgery had reached a perfection hitherto unattained in the annals of science. The human brain had been probed and altered so that by means of safe and simple operations criminal tendencies could be eradicated and the channels of higher thought opened for the expression of latent genius. But no such altruistic motive guided the scalpels of the hired surgeons of the Industrial Dictators. To make a long story short, this is what they were employed to do.

"First under the guise of 'vocational treatments,' and later brazenly and openly under the name of 'vocational operations,' they compelled every applicant for employment to submit to cerebral surgery. The aim of the operation was twofold: to block the brain paths of creative thinking, and to concentrate all the energies of the mind on the particular task for which the victim was selected.

"This began the creation of a race of human robots, each a highly specialized machine for the performance of his appointed task, incapable of thinking on any other subject, and hence incapable of revolt or even discontent.

"This horror of the ages might have gone on until the humanity of our planet had become a soulless menace to the universe had not youth intervened. Even in your time the Revolt of the Youth was beginning to assume alarming proportions. Toward the false psychology that had been deliberately foisted on the credulous masses through the channels of a corrupted press, a tainted educational system, and a fossilized religion, the younger generation maintained a mocking indifference. If pressed too far this indifference flared into open rebellion. The age-old fetishes of the flag, the altar, and the home were discarded by these clear-eyed, strong-limbed, clean-minded youngsters, along with their belief in storks and Santa Claus. They had seen the flag used as an appeal to selfish interests, they had seen Mammon enthroned on the altar of God, they had seen the home desecrated and broken by the force of economic pressure.

"Between the youngsters and the elders of that day a gap in evolution yawned and widened. The thinking processes of these youths were as logical as those of their elders were muddled. Their minds drove straight to conclusions, exposed in the subtlest motives, and laughed in the face of superstition. In the dawn light of their awakening they said that the idols of the elders had brought them nothing but chains and slavery. They boldly stated that if life were nothing more than a senseless circle of its own perpetuation, that if man's sole duty was to reproduce his kind, foregoing all happiness for the sake of those who must likewise forego all happiness for the generation that should follow them and so on *ad infinitum*, then life was not worth living. They looked *back* on the life process and found its meaning. They proclaimed the gospel of human happiness as the purpose of life and the perpetuation of happiness as the *reason* for perpetuating life.

"They went too far, of course, in their rebellion. In their resentment against the old they often discarded principles that might have strengthened the fabric of the new. In their hatred of pain they often grasped the transitory pleasures of the moment rather than building for permanent and enduring contentment. In time, however, they swung back to normal and by the time that the first cerebral 'vocational operations' were performed they had settled down grimly to the business of consistent, organized revolt. Everywhere that youth flaunted itself, rebellion flared—and youth was everywhere. Swelling the ranks of the army and navy, in the fields of scientific research, even under the parental frown of the Industrial Dictators—everywhere, rebellion spread like wildfire. The cerebral specialists were hunted down like rats and death, swift and untraceable, met them at every turn. It was a case of father against son, of mother against daughter. The hypnotized elders had been thoroughly convinced that youth's rebellion against 'sacred institutions' was a contagious insanity that only the surgeon's knife could cure. Still bound hand and foot by creeds of fire and brimstone, they were inflamed by the hired ministers of Mammon to make a sacrifice of their children's splendid intellects, to save their souls from Hell.

"But youth was not alone in its conflict, for many true reformers, scientists, and radicals rallied to its side. Yet it must be borne in mind that it was the oncoming tide of youth that engulfed these movements rather than that youth enlisted under their banners. This accounts for the synthesis of thought that emerged from the fusion of these various philosophies into one mighty movement that was broad enough to include them all, and to unite them for one purpose.

"Then came war! Revolution, bloody and horrible beyond the dreams of Hell! Inventions of diabolic destructiveness were loosed on both sides, but it was a young scientist of the rebellion who perfected the disintegrating ray.

"In the wake of this crumbling terror, vengeance followed swift and merciless. Armies melted into atoms, cities crumbled into dust, and mountains toppled in the sea. It all culminated with that ghastly midnight carnage known as the Slaughter of the Ancients. Horrible and unnatural as it may seem, this annihilation of one generation by its offspring, it was a thing that had to be. Again the Inexorable Law had spoken. Nature herself had entered the lists on the side of progress and the fittest had survived.

CHAPTER 4
The New Chivalry

"In the year 1955, peace was restored to the stricken planet, reconstruction began, and the World-State elected a woman, known as the World President, as its chief executive. This was before the establishment of the monarchy.

"Any narration of the Great Revolt would be incomplete without a description of the changes that took place in the status of woman. In your day woman was just beginning to demand and attain economic equality with man. Shortly afterward she demanded and secured the establishment of a single code of morals. Man met these demands sullenly and retaliated for every inch of ground that he was forced to yield by a lessening of his chivalry. This only proved to woman that his chivalry was without any foundation save that of a sneering deference to weakness. The knighthood of the ages was but a sugar-coated pill that concealed a soul-killing poison, an opiate to drug the intellect. This discovery embittered woman and almost caused a war among the sexes. The ultra-feminists began to acquaint the world with the true status of the case. They began to demand chivalry, but not as an opiate to lull the reason into submission to a sex whose last claim to superiority had been undermined. They demanded it as a tribute still due to those who were *more* than equals because of the sacrifice they still endured in giving birth to man. Man met this demand with taunts and insults. Woman gave him his choice between the restoration of chivalry and the surrender of his ancient privileges, even the surrender of his parenthood. She grimly stated that it were better for humanity to die painlessly through the ceasing of birth than to commit suicide through the continuance of manmade institutions.

"Chivalry was restored. There was nothing else to do. Notwithstanding, woman in her new bigness that had come to her through the broadening influences of her new freedom was not inclined to add humiliation to her victory. She sweetened man's defeat with such queenly graciousness that eventually the new chivalry came to have a real foundation. Men, casting aside the childishness that had always made woman regard them maternally rather than as comrades, became real men, men who were big enough to give honor where honor was due, and in addition to chivalry came also mutual respect. Today in our newfound immortality, with the burden of childbearing practically lifted, woman is still accorded chivalry. This is necessary because of her more delicate organism, whose very delicacy must be conserved and perpetuated if she is to exercise, for the benefit of all humanity, her finer sensibilities. Woman has found her compensation for motherhood as the mother of the World-State. She is supreme in the realm of the government. She has enlarged the scope of maternity and the four walls of her home to include the spiritual and intellectual guidance of our planet, the home of the human race.

"Naturally, the functions of government today are, as you have already learned, vastly different from its functions in your time. Concerned now with education, with the patronage of art, science, and literature, with the beautification and spiritualization of all life, it finds in woman its ideal director. Man still leads in invention, mechanics, mathematics, and the more strenuous sports. Woman has ceased to imitate man, being content in her own sphere. She has intensified her femininity, wherever it can be done without a sacrifice of her health and freedom. Thus she has preserved that pleasing contrast in the sexes which perpetuates their appeal for one another.

"All this is a digression and a glimpse into times far beyond the Revolution but it will enable you to understand our present social values. This feminist movement was not distinct from the Revolt of Youth, but was concurrent with it. There might have been an open war between the sexes had woman not played such a glorious part in the Revolution and had not the memory of sufferings shared together in the Great Rebellion softened the bitterness of the sex strife.

"With youth triumphant a glorious era was ushered in and true Socialism was established. The soul, the higher nature of man, with infinite leisure to unfold, blossomed in beauty and soared to heights of achievement hitherto undreamed of. Forever casting off the old puritanical idea that earthly happiness is a thing to be rejected in order to purchase a hypothetical paradise beyond, man reached forth his hand and gathered the joy and plenty that have always lain within his reach. Disease and death yielded before the 'consciousness of immortality'; crime and repression vanished simultaneously with the 'consciousness of sin' and the lifting of poverty. Great inventions were perfected, making life's necessities attainable by a maximum of two hours' daily labor, and man, freed from the ancient curse of toil, raised his head from the ground and began to explore the infinite."

"You spoke of the monarchy," I interrupted. "Was the United States willing to surrender its long-cherished ideals of democracy? In fact, very few nations had any time for kingdoms and for kings even in my day. I must admit, however," I added shamefacedly, "that we had very little real democracy."

A New World

"When the world came under one government, England insisted that the highest officer in the Federation should bear the title of King. Since all the powers were making concessions to each other in order to end conflict forever, England had her way in this. She explained, and rightly too, that a King was a beautiful tradition that would add majesty and dignity to a world whose late sordid utilitarianism had starved the race for beauty. The title didn't make much difference anyway, since the first King was an American, and it *does* keep alive the spirit of romance and the glamour of pageantry.

"What we really have is a hierarchy, a perfect system in which each officer is supreme in his own jurisdiction and responsible only to his immediate head. Each officer is an expert in the duties of his office and only experts in a given sphere are eligible for offices embracing duties in that sphere. All officers are selected by popular suffrage, the vote being confined, of course, to candidates who under our rigid educational tests have qualified as experts for the offices to which they aspire. All elections are yearly, even that of King. Each officer has an assistant, a vice-officer, who serves under him. It is really the vice-officers who are elected each year, as each incumbent is succeeded by his assistant. This prevents confusion due to frequent changing of officials as each incoming officer has had a year's thorough training under his predecessor. The King may assume autocratic power in any crisis, but normally he is simply head of the Supreme Council composed of ex-Kings, in which body he casts the deciding vote.

"As I have already mentioned, we have very little government as you would conceive it, but its functions have enlarged tremendously to embrace spheres of jurisdiction outside of what your age would have considered expedient. Crime has practically vanished and with it the complex systems of jurisprudence, save as councils of arbitration and advice. Health is perfect, as no sane person would think of violating its laws; hence any supervision in that respect would be superfluous. There is no longer any need of armies and navies and even the International Police Force has survived only because it adds dignity and smoothness to our functions.

"The government's chief and holiest responsibility is the direction of education, which, however, has become greatly simplified. Knowledge is now conveyed to the mind during sleep by radiographic or phonographic lectures. The subject matter is indelibly imprinted on the subconscious mind, whose memory is eternal. During waking hours the objective mind is trained by great psychologists to recover at will any detail that has been impressed on the unconscious. Since all industry is controlled and all art is created by thought-power, our chief technical training is in thought-control and direction. Great stress is laid upon athletics, for a perfect mind can function adequately only through a perfect body.

"Our college course, which is compulsory, also embraces a year's voyage on one of our floating universities as a training for world citizenship. Our students, under the guidance of their instructors, visit all nations that the bonds of human understanding and world brotherhood may be strengthened. Since our lives are practically endless and since knowledge is also endless, it is arranged that after every five years of service to the State, each citizen again enters school for the purpose of adding to his education such branches of learning as he may have neglected and such new wisdom as may have been added to our racial store. International marriages are encouraged, since long before we attained immortality, we had weeded out undesirable racial strains by wholesale sterilization. The carefully preserved superior strains in the various races have united to form a super-race. Children are still born occasionally whenever a marriage is consummated wherein the contracting parties possess qualities of genius that we desire to see multiplied. However, the case must be exceptional, as we must avoid overpopulation.

"We cherish spaciousness too well to permit even the suggestion of over-crowding. Birth is entirely different from the horror that it was in your day. The embryo is removed from the womb shortly after conception and brought to perfect maturity in an incubator. The old relations of the sexes except for purposes of procreation have practically ceased. The great energy back of the wasteful reproduction that led at last to death has been turned into the channels of rejuvenation. This does not imply that men and women do not love and live with their chosen mates in perfect comradeship. It does not even mean the absence of sex attraction, for, as I have told you, all our emotions have been preserved and intensified. It does mean that the divine ecstasy generated by our love for one another is transmuted to the higher planes of soul expression, whence it returns to us as children of inspiration, as the materialization of our dreams of beauty.

"We have preserved the institution of monogamy and marriage but not in an arbitrary manner, as there always have been and always will be minds who do not adapt themselves to it. On the whole, however, you will find our world a world of homes and our marriages enduring. Why should they not be, since with the removal of all pressure, economic or spiritual, they are based on love alone? Reading each other's inmost thoughts with our powers of thought-discernment, with no emotions to conceal, no impurity to hide, no selfish motives to attain—we *know* when the spark has flashed between us."

As she spoke of the *spark*, her voice trembled—faltered—then raising her glorious eyes, she looked straight into mine, searching—finding—and unafraid. Waves of ecstasy surged through and over me, and though many centuries flowed between us, I knew and loved and understood this woman, and her soul flowed into mine above the barriers of sensual limitation.

A World Freedom

Her voice regained its power and she continued:

"Though I have digressed to explain our marriage system to you, the supervision of marriage and the selection of mates is not a function of government. It is left purely to individual choice. There was a time, far back, when in order to weed out inferior strains, sterilization was resorted to, but there are no longer any unfit. When highly superior couples meet and mate, the government may suggest that they bear a child or children. On the other hand, couples really desiring offspring may apply to the government for a permit to bear them. Such requests are usually granted, for the depletion of population during the Great Revolt, and the further depletion resulting from the weeding out of the unfit, leaves room for the addition of several millions more to our population. Good judgment is always exercised by our people and there is not among them that mad desire to reproduce themselves which was, after all, only a magnificent gesture of defiance to death.

"An important function of our government is the supervision of popular entertainment, the judicious direction of the great leisure which we now have at our disposal, so that it may be employed constructively as well as joyously. This means so much more to us than you can realize. In your age men plunged madly into pleasure to drown the sense of frustration, the monotony of coarsening toil and the degrading conditions surrounding it. In your age pleasure was an escape from reality; with us it is the jewel in the crown of realization. Two hours we spend in the acquisition of knowledge, which does not include our training during sleep. Three hours we spend in bathing, exercises, and the care of our bodies. The balance of our time we pass as we see fit, either in the quiet contentment of our homes or in our wonderful diversions that include the drama, music, the art galleries, the astronomical observatories, and above all—dancing.

"Our young people, too," I mused aloud, "were also fond of dancing."

"Yes, and why not? Is not all life the mystic dance of atoms to the music of the spheres? What higher form of worship can there be than taking part in that eternal ritual?"

"I don't think that our younger generation interpreted the dance in quite that beautiful manner." I smiled, thinking of the horrible rhythms of the jazz age.

"No doubt their minds were partially corrupted by the impure thoughts of their elders," responded Iris. "Yet the eternal urge was there, impelling them by means of rhythm to the harmonization of their spirits with the Undeviating Plan."

"Is that your religion?" I asked.

"This is knowledge. We have no religion. The very word 'religion' means 'to bind' and we are free. Religion was a ladder by which men hoped to scale the walls of heaven. We have attained that goal in this, our earthly paradise. We have thrown away the ladder. Faith has blossomed into certainty."

"But you have no system of belief—no form of worship?"

"We do not *believe* in God, the Universal Essence; we *know* that it is within and without us. It pulses through our veins in the passion and the ecstasy of life. Worship? Is not our whole life worship, is not every new attainment but a new prostration of the soul before the altar of the yet-to-be-attained!"

"Surely, this is heaven I have found," I told her, "instead of the same old Earth eight hundred years beyond my time."

"There was One who said, 'The kingdom of heaven is within the heart.' Truly it is like that. A sage once sought in distant countries to find an exotic blossom, to discover it had been blooming all the while beside his cottage door."

An ugly doubt assailed me like a serpent crawling through the fields of Eden.

"Still, are you sure, *can* you be sure," I questioned, "that this seeming perfection, this supreme contentment is not really the beginning of decadence? May it not be that humanity has reached the mountaintop and is going gracefully down the other side?"

"The other side!" She laughed musically. "Why, we have barely set our feet upon the first slopes! We have just come through the Valley—the Valley of Illusion—and raised our eyes to glimpse the splendor of the mountaintop. We have scarcely conquered ourselves and our own planet—as yet. Beyond us lies—the Infinite—worlds innumerable, space illimitable—room for the soul to grow until it includes all life, all time and all being. Why, we have only recently established communication with Mars and Venus. The beginning of decadence! We have reached only the beginning of wisdom—in the realization of our littleness as compared to this Vastness." She pointed to the firmament and all at once I knew that these people would never know decadence. A deep shame swept over me that, in my crude materialism, I had been so beast-minded as to believe that the lifting of the burden of toil would quench the spark of human ambition.

CHAPTER 5

The New City

Therius broke the thread of my self-reproach. "We are coming into the harbor," he reminded us. "The tale is ended, and so is our journey. The rest you can learn from observation."

I raised my eyes to the scene we were approaching. It was the port of Corpus Christi beyond a doubt. The coastline had changed but little in eight hundred years. But I was totally unprepared for the splendor of the royal city that rose before me like Venus from the waves. Ivory spires and fairy minarets flung themselves against the Italian blue of the heavens. Golden domes caught and scattered jewels of sunshine in crystal showers of light. Spacious avenues paved with varicolored glass and bordered by towering trees of tropic foliage led away from the water's edge into seemingly infinite distances. Seductive music floated out through fretted casements, and above us graceful aircraft dipped and circled or hung motionless above the radiant Earth.

Iris touched my arm. "This is Nirvania," she told me rapturously, seeming to drink its fragrance into her soul. "Nirvania the beautiful!"

Heriod laughed teasingly. "That's what they call it now," he explained. "Used to be Corpus Christi. Iris thinks it's marvelous because she was born there, but it's just what it always was, a charming little seaport town. Just wait till you see my city—New York."

Somehow I was glad to find that mankind was still human enough to have local pride. The pleasing touch of nature brought me to Earth again and we went about the business of landing.

Quite a crowd had gathered to meet us. Therius informed me that this was due to the fact that he had sent a "thought-message" ahead telling all about myself. The throng crowded about us like the happy children that they were. Without any introduction they shook hands with me and embraced me as an old friend from whom they had been long parted. I could not help noticing that there was considerable restrained mirth because of my drab-colored, uncomfortable garments, but be it said to their credit, their mirth *was* restrained.

Therius, Iris, and several erstwhile companions conducted me straight to the mayor's residence, which was some little distance from the pier. They made no suggestion of entering any of the numerous vehicles of transportation that were at hand, and from the number of people that were sauntering along the streets, I decided that these people enjoyed walking.

All around me were evidences of a higher culture than I had ever dreamed possible on Earth. It came to me that the keynote of their whole civilization could be expressed in three words: beauty — simplicity — spaciousness. There were no signs of the unsightly utilitarian structures of my day, no smoking factories, no ugly office buildings, no malodorous warehouses, no towering masses of iron and steel. Instead I saw a city of airy homes nestling in the midst of cool and verdant parks. Here and there at pleasing intervals were scattered the spires and domes of dignified public edifices that evidently served as schools, theatres, libraries, and museums of art. There was no heavy traffic on the streets. Leisurely moving bright-colored passenger vehicles skimmed along, keeping a foot or so above the pavement as though held to that position by some gravity-controlling device. There were numbers of people who actually flew through the air, equipped with artificial wings of gorgeous plumage that gave them the appearance of great birds. A surprising number were walking, considering the ease of transportation. Multitudes were singing and dancing in the grassy spaces or on smooth glassy platforms, to the sound of invisible music.

The absence of the frantic speed, so nerve-wracking in my time, struck me as unusual. I remarked about it to my companion, mentioning the mad velocities of 1930.

"What was their particular hurry?" said Iris so seriously that I knew she intended no sarcasm.

Therius with his usual professorial habit of taking the answer out of one's mouth, replied for me:

"They were hurried," he said, as though settling the question for all time, "because of the brevity of life in that day. One cannot blame them for wanting to crowd as much experience as possible into their brief span. Add to this the fact that they didn't believe in their religions, as their actions repudiated any hope for a hereafter."

"Didn't believe in their religions?" I asked curiously.

"Can you imagine a sane person believing in the immortality of the soul, grieving over the dead and rushing along at 200 miles per hour?"

Come to think about it, I couldn't. "Do *you* believe in immortality?" I asked him.

He smiled. "We don't have to believe in it, we *have* it."

Further conversation was interrupted by our having reached our destination.

The Mayor of Nirvania

Wide marble steps that would have done credit to a Doric temple led up to the mayor's palace. A great glass door swung noiselessly open as Therius pressed a button. We found ourselves in a colossal patio covered with movable skylights. It was paved with transparent glass beneath which flowed crystal waters in whose depths innumerable fragile fish of tropic waters disported themselves, trailing their filmy veils amid waving fernlike sea plants and through the apertures of miniature castles. The walls were simply magnificent mirrors broken by panelings displaying paintings whose genius was supreme, and occasional niches containing statuary unsurpassed by the artistry of Greece and Rome. A singing fountain tossed its white spray into a pool in the center of the court and here the fishes came to the surface.

The only furnishings were low Oriental couches, a great profusion of velvet and silken cushions, a few low stools with Oriental carvings and quite a number of rare plants and palms. A delicious perfume hung in the air and a cool breeze was set in motion by invisible fans. Several magnificent Persian cats of an inconceivable size stretched themselves lazily in the warm glow that filtered through the skylights and a beautiful shepherd dog rose to greet us. I received quite a fright as a shaggy, majestic African lion rose from a cushion and sauntered curiously towards me, but Therius allayed my fears by patting him on the head and informing me that there were no more wild animals. A few uncaged canary birds and some humming birds flew freely about the patio unharmed and unnoticed by the giant cats. The whole scene was as beautiful as a vision of the Golden Age. Liberty and light and laughter had come at last to the Earth and our children's children had come into their own.

To my left a door swung noiselessly open and a young man joined us. He was tall, lithe, and splendidly proportioned, as were all this super-race. His features portrayed a subtle blending of the noblest qualities of the ancient Greek, the North American Indian, the Oriental, and the Anglo-Saxon. The aquiline nose was unquestionably Grecian, the high cheekbones were those of the Indian, the soft, mysterious eyes held all the charm of Hindustan, yet something flashed in their depths that betrayed the keen alertness of the modern American. In him as in all his contemporaries, the highest traits of all races were fused into a sort of sculptured harmony of face and form.

He was dressed very much like my other companions in a short, belted tunic of shimmering golden scales. A cloak of royal purple lined with gold was fastened at one shoulder by a jeweled clasp, leaving one arm bare. Around his head was a golden circlet set with a precious stone that resembled a sardonyx. His sandals might have been fashioned of flexible gold. On the front of his tunic glittered a symbol that must have been the insignia of his office, for he was introduced to me as the mayor of Nirvania. Judged according to his youth and his general air of quiet culture coupled with enthusiasm, he might have been a college freshman.

He greeted me as naturally as though receiving visitors from past ages was part of his daily routine. Placing his palm upward in an outstretched arm, I laid my palm on his. Smiling into my eyes, he offered me the freedom of the city in a few well-chosen words. My companions then took leave of me, somewhat reluctantly, I thought, and I was left alone with the mayor.

With something of an Old World courtesy he motioned me to a low divan and placed himself beside me. He pressed a button and a handsome young man entered bearing a low table which contained a couple of jeweled food flakes, a sparkling beverage, and some foamy concoctions that would have temped the appetite of a Sybarite. As though it were the most natural thing in the world to introduce one's servants to one's guests, the mayor presented the young man to me. This charming boy, whose name was Adrian, remarked during the course of our short conversation that he was serving this year in the mayor's home but that next year he would enter his chosen vocation — aviation. I gathered that everybody takes turns at performing essential household tasks that, by reason of the marvelous laborsaving devices, are rendered extremely light. Since it occurs that the servant in one's household today may be the ruler of the State tomorrow, no stigma is attached to the performance of any necessary labor.

The young gentleman seated himself familiarly on a cushion, inhaling from his own food flask and chatting with us while we ate. When we had finished, he departed, taking the serving stool with him. I must have talked two hours with the mayor, mostly answering his questions regarding my era, for he belonged to that alert, curious type of intellect that never rests until it has exhausted all possibilities of knowledge from any given subject. The room was filling with the shadows of twilight, as the whole patio was suddenly flooded with a soft radiance that seemed to be reflected from the stately mirrors and to run along walls in quivering streams of rosy, liquid light. I was about to inquire into the source of this mysterious lighting as the mayor remarked that my unusual experiences must have fatigued me greatly and all at once I realized that I was really very tired and drowsy. He rose saying that he would conduct me to my sleeping quarters. I was somewhat surprised to observe that he was leading me up a spiral glass stairway that ended on the roof.

A Night in Nirvania

He told me that the roof space of practically all the dwellings in tropical lands was converted into parks and gardens in which were constructed glass sleeping porches. On stepping onto the roof, I was enraptured with the woodland beauty that lay before me. Rich grass interspersed with clusters of wild flowers carpeted the entire space. Graceful trees and fernlike shrubbery half-concealed several sleeping porches whose mirrored walls threw back the beauty of the scene. Little streams of water purled through glassy channels fed by an immense swimming pool in the center of the artificial aerial forest. From the middle of this pool rose to a great height the shimmering rainbow cascade of an illuminated fountain. This, I saw, was only one of the many fountains that, ascending from neighboring housetops, lit the sky with pyrotechnic splendor.

I gazed enchanted on the vision of Nirvania as it lay spread out below me, Nirvania the beautiful! The mayor opened the door of one of the mirrored enclosures and bid me enter ahead of him. I saw that the walls were composed of mirrors within as well as without. The monotony of glass was agreeably broken by panels containing rare paintings. The porch was roofless but the mayor showed me how by moving a lever the whole covering would slide into place. There were several airy windows but no shades or curtains. In one corner was the bed, a luxurious, low divan piled high with silken coverings. A soft carpet resembling natural grass covered the floor in the middle of which was set a commodious glass pool filled with sparkling water. A button at the right, just under a thermometer, could be pressed, the mayor told me, to bring the water to any desired temperature. Another at the left released the water and still another filled the pool with a fresh supply. An immense glass floor chest contained, he told me, towels, a night robe, and a change of clothing for the morning. A food flask and a crystal water bottle reposed on a low stool at my bedside and on another stool were placed a number of beautifully bound books. In one corner stood a magnificent cabinet whose mechanism the mayor explained to me. By pressing various buttons near the head of my bed, music could be played, the news of the day recited, views of distant places flashed upon the large wall mirrors, or thought-communication established with any person on the planet.

"But," admonished the mayor, "this must be taught you, and tonight I would suggest that after your bath you press this button and turn on the sleep-producing music. This music we have so perfected that by means of its vibrations sleep is immediately induced."

He now bade me a cordial good night and left me. Determined to heed his advice and get a good rest so that I might be fresh for the marvels that lay before me on the morrow, I disrobed and plunged into a warm, refreshing bath. Deliciously rejuvenated, I gave myself a vigorous rubbing with an immense bath towel that I found in the glass chest and dressed myself in the silken night robe that had been provided for me. I sought my kingly divan and tried to sleep but the mental exhilaration of the day had been too much for me. Doubting seriously that any music could quiet the mad havoc of my raving thoughts, I pressed the music button. Immediately a seductive, languorous strain floated from the instrument into my throbbing brain, lulling its wild pulsations and steeping my entire being in a sea of slumber. Waves of peace flowed through and over me. My eyes closed but my spirit floated ecstatically through Nirvanian spaces exploring dim cool caves of sleep and shadowy star pavilions tapestried with dreams. But through it all the face of Iris smiled—the hand of Iris beckoned.

CHAPTER 6

Morning Sport

When I awoke it was radiant dawn. The bright sunshine was stream-ing in through the windows and the melodious warbling of a thousand birds floated in from the trees outside. It was fully five minutes before I could ori-ent myself, before I could realize that the events of the last twenty-four hours were not a fantastic dream. The door opened and Adrian entered the room, bidding me a pleasant good morning. He had come in without the formality of knocking and, I must also add, without the formality of clothes. He seemed utterly unconscious of any oversight, remarking that he was glad that I had not yet bathed because he felt sure that I should enjoy a plunge in the swim-ming pool with the rest. He added, with a significant smile, that Iris—who, he informed me, was the mayor's sister—had sent him for me.

At this welcome news I scrambled out of bed and began a hurried toilet while Adrian waited. "You can just grab up your garments and take them along," he suggested. Not relishing the prospect of traversing the roof garden clad only in the glittering sunlight, I politely ignored this suggestion by ran-sacking the chest. There I found a glittering tunic of cloth of gold with a gor-geous purple cape that fastened at the shoulder with the usual jeweled clasp. I found also golden sandals with jeweled buckles and a golden circlet for my head. The single undergarment was of closely woven silk of a marvelous tex-ture. I was glad indeed that I should no longer be compelled to offend the pub-lic taste with my old uncomfortable garb of 1932. With Adrian's help I soon arrayed myself in regal splendor, discovering that my garments, for all their richness and beauty, were designed with the utmost simplicity. My toilet com-pleted, I surveyed myself before a mirror.

I was proud indeed of my reflection, and Adrian's frank smile of approval convinced me that, after all, there was not so much difference between my ap-pearance and that of the other young people of this paradise. With the exception of my short hair, which a month's growth would remedy, I could almost say there was no difference at all. Without being vain, I can truthfully say that I had always been considered a good-looking chap. A passion for athletics and my four years in the navy had so developed my body that my figure was nothing to be ashamed of. Add to this my luxuriously simple and revealing costume and the picture was all that could be desired. My companion now led me to the magnificent pool from which rose the rainbow fountain that I had so admired the night before. Many heaps of silken clothing lay scattered on the grassy banks or spread carelessly on the shrubbery.

In the crystal pool itself twenty or thirty joyous bathers of both sexes were plunging and swimming through the sparkling water. I observed with embarrassment that not a single garment concealed the shining perfection of their glorious forms. Shamefacedly, with all the false modesty of my age, though I had once thought that we had cast it all aside, I asked Adrian if it were customary to "go in" without a bathing suit.

"What is a bathing suit?" he questioned so wonderingly that I realized that so innocent and frank were these people that they had forgotten that such superfluities had ever been worn.

"Oh, it's all right," I assured him hastily. "I won't need one."

I quickly stripped off my clothing and we plunged in together. Several young girls, among them Iris, swam gracefully toward me and challenged me to a game of water ball. I soon forgot my prudishness and entered boyishly into the spirit of the fun.

Finally I came out of the pool refreshed, glowing, and feeling as though I had bathed in the fountain of youth.

Iris came up to me on the bank, swinging her garments in one hand and shaking the shining water drops from her glorious hair. Her unveiled beauty made me gasp with wonder and her utter innocence caused my soul to kneel in reverence before her white virginity.

"Oh, you are beautiful!" I gasped, unable to restrain my admiration. "Beautiful as a sea goddess!"

Frankly her eyes met mine. "Why—yes, I am beautiful," she agreed with disarming veracity. "All of us are so. You, too, are very handsome and—a poet as well. Tell me—" she queried with a touch of feminine coquetry as old as Eden, "do you like the color of my hair?"

I raised my eyes to her shimmering ringlets, green as the ocean on an Indian summer's day and throwing back the light like emeralds.

"It is beautiful," I murmured, "and utterly in keeping with one who, to me, will always symbolize the glamor and the agelessness of the eternal sea. The sea, you must know, has always been my ladylove—till now."

Afraid of my own daring, I abruptly changed the subject. "How did your people discover this wonderful hair coloring? I see that your hair is entirely unharmed by the process."

"We treat the pigment cells themselves and thus attain permanently any shade we desire. You see, we grew tired of the same old colors and decided to improve on nature."

"By the way," she continued, deftly slipping into her garments, "my brother, the mayor, wants us to have breakfast with him. After breakfast he desires me to show you around the city, or rather," she confessed frankly, "I asked him to let me be your guide. He was born in New York, you see, and he doesn't really see the charm of Nirvania. But I love it and I want you to see it as I see it."

"You won't have any trouble impressing me with the beauties of Nirvania. You see, it was my city too. At least we have that bond of kinship between us—you and I—though you are eight centuries beyond me in evolution."

An Inspection Tour

"You think that?" she asked incredulously. "What a mistake you are making. Why, even the scientists of your day had to admit that the brain-stuff of the human race, the human mind's innate potentiality, alters but little through the centuries. The mental capacity of the Egyptian Pharaohs was as high as that of the sages and financiers of your day. We have no more *capacity* to learn than you—we have simply unfolded more of the powers that have always been latent in man. You can do likewise—in time."

"You mean, then, that the gulf between us is not so impassable after all, that I may someday become like your people? Oh, I promise you," I told her eagerly, humbly, "that I shall strive, study, labor unceasingly if only I may hope that someday I may dare to tell you what is in my heart."

She laughed and from the delicate blush that suffused her features, I knew that she was not unaffected by my evident devotion. "You are overestimating your handicaps," she told me, "and underestimating yourself. With our educational methods that have speeded up the process of acquiring and using knowledge beyond the dreams of your educators, a few months will witness the unfoldment of your unused capacities. Besides," her voice grew more intense—"do you not realize that had there not been in you that *something* that responded to our ideas you would never have been captured in the thought-net that we spread out yonder in the sea?"

"You mean that even Therius's wonderful invention could not have drawn me into this dimension had I not, in some degree, belonged here?"

"I mean just that. The keynote of the whole invention is attunement. Unless the rate of vibration of the thought projected is attuned to the rate of

vibration of the thought it contacts, there can never be that union of energies that would produce sufficient force to draw one from one age, from one
dimension, into another."

"Oh, I am glad—glad—to know this!" I told her eagerly. "Now I can hope!"

She dropped her eyes before the eager passion of my own and with girlish abandon caught my hand and raced with me across the garden and down
the glass stairway to the mayor's breakfast room. After a delicious breakfast
interspersed with joyous conversation, the mayor excused himself, wishing
us much adventure on our tour of inspection through the city. He added jocosely that since life was eternal it would be just as well if I didn't try to see
everything at once. He also remarked that after I had browsed around the
city for a few days and rested and adjusted myself, the people would like to
hear me tell them all about my age and time. This pleasing task I gratefully
promised to undertake, and hand in hand with Iris the adorable, I started
off with a light heart on my expedition into Paradise. Had I only known that
journey's end! Had I only foreseen what would happen through my own damnable curiosity.

I saw so much in my short journey that ended so disastrously that it is impossible to give anything like a connected account of it. It would take years to
acquire a technical knowledge of the marvelous inventions that surrounded
me on every hand. Yet a single simple process was common to all: the application of the power of thought to the powers of nature. Iris informed me that
only the experts bothered about the technicalities of their own trade. Each
individual, after acquiring a liberal education in the arts and sciences, special-
izes in his chosen field. An architect, for instance, studies for his profession
much as an architect would do in our day, except that he need not take into
account actual construction. He learns to draw his model and then, by intense
concentration with the picture of his model ever before him, he transfers
every detail of the picture to the marvelous crystal that reflects it back to him.
Then when the image in the crystal is perfect, he removes the crystal from its
tripod and resets it in the projection machine. Again with the aid of thought
he releases from his brain an energy that literally assists the mental image
toward its materialization. It is clothed in substance by appropriating the
eternal creative energies that forever surround us, by attracting the free elec-
trons that are continually seeking a positive nucleus around which to revolve.

"It is not really creation," Iris explained. "The very word 'creation' implies
making something out of nothing—an obvious absurdity. That would contra-
dict the first law of physics that nothing in the universe is ever created or destroyed by the action of forces that we know nothing about. Our inventions
simply utilize a process as old as nature, the transformation of energy into

matter. Someday, when there is building going on, I shall show you this marvelous process in operation."

"This accounts, then, for the absence of factories and complicated machinery?"

"Oh yes," she answered inclusively, "it accounts for everything."

The Strange Tower

Everywhere we wandered was beauty, dignity, simplicity. Everywhere the happy, laughing people walked in the sunshine, soared through the air like birds of paradise, or sped along the glassy highways in their graceful vessels. I noted that some of these vehicles were shaped like giant swans, others liked winged horses, and still others like fairy vessels of the sea. Everywhere beauty and utility were harmonized into one synthetic whole. The thing that impressed me most was the frequency of laughter: low, musical, heart-free laughter that filled the air like the melody of birds. The Happy, Laughing People—I shall always call them that. I recalled that the wild young generation of my day was also a happy, laughing folk, though heaven knows they had little to laugh about. Oh, could they only have foreseen the sublime vindication of laughter that endures through tears—through heartbreak—through misunderstanding.

Having wandered more or less aimlessly through all these marvels for the greater part of the day, Iris and I came about sundown to a high hill crowned with what seemed to be a fortress of the Middle Ages. There was something vaguely familiar about it to me and something that filled me with a strange foreboding. Gloomy and ominous, it loomed over us like the shadow of ancient evil. Sardonically and irresistibly it beckoned us, and humanlike we came.

"That's one of the old landmarks," said Iris. "We have preserved a few of them because of their picturesqueness. We call this place the Hill of the Mad Inventor. Why, he lived in your own time, I believe. He was immensely wealthy and he built this castle in the style of a medieval stronghold. It is said that its very stones were brought from abroad, recovered from the demolition of an ancient castle of which this is the exact replica. The older castle was itself the outpost, they say, of a Black Magician, who of course was probably nothing more than a scientist too advanced for his time.

"The mad inventor was once a brilliant scientist, adding much to the world's store of knowledge, but in his old age his mind became unbalanced. In his madness he was supposed to have performed weird and murderous experiments, but—" she interpolated sagely—"he might not have been mad after all. Your people had a habit of classifying as insanity everything beyond their range of comprehension. However, whether merited or not, the appellation stuck and so we still call this the Hill of the Mad Inventor. His name, I believe, was Peter—Peter Holden."

"Peter Holden!" I burst out explosively. "Why, I knew him! He was a professor of chemistry before he began acting queer and was asked to resign from the university. Shortly after that he either inherited or obtained by some means an immense fortune and immediately began the construction of this—this monstrosity. Thereafter all he did was to shut himself up in that crazy tower room, where he was reputed to be trying to explore the Fourth Dimension."

"All of which," commented Iris, "was not so crazy, after all. You, yourself, are now actually exploring what to you is the Fourth Dimension."

"It may not be crazy now," I admitted, "but it was then, in view of the limited resources we had to work with. However, let's explore the tower room and see what's left of old Peter's laboratory. I've always wanted to see it, but he'd doubtless turn over in his grave if he knew anyone was going to enter it."

"I'm afraid there's not much there that we could fathom," said Iris, strangely reluctant to go, I thought. "There's just a lot of complex machinery that we know nothing about, but we have left it intact and it's all in an excellent state of preservation."

"Well, maybe I'll know something about it," I boasted, overruling her hesitation, or more likely taking advantage of her courtesy.

The Time Powder

Outwardly bold, yet at the same time conscious of an ugly premonition hammering in my brain, I led her inside the crumbling ruin. Everywhere there was the odor of decay and strange batlike creatures flitted around in the half light, adding a special terror all their own. The tower room being my main objective, as it was the true lair of the Mad Inventor, I guided Iris up the narrow spiral stairway that led up to it. Looking back upon that mad adventure I cannot but admire the courage of this angel of the Golden Age when confronted by terror that actually oozed from the very walls of this charnel house of antiquity. There were suggestions lurking there like ghosts in every corner, suggestions of the sordidness and the ugliness that have passed away forever. If they even leered and gibbered at me, so shortly separated from that time, how much more so must they have terrorized the sensitive soul of Iris. But she gave no sign of fear, save to cling a little closer to me.

Finally we entered the tower room itself, the scene of Peter Holden's mad experiments. It looked like the den of a medieval alchemist, doubtless because of its forbidding setting, but the equipment of his laboratory was expensive and up-to-date enough in my day. I could make neither head nor tail of it, however, for I'm no scientist, and Iris, though possessing a keener brain than many an expert of 1930, was equally at a loss to explain this complex mass of wires and tubes. A curiously carved box on a table by itself attracted my attention. Oh, how I have cursed the hour that I saw it!

"I wonder what's in that old box?" I asked her.

"I don't know. We tried to open it one day, but the combination failed to respond to our thought-vibrations. We know nothing of keys. We hated to break the lock, as the box is very rare, so we decided to wait until somebody could open it. Afterwards—we forgot all about it."

Some satanic curiosity prompted me to open that box—to see what it contained. There was something sinister about it—something about the grinning gargoyles that were carved upon it that literally challenged me to defy their hellish guardianship. I saw at a glance that the lock was not intricate, and having once learned something about opening locks from a clever shipmate, I jerked up a piece of wire from an adjoining table and after five minutes had the thing open. At first I thought that it contained nothing but a curious sort of packing that fell to dust at the touch of my hand. Finally I touched something solid and gleaming. It was a small tube made of something that resembled aluminum, but unlike the packing, the passage of time had not seemed to affect it.

Forgetting the adage that fools rush in where angels fear to tread, I unscrewed the tap and poured into my hand its full contents, a small pile of glittering yellow powder. Iris watched my every movement with a proud smile on her beautiful face. She was enormously pleased at my prowess in mastering the intricacies of a mechanism that her people had failed to fathom.

To further satisfy my hellish curiosity I raised the powder to my nostrils, and idiot that I was, I sniffed it.

The next thing I knew, a swift dizziness rushed over me, blinding me, nauseating me—a current ran through my veins like liquid fire—a thousand electric needles seemed to prick and torture me. Through it all I felt soft arms envelop me—soft lips press mine—and a despairing voice call my name, pleadingly—fearfully and rising at last to a vibrant crescendo of terror. In spite of my almost superhuman efforts to respond to that call, I slipped painlessly into a white sea of unconsciousness.

When I awoke I found myself still in the tower room, lying on a narrow couch with old Peter Holden bending over me—shaking me, and raving like a maniac.

"You would steal into my laboratory, you young whippersnapper," he shrieked, "though how you got through that locked door would baffle the fiends! You would open my box and steal my powder—my Fourth Dimension powder!"

He was raving now in earnest—frothing at the mouth, but I too, now in full possession of my senses, also went raving mad, and my own outburst silenced his.

"Damn you and your Fourth Dimension powder!" I yelled, rising to my feet and almost throttling him. "But for you—but for your damnable powder, I should now be where your old bones have crumbled into ashes and your satanic laboratory is but a blot on the landscape, a cancer in a healthy world. You're responsible for my being here!" I shrieked in mad unreason, "and by Heaven, you'll send me back or I'll kill you!"

A look of utter astonishment came into my victim's eyes in spite of his evident terror.

"Let me go, you fool!" he gurgled. "Quiet yourself, and tell me exactly what you are talking about."

Reason came to me at these words. At least the realization was borne in upon me that it was no fault of Peter's but my own insatiable curiosity that was responsible for my plight.

So I sat there in the waning, spectral light of the old tower room and told him everything. Be it said to his credit, he never expressed a single doubt of my sanity, once he had fixed his eyes upon my strange apparel. His scientific mind must have told him at a glance that an art was used in the manufacture of my garments that was beyond the science of his age.

When I had finished my fantastic tale, he jumped to his feet like a schoolboy and danced up and down in unrestrained glee.

"So it worked!" he yelled. "It worked! Eureka! Eureka!"

"Undoubtedly it worked," I commented bitterly, "but it worked backwards."

"You poor young fool!" he exclaimed with frank contempt. "Can't you see that it worked according to the way you took it?"

The Return to Nirvania

Enlightenment began to dawn. "Then that means that had I taken it here in this age, it would have transported me—there?"

"Beyond the shadow of a doubt! And since I have the formula, I can make more of it. I'll admit that I was a little hasty and cut up over losing the powder that I had on hand as I meant to have tried it out in a few days, as soon as I had found a subject for the experiment. You, thank Heaven, are the God-given *willing* subject I've been looking for."

"But how do you know that I shall be transported to that particular age instead of to another epoch infested by God knows what horrors?"

"I think I can put your faith in the same principle by which you came *back* exactly eight hundred years instead of six hundred or a thousand hundred. You see the quantity of the substance determines the length of the voyage through time, the Fourth Dimension. It only remains to fill the tube again with the exact quantity that it contained before."

I must admit that my faith in this exactitude of his computations was anything but unwavering. But in my soul I knew that Iris was worth the risk. Like that other Anthony whom she so admired, I was prepared to lose the world for love.

"How long did you say," I asked eagerly, "that I must wait?"

"Fully three weeks, you young thief!" he retorted, his anger rising with my impatience. "And meanwhile—you get out of here, and don't show your prying nose around this place until the time is up. You can write your story while you're waiting and send it to some fiction magazine. The consummate idiots of this asinine age would never accept it as fact—but it may give someone an idea—if there is a mind big enough to hold it."

"But," I stammered, curiosity again mastering me, "won't you tell me the principle of this—Fourth Dimension powder?"

The old man glared at me sardonically, "I can furnish you the information, young man, but I can't endow you with the intelligence to understand it. However, your desire to know something is commendatory, so to get rid of you, I'll outline the principle, trying to put it in terms that your intellect can grasp." I made a mental comment that Prof. Holden's opinion of my intellect had always been biased doubtless by the grades I had made in chemistry.

"This powder," he began painfully, as though seeking adequate terms, "is manufactured from a combination of certain Oriental drugs which acts directly upon the cerebral tissues, slowing down or speeding up the vibrations of thought. These thought-vibrations, freed from the dominance of the objective senses, which are completely paralyzed at the first whiff of the powder, change the rate of vibration of the atoms of the body. Since any given organism is held together only by the affinity of its atoms, it follows that the atoms of an organism whose rate of vibration is speeded up—say, to correspond with that of organisms 500 years hence—would no longer have an affinity for the predominant rate of vibration of this age. Since every atom automatically seeks the rate of vibration for which it has affinity, it follows that any organism or combination of atoms acted upon by this powder will travel through time until it encounters the rate of vibration that corresponds with its new scientifically induced rate. The influence of certain Oriental drugs on the sense of time has long been a matter of common knowledge. Working from that point I have effected a combination that affects not only the mind, but changes the rate of vibration of the atoms of the body. And now—" he broke off angrily—"will you get out of here? But wait! Put on what the world calls a decent suit of clothes before you go, or you'll spend your next three weeks in jail."

After helping myself to old Peter's wardrobe I at last departed, much to his grim satisfaction. After the old hermit's lucid explanation, I went with a hope in my heart and a song on my lips.

That song soon changed to sorrow when I found myself again confronted with the bitterness, the heartache and the mad acquisitiveness of an age that, even in a few short hours of Paradise, had already become to me a horrid nightmare. I was already sorrowful when I realized that the remedy was all so simple, too simple. It needed nothing more than the realization that human brotherhood is the only remedy even from a selfish standpoint. Unwittingly I spoke my thoughts to some of my old acquaintances, only to be sneeringly asked what kind of home brew I had been using. I gave it up and surrendered myself to my dreams and the compilation of this narrative.

Now at the end of my probation I am mailing this story to my aunt. She will understand it, and she will know what to do with it. I have settled my affairs and after a few more interminable hours I shall be on my way to the tower room. My tryst may be a rendezvous with death or the key to life eternal. If it is death that awaits me at the end of the trail he comes too late—too late to rob me of that consciousness of immortality that shall survive the transition of form. If it is life everlasting—life unbroken by the periodical specter of the Ancient Foe—then I shall live it reverently, gloriously.

If old Peter is ready for me tonight, he will put a light in the tower room. The shadows are deepening, creeping around me languorously, caressingly, bidding me farewell. Even now I would turn back—were men not blind, would they only listen. For I have known a love that has taught me that even its own surrender is preferable to a duty cast aside. But the time has not yet come for the message to peal forth from the inner temples of the heart. Many Christs must still be crucified, many sages must go down to death, before man, the eternal prodigal, returns from his weary journey among the husks and ashes to find the flower that he has sought in a far country, before his very door.

Ah! It is there! The light! But it is more than a light to me—it is a summons from the infinite. It is a challenge to plunge into the fathomless—to dare the Causeless—to live beyond the Law. More than all this, it is the call of Love. Across the deeps of time I hear the voice of Iris—the welcome of the Happy Laughing People, and I come! Bride of the centuries—I come!

Take me to you.

L(UCILE) TAYLOR HANSEN (1897–1976) was an American SF author and science journalist who published with *Amazing Stories* from 1929 to 1949. She was born in Fort Niobrara, Nebraska, and lived with her grandfather in Missouri before moving to Los Angeles to be with her mother and stepfather. In 1915 she matriculated at the University of Illinois, receiving her degree and then returning to the West Coast to study archaeology, anthropology, and geology at UCLA. She married A. Fred Hansen in 1924 and kept his name when they divorced a few years later. Hansen began writing SF to make ends meet, publishing a handful of stories in 1929 and 1930. She left the SF community for almost a decade, during which time she traveled extensively throughout the United States and Mexico, bore her daughter, Ione Athena Pantazos, and married Ione's father, Iwanne Pantazos.

When Hansen returned to SF in 1941, she wrote primarily as a journalist for Raymond A. Palmer at *Amazing Stories*, developing a reputation for expertise in ancient mysteries for which she is still remembered (for more details, see the entry on Hansen in chapter 4, "Journalists," of this anthology). After leaving the SF community again in 1949, Hansen continued researching and writing about Native American storytelling traditions, with particular emphasis on the recurrent figure of the Christ-like "Great White Prophet." Her 1963 book on this subject, *He Walked the Americas*, remains popular today and has inspired an eighteen-part dramatization on YouTube (https://www.youtube.com /watch?v=veVmaC9eQco).

Like many other women involved with the early SF community, Hansen achieved several firsts: she was the first woman to work across areas of production in a professional SF magazine, and she was one of the first SF specialist authors to capitalize on popular pseudoscientific fads in her writing. Most notably, however, Hansen is remembered as one of the first major women writers to successfully masquerade as a man in the SF community. While many women who wrote SF in the early twentieth century used androgynous names or initials in their bylines, most allowed their editors to print biographies and pictures that made their sex evident. But the illustration accompanying Hansen's 1930 story "The City on the Cloud" is clearly that of a young man, and Hansen's letter in the July 1943 issue of *Amazing Stories* bears the title "L. Taylor Hansen Defends Himself." Meanwhile, Hansen further muddied the waters by telling SF fan Forrest J Ackerman that she had never done any SF writing, but simply handled stories for her brother (Bleiler and Bleiler 164).

Scholars debate the reasons for Hansen's masquerade, citing everything from her desire to conform to the emergent conventions of a male-oriented popular genre to her fear that association with SF would destroy her science-writing career.[9] Whatever her motivation, Hansen was not alone in her experiments with sex and gender identity. Stories by other early women SF authors (including Leslie F. Stone's "Out of the Void" and C. L. Moore's "Shambleau," reprinted in this anthology) revolve around sex- and gender-based misperceptions. Meanwhile, the technique of framing stories as letters written by the acquaintance of the purported author or narrator extends back to Mary Shelley's *Frankenstein* (1818) and plays a crucial part in early SF magazine stories such as Lilith Lorraine's "Into the 28th Century" (1930). Thus it seems Hansen created an SF persona for herself that was extrapolated from the conventions of her chosen genre, especially as interpreted by other women writers.

"The Man from Space" demonstrates Hansen's ability to craft an SF story that is every bit as careful and compelling as her public identity. The author's third sale, which appeared in the February 1930 issue of *Amazing Stories*, relates the adventures of two college students, their astronomy professor, and an unnamed alien among the stars. As such, it evinces two of the major characteristics that Gernsback associated with good SF: it provides readers with a "charming romance" that is also "interwoven with scientific fact" ("New" 3). That "The Man from Space" does not fulfill Gernsback's third requirement for good SF (because it does not offer "prophetic vision" of future technologies) illustrates Hansen's sensitivity to the requirements of different editors. By the time she sold "The Man from Space" to *Amazing*, the retired natural history professor T. O'Conor Sloane, who had a slightly different vision for the genre than his predecessor, had replaced Gernsback. While he embraced the use of scientific facts and technical explanations to educate the public, Sloane was skeptical that SF could inspire inventors and he dismissed the possibility of space travel as outright fantasy. Accordingly, Hansen frames her story as a classic dream vision, transporting her characters from classroom to outer space through the vehicle of the narrator's unconscious imagination rather than by means of an actual rocket. As such, "The Man from Space" pays homage to the ideals of both Gernsback and Sloane, using an epic journey through space to teach scientific facts in a manner that no classroom lecture could hope to match without violating the ideas of the scientific community's more conservative members.

But Hansen's story is more than just a clever synthesis of differing editorial ideas about good SF; it is also one of the earliest sympathetic treatments of the alien other. In an era when U.S. authors typically represented aliens as "quasi-humans . . . under threat from predatory monsters" or as "conquistadors" engaged in a Darwinian struggle for survival with all other species, Hansen's alien adventurer is different (Killheffer and Stableford). While he is indeed a humanoid being with a tragic past, Hansen's alien does not need to be rescued by humans;

instead, he has set out on his current journey to save other races from suffering the same sad fate as his own. As such, he is a friendly teacher disseminating knowledge rather than an enemy warrior competing for scarce resources. This revised story of the encounter between the scientifically inclined, open-minded young human and the equally rational but tragically older and wiser alien would play itself out again in Hansen's later SF science journalism, where contact between the young white scientist-adventurer and the older Indigenous shaman leads the former to reevaluate her assumptions about the latter—and, in turn, to generate new perspectives on the world as a whole.[10]

....

"The Man from Space"

Amazing Stories, February 1930

"From the days of superstition, when the sudden appearance of a new star portended the birth of a great man or a terrible destruction by war and plague, up to the present time, when these phenomena are studied with telescope and spectroscope, the brilliant flashing bursts of novae continue to interest mankind."

Professor Kepling hesitated and glanced suspiciously over his class. It was a warm afternoon—languorously warm. I yawned and looked at my frat brother, Jim Turner. We had been to the same dance the night before and I was wondering if he would manage to fight off the tendency to go to sleep as well as I was doing so far. To my surprise Jim was leaning forward eagerly, drinking in every word. I remembered then that he was a sort of "bug" on astronomy, nursing a hopeless wish that he had been born a century or two later so that he might travel to other worlds. I shrugged my shoulders as the cultured voice of the gray-haired professor droned on.

"History has recorded many instances of the appearance of novae, but the first one to be studied by a mind more scientifically than superstitiously inclined was observed by Tycho on the evening of November 11, 1572. It seems that in going toward his home on that night, the celebrated Danish astronomer saw people standing out in the streets, staring and pointing at the sky directly overhead, where he was astonished to see an unknown star of surpassing brilliance. The new star even outshone the planet Jupiter. In fact, there was not another star in the whole heavens that could be compared to it.

"He had, of course, only imperfect instruments with which to study it, but with these he determined as best he could its exact location, and faithfully followed its subsequent changes. It kept on brightening until at last it even shone in the daytime. Finally, however, it began to fade, turning red as it did so. In March it disappeared from the interested astronomer's searching sight and has never been seen since."

My eyelids were getting heavy. I jerked them open, determined to get the points of the lecture, for I knew by Jim's fascinated stare that he would be "raring to go" for a good discussion as soon as the bell rang.

"There have been others of less brilliance," the well-modulated tones droned on, "but the next famous nova occurred on the evening of February 22, 1901. An amateur astronomer in Edinburgh was the first man to see the new star blazing in the constellation of Persei. He telegraphed the news over the world. Luckily, the heavens had been photographed on February 19th and the spot where the star now shone showed no trace in the photograph.

"Within a few hours of its discovery, however, it was ablaze—outshining Capella and exceeding first magnitude. But like a terrible conflagration, it burned only a few days and then began to die away with a red glow, its light diminishing and then flaring up again spasmodically every few days, though none of these revivals equaled the splendor of the first outburst. Finally it died away to the ninth magnitude.

"This time, however, there was a sequel to the story. Some six months later photographs showed that the star was now surrounded by a spiral nebula, which spread from it like an expanding wave. Four condensations seemed to gather in this fiery ring and revolve about its main nucleus of sun, but in time these condensations faded from sight and the nova became only a fairly nebulous star of less than ninth magnitude."

I caught myself nodding and straightened quickly. If only that man could speak more roughly, but the combination of late hours and a lulling voice was liable to get me yet . . .

"The question naturally arises—how do these terrible conflagrations come about? In answer, several theories have been advanced. The first one proposed was that two suns traveling in opposite directions through the uncharted realms of space had collided. A direct head-on collision would of course be rather rare, though quite possible. But novae are not rare spectacles. Every year the telescope brings us the tale of more novae, even though most of them are at far too great a distance to be seen with the naked eye.

"Let us suppose, however, that some of these suns, instead of actually colliding with each other, simply pass a little too close. Large bodies such as suns are extremely dangerous to each other. They have terrible tidal pulls. Suppose that each should come close enough for the tidal pull of the other to tear open its photospheric envelope. The result would be that the incandescent central masses would collide like two terrific clashing waves of fire.

"A second theory, advanced by Seeliger of Munich, was that a collision between a blazing star or sun and a vast dark nebula or swarm of meteors—remnants of some destroyed system—would cause such a spectacle as a nova presents. This theory underwent modifications from others until it was finally proposed that a dark or burnt-out sun, plunging into a swarm of meteors, would have its dead surface heated to incandescence, and if the sun were of vast size, it would then appear as a new star.

"A third theory supposed that a huge dark star had struck a sun surrounded by planets and that each successive rekindling of the blaze was the running down of a new unfortunate planet.

"In a fourth theory, however, the French astronomer Janssen discards all collision theories and puts forward the idea of an explosion of the sun caused by chemical changes within the sun itself. If oxygen exists in the sun's chromosphere, and we know that it does, then should the temperature tend to drop to a critical point, the combination of oxygen and hydrogen would cause a terrific explosion. We know that the temperature of our own sun keeps varying from day to day. It makes us shudder to think what would happen if our sun should be suddenly transformed into such a laboratory."

Jim was leaning forward with strained attention. I didn't blame him. Those last words made me glance almost involuntarily at a shaft of sunlight, which was lazily streaming across the floor . . . The soft voice continued:

"In any event we can imagine a terrific flash, blinding all human sight forever, and then within ten minutes a wave of all-enveloping flame . . ."

I glanced back at the lazy yellow shaft of sunlight—but this time my eyelids drooped in spite of me as I heard the lulling voice droning on from a greater and greater distance. Finally I shook off the tendency to doze and opened my eyes. The first thing that they fell upon was the lazy shaft of sunlight. Somehow it looked different. I rubbed my eyes and stared again. There was certainly something queer about the color, but when I touched Jim's sleeve, he only shook me off impatiently. I did not have long to puzzle over it, however, when the bell rang and Jim fairly leapt over the space between us, grabbing my arm and jerking me to my feet.

"What a lecture! But what do you think caused the nebulous ring and the condensations?"

"Don't know," I murmured as we pressed out past the other students into the hall. "But I do know that I was sleepy. I had to fairly fight myself, and that in spite of the interesting facts of the lecture."

"You would," he laughed. "But what a sight that would be from a ringside seat."

"Might have an uncomfortable resemblance to those warm regions some of us are supposed to visit sometime without the wishing."

"But joking aside, Bob, that would put a sure and sudden end to our little planetary system, wouldn't it?" he laughed.

"By the way," I remarked as casually as possible, "doesn't the sun look a little peculiar?"

Jim snorted.

"So old Kepling has you worried?"

"I mean it. I didn't go to lab yesterday, so I'm asking you if there is some unusual atmospheric condition such as a big fire somewhere near that would cast an ash veil. It just looks—well—strange!"

"Then the trouble is with your eyes. If you took a sip from Brown's hip flask last night, I would advise you to lay off."

We walked the rest of the way toward the house in silence. I did not have a class for the rest of the day, but Jim, I remembered, had mentioned a quiz in calculus. Finally, on the porch, I touched his arm.

"I suppose you will be studying instead of playing a set of tennis with me as usual?"

"No, the quiz has been called off."

"Called off?"

"Yep. Somebody stole the questions."

"Holy cats! Who'd be fool enough to do a thing like that? Somebody doesn't care much about his diploma."

"Don't know. Lots of things have been disappearing around the laboratories. Kenny says that it is a ghost."

"Well, he's kind of nutty anyway. I suppose that he claims to have seen it?"

"Yes, he did. He says that he came upon something silverish and shining the other day hanging over the botany microscopes, and that the thing, which he could see right through, just faded out when he came into the room."

"Well, whoever heard of a ghost taking up its residence in a scientific laboratory and stealing calculus questions? Evidently my eyes are not the only ones around this place that are in need of an examination!"

It was well toward midnight that evening when I next saw Jim. Then he came bursting into my room with his eyes fairly popping out of his head.

"You remember what I told you about the calculus questions?" he asked when he could get his breath.

"Yeah," I yawned.

"Well, I can't tell you about it, but you must come with me right away. Kepling's in his office, waiting for you."

"Say, now listen. I don't know anything about those questions. Besides that, I don't take calculus."

"Oh dry up! No one is accusing you. Kepling isn't a mathematician."

"All right," I grinned with better humor, "I suppose it's about the ghost then."

For all my teasing, however, the information that I could get out of Jim as to why Kepling had sent for me was extremely unsatisfactory. I simply had to smother my curiosity and follow my friend in silence as he made his way past the night watchman and through the darkened halls of the science building to where the lights shone through the transom of Kepling's office.

"Come in," answered the cultured voice behind the door in response to Jim's knock.

"Did you see it again, Doc?" my friend's voice inquired anxiously as he stepped through the doorway in front of me.

The silver hair of Kepling's head tossed in a negative answer as he turned around in the glow of the student lamp that streamed down upon him and motioned us to a seat.

"Mr. Hunt," looking from Jim's anxious face to my puzzled one, "I asked Mr. Turner here to bring me his most trusted friend, but to give him no information as to why he had been summoned."

"He was mum all right," I grunted, hardly realizing in that moment the great compliment that Jim had paid me.

"He told me that he had already informed you about the strange presence which seems to have been hovering about this science building for some time."

I nodded silently.

"He also told me that he had informed you about the main irregularities that have been discovered."

I nodded again, wondering what the man was driving at.

"It was not until tonight that I saw the creature. In fact, we both saw it. Mr. Turner was discussing the subject of novae with me here at my desk—and in particular the most interesting Nova Persei. I had just been sketching the star with its nebula and the condensations, in illustrating what is to my belief a theory of planetary conception, when we were disturbed by the feeling that we were not alone. Glancing up, we were both somewhat startled to see a tall, shining, indescribable thing before us.

"I put out my hand and touched it.

"My fingers were resisted by a soft, damp, or clammy substance which moved away sharply under my hand as if that touch had hurt it, though the movement of my hand was exceedingly gentle.

"It is my belief now that the creature would undoubtedly have tried to get into communication with us, if I had not taken the initiative. Instead, it faded from our astonished sight—leaving the room absolutely empty."

"But surely, sir, you do not believe . . ."

"That it was a ghost? No. But I do believe that we are entertaining an extra-terrestrial visitor."

"You mean," I gasped, a thrill creeping coldly up my spine, "you mean a man from . . . space?"

"Yes."

"But why?"

"Because of the strange composition of the creature in the first place, its method of locomotion, and its ability to fade from sight. In the second place, I would say because of the interest which it takes in such things as microscopes, astronomy charts, calculus questions, and my poor drawings of Nova Persei."

I nodded slowly.

"Cast here among the creatures of an unknown civilization, this being is just as cautious, as curious, and as half-frightened as we would be in similar circumstances."

"Did it look man-like?" I asked thoughtfully.

"No. Not at all. But that does not mean that it lacks intelligence. Remember that we are entirely the product of our own planet, from our lung capacity to the pressure that we can bear upon our bodies. Then take note of all the types of life that this single Earth has evolved. We are forced to the conclusion that nature is very generous with her patterns. By the law of averages alone, we would probably search far among types of life on other planets for a pattern just like ours."

"Of course, I hadn't thought of that."

"But let's figure out a plan, Doc," Jim's voice put in impatiently.

"Yes, what shall we do about it?" I asked. I was never very long on the arguments. That was Jim's strong point. Mine was action. And here he was voicing my sentiments.

"I have not outlined a very definite plan . . ." Kepling began.

"Suppose Jim and I catch it!"

The white hair tossed a quick negative.

"Such a proceeding would not only destroy all the confidence which it has gained by watching us, but would be liable to be highly dangerous as well, because we do not know what weapons it might have."

I nodded regretfully. It was good advice, but I couldn't help wishing that he hadn't thought of that. "Besides," he continued, "I have an odd feeling that this thing may know the secret of invisibility, thought-reading or possibly the fourth dimension. In fact, young gentlemen, when dealing with extraterrestrial intelligence we must expect to meet with something beyond or undiscovered by our present knowledge limit. For we are but the ignorant offspring of our own planet and once out of that pale we are adrift on an unknown sea."

"Then what shall we do?" I asked.

"In view of the fact that this being was attracted by our little discussion of Nova Persei, I propose that we continue the talk and further it by more charts and drawings. Possibly this will bring him back."

"But after he gets here?" I persisted.

"We will attempt to communicate with him."

I nodded slowly, noting that the doors were closed. Kepling had said something about the fourth dimension. I looked at Jim skeptically, but his eyes were on the old professor, and he seemed to have forgotten my presence utterly in that rapt mood, which I had seen come over him so often during an interesting lecture.

"It won't be hard for me to talk about Nova Persei, for that is one of my hobbies, just as novae are one of my special fields of research. Perhaps it will become more fixed in your mind if I point it out on our large chart, while the action of so doing may also serve the double purpose of attracting our strange visitor."

Adjusting his glasses, Kepling peered through some charts scattered over his desk and selected one of the largest, unrolling it slowly and running one thin, sensitive finger along the Milky Way.

"Here it is in the constellation of Perseus," he nodded, the finger stopping over a dot and then dropping back to another dot.

"This is Argol. You remember my lecture on Argol, sometimes called the 'Demon Sun' because of the huge planet that eclipses its full light at regular intervals?"

I nodded, recalling the interesting discussion that Jim had hurled at me right after that lecture.

"The ancients thought, of course, that Argol winked—in fact . . ."

The sensitive finger curled up from the chart and the white head was raised slightly as if listening . . . Then suddenly I noticed a strange silvery light that seemed to shine on the wall above the desk, over the shaded portion of the student lamp.

"Slowly . . . turn slowly!" Kepling warned me as I started to whirl around in response to that instinct which made one search immediately for the cause of an unexplained fact. "Remember, it must not be frightened away again."

I checked my startled movement with an effort, and turned slowly only to gasp in amazement. For the thing that glowed just beyond the circle of light rays from the lamp was one of the most grotesque creatures that one could conceive. It stood perhaps seven feet high—or rather, I should say floated, because apparently it had no method of support, but moved as if our atmosphere had been so much heavy liquid. Like one of those beautiful self-luminous denizens of the deep seas, it glinted with a faint silvery light, its nine tentacles hanging down like a drooping flower whose long, faintly waving petals faded out into shadow. At the same moment, I was aware of a strange, heavy perfume that seemed to suddenly fill the air of the little room and engulf me like a tidal wave from the sea. I put out a hand to touch Jim's sleeve to warn him about that peculiar odor, but my arm seemed to become unbearably heavy. It dropped limply back to my side, Jim leaning forward in his chair, the white head of Kepling lit by the streaming rays of the student lamp, and the silvery thing which floated just beyond the circle of light, all became fixed like figures of wax or the sketches of a madman on an illumined canvas and then suddenly swam together in a crazy whirl, as I fell forward into the dark pit of unconsciousness.

It must have been days before I again came to. Perhaps because of my un-expected movement, I received more of the mysterious drug than either of my two companions. At any rate, when I next opened my eyes, their anxious faces were bending over me. I glanced at them and smiled, when suddenly I caught sight of our strange surroundings, and the smile faded into an expression of wonder.

"Yes, we looked the same way when we first glanced around," Jim grinned.

"But . . ."

"See, Doc, he is getting interested. I said he would come around all right."

"The coming around isn't the point in question!" I answered, sitting up and staring at the glass palace surrounding us—my eyes roving from the lustrous, silver mattress-like rug upon whose tufted fibers of moonlit cobwebs I had been resting, to the glowing draperies above our heads that twined backwards like so much gossamer-thin spun glass, glistening as they moved in an unfelt breeze.

"Doc thinks that the machinery which propels her is up there, but we can't find any way of getting up," Jim volunteered.

My eye dropped back down the sheer glass-like walls that glowed with the same weird silvery light that our visitor had emitted in the office of Dr. Kepling.

"But how in . . ."

"We know nothing more than you do," the cultured voice of the old professor assured me. "We were also drugged in the office. We both saw you fall but were already powerless ourselves. During our state of unconsciousness we were evidently kidnapped."

"He might have invited us to go," I grunted resentfully. "I have a notion to smear him up."

"That would be most unwise," Kepling said quickly. "In the first place, he has not harmed us, and in the second place, even if you should succeed in overpowering him with his strange drugs, we have not the remotest chance of getting back to Earth."

"You mean that we are in space right now—off the Earth?"

"Exactly."

"And this is a spaceship?"

"Nothing else but!" Jim grinned gleefully.

"But where did he have it when he was hanging around the Science Building?"

"Undoubtedly he had it stationed in the upper atmosphere, and he conveyed us to it in some mysterious manner."

"Suppose we ask him?"

"I have tried to communicate with him but my efforts have been unsuccessful. However, I believe I can enlighten you both on one point. My observations tend to the prophecy that we are speeding toward the constellation of Perseus or Andromeda at a terrific rate."

"Well, that is the best news I have heard since the calculus questions were stolen," Jim grinned.

"But what about our Earth?" I asked. "Is it still visible?"

"No, the Earth dwindled away some time ago and now even our sun has shrunk to a star of the first magnitude."

"That ought to be an interesting sight," I said, starting to rise.

"Take it easy, Mr. Hunt. The sensation of weightlessness may not make you any too steady on your feet for awhile."

———

I arose awkwardly. Outside of being slightly dizzy, which I laid to the lack of gravity, I managed to follow the white-haired figure of Kepling without any mishaps, although my eyes were busily roving over the fantastic building, which Jim later told that he had nicknamed "the Temple of the Stars." It was formed of a type of composition that at first glance resembled glass, but although it was transparent, yet it glowed with a silver luminosity, giving the effect of diffused moonlight.

As soon as Kepling reached the edge of this strange palace and pointed back to a bright yellow star below us, the luminosity of the floor and walls, which I will continue to call glass for the want of a better name, faded out, and the stars glowed through the black abysses of space at us from all sides like millions of varicolored lights. How aptly Jim had named the ship! I was so awestruck at the gorgeous spectacle they presented that I failed to note the puzzled frown that had crept over the placid features of the white-haired scientist.

"Something is the matter with the sun—I mean our sun," he announced, his usually quiet voice vibrating with a note of alarm.

"I expected as much," I heard myself saying.

"What?"

"Well, I mean it's a hunch that came to me yesterday, or day before, or last week—or whenever it was that you gave your lecture on Nova Persei."

"Then why didn't you mention it in the office?"

"Forgot it, I suppose. So much was happening. Then, too, Jim had kidded me. He had suggested . . . oh, certain disagreeable possibilities."

But Kepling was no longer listening to me.

"Look!" he cried, his voice trembling with excitement.

My eyes turned unwillingly—almost fearfully—back to that little yellow star. It was ablaze. Its dazzling glory seemed to expand—eclipsing the more feeble lights of its nearest neighbors.

Then again I felt that strange presence near me, and turning around, I saw the flower-like being floating near us in all its ghostly, silver beauty. One long, radiant tentacle slowly separated itself from the others and pointed to a great opaque globe that began to glow with a ruby light.

"Look, a new type of telescope, I suppose," I said as Kepling's horror-stricken eyes followed my pointing finger.

Slowly the ruby light began to shrink, turning to a glaring white as it concentrated in a spot of terrific brilliance.

"He is showing us the sun—our sun . . ." The old astronomer's voice ended in a groan.

Then suddenly I saw it—that wave of fire—spreading . . . on every side . . . spreading. Jim covered his eyes as if to shut out the horror of it. Beside me the flower-thing floated silently, his phosphorescence touching the scene with a detached, unearthly shimmer. Perhaps he lingered there with unexpressed and inexpressible sympathy!

The wave of flame spread on and succeeding waves followed it, until the glare of the flaming disc became unbearable. But the globe followed the first wave of fire, and slowly the gleaming nucleus drifted to the edge and out of sight.

Jim uncovered his eyes again and stared as a hypnotized man might stare at the globe.

Flashing in a trillion sparkles, the wave of white-hot gas was reaching for its first planet . . .

"Mercury!" Kepling gasped, even as the wave engulfed it and turned it into a tiny torch.

The light of the conflagration seemed to intensify as it spread, and again the globe followed its expanding edge. I felt my throat tighten as Venus swept into view. But almost immediately it was caught up in the veil of fire, seemed to actually explode in hissing steam and slowly swung toward the edge of the globe as the third planet accompanied by its tiny silver bubble of a moon came into the path of the fiery death.

Kepling groaned, while Jim stared like one turned to stone. In that moment of horror, as we watched in helpless misery the luminescent wave creeping upon our little world, I seemed to be able to see with my mind's eye the streets of the cities with their floods of terror-stricken faces turned skyward—some groping with blind stares from which sight had been forever blasted, and others glaring with pupils from which the light of reason had vanished . . .

But the wave of death swept on—engulfing the planet and causing it to gleam suddenly like a large diamond thrown into a strong light.

Kepling slumped limply to the floor. That movement startled Jim from his frozen state, and he bent over the old gentleman with white, drawn features. But I staggered back away from the globe, closing my hands over my face as if to shut out its terrible message. My foot struck a bench and on this I sank, dropping my head into my hands.

Infinite moments went by. Finally I felt a hand on my shoulder and heard Kepling's voice murmuring, "I know, my boy, that it is easier to face the most horrible death oneself than to realize that everything one has loved and lived for has been swept away in one moment of unspeakable terror, but the past is past while we are still alive and must go on."

"As wanderers of space."

"Yes, as wanderers of space," he nodded, gripping my shoulder harder with his slender fingers. "For without the need of words it has been revealed to us why we were kidnapped."

"Perhaps he too . . . he seemed sort of helplessly sympathetic when it happened," I murmured, noting that the globe had turned black and that the silver luminosity had come back into the floor and the walls.

"Perhaps," the white head nodded. "It is a cruel, unbelievable fact to face but we must realize that not only our friends, but also all art, all history and literature, all the sciences—everything which we call our civilization—has been swept like a gnat into nothingness. For when we three die, our race will be no more."

"Don't!" Jim begged in a whisper, instinctively using the hushed tones that one falls into in the presence of death.

————

So it was that our great adventure was begun upon the ashes of tragedy, and this was why the bitterness of that tragedy never entirely forsook our minds. For though in the days which followed, we did much to regain our zest for life, yet behind it always loomed that terrible knowledge that the past was blotted out—making the future but a hopeless blank, even as those dark apertures torn in the star-clouds of the heavens are a blank, through which we seem to look into endless nothingness . . .

And now time slipped by, almost without the realization that it was passing. Kepling worked almost unceasingly upon copying what he could remember of scientific books, while Jim and I spent hours at the glass wall looking out at the stars that gleamed around us like endless swarms of fireflies.

We saw our host but seldom, although he seemed to anticipate our wishes in a most extraordinary manner, the objects we had desired always appearing to materialize from nowhere. He himself, however, kept out of sight—either preferring to stay invisible or else remaining in the upper part of the palace-ship that we had never seen. We often commented upon him, wondering where he had come from, where he was going and, again, if he, too, was the victim of one of those catastrophes that astronomers have called novae—an exile without a parent civilization—a wanderer through space.

This feeling was intensified when, passing near to Algol, he distracted our attention from the "Demon Sun" by pointing one gleaming tentacle to the nebulous rotating ring of Nova Persei, which was looming up like a strange Saturn among the stars and then slowly fading away again into darkness. Jim was the first to voice his opinion.

"You were right, Doc. This man from space is certainly interested in Nova Persei."

Kepling nodded thoughtfully.

"Wanted: one Sherlock Holmes," I grinned.

"Well, I don't know why it should, but it gives me the creeps to think that he might have come from Nova Persei," Jim murmured with a shrug.

"And the way he has of fading away into nothingness gives me the creeps," I added.

"It is equally possible that our methods of locomotion give him the creeps," Kepling smiled. "Personally, I am of the opinion that his method has innumerable advantages."

Jim laughed.

"Especially in some of the exploring expeditions that we probably have in store for us!"

"Look!" Kepling interrupted. "The nebula around Nova Persei is pretty plain now because of our nearness—but the condensations—they are easily distinguished."

"You know, Doc," Jim said thoughtfully, "they do look like the remains of planets. Not that I'm upholding the theory that they were run down by a dark star, but merely overtaken by the wave of fire."

Kepling's eyes sparkled suddenly as the idea took hold of him.

"Possibly they are. I wish I could turn the globe back to our sun and observe what has happened," he said earnestly, the scientist in him fully aroused over the conception of a new theory.

He had no sooner uttered the wish than the globe clouded with showers of stars and comets, until at an immeasurably further distance than we had viewed it before, a flaming sun flashed upon the screen. Surrounding it was a very faint nebulous haze and dimly marked were four tiny condensations— somewhat brighter than the luminescent veil that surrounded them.

"Why only four?" I asked in surprise.

"We are evidently too far away to see the four minor planets and those are the major four."

"Good reasoning, Jim," Kepling smiled affectionately.

"But it does have an uncanny resemblance to Nova Persei," I put in.

"Except the positions are about reversed," Jim added.

"Of course, there is no need of forming theories any more, but the habits of a lifetime are hard to break." The white-haired figure smiled wistfully as I turned away from the globe. Somehow, the sight of that gloriously beautiful funeral pyre hurt me more than the lash of a whip. Disconsolately I turned away, walking toward the opposite wall and looking off through the myriad swarms of stars that glowed in through the darkened sides of the ship. Then suddenly I stopped and stared. For out of the tail of my eye I had caught sight of an enormous colored light ahead of us that loomed up like a vast comet. I looked up quickly. The new object, which seemed have appeared from behind the hidden prow of our spaceship as if we had been steering toward it and now were swerving to one side, was a brilliant blue sun, the lower third of which was covered by its reddish-yellow companion. I had often viewed binary or double stars back in the old university telescope, so the sight was not unusual, but the nearness of this pair made me gasp at the splendor of the spectacle they presented.

"Come quickly!" I called out with excitement.

Jim was the first one to reach my side, but the white-haired astronomer was not far behind him.

"Look at the blue sun up there with its companion that looks like a huge luminous orange."

"Must be Almack," Kepling said thoughtfully.

"Almack?" I asked, trying to place the familiar name.

"Yes. You will remember that in my lecture on multiple suns, I mentioned this group of three."

"Three?" I said quizzically, taking another look at the apparent double.

"Yes, three. Behind the orange sun, you will see the thin green outline of the third. Like all multiple suns, you will remember that they revolve around their common center of gravity."

"Did you say the third sun was green?" I asked, trying to separate it from the red corona of the orange.

"Don't you remember our discussion of that very group?" Jim grinned at me. "You were trying to figure out the sunset effects."

"Sounds more like your ideas. You were the interplanetary bug of our group."

"Perhaps so. But, oh, how I would like to take a peek at a world lit by this trio of colored suns!"

"That is a wish that I have secretly nursed all of my life," Kepling admitted softly.

—————

Hardly had the words left his lips than the three jewel-like suns swung back toward the prow, becoming eclipsed at last by the forepart of the ship.

"He is going to take us there," I laughed. "How's that for thought-reading?"

"Well, the wish was double," Kepling smiled, "and therefore doubly strong."

"Triple," I corrected.

Jim laughed as the silver luminosity came back into the walls. It was the first real laugh I had heard from him since the days on Earth.

"I am only hoping that our entertaining host has adequate means of breaking the speed of the ship," the old professor murmured with a worried frown.

"But if we really wanted to worry, Doc, we wouldn't have to go very far. A whole host of funny ideas would come trooping in," Jim grinned. "For instance, we might begin to wonder about the air and if its content would agree with our lungs, or we might wonder if the planet is too small and the atmospheric pressure would burst us, as the deep-sea fish burst when they come into the air; or we might wonder if the planet is so large and the atmosphere so dense that we would be crushed . . . or . . ."

"That will do for the present," I put in.

"Besides, we haven't any weapons . . ." he continued.

"Young gentlemen, I for one have full confidence in the good judgment of our host."

"So have I. Even if I did start out wanting to kill him off."

"I tell you—he's a great animated flower," Jim agreed.

"But the most practical thing," I interrupted, "would be to get some sleep before we get too close, because we will be too interested in the landing of the ship to even think about such a thing later on, while we do not know what dangers or hardships may await us on the new world."

Both of my companions agreed on the wisdom of this suggestion, each throwing himself down on his particular tufted mattress-like rug. For a long time, however, sleep would not come to me. I lay awake wondering to what weird civilizations this man from the unknown was carrying us. To what destinations were we ultimately bound? What adventures awaited us on the morrow? How long would we stay on this world with its colored suns—and after that—what?

The first thing that I noticed after I had awakened was the glow of the colored suns upon the silver luminosity of the walls. A green light blended into lavender and then purple was followed by orange in unending splendor.

I sat up and drank in the cubistic beauty of the crystal palace under these changing rays. When I stirred, Jim immediately sat up and called out, "How are these for stage effects? If I could transport them to Broadway, we'd both be rich."

But my laugh that followed this apparently thoughtless remark died in my throat.

"Come now. I'm sorry. No gloomy thoughts today."

I nodded with a smile, walking over toward the walls. As usual, this movement on our part was the signal for the luminosity to die out, but this time the light which shone through from the colored suns was even more intense than the silver which up to now had seemed to act as a screen.

Suddenly Kepling's voice sounded softly behind us.

"Look toward the prow of the ship."

We turned our faces upward almost simultaneously, and gasped to see the disc of a planet swinging between us and the star-spangled blackness of space. It was tinted green and orange—one side of a mountain chain being of a greenish hue and the other a reddish-orange.

"What about the pressure?" Jim asked anxiously.

The cultured voice droned a low reply that might have been part of a class-room lecture.

"The size of the body is close to that of our own Earth and so the pressure is about right, while it is far enough from its suns to give a very pleasant temperature."

"What did I say about our ghost-like friend?"

"Was it you who said it?" I teased Jim. We hadn't completely overcome our earthly habit of annoying each other's peace of mind, even with the ever-present example of gentle manners we had in the old professor.

"I didn't believe that our host would knowingly lead us into danger," Kepling put in innocently. "Concerning the contents of the atmosphere, however, we can only take a chance."

"I am only waiting for the opportunity to take it," Jim grinned.

"Don't be so sure about the chance," I nodded. "It looks very much as if our engineer has decided to give the planet the go-by."

Indeed, the disc was rapidly swinging toward our stern. Kepling watched for a few moments in silence and then smiled.

"He is turning the ship around. In other words, he is going to lower us stern first upon the planet."

"But what is the idea, Doc?"

"He probably has noted our interest and intends to allow us unobstructed observation."

After a moment it was quite plain that this was indeed just what was happening. As the great globe rushed up toward us, lit by its sinking green and rising orange sun, we kneeled down and finally threw ourselves prone upon the floor as the mountain chains took more definite form. Kepling was the first to point out the vast moon-like craters that dotted the face of the planet and lifted jagged crags skyward from the level of what appeared to be a dead plain.

"Evidently very little water," the astronomer commented tersely.

"The seas do appear to be dried up — very much like the state on the moon," Jim agreed.

The green sun had dropped from sight when at last we decided that the light patches on the mountaintops were snow. It was an orange world that we now rapidly lowered ourselves upon, hovering sometimes and again seeming to waver along sideways as if seeking a particular spot which the engineer had admired during a previous visit. Jim was the first one to suggest this possibility, and once the idea was planted, it grew upon us.

We finally passed a part of the wildly mountainous country that began to be lit by the blue sun on one side and the orange on the other. At this point the ship ceased to waver and began to drop rapidly toward the mountains, landing with a scarcely perceptible jar on a level plateau that was just opposite a tremendous talon-like range of peaks. The little plateau upon which we found ourselves seemed to be itself the peak of a mountain, though not as high as the chain opposite—nor could we look down the other side, for another glance showed us that our resting place was not quite the top, but a small ridge had to be climbed first. For a moment now, we rested in shadow, but it was a weird twilight, the greenish tint lingering in the heavens only as a kind of afterglow, giving the effect of strangeness which I have sometimes noted on Earth, after a wild storm has momentarily torn a cleft in the clouds for the zodiacal light to peer through.

Then as we stood there by the glass walls, our specter-like host floated down toward us from the shimmering upper drapes, and pointing with one of his lustrous tentacles, he called our attention to an open doorway, through which a cool breeze sprang into the ship.

————

Jim was the first one through, landing in the moss-like growth of the plateau with one long jump. I followed. Bounding along like a puppy that has been held in confinement, he ran with long leaps and jumps toward the edge of the cliff, where he stopped and waved like a maniac. I caught up with him with such a leap that I almost went over the cliff, while the white-haired figure of the scientist followed with more dignity. But when I looked down into the valley, the unearthly character of this moonscape left me gasping.

Imagine, if you can, a range of huge silt mountains from which ever-tumbling veils of snow and rock dropped intermittently into a gorge four times deeper than the Grand Canyon with a dull roar. It seemed as I stood there that I was gazing upon a staircase for giants leading down to a bottomless pit of half-fluid mud, and then over it all that weirdly changing sky and finally the first gleams of the blue sun, as it climbed through a knife-slashed pass.

I was still looking in awestruck silence when Kepling's voice murmured, "I believe that the scene on the other side just over the ridge is perhaps equally interesting!"

"How can it be?" Jim gasped.

"Such is the judgment of our host at any rate. He pointed up that way but you two rushed off too vigorously to even notice his instructions."

"Well, we can go up there, but Doc, just look at that pit."

"The region is evidently still volcanic," Kepling mused, picking up a rock.

"Some push certainly heaved up those mountains. But look at that swamp," Jim persisted.

Kepling nodded thoughtfully.

"I bet it's full of funny-looking monsters," I laughed.

"Not so funny close up," Jim interrupted. "But let's take that look at the other side. Personally, I feel like getting some exercise. The only trouble with space travel is that there are so few stopovers and those are so far apart!"

So with Jim leading the way, we climbed up the rocks leading toward the ridge. Once over the top, however, our leader did a war dance to convince us of his approval of the view, while I turned and smiled at Kepling. The old scientist waved away my offer of assistance, and I, too, leaped over the intervening rocks, where I stopped and slumped down with awestruck eyes. For yawning below us was the cavernous depths of a vast crater where a molten lake boiled and bubbled—the living lava splashing up with livid spurts of hellish splendor in the glowing pit—miles below us. Across from us the opposite walls of the crater were outlined blackly against a carmine sky, the sinking rays of the setting orange sun giving the appearance of a huge conflagration raging down the unseen slopes of the other side, which, having swept through the crater, had left this lake of glowing embers behind.

Overhead the sky was turning a reddish-purple, while over to one side a huge purplish moon, half-ruby and half-blue, was rising.

Kepling stopped for a moment on top and then stepped over to the very edge and looked down. I was just admiring the old scientist's nice sense of balance when I heard him give a sharp cry, saw him throw his body around as if to catch himself, and then go plunging down through the darkness toward that glowing pit. I started to my feet in horror when a sudden convulsion of the rocks made me look down. Imagine my terror to realize that what we had mistaken for a ridge of rocks in our delight at the scene before us was a sleeping dragon—a huge armored creature that had been taking a nap on the crater's rim. Kepling had been standing on the thing's back, and therefore had been the first to fall as it moved. So perfectly matched to the rocks had been his protective coloring that we had not noticed him!

I leapt to his tail, intending to then jump to some lava projections and try to get a glimpse of the old professor before the monster turned on me, but I was too slow. He swished his tail, hurling me unceremoniously into space whence I dashed helplessly against some rocks and started to slide down the cliffs toward that red, bubbling horror. Miraculously, I don't know how, I kept my senses, digging my heels and fingers into the earth to stop me and clutching what plants I could grasp. At last I caught a gnarled plant growing at the very edge of the long drop into the cauldron. There I swung between the lava cliff and the burning lake, with only one toehold with which to climb back.

When at last, shivering and perspiring, I finally pulled myself up and lay limply on the black rock, a wail and a roar sent my eyes back to the monster.

Something was being pulverized into nothingness under the maddened stamps of the great beast, whose gleaming red eyes did not note that a new menace flew through the air at him until it was too late, and a silvery-gleaming, flower-like creature with shimmering tentacles lit upon his back like a giant insect of some terrible, malignant type. With a roar of agony that reverberated from cliff to cliff through that glowing crater, the great animal leaped into the air and headed straight for me—maddened into frenzy by the stinging thing that he could not shake off. Each leap shook the whole mountain as those tons of animal flesh crashed to earth.

Then, suddenly, with a more ominous roar, I felt the whole cliff tremble, and leaped back just as the entire face of the mountain gave way, carrying with its rush of rocks, like a struggling ant, the brown dragon and the silver thing that still clung to its quivering flanks like a phosphorescent flower . . .

———

For a moment I was too much concerned with racing the breaking rocks on the top of the slide to catch more than a glance of the dragon that roiled under the thunder of the avalanche, but after the dust had at last cleared away from the freshly glowing lava lake, I sat down on the tip of the rim and stared with unseeing eyes into the cauldron.

Behind me, with its glass walls glittering in the rising rays of the blue sun, the palace-ship, which Jim had nicknamed "the Temple of the Stars," stood peacefully, waiting for the gleaming master, which would never return. Before me, the ruby color of the cauldron changed subtly through all the shades of lavender to purple as the blue sun climbed higher and the orange sun deepened its glow to the red of a deep garnet. Before me, a few loosened rocks still bounded hollowly down the cliffs . . .

Of my companions who had accompanied me over the rim in such high spirits, not a shred remained to tell that they had ever lived. Indeed, seated here upon a giant crater—like a gnat that surveys a mountain gorge—to what end had I struggled so madly to preserve my life, doomed as I was to die on this wild, weird world—or in case I did learn the secret of the ship's propulsion and fuel—then to wander through space forever alone—the last living creature of my kind?

———

"Bob Hunt! Will you wake up, or shall I have to carry you out of here?" I heard Jim's voice asking impatiently. I opened my eyes suddenly, looking in consternation from the streak of yellow sunshine that was lazily streaming over the classroom floor, back to the very amused eyes of Dr. Kepling.

"But I thought . . ."

"Never mind what you thought! Come on and get moving!"

"But Jim! We're still on Earth! And our sun . . . why, it's all right! It's normal—isn't it?"

A deep horselaugh greeted this statement from the vicinity of the doorway, where a number of amused students were lingering.

"Make a fool of yourself if you wish—but count me out!" Jim snapped starting toward the door.

I picked up my books sheepishly and followed him, apparently deaf to a number of wisecracks that were hurled at me. Only when we were nearing the house did he deign to notice me.

"You picked out one of the most interesting lectures of the year to sleep on, you poor nut."

"I know—it was about Nova Persei."

"Oh, you did hear some of it, did you?"

"Of course I did." Then after a moment, "You know, Jim, I have a funny hunch that those condensations were the remains of planets which were consumed by the wave of fire which the main sun threw off when it exploded."

"Sleep all through a lecture and then presume to know something about it, eh? Well, Mr. Would-Be Scientist, get this—the collision theories fit the facts of Nova Persei better than the explosion theory."

After that I subsided. Only in front of the house, I laid a hand on his arm.

"Are you still too peeved to play our usual set of tennis this afternoon?"

"Sorry, old sleepyhead, but I have that calculus quiz coming off this afternoon."

"Oh, the questions—no one stole them?"

"Well, aren't you just brimming over with the most amazing ideas? Who would be fool enough to steal calculus questions?" Then with a laugh—"Say, boy, I only wish that I could answer that dumb question in the affirmative—but there is *no such luck*."

[Author's note: I realize that there are inconsistencies in this dream of Bob Turner's, but who has ever heard of an entirely consistent dream?]

C(ATHERINE) L(UCILLE) MOORE (1911–87) was an American writer who authored and coauthored more than seventy-five stories in SF magazines between 1932 and 1956. She was born in Indianapolis, Indiana, in 1911 and "picked up an early love of reading from her mother" (Bloom 141). Moore was particularly fond of SF and fantasy, especially the John Carter and Tarzan novels of Edgar Rice Burroughs and *Alice in Wonderland* by Lewis Carroll (Elliot 46). As a literature student at Indiana University, Moore contributed frequently to the *Vagabond*, a student-run magazine, and fellow contributors praised her as "the most promising prose writer who has been at Indiana for some time" (Liptak, "Many"). Eventually, the Great Depression forced her to exchange college for business school and then to pursue work as "the secretary to the vice president of the Fletcher Trust Co.," a bank in downtown Indianapolis (Davin, *Pioneers* 77). Moore rediscovered SF in 1931 when she came across a copy of *Amazing* during a lunch break. It wasn't long before she published her first story, "Shambleau," in the November 1933 issue of *Weird Tales* under the name C. L. Moore. According to Moore, "I used the initials, 'C. L.,' simply because I didn't want it to be known at the bank that I had an extra source of income," something that could have led to the termination of her employment during the Depression (Elliot 47).

In the 1940s, Moore became one of the few women to make her living from SF writing. Her success was enhanced by her partnership with Henry Kuttner, a fellow genre author who "wrote a fan letter to Mr. C. L. Moore," only to learn that Moore was a woman (Bloom 141). The correspondence between Moore and Kuttner led to both an artistic and a romantic collaboration. The couple published their first coauthored story, "Quest of the Starstone," in the November 1937 issue of *Weird Tales*. After marrying in 1940, they "decided to write on a full-time basis," combining their earnings and making just "enough to get by" (Elliot 46). Living in Los Angeles and writing under their own names as well as pseudonyms, including Lawrence O'Donnell and Lewis Padgett, Moore and Kuttner greatly increased their output and, through shrewd negotiations with various SF editors, also increased the amount they were paid for their stories. When word rates for SF authors began to stagnate in the 1950s, Moore and Kuttner attended the University of Southern California, where they completed their degrees before taking on work as scriptwriters for Warner Brothers. After Kuttner's death in 1958, Moore continued working for Warner until 1963, when she married Reggie Thomas and retired from professional writing.

Unlike many other early SF authors, Moore was never lost from SF history. Even after she quit writing she was a regular participant in the Tom and Terri Pinckard SF literary salon, whose members included A. E. Van Vogt, Robert Bloch, Larry Niven, and Norman Spinrad. In 1973 the Los Angeles Science Fiction Society honored her with a Forry Award, and four years later she received a Count Dracula Society Award for Literature. In 1981 Moore won the World Fantasy Award for Lifetime Achievement and the Gandalf Grand Master Award, thereby becoming the eighth and final Grand Master of Fantasy. She was nominated as a Grand Master of Science Fiction, but her husband asked that the nomination be withdrawn due to Moore's advanced Alzheimer's disease. In 1998 she was inducted posthumously into the Science Fiction and Fantasy Hall of Fame, and in 2004 she and Kuttner received the Cordwainer Smith Rediscovery Award.

Moore's stories for *Weird Tales* in the 1930s proved to be some of the most highly regarded the magazine ever published. This is particularly true of "Shambleau." Legend has it that the editor, Farnsworth Wright, "closed *Weird Tales'* offices for the day in celebration" upon reading Moore's story (Liptak, "Many"). In the May 1937 issue of his magazine, Wright noted that "Shambleau" was one of the most important discoveries he had ever made, and, in a letter printed a few pages later, a reader named David Beams enthused that Moore's tale "was equal to Edgar Allen Poe at his best" (638). The appeal of "Shambleau" to *Weird Tales* readers seems relatively straightforward. The multi-genre magazine specialized in bizarre SF stories that explored the dark side of the engineering paradigm central to both SF and the greater American imagination at that time. Following, as it does, the misadventures of a human adventurer whose attempt to rescue a Martian damsel in distress goes disastrously awry, "Shambleau" warns readers that the dream of human control over the material world is, at best, just that—a dream that will inevitably be undone by the complexities of a vast and potentially hostile universe.

But "Shambleau" is more than just a well-crafted parable about the dangers of scientific pride; instead, much of the story's horror derives from its critique of assumptions about sex and gender roles. Moore famously noted that her story's title character was a version "of the self I'd like to have been": red-haired, physically powerful, and intoxicatingly desirable ("Footnote" 368). But Moore's Shambleau is more than just a superwoman; she is "an alien who is truly *alien*" (Del Rey x). In one sense, Moore's extraterrestrial "might represent a separate female culture that is beyond our known words and worlds" (Gubar 19). At the same time, her description of Shambleau as a Medusa-like being with living tresses that penetrate victims while sending them into sexual ecstasy frustrates straightforward readings of Moore's antagonist as either male or female, thereby displacing the extraterrestrial—and, for at least a brief time, Moore's protagonist and readers—from "the heterosexual economy" that drives the broader story (Hollinger 147). As such, "Shambleau" can be understood as a science fictional updating of the female Gothic in which characters experience the sublime as "an aesthetic that multiplies difference" and undermines patriarchal understandings of social and sexual order (Heiland 5). Thus Moore provides readers with one of the genre's most celebrated and anthologized stories, drawing on the new tools of SF and the rich history of the female Gothic to craft a subversive feminist story that has only become more compelling with time.

....

"Shambleau"

Weird Tales, November 1933

Man has conquered Space before. You may be sure of that. Somewhere beyond the Egyptians, in that dimness out of which come echoes of half-mythical names—Atlantis, Mu—somewhere back of history's first beginnings there must have been an age when mankind, like us today, built cities of steel to house its star-roving ships and knew the names of the planets in their own native tongues— heard Venus's people call their wet world "Sha-ardol" in that soft, sweet, slurring speech and mimicked Mars's guttural "Lakkdiz" from the harsh tongues of Mars's dryland dwellers. You may be sure of it. Man has conquered Space before, and out of that conquest faint, faint echoes run still through a world that has forgotten the very fact of a civilization that must have been as mighty as our own. There have been too many myths and legends for us to doubt it. The myth of Medusa, for instance, can never have had its roots in the soil of Earth. That tale of the snake-haired Gorgon whose gaze turned the gazer to stone never originated about any creature that Earth nourished. And those ancient Greeks who told the story must have remembered, dimly and half believing, a tale of antiquity about some strange being from one of the outlying planets their remotest ancestors once trod.

————

"Shambleau! Ha . . . Shambleau!"

The wild hysteria of the mob rocketed from wall to wall of Lakkdarol's narrow streets and the storming of heavy boots over the slag-red pavement made an ominous undernote to that swelling bay, "Shambleau! Shambleau!"

Northwest Smith heard it coming and stepped into the nearest doorway, laying a wary hand on his heat gun's grip, and his colorless eyes narrowed. Strange sounds were common enough in the streets of Earth's latest colony on Mars—a raw, red little town where anything might happen, and very often did. But Northwest Smith, whose name is known and respected in every dive and wild outpost on a dozen wild planets, was a cautious man, despite his reputation. He set his back against the wall and gripped his pistol, and heard the rising shout come nearer and nearer.

Then into his range of vision flashed a red running figure, dodging like a hunted hare from shelter to shelter in the narrow street. It was a girl—a berry-brown girl in a single tattered garment whose scarlet burnt the eyes with its brilliance. She ran wearily, and he could hear her gasping breath from where he stood. As she came into view he saw her hesitate and lean one hand against the wall for support, and glance wildly around for shelter. She must not have seen him in the depths of the doorway, for as the bay of the mob grew louder and the pounding of feet sounded almost at the corner she gave a despairing little moan and dodged into the recess at his very side.

When she saw him standing there, tall and leather-brown, hand on his heat-gun, she sobbed once, inarticulately, and collapsed at his feet, a huddle of burning scarlet and bare, brown limbs.

Smith had not seen her face, but she was a girl, and sweetly made and in danger, and though he had not the reputation of a chivalrous man, something in her hopeless huddle at his feet touched that chord of sympathy for the under-dog that stirs in every Earthman, and he pushed her gently into the corner behind him and jerked out his gun, just as the first of the running mob rounded the corner.

It was a motley crowd, Earthmen and Martians and a sprinkling of Venusian swampmen and strange, nameless denizens of unnamed planets—a typical Lakkdarol mob. When the first of them turned the corner and saw the empty street before them there was a faltering in the rush and the foremost spread out and began to search the doorways on both sides of the street.

"Looking for something?" Smith's sardonic call sounded clear above the clamor of the mob.

They turned. The shouting died for a moment as they took in the scene before them—tall Earthman in the space-explorer's leathern garb, all one color from the burning of savage suns save for the sinister pallor of his no-colored eyes in a scarred and resolute face, gun in his steady hand and the scarlet girl crouched behind him, panting.

The foremost of the crowd—a burly Earthman in tattered leather from which the Patrol insignia had been ripped away—stared for a moment with a strange expression of incredulity on his face overspreading the savage exultation of the chase. Then he let loose a deep-throated bellow, "Shambleau!" and lunged forward. Behind him the mob took up the cry again, "Shambleau! Shambleau! Shambleau!" and surged after.

Smith, lounging negligently against the wall, arms folded and gun-hand draped over his left forearm, looked incapable of swift motion, but at the leader's first forward step the pistol swept in a practiced half-circle and the dazzle of blue-white heat leaping from its muzzle seared an arc in the slag pavement at his feet. It was an old gesture, and not a man in the crowd but understood it. The foremost recoiled swiftly against the surge of those in the rear, and for a moment there was confusion as the two tides met and struggled. Smith's mouth curled into a grim curve as he watched. The man in the mutilated Patrol uniform lifted a threatening fist and stepped to the very edge of the deadline, while the crowd rocked to and fro behind him.

"Are you crossing that line?" queried Smith in an ominously gentle voice.

"We want that girl!"

"Come and get her!" Recklessly Smith grinned into his face. He saw danger there, but his defiance was not the foolhardy gesture it seemed. An expert psychologist of mobs from long experience, he sensed no murder here. Not a gun had appeared in any hand in the crowd. They desired the girl with an inexplicable bloodthirstiness he was at a loss to understand, but toward himself he sensed no such fury. A mauling he might expect, but his life was in no danger. Guns would have appeared before now if they were coming out at all. So he grinned in the man's angry face and leaned lazily against the wall.

Behind their self-appointed leader the crowd milled impatiently, and threatening voices began to rise again. Smith heard the girl moan at his feet.

"What do you want with her?" he demanded.

"She's Shambleau! Shambleau, you fool! Kick her out of there—we'll take care of her!"

"I'm taking care of her," drawled Smith.

"She's Shambleau, I tell you! Damn your hide, man, we never let those things live! Kick her out here!"

The repeated name had no meaning to him, but Smith's innate stubbornness rose defiantly as the crowd surged forward to the very edge of the arc, their clamor growing louder. "Shambleau! Kick her out here! Give us Shambleau! Shambleau!"

Smith dropped his indolent pose like a cloak and planted both feet wide, swinging up his gun threateningly. "Keep back!" he yelled. "She's mine! Keep back!"

He had no intention of using that heat-beam. He knew by now that they would not kill him unless he started the gun-play himself, and he did not mean to give up his life for any girl alive. But a severe mauling he expected, and he braced himself instinctively as the mob heaved within itself.

To his astonishment a thing happened then that he had never known to happen before. At his shouted defiance the foremost of the mob—those who had heard him clearly—drew back a little, not in alarm but evidently surprised. The ex-Patrolman said, "Yours! She's *yours*?" in a voice from which puzzlement crowded out the anger.

Smith spread his booted legs wide before the crouching figure and flourished his gun.

"Yes," he said. "And I'm keeping her! Stand back there!"

The man stared at him wordlessly, and horror and disgust and incredulity mingled on his weather-beaten face. The incredulity triumphed for a moment and he said again, "*Yours!*"

Smith nodded defiance.

The man stepped back suddenly, unutterable contempt in his very pose. He waved an arm to the crowd and said loudly, "It's—his!" and the press melted away, gone silent too, and the look of contempt spread from face to face.

The ex-Patrolman spat on the slag-paved street and turned his back indifferently. "Keep her, then," he advised briefly over one shoulder. "But don't let her out again in this town!"

Smith stared in perplexity almost openmouthed as the suddenly scornful mob began to break up. His mind was in a whirl. That such bloodthirsty animosity should vanish in a breath he could not believe. And the curious mingling of contempt and disgust on the faces he saw baffled him even more. Lakkdarol was anything but a puritan town—it did not enter his head for a moment that his claiming the brown girl as his own had caused that strangely shocked repulsion to spread through the crowd. No, it was something deeper rooted than that. Instinctive, instant disgust had been in the faces he saw—they would have looked less so if he had admitted cannibalism or *Pharol*-worship.

And they were leaving his vicinity as swiftly as if whatever unknowing sin he had committed were contagious. The street was emptying as rapidly as it had filled. He saw a sleek Venusian glance back over his shoulder as he turned the corner and sneer, "Shambleau!" and the word awoke a new line of speculation in Smith's mind. Shambleau! Vaguely of French origin, it must be. And strange enough to hear it from the lips of Venusians and Martian drylanders, but it was their use of it that puzzled him more. "We never let those things live," the ex-Patrolman had said. It reminded him dimly of something . . . an ancient line from some writing in his own tongue . . . "Thou shalt not suffer a witch to live." He smiled to himself at the similarity, and simultaneously was aware of the girl at his elbow.

She had risen soundlessly. He turned to face her, sheathing his gun, and stared at first with curiosity and then in the entirely frank openness with which men regard that which is not wholly human. For she was not. He knew it at a glance, though the brown, sweet body was shaped like a woman's and she wore the garment of scarlet—he saw it was leather—with an ease that few unhuman beings achieve toward clothing. He knew it from the moment he looked into her eyes, and a shiver of unrest went over him as he met them. They were frankly green as young grass, with slit-like, feline pupils that pulsed unceasingly, and there was a look of dark, animal wisdom in their depths—that look of the beast that sees more than man.

There was no hair upon her face—neither brows nor lashes, and he would have sworn that the tight scarlet turban bound around her head covered baldness. She had three fingers and a thumb, and her feet had four digits apiece too, and all sixteen of them were tipped with round claws that sheathed back into the flesh like a cat's. She ran her tongue over her lips—a thin, pink, flat tongue as feline as her eyes—and spoke with difficulty. He felt that that throat and tongue had never been shaped for human speech.

"Not—afraid now," she said softly, and her little teeth were white and pointed as a kitten's.

"What did they want you for?" he asked her curiously. "What had you done? Shambleau . . . is that your name?"

"I—not talk your—speech," she demurred hesitantly.

"Well, try to—I want to know. Why were they chasing you? Will you be safe on the street now, or hadn't you better get indoors somewhere? They looked dangerous."

"I—go with you." She brought it out with difficulty.

"Say you!" Smith grinned. "What are you, anyhow? You look like a kitten to me."

"Shambleau." She said it somberly.

"Where d'you live? Are you a Martian?"

"I come from—from far—from long ago—far country—"

"Wait!" laughed Smith. "You're getting your wires crossed. You're not a Martian?"

She drew herself up very straight beside him, lifting the turbaned head, and there was something queenly in the poise of her.

"Martian?" she said scornfully. "My people—are—are—you have no word. Your speech—hard for me."

"What's yours? I might know it—try me."

She lifted her head and met his eyes squarely, and there was in hers a subtle amusement—he could have sworn it.

"Someday I—speak to you in—my own language," she promised, and the pink tongue flicked out over her lips, swiftly, hungrily.

Approaching footsteps on the red pavement interrupted Smith's reply. A dryland Martian came past, reeling a little and exuding an aroma of *segir-*whisky, the Venusian brand. When he caught the red flash of the girl's tatters he turned his head sharply, and as his *segir*-steeped brain took in the fact of her presence he lurched toward the recess unsteadily, bawling, "Shambleau, by *Pharol*! Shambleau!" and reached out a clutching hand.

Smith struck it aside contemptuously.

"On your way, drylander," he advised.

The man drew back and stared, blear-eyed.

"Yours, eh?" he croaked. "*Zut!* You're welcome to it!" And like the ex-Patrolman before him he spat on the pavement and turned away, muttering harshly in the blasphemous tongue of the drylands.

Smith watched him shuffle off, and there was a crease between his colorless eyes, a nameless unease rising within him.

"Come on," he said abruptly to the girl. "If this sort of thing is going to happen we'd better get indoors. Where shall I take you?"

"With—you," she murmured.

He stared down into the flat green eyes. Those ceaselessly pulsing pupils disturbed him, but it seemed to him, vaguely, that behind the animal shallows of her gaze was a shutter—a closed barrier that might at any moment open to reveal the very deeps of that dark knowledge he sensed there.

Roughly he said again, "Come on, then," and stepped down into the street.

———————

She pattered along a pace or two behind him, making no effort to keep up with his long strides, and though Smith—as men know from Venus to Jupiter's moons—walks as softly as a cat, even in spaceman's boots, the girl at his heels slid like a shadow over the rough pavement, making so little sound that even the lightness of his footsteps was loud in the empty street.

Smith chose the less frequented ways of Lakkdarol, and somewhat shamefacedly thanked his nameless gods that his lodgings were not far away, for the few pedestrians he met turned and stared after the two with that by now familiar mingling of horror and contempt which he was as far as ever from understanding.

The room he had engaged was a single cubicle in a lodging-house on the edge of the city. Lakkdarol, raw camp-town that it was in those days, could have furnished little better anywhere within its limits, and Smith's errand there was not one he wished to advertise. He had slept in worse places than this before, and knew that he would do so again.

There was no one in sight when he entered, and the girl slipped up the stairs at his heels and vanished through the door, shadowy, unseen by anyone in the house. Smith closed the door and leaned his broad shoulders against the panels, regarding her speculatively.

She took in what little the room had to offer in a glance—frowsy bed, rickety table, mirror hanging unevenly and cracked against the wall, un-painted chairs—a typical camp-town room in an Earth settlement abroad. She accepted its poverty in that single glance, dismissed it, then crossed to the window and leaned out for a moment, gazing across the low roof-tops toward the barren countryside beyond, red slag under the late afternoon sun.

"You can stay here," said Smith abruptly, "until I leave town. I'm waiting here for a friend to come in from Venus. Have you eaten?"

"Yes," said the girl quickly. "I shall—need no—food for—a while."

"Well—" Smith glanced around the room. "I'll be in sometime tonight. You can go or stay just as you please. Better lock that door behind me."

With no more formality than that he left her. The door closed and he heard the key turn, and smiled to himself. He did not expect, then, ever to see her again.

He went down the steps and out into the late-slanting sunlight with a mind so full of other matters that the brown girl receded very quickly into the background. Smith's errand in Lakkdarol, like most of his errands, is better not spoken of. Man lives as he must, and Smith's living was a perilous affair outside the law and ruled by the ray-gun only. It is enough to say that the shipping-port and its cargoes outbound interested him deeply just now, and that the friend he awaited was Yarol the Venusian, in that swift little Edsel ship the *Maid* that can flash from world to world with a derisive speed that laughs at Patrol boats and leaves pursuers floundering in the ether far behind. Smith and Yarol and the *Maid* were a trinity that had caused the Patrol leaders much worry and many gray hairs in the past, and the future looked very bright to Smith himself that evening as he left his lodging-house.

Lakkdarol roars by night, as Earthmen's camp-towns have a way of doing on every planet where Earth's outposts are, and it was beginning lustily as Smith went down among the awakening lights toward the center of town. His business there does not concern us. He mingled with the crowds where the lights were brightest, and there was the click of ivory counters and the jingle of sil-ver, and red *segir* gurgled invitingly from black Venusian bottles, and much later Smith strolled homeward under the moving moons of Mars, and if the street wavered a little under his feet now and then—why, that is only under-standable. Not even Smith could drink red *segir* at every bar from the Mar-tian Lamb to the New Chicago and remain entirely steady on his feet. But he found his way back with very little difficulty—considering—and spent a good five minutes hunting for his key before he remembered he had left it in the inner lock for the girl.

He knocked then, and there was no sound of footsteps from within, but in a few moments the latch clicked and the door swung open. She retreated soundlessly before him as he entered, and took up her favorite place against the window, leaning back on the sill and outlined against the starry sky beyond. The room was in darkness.

Smith flipped the switch by the door and then leaned back against the panels, steadying himself. The cool night air had sobered him a little, and his head was clear enough—liquor went to Smith's feet, not his head, or he would never have come this far along the lawless way he had chosen. He lounged against the door now and regarded the girl in the sudden glare of the bulbs, blinding a little as much at the scarlet of her clothing as at the light.

"So you stayed," he said.

"I—waited," she answered softly, leaning farther back against the sill and clasping the rough wood with slim, three-fingered hands, pale brown against the darkness.

"Why?"

She did not answer that, but her mouth curved into a slow smile. On a woman it would have been reply enough—provocative, daring. On Shambleau there was something pitiful and horrible in it—so human on the face of one half-animal. And yet . . . that sweet brown body curving so softly from the tatters of scarlet leather—the velvety texture of that brownness—the white-flashing smile . . . Smith was aware of a stirring excitement within him. After all—time would be hanging heavy now until Yarol came . . . Speculatively he allowed the steel-pale eyes to wander over her, with a slow regard that missed nothing. And when he spoke he was aware that his voice had deepened a little . . .

"Come here," he said.

She came forward slowly, on bare clawed feet that made no slightest sound on the floor, and stood before him with downcast eyes and mouth trembling in that pitifully human smile. He took her by the shoulders—velvety soft shoulders, of a creamy smoothness that was not the texture of human flesh. A little tremor went over her, perceptibly, at the contact of his hands. Northwest Smith caught his breath suddenly and dragged her to him . . . sweet, yielding brownness in the circle of his arms . . . heard her own breath catch and quicken as her velvety arms closed about his neck. And then he was looking down into her face, very near, and the green animal eyes met his with the pulsing pupils and the flicker of—something—deep behind their shallows—and through the rising clamor of his blood, even as he stooped his lips to hers, Smith felt something deep within him shudder away—inexplicable, instinctive, revolted. What it might be he had no words to tell, but the very touch of her was suddenly loathsome—so soft and velvet and unhuman—and it might have been an animal's face that lifted itself to his mouth—the dark knowledge looked hungrily from the darkness of those slit pupils—and for a mad instant he knew that same wild, feverish revulsion he had seen in the faces of the mob . . .

"God!" he gasped, a far more ancient invocation against evil than he realized, then or ever, and he ripped her arms from his neck, swung her away with such a force that she reeled half across the room. Smith fell back against the door, breathing heavily, and stared at her while the wild revolt died slowly within him.

She had fallen to the floor beneath the window, and as she lay there against the wall with bent head he saw, curiously, that her turban had slipped—the turban that he had been so sure covered baldness—and a lock of scarlet hair fell below the binding leather, hair as scarlet as her garment, as unhumanly red as her eyes were unhumanly green. He stared, and shook his head dizzily and stared again, for it seemed to him that the thick lock of crimson had moved, *squirmed* itself against her cheek.

At the contact of it her hands flew up and she tucked it away with a very human gesture and then dropped her head again into her hands. And from the deep shadow of her fingers he thought she was staring up at him covertly.

Smith drew a deep breath and passed a hand across his forehead. The inexplicable moment had gone as quickly as it came—too swiftly for him to understand or analyze it. "Got to lay off the *segir*," he told himself unsteadily. Had he imagined that scarlet hair? After all, she was no more than a pretty brown girl-creature from one of the many half-human races peopling the planets. No more than that, after all. A pretty little thing, but animal . . . He laughed a little shakily.

"No more of that," he said. "God knows I'm no angel, but there's got to be a limit somewhere. Here." He crossed to the bed and sorted out a pair of blankets from the untidy heap, tossing them to the far corner of the room. "You can sleep there."

Wordlessly she rose from the floor and began to rearrange the blankets, the uncomprehending resignation of the animal eloquent in every line of her.

———

Smith had a strange dream that night. He thought he had awakened to a room full of darkness and moonlight and moving shadows, for the nearer moon of Mars was racing through the sky and everything on the planet below her was endued with a restless life in the dark. And something . . . some nameless unthinkable *thing* ... was coiled about his throat ... something like a soft snake, wet and warm. It lay loose and light about his neck ... and it was moving gently, very gently, with a soft, caressive pressure that sent little thrills of delight through every nerve and fiber of him, a perilous delight—beyond physical pleasure, deeper than joy of the mind. That warm softness was caressing the very roots of his soul with a terrible intimacy. The ecstasy of it left him weak, and yet he knew—in a flash of knowledge born of this impossible dream—that the soul should not be handled ... And with that knowledge a horror broke upon him, turning the pleasure into a rapture of revulsion, hateful, horrible—but still most foully sweet. He tried to lift his hands and tear the dream-monstrosity from his throat—tried but half-heartedly; for though his soul was revolted to its very deeps, yet the delight of his body was so great that his hands all but refused the attempt. But when at last he tried to lift his arms a cold shock went over him and he found that he could not stir ... his body lay stony as marble beneath the blankets, a living marble that shuddered with a dreadful delight through every rigid vein.

The revulsion grew strong upon him as he struggled against the paralyzing dream—a struggle of soul against sluggish body—titanically, until the moving dark was streaked with blankness that clouded and closed about him at last and he sank back into the oblivion from which he had awakened.

Next morning, when the bright sunlight shining through Mars's clear, thin air awakened him, Smith lay for a while trying to remember. The dream had been more vivid than reality, but he could not now quite recall ... only that it had been more sweet and horrible than anything else in life. He lay puzzling for a while, until a soft sound from the corner aroused him from his thoughts and he sat up to see the girl lying in a cat-like coil in her blankets, watching him with round, grave eyes. He regarded her somewhat ruefully.

"Morning," he said. "I've just had the devil of a dream ... Well, hungry?"

She shook her head silently, and he could have sworn there was a covert gleam of strange amusement in her eyes.

He stretched and yawned, dismissing the nightmare temporarily from his mind.

"What am I going to do with you?" he inquired, turning to more immediate matters. "I'm leaving here in a day or two and I can't take you along, you know. Where'd you come from in the first place?"

Again she shook her head.

"Not telling? Well, it's your own business. You can stay here until I give up the room. From then on you'll have to do your own worrying."

He swung his feet to the floor and reached for his clothes.

Ten minutes later, slipping the heat-gun into its holster at his thigh, Smith turned to the girl. "There's food-concentrate in that box on the table. It ought to hold you until I get back. And you'd better lock the door again after I've gone."

Her wide, unwavering stare was his only answer, and he was not sure she had understood, but at any rate the lock clicked after him as before, and he went down the steps with a faint grin on his lips.

The memory of last night's extraordinary dream was slipping from him, as such memories do, and by the time he had reached the street the girl and the dream and all of yesterday's happenings were blotted out by the sharp necessities of the present.

Again the intricate business that had brought him here claimed his attention. He went about it to the exclusion of all else, and there was a good reason behind everything he did from the moment he stepped out into the street until the time when he turned back again at evening, though had one chosen to follow him during the day his apparently aimless rambling through Lakkdarol would have seemed very pointless.

He must have spent two hours at the least idling by the space-port, watching with sleepy, colorless eyes the ships that came and went, the passengers, the vessels lying at wait, the cargoes—particularly the cargoes. He made the rounds of the town's saloons once more, consuming many glasses of varied liquors in the course of the day and engaging in idle conversation with men of all races and worlds, usually in their own languages, for Smith was a linguist of repute among his contemporaries. He heard the gossip of the space ways, news from a dozen planets of a thousand different events; he heard the latest joke about the Venusian Emperor and the latest report on the ChinoAryan war and the latest song hot from the lips of Rose Robertson, whom every man on the civilized planets adored as "the Georgia Rose." He passed the day quite profitably, for his own purposes, which do not concern us now, and it was not until late evening, when he turned homeward again, that the thought of the brown girl in his room took definite shape in his mind, though it had been lurking there, formless and submerged, all day.

He had no idea what comprised her usual diet, but he bought a can of New York roast beef and one of Venusian frog-broth and a dozen fresh canal-apples and two pounds of that Earth lettuce that grows so vigorously in the fertile canal-soil of Mars. He felt that she must surely find something to her liking in this broad variety of edibles, and—for his day had been very satisfactory—he hummed "The Green Hills of Earth" to himself in a surprisingly good baritone as he climbed the stairs.

The door was locked, as before, and he was reduced to kicking the lower panels gently with his boot, for his arms were full. She opened the door with that softness that was characteristic of her and stood regarding him in the semi-darkness as he stumbled to the table with his load. The room was unlit again.

"Why don't you turn on the lights?" he demanded irritably after he had barked his shin on the chair by the table in an effort to deposit his burden there.

"Light and—dark—they are alike—to me," she murmured.

"Cat eyes, eh? Well, you look the part. Here, I've brought you some dinner. Take your choice. Fond of roast beef? Or how about a little frog-broth?"

She shook her head and backed away a step.

"No," she said. "I cannot—eat your food."

Smith's brows wrinkled. "Didn't you have any of the food-tablets?"

Again the red turban shook negatively.

"Then you haven't had anything for—why, more than twenty-four hours! You must be starved."

"Not hungry," she denied.

"What can I find for you to eat, then? There's time yet if I hurry. You've got to eat, child."

"I shall—eat," she said, softly. "Before long—I shall—feed. Have no—worry."

She turned away then and stood at the window, looking out over the moon-lit landscape as if to end the conversation. Smith cast her a puzzled glance as he opened the can of roast beef. There had been an odd undernote in that assurance that, undefinably, he did not like. And the girl had teeth and tongue and presumably a fairly human digestive system, to judge from her human form. It was nonsense for her to pretend that he could find nothing that she could eat. She must have had some of the food concentrate after all, he decided, prying up the thermos lid of the inner container to release the long-sealed savor of the hot meat inside.

"Well, if you won't eat, you won't," he observed philosophically as he poured hot broth and diced beef into the dish-like lid of the thermos can and extracted the spoon from its hiding-place between the inner and outer receptacles. She turned a little to watch him as he pulled up a rickety chair and sat down to the food, and after a while the realization that her green gaze was fixed so unwinkingly upon him made the man nervous, and he said between bites of creamy canal-apple, "Why don't you try a little of this? It's good."

"The food—I eat is—better," her soft voice told him in its hesitant mur-mur, and again he felt rather than heard a faint undernote of unpleasantness in the words. A sudden suspicion struck him as he pondered on that last remark—some vague memory of horror-tales told about campfires in the past—and he swung round in the chair to look at her, a tiny, creeping fear unaccountably arising. There had been that in her words—in her unspoken words, that menaced . . .

She stood up beneath his gaze demurely, wide green eyes with their pulsing pupils meeting his without a falter. But her mouth was scarlet and her teeth were sharp . . .

"What food do you eat?" he demanded. And then, after a pause, very softly, "Blood?"

She stared at him for a moment, uncomprehending; then something like amusement curled her lips and she said scornfully, "You think me—vampire, eh? No—I am Shambleau!"

Unmistakably there were scorn and amusement in her voice at the suggestion, but as unmistakably she knew what he meant—accepted it as a logical suspicion—vampires! Fairy-tales—but fairy-tales this unhuman, outland creature was most familiar with. Smith was not a credulous man, nor a superstitious one, but he had seen too many strange things himself to doubt that the wildest legend might have a basis of fact. And there was something namelessly strange about her . . .

He puzzled over it for a while between deep bites of the canal-apple. And though he wanted to question her about a great many things, he did not, for he knew how futile it would be.

He said nothing more until the meat was finished and another canal-apple had followed the first, and he had cleared away the meal by the simple expedient of tossing the empty can out of the window.

Then he lay back in the chair and surveyed her from half-closed eyes, colorless in a face tanned like saddle-leather. And again he was conscious of the brown, soft curves of her, velvety—subtle arcs and planes of smooth flesh under the tatters of scarlet leather. Vampire she might be, unhuman she certainly was, but desirable beyond words as she sat submissive beneath his slow regard, her red-turbaned head bent, her clawed fingers lying in her lap. They sat very still for a while and the silence throbbed between them.

She was so like a woman—an Earth woman—sweet and submissive and demure, and softer than soft fur, if he could forget the three-fingered claws and the pulsing eyes—and that deeper strangeness beyond words . . . (Had he dreamed that red lock of hair that moved? Had it been *segir* that woke the wild revulsion he knew when he held her in his arms? Why had the mob so thirsted for her?) He sat and stared, and despite the mystery of her and the half-suspicions that thronged his mind—for she was so beautifully soft and curved under those revealing tatters—he slowly realized that his pulses were mounting, became aware of a kindling within . . . brown girl-creature with downcast eyes . . . and then the lids lifted and the green flatness of a cat's gaze met his, and last night's revulsion woke swiftly again, like a warning bell that clanged as their eyes met—animal, after all, too sleek and soft for humanity, and that inner strangeness . . .

Smith shrugged and sat up. His failings were legion, but the weakness of the flesh was not among the major ones. He motioned the girl to her pallet of blankets in the corner and turned to his own bed.

From deeps of sound sleep he awoke, much later. He awoke suddenly and completely, and with that inner excitement that presages something momentous. He awoke to brilliant moonlight, turning the room so bright that he could see the scarlet of the girl's rags as she sat up on her pallet. She was awake, she was sitting with her shoulder half-turned to him and her head bent, and some warning instinct crawled coldly up his spine as he watched what she was doing. And yet it was a very ordinary thing for a girl to do—any girl, anywhere. She was unbinding her turban . . .

He watched, not breathing, a presentiment of something horrible stirring in his brain, inexplicably . . . The red folds loosened and—he knew then that he had not dreamed—again a scarlet lock swung down against her cheek . . . a hair, was it? a lock of hair? . . . thick as a thick worm it fell, plumply, against that smooth cheek . . . more scarlet than blood and thick as a crawling worm . . . and like a worm it crawled.

Smith rose on an elbow, not realizing the motion, and fixed an unwinking stare, with a sort of sick, fascinated incredulity, on that—that lock of hair. He had not dreamed. Until now he had taken it for granted that it was the *segir* that had made it seem to move on that evening before. But now . . . it was lengthening, stretching, moving of itself. It must be hair, but it *crawled*; with a sickening life of its own it squirmed down against her cheek, caressingly, revoltingly, impossibly . . . Wet, it was, and round and thick and shining . . .

She unfastened the last fold and whipped the turban off. From what he saw then Smith would have turned his eyes away—and he had looked on dreadful things before, without flinching—but he could not stir. He could only lie there on his elbow staring at the mass of scarlet, squirming—worms, hairs, what?—that writhed over her head in a dreadful mockery of ringlets. And it was lengthening, falling, somehow growing before his eyes, down over her shoulders in a spilling cascade, a mass that even at the beginning could never have been hidden under the skull-tight turban she had worn. He was beyond wondering, but he realized that. And still it squirmed and lengthened and fell, and she shook it out in a horrible travesty of a woman shaking out her unbound hair—until the unspeakable tangle of it—twisting, writhing, obscenely scarlet—hung to her waist and beyond, and still lengthened, an endless mass of crawling horror that until now, somehow, impossibly, had been hidden under the tight-bound turban. It was like a nest of blind, restless red worms . . . it was—it was like naked entrails endowed with an unnatural aliveness, terrible beyond words.

Smith lay in the shadows, frozen without and within in a sick numbness that came of utter shock and revulsion.

She shook out the obscene, unspeakable tangle over her shoulders, and somehow he knew that she was going to turn in a moment and that he must meet her eyes. The thought of that meeting stopped his heart with dread, more awfully than anything else in this nightmare horror; for nightmare it must be, surely. But he knew without trying that he could not wrench his eyes away—the sickened fascination of that sight held him motionless, and somehow there was a certain beauty . . .

Her head was turning. The crawling awfulnesses rippled and squirmed at the motion, writhing thick and wet and shining over the soft brown shoulders about which they fell now in obscene cascades that all but hid her body. Her head was turning. Smith lay numb. And very slowly he saw the round of her cheek foreshorten and her profile come into view, all the scarlet horrors twisting ominously, and the profile shortened in turn and her full face came slowly round toward the bed—moonlight shining brilliantly as day on the pretty girl-face, demure and sweet, framed in tangled obscenity that crawled . . .

The green eyes met his. He felt a perceptible shock, and a shudder rippled down his paralyzed spine, leaving an icy numbness in its wake. He felt the gooseflesh rising. But that numbness and cold horror he scarcely realized, for the green eyes were locked with his in a long, long look that somehow presaged nameless things—not altogether unpleasant things—the voiceless voice of her mind assailing him with little murmurous promises . . .

For a moment he went down into a blind abyss of submission, and then somehow the very sight of that obscenity in eyes that did not then realize they saw it was dreadful enough to draw him out of the seductive darkness . . . the sight of her crawling and alive with unnamable horror.

She rose, and down about her in a cascade fell the squirming scarlet of—of what grew upon her head. It fell in a long, alive cloak to her bare feet on the floor, hiding her in a wave of dreadful, wet, writhing life. She put up her hands and like a swimmer she parted the waterfall of it, tossing the masses back over her shoulders to reveal her own brown body, sweetly curved. She smiled, exquisitely, and in startling waves back from her forehead and down about her in a hideous background writhed the snaky wetness of her living tresses. And Smith knew that he looked upon Medusa.

The knowledge of that—the realization of vast backgrounds reaching into misted history—shook him out of his frozen horror for a moment, and in that moment he met her eyes again, smiling, green as glass in the moonlight, half-hooded under drooping lids. Through the twisting scarlet she held out her arms. And there was something soul-shakingly desirable about her, so that all the blood surged to his head suddenly and he stumbled to his feet like a sleeper in a dream as she swayed toward him, infinitely graceful, infinitely sweet in her cloak of living horror.

And somehow there was beauty in it, the wet scarlet writhings with moonlight sliding and shining along the thick, worm-round tresses and losing itself in the masses only to glint again and move silvery along writhing tendrils—an awful, shuddering beauty more dreadful than any ugliness could be.

But all this, again, he but half realized, for the insidious murmur was coiling again through his brain, promising, caressing, alluring, sweeter than honey; and the green eyes that held his were clear and burning like the depths of a jewel, and behind the pulsing slits of darkness he was staring into a greater dark that held all things . . . He had known—dimly he had known when he first gazed into those flat animal shallows that behind them lay this—all beauty and terror, all horror and delight, in the infinite darkness upon which her eyes opened like windows, paned with emerald glass.

Her lips moved, and in a murmur that blended indistinguishably with the silence and the sway of her body and the dreadful sway of her—her hair—she whispered—very softly, very passionately, "I shall—speak to you now—in my own tongue—oh, beloved!"

And in her living cloak she swayed to him, the murmur swelling seductive and caressing in his innermost brain—promising, compelling, sweeter than sweet. His flesh crawled to the horror of her, but it was a perverted revulsion that clasped what it loathed. His arms slid round her under the sliding cloak, wet, wet and warm and hideously alive—and the sweet velvet body was clinging to his, her arms locked about his neck—and with a whisper and a rush the unspeakable horror closed about them both.

In nightmares until he died he remembered that moment when the living tresses of Shambleau first folded him in their embrace. A nauseous, smothering odor as the wetness shut around him—thick, pulsing worms clasping every inch of his body, sliding, writhing, their wetness and warmth striking through his garments as if he stood naked to their embrace.

All this in a graven instant—and after that a tangled flash of conflicting sensation before oblivion closed over him. For he remembered the dream—

and knew it for nightmare reality now, and the sliding, gently moving caresses of those wet, warm worms upon his flesh was an ecstasy above words—that deeper ecstasy that strikes beyond the body and beyond the mind and tickles the very roots of the soul with unnatural delight. So he stood, rigid as marble, as helplessly stony as any of Medusa's victims in ancient legends were, while the terrible pleasure of Shambleau thrilled and shuddered through every fiber of him; through every atom of his body and the intangible atoms of what men call the soul, through all that was Smith the dreadful pleasure ran. And it was truly dreadful. Dimly he knew it, even as his body answered to the root-deep ecstasy, a foul and dreadful wooing from which his very soul shuddered away—and yet in the innermost depths of that soul some grinning traitor shivered with delight. But deeply, behind all this, he knew horror and revulsion and despair beyond telling, while the intimate caresses crawled obscenely in the secret places of his soul—knew that the soul should not be handled—and shook with the perilous pleasure through it all.

And this conflict and knowledge, this mingling of rapture and revulsion all took place in the flashing of a moment while the scarlet worms coiled and crawled upon him, sending deep, obscene tremors of that infinite pleasure into every atom that made up Smith. And he could not stir in that slimy, ecstatic embrace—and a weakness was flooding that grew deeper after each succeeding wave of intense delight, and the traitor in his soul strengthened and drowned out the revulsion—and something within him ceased to struggle as he sank wholly into a blazing darkness that was oblivion to all else but that devouring rapture . . .

The young Venusian climbing the stairs to his friend's lodging-room pulled out his key absentmindedly, a pucker forming between his fine brows. He was slim, as all Venusians are, as fair and sleek as any of them, and as with most of his countrymen the look of cherubic innocence on his face was wholly deceptive. He had the face of a fallen angel without Lucifer's majesty to redeem it, for a black devil grinned in his eyes and there were faint lines of ruthlessness and dissipation about his mouth to tell of the long years behind him that had run the gamut of experiences and made his name, next to Smith's, the most hated and the most respected in the records of the Patrol.

He mounted the stairs now with a puzzled frown between his eyes. He had come into Lakkdarol on the noon liner—the *Maid* in her hold, very skillfully disguised with paint and otherwise—to find in lamentable disorder the affairs he had expected to be settled. And cautious inquiry elicited the information that Smith had not been seen for three days. That was not like his friend—he had never failed before, and the two stood to lose not only a large sum of money but also their personal safety by the inexplicable lapse on the part of Smith. Yarol could think of one solution only: fate had at last caught up with his friend. Nothing but physical disability could explain it.

Still puzzling, he fitted his key in the lock and swung the door open.

In that first moment, as the door opened, he sensed something very wrong . . . The room was darkened, and for a while he could see nothing, but at the first breath he scented a strange, unnamable odor, half-sickening, half-sweet. And deep stirrings of ancestral memory awoke within him—ancient, swamp-born memories from Venusian ancestors far away and long ago . . .

Yarol laid his hand on his gun, lightly, and opened the door wider. In the dimness all he could see at first was a curious mound in the far corner . . . Then his eyes grew accustomed to the dark, and he saw it more clearly, a mound that somehow heaved and stirred within itself . . . A mound of—he caught his breath sharply—a mound like a mass of entrails, living, moving, writhing with an unspeakable aliveness. Then a hot Venusian oath broke from his lips and he cleared the door-sill in a swift stride, slammed the door and set his back against it, gun ready in his hand, although his flesh crawled—for he *knew* . . .

"Smith!" he said softly, in a voice thick with horror. "Northwest!"

The moving mass stirred—shuddered—sank back into crawling quiescence again.

"Smith! Smith!" The Venusian's voice was gentle and insistent, and it quivered a little with terror.

An impatient ripple went over the whole mass of aliveness in the corner. It stirred again, reluctantly, and then tendril by writhing tendril it began to part itself and fall aside, and very slowly the brown of a spaceman's leather appeared beneath it, all slimed and shining.

"Smith! Northwest!" Yarol's persistent whisper came again, urgently, and with a dream-like slowness the leather garments moved . . . A man sat up in the midst of the writhing worms, a man who once, long ago, might have been Northwest Smith. From head to foot he was slimy from the embrace of the crawling horror about him. His face was that of some creature beyond humanity—dead-alive, fixed in a gray stare, and the look of terrible ecstasy that overspread it seemed to come from somewhere far within, a faint reflection from immeasurable distances beyond the flesh. And as there is mystery and magic in the moonlight, which is after all but a reflection of the everyday sun, so in that gray face turned to the door was a terror unnamable and sweet, a reflection of ecstasy beyond the understanding of any who have known only earthly ecstasy themselves. And as he sat there turning a blank, eyeless face to Yarol the red worms writhed ceaselessly about him, very gently, with a soft, caressive motion that never slacked.

"Smith . . . come here! Smith . . . get up . . . Smith, Smith!" Yarol's whisper hissed in the silence, commanding, urgent—but he made no move to leave the door.

And with a dreadful slowness, like a dead man rising, Smith stood up in the nest of slimy scarlet. He swayed drunkenly on his feet, and two or three crimson tendrils came writhing up his legs to the knees and wound themselves there, supportingly, moving with a ceaseless caress that seemed to give him some hidden strength, for he said then, without inflection, "Go away. Go away. Leave me alone."

And the dead, ecstatic face never changed.

"Smith!" Yarol's voice was desperate. "Smith, listen! Smith, can't you hear me?"

"Go away," the monotonous voice said. "Go away. Go away. Go—"

"Not unless you come too. Can't you hear? Smith! Smith! I'll—"

He hushed in mid-phrase, and once more the ancestral prickle of race-memory shivered down his back, for the scarlet mass was moving again, violently, rising . . .

———

Yarol pressed back against the door and gripped his gun, and the name of a god he had forgotten years ago rose to his lips unbidden. For he knew what was coming next, and the knowledge was more dreadful than any ignorance could have been.

The red, writhing mass rose higher, and the tendrils parted and a human face looked out—no, half-human, with green cat-eyes that shone in that dimness like lighted jewels, compellingly . . .

Yarol breathed, "Shar!" again, and flung up an arm across his face, and the tingle of meeting that green gaze for even an instant went thrilling through him perilously.

"Smith!" he called in despair. "Smith, can't you hear me?"

"Go away," said that voice that was not Smith's. "Go away."

And somehow, although he dared not look, Yarol knew that the—the other—had parted those worm-thick tresses and stood there in all the human sweetness of the brown, curved woman's body, cloaked in living horror. And he felt the eyes upon him, and something was crying insistently in his brain to lower that shielding arm . . . He was lost—he knew it, and the knowledge gave him that courage which comes from despair. The voice in his brain was growing, swelling, deafening him with a roaring command that all but swept him before it—a command to lower that arm—to meet the eyes that opened upon darkness—to submit—and a promise, murmurous and sweet and evil beyond words, of pleasure to come . . .

But somehow he kept his head—somehow, dizzily, he was gripping his gun in his upflung hand—somehow, incredibly, crossing the narrow room with averted face, groping for Smith's shoulder. There was a moment of blind fumbling in emptiness, and then he found it, and gripped the leather that was slimy and dreadful and wet—and simultaneously he felt something loop gently about his ankle and a shock of repulsive pleasure went through him, and then another coil, and another, wound about his feet . . .

Yarol set his teeth and gripped the shoulder hard, and his hand shuddered of itself, for the feel of that leather was slimy as the worms about his ankles, and a faint tingle of obscene delight went through him from the contact.

That caressive pressure on his legs was all he could feel, and the voice in his brain drowned out all other sounds, and his body obeyed him reluctantly—but somehow he gave one heave of tremendous effort and swung Smith, stumbling, out of that nest of horror. The twining tendrils ripped loose with a little sucking sound, and the whole mass quivered and reached after, and then Yarol forgot his friend utterly and turned his whole being to the hopeless task of freeing himself. For only a part of him was fighting, now—only a part of him struggled against the twining obscenities, and in his innermost brain the sweet, seductive murmur sounded, and his body clamored to surrender . . .

"*Shar! Shar y'danis . . . Shar mor'la-rol—*" prayed Yarol, gasping and half-unconscious that he spoke, boy's prayers that he had forgotten years ago, and with his back half-turned to the central mass he kicked desperately with his heavy boots at the red, writhing worms about him. They gave back before him, quivering and curling themselves out of reach, and though he knew that more were reaching for his throat from behind, at least he could go on struggling until he was forced to meet those eyes . . .

He stamped and kicked and stamped again, and for one instant he was free of the slimy grip as the bruised worms curled back from his heavy feet, and he lurched away dizzily, sick with revulsion and despair as he fought off the coils, and then he lifted his eyes and saw the cracked mirror on the wall. Dimly in its reflection he could see the writhing scarlet horror behind him, cat-face peering out with its demure girl-smile, dreadfully human, and all the red tendrils reaching after him. And remembrance of something he had read long ago swept incongruously over him, and the gasp of relief and hope that he gave shook for a moment the grip of the command in his brain.

Without pausing for a breath he swung the gun over his shoulder, the reflected barrel in line with the reflected horror in the mirror, and flicked the catch.

In the mirror he saw its blue flame leap in a dazzling spate across the dimness, full into the midst of that squirming, reaching mass behind him. There was a hiss and a blaze and a high, thin scream of inhuman malice and despair—the flame cut a wide arc and went out as the gun fell from his hand, and Yarol pitched forward to the floor.

———

Northwest Smith opened his eyes to Martian sunlight streaming thinly through the dingy window. Something wet and cold was slapping his face, and the familiar fiery sting of *segir*-whisky burnt his throat.

"Smith!" Yarol's voice was saying from far away. "N.W.! Wake up, damn you! Wake up!"

"I'm—awake," Smith managed to articulate thickly. "Wha's matter?"

Then a cup-rim was thrust against his teeth and Yarol said irritably, "Drink it, you fool!"

Smith swallowed obediently and more of the fire-hot *segir* flowed down his grateful throat. It spread a warmth through his body that awakened him from the numbness that had gripped him until now, and helped a little toward driving out the all-devouring weakness he was becoming aware of, slowly. He lay still for a few minutes while the warmth of the whisky went through him, and memory sluggishly began to permeate his brain with the spread of the *segir*. Nightmare memories . . . sweet and terrible . . . memories of—

"God!" gasped Smith suddenly, and tried to sit up. Weakness smote him like a blow, and for an instant the room wheeled as he fell back against something firm and warm—Yarol's shoulder. The Venusian's arm supported him while the room steadied, and after a while he twisted a little and stared into the other's black gaze.

Yarol was holding him with one arm and finishing the mug of *segir* himself, and the black eyes met his over the rim and crinkled into sudden laughter, half-hysterical after that terror that was passed.

"By *Pharol*!" gasped Yarol, choking into his mug. "By *Pharol*, N.W.! I'm never gonna let you forget this! Next time you have to drag me out of a mess I'll say—"

"Let it go," said Smith. "What's been going on? How—"

"Shambleau." Yarol's laughter died. "Shambleau! What were you doing with a thing like that?"

"What was it?" Smith asked soberly.

"Mean to say you didn't know? But where'd you find it? How—"

"Suppose you tell me first what you know," said Smith firmly. "And another swig of that *segir*, too, please. I need it."

"Can you hold the mug now? Feel better?"

"Yeah—some. I can hold it—thanks. Now go on."

"Well—I don't know just where to start. They call them Shambleau—"

"Good God, is there more than one?"

"It's a—a sort of race, I think, one of the very oldest. Where they come from nobody knows. The name sounds a little French, doesn't it? But it goes back beyond the start of history. There have always been Shambleau."

"I never heard of 'em."

"Not many people have. And those who know don't care to talk about it much."

"Well, half this town knows. I hadn't any idea what they were talking about, then. And I still don't understand, but—"

"Yes, it happens like this, sometimes. They'll appear, and the news will spread and the town will get together and hunt them down, and after that— well, the story doesn't get around very far. It's too—too unbelievable."

"But—my God, Yarol!—what was it? Where'd it come from? How—"

"Nobody knows just where they come from. Another planet—maybe some undiscovered one. Some say Venus—I know there are some rather awful legends of them handed down in our family—that's how I've heard about it. And the minute I opened that door, awhile back—I—I think I knew that smell . . ."

"But—what *are* they?"

"God knows. Not human, though they have the human form. Or that may be only an illusion . . . or maybe I'm crazy. I don't know. They're a species of the vampire—or maybe the vampire is a species of—of them. Their normal form must be that—that mass, and in that form they draw nourishment from the—I suppose the life-forces of men. And they take some form—usually a woman form, I think, and key you up to the highest pitch of emotion before they—begin. That's to work the life-force up to intensity so it'll be easier . . . And they give, always, that horrible, foul pleasure as they—feed. There are some men who, if they survive the first experience, take to it like a drug— can't give it up—keep the thing with them all their lives—which isn't long— feeding it for that ghastly satisfaction. Worse than smoking *ming* or—or 'praying to *Pharol*.'"

"Yes," said Smith, "I'm beginning to understand why that crowd was so surprised and—and disgusted when I said—well, never mind. Go on."

"Did you get to talk to—to it?" asked Yarol.

"I tried to. It couldn't speak very well. I asked it where it came from and it said—'from far away and long ago'—something like that."

"I wonder. Possibly some unknown planet—but I think not. You know there are so many wild stories with some basis of fact to start from that I've sometimes wondered—mightn't there be a lot more or even worse and wilder superstitions we've never even heard of? Things like this, blasphemous and foul, that those who know have to keep still about? Awful, fantastic things running around loose that we never hear rumors of at all!

"These things—they've been in existence for countless ages. No one knows when or where they first appeared. Those who've seen them, as we saw this one, don't talk about it. It's just one of those vague, misty rumors you find half hinted at in old books sometimes . . . I believe they are an older race than man, spawned from ancient seed in times before ours, perhaps on planets that have gone to dust, and so horrible to man that when they are discovered the discoverers keep still about it—forget them again as quickly as they can.

"And they go back to time immemorial. I suppose you recognized the legend of Medusa? There isn't any question that the ancient Greeks knew of them. Does it mean that there have been civilizations before yours that set out from Earth and explored other planets? Or did one of the Shambleau somehow make its way into Greece three thousand years ago? If you think about it long enough you'll go off your head! I wonder how many other legends are based on things like this—things we don't suspect, things we'll never know.

"The Gorgon Medusa, a beautiful woman with—with snakes for hair, and a gaze that turned men to stone, and Perseus finally killed her—I remembered this just by accident, N.W., and it saved your life and mine—Perseus killed her by using a mirror as he fought to reflect what he dared not look at directly. I wonder what the old Greek who first started that legend would have thought if he'd known that three thousand years later his story would save the lives of two men on another planet. I wonder what that Greek's own story was, and how he met the thing, and what happened . . .

"Well, there's a lot we'll never know. Wouldn't the records of that race of—of things, whatever they are, be worth reading! Records of other planets and other ages and all the beginnings of mankind! But I don't suppose they've kept any records. I don't suppose they've even any place to keep them—from what little I know, or anyone knows about it, they're like the Wandering Jew, just bobbing up here and there at long intervals, and where they stay in the meantime I'd give my eyes to know! But I don't believe that terribly hypnotic power they have indicates any superhuman intelligence. It's their means of getting food—just like a frog's long tongue or a carnivorous flower's odor. Those are physical because the frog and the flower eat physical food. The Shambleau uses a—a mental reach to get mental food. I don't quite know how to put it. And just as a beast that eats the bodies of other animals acquires with each meal greater power over the bodies of the rest, so the Shambleau, stoking itself up with the life-forces of men, increases its power over the minds and the souls of other men. But I'm talking about things I can't define—things I'm not sure exist.

"I only know that when I felt—when those tentacles closed around my legs—I didn't want to pull loose, I felt sensations that—that—oh, I'm fouled and filthy to the very deepest part of me by that—pleasure—and yet—"

"I know," said Smith slowly. The effect of the *segir* was beginning to wear off, and weakness was washing back over him in waves, and when he spoke he was half meditating in a low voice, scarcely realizing that Yarol listened. "I know it—much better than you do—and there's something so indescribably awful that the thing emanates, something so utterly at odds with everything human—there aren't any words to say it. For a while I was a part of it, literally, sharing its thoughts and memories and emotions and hungers, and—well, it's over now and I don't remember very clearly, but the only part left free was that part of me that was all but insane from the—the obscenity of the thing. And yet it was a pleasure so sweet—I think there must be some nucleus of utter evil in me—in everyone—that needs only the proper stimulus to get complete control, because even while I was sick all through from the touch of those—things—there was something in me that was—was simply gibbering with delight . . . Because of that I saw things—and knew things—horrible, wild, things I can't quite remember—visited unbelievable places, looked backward through the memory of that—creature—I was one with, and saw—God, I wish I could remember!"

"You ought to thank your God you can't," said Yarol soberly.

———

His voice roused Smith from the half-trance he had fallen into, and he rose on his elbow, swaying a little from weakness. The room was wavering before him, and he closed his eyes, not to see it, but he asked, "You say they—they don't turn up again? No way of finding—another?"

Yarol did not answer for a moment. He laid his hands on the other man's shoulders and pressed him back, and then sat staring down into the dark, ravaged face with a new, strange, undefinable look upon it that he had never seen there before—whose meaning he knew, too well.

"Smith," he said finally, and his black eyes for once were steady and serious, and the little grinning devil had vanished from behind them, "Smith, I've never asked your word on anything before, but I've—I've earned the right to do it now, and I'm asking you to promise me one thing."

Smith's colorless eyes met the black gaze unsteadily. Irresolution was in them, and a little fear of what that promise might be. And for just a moment Yarol was looking, not into his friend's familiar eyes, but into a wide gray blankness that held all horror and delight—a pale sea with unspeakable pleasures sunk beneath it. Then the wide stare focused again and Smith's eyes met his squarely and Smith's voice said, "Go ahead. I'll promise."

"That if you ever should meet a Shambleau again—ever, anywhere—you'll draw your gun and burn it to hell the instant you realize what it is. Will you promise me that?"

There was a long silence. Yarol's somber black eyes bored relentlessly into the colorless ones of Smith, not wavering. And the veins stood out on Smith's tanned forehead. He never broke his word—he had given it perhaps half a dozen times in his life, but once he had given it, he was incapable of breaking it. And once more the gray seas flooded in a dim tide of memories, sweet and horrible beyond dreams. Once more Yarol was staring into blankness that hid nameless things. The room was very still.

The gray tide ebbed. Smith's eyes, pale and resolute as steel, met Yarol's levelly.

"I'll—try," he said. And his voice wavered.

DOROTHY GERTRUDE QUICK (1896–1962) was the pen name of Dorothy Gertrude Quick Mayer, a prolific writer of horror, detective fiction, poetry, and nonfiction. Born in Brooklyn to a wealthy family, Quick met Samuel Clemens (a.k.a. Mark Twain) in 1907 while on board the SS *Minnetonka*, and the two became close friends. Later, Quick gave credit to Twain for encouraging her to write, and she lectured extensively on their friendship. Her 1961 memoir of the great American author, *Mark Twain and Me*, was the basis for a 1991 Disney television movie of the same name. Quick married John Adams Mayer in 1925 (a society event noteworthy enough to merit mention in *Time* magazine's "Milestones" column) but published under her maiden name throughout her life. She made her first genre fiction sale to Farnsworth Wright, the editor of *Oriental Stories*, in 1932 and went on to contribute stories and poems to Wright's more successful editing venture, *Weird Tales*, for more than twenty years.

Most of Quick's early genre work was standard horror fare, but in the mid-1930s she began experimenting with more science fictional offerings. In 1938 the *New York Post* announced the publication of her first novel, a planetary romance called *Strange Awakenings*, which, as the unnamed author of the article enthusiastically notes, "curiously enough is not biographical" but instead relates the "fantastic tale of a young woman who wakes up to find herself on the planet Venus, something in the manner of some of Jules Verne's heroes" ("Mrs. John Adams Mayer" 7). Other notable SF works from Quick include the Patchwork Quilt sequence, a series of short stories written for *Unknown* between 1939 and 1945 "whose potential seems obvious, [but] may have suffered" from that magazine's demise, and her first SF sale, "Strange Orchids" (Clute).

"Strange Orchids" appeared in the March 1937 issue of *Weird Tales* accompanied by a cover that celebrated genre artist Margaret Brundage painted for the story (see chapter 5, "Artists," of this anthology for more details). It is a Gothic tale characteristic of the "weird-scientific" style that Wright preferred for his magazine. Like other stories of this type—including Clare Winger Harris's "The Evolutionary Monstrosity," featured elsewhere in this anthology—"Strange Orchids" explores the dark side of Enlightenment rationality, especially as it is figured in the character of the physically and socially isolated mad scientist. However, while other authors associated with this tradition (including Mary Shelley, H. G. Wells, and Harris) endowed their mad scientists with extraordinary and almost admirable ambition to create new races or conquer evolution, Quick's protagonist is more decadent than grand in his scheme to create the perfect hothouse flower. As such, her story seems to comment on the instrumental ends to which much scientific theory is applied and the horror that ensues when human lives are sacrificed in the process.

Quick's story also pays homage to two other traditions of popular women's writing that flourished in the nineteenth and early twentieth centuries: the female Gothic and domestic fiction. In an era when most SF stories were narrated from the perspective of a male character, Quick draws on the rich history of the female Gothic to cast her female narrator as both victim and heroine of the story. She also invokes the conventions of domestic fiction by pitting her vain and condescending mad scientist—who, incidentally, claims to love Quick's narrator but then treats her like a slow child—against the levelheaded, confident government agent who knows his own limits and actively enlists the narrator to help him stop their evil nemesis. In doing so, Quick makes clear the type of new man who is appropriate to accompany the New Woman of the twentieth century on even her most dangerous adventures.

"Strange Orchids"
Weird Tales, March 1937

If I had not gone to Muriel's party, I wouldn't have met Angus O'Malley and I would have been spared the horror and despair of the tragic events in which the strange orchids played so terrible a part.

Often as I look at my white hair—the legacy that those happenings left me—I wonder if my life would have been happier had I followed my first impulse and remained away from Muriel's. But almost instantly the question is answered for me and I know that despite the white hair—despite the horror that put it there—I am glad I went to Muriel's.

For even if I did meet Angus O'Malley that night, I also met Rex Stanton, and if the one brought me terror beyond comprehension the other brought me such joy that it overbalanced everything else. And the very fact that neither Rex nor I can quite forget the things that happened has only served to bring us closer together.

The reason I hesitated about going to Muriel's was that one never knew whom one would meet at her studio. I'm not a snob, but I do dislike being thrown into close contact with a gangster or the leading female impersonator who talks with a lisp and rouges his cheeks. I had on previous occasions been introduced to both at Muriel's. On the other hand, there were rumors that Splondowski would be at the party with his violin, and it was because of Splondowski that I finally went. I couldn't resist hearing him play even though I had to sit next to Public Enemy Number 1 to do it.

It was while I sat listening to the magic notes of Splondowski that I saw Angus O'Malley for the first time.

He was standing near the door when I happened to look up. His eyes caught mine and held them with strange magnetism. I felt as though they were stripping my body bare of the Paris gown I was so proud of—as though I must snatch something to cover myself with, even though I knew I was perfectly clothed. The impulse was almost overpowering, but much as I wanted to give in to it, I couldn't. His eyes, deep black like a mysterious unfathomed pool, would not have let me. I sat staring into them as though I had been a bird fascinated by a snake.

Then an even worse thing happened. I felt as though he had exhausted the possibilities of my body, that now that he knew every line I possessed he must probe still further. With a kind of mental anguish I felt him probing my soul, until eventually he knew that, too. Then he released my eyes and I was completely myself again.

At the same time I realized that Splondowski had played at the most only four bars of music, although it seemed ages ago that I had first looked up at the handsome stranger. I told myself I was a fool with an overactive imagination. The music got me all stirred up and I began feeling things, I thought, and out of the corner of my eye stole another glance at the man who had produced such an extraordinary effect upon me. He was very tall and very slim, with thick black hair that waved back from a rather low forehead. He wore it longer than most men, and there was a suspicion of curl at the end that gave him a Byronic look. His eyes were, as I have said, black under heavy brows and lids. His nose was fine, chiseled Greek, as were the lines of his face. His mouth was well cut, but easily the most sensuous I have ever seen. Was it this that had made me imagine things? If so, I'd better consult a psychiatrist immediately. Nice, well brought up girls of twenty shouldn't have such thoughts of their own volition. I'd never had them before, but I'd never seen anyone like Angus O'Malley, either. I noticed that his skin was very white, extraordinarily fine in texture for a man, and his hands were slender—the hands of an artist or a dreamer. I wondered who he was, and then remembered how I had felt looking into his eyes and decided I didn't want to know.

———

A few minutes later Splondowski had finished playing and Muriel came up to me, the man I didn't want to know beside her.

"Mr. O'Malley wants to be presented," Muriel said as if Mr. O'Malley were the King of England conferring a favor.

Muriel made the necessary remarks, "Louise Howard, Angus O'Malley," and rushed away.

Angus O'Malley extended his hand. Reluctantly I put mine into it. He bent low over my fingers and touched them with his lips. It was as though a flame had brushed across my hand.

"You are lovely," he said, and his voice was deep and beautiful. "There is nothing unusual about you, but nevertheless you are lovely."

It was an odd compliment, especially as he said it rather regretfully.

I drew my hand away.

"Do you like unusual things?" I asked. I somehow wanted to be impersonal with this man.

"It is only the unusual that gives zest to life. See." He touched his coat lapel, and for the first time I noticed that it contained, instead of a carnation that from a distance I had credited him with wearing, a single lavender orchid. It was an exquisite flower, a very pale shade with a purple heart. Even as I admired it I thought what an odd thing it was for a man to wear in his buttonhole.

O'Malley continued speaking almost as though he guessed my thought. "I wear orchids because they are not commonplace. I wear unusual ones when I can; otherwise I content myself with the better-known varieties. Just now I have nothing worth exhibiting, but someday I shall show you my orchids."

He took it for granted that I would want to see them, which I emphatically did not.

"That flower seems exquisite to me," I said.

"It gives me nothing," he shrugged. "Still, it will do until another blooms."

There was the anticipation of a true collector in his eyes for a few seconds; then it died away as they concentrated on me.

"But we waste time talking of something that does not interest you. Besides, I want to tell you that I am attracted to you. I have looked upon you and searched your inmost thoughts, and you please me."

Again the king-like touch—Louis XIV condescending to a peasant; more than that, for it came to me that he was expressing in actual fact the feelings I had had while Splondowski played. A panic swept over me. I wanted to run away.

He leaned toward me. "Look at me," he commanded.

I was afraid. I didn't dare meet his gaze again. I looked about the room, hoping to catch the eye of someone I knew. Everyone I could have signaled was looking the other way. Then, out of a mass of unfamiliar faces, one looked into mine—a kindly, straightforward face, bronzed skin, steady blue eyes and brown hair, and a humorous mouth that was both firm and tender. His tall, well-knit, muscular body stood out above the others by sheer force of personality. I smiled in his direction, hoping my need for his help would somehow or other miraculously be conveyed to him.

"Look at me." O'Malley's voice was in my ear and it seemed to be weaving a spell around me. I knew in another minute or two I should meet his eyes, and I was afraid—afraid of what might happen when I did.

Just then the miracle happened—a new voice broke the tension between us—a gay, cheerful voice that was like a mountain stream running over stones, crystal clear. "I'm *so* glad to see you again."

I looked up into the blue eyes of the young man to whom I had sent the S.O.S. and was able to forget the deep black ones I was so anxious to evade.

"I'm glad to see you." I gave him both my hands.

I think it was at that instant I fell in love with Rex Stanton, and he swears that when he took my hands and felt them tremble in his he knew I was the girl he wanted to marry. I didn't know then, but my subconscious self must have, for it was an electric moment.

Angus O'Malley broke into it. "Will you not present me to your friend?" There was a depth and malice in his voice that made me realize I didn't know the name of my rescuer.

He saved me again. "Surely you remember me, Rex Stanton, Mr. O'Malley. I've had the pleasure of meeting you before."

O'Malley's full lips curved oddly. "My memory is, for once, at fault."

"Well, not being an unusual type, I'm afraid I'm easy to forget." Rex Stanton smiled charmingly.

That word again—*unusual*. It seemed odd that both men should emphasize the word.

O'Malley ignored Rex and turned to me. Taking my hand, he bent over it. Once more I felt the touch of his hot lips and experienced the same sensations. As he straightened up he whispered in my ear, "A captive bird may beat its wings against the net, but it is of no avail." Then louder, "I shall give myself the pleasure of calling upon you tomorrow." And without a word to Rex he was gone.

I began to shake with convulsive tremors that I couldn't control.

Rex Stanton put his arm around me. "He's a strange person, but he's not quite as bad as all that. You did want me to come over, didn't you?"

I leaned against him, and nodded. Almost before I knew it he had piloted me out through the crowd into a quiet corner of Muriel's library, which fortunately was entirely deserted. Then almost without my own volition I was telling him all about everything, even my imagined feelings while Splondowski played.

By the time I'd reached the end of my recital I was calm again.

Rex looked grave. "The man seems slightly goofy to me," he commented.

"Of course I'd never met him before, but luckily I had inquired who he was. He rather stands out in an assemblage—with his orchid boutonnière! Oh well, I guess he's safe enough—probably just a little touched. Still I'd like to be there tomorrow when he calls."

"Will you?" I cried. Already I was sure that if Rex was on hand nothing could go wrong.

"If you want, I'll come early and stay late. That's a bargain and my good luck."

We shook hands. Then he said, "You're not one of Muriel's types?"

"We went to school together. I came to hear Splondowski. Why did you come? You're not her type, either."

He grinned. "Touché. I knew her first husband. I came because, frankly, I knew she accumulated odd people, and I'm investigating the disappearance of Lucia Trent."

"I knew Lucia." I felt suddenly saddened as I remembered her bright beauty. Lucia had golden hair of the color that is formed in the water lily's heart, brown eyes with tiny yellow flecks in them, a tawny skin the shade of honey and a body full of slim curves that were lovely to behold. She was only seventeen when she walked out of her house to go and see her best friend. Her mother had waved good-bye to her laughingly and sent messages, but they had never been delivered, for Lucia had vanished as completely and utterly as though she had never existed. No one ever saw her again. It was a terrific mystery, and it had brought sorrow to us all.

"You're just the person for me, then." Rex brought me back into the present. "Tell me, was there anything"—he started to say "unusual," then in the light of my recent confession changed it to—"*different* about her?"

"Do you think it could have been white slavers?" I advanced the most popular theory.

"I wonder. Was there any particular man?"

"At least fifteen boys. Lucia was popular. But none of them knew anything. They all adored her—everyone did—but she hadn't any secret passion, if that's what you mean." I was almost caustic. It seemed so silly to associate Lucia with intrigue.

"I only asked. One has to cover every contingency, you know."

"How did you—" I began.

He cut me short. "I was coming to that. Your friend Lucia isn't the first girl to disappear completely with no trace."

"You mean Dorothy Arnold?" Everyone had been comparing the two cases.

"That's ancient history. I mean in the last year. Outstanding disappearances. In this city, of course, there are always a number of missing girls, but there is generally some kind of a lead. Too, the girls are usually from the lower classes, especially girls without anyone to be interested in what becomes of them. These disappearances I've been investigating haven't been like that. They've all been girls like Lucia, young, beautiful and intelligent and from good families, which doesn't interest white slavers ordinarily. After about eight such disappearances the coincidence struck the police. Eventually I was called in from Washington."

A G-man! No wonder I had felt confidence in him.

He went on. "There have been sixteen cases—no, your friend was the seventeenth. Seventeen girls snatched into thin air—gone without a trace. They've all left their homes for some normal reason and not one of them has been seen again. God help me, I haven't been able to find a single clue. I've been clutching at straws. That's why I came here tonight—a futile gamble, but it brought me something very wonderful."

"What?" I asked point-blank because I had to know.

When he answered, "You," I was content.

The next afternoon Angus O'Malley came to find Rex and me chatting cozily over the tea table. He remained to join in the talk. It was all very commonplace. I began to think I had dreamed the night before, until once he caught my eyes and held them and it seemed to me that a message came from his brain to mine. "Flutter your wings if you like, but remember only I can open the net." Then there came into my vision the lavender edges of the orchid he was wearing. A slight movement of the petals drew my eyes away from him.

He hadn't touched my hand in greeting, and he did not do so in farewell, but just as he took his departure he said, "I shall come again. In a few days my new orchid will bloom, and I want you to see it." There was a touch of malice as he bowed slightly toward Rex—"Perhaps the good Mr. Stanton will be here too."

"I *would* like to see the orchid." Rex ignored the malice.

"Unfortunately I can set no date. My flowers are capricious, but when it blooms I will come."

Another bow, this time in my direction, and he was gone. From the other side of the front door we heard something that from anyone else would have been a chuckle but from Angus O'Malley seemed sinister.

Rex said, "We're all washed up about that man. Except for the orchid and his Oscar Wildish appearance he's all right."

"Except for the orchid." If Rex had only known—if I had only guessed—but we didn't. I said, "I hope you're here when he comes." And when Rex began to tell me how much he wanted to be, I dismissed Angus O'Malley from my mind.

———

Three days later I was sitting out under the trees with a book Rex had sent me when suddenly a shadow fell upon it. I looked up and there was Angus O'Malley smiling down upon me. In his buttonhole was the most exquisite orchid I had ever seen. Its petals were the yellow color of honey and its heart was deep brown with little golden flecks.

"Oh!" I exclaimed, forgetting my fear of him in my admiration of the orchid. "I have never seen an orchid like that."

He knew what I meant. "You never will again—unless I am so fortunate as to find—the same colors—once more. See," he took it from his coat and held it out to me, "I have brought it for you. Will you wear it?"

I touched the flower, and one of the petals curled around my finger as though it had been a living thing.

"May I pin it on?" he asked, and before I could either assent or refuse he was fastening the great golden flower on my dress near my shoulder, where the petals brushed against my cheek. "Speak to her, my flower," he whispered; "tell her the things I have told you to tell her. Sing to her of my love in the daytime and at night tell her of the joys to be found in my arms."

I shrank back. He caught my hands in his. "You are not beautiful, your hair has no vivid color, but you can be a companion with whom to share my secrets, someone to know and understand my work. I would see that you understand. Surely I, who thought never to know love, have been pierced by the arrow of the blind god. Give yourself to me."

All this time he had been pulling me closer until now I was in his arms and his full lips were near mine.

"No, no!" I tried to push him away.

"Then will you marry me?" he laughed wildly. "Yes, I, Angus O'Malley, chosen of the gods, I who can make and unmake souls, ask you to be my wife."

I shook my head. I could not command my voice.

His lips crushed mine. At first I thought I would die of sheer repugnance, and then my will seemed caught up into his—the repugnance went away and in its stead came response to his kisses.

Suddenly the orchid petals brushed against my cheek and a small stifled voice whispered in my ear. "Send him away. Send him away. Danger! Danger!" The small voice went on and on, growing stronger as it seeped into my consciousness. "Send him away. Danger! Danger!"

The voice seemed vaguely familiar, yet I could not place it, but it brought me back to my senses. With enormous effort I twisted from his arms and wiped his kisses from my lips with the back of my hand.

"Go—please go. I never want to see you again!" I cried.

His eyes narrowed. "Yet you responded to my kisses."

The still small voice was silent now. I must have imagined it. I told myself sternly that flowers couldn't speak. But I remembered how I had returned his kiss, and a wave of shame swept over me until my cheeks burned.

"You are afraid. The little white dove trembling before the eagle. But the eagle can be kind—to his mate. Do not tempt me to be otherwise—for if you do—" His voice died away without putting his thoughts into words, yet I understood that he was threatening me.

And then like the sunlight breaking through thunderclouds came Rex Stanton's voice: "Louise. Louise. Where are you?"

"Down by the willows," I called.

"The guardian angel," O'Malley sneered, then bent down close to me. "I am going away, but I will come back, and when I do, you must make up your mind which it is to be, love or hate—and I warn you I can hate even better than I can love."

The small voice whispered again, "Danger! Danger!" and the orchid petals touched my cheek, gently, pityingly.

"My flower will tell you of my love," O'Malley said, and then he strode off across the lawn past Rex, who had just come into sight.

"Wow!" Rex exclaimed; "not even a greeting did I get. I felt as though a storm cloud sailed by. I take it that all is not serene on the horizon."

Once more I unburdened my mind of everything that happened.

———

Rex made no comment until I had finished; then he said, "You can't marry O'Malley, because you're going to marry me."

He held out his hand. I put mine into it, and that was that. We didn't speak of love; it wasn't necessary. He didn't kiss me then. But the look in his eyes was a caress and we were both happy with the deep contentment of perfect love. It was a wonderful moment between us.

Rex broke the spell. "Let me see the orchid. It's different in color from any I've ever seen."

With unsteady fingers I unfastened it and put it in his hands, and as I did so it seemed to me I heard a sigh.

Rex heard it too. He looked at me sharply. "'There are more things in heaven and earth than are dreamt of in your philosophy,'" he quoted. "Perhaps we're up against magic."

I laughed, but my laugh died away as quickly as a sudden breeze on a still day, for the flower in Rex's hand bent over as though it were nodding—and there was no wind!

I shivered. "Rex, I'm afraid."

"If the flower has life, a strange life of some kind we don't understand, at least it is your friend," Rex said calmly. "It warns you of danger. It confirms my suspicion that we're up against something incomprehensible."

"He said he would make me understand—perhaps that's what he meant—"

Then suddenly something Rex had said beat itself into my brain: "Your friend." I looked down at the flower—saw the lovely golden honey color, the deep brown heart with yellow flecks—

"Lucia! Lucia Trent!" I exclaimed. "The orchid—it's like Lucia—the same coloring!"

I stopped aghast at my own thought—but once more the flower bowed as though in assent and swayed toward me as though it wanted to touch.

"Good heaven!" Rex stared at the flower. "You're sure?"

"She had those same golden flecks in her brown eyes."

"There might be a connection, but what? What?"

"I saw a movie in which a scientist reduced people to dolls. Then he hypnotized them into doing whatever he wanted—sent them forth to slay." Lionel Barrymore's acting was still vivid before me.

"My God! Perhaps—" Rex stared at the orchid.

The flower swayed back and forth as though it were trying to say no.

"The orchid—whatever—whoever—it is, is my friend," I said solemnly, and the flower nodded. "It's uncanny—it knows what we say."

"It's against all the laws of nature," Rex protested.

"It may only be a law we don't understand. O'Malley said the orchid would tell me of his love. He may have given it power to say what he wanted it to."

"And because Lucia was your friend the flower spoke of its own accord."

The orchid bent over again. We knew it meant yes, and we were silent before a marvel we couldn't comprehend.

Finally Rex spoke. "What do you know about O'Malley?"

"Nothing that I haven't told you."

"Muriel said he bought a magnificent old place at Riverdale-on-Hudson about two years ago and installed wonderful orchid houses. He drives a Rolls Royce and has a yacht. He sometimes takes people on cruises, often has parties at his estate. Could you find out if Lucia knew him?"

"I could ask her mother."

"Do—and I'll try to get more of a line on him. Find out if there's any connection with any of the other girls. Of course it's utterly fantastic, and I can't for the life of me think Lucia's soul is imprisoned in that flower. Still, it's the only lead I've had, and I told you I was clutching at straws."

Rex gave back the orchid to me and once more I fastened it to my shoulder.

"He said he could make and unmake souls." I hesitated, then went on: "Perhaps tonight—"

"I'm afraid for you. May I come and stay outside your door?"

I shook my head. "If Lucia is in any way connected with the orchid, I'm not afraid. Besides, O'Malley gave me until he came back to decide. I'm not afraid of *him—now*!"

Rex took my face in his two hands and kissed me gently. My arms stole around his neck. This time there were no warning whispers.

———

Rex came early the next morning to hear what had happened. I told him that I had slept remarkably well with the orchid in a vase on the night table beside my bed, that toward morning I had had a confused dream in which Lucia with tears streaming from her eyes stood in front of a curious iron-studded door and shook her head, warning me that I must not go inside.

Neither of us could make anything of it. Then Rex asked, "Did you check up on O'Malley and Lucia?"

"Mrs. Trent had never heard of him, but finally after I kept pressing her she did remember Lucia speaking of an unusual-looking man she had met at a party, who had raved about her looks. Lucia had been a little excited by his fulsome admiration and rather wondered why he hadn't made any effort to date her. It was the day after that she disappeared." I reeled off the information I had gathered.

"It could be O'Malley. I had all the other girls' families approached, with no results except that one father remembered his daughter telling him practically the same thing you've just reported, only he recalled the man's name. It *was* O'Malley. It's the first definite link we've had, but where it will lead to I've no idea. I can't see my way clear." Rex drew his brows together.

"Do you suppose Lucia's still alive?" I asked.

"Can't be, if your theory's right and her spirit is imprisoned in the flower."

"The dolls were."

"I don't know. I don't know anything. This whole thing's a labyrinth through which I can't find my way," Rex groaned. "The only clue I've got is in your hands, and it's dynamite. Still I have to use it. If you're willing—"

"I'll do anything," I said, little dreaming what was in his mind.

"There's danger, a very real danger, but I'll be around. I hate even to ask you, but seventeen girls have disappeared. It may be we can save them, or if not, others—" He broke off abruptly, then went on. "There's only one way to go about it. Could you bear to be nice to O'Malley?"

"Nice to O'Malley?" That was the last thing I had expected.

"Yes, lead him on. He's in love with you. Why, if he really is connected with these disappearances, you haven't been spirited away I can't fathom. Perhaps, like Eastern potentates, he keeps a harem for his pleasure, but looks on you as the Ranee that must be really won according to Hoyle, or something like that. There's only one way to find out, as I see it. Lead him on, humor him until he gives himself away or we find a path through the labyrinth."

"You mean let him kiss me?" I gasped. "I'm afraid. Suppose there isn't a flower to save me."

"Wear the orchid. Somehow I feel that with it you're safe, and I'll be right on the job. Tell him you don't like me but I'm hard to shake. I'll have my men on constantly covering us." Rex was more serious than I had ever seen him.

"He'll read my thoughts," I protested, remembering only too well the feelings I had experienced while Splondowski played.

"You must make your mind a blank so he can't get inside it. Will you do it, Louise—for humanity?"

"I'll do it—for you." I said fiercely. I knew how much Rex wanted to succeed with this particular assignment and what it would mean to his future if he did.

Four days passed with no sign from O'Malley, and on the fifth day a new sensation struck the city—another girl vanished, the eighteenth, Helen Ferguson. Again there was no trace of any kind. She had left her house to do some shopping. The whole thing was inexplicable.

Rex investigated at once, but found nothing. "It's incredible that no passerby noticed anything," he told me, "and to make matters worse it gives O'Malley a clean bill of health, so far as I can see. He wasn't off his place. I've had it watched. Nothing unusual happened on the estate. The men I've got posted all around reported."

"No one went in?" I asked.

"Nothing passed the gates but his own Ford delivery truck, which went to market and returned full of provisions. It goes every other day. He has a retinue of servants and evidently buys largely."

"What was Helen Ferguson like?"

"Beautiful—auburn hair, greenish eyes, and a lovely complexion—noted for her skin, which was like a pale pink rose petal."

"I'm glad I'm not beautiful," I said, and shuddered.

"You are to me. I love your sweet little face." Rex leaned over and kissed me to emphasize his point, and we forgot the problems for the time being.

Two more days went by, and it was practically a week since I had seen O'Malley, and the orchid was still as fresh as when he had given it to me. I wore it constantly, and kept it in water at night near my bed. But it gave no more signs of being anything but a flower; there were no whisperings, no assents or denials when I addressed questions to it, and I began to think there never had been.

On the morning of the eighth day I received a note. It was written on green paper with green ink. In one corner was engraved an orchid, and below it:

ORCHID HOUSE
RIVERDALE
NEW YORK

It was the type of paper a luxury-loving woman would have, but it was Angus O'Malley who had written the note:

Come to see my orchids Wednesday at four. I am asking Muriel and some others. Bring the good Mr. Stanton if you wish. I shall expect you—and my answer.
Angus O'Malley

That was all. There was no beginning.

I phoned Rex. He was delighted.

"So much easier than I thought!" he crowed. "In a crowd you'll be perfectly safe."

If he had only known! But he didn't.

All the way up to Riverdale we laughed and joked and planned our future. It was only when we drew up before the great iron grille gates of Orchid House that I began to be afraid and the flower on my shoulder trembled as though it too echoed the wild beating of my heart.

"It's like a prison," I said, as the gates clanged shut behind us.

Rex was silent as we drove up the long wooded road.

"He must own acres," he remarked at last.

Just then the house came within our range of vision. It was like a feudal castle—one of the German ones out of a fairy tale. From any of the four towers Rapunzel might have let down her golden hair—or the fairy Melusine woven her spells.

"Don't worry," Rex's steady and cheerful voice broke into my thoughts, "I'll be right beside you; I'm armed, and I've men all around the outside."

I touched his hand, where it rested on the wheel. Then I assumed the bored air we had agreed upon. It was a good thing I did so, for when we drove under the porte-cochere and stopped it was Angus O'Malley who opened the car door for us. He greeted Rex with exaggerated courtesy. He kissed my hand lingeringly before he guided us into the house.

———

When we passed through the doors we went back centuries into medieval England, to a great room that was vaguely familiar.

"The Hall of Elthaue," our host said. "I had it copied; only I have heat and electricity."

There were about forty people in the hall, most of whom I knew. O'Malley was a charming host. He gave us tea—an utterly commonplace tea—and then took us all over the house and the conservatories, which were full of the most beautiful orchids I have ever seen. None of them, however, was like the yellow one I wore.

"Where is the plant this came from?" I asked him.

For a second he hesitated, then pointed to a moss-like ball with no bloom upon it. Somehow I felt he lied, but I could not dispute him.

When we returned to the house after our tour of the conservatories I looked for Rex. Muriel had him in one corner. Someone came up to O'Malley and engaged him in a long discussion. I decided to slip off by myself and explore a little, for I had noticed that O'Malley had not taken us into one of the towers, although he had meticulously shown us everything else—even his own sleeping quarters, which were in one of the towers but completely modern and fantastic with mirrored walls.

I made my way to where I thought the entrance of the tower would be, judging by the others I had seen. A tapestry covered the wall where the door should have been. I pulled it back and stepped inside to the circular room all the other towers had had, looked up at the same stone stairway, but in the tower halfway up the stairs barring the ascent was a door—a curious iron-studded door—the same door I had seen in my dreams!

"Are you Pandora or Bluebeard's wife?" O'Malley's voice was in my ear. He was standing right behind me. I swung around, deciding quickly that this was an emergency that called for the truth.

"I noticed you didn't show us one tower, and I confess to curiosity." I actually managed to be coy.

"These are my private rooms. Someday I will show them to you. But now, little white bird, you must tell me, is it love or hate?" His eyes searched mine.

I followed Rex's instructions. I made my mind a blank before I answered. Then I said shyly, "I wouldn't want you to hate me."

Joy leapt into his face for the moment, transfiguring it from a Brenda mask into something closer to humanity.

"Then it is love!" He caught my hand.

I held him off a little. "Perhaps, but you must be patient with me for a little. This has all been so quick. I am attracted to you, but I need time. You"—I hesitated, then rushed on—"you frighten me sometimes. You are not like other men."

I had struck the right note. His colossal ego was touched.

"You have spoken more of a truth than you know. See, I will be gentle. I will be kind." He took me in his arms tenderly and caressed me as though I had been a child. "In your arms I will forget that I am a lonely god."

He kissed me then, and I did not resist, though the small, still voice of the flower was again whispering, "Send him away," over and over in my ear.

Eventually he let me go. "We will announce our engagement immediately. I want to watch the good Mr. Stanton's face." Nero at the circus turning his great emerald for all to see.

Rex—the mention of his name brought him before my eyes and for one second made me forget the guard I was keeping on my mind. Only one second, but it was enough.

"So!" O'Malley's lips drew back from his teeth in a bestial snarl. "So it's the good Mr. Stanton you love and you are tricking me for his sake!" With unerring precision he hit the nail directly on the head. "So—you wanted to find out my secrets. Well, you shall."

He caught me by the wrist and dragged me toward the stairs. I screamed, but the sound died in my throat as he struck me on the side of the head with terrific force. He caught me as I fell, and then I knew nothing more.

When I came to, my head ached terribly and for a second I didn't know what had happened. Then I remembered and looked about for O'Malley. To my great relief I found that I was alone.

My dress was gone. I was wrapped in a lovely blue satin kimono, and I was lying on a long couch that took up one side of a barren, cell-like room. There was no other furniture. The walls were of stone and there was no window. High up in the ceiling, which must have been at least twenty feet away, were a few round holes which evidently afforded ventilation. There was a carved wooden door, which I tried although I knew it would be locked. I was a prisoner. I could scream and yell, but no one would hear. But of course Rex would rescue me. I pinned all my hopes to that, and didn't even let myself think how impossible it would be.

Two more things I noticed. The yellow orchid I had worn was lying crushed to a pulp on the floor, as though it had been stamped upon, and there were little crimson spots all over that looked like blood. To take my eyes from it I looked at my wristwatch. Seven-fifteen. It must have been nearly six when I had started exploring, so I had been here in this prison for over an hour. Surely I must be missed. Surely Rex—My thoughts died away in agonized fear.

———

I waited for what seemed an eternity but was actually only twenty minutes. Then I heard the sound of a bolt being shot back. A second later the heavy door swung upward and Angus O'Malley stood on the threshold.

He was dressed in a long Chinese robe that made him look more exotic than ever.

"Mr. O'Malley—" I began.

He held up his hand. "You little fool. Did you think you could fight me? That I who know the secrets of Cagliostro, of Nicodemus—yes, even of Merlin himself—could be deceived by a girl? Your friends have gone. The good Mr. Stanton has gone. I told them you were taken ill and asked me to send you home. I actually sent a car with a girl in it through the gates. Later that car will be discovered a complete wreck; the girl dressed in your clothes will be found dead, her face mutilated beyond recognition. No one will look for you after that."

With a sickening sensation I listened to him. All hope died away, for even Rex would accept such overwhelming evidence.

"What are you going to do with me?" I faltered. My lips were dry.

He looked at me and smiled, and there was more menace in that smile than in any words he had ever uttered.

"First I am going to show you my orchids—the rare ones," he said slowly.

An unholy light shone in his eyes as his fingers locked around my wrist like iron bands. He half led me, half pulled me through the door out into a hall, then up the stone stairway to another iron-studded door. I contemplated screaming, but quickly realized how futile that would be.

"You are wise," he said, reading my thoughts easily. "No one could hear. This tower is soundproof, and only I know the secret of the door below."

He pressed part of the iron decoration and the door swung open. He pulled me into a room that was very hot. It was full of laboratory apparatus. There were several long tables or benches, covered with sheets. He led me to the far end, where there was a particularly long table with a complicated series of tubes and retorts suspended above it. Most of the table was covered with heavy linen of a peculiar blue shade that was tent-like in appearance, but at one end free from the cover I could distinguish a girl's head; beautiful auburn hair, a pale rose-leaf skin, and tortured brown eyes that looked into mine pleadingly.

"Helen Ferguson!" I gasped.

"Helen Ferguson," O'Malley repeated and held up the blue linen on the side so that I could see under the tent-like arrangement.

It was that moment I think my hair turned white; for growing from her lovely body was the dark mass of an orchid plant!

I would have fainted, but O'Malley held me and forced me to listen by the sheer power of his will. "You alone are privileged to look at the miracle of the age. Only I can work such a miracle—a flower that lives, that absorbs the color, the beauty of whatever subject I select—a flower that I can talk to, that answers all my need for beauty, for love. Imagine wearing the beauty all men desire in my buttonhole. Truly in such moments I am a god."

"A god! You are a beast! That poor girl—is she alive?"

"Of course. The plant thrives on her life. It absorbs her color, her brain, her very soul into itself, and then when it has exhausted all she has to give, it blooms, and lives as long as I can keep what is left of the body intact."

"Dear God, how she must suffer!" I turned my face away from those anguished brown eyes and the terrible growth in her breast.

"Only so far as she knows her condition before the orchid absorbs her brain entirely. Of bodily suffering there is none. I sever the nerves when I implant the roots. I will explain—"

"No! No! I can't bear any more."

He laughed—an eerie macabre laugh that pierced my soul.

"But you must. You wanted to see the plant from which the yellow orchid came; so look."

He dropped the blue linen back into place and swung me around until I faced another table, which he uncovered. There lay the body of my friend Lucia Trent, and it was horrible to see, for all the color had been drained from it. The shape, the features were still hers, but it was all shadowy—the hair that had been golden had the same pallor as her cheeks. She was like a vegetable from which the juice and pulp have been extracted.

"It's horrible!" I moaned. "Oh, Lucia, Lucia!"

"So she was your friend! That explains why she did not do my bidding. Her love for you was stronger than my commands."

His face was concentrated fury. If there had been any life in that pale shadowy form he would have stamped it out—just as he had destroyed the orchid.

"Take me away," I pleaded, "before I go mad."

He shook his head. "No, you are to stay. You have cheated me of a flower— you must replace it—look."

He threw open a door. Behind it on shelves in glass vases were sixteen strange orchids of colorings and forms never seen before. O'Malley leaned toward them and they suddenly became animated with life. They swayed to meet him, touching his cheeks, his lips, his eyes—caressingly. It was obscene and terrible to behold, and all the while there was a strange whispering that was even more terrible.

"They are my darlings—all I have asked from life until I met you—you who I thought would sit at my feet and learn wisdom, who would be my companion, sharer of my secrets, my mate"—he looked at me as though he were seeing me for the first time—"why, I cannot understand. Of course I knew you hadn't the color for a flower, and something in you touched me so that for a little while I became a man, but now I have reverted to my godhead."

The man was a raving maniac!

"I no longer desire you as a woman—and fortunately you will make a lovely orchid—a white orchid! See, in all my sixteen blossoms there is not a white one. I have never tried a young woman before with white hair."

I did not know my hair was white. I thought him crazier than ever, but I did comprehend the fate that awaited me. I had given up hope of rescue. Rex would believe me dead. I could not escape, but I must put off the terrible moment. I could at least keep him talking—perhaps dissuade him from the awful thing he contemplated, from which my whole being revolted.

"How—how," I stammered, "could you get these girls here without leaving any trace?"

He smiled conceitedly. "The obvious is never noticed. I merely drove up beside them in an inconspicuous car when no one was near and offered a lift—I had of course met each girl before. Once inside the car, a quick hypodermic with a little serum of my own and they were under my control. Then I put a hat with a mourning veil on them and drove out into the country, where I changed cars."

"But no one ever saw them go through your gates!" I remembered Helen Ferguson and thanked God I could still keep him talking.

"My Ford delivery truck came through with supplies—an inanimate woman can easily be made into a bag of potatoes. Sometimes I drove it disguised as my chauffeur." He answered my question, then turned to the orchids.

"Good-bye for the present, my little darlings. Soon you shall have new companions." He shut the door and turned to me. "I shall wear you in my buttonhole—flaunt you in the eyes of the good Mr. Stanton, and you will caress me as the others do—my white orchid."

"No, no!" I screamed. "Kill me outright—anything but that."

As long as I live I will hate myself for being such a coward, but the horrors with which I was surrounded were too much for me. I begged, I pleaded, but he only laughed at me. Finally he flung me into a chair and tied my wrists to its arms.

"I must prepare for the operation," he said.

He went away and presently returned with a dark ball of fungus root. Soon those hideous things would be feeding upon me. The thought was so horrible that I must have fainted, for the next thing I was conscious of was O'Malley dressed in a white surgeon's gown standing before a perfectly equipped operating table that he had wheeled into the room. Near it was a long table fixed like the one on which Helen Ferguson lay. Soon I would be like her, unable to move, or to speak, or to suffer anything except the most terrible mental anguish.

O'Malley was adjusting a tray of instruments now. It seemed to me that I couldn't see him quite so clearly. Was terror making me blind? Through the heat of the room I noticed a sweet, sickly smell. Was it some kind of anesthetic O'Malley was using? Was this the end? Vaguely I saw him pick up a hypodermic syringe and start toward me. As he came it seemed to me that he swayed. The sickly sweet smell was overpowering me. This was the end. The blackness engulfed me and even the horror was gone.

From far off I seemed to hear Rex's voice calling. "Darling, darling," it was saying over and over.

I wanted to open my eyes, but I couldn't. There seemed to be weights on them. At last I managed to flutter my lids, and looked up into Rex's face. It seemed to have aged. There were strained lines I had never seen before.

"Thank God she's coming around!" he said.

I was immediately conscious of other men bending over me and the murmuring rustle that the wind makes through the leaves of trees. Perhaps I had actually died and was in heaven, only then Rex—

"Rex," I whispered weakly. "It is really you—am I alive?"

"My darling!" He gathered me in his arms convincingly. "You are all right. Thank God! It was a close thing."

"O'Malley didn't—" I didn't dare look down at myself.

"No, no—we were in time. Oh, my dear!" He buried his face in my neck as though overcome with emotion.

One of the men spoke. "I think we should get Miss Howard to the hospital. She needs treatment and rest."

Rex pulled himself together. "I'll carry her to the car," he said and picked me up.

"Where are we?" I was tremendously weak and helpless but my head was clear.

"She should be quiet," the same man spoke.

"I must know what happened," I whispered to Rex.

"We're leaving the grounds of Orchid House," Rex answered.

"O'Malley?" I shivered convulsively.

"He will never trouble you again. O'Malley is dead," Rex assured me with a tone of finality in his voice.

————

When we were in the car and I was resting in Rex's arms with the cool night air reviving me more and more, I asked him to tell me what had happened, and he, knowing I could not rest until I knew, satisfied my curiosity.

"When O'Malley said you had been taken ill and he had sent you home, I knew he lied. You would never have gone off like that without a word to me! I knew something was wrong. I left almost at once and contacted one of my men who had been watching the gate. He had seen the car leave and a girl in it. He recognized your clothes but was sure the girl wasn't you; he'd seen you on the way in. I'd known that if O'Malley was actually connected with the disappearance we would have to raid Orchid House, so I was prepared with a new kind of gas that paralyzes. If an antitoxin is given within a certain length of time it is harmless; otherwise the person who inhales it dies. I knew O'Malley would do nothing while the guests were there, so I waited and got ready. As soon as everyone had left, my men and I, fully protected with masks, entered Orchid House, spraying the gas as we went. It is very powerful and travels so fast that a little is sufficient. By the time we'd reached the house the servants and guards were overcome.

"I had noticed that O'Malley hadn't shown us the fourth tower. I made for it and we sprayed the gas under the door. Then we tried to open it. You'll never realize the agony I went through when we couldn't. It was so awful; I lived a thousand years in a few minutes. You might already be dead, but if we were in time to save you from O'Malley, unless we got through that door before long it would be too late for the antidote, and the gas would kill you. Finally, as a last resort, we blew off the door, and got to you just in time to administer the serum and carry you out into the open air."

Rex paused and brushed my hand against his cheek. The miracle had happened—I had been snatched back from the brink of unutterable horror just in time.

"I had the strange orchids destroyed—O'Malley and the girl were paralyzed. They died long before you came around. We didn't try to save them."

"I'm so glad—oh, Rex, Rex, I'll never forget her eyes!" I clung closer to him for comfort.

"My dear, my dear, I know. I've seen your hair. Someday you will tell me everything, but not now—now you must forget what's happened and rest and recover from all this. I will do my best to help and make you happy." He leaned down and kissed me tenderly.

———

The years have passed. Rex has kept his promise. We have known happiness too great for words to describe. But even that happiness has never been able to wipe away the memory of the affair of the Strange Orchids.

AMELIA REYNOLDS LONG (1904–78) was an American author who wrote SF, fantasy, and detective stories for early-twentieth-century genre magazines. Long grew up loving William Shakespeare's *Macbeth* and the work of Edgar Allan Poe, eventually bringing her affinity for the weird to her writing career. She lived most of her life in Harrisburg, Pennsylvania. She graduated from Harrisburg High School in 1922 and then attended the University of Pennsylvania, earning her BS in education in 1931 and her MA in the same field in 1932. She was a talented writer who published SF in professional and amateur publications alike. While Long usually sold SF under her full given name, F. Orlin Tremaine shortened her byline to "A. R. Reynolds" for *Astounding*, and Long herself occasionally employed the pseudonym Mordred Weir to ensure that she did not saturate the market with too many stories published under her real name.

Long made her first SF sale to *Weird Tales* in 1928 and went on to publish nineteen more genre stories in venues that included *Amazing Stories*, *Astounding*, and *Stardust*. Her tales tend to focus on science professors who get into comic situations involving some combination of hypnosis, romance, and experiments gone awry. Her works were popular with editors and fans alike, and her 1930 short story "The Thought Monster" was made into the low-budget SF monster movie *Fiend without a Face* (1958). By the mid-1930s, Long had become disenchanted with SF because she felt the genre had "lost its wonder through the sheer extravagance of mechanical magnitudes" ("Time" 122). Around that same time she began to establish herself as an Agatha Christie–style mystery novelist, using her own byline and the pen names Peter Reynolds, Patrick Laing, and Adrian Reynolds. She published more than thirty mystery novels between 1936 and 1952 and then switched to poetry for the rest of her life. During this period she also worked as a textbook editor at Stackpole Books and as a curator at Harrisburg's William Penn Museum. Today, Long's name lives on in the Pennsylvania Poetry Society's Amelia Reynolds Long Memorial Award.

Although Long was somewhat skeptical about the merits of SF in general by this time, her 1937 short story "Reverse Phylogeny" is an outstanding example of what Tremaine called "thought-variant SF." As he explained in the December 1933 issue of *Astounding*, this mode of SF was characterized by the development of an idea that "has been slurred over or passed by" in other, more action-oriented tales (qtd. in Langford, "Thought-Variant"). In Long's story, Professor Aloysius O'Flannigan performs a public experiment in which he hypnotizes a group of volunteers to establish a scientific basis for the existence of Atlantis. As such, "Reverse Phylogeny" capitalizes on the early-twentieth-century fascination with ancient mysteries, especially, as they articulate, with what were then the new sciences of anthropology and archaeology. While the individual experiences related by the volunteers provide plenty of action for readers, they are not the point of Long's story. Instead, O'Flannigan treats them as pieces of evidence that will settle scientific debates over the reality of Atlantis once and for all.

"Reverse Phylogeny" also demonstrates Long's skill at infusing genre fiction with humor. Like other comic SF authors, Long often "mocks or satirizes standard SF conventions" in her fiction, and "Reverse Phylogeny" is no exception ("Comic Science Fiction"). O'Flannigan is very much a parody of the traditional SF scientist, one who takes his work seriously but whose experiments lead to comic chaos rather than great triumph or great tragedy. In this particular story, O'Flannigan is trying to settle an academic debate, and the confused narrator underscores the fickle nature of such debates when he complains, "You have the darndest way of switching from one side of a question to another!" In what is likely to strike readers as a less fortunate aspect of her story, Long turns to racial stereotypes for laughs: her protagonist O'Flannigan, the silver-tongued Irish scientist who spoils for a good (intellectual, if not physical) fight, and the character Chief Rain-in-the-Face, a laconic savage who lapses into bouts of scalping and other menacing behaviors. But though—or perhaps because—it features such elements, "Reverse Phylogeny" provides readers with an excellent snapshot of comic SF as it was first written in the early twentieth century, especially as it anticipates the explosion of comic SF written by Henry Kuttner, L. Sprague de Camp, and Arthur K. Barnes in the 1940s and the proliferation of comic SF across media today.[11]

....

"Reverse Phylogeny"
Astounding Stories, June 1937

Once more I have before me the task of explaining to the public another of the escapades of my friend, Professor Aloysius O'Flannigan. Not that Aloysius has asked me to do so; he is far too proud for that. But when—because of a minor incident that had no place in his original plan, and for which he can in no way be held responsible—remarks are made that the whole experiment concerning the lost continent of Atlantis had a decidedly fishy flavor, and when certain malicious-tongued individuals begin to accuse an inoffensive, peace-loving man like Aloysius of deliberately attempting to drown Mr. Theophilus Black on dry land, it seems to me that in mere fairness something ought to be done about it.

It all began with a series of articles of a well-known science magazine, of which Aloysius is an ardent reader. Dropping into his library one day, I found him sitting cross-legged upon the floor, with several copies of the magazine strewn around him. As I entered, he glanced up, made a dive for one of the magazines, and thrust it at me.

"Eric, I want you to read this!" he exclaimed, his eyes gleaming behind his thick-lensed spectacles. "Then tell me what you think of it."

He had turned this magazine open at an article entitled: "Atlantis: Proof of Its Existence," written by a Mr. Theophilus Black. It was a well-constructed article, exhibiting excellent imaginative qualities and, to my mind at least, quite a bit of erudition on the part of its author. As I finished it and was about to comment, Aloysius pushed a second article into my hand.

"Read this before you say anything," he directed. "Then give me your reaction to both of them."

The article in the second magazine was called "Atlantis Debunked," and it lived up to its title. I read it as Aloysius directed and, whereas only a few minutes before, Mr. Black had me willing to swallow the whole continent of Atlantis, Mr. Kenneth McScribe, the author of the second article, now had me gagging on the first pebble. I looked helplessly at Aloysius, feeling a trifle groggy.

"There are several other articles here, but you needn't go into them," he said understandingly. "But what do you think of the Atlantis theory as a whole?"

"I hardly know," I answered, trying to sort out my jumbled reactions. "There seem to be equally good arguments on both sides."

"That's what I felt, too." He nodded. "Mr. Black's logic is excellent, but he builds it upon a rather porous situation, upon which Mr. McScribe has very cleverly turned a microscope. But, in his enthusiasm, Mr. McScribe has used too powerful a lens and blurred matters a little. For example"—he picked up one of the magazines and selected a particular paragraph—"Mr. McScribe would throw out the evidence of the air-cooled volcanic rocks found in the Atlantic Ocean because Mr. Black cannot quote their geological age. I fail to see where their age has a great deal to do with it. After all, the question is not *when* Atlantis might have existed, but *whether* it existed at any time."

"True," I agreed hopefully. "And the very existence of those rocks is a strong indication—"

"Not so fast!" he broke in. "The existence of those rocks need indicate nothing more than a now-submerged island; and it's going a little strong to construct a whole continent out of that—a little like making a mountain out of a molehill, on an exalted scale."

"You have the darndest way of switching from one side of a question to another!" I complained. "A fellow can't tell whether you actually turn the corners, or just wander in a circle."

"I'm afraid you haven't got the scientific mind, Eric." He sighed. "What I'm trying to do is sift the evidence."

"And what have you found so far?" I inquired with a touch of sarcasm.

"Not much, I'm afraid," he admitted. "You see, both Mr. Black and Mr. McScribe have made the same error of arguing over material evidence: such things as similarity of place names on both sides of the Atlantic, prehistoric remains, social development, and the like. They should look for psychological indications: racial characteristics or instincts in man himself that would either prove or disprove his descent from inhabitants of a continent—"

————

He broke off in midsentence, and a rapt expression came over his face. "Divil an' all!" he exclaimed, slapping his right fist into the palm of his left hand. "I believe it could be done; I'm going to try it!"

"Now what?" I asked a little fearfully, knowing from past experience that when Aloysius used that tone anything might be expected to happen.

"I'm going to awaken racial memory," he replied. "After all, our so-called instincts are nothing more than inherited race memory, as any psychologist will tell you. If those dormant memories can be aroused, brought up from the unconscious into the conscious mind and—"

"But how can it be done?" I wanted to know.

"Through hypnotism, of course," he answered. "I could turn the mind of a subject back through the deep strata of instinct bequeathed to him by his ancestors, inducing him to relive them as if they were a part of his own experience, until we had discovered whether there was or was not an Atlantean layer. Why, we might even settle the mooted question of whether mental traits can be inherited!"

There are times, I reflected, when nothing else in the English language is so expressive as the single word "Nuts." But I said nothing, hoping that he would work off his enthusiasm by writing a letter to the magazine. I should have known better.

It was only a week later that he sent for me to come around again. Upon arriving at his house, I found that he already had three other guests: two very scholarly looking gentlemen and a full-blooded Indian, feathers and all.

"Eric," he said, "I want you to meet Mr. Black, Mr. Scribe, and Chief Rain-in-the-Face. Gentlemen, my friend and sometimes colleague, Mr. Dale."

Mr. Black and Mr. McScribe acknowledged the introduction with the usual polite phrases.

Chief Rain-in-the-Face (ah! The appropriateness of that name!) confined himself to a noncommittal "Ugh."

As for me, I'm afraid I let my jaw fall open rather foolishly.

"I wrote to Mr. Black and Mr. McScribe about my planned experiment to settle the Atlantis question," Aloysius went on, "and they very graciously consented to act as subjects. The fact that they are on opposite sides in the debate will give added significance to our findings."

"I see," I managed a trifle weakly. "And where does—er—Chief Rain-in-the-Face come in?"

"In order to prove or disprove Mr. Black's contention that the first settlers on the American continent were from Atlantis, it was necessary that a genuine Indian take part in the experiment," he explained. "Of course, in order to be really scientific, we should have an Egyptian as well but none was procurable. However, Mr. Black is convinced that his earliest forbears were Atlanteans; so that will have to suffice.

"And now, gentlemen," he continued, "if you are ready, we will begin the first step. Eric, you will act as witness and recording secretary."

He lined his subjects up in chairs facing him and, after a few minutes, succeeded in placing all three of them in a state of deep hypnosis. He then undertook, by suggestion, to turn their minds backward through layers of inherited instinct, making them relive their "race memories," as he called them, as actual experiences.

I will say this much for what followed: It was extremely interesting, and would have convinced the Reincarnationists that their day of justification had arrived. During the next two hours, Chief Rain-in-the-Face told us all about what happened to Henry Hudson after he had sailed on his last voyage up the river that now bears his name, while Mr. Black and Mr. McScribe furnished us with some interesting sidelights in the lives of several prominent personages at the courts of Louis XIV and Henry VIII respectively. All in all, it was a morning well spent.

———

Upon being awakened, none of the three men retained any memory of their mental experiences while in the hypnotic state; and they were exceedingly surprised when I read my notes to them. At Aloysius's request, they all promised to return the next day, when the experiment would be continued.

"Of course, today was only the beginning," Aloysius said when we were alone. "A mere scratching of the surface. Tomorrow we will go deeper, and the next day deeper still, until, eventually, we reach the level that will prove conclusively from what source these races have sprung."

"I hope you're not claiming that today's performance had anything to do with instinct," I remarked. "Why, the very latest of our instincts was developed long before the sixteenth and seventeenth centuries. Moreover, according to your own statement, instinct is *race* memory. What these men related today were the experiences of single individuals."

"I know that," he admitted unperturbed. "But it only goes to verify another theory of mine. For a long time I have believed that the life experiences of our not-too-distant ancestors are inherited in certain cells of the brain, just as their physical characteristics are duplicated in our bodies. They bear the same relationship to racial memory that family resemblance bears to racial resemblance. For example, it—"

"Never mind the example," I cut in. "I'll probably understand better without it. And now, if I may speak figuratively, how long in this experiment of yours before we get through the topsoil and strike bedrock?"

"Oh, about two weeks," he replied. "Incidentally, I like your metaphor. It has such a—er—archaeological flavor."

I will not go into a detailed account of all the subsequent steps in the experiment, but will note only the highlights. There was, for instance, the time when Chief Rain-in-the-Face went on the warpath, and attempted to translate his mental experience into physical action with the aid of the table lamp and a letter opener. He entirely wrecked the experiment for that day, and had to be brought out of his hypnotic trance by the somewhat crude means of a crack over the head with a volume of the encyclopedia.

Then there was the time when Mr. McScribe thought he was with Joshua before the walls of Jericho, and insisted upon going out and marching around the block until the policeman on the beat picked him up as a suspicious character.

It was this incident, together with the explanation it entailed, that was responsible for bringing the whole affair to the public. When we went to the police station to collect Mr. McScribe, an over-enterprising reporter was present and that evening the story, embellished with lurid details, appeared in his paper. The result was that the next morning representatives of every newspaper in the city descended upon us.

Now Aloysius is retiring by nature, and at first he refused to have anything to do with them. But it is easier to rid oneself of dandruff than the gentlemen of the press. By sheer persistence, they wore him down, until at last he consented to their being present at the next experiment.

By this time he had got back to the early Egyptian period and had actually begun to accomplish things with race memory. The reporters were duly impressed, and when their stories appeared, the reading public got its money's worth. Interest in the subject became so acute that the editor of the paper that carried the first story got the brilliant idea that the remainder of the experiment be put in a public auditorium, the affair to be sponsored by his newspaper.

Naturally, Aloysius would have refused anything so spectacular, had not both Mr. Black and Mr. McScribe intervened. What weight, they argued, would our findings carry if they could be attested to by only one or two men? For the sake of science, the final steps should be taken before a sufficient number of witnesses, so that the outcome could never be doubted. The argument undeniably had its points, and at last, in spite of his better judgment, Aloysius gave in.

It was arranged for the final stage of the experiment to be conducted in the city's largest auditorium. Free tickets could be had by taking a year's subscription to the sponsoring newspaper, and the public's response would have turned Barnum green with envy. Within three days every seat in the house had been taken, and tickets for standing room were being issued on six month's subscriptions.

At last the fatal night came, when, according to the best calculations, the Atlantean strata in the unconscious minds of the three subjects should be reached. Aloysius had planned to skip a few thousand years in order to get, if possible, a description of Atlantis in its heyday, then to work up gradually to the great inundation. It would, he explained, make the experiment more understandable to the audience.

I think that, of the two of us, I was the more nervous. Experience had taught me that Aloysius's experiments quite frequently ended in unforeseen results, and I did not relish the thought of how so large an audience might react in such a case. I even urged him to have a sort of dress rehearsal in private, but he refused.

"No, Eric," he said firmly. "If I did that, tonight's performance would not be a true experiment, but merely a demonstration of something already proven. I am a man of my word, and must give these people what I promised."

"But suppose there was no continent of Atlantis," I argued. "Then what?"

"In that case," he replied, unruffled, "we will have proven Mr. McScribe's contention."

I saw that there was nothing I could do, so I gave up.

Promptly at eight o'clock, Aloysius stepped out upon the stage, and explained to a packed and eager house what he proposed to do. He was followed by Mr. Black and Mr. McScribe, who, in turn, stated their positions in the matter.

Chief Rain-in-the-Face, upon being introduced next, confined himself to the usual, noncommittal "Ugh," since the purpose of the whole affair was still a little hazy in his mind.

Amid a silence heavy enough to be weighed, Aloysius proceeded to place his three subjects in a state of hypnosis. He had explained that the best results might be expected from Mr. Black since he alone, once the mental transfer to the remote past had been made, seemed able to translate his awakened race memories into the language of the present. Chief Rain-in-the-Face, when under the hypnotic influence, spoke his native Indian language while on the last two occasions, Mr. McScribe had emitted a kind of unintelligible jabbering suggestive of an anthropoid ape.

As soon as the hypnotic trance was deep enough, Aloysius addressed the three collectively, informing them that they were now living before the dawn of recorded history, in approximately the year 20,000 BC, and directing them to describe their experiences. There followed a minute of tense expectancy, during which a subtle change seemed to take place in all three men.

Then Chief Rain-in-the-Face rose and delivered a spirited oration in a language that resembled none known on Earth today; after which he bowed formally and resumed his seat.

The audience understood not a word of what he said, and accordingly looked duly impressed. Aloysius raised his hand to check applause he saw was about to break forth, and turned to Mr. Black.

"Now, Theophilus Black, tell us where you are and what you see."

The reply came at once; but the words were spoken slowly, as if the speaker was obliged to translate his thoughts into a tongue with which he was unfamiliar:

"I am in a great city—the capital of the civilized world. On all sides, tall, white buildings rear themselves toward the sky, while the streets are thronged with busy people. There are also many horse-drawn chariots; but each year those grow fewer, for recently there has been invented a chariot that runs without horses. Since the invention of this horseless chariot, the pedestrians, too, have grown fewer. The land is rich and powerful, and its scientists are the greatest the world has ever known."

"What is the name of this land?" Aloysius put in, endeavoring to control his excitement. So far, results were turning out far better than they had before.

There was a brief pause; Mr. Black said then, "Its native name would mean nothing to you, but it has come down to you in legend as Atlantis."

———

A unanimous gasp arose from the audience. The authenticity of the mythical Atlantis was actually being proven! At this very moment, the man before them had returned there mentally through awakened race memory! No wonder they were excited and thrilled. I was myself.

"I have said that our scientists are the greatest the world has ever known,"

Mr. Black went on in the same hesitant, rather monotonous voice. "But recently they have fallen into disrepute; and all because they have predicted that which does not please the people to believe.

"For many years we have known that the ocean bottom is rising. Our own coastal plains have been sinking, while our mariners report that in distant reaches of both the eastern and western oceans, strange new islands have appeared. Our scientists have studied these reports and announced that the appearance of the islands marks the beginning of a great cataclysm of nature, which will raise new continents from the ocean bottom, pouring the waters that now cover them over Atlantis, burying it forever. Naturally, the people are loath to accept such a prediction, for it seems to them impossible that Atlantis, the wise and beautiful, could ever perish."

"Does no one believe the scientists?" Aloysius asked.

"None but a few religious sects, who believe that the end of the world has been predicted. One of our merchants has taken advantage of their credulity, and has advertised in his shop a special sale of fine linen for ascension robes."

"When do the scientists predict that this great catastrophe will take place?"

"They say that it will occur about ten years from now."

Aloysius waited several seconds before speaking again. Then he said, "Six years have passed. The catastrophe is only four years away. Tell us what is happening in Atlantis now."

The reply came promptly. "Earthquakes have begun to shake our land. Two volcanoes have become active. The ocean bottom to the east and west is rising rapidly."

"Do the people still doubt the predictions of the scientists?"

"A few more have ceased to doubt. These are building large boats in which, if the water begins to rise over the land, they will flee to the small, barbarous continent of Yropa to the northeast. The boats are very large. They will carry animals and supplies as well as men and women."

"Blast me eyes!" exclaimed an awed British voice from the balcony. "A whole fleet of bloomin' Noah's arks!"

Aloysius gestured sternly for silence, and returned to his subject. "Now three more years have gone by. The disaster is only one year away."

The audience leaned forward breathlessly to catch the answer. This time the voice that delivered it was strained and tense.

"The sky is dark with the ashes from the volcanoes. Whole cities have been destroyed by earthquakes. Reports reach us that the sea has rushed in over a portion of Yropa, creating a large island off the west coast, where before was a peninsula. Also, a large tract of land shaped like a boot has arisen out of the sea on the south of Yropa.

"At least the people of Atlantis believe that the scientists predicted correctly, but now it is too late. Most of the boats have already departed to establish colonies in Yropa and other barbarous places. As for the others, their captains grow rich conducting one-way excursions to the new islands. Atlantis is a doomed continent."

The voice moaned away into silence, like the last gasp of the dying civilization it described. It was echoed by the audibly released breath of the gallery.

From my place in the wings, I tried to catch Aloysius's eye. Surely the experiment had gone far enough and it was now time to awaken the subjects. Besides, during the last few minutes, Chief Rain-in-the-Face had shown distinct signs of restlessness, as if he was passing through the same mental experiences as Mr. Black, but was unable to express himself. To keep him in the hypnotic state much longer might lead to complications.

But Aloysius had not yet finished. A gleam came into his eyes that I knew only too well; he braced himself to launch the real climax of his experiment. "The hour of catastrophe has come!" he cried in ringing tones. "Atlantis is sinking! The waters are closing over it! Tell me what you see."

———

There was a moment of electric tension so strong it could have charged a battery. Then the answer came, but this time it was not in words, but in actions.

Before anyone fully realized what was happening, Chief Rain-in-the-Face had leaped from his chair. The next instant he was heading for the edge of the platform, while his arms flailed about in perfect imitation of an English Channel swimmer. Pausing on the platform's edge for only a split second, he executed a perfect swan dive into the lap of an obese lady in the front row!

Instantly pandemonium broke loose. Women screamed and men shouted. There was a mad stampede for the exits, in which everybody seemed to get in everybody else's way. One well-meaning soul, attempting to switch on more lights, pressed the wrong button—with the result that he turned on the emergency fire sprinkler instead, and streams of water began to spurt in all directions. We learned afterwards that this caused several people to believe that the entire company had actually been translated bodily as well as mentally to sinking Atlantis and were going down with it.

In vain, Aloysius entreated the crowd to be calm, assuring them that everything was all right. However, those people had but one thought in mind: to get out of there—quickly, while they still had their scalps.

In the excitement, the two other subjects of the experiment had been completely forgotten, and it is painful to contemplate what might have been the fate of at least one of them had not a faint, gurgling sound attracted my attention. I went to investigate. There was poor Mr. Black flapping helplessly in his chair, emitting the most awful gaspings and groanings, like a man in the last stages of drowning.

"Aloysius!" I bellowed, striving to make myself heard above the surrounding din. "You've got to get Black out of the Atlantis period, quick! The poor devil can't swim!"

Leaving the auditorium attendants and the police, who had arrived by this time to look after the commotion in the front, we rushed to the assistance of Mr. Black while Mr. McScribe peered at us from beneath the speaker's table, a perfect example of the atavistic cave man gone to cover. Our star subject was in pretty bad shape, and even after he had been awakened from the hypnosis, it was necessary to administer artificial respiration.

After the excitement was all over, and Aloysius had been warned, by an irate police sergeant, that, "if there's any more av this foolishness, Professor O'Flannigan, ye'll find yerself in a cage with the rest of the monkeys," we were allowed to go home.

To my surprise, Aloysius was not nearly so downcast as I had expected. "I'll admit that matters did get a little out of hand toward the end," he said philosophically. "But, in spite of that, the experiment was a success. We certainly proved the onetime existence of Atlantis."

"I'm not so sure," I replied sourly. "I heard a couple of reporters say that the whole thing could be explained by pure mental suggestion."

Aloysius merely smiled. "Of course, there will always be skeptics," he said. "But I have material proof that cannot be explained away."

"*Material* proof?" I repeated. "What in the world do you mean?"

"For a long time," he began, "certain scientists have maintained that there exist ultra-dimensions in time and space, which, if they were thoroughly understood, could be passed through physically as well as mentally. Now don't ask me how, for I'm not a mathematician. All I know is that, in some way, Mr. Black's mental rapport with the past became so strong that he was able to draw through these dimensions an actual, material specimen from the sinking continent of Atlantis. I took it from his mouth when we were reviving him. Here it is."

He put his hand into his pocket and drew out—by the tail—a little dead fish!

I stared at it incredulously. "Holy mackerel!" I gasped.

Aloysius shook his head. "No, Eric," he corrected, with his usual care for scientific accuracy, "just a sucker."

LESLIE PERRI (c. 1920–70) was the pen name of Doris Marie Claire "Doë" Baumgardt, an author and artist who published widely in SF fanzines and made three professional story sales between the late 1930s and 1950s. According to census records, her parents, Fritz and Marie Baumgardt, were German immigrants who settled in New York in the mid-1910s, and Doris Baumgardt was born sometime in late 1920 or early 1921. Her interest in SF developed after she met Frederik Pohl through a mutual friend in high school. The two began dating, and Pohl "persuaded her after six months to attend a Futurian Society meeting" for the group of New York–based fans who aspired to become SF authors, editors, and artists (Knight 33). She adopted the name Leslie Perri as her byline in the many Futurian fanzines where she published, garnering a reputation for "remarkably perceptive" character sketches of her fellow SF fans (Davin, *Partners* 101). As she wrote of Cyril Kornbluth in *Vombiteur Littéraire*: "[He] is a man of a second's acquaintanceship, we are biased in our approval of him. He likes our art endeavors . . . nevertheless, steeling ourselves to an abstract observation, Kornbluth is a ponderous manifestation of aesthetic appreciation, a bull with daisy wreaths strung around his ears" (qtd. in Rich 38). Perri also gained national recognition for her work as a founding member of the Fantasy Amateur Press Association and was one of just five Futurians who were allowed to attend the first World Science Fiction Convention in 1939.[12]

Perri's Futurian connections enabled her to break into the professional genre magazine community as editor of *Movie Love Stories*, where she "practically wrote" much of the content (Knight 90). Another Futurian, Robert A. W. Lowndes, solicited her first professional SF story sale, "Space Episode," for the December 1941 issue of *Future*. After briefly marrying and divorcing Pohl in the early 1940s, Perri went on to marry the painter Thomas Owens (with whom she had her daughter, Margot) and then Futurian Richard Wilson (with whom she had her son, Richard). During this period she made two other professional SF sales before embarking on a career as a reporter and journalist. Perri died of cancer in 1970, but her name lives on through the memoires of other Futurians and through "Space Episode," which was reprinted in the May 1954 issue of *Space Fact and Fiction* and in Janrae Frank, Jean Stine, and Forrest J Ackerman's 1994 edited anthology *New Eves*.

"Space Episode" shows Perri's intelligence—which Pohl described as "humorous" and "deprecatory" (*Way* 74)—as she takes the familiar tale of heroic space travel and turns it on its head. Like other SF writers of the late 1930s and early 1940s (such as Amelia Reynolds Long and Dorothy Les Tina, both of whom are featured in this anthology), Perri seems to have been influenced by F. Orlin Tremaine's concept of the thought-variant tale, which emphasizes a speculative idea rather than gadgetry or adventure. Although "Space Episode" certainly includes both of these narrative elements—revolving, as it does, around the first flight into outer space and the mechanical disaster that nearly prevents the space ship from returning to Earth—the real force of Perri's story comes from the personal interactions of its mixed-sex crew. Much of this is conveyed by her female narrator, Lida, who recognizes both the potential of the womblike spaceship to foster new modes of gender relations and the need for women to actively break free of patriarchal stereotypes. As such, "Space Episode" also pays homage to the female Gothic tradition that depicts women as both victims of men and the heroines of their own stories—indeed, Lida's last thought as she leaves the ship is that her heroic actions will make for great newspaper copy.

"Space Episode" sparked polarized responses from readers that dramatized the battle of the sexes as it occasionally flared up in early genre magazines.[13] The letter pages of the February 1942 issue included a tirade against Perri's story by Victor Mayper, Jr., which concluded, "Of all the hacky, sour, limping stories, this tops them all. Bah! Triple bah!" (108). On the same page, a letter from Virginia Combs gushed that "Space Episode" was "good, fine, and super. The last story in the magazine rated first with me. Call it loyalty to my sex or what you will but I still like it best. It was swell. More!" (108). The debate spilled into the letter pages of the April 1942 issue as well, where editor Lowndes noted that he considered the story a success—despite the fact that it was the lowest-rated story in the issue based on readers' scores—because "ardent feminists plugged it roundly" and "it served to show, if nothing else, that quite a few girls read *Future*" (102–103). As a provocative reinterpretation of the classic space story, "Space Episode" anticipates the feminist SF of James Tiptree, Jr., and Joanna Russ, whose strong women have no patience for male conceits about valor and heroism.

....

"Space Episode"

Future Combined with Science Fiction, December 1941

She stared at her two companions for a moment and then a sickening revulsion replaced fear, the fear that held each of the three in a terrible grip of inertia. Her slim hands bit hard into the back of one of the metal seats. The tiny rocket ship was plummeting to destruction, careening dizzily through space. Here, in the atmosphere-less void, their motion was negligible to them, but instruments told a grim story: unless they could blast the forward rockets very soon they would be caught in the Earth's titanic grip and drawn with intensifying acceleration to its surface. They would come screaming down like some colossal shell and the planet's surface would become a molten sore where they struck. And now, while precious seconds fled, the three of them stood transfixed, immobile.

What had happened? A simple thing, an unimportant thing in space. They had encountered a meteor swarm, one utterly infinitesimal in the sight of the looming worlds about them. But it had left one of its members jammed in their forward rocket nozzles, the tubes that determined whether they would land safely or crash in a blaze of incandescence. They had turned off their operating power rather than wreck the ship completely; with no escape for rocket blasts, their motors would be smashed to pieces.

The first they knew of disaster, striking unheralded from space, was the ear-shattering impact of the meteor. No sound, just concussion that was worse than any deafening crash. Then the power generator dial shot to the danger line; the ship began to plunge, teleplate showing the universe seemingly turning fast somersaults as their ship careened end over end. The truth was evident at once: that impediment must be removed from the forward tubes. One of them must volunteer to clear away the obstruction, or all were doomed.

A time for heroics, this, but none of them felt like heroes. Erik and Michael stood side by side, a sort of bewildered terror on their faces—a "this can't happen to us" look. Neither had moved or spoken a word since the first investigation. Erik, upon discovering that the outer door was gone, had flung his space suit to the floor with an impotent curse. For that shorn-off door meant that whoever left the ship now could never return; it was a one-way passage. The taller of the two men played with the instruments, spinning them this way and that, then stood waiting. Waiting for heaven alone knew what miracle to happen.

Lida found her confidence in them, that fine confidence she had known up to now, dissolving away, leaving her with an empty feeling that was greater than any fear could have been. She could not square them, as they were now, with the men she had known before—through innumerable Terrestrial dangers on land, sea, and in the clouds. The three had had a planet-wide reputation as reckless and danger despising. And now . . .

"Erik!" she cried suddenly. "Damn it, this is not a tea party! We have to do something now. Toss coins or draw lots. Either one of us goes out there now, or we all crack up."

Michael glanced at her dully as she spoke, his tongue moving over dry lips. Erik closed his eyes, brushing his hair with a limp gesture. Lida's hands tightened on the back seat; what was wrong with them? She bent forward slightly, her heart beating like a dull and distant drum. The dials on the control board frightened her; she whispered now. "You see what little time we have left? Nothing's going to happen unless we make it happen. We're falling, falling fast."

Michael slumped in his seat, dropped his head to his knees groaning. Erik looked at her vaguely for a long second, then turned his eyes to the teleplate. Cold perspiration stood on his forehead. This was the dashing Erik Vane, one-time secret dream hero, close companion since that day, years back, when he and Mike had fished her out of the wreck of her plane somewhere in the Pacific. Suddenly, it all seemed amusing to her; the question of sacrifice lay between Michael and Erik—this was strictly men's work. But they were finding life a sweet thing—a sudden burst of laughter overcame her. There was such an amusing impotency to Erik's strength and the dash of his clothes; the knuckles stood white on his hands, cold damp fear glittering on his forehead.

––––––––

And what of Michael, the gallant? He slumped in his seat, holding his face in his shaking hands. Could this be the same man who had saved them all by scaling what was virtually a sheer cliff by night and obtaining help from neighboring aborigines? All the dangers they had faced together and overcome together now crowded in her memory, one piling upon another. Scores of times one of them had unhesitatingly faced unpleasant death for the sake of all; she had been no exception.

And there was another picture that made her laugh, too, but it wasn't a gay laugh. The picture of Michael opening the outer door of the rocket on the night they left, bowing gallantly, speaking extravagantly dear words of welcome to her on their first space flight. Lida clung to a chair, eyes blurring, as she gazed at the control panel, now a welter of glittering metal, polished and useless.

Michael's head shot up suddenly. "Stop laughing! Stop it!" He covered his face with his hands and Lida felt sick; he was crying.

She paused, her eyes filled with bitterness and contempt. Then she smiled wearily, feeling strangely akin to the vacuum outside them. There was only a sudden decision and she made it. This was her exit and to hell with heroes!

She bowed to them scornfully, waving aside their fears with a flippant sweep of her hand. Only one regret remained now. They could have chosen fairly, made a pretense of flipping a coin. She looked cocky and defiant now, gathering tools for her job. A grin twisted her mouth into a quivering scarlet line. Would she make a television headline? Would they name a ramp after her or, perhaps, someday, a rocket division? There were several photos of her in newspaper files; she hoped they would pick a good one when they ran the story. Oh, hers would be a heroic end.

She put aside the word "end" mentally and turned her attention to what had to be done. Her decision made, she would have to act swiftly or the sacrifice would be useless. The cabin's interior was becoming unreal and horrible with apathy. She ignored the others; they were like figures in a nightmare. The outer door had been destroyed, no doubt about that. Erik was almost blown from the cabin when he opened the inner door. She would need magnetic clamps from the outset; the neutralizing effect of the airlock between the two doors was gone—that spelled doom for the one who ventured beyond the cabin. Once out, there was no returning. The force of escaping air would not permit it.

On the black, glistening floor of the cabin laid Erik's glittering, iridium-woven spacesuit. He had ventured that much at least, pulled it from a locker and tossed it to the floor. Fortunately the gyroscopes were working. She stepped into the suit, smiling grimly. It was much too long and wide all over. Her fingers were swift and sure, adjusting the steel clamps.

Michael was still in a semi-coma. Erik was watching her reflection. He knew what she was doing. His shoulders were rigid now, but he made no move to stop her. And now memory played the final ironic trick. She recalled Michael saying, with his arm around her shoulders, "When we get to Mars, you'll be the glamor girl of the planet. It'll be wonderful, Lida—just the two of us." His eyes had hinted at things he did not put into words, and even though she knew that nothing of the kind would happen as long as there were three of them, she had been glad for him then.

She jerked up the front zipper, trying to close her memories with the same motion. There weren't many seconds to spare now. She fastened the tools to her belt, checked them and with them her signal-sending button with the receiving set on the instrument board. Then, with shaking hands she could not help, she picked up the helmet.

Michael looked up suddenly, incredulity filling his eyes. Erik wheeled around from the teleplate.

"Lida!" he said, his voice hoarse.

Gone were the bitterness and contempt now. "So long, Erik," she replied softly. "I'll do the best I can. Watch for the signal on the control board. I'll send it through when the rocket nozzles are clear—that is, if I'm not blown from the ship."

He swayed for an instant, lurched over to where she stood. "I can't let you do it. Give me the suit, Lida. I'll go." She looked at him, cynical and proud, her eyes glittering like steel and her small chin thrust forward determinedly. These words he had said—what were they but words he flung from him, reaching out to pull together the tatters of his self-respect? She pitied him.

"There's no time for that now," she replied crisply. "Good luck."

On a sudden impulse she darted over to Michael and struck him sharply across the face. He looked up suddenly, his eyes widening in amazement. "Aren't you going to say—good-bye?"

"Lida," he muttered, "don't go. Don't leave us now; it won't do any good, Lida. Take off the suit and we'll all go together."

————

She shook her head defiantly. "No! There's still time. Good-bye, Michael." She fastened on the helmet, her hands cold. Steeling herself against the sudden chill of terror that was seeping through her, she forced herself to the inner door. She pressed the electric release, her hands, heavily swathed, clinging to the steel ring. The panel slid open slowly; a buzzing sound would be filling the cabin now, but she could not hear it. She could feel their eyes on her. With a magnetic clamp in readiness, she waited for the moment when the aperture would be wide enough. Then suddenly, pressing the button in reverse, she plunged through and was hurtled against the wall of the air lock. The magnetic clamp held!

Breathing a deep sigh of relief, Lida glanced around her. The inner door was shut already; this, then, was her final good-bye. There would be no returning to the cabin. She was conscious of a dull, throbbing pain in her arm. It was numb from the impact. Frantically, trying to save time, she worked it up and down until gradually life returned to it. Then she made her way to the ragged-edged gash in the hull. Nothing remained of the outer door. Clinging to a large metal splinter, she made a hurried survey.

The path of the meteor and the damage it had done were clearly visible. It had ploughed a deep welt-like furrow in the side of the ship and piled melted metal and large chunks from the side over the nozzle ends. There were probably meteor fragments as well. But her job would be easy even so. Judicious blasting with the torch would take care of everything. Placing a heavily padded foot in the still-glowing furrow, she detached a magnetic clamp from her belt.

Space lay around her and, as she worked, she felt a nameless dread seep into her being. The face of the planet was directly *above*. Desperately, she tried not to look at it. Despite her efforts, she could not help but glance upward at its looming immensity, cringing as she did so. It was so horribly large—falling on her. It seemed to be drawing her *up*, the way an electromagnet catches a piece of scrap iron. And around her was space, space filled with pinpoints, billiard balls, and footballs of light. She knew she must not stop to look at them. They would charm away her senses and burn out her eyes. She knew this without ever having been told. There was a horror in space, not anything alive, but a dread that chilled and stole away one's life.

Slowly, carefully, she made her way up the side of the ship, using her torch, when necessary, to clear obstructions. Finally she reached the nose, rested against the boldly painted nameplate *Ares*. A sense of the horrible irony of the situation struck her. If they had immediately fired the forward rockets when the meteor struck, the tremendous blast furnace would have melted the obstruction, for, she saw now, it was very slight. Given a chance to harden, however, it was a different story; to blast now, with it there, would blow out the tubes.

She understood, now, why men who had faced all manner of Terrestrial dangers had become weak and helpless here. They had been fools, all of them, to come on this flight without conditioning — space was no place for humans unless they had been conditioned to it gradually. And they had thought themselves so clever in the way they had evaded the requirements for a license.

She pressed the signal button at her waist as the last trace of the obstruction was eaten away. An instant later, there was an answering flash in the small metal tube next to it; they had been watching the control button. A single tear ran down her nose as she thought, "I hope they go to hell, damn them."

Pulling her hand from the magnetic clamp, she straightened up stiffly, and with a hard, quick push jumped clear of the ship. It swerved suddenly and with dizzying violence knocked her clear of their rockets. She had not considered the imminence of them before. The thought of being charred . . .

Earth loomed above her. She had not the acceleration of the ship. Soon it would leave her behind. She would float out here in an orbit of her own, a second moon. Perhaps a meteor would strike her someday; perhaps in the future space voyagers would find her and bring her home. Soon, within an hour at the most, there would be no more air. But why wait hours? With a sudden movement, she threw open the helmet of her suit.

The ship was gone now. Michael and Erik were safe. And something tenuous had clamped itself over her nose and mouth so that she could no longer breathe. For an instant she struggled, lungs bursting, as in the throes of a nightmare. Her thoughts cried out, "Michael! Michael!"

The darkness gathered her in.

DOROTHY LOUISE LES TINA (1917–2003) was an American author and artist who published two short stories and contributed interior art to SF magazines, including *Astonishing Stories*, *Science Fiction Quarterly*, and *Future Fantasy and Science Fiction* in the 1940s (see the entry on Les Tina in chapter 5, "Artists," of this anthology for more details regarding her illustration work). As a young girl, Les Tina moved with her family from her birthplace in Chicago to San Diego, where she eventually graduated from San Diego State Teacher's College. She moved to New York City after her first marriage ended and landed a job as a clerical assistant on the war-depleted staff of Popular Publications in 1942, where she worked her way up to a position as assistant editor and met her second husband, the SF author and editor Frederik Pohl. Pohl introduced her to his network of friends, including various members of the Futurian fan group. Soon after this, Les Tina began contributing interior art and short stories to the SF magazines edited by the Futurian Robert A. W. Lowndes. She joined the military in 1943, serving as an officer in the Women's Army Corps. Her mother joined the Corps a year later, and they "became the first, and to date, the only mother–daughter team to actively serve together" (Romubio).

Les Tina held her military post until 1967, using her writing and organizational talents to serve as a public relations officer and the producer of Soldier Shows in Europe. She married and divorced Pohl in the mid-1940s, taking classes in "theater and paranormal psychology" before settling down with her third husband, Major Raymond E. Johnson, in 1952 (Pohl, *Way* 152–53). During this period Les Tina established herself as an author of romance, domestic comedy, and children's novels while teaching elementary and adult classes on psychical research and creative writing. When Johnson's work took them to Tunisia and Iran, she researched and published a college textbook on the Armenian people. In the 1980s Les Tina and her husband returned to San Diego, where she remained involved with gardening and amateur astronomy until a "short, courageous battle with cancer" ended her life in 2003 (Romubio).

Les Tina's first professional SF sale—"When You Think That . . . Smile!"—is both a classic SF thought-variant tale and an incisive feminist critique of gender relations. Revolving around one man's reaction to the magical tobacco that endows him with telepathy, "When You Think That . . . Smile!" draws on psychology and sociology to consider the complexities of subjectivity that lie beneath the civility and incivility of everyday life. Like her fellow Futurian Leslie Perri in "Space Episode," Les Tina takes particular advantage of the thought-variant story's speculative nature to assess contemporary gender relations with a critical eye. As the narrator's favorite domestic ritual, pipe smoking, is transformed by his special new tobacco, so too are his perceptions of the people who surround him. In particular, Les Tina is careful to map the narrator's changing relations to his wife and the institution of marriage as a whole, providing readers with an object lesson about the interdependencies of families and the need to respect women's work maintaining them. In many ways, then, "When You Think That . . . Smile!" is a bridge between the feminist-socialist utopian works of early-twentieth-century authors such as Leslie F. Stone and Lilith Lorraine, which explored how new domestic technologies might transform gender relations, and the midcentury "women's SF" pioneered by Judith Merril and Alice Eleanor Jones that treated the family and the home as a focusing lens through which to explore the relations of science, society, and sex.

....

"When You Think That . . . Smile!"

Future Fantasy and Science Fiction, February 1943

It began the night I suddenly looked up from my newspaper and stared accusingly at my wife, Martha. I took my pipe out of my mouth.

"Hey," I said.

She looked up. She had been knitting a sweater—now she knitted her brows.

"What's the idea thinking that about *my* mother?" I snapped. "Yours is no prize, not even at a rummage sale."

"Well!" Martha exploded. "Well, that's nice! I haven't said a word, just sat here inhaling your pipe's b.o., all evening, keeping busy—"

"Your mind's been busy, all right! I know you don't like my mother, but at least you might quit picturing her in your mind as being tied to a stake while you jab her with your knitting needles—"

My wife was speechless. Which was unusual in itself. But the unaccustomed quiet didn't warn me—I only saw with oratorical relish that the wavelength was clear for my continued broadcast.

"And another thing," I went on severely, "I know you're planning on some more pants-pocket piracy tonight after I'm asleep. So you lost your allowance at the bridge game yesterday. Why don't you tell me you're broke? Why not be honest about it? And, by the unhappy way, why didn't you mention having scraped the fender of the car today—"

Martha suddenly found her voice. Or maybe it was somebody else's . . . It didn't sound like hers.

"How do you know all those things?" she asked in an awed whisper.

"Why, I . . . I—" I broke off and looked at her. Yes, how *did* I know about them? She hadn't told me. I hadn't even seen the car—but still I knew what had happened.

"I don't know how I know what I know," I finished lamely. I looked up at her and added, "No, I didn't call up the bridge girls to find out if you lost. And my mother hasn't been talking to me about you. And—"

My voice jolted to a halt. Martha's eyes were round and panicky.

"You're saying what I'm *thinking*," she said in a low voice. "You're reading my mind . . ."

"Nonsense," I told her gruffly.

I knocked the ashes out of my pipe into the tub that held our rubber plant and filled up the bowl again from my tobacco pouch. The pungent odor of the shredded leaf pleased me. It was good tobacco. A new blend. I liked it. Little, insignificant thoughts like these wheeled around in my brain. Because I didn't want to think the truth. I didn't want to believe what Martha had said.

But I looked at her again, and knew that she was annoyed that I had put my pipe ash in the tub, and also that she was frightened and confused.

"All right," I said slowly, "so I read your mind. Haven't you ever heard that people who live together a long time get—well—in tune mentally, or something like that, and they can guess what the other person is thinking?"

"You didn't guess . . . You *knew*!" Martha pointed out.

She had me there.

Shades of Houdini, I thought, what's happened to me? I fixed Martha with an eye I tried to keep steady.

"Think of something, anything," I ordered. "As peculiar as you can."

She thought of eating broiled lobster for breakfast. That did it. There was no getting around it, after that. I definitely, uncomfortably, could read her mind.

I told her so, laughing a little shakily. I found I could sense every shade of her thoughts.

I tried to imagine what it would be like meeting people. They wouldn't know about me—and no matter how polite they were, no matter how gracious . . . they wouldn't be able to make their minds polite. The thing had possibilities. But how had it happened? I'm no mystic . . . The closest I've ever been to a séance is a Ouija board. I'm not a student of the occult. Or any other cult, for that matter.

"Think of something else," I asked Martha.

She thought of taking me to a psychiatrist.

"None of that," I told her. "You're not going to get me under a microscope.

This thing has happened, no matter how, and I'm not going to have somebody poking around in my subconscious."

"In fact," I went on, thoughtfully drawing on my pipe, "the only thing to do is take a philosophical attitude about it. It'll come in mighty handy. Say, wouldn't I make a lawyer, though? Or a detective? I'll have to think that over. I could even go into vaudeville. I wouldn't need any stooge to give me hidden clues . . ."

I mused a bit. I was bewildered but excited. This was *something* indeed!

"I still can't believe it. Maybe it will go away," Martha said hopefully.

"Why do you want it to go away? I'm not such a tremendously gifted man that I can punch a sixth or seventh sense, or whatever this is, in the nose."

"I wish it hadn't happened!" Martha's voice was brittle. Martha was not pleased.

"If wishes were Holsteins we'd all have cream on our cornflakes," I observed airily. "Hah, you won't be able to keep *anything* from me anymore!"

"That's what I mean," she answered. "I won't even be able to *think* in private."

I sucked on my pipe's stem, found it was out, dropped it into my coat pocket, went to the closet and got my hat.

I wriggled my fingers at Martha.

"I'm going out for a while—want to find some new victims," I told her. "Keep your mind out of the gutter . . . Remember, I'm the original know-it-all."

"Yes, you're a know-it-all, all right," she observed. She said it with a strained laugh. But there was fear in her eyes. "I can't understand your taking it so calmly."

"I'm hardly calm," I said. "And you can stop thinking about that new fur coat. We can't afford it—"

With that I went out and shut the door softly behind me, neatly severing in two Martha's outraged voice.

I stabbed the button for the elevator, and rocked back and forth on my heels while I waited. I thought about how nice it was to live in an apartment and have no lawn to cut. After I had exhausted that subject mentally my mind began to pick at the problem again. I mean, *the* problem. How and when had I changed from being an ordinary person into . . . Well, what had I changed into?

I heard the elevator slowly and leisurely drawing itself up to my floor hand over hand. Or, I guess I should say, wheel over pulley.

Sam, the milk-chocolate elevator boy, was sleepy. I caught a glimpse of a toothy yawn as the doors slid open. I stepped into the cube.

"Good evening, Sam," I said warily, "how are you tonight?"

He was my first prospect.

"Fine," he said. He hunched his shoulders and yawned again.

———

I knew he was not fine, I knew that he was sleepy, that he was hungry, and that he had lost six dollars in a crap game. The first two I might have guessed—but not the last.

So, when we arrived at the lobby, I smiled innocently and asked, "Why didn't you get out of the game when you were a ten-dollar winner, Sam?"

He looked at me dolefully. "That was mah big mistake. Ah bin thinkin' about that—"

He broke off sharply and his chocolate bon-bon eyes showed a white edge.

"How'd you know?" he asked in a furry whisper.

I smiled. I was enormously pleased with myself.

I produced that venerable, creaking saw that time has mellowed past the point of cleverness.

"Sam," I said, and winked, "a little bird told me."

I left him, then, and stepped confidently out onto the street.

I had walked a block when a beggar stopped me, with that old wheeze about a nickel for a cuppa coffee. Ordinarily I would have given him a coin; now I gimleted him with my eye.

"My good man, you have more money in the bank than I have. Let's see . . . One thousand, two hundred and thirty-nine dollars, if I'm not wrong. And six cents," I added, as he thought of it.

The sidewalk might have been a magnet and his shoes metal to judge by the way he stood perfectly still and stared after me as I walked away. I had suspended his animation, temporarily.

I filled up my pipe, saw that my tobacco was gone, and made a mental reservation to get more, if I could find the same little smoke shop. I sauntered along, puffing gently, like a locomotive on an easy grade.

A swinging-hipped girl passed me. Her eyes were quick and bright and her lips were very red.

"Nuh uh," I murmured, and was gratified to see her nose elevate.

Hey, this thought-reading business had its brighter side.

I walked on, amusing myself by dabbling in the minds of the people who, unhappily for them, shared the sidewalk with me. I learned a lot about human nature. Too much. Some of it I didn't like. I hadn't known people thought such things. Well . . . not in just that way, anyway.

I sighed and shook myself a little. Sometimes it's better not to be too wise. The minds I read, on the whole, were not happy ones. Many of them were mean, selfish. Little minds. It was depressing.

I decided to go home. I was weary of the game. I wanted to see Martha. I felt moody, restless.

The apartment was quiet when I unlocked the front door and walked in.

"Hi, Martha," I called, "the mastermind is back!"

—————

No answer. And for a very good reason. There was no Martha. Instead there was a note pinned to one of the rubber plant's leaves.

I read it twice. And then I sat down and stared at it. But I wasn't seeing it. I was seeing Martha's eyes just before I left. The note was written hastily and to the effect that though I had been a dandy husband in the past . . . I wasn't such great shakes at present. The gist of the thing was that no woman wants a man knowing what she's thinking.

So there I was—a louse without a spouse. And all because my brain cells had gone on a bender. It wasn't fair. It wasn't my fault. I didn't deliberately short-circuit myself.

She wasn't very original. She had gone home to mother. But I wasn't thinking about that. All I knew was that I missed her. More than I thought possible. I tried to call her—and got a phone hung up in my ear.

I stood the emptiness of the apartment for about a half hour and then went out again. I was conveyed down in the elevator, as I had been conveyed up, by a respectful Sam.

I made a mental note of his thoughts, but without interest. I didn't care about anything but having Martha come back. And yet I was certain she wouldn't as long as I stayed the way I was. But, for all I knew, I would never change. I thought of going to a doctor, but somehow I felt that wouldn't help. What could I do, then?

I slouched disconsolately along the street. Every time a person came near I drew back mentally. I didn't want to know what they were thinking about. I had enough thoughts of my own to keep me busy.

I took out my pipe, remembered I was out of tobacco, and put it away. Then I decided to find the smoke shop where I had bought it.

I wandered up one street and down another. What to do? Wryly I decided that I would rather not be a mental giant if wifelessness went with it.

Then I saw the tobacco shop across the street. I jaywalked and almost found myself in the market for a pair of wings and a secondhand harp. (I hear new harps come high.) The driver missed me, however, and I picked up some brand new certain-type words out of his mind.

The shop was still open. It was a little place, wedged in between two many-storied buildings. It was lit by a single bulb in the ceiling.

I pushed open the door and went inside. From the back hurried the small, wrinkled, Egyptian-looking owner.

"Hello," I said, "remember me? I bought some tobacco in here a couple of days ago. I'd like some more. It was a special blend, you said."

I looked at him with lackluster eyes. Idly I wondered what went on in the mind of such an odd-looking person. In a minute I would know. But nothing happened. Nothing at all!

My heart took one leap and then settled down to a steady rhumba. I wasn't able to read his mind! I had blown a fuse, or something.

But he was talking fast, not giving me time to more than nod.

"You the man?" he demanded. "You the man who bought that tobacco? That was a terrible thing I did. I made a mistake. That tobacco is very rare—imported from Turkey—and should not be smoked by everyone. Sometimes it affects them strangely. It's unpredictable. A man can smoke it for a while without anything happening . . . And then, poof!" He made a motion with his hands. "Are you all right—no effects from it?"

I smiled at him. "No," I said cautiously, "I noticed nothing, only that I liked it. You can see for yourself. Will you sell me some more?"

He looked relieved. Then doubtful. But I relied on the fact that not only does money talk—it gives an oration when there's enough of it.

So it was over. I could explain to Martha. I could prove to her, some way, that the gift was gone. She would be able to tell by my relief, if nothing else.

For myself, I was glad I would be able to look at a person again and take him at his face value. I didn't want to know right off what he thought—I wanted to find out a little at a time. It was easier on the nerves. And the illusions.

Why, then, did I want more of the stuff? Well, they say it takes a smart man to understand a woman . . . Anytime Martha puzzled me overly . . . Well, there would always be my pipe . . . and the tobacco . . .

....

Speculative poetry—including SF, horror, fantasy, dark fantasy, speculative, and science verse—has long been part of the SF genre. It appeared in nearly every professional and amateur publication of the 1920s, 1930s, and 1940s, a period that also marked the publication of the first two genre poetry anthologies: August Derlith's edited *Dark Side of the Moon: Poems of Fantasy and the Macabre* (1947) and Lilith Lorraine's single-author chapbook, *Wine of Wonder* (1952). As the prominence of Lorraine's name in this short history suggests, women made significant contributions to the development of speculative poetry. It was in poetry, perhaps more than anywhere else in the SF community, that women were recognized as tastemakers in the field. It was also in poetry—again, perhaps more than anywhere else in SF—that women made meaningful connections with one another. These connections crossed both space and time. Whether they wrote light verse or dark elegy, early women speculative poets often used the techniques first developed by their nineteenth-century predecessors to explore the most pressing scientific and social issues of their time. In doing so, they articulated the issues of gendered aesthetic vision and power relations that are still central to feminist speculative poetry.

The term "speculative poetry" covers many modes of poetic creation, and members of the SF community continue to debate the exact definition of this term. Generally speaking, however, they agree with the Science Fiction Poetry Association founder Suzette Haden Elgin's description of such poetry as that which is "about a reality that is in some way different from the existing reality" and that contains elements of both science and narrative or "story" (12). They also agree that while the history of fantastic poetry, broadly defined, extends back to the *Odyssey* and *Beowulf*, modern speculative verse emerged in the nineteenth century in tandem with widespread literacy, the professionalization of science, and the massive expansion of industrialism. For example, William Blake, Samuel Coleridge, and Edgar Allen Poe experimented with new patterns of accentual verse to produce a sense of wonder (and sometimes dread) about the modern world; Walt Whitman pioneered the use of free verse to articulate his cosmic visions; and Charles Baudelaire employed symbolism to create what he called the atmosphere of modernity. Elsewhere, Robert Burns incorporated dialect into his fantastic poetry to make his world-building more persuasive, while George Gordon, Lord Byron, and John Keats updated mythic heroes and villains for modern readers.[1]

Like their male counterparts, the dozens of (often wildly popular) women writers who wrote nineteenth-century fantastic verse experimented with form, dialect, and character development. They also contributed to their chosen genre in two other ways. Authors including Felicia Hemans, Laetitia Elizabeth Landon, and Adelaide Proctor drew on the "hidden world of the nineteenth-century woman" to demonstrate the power of imagination, especially as it enabled middle-class women with limited education or travel opportunities to cast themselves as the heroines of fantastic adventures (Spivack 63). For example, the female narrator of Proctor's "Pictures in a Fire" both capitalizes on and transcends her life as a domestic angel by looking into the hearth with her child and seeing, among the flames, fantastic worlds populated by adventurous knights and powerful fairies. Here then, the narrator—and, by extension, Proctor herself—asserts both her authority to craft strange new worlds and the value of drawing on subject matter from the private sphere of the home to do so.

In a related vein, nineteenth-century women writers such as Sara Coleridge, Jean Ingelow, and Christina Rossetti used the fantastic worlds of speculative poetry to articulate their discontent with the here and now while imagining other times and places where women become the heroes of their own stories. As the fantasy scholar Charlotte Spivack explains, "For these women, fantasy was not merely a subject but also a language. Unable to participate actively in the political and economic life of their time and unable to communicate with anyone about their hidden dreams and desires, they expressed their subjective experience of reality in the literary language of fantasy" (63). Rossetti's often-anthologized "Goblin Market" is particularly important in this respect, as it celebrates the adventures of two young women whose journeys through the fantastic space of the goblin market allow them to test (and, in the case of the second sister, prove) the claim that feminists of their own time made regarding the ability of women to succeed in the masculine world of the public sphere.

Given the diversity of nineteenth-century experiments with speculative verse—not to mention the prominence of the authors who engaged in them—it is no surprise that early-twentieth-century genre magazines featured poetry on a regular basis. Such poetry generally took one of two forms: light SF verse in which authors celebrated human control over nature, especially with "visions of voyaging outward among bright destinations," or dark fantasy and horror poems in which authors spun tales of "frightful creatures and happenings" that revealed the helplessness of humans in the face of natural and supernatural forces alike (Sneyd, *Fierce* 4). Hugo Gernsback introduced the use of light SF verse as filler in his early radio magazines and continued this practice in *Amazing Stories* and other SF publications. Meanwhile the editors Edwin Baird, Farnsworth Wright, and Dorothy McIlwraith all prominently featured darker, more experimental forms of poetry in the pages of *Weird Tales*, a magazine dedicated to showcasing the best in genre fiction across forms.[2]

The opening decades of the twentieth century also marked the appearance of SF's first poetry group, the Cosmic or Stellar poets. Influenced by the mainstream poet George Stirling's 1902 opus, *The Testimony of the Suns*, Clark Ashton Smith, Stanton A. Coblentz, and Lilith Lorraine worked both separately and together to produce a new mode of verse that would use "powerfully colorful imagery" to "express strong, and strangely universe-conscious, emotional reactions to the vastness of time and space, to futures wondrous or terrible" (Sneyd, *Fierce* 13). Although largely forgotten now, the Cosmic poets inspired their midcentury successors to create the first generation of SF poetry magazines, including Lorraine's small-press publication *Challenge* and Orma McCormick's fanzine *Starlanes*, where even letters to the editor were written in verse. They also influenced the careers of another prominent midcentury SF group: the Futurians, who counted among them the would-be authors and editors Isaac Asimov, Frederik Pohl, and Judith Merril. Many Futurians tried their hand at poetry before establishing themselves in other areas of SF. Indeed, at least two — Pohl and Merril's sometime-housemate Virginia Kidd — made their debuts with speculative verse.

Like their nineteenth-century predecessors, twentieth-century women writers were active participants in all kinds of speculative poetry, and, indeed, their work often paid homage to those who came before them. Gernsback was particularly well known for supporting women's participation in the SF community, so it is no surprise that he and his editorial staff featured about half a dozen women poets in the pages of *Amazing* and its sister magazines. The most prominent of these was Julia Boynton Green, an American poet whose accomplishments were celebrated in Frances Elizabeth Willard and Mary Ashton Rice Livermore's 1897 treatise, *American Women: Fifteen Hundred Biographies with over 1,400 Portraits — A Comprehensive Encyclopedia of the Lives and Achievements of American Women in the Nineteenth Century*. In poems such as "The Night Express," Green depicts the march of technocultural progress in a thoroughly Gernsbackian way without reference to sex or gender. However, in "Radio Revelations" and "Evolution," she also pays homage to the female speculative poets who preceded her with poems that employ domestic settings and motifs as the starting point for fantastic adventures.

By way of contrast, the poems published by Leah Bodine Drake in *Weird Tales* present readers with dark worlds where women reject human society to embrace dreadful but liberating supernatural forces. While Drake's poetic voice pays homage to Burns and her modernization of mythic figures (especially the witch and the werewolf) is clearly in dialogue with that of Byron and Keats, she departs from her predecessors by refusing to import the values of patriarchy into her fantastic worlds. For Drake, female mythic figures are not a threat to or reward for heroic men. Rather, the heroines of "They Run Again" and "The Wood-Wife" are fully realized people who reject the company of human men for that of werewolves and demons. Like Green, Drake wrote poems, such as "Sea-Shell," that invoked the work of her nineteenth-century female predecessors, particularly in their evocation of mundane objects that trigger fantastic flights of imagination. Taken together, Green's and Drake's poems illustrate the unique contributions that women made to the two poles of speculative verse most frequently featured in early-twentieth-century genre magazines.

Women's work as tastemakers in the ongoing development of speculative poetry is perhaps best represented by Lilith Lorraine, the pioneering SF author, editor, and publisher who is often credited with having published the first magazine dedicated entirely to SF poetry (*Challenge*) and the first book of SF verse (*Wine of Wonder*). A Christian socialist feminist and self-described Leonarda who won numerous prizes for her contributions to the arts, Lorraine began her career as a prose fiction writer for the Gernsbackian pulps before transferring her allegiance to "prophetic" poetry, which, she claimed, "is not an escape but a challenge, not a daydream but a blueprint, not the Swan-Song of an old world but the Dawn-Song of a new" (qtd. in "Lilith Lorraine"). The diversity of Lorraine's literary experience is reflected in the diversity of her verse: while poems such as "Earthlight on the Moon" provide readers with thoroughly Gernsbackian celebrations of human progress, others such as "The Acolytes" demonstrate her skill at conveying a sense of cosmic horror. Still other Lorraine poems, such as "Men Keep Strange Trysts," demonstrate her belief that SF can and should provide political critique as well.

Women poets were also active participants in fan culture. When genre readers began to produce fanzines in the 1930s, "the presence of poetry in the pulp magazines they read . . . made the idea of using poetry in their own publications seem . . . natural" (Sneyd, *Elsewhen* n.p.). Moreover, the prominence of women poets in the pulp magazines seems to have made the idea of featuring them in amateur publications natural as well. Following in the footsteps of Green and Lorraine, Virginia Kidd dreamed in verse of young people, scientists, and other visionaries working together to build better futures for all. Like other Futurians, Kidd published just one short, untitled SF poem early in her career before moving on to work as a literary agent and editor. But she carried the lessons she learned from Lorraine and other female speculative poets with her throughout her career. Kidd is often celebrated for her advocacy of strong-minded female (and often overtly feminist) authors, and she was instrumental in publishing the new generation of literarily trained and politically active poets who emerged in the 1960s and 1970s as part of the New Wave movement.

Meanwhile, the poems published in the *Acolyte* by Tigrina—the pen name of the SF fan and pioneering lesbian journalist Edith Eyde—present readers with dark worlds where supernaturally talented women are persecuted for their differences. Like Drake, Tigrina continues the tradition of updating mythic figures to reflect feminist rather than patriarchal values. But she takes this process a step further than her professional counterpart. When Tigrina's witches and vampires reject human men, they do not turn to their supernatural male counterparts for comfort or company. Instead, in "Defiance" and "Affinity," they seek out one another to create communities of like-minded women. In this respect Tigrina's poetry is much like that of Sara Coleridge and Christina Rossetti before her, using fantastic spaces contiguous with the real world to critically assess how women are prevented from exercising power while imagining how they might use their unique talents to overcome oppression and become the heroines of their own life stories. Taken together, the women featured in this chapter of *Sisters of Tomorrow* serve as an important bridge between nineteenth-century experiments with speculative verse and modern SF poetic practice. Writers such as Green, Drake, and Tigrina updated the poetic techniques first developed by Byron, Keats, Proctor, and Rossetti to assert women's scientific and social authority in the modern world. Meanwhile, Lorraine and Kidd incorporated the youthful energy and expansionist vision of the Gernsbackian pulp magazines into their own verse, demonstrating how poets might join scientists and prose SF authors in the shared project of preparing readers for what was sure to be an increasingly technological and global future. While the rhymed and metered verse in which these early-twentieth-century poets wrote has fallen out of favor in modern SF poetry, the themes they addressed—including the promises and perils of technology, the wonder of the universe beyond everyday human experience, and the role of women in the creation of brave new worlds—are still central to SF in all its forms today.

JULIA BOYNTON GREEN (1861–1957) was an American poet whose light verse epitomized the sense of wonder often associated with early magazine SF. Born in Boston, Green briefly attended college at Wellesley and studied art in London before returning home to care for her sick mother. At this time Green began publishing poetry in local journals and the *Boston Transcript*. Her first book of verse, *Lines and Interlines*, appeared in 1887 and was described as "strikingly excellent" in Frances Elizabeth Willard and Mary Ashton Rice Livermore's *American Women . . . A Comprehensive Encyclopedia of the Lives and Achievements of American Women in the Nineteenth Century* (1897).

Subsequent life events—including marriage, an extended tour of Europe, and a permanent relocation to California in 1893—delayed Green's next book for more than forty years. The publication of *This Enchanted Coast: Verse on California Themes* in 1928 (followed by *Noonmark* in 1936) established Green as one of what the poet Brian Kim Stefans calls a "lost generation" of poets who participated in the tradition of "Los Angeles boosterism" to encourage emigration (n.p.). But while other artists associated with this tradition uncritically celebrated the merits of West Coast life, Green's often fantastic but always thoughtful explorations of human and technological encroachment on California's native landscape set her apart from her peers and, in Stefans's estimation, "could have [earned her] a national audience" (n.p.).

Green found this national audience with her poetry for *Amazing Stories* and *Amazing Stories Quarterly*, where she was the second most frequently published poet of her day.[3] The founder of *Amazing*, Hugo Gernsback, introduced the use of light verse (i.e., brief, often humorous poems featuring word play, striking rhyme schemes, and heavy alliteration) as filler in his radio magazines, and he continued this tradition with his SF publications. In formal terms, Green's verse was ideally suited for such purposes. Green was an anti-modernist who railed against free verse, "and so her poetic style never much transcended what she had already developed in her youth; [her] taste for sonnets, ballads and rhyming couplets persists well into the 20th century" (Stefans n.p.). Her work was also a good match to the *Amazing* franchise in terms of content. Poems such as "Evolution" and "Radio Revelations" celebrate human mastery over time and space in the playful, optimistic manner often associated with Gernsbackian SF. Even Green's more critical offerings, such as "The Night Express," speculate about the future of human–machine relations in a thoroughly science fictional manner. By asking readers to consider what might happen if our creations became more lively than we are, Green establishes herself as part of a speculative tradition that begins with Mary Shelley's *Frankenstein* (1818) and continues with writers of cyberpunk and post-singularity SF today.[4]

While Green wrote about the same range of scientific and technological topics that fascinated her male counterparts, she often used the techniques of her nineteenth-century female predecessors to stake claims for women in the modern world. Like poems written by Felicia Hemans and Adelaide Proctor nearly one hundred years earlier, Green's "Radio Revelations" uses the encounter with an everyday domestic object as the occasion to exercise a truly fantastic female imagination. However, while Hemans and Proctor seized upon traditionally feminine objects such as laundry and the hearth to enable their flights of proto-feminist fancy, Green explores how feminine encounters with masculine objects (such as the titular radio) might enable women to imaginatively recast the entire universe as domestic comedy. Green also follows the precedent set by authors such as Jean Ingelow and Christina Rossetti by making women the heroes of their own adventures. This is most obvious in "Radio Revelations," but it is also central to "Evolution," which asks readers to accept modern theories of human development based not on intellectual fads that come and go but on the lasting gut instincts of the narrator herself. Thus Green makes the female poet with sensibility—rather than the male scientist with sense—the true champion of modernity. This was certainly true of Green as a poet herself: while contemporary readers might find her writing style and celebration of domesticity to be distinctly old-fashioned, Green's insistence on playing with shifts in perspective and questions of gendered authority are very much at the heart of modern feminist SF poetry as it is written by Ursula K. Le Guin, Margaret Atwood, and Jane Yolen today.[5]

"The Night Express"

Amazing Stories, July 1931

Man's scanty merits from his faults I sift
    Disheartened at the residue. When—hark!
    There goes the night express, nicknamed "The Lark"!
I feel my heart grow big—grow light—and lift!
Our sinner still has wonders in his gift.
    Listen to that racing engine's joyous bark—
    A steel-thewed greyhound speeding through the dark,
Staunch, steady, proud, magnificently swift!

The erring human gentles to his need
    Wind, water, lightning; will he miss the goal
Of mental strife? Or being of the breed

Of conquerors will he lose his grip of soul?
Master of metals, motors, wheels, and wings,
Will Man descend to be the thrall of Things?

. . . .

"Evolution"
Amazing Stories, August 1931

Long have wise folk a baffling secret sought—
The mystery of human origins.
A theory rises—sinks; another wins
A transient credence. Some men will have naught
Of simian kin, nor bear the shocking thought
Of simple earthly sources of our sins
And virtues. These are valiant paladins.
But by slight hints may not deep truths be taught?

Often when strolling idly out of doors
The joy of upright carriage thrills me through—
As though in some dim past I'd gone "all-fours"!
And often speech, or victory in some test
Of wits, stirs quick surprise, a wonder new,
As though I'd once lacked language, groped,
    and guessed!

. . . .

"Radio Revelations"
Amazing Stories Quarterly, Fall–Winter 1932

Before John's new receiving set
I listened, half expecting
The music of the spheres to get,
Some stellar fugue or canzonet,
Man's chatter intersecting.
Instead, from empyrean heights
Celestial gossip drifted;
The greater and the lesser lights
It seems have frolics, feuds, and fights,
Even as the less uplifted.

"It's scandalous how Orion goes,"
Quoth Vega in high dudgeon,
"Can't he afford some pants and hose?
"Or is it that he loves to pose
"In just his belt and bludgeon?"
Then Vesta scolded, "Listen, pray!
"Those wild beasts—where's their cager?
"As I went down the Milky Way
"To get my Pasteurized Grade A
"He *bit* me—Ursa Major!

"Of course, surprised, I had no show—
"I whacked him with my slipper,
"But Aries, Serpens, Scorpio
"And Taurus joined the scrap and so
"I brandished the Big Dipper.
"Then pranced up Sagittarius
"And shot them! How I kissed him!
"We two then harnessed Pegasus
"To Charles's Wain—absurd old bus—
"And ranged the Solar System.

"Now don't tell, Dearie, on your word
"Of honor as a planet;
"The cause of Mars' red face I've heard
"*Is booze!* He's sure the gay old bird—
"It's years since he began it."
Then burst forth Vega, "What's the use
"Of Luna's mad endeavor
"To change her figure and 'reduce'
"When in one month—the silly goose—
"She'll be as round as ever?

"There's Berenice! She's marcelled her hair!
"Her cute dog star she's leading.
"Here kid—take Cassiopeia's Chair.
"What news?—You don't say! Did they dare?
"*Young Comet pinched for speeding?*
"Well! Well! I've, too, a tale to stir;

"Now Venus is no pattern,
"We all know that, but Jupiter
"Is worse—I'm not much blaming her—
"*She has eloped with Saturn!*

"Of course she's flirted lots, my dears,
"But Saturn's been her 'steady.'
"He has a bad 'case' it appears,
"Old softy! Why he's had for years
"A *choice of rings* all ready!"

"This Radio," I rejoiced, "what fun!
"And cheaper than a movie."
Just then John's voice boomed like a gun,
"Wake up, old girl—it's half past one.
"And put the cat out, Lovey."

VIRGINIA KIDD (1921–2003) was a Pennsylvania-born literary agent, editor, and author who influenced the development of American SF over the course of the twentieth century. Trained in Spanish, Italian, Latin, French, and German at the Berlitz School of Languages, Kidd began reading her brother's SF magazines at the age of nine and, by the age of eleven, was sending letters to the editorial columns of those magazines on a regular basis. She quickly became close friends (by correspondence) with SF fans across the country and, at the age of sixteen, was engaged briefly (again, by correspondence) to the Futurian Robert A. W. Lowndes. During World War II Kidd relocated to New York, where Lowndes introduced her to other Futurians, including her soon-to-be housemate, Judith Merril, and her future husband, James Blish. In 1945 Kidd helped the Futurians create the Vanguard Amateur Press for the dissemination of SF fanzines; a decade later, she collaborated with Blish and Damon Knight to establish the Milford Writers Workshop, which still takes place annually.[6]

Kidd published her own SF fiction and poetry sporadically throughout the midcentury decades but was, as she herself put it, mostly a "writer in the cracks" who excelled at putting other authors in touch with the right editor or press (qtd. in Liptak, "Clients"). Accordingly, in 1965 she established the Virginia Kidd Literary Agency, where she represented such writers as Judith Merril, Gene Wolfe, Anne McCaffrey, and Ursula K. Le Guin. Kidd was the first female literary agent in the SF community and an ardent advocate of New Wave and feminist experiments in SF. In 1970 Kidd launched the poetry magazine *Kinesis* and, with it, the mainstream poetry career of SF author Sonya Dorman. Later that decade, she edited several important speculative fiction anthologies, including *Saving Worlds: A Collection of Original Science Fiction Stories* (1973, with editor and author Roger Elwood), *Millennial Women* (1978, which earned Kidd a Locus Award), and *Edges: Thirteen New Tales from the Borderlands of the Imagination* (1980, with her client and friend Le Guin). Kidd continued writing "in the cracks" throughout her life, publishing her last short story, "Ok, O Che? by K.," in 1995 and her last poem, "Argument," in 1998. Kidd was also an active member of First Fandom (an organization for fans who were active in the SF community before the first WorldCon in 1939) until her death in 2003.

Kidd is remembered primarily for her accomplishments as an agent and editor, but she was quite literally first and last an SF fan and poet. The short untitled poem included here—first published in the *Fantasy Fan* when Kidd was just twelve years old—captures the energy of both the young Kidd in particular and the nascent SF fan community in general. As the SF poet and historian Steve Sneyd notes, the first generation of fan poets (including Kidd and fellow Futurians Frederik Pohl and Cyril Kornbluth) found it "natural" to emulate the style and content of their professional counterparts (*Elsewhen* n.p.). Kidd was no exception. In six short lines, she cheerfully projects a world where young people make a clean break with the past, using "science and knowledge" to build a fantastic new future. This vision of youth-driven technocultural progress is very much in line with that of Hugo Gernsback and many of the authors associated with the *Amazing* franchise, including Lilith Lorraine and Leslie F. Stone (both of whom are featured in this anthology). Meanwhile, Kidd's use of light verse is reminiscent of the stylistic techniques employed by one of *Amazing*'s most popular poets, Julia Boynton Green (also featured in this anthology). Indeed, while Lorraine, Stone, and Green can be seen as transitional figures who used the techniques of nineteenth-century women fantasy poets to explore twentieth-century technocultural hopes and fears, Kidd can be seen as a figure whose career connects the practices of women writing SF in the early twentieth century to those who are doing so today.

"Untitled"
Fantasy Fan, December 1933

Science and Knowledge,
And strong youth and power—
Science, the creed of a nation!
New customs for old,
New ways, a new mold—
The tale of the New Generation!

LEAH BODINE DRAKE (1904–64) was a Kansas-born poet, editor, and critic. She attended the Hamilton College for Women in Kentucky and worked briefly as a dancer for the American impresario Billy Rose of Ziegfeld Follies fame before turning her attention full time to literary endeavors. Drake sold her first poem to *Weird Tales* in 1935 and became the second-most-published poet in that magazine (following Dorothy Quick, featured elsewhere in this anthology). Her verse appeared in August Derleth's groundbreaking genre anthology, *Dark of the Moon* (1947), as well as prestigious mainstream venues including the *Poetry Chapbook*, the *New Yorker*, and the *Saturday Evening Post*. Drake published three collections of poetry (the last appearing posthumously), served as a poetry critic for the *Atlantic Monthly*, and earned prizes that included two Borestone Mountain Poetry Awards and several Poetry Society of America Awards. She was proud to count herself among the Daughters of the American Revolution—her ancestors included Davy Crockett—and was listed in *Who's Who in American Poetry* as well as the 1958 supplement to *Who's Who in America*.[7]

Given Drake's heritage, it is perhaps no surprise that her poetry is part and parcel of the American weird tradition extending back to Edgar Allen Poe and Nathaniel Hawthorne. As the SF poet and historian Steve Sneyd explains, early European settlers on the American East Coast gravitated toward what we would now call weird or horror storytelling as a way of managing anxiety about what they perceived to be the suffocating vegetation, dangerous animals, and alien—even demonic—native inhabitants of their new home (*Fierce* 6). In a similar vein, the short biography included on the dust jacket of Drake's first book of verse, *A Hornbook for Witches* (1950), notes that the author's "choice of the macabre in poetry comes naturally, for her earliest memories include the tremendous silences of the Navajo country, the woods and swamps of the deep South, and tales of 'ha'nts' told by Aunt Coopie, a Negro member of the household." And indeed, while the narrators of poems such as "They Run Again" and "The Wood-Wife" speak in watered-down versions of the rural British dialects popularized by Robert Burns a century earlier, the heavy oaks, fern-thick forests, and supernatural animal-human hybrids that inhabit them are clearly indebted to the American landscapes with which Drake was most familiar.

Like the creative output of many other women associated with the early genre magazine community, Drake's poetry can be seen as a bridge between the practices of her nineteenth-century predecessors and the sensibilities of contemporary feminist SF authors. This is particularly apparent in "Sea-Shell," which, like the poems of Felicia Hemans and Adelaide Proctor, uses the narrator's encounter with an everyday object as the occasion to imagine strange new worlds and celebrate the female poet's creative agency. But while Hemans and Proctor focus on the domestic objects of the nineteenth-century middle-class housewife's domain, Drake's narrator draws inspiration from the wider natural world through which she roams. The refusal of women to be confined by enclosed domestic spaces and the traditional gender roles associated with them is a common thread throughout Drake's work, informing the actions of the heroines in both "The Wood-Wife" and "They Run Again." In these poems, women refuse the safety of good homes and well-established men, preferring instead to take their chances with treacherous terrains and supernatural creatures. As such, Drake's verse tells a tale about the lengths to which women will go in their attempts to escape patriarchy, a tale that informs a number of twentieth-century feminist SF stories, including Lilith Lorraine's "The Celestial Visitor" (1935) and James Tiptree, Jr.'s celebrated classic, "The Women Men Don't See" (1973).

....

"They Run Again"
Weird Tales, June–July 1939

Beyond the black and naked wood
In frosty gold has set the sun,
And dusk glides forth in cobweb hood . . .
Sister, tonight the werewolves run!

With white teeth gleaming and eyes aflame
The werewolves gather upon the howe!
Country churl and village dame,
They have forgotten the wheel and plow.

They have forgotten the speech of men;
Their throats are dry with a dreadful thirst;
And woe to the traveller in the glen
Who meets tonight with that band accurst!

Now from the hollows creeps the dark;
The moon like a yellow owl takes flight;
Good people on their house doors mark
A cross, and hug their hearths in fright.

Sister, listen! The King Wolf howls!
The pack is running! . . . Drink down the brew.

Don the unearthly, shaggy cowl, —
We must be running, too!

....

"The Wood-Wife"
Weird Tales, March 1942

In a hollow oak tree
  I live by the wood,
A bit more than human
  And far less than good.

I've queer spells, and potent spells,
  That I went to learn
From the goat-hooved and shaggy ones
  Who hide in the fern.

The good-wives, the house-wives
  They shudder at my sin:
But much they'd give to learn to weave
  Cloth of spider's-spin!

My pet fox, my russet fox,
  He ravishes their geese:
Yet none dare call out the hounds
  If they would know peace!

On a day of falling leaves
  I met the young Squire.
I gave him a sideways look
  That set his face afire.

The bonny young Squire,
  He dreams in a spell;
But not of golden curlylocks
  Of Parson Jones' Nell—
But of red hair, and green eyes
  That have looked on hell!

Dream, pretty Squire-kin!
  It's small use to burn!

For when the moon is up
    The wood-wife will turn

Three times widdershins,
    And greet where you stood
The shagged-men, the satyr-men
    Who creep from the wood!

....

"Sea-Shell"

Weird Tales, September 1943

Stranded upon the sand
    Here is a twisted shell:
    Lift it within your hand,
    Press it against your ear;
    Listen! . . . And you will hear
    Echo of deep-sea bell
Ringing in belfry beneath the brine,
Where mermaidens, scaled with tourmaline,
    Toll a dolorous knell.
'Tis the voice of a city beneath the sea!
Gold-eyed fishes stare endlessly
At turrets and ramparts of porphyry
    Drowned in the gold-green well.

Who built that city forlorn?
    What was its perilous fame
    That tymbal and gong and horn
    Blared from the torch-lit wall?
    When did its doom befall?
    What was the reason it came
Crashing down over palace and keep,
A sea that rose like a mountain steep,
    Quenching the living flame?
Hark! Does the sea-shell's echoes tell
The name of that city before she fell?
Ah no! I can hear its cry, its bell,
    But never its fabulous name!

TIGRINA is one of several pen names used by the American editor, author, and singer-songwriter Edith Eyde (b. Edythe Eyde in 1921). Eyde grew up on an apricot ranch in Fremont, California, where she studied violin. In 1945, after two years of college and a secretarial course, she relocated to Los Angeles and took on work as a secretary at RKO studios. By that time Eyde was already an active participant in the Los Angeles Science Fiction Society, where she was nicknamed Tigrina by her good friend and writing partner, Forrest J Ackerman. As Tigrina, Eyde published *Hymn to Satan* (the first fanzine dedicated to filk, or SF and fantasy music), served as an associate editor of the Detroit-based SF fanzine the *Mutant*, and wrote poetry and stories (some coauthored with Ackerman) for a number of other amateur genre publications.

While Eyde's involvement with SF fandom did not lead to a career as a professional SF writer, it had a profound influence on her work as a pioneering lesbian journalist. When Eyde came out in 1946, she drew upon her experience with fanzine culture to produce and distribute *Vice Versa*, the first publication in the world devoted to lesbian issues.[8] *Vice Versa* ran for more than ten years and, as the media historian Rodger Streitmatter argues, its provocative mix of editorials, book and movie reviews, and SF stories "set the agenda that has dominated lesbian and gay journalism for fifty years" (2). When *Vice Versa* folded in 1958, Eyde took the pen name Lisa Ben (an anagram for "lesbian") and became a journalist for the *Ladder*, the first nationally distributed lesbian magazine.[9] In 1972 Eyde was formally honored by the gay rights organization ONE, Inc., for the creation of *Vice Versa*. Since then she has appeared in numerous documentaries, including the 1984 film *Before Stonewall*. In 1997 Eyde was honored as a founding member of the Los Angeles LGBT community, and in 2010 she was inducted into the National Lesbian and Gay Journalists' Association Hall of Fame.

Given the influence of SF fandom on her career as a lesbian journalist, it is no surprise that Eyde explores LGBT themes in her speculative poetry. While SF writers rarely included out LGBT characters or worlds founded on alternative modes of sexuality until the advent of New Wave and feminist SF in the 1960s, the SF author and editor Nicola Griffith argues that LGBT readers (and writers) have a certain affinity with the mutants, aliens, and other outsider characters found in speculative fiction because "in a largely heterosexual society we are, after all, often treated as aliens" (7). This certainly seems to be true of Tigrina's "Affinity" and "Defiance," both of which sympathetically depict vampires and witches as brave outsiders in search of a like-minded community. In many ways, Tigrina's poems seem to pay homage to *Weird Tales* veterans Dorothy Quick and Leah Bodine Drake, both of whom regularly featured strong, supernaturally talented women in their weird verse (for further discussion, see the entries on Quick and Drake in this anthology). But while their association with the paranormal sometimes destroys Quick's heroines and Drake's protagonists ally themselves with preternatural men, the women of Tigrina's worlds survive persecution by forming bonds with one another across space and time. As such, her poems anticipate the kinds of stories told today by Elizabeth Lynn, Mercedes Lackey, and the dozens of authors featured in Nicola Griffith and Stephen Pagel's award-winning *Bending the Landscape* anthology series.

....

"Defiance"

Acolyte, Winter 1945

The church bells toll on sabbath morn
And I must don my finest gown,
And with my family sally forth
To go to church in Hilltop-town.
Yes, I must step through yawning doors
Into that holy atmosphere,
While all within me crawls and cringes,
Half in loathing, half in fear.
And I must sit with folded hands
Sedate and prim within my chair,
And listen to the preacher's drone
And bow my head in humble prayer.
And I must sing their foolish hymns
And raise my voice in harmony.
But I insert a word or two
And change it to a blasphemy.
At all these good and holy things
My inward spirit doth rebel,
And fervently, though silently,
I call upon the King of Hell.
I pity these poor simple folk
Who spend their lives on bended knee.
Uninteresting people they,
How boring paradise must be!

You ask, do I not dread the day
When I must for my sins atone?
Ah no, Hell is a welcome place.

I know the Devil loves his own!
My family is a pious lot,
And by their laws I must abide,
But they forget. In Salem-town
Some of their forebears lived and died.
My great-great-grandma, long ago,
Was burned for deeds that she had done.
'Tis said that I resemble her.
I do . . . and in more ways than one!

．．

"Affinity"
Acolyte, Spring 1945

You, too, are tainted with the Vampire strain
The same blood surges through us both, like wine.
No wonder that our thoughts and moods combine
And merge beyond the common, earthly plane.
Forbidden arts, weird rites, and devil lore,
Such things are legends now, but they have been
Reality beyond mere human ken,
And they shall flourish in this world once more.

No longer must I walk the earth alone.
Together we shall prowl in ebon nights
And share our secret joys and dark delights
While venturing into the vast unknown,
Flesh of my flesh, blood of my blood, thou art
My shadow, twin, and living counterpart.

LILITH LORRAINE (1894–1967) was a pioneering American SF author, poet, and editor (for more details about her life, see the entry on Lorraine in chapter 1, "Authors," of this anthology). While she was involved in nearly every aspect of early SF production, her contributions to the development of genre poetry were particularly noteworthy. When she began publishing short stories in the early 1930s, Lorraine described herself as a "sometimes poet," but by the end of the decade she was almost exclusively writing and publishing verse. August Derlith featured her work in the weird poetry anthology *Fire and Sleet and Candlelight* (1961), and Lorraine's own *Wine of Wonder* (1952) was touted as the first anthology of SF verse. In the 1940s Lorraine created the Avalon World Arts Academy as a training ground for mainstream and speculative poets alike, many of whom were featured in the two little magazines she began publishing at that time: the *Raven*, a zine dedicated to Edgar Allen Poe, and *Different*, a publication devoted to politically engaged fantastic fiction and poetry. In 1950 she brought out *Challenge*, the first dedicated SF poetry magazine. *Challenge* folded after just four issues, but Lorraine continued to edit the *Raven* and other SF poetry magazines and anthologies until her death in 1967. Over the course of her career, she received several prizes, "including the Arizona State Poetry Prize, a Gold Medal and citation from the Governor of Morelos, Mexico, and the Old South Award from the Poetry Society of Texas" (Wagner, n.p.).

Along with fellow genre poets Clark Ashton Smith and Stanton A. Coblentz, Lorraine led the Cosmic or Stellar poetry movement, advocating the use of "powerfully colorful imagery" to convey to readers "the vastness of time and space [and] futures wondrous or terrible" (Sneyd, *Fierce* 13). As a political progressive and the only Cosmic poet who began in SF rather than weird fiction, it is perhaps no surprise that Lorraine often celebrates in her verse the possibility of collective human action leading to the end of scarcity and the beginning of human dominion over the universe, as in her first professional SF poem, "Earthlight on the Moon" (1941). But Lorraine was nothing if not multidimensional, and in poems such as "The Acolytes" (1946), she projects futures where eldritch powers gain dominion over Earth—much to the delight of the narrator, who welcomes any change in the human status quo. Elsewhere, Lorraine's poetry more directly criticizes capitalist greed, as in the 1946 poem "Men Keep Strange Trysts," which was included in Lorraine's FBI file as proof of her suspect politics. Taken together, these works illustrate Lorraine's belief that poetry "is the atomic energy of the soul, which exploded against the battlements of hate and terror will level them in the dust of oblivion and leave the liberated soul free in an expanding universe" (Lorraine, "Story" 4).

"Earthlight on the Moon"
Stirring Science Stories, June 1941

Yes, we shall see them, men against the stars,
A federated planet, proud and free;
When grown aweary of their pygmy wars,
They hurl their legions through eternity.

Yes, we shall see their silver starships daring
Wherever worlds are waiting to be won,
Against the battlements of darkness faring,
Against the flaming fortress of the sun.

And then at least when against their gods of greed they leaven,
And glorify the man of simple worth,
Then we shall see them pluck the stars from heaven,
And set them in the diadem of Earth.

Yes, poets at last shall sing and lovers croon
Beneath the emerald Earthlight on the moon.

"The Acolytes"
Acolyte, Spring 1946

The Elder Ones are stirring as the red
Stallions of chaos champ their bits with rage;
And they have sent their messengers ahead
Proud with the knowledge of their alienage.

They walk apart from men, the Acolytes,
By stagnant pools and rotting sepulchers,
Whispering of dark, delirious delights,
As young gods die among their worshippers.

They dream of dim dimensions where the towers
Of Yuggoth pierce the decomposing dome
Of skies where dead stars float like evil flowers
Afloat on tideless seas of poisoned foam.

Black tapers glow on many a ruined shrine,
The patterns coalesce—the good, the bad—
The old familiar stars no longer shine—
And I—and I—am curiously glad.

....

"Men Keep Strange Trysts"

Different, June–July 1946

Men keep strange trysts before the Judgment Day;
Meet many a Dark Companion face to face;
Sign fearful covenants, the crimson way,
Beneath the thick veil of the commonplace.

Covens more colorful but less accursed
Profaned the dawn-world—demon-wings were wide—
They cast a fearful shadow at their worst,
But seared no offending countryside.

Gone are the lost, ineffable delights
Evoked from witches' urn and wizard-spell—
But nations sell their souls in scarlet rites,
And gold is still the currency of hell.

3 JOURNALISTS

SF and science journalism have long been intertwined. One of the first modern science journalists was H. G. Wells, and many of the newspapers and magazines that first published science columns published SF stories as well (*History*). Conversely, science writing has been part of genre magazine culture since its inception. As in other areas of SF, women contributed to the development of this tradition in diverse ways, producing everything from short filler pieces on basic science to lavishly illustrated and densely researched serial columns on controversial topics, including race, gender, and evolution. For the most part, these authors followed the new rules for science writing developed by the newspaper publisher E. W. Scripps's Science Service. But their writing was also characterized by a willingness to redefine the process of scientific discovery, a desire to assert lay authority, and a celebration of the fine line between fact and fiction that was characteristic of the early SF community and that anticipates new styles of science journalism today.

Modern science journalism emerged at the turn of the century in tandem with the professionalization of both science and newspaper publishing. Following the "information" versus "story" models of reporting that were fashionable at the time, early forays into science journalism were either dry and technical or sensational and derisive of science as an egghead endeavor (Roggenkamp xii). Wells — who wrote science essays for *Nature*, the *Fortnightly Review*, and the *Pall Mall Gazette* — was one of the first writers to propose a way out of this dilemma. As he argued in an 1894 issue of *Nature*, "The fundamental principles of construction that underlie stories such as Poe's 'Murders in the Rue Morgue' or Conan Doyle's 'Sherlock Holmes' series are precisely those that should guide a scientific writer" (qtd. in Rensberger 1055). For Wells, it was not a matter of choosing between information and story-based modes of reporting. Instead, science journalists could help readers better appreciate science and technology by presenting information in a narrative form modeled on one of the most popular modes of storytelling in Wells's day: detective fiction.[1]

The kind of change that Wells envisioned occurred with the creation of Science Service in 1921. Founded by the newspaper publisher Edward W. Scripps, the zoology professor William E. Ritter, and representatives from the National Academy of Science, the National Research Council, and the American Association for the Advancement of Science, Science Service was created to maintain government support for scientific endeavors begun during World War I, combat public fascination with pseudoscience, and even facilitate the workings of democracy. As the journalism historian David J. Rhees explains, facilitating the democratic process was particularly important to Scripps, who believed that "the task of popularization was to 'democratize' science and bring it within the reach of many." By translating scientific ideas into "plain United States" English, citizens would have "the basis for forming intelligent opinions on matters of national importance." Scripps's timing could not have been better: the events of World War I and the development of new domestic, communication, and transportation technologies made Americans curious about everything from chemistry to psychology to automobile production. By 1929 Science Service provided content to more than a hundred newspapers while experimenting with novel services, including public radio broadcasts, earthquake forecasting, and on-site fact checking for archeological finds.

Science Service's success derived in large part from the innovative writing techniques developed by Scripps. The first newsletters produced by the editor-in-chief, Edwin E. Slosson, were very much in line with the dry style of technical reporting that had become fashionable just a few decades earlier. Scripps recognized Slosson's expertise but believed that "there is no better propaganda for science than the romantic facts of research and discovery" (Rhees). Accordingly, he encouraged Slosson and his writers to use eye-catching headlines while explaining scientific and technological developments in a tempered manner and to provide "human interest angles whenever possible [by] relating scientific concepts to everyday life" (Foust 61). He also encouraged them to capitalize on the popularity of scientific luminaries such as Albert Einstein and Marie Curie as a way of introducing their work to the public and to cast all scientists as intrepid pioneers who braved new frontiers for the betterment of humanity every day (Rhees). By thinking in terms of the mass audience for which they were writing, as well as the scientists they sought to represent, the writers of Science Service proved that science journalism could be both entertaining and informative.

Anglophone women have participated in the practice of science popularization since the Enlightenment, so it is not surprising that they sought work as science journalists in the opening decades of the twentieth century.[2] As a whole, journalism was relatively welcoming to women at this time. In 1901 9 percent of all American reporters were women, and by 1931 that number had risen to 17 percent (Franks 2). While many of these reporters wrote for society pages or women's magazines, a few trailblazers made their names in sports, politics, investigative reporting, and, of course, science journalism.[3]

In the first decade of its existence, Science Service hired half a dozen female reporters with "background[s] in science and a love of writing" (Tressider). Some of these women were formally trained in basic scientific subjects such as chemistry. Others were experts in the new social sciences (including anthropology, sociology, and psychology) that Scripps believed would be central to the future development of society (Rhees). Taken together, they were instrumental in changing popular perceptions of both science and women in science reporting.

While the first generation of SF editors often addressed scientific and technological issues in their editorial columns, modern science journalism did not appear in SF magazines until the late 1930s, when a new generation of editors took over the genre's major publications. It was particularly central to *Amazing Stories* and its sister publications under the leadership of Raymond A. Palmer, who was hired by Ziff-Davis in 1938 to resuscitate the then-failing franchise. Palmer, an active SF fan from the late 1920s who is credited as co-founder of the first SF fanzine, was delighted to take on the challenge: "Here at last I had the power to do to my old hobby what I had always had the driving desire to do to it. I had in my hands the power to change, to destroy, to create, to remake, at my own discretion" (qtd. in Nadis 31). Encouraged by his employers to target a young male audience, Palmer exchanged stories that were carefully extrapolated from current scientific and social trends for action-packed intergalactic romps; hired new artists to increase the sex appeal of *Amazing*'s covers; and replaced the "courtly and reserved" editorial tone set by his predecessor, the eighty-something T. O'Conor Sloane, with a "brash, silly, and chummy" one much like that of the fan community from which he came (Nadis 32). While longtime readers decried these changes, there was no doubt that they were successful. When Palmer took over *Amazing*, its circulation was below 40,000; within a decade he had increased it to 250,000 while founding the companion magazine *Fantastic Adventures* and laying the groundwork for a whole new cluster of paranormal publications.

As he transformed *Amazing Stories*, Palmer transformed the way SF magazines presented science itself. Like E. W. Scripps, the *Amazing* founder Hugo Gernsback dreamed of bringing science to the masses in an accurate but easily digestible manner. Accordingly, he hired as many science and engineering PhD's as possible to help shape his magazine. Sloane—a retired professor, inventor, and former *Scientific American* editor with a PhD in electrical engineering who wrote dozens of popular science books—was involved with *Amazing Stories* from its inception, beginning as Gernsback's managing editor in 1928 and then assuming the role of editor just a year later ("T. O'Conor Sloane"). Sloane advocated the information model of science writing and began each issue of *Amazing* with a "long, thorough, but rather dull treatise on a topic such as the history of printing technology or the chemical composition of the Earth's atmosphere" (Nadis 30). Palmer transformed this opening column into a casual, entertainment-oriented affair where he speculated goofily about new scientific developments—wondering, for instance, "what a space explorer [in a new invention called 'the space suit'] would do to scratch an itch" (Nadis 32). For Palmer, scientific and technological development might indeed be amazing, but it should be amusing as well, something that all intelligent people could play with in the laboratory of their minds.

After doing away with the Victorian model of science writing embodied by Sloane, Palmer hired scores of writers to produce modern science journalism for *Amazing*, including everything from basic science filler material to one-shot science history essays to illustrated serial columns. While many of these new features were written along the lines of their mainstream counterparts, others were not. Palmer seems to have been particularly keen to upset what Rensberger calls the hierarchical "Gee-Whiz" model of science reporting, in which science journalists respectfully translate the complex ideas of godlike scientists for an equally respectful audience (1055). Instead, his formative experiences with a boisterous fan community confident in its own intellectual abilities led Palmer and his writers to challenge scientific authority just as often as they celebrated it. Furthermore, the editor's interest in the occult and pseudoscience (combined, perhaps, with his love of a good joke) led him to publish a number of weird science pieces that encouraged readers to actively debate the relations of fact and fiction and science journalism versus science hoax.

Palmer was well known for patronizing women writers and hired many as science journalists. When he began publishing science journalism in *Amazing* and *Fantastic Adventures*, about 10 percent of his science writers were women; by the time Palmer left Ziff-Davis in 1949, that number had risen to 25 percent. Moreover, two of the five most prolific science writers for his magazines were women. The first of these was L. Taylor Hansen, who produced sixty-two essays on anthropology and geology for *Amazing Stories*, fifty-five of which were featured in the lavishly illustrated "Scientific Mysteries" column. The second was Lynn Standish, who wrote forty-seven articles on a wide range of subjects and was the primary author associated with *Amazing*'s "Scientific Oddities" column in the 1940s and its "Facts of the Future" column in the 1950s.[4]

Like their professional counterparts, women who served as science reporters for Palmer often wrote in the standard Science Service manner. For example, articles such as Henrietta Brown's "Marine Engineering in the Insect

World" and Standish's "Battle of the Sexes" feature eye-catching headlines while providing readers with sober, scientifically accurate accounts of their subject matter. In a similar vein, Standish cites sources in text for all the items featured in "Scientific Oddities" and Hansen, who was formally trained in the subjects she wrote about, provides end notes for her "Scientific Mystery" columns. Authors also foregrounded the human interest angle in their science reporting, although some did this more gracefully than others: in the early short piece "Natural Ink," Ellen Reed rather awkwardly attaches a final sentence connecting the squid and its natural defense systems to human writing technologies; later authors such as Brown, Fran Miles, and Laura Moore Wright more successfully integrate their subject matter with the concerns of World War II. Finally, Standish and Hansen emphasize the drama of discovery and the role of the scientist as an intellectual pioneer in their science columns. This is particularly evident in "Scientific Mysteries," where Hansen (with Palmer's help) casts herself as "something of an Indiana Jones figure" fighting the evils of racism both within and without the scientific community (Nadis 111).

Even as they imported the techniques of modern science journalism into the SF magazine community, women modified them to better suit their community's needs. In some cases, this meant acknowledging readers as critical thinkers in their own right. Both Standish and Hansen forsake the tendency of science writers to address readers as a passive "you" distinct from the active scientist and science journalist. Instead, they employ a more inclusive "we" to collapse the hierarchical distance between expert and layperson and include all scientifically inclined people in the process of discovery and invention.

Women writing for *Amazing* and *Fantastic Stories* also departed from the role of science journalist as translator by asserting their own opinions on the topics they covered. This is particularly evident in Wright's "Sunlight," where the author explores facts that she suggests are unknown to the scientists but will change nuclear research forever, and in Standish's "Scientific Oddities" vitamin vignette, where the medical reporter usurps the role of the doctor by providing her own health advice to readers. SF science writers further asserted both the collaborative nature of discovery and their own authoritative contributions to it with anecdotes about their involvement in ongoing scientific debates. In cases such as Standish's "Scientific Oddities" essay on animal biology, the debates are relatively low-stake, casual affairs about surprising but noncontroversial facts. In other cases, such as Hansen's "The White Race: Does It Exist?" and "Footprints of the Dragon," the debates over evolution and racial difference are highly charged and formally documented to better underscore Hansen's own paradigm-shattering place within them.

Finally, while the women who wrote science journalism for *Amazing* and *Fantastic Adventures* seem to have taken their writing quite seriously, at least one, L. Taylor Hansen, collaborated with Palmer to provoke debate over the relations of science writing and science hoax. Palmer's interest in occult matters led him to experiment with "graft[ing] science fiction to studies of 'strange mysteries'" throughout his tenure at Ziff-Davis (Nadis 111). Indeed, *Amazing*'s circulation peaked at 250,000 in the mid-1940s when the editor encouraged fans to debate the merits of the Shaver Mystery, a series of stories based on letters from a Pennsylvania factory worker, Richard Shaver, who claimed to have discovered an ancient, evil, and technologically advanced civilization located in caverns under the earth. But Palmer's earliest experiment in this vein occurred several years before in cooperation with Hansen, whose "Scientific Mysteries" column presented readers with a mixture of "mythological lore and anthropological reports" that upset the widespread American belief in white supremacy (Nadis 111). While debate over Hansen's claims never reached the epic proportions of those associated with the Shaver Mystery, fans did indeed engage critically with her ideas, debating both their scientific accuracy and their aesthetic merit.

Much like their Science Service counterparts, women who worked as science writers in the early SF magazine community wrote about a wide range of technoscientific topics in both informative and entertaining ways. In doing so, they helped shape new understandings of women as scientific and technological experts. They also anticipated changes occurring in science writing today. As science journalism migrates online, audiences respond more quickly and publicly to science stories, reframing them to better express their own interests and needs. Accordingly, science writers find they must relinquish traditional models of science communication that treat readers as passive blank slates, instead approaching "the audience as a 'growth medium' in which the seeds planted by individual stories can grow into two kinds of knowledge: knowledge of the sort imagined by the story writers, and knowledge nurtured by the community itself" (Lazlo, Baram-Tsabari, and Lewenstein 865). The women who wrote about science for *Amazing* and *Fantastic Adventures* already knew this was the case, and so while authors such as Reed, Miles, and Brown hewed to the conventions of modern science journalism to encourage interest in the knowledge generated by scientists and science writers, others—including Standish and, most spectacularly, Hansen— pushed the limits of those conventions to encourage knowledge production on the part of the SF community itself.

ELLEN REED, FRAN MILES, HENRIETTA BROWN, LYNN STANDISH, AND LAURA MOORE WRIGHT

With the notable exception of L. Taylor Hansen (featured elsewhere in this anthology), very little is known about the first generation of women who worked as science journalists for the SF community. What information is available comes from their publishing patterns in *Amazing Stories* and *Fantastic Adventures* and the occasional comment from the editor, Ray Palmer. Biographical details are particularly scarce for Ellen Reed, Fran Miles, and Henrietta Brown, all of whom sold one or two short pieces to Palmer before disappearing from the SF community and the historical record altogether. Similarly, while it is possible that the Laura Moore Wright featured in the May 1946 issue of *Amazing* is the mid-century Canadian poet of the same name, there is currently no concrete evidence to prove that they were one and the same.[5] Even Lynn Standish—one of Palmer's most frequent science contributors, whose name was associated with two regular science columns—is shrouded in mystery. SF historian Eric Leif Davin confirms that Standish was one of the many women who published with Palmer in *Amazing* and *Fantastic Adventures* but provides no other information about her (*Partners* 115). Palmer himself provides one tantalizing clue when he celebrates "Lt. Lynn Standish [stationed] in New Guinea" as one of the many SF writers who deserves recognition for serving both SF and the greater American community in a time of war ("Observatory" 6). However, there seems to be no record of Standish's service beyond this one comment, and indeed, given that in the same editorial Palmer celebrates the military exploits of "Sgt. Morris J. Steele," which was a house pseudonym used by Palmer and many other writers, it is difficult to know whether Standish's service was fact or fiction.

None of the women featured in this chapter rose to great fame or fortune on the basis of their literary endeavors, but they were instrumental in shaping modern science journalism for the SF magazine community. Like their counterparts at Science Service and the other science news writing organizations that flourished in the first half of the twentieth century, Brown, Miles, and Standish used catchy headlines such as "Marine Engineering in the Insect World," "Oil for Bombing," and "The Battle of the Sexes" to get their audiences interested in what might be otherwise mundane facts about bugs, oil production, and human biology. Furthermore, regular contributors such as Standish could depend on provocatively titled monthly columns such as "Scientific Oddities" to catch readers' attention. Once they had this attention, authors attempted to maintain it by emphasizing the human interest angle in each story. Reed, Brown, and Standish (particularly in "The Battle of the Sexes") accomplished this by tacking on a single sentence connecting the scientific phenomenon under consideration to everyday human life. Miles and Wright wove together stories of scientific discovery or technological accomplishment with the unfolding drama of World War II itself.

Also like their mainstream counterparts, some women who wrote about science and technology for the SF magazine community employed a variant of Rensberger's "Gee-Whiz" model of reporting. This is most evident in Standish's "Scientific Oddities" column, which celebrates scientists as "miracle" workers while personifying science as a benevolent force naturally allied with doctors and other "famine fighters" in the quest to identify the "magic chemicals" that will produce "greater vigor, increased longevity, and higher cultural development" for all. But it is also apparent in Reed's filler piece on the sea pigeon, which is, in essence, a verbal translation of a visual display constructed by the curators of the New York Aquarium. Meanwhile, Miles relies heavily on quotations from technologically savvy politicians, and Brown employs passive verb constructions such as "we are told" to reinforce the respectful distance between layperson and scientific expert.

Even as they hewed to many of the science writing conventions developed in the opening decades of the twentieth century, SF science journalists adapted those conventions to better meet the needs of an audience that saw itself as distinct from other laypeople by virtue of its intellectual ability and engagement with new sciences and technologies. The difficulty of negotiating these two different conceptions of audience is particularly evident in Brown's writing, which swings back and forth between the use of passive verb constructions to separate scientific experts from their lay counterparts and the use of active ones such as "we find" to involve readers in the process of scientific observation and discovery. Meanwhile, Standish's "Scientific Oddities" column complicates the relations of scientist and science journalist by beginning with an anecdote that makes the science journalist an equal partner in scientific debate and ending with the dispensation of medical advice, not by "science" or its partner "famine fighters," but by the science reporter herself.

But perhaps the most interesting contribution in this respect is that of Wright, who takes on the role of scientist-instructor by guiding her readers through a series of exercises designed to help them understand the scientific phenomenon under consideration in the comfort of their own homes. Wright's confidence in the layperson's ability to observe the material world both accurately and imaginatively leads her to generate her own scientific hypotheses regarding spontaneous combustion and the development of nuclear weaponry. While she does so as respectfully as possible—she is careful to present her hypotheses as speculative questions rather than definitive answers—Wright is also confident in her ability to discover amazing new facts "which I felt should be made known, if [they are] already not known amongst scientists." As such, she unsettles the then-fashionable model of top-down scientific discovery and knowledge dissemination, replacing it with a more democratic one in which anyone with a good eye and open mind can participate in these processes on his or her own terms. Thus SF science writers such as Reed, Brown, Miles, Standish, and Wright demonstrated both the potential and limits of science journalism as it developed in the opening decades of the twentieth century.

....

Ellen Reed, "Natural Ink"
Fantastic Adventures, June 1942

One of the strangest of many curiosities at the New York Aquarium is the snail-like sea pigeon. The sea pigeon is a shell-less snail, less than a foot long, with a dark reddish-brown color. It moves in the water by means of a pair of wing-like appendages. Its resemblance to a pigeon flying through the water accounts for its name.

The sea pigeon lives upon sea lettuce, consuming about a teacup-ful every day. The young of the sea pigeon are deposited in long strings of bright yellow eggs composed of a mucous-like substance that hardens into a stiff jelly very quickly. Each string of eggs numbers about one-half million eggs.

Probably the most interesting fact about the sea pigeon is its means of a defense in case of attack. When danger approaches, the sea pigeon releases a large quantity of dark, inky fluid that covers up its escape. The fluid thus secreted has been found to be as good as our own manufactured ink and will make a durable record on writing paper.

....

Fran Miles, "Oil for Bombing"
Fantastic Adventures, October 1944

The opening of a new aviation gasoline refinery on Aruba by the Lago Oil Company, Standard Oil of New Jersey subsidiary, was cited by Governor Pieter A. Kasteel of Curacao as the latest example of "the splendid cooperation between the United States and the Netherlands for the prosecution of the war."

Speaking at the opening ceremony, the Governor said: "Lago Oil will continue to be most important for our whole territory, for the prosecution of the war and the development of our common task after victory is won. You supply in ever-increasing quantities the vital fuel without which Allied planes cannot fly. It is all a question of teamwork—you over here and the air-men over there working together with all your might to crush forever the ugly monsters of Hitlerism and Japanese aggression."

....

Henrietta Brown, "Marine Engineering in the Insect World"

Fantastic Adventures, July 1945

We read of floods and how humans fare when at the mercy of the elements. Our hearts are filled with pity for the suffering and the homeless. We watch with interest on the movie screen the humorous antics as well as the narrow escapes of people caught in flooded areas. We are apt to forget that there are other than human lives involved in the chaos.

Insects are plagued by floods many more times during the year than humans. A sudden heavy rain will cause a patch of lawn, a meadow, or a field to be vacated by thousands of tiny six-legged creatures. Butterflies, ladybirds, tiger beetles, grasshoppers, ants, and a host of others find themselves flood-bound on tiny islands after a downpour. They must make their escape—but how?

With the various peculiar, but convenient, features of their anatomies, they travel across the flood by all of the three possible routes—the air, the surface, and the underwater route. The insects that can fly, of course, take the air route. The grasshopper is able to leave his island by taking an enormous jump.

Some insects cannot fly, but can swim. We are told that ants, for example, make real swimming movements, rowing with their six legs as if they were six-oared boats and steering to the right or left just as the oarsman steers, by varying the strokes of the starboard and larboard oars.

In contrast to these slow-going ants we find insects that can actually walk and run on the surface of the water. Their tiny legs are supported on the surface film, just as an oily needle if you lay it gently on the water in a glass will rest on the surface film without even getting wet. Since these insects move not through the water, but over it, they encounter no resistance from it, and they can run very rapidly. In this respect they may be compared to our broad, flat motorboats, which, when they are going at full speed, rise up and skim over the surface, thus avoiding the resistance of the water and shooting along at a prodigious rate.

A fourth group of insects, which includes the heavy and clumsy beetle, cannot escape by any of the three foregoing methods. They fly but poorly or not at all; they cannot swim, and they are not built for walking on the surface of the water. These beetles boldly embark upon the submerged route. They crawl down into the water and walk along the bottom. They probably carry with them a small supply of air in the form of bubbles on the surface of their body. They are able to travel a considerable distance under water before they find it necessary to crawl up on a stick or a grass blade for fresh air.

Thus Mother Nature has equipped the lowliest of inhabitants of this planet with the means of survival.

....

Lynn Standish, "The Battle of the Sexes"
Amazing Stories, April 1943

Which sex has the edge on the other? Here are a few facts on the subject that answer (?) the question.

Universally a topic of heated discussion is the question of the superiority of one sex over the other in a particular field. Unfortunately, of course, emotion has dominated reason in these arguments—and entirely unwarrantedly, for there exists today a great body of knowledge based upon scientific experiments on the differences between men and women in various types of behavior.

The first such study, made almost 50 years ago, showed that men did better in motor tests of speed and accuracy of movement and quickness in solving problems designed to test "ingenuity." Women did better in the same motor tests of speed and accuracy when colored cards were used instead of other objects, and they did better in tests of rote memory. In tests of taste, smell, pitch discrimination of sounds, and in the accuracy of judging weights, there were slight or no differences.

In a later series of tests, school people were rated by teachers on athletic aptitude, intelligence, shyness, conscientiousness, and good temper. Boys were found to be more athletic, more noisy, more self-conscious, and quicker-tempered than girls. Girls were found to be shy and more conscientious. And, as rated by their teachers, no difference in intelligence was noted.

Hundreds of studies of sex differences have followed these pioneer attempts. Of course, many fields were found where there were no differences or where the differences were too slight to be significant. But major and reliable findings have been published about the topics of differences in physical characteristics, differences in the ability to use the senses, differences in motor and mechanical abilities, and differences in mental and emotional traits.

The following have been proved by experiment:

Until puberty (and usually even throughout early adolescence), girls advance more rapidly in height, weight, dental growth, anatomical maturity, and physiological development. The female's brain is smaller than the male's but is heavier in proportion to the total body weight. Women's hearts beat faster and their simple reflexes (like the knee jerk and the dilation of the pupil) are usually quicker. Men have larger muscles than women and excel them in endurance, physical strain, and athletic achievement.

In the field of sensory discrimination, women test consistently faster in finding differences among colors and in rapidity of perceiving objects. Men endure pain better and usually judge differences in weight somewhat better than women do.

In tests where the aim is to cancel designated items, women are consistently faster. Other tests of differences in motor and mechanical traits show that boys do better in performances where manipulation of objects, tracing mazes, or visualizing spatial relations are involved. Tests of mechanical aptitude, mechanical construction, and knowledge of mechanical things show, too, that boys do better than girls. In simple tests of tapping and tracing, no differences have been found.

In tests of difference between the sexes in mental and emotional traits, several significant facts have been discovered. Women do better than men in nearly all measures of memory. They do better on vocabulary tests, on tests of language usage, and on other tests where verbal association and literal rather than numerical items are involved. Men, however, do better in tests involving numbers, geometric ideas, or arithmetic reasoning and computation. On general information tests, too, such as those on current events, scientific discoveries, and historical facts, men score consistently better.

In mental traits, the male sex has been found to be more variable; hence there are more male geniuses than female geniuses—and, by the same token, more males in the feeble-minded class. Girls, as a rule, make higher school marks than boys. But this has been attributed to the slower physical development of younger boys and to the greater docility of the girls. Boy rebels make poor scholars!

Studies in the realms of emotional and temperamental traits have reported women to be more interested in persons and personal problems, while men are more intrigued by mechanical things and abstract activities. Women's thoughts were found to stray to subjects associated with personal ornament and to concrete, everyday problems, usually related to the individual human being. Men's associations wander to business relations, to moneymaking activities, and to matters of general and abstract interest. In tests of honesty, no differences were found, although schoolgirls excelled schoolboys in tests of moral knowledge and social attitudes.

When appraising these differences it must be remembered that when the words "is better" were used, the meaning intended was "is better on the average," since overlapping occurs, of course. Even with this consideration in mind, let's expect to have a more scientific argument tomorrow morning at the breakfast table when the wife says, "Men are dumbbells." Many a home can restore its tranquility with Dr. Science at the helm, you see.

....

Lynn Standish, "Scientific Oddities"
Amazing Stories, December 1945

AN AMAZING ANIMAL

My friends and I got to talking about camels the other day (animals to you) and I really learned some facts about these strange creatures that I would like to pass on to you.

The modern camel is a most remarkable case of adaptation to environment. The foot consists of two elongated toes, each tipped with a small nail-like hoof. The leg does not rest on this hoof but on the elastic pads or cushions under and back of them. In the Asiatic variety the toes are united by a common sole, thus presenting one broad pad for support on the loose sand of the desert.

The thighbone is unusually long, and the hind leg lacks that powerful muscular connection with the barrel of the animal that is so prominent a feature in the anatomy of the horse. In fact, the leg is almost disconnected from the body. In consequence, if the sand under the rear foot of a camel gives away, his body is not dragged down with it, as that of a horse would be, unless the other foot is undermined.

Still more wonderful as an adaptation is the stomach. The camel is a ruminant and chews the cud. Like all others of this order the digestive organ is divided into four parts or chambers. Two of these in the camel are connected by separate passages with the mouth, into one of which the animal sends the solid food it gathers in the field, and into the other the water it drinks, though it has also the power to pass water into either at will.

Both of these divisions of the stomach, but principally the one to which liquid food is generally sent, are provided with a number of pouches or cells in their linings, with muscular walls, and with orifices that can be opened or closed as desired. When water is available in plenty these are all filled to distention, and when the liquid is needed it is allowed to exude and mingle with the solid food, until enough has been provided for the time being for digestive and other bodily functions. By this arrangement a camel can live and travel without too serious discomfort for from five to seven days without drinking.

BERYLLIUM — NEWEST METALLURGY MIRACLE

Perhaps you have never seen any beryllium, yet you probably have occasion to use it every day; and it makes a big difference in your comfort, safety, and pocketbook.

Your new vacuum cleaner, refrigerator, or thermostat will last four or five times as long as the old one, because of beryllium.

We think of the properties of a metal as being eternal, but all metals get tired under strain. Instruments and gauges of all kinds, in hospitals, laboratories, factories, electric power plants, and on ships, use springs and diaphragms made of beryllium-copper. Beryllium is beginning to be used in autos, radios, electric motors — wherever there are higher speeds or exceptional strains.

Beryllium had been discovered as a chemical element and identified as a metal as early as 1827. Andrew J. Gahagan and J. Kent Smith experimented with beryllium in a small laboratory in Detroit.

Since 1929 the price of beryllium has dropped from $200 to $15 per pound and will undoubtedly come down further to meet the popular demand. The ore occurs along scattered localities from Maine to Georgia, in North and South Dakota, Utah, Wyoming, Nevada, California, New Mexico, and Arizona. Argentina and Brazil produce beryl and used to supply Germany before the war.

The whole field of research in this metal is pregnant with latent marvels. Used mainly now as an alloy, the pure metal itself has countless untried possibilities.

Pure beryllium is transparent to X-rays, and is used for windows in X-ray machines. The tube of your fluorescent lamp — the closest thing to sunlight man has produced — is coated with beryllium oxide. So is the magic screen of new television sets. And Dr. Sawyer has discovered that when kilns are lined with beryllium silicate bricks, the beryllium in some mysterious way imparts strength to porcelain.

What surprises the future may hold with beryllium can no more be imagined than Fulton could have visualized an airplane operated from the ground by radio.

VITAMINS FOR ALL

We used to think of vitamin deficiency as the curse of people too poor or too ignorant to buy the lean meat, milk, vegetables, oranges, and cereals that prevent chemical famine. But this deficiency disease pops up among intelligent people with plenty of money to provide the so-called well-balanced diet. Many people are listless, forgetful, and jittery; they don't know why but these symptoms have been diagnosed as vitamin deficiencies.

Many doctors watched people develop deficiency disease, and tried to find the clues to this riddle.

Our chemists were building crystal-pure B vitamins; their new chemicals—thiamin, riboflavin, and nicotinic acid, which soothed the hidden hunger of people in extreme agony of pain, saving them from the verge of blindness as well as rescuing those about to die. But this was only part of the strange power of these magic chemicals. Then the famine fighters began shooting huge doses of vitamins into human beings unaccountably sick but not suspected of malnutrition.

Thus the magic chemicals became more than curative. The well-balanced diet, though good, may not be enough. You may eat the best-balanced diet in the world, and still be unable to absorb your food; or maybe you can absorb it, but the cells of your body cannot use it.

If you're not feeling well, go to your doctor for your vitamins; do not risk asking the drugstore clerk for vitamin preparations for loss of weight and pep because these symptoms may be the warning signal of a hidden malady.

Doctors can try nicotinic acid on crackpots now referred to them by psychiatrists. They can test riboflavin on eye troubles that are the despair of eye specialists. They can follow the effects of this or that B vitamin on baffling digestive jangles. At worst, no harm done. At best, another triumph for vitamins.

In the past, science has conferred on those people who have availed themselves of the newer knowledge of infectious diseases better health and a greater average length of life. In the future it promises to those races that will take advantage of the knowledge of nutrition greater vigor, increased longevity, and higher cultural development.

....

Laura Moore Wright, "Sunlight"

Amazing Stories, May 1946

There are myriads of light-reflecting particles all through the air. They are not dust, but are of a substance that is not ordinarily visible to human eyes, as they would interfere with the clearness of our vision. There are, without doubt, many things around us that our eyes are not adjusted to see. However, these light-reflecting particles can be seen by focusing one's eyes on the air—not looking through it as we naturally do.

The best place to observe these light-reflecting particles is from an open veranda. Standing well back under the roof, look towards the sky, but at the air a short distance away, as though the veranda were closed in and you could not see beyond the edge of it. Shortly, you will see tiny circles. Watch these circles, and observe their motions, as that will help you to focus your eyes on the air. Within a very few minutes, you will perceive specks of light in the air.

As you observe these specks of light, you will see that they extend far into the distance—as far as the eye can see. At first they are almost too bright for one's eyes. They should not be looked at too much, as they would interfere with one's ordinary vision.

These specks of light seem to be possessed of independent motion, and dance about hither and thither in the air. When the sun is shining, they look like specks of light. When the sun is not shining, they are of a silver color.

The brighter the sunshine, the larger are the flame-like specks, or perhaps it is the other way around. On a very bright day, a flame like a shooting star may shoot across the air—evidently a number of them clash together. Perhaps that may be the cause of many mysterious fires.

The existence of these light-reflecting particles is a scientific fact, which I have felt should be made known, if it is not already known among scientists. I am now wondering if it may not contain the answer to the control of the Atomic Bomb?

L(UCILE) TAYLOR HANSEN (1897–1976) was a pioneering SF author and science popularizer, as well as one of the first women to intentionally masquerade as a man in the genre community (for more details about her life, see the entry on Hansen in chapter 1, "Authors," of this anthology). Hansen's scientific interests and penchant for self-creation came together in her SF science journalism. This is particularly true of the fifty-five "Scientific Mystery" articles she produced for *Amazing Stories* between 1941 and 1949, in which she marshals both firsthand observation and secondary research to challenge popular notions of white superiority. Over the course of her eight years as the author of this column, Hansen drew on her knowledge of anthropology, archaeology, and geology to contend that Indigenous Americans (rather than Eurowestern Caucasians) were the true source of humanity's physiological and cultural development.[6] As she built this argument, Hansen also built a particular image of herself as a visionary male scientist-adventurer. She was careful to steer clear of gendered pronouns in her writing, describing herself in "Footprints of the Dragon," for instance, as simply "the present writer." However, she regularly presented herself as engaged in masculine scientific activities with male experts of all races, creeds, and colors. Accompanied as they were by detailed illustrations of these experts, it would have been natural for readers to assume that Hansen was also a man.

Meanwhile, Hansen's editor and good friend, Ray Palmer—who enjoyed making up false author biographies, complete with pictures of himself in whatever costume seemed appropriate—perpetuated the ruse more aggressively. In an exchange between Hansen and a group of irate fans led by H. Malamud (reprinted in this anthology), Palmer announces that Hansen will defend "himself" against his detractors, and then, when Hansen does just that, Palmer responds with an enthusiastic "Atta-boy!" Elsewhere, Palmer describes Hansen as a rugged scholar-adventurer who has traveled to the four corners of the earth in the quest to discover humanity's true origins (Nadis 111). The picture of Hansen that emerges at the intersection of all this authorial, artistic, and editorial activity is that of what Brian Attebery describes as the "typical" early magazine SF hero: a "youthful scientist" who is "undervalued by society" but who wins the day "by dint of his ingenuity and scientific knowledge" ("Cultural" 347). Given that Palmer grew up on this image of the heroic scientist and that Hansen herself helped shape it in her earlier fiction writing, it seems entirely appropriate that the two would collaborate to present her in this light.

Even as Hansen was cast (or allowed herself to be cast) as a variant of the early SF magazine hero, she wrote as a modern science journalist. Like her Science Service counterparts, Hansen employed the conventions of modern science writing to both entertain and inform her readers. If the title of her

210

3.1. Illustration by Joe C. Sewell that accompanied L. Taylor Hansen's "Scientific Mysteries" column in the July 1942 issue of *Amazing Stories*.

THE WHITE RACE—DOES IT EXIST?

By L. TAYLOR HANSEN

When we speak of the races of earth, is there really such a race as the white race? Is the color of a man's skin indicative of his origin?

THERE is no subject upon which more scientific nonsense, or rather let us say nonsense purporting to be science, has been written than upon the subject of race. The reason is not hard to find. Each man prefers his own type and considers his to be the highest. It is a subject which is more bound up with emotion than with reason, and the average man is still essentially an emotional animal.

Since the start of history, the question of a desirable racial type has run through as many fashions as women's clothes. The Germans, in preferring blonds, are not the first peoples to set a racial style. The Mayans admired slanting foreheads (and strangely enough, their ironed-out foreheads, done in infancy, did not affect their intelligence), the Incas admired large ears, certain African tribes large lips, the Turks once admired excess fat and the Medieval artists thought excessively long necks were desirable.

The ideas of race which were popular during the days of our fathers, are at present giving place to other standards of differentiation. If the tendency continues to its inevitable conclusion, we are going to discover that there is no such thing as a white race. For the standards of color by which our parents learned to classify mankind are far too superficial for the most advanced anthropologists. Today the scientists are busy pointing out that skeletal differences are far more important than the shade of the subject's skin.

Modern science regards the white, yellow, black, red and brown, even when the latter is eliminated or classified with the red as a sub-group under the yellow, with profound distrust. Thus the deeper structural differences are leading the foremost thinkers to suspect the old classifications so strongly that they are going out of fashion in any scientific discussions worthy of the name.

For example, Huntington contends that skin-color is now distributed over the earth's surface according to the strength of the sun's rays, and is only man's reaction to his environment. Dixon of Harvard University, argues that all men are to be divided by skeletal differences into round-heads with narrow noses, round-heads with broad noses, long-heads with narrow noses, etc., completely ignoring hair-texture and the color of the skin. Both of these eminent scientists have agreed that the negro is not a primitive, but a recently-evolved tropical type. In other words, a group of the long-heads, finding themselves in a tropical environment, evolved the spreading nostrils, thicker skull and blacker skin of the negro. Thus the negro is a late adaptation of Modern Man to a tropical environment.

NOW it is interesting to note that mankind may be divided into two rather distinct types which are called "harmonics." One is a long-headed, long-faced, individual with long eye-sockets. The hair in cross-section is inclined to be very oval, thus giving it a tendency to curl. The type is the Ancient Egyptian. Let us call him the "proto-negroid" because in its extremity, the type becomes more negroid, the hair becoming exaggeratedly curly, etc. The negro is a late branch from the type. In its earlier form, the skin is a tan shade and the eyes are long and deep-sunken, the nose delicate, the lips not too full. The stature is slight and slender. The hands and feet slender and delicate.

The "proto-negroid" is sometimes called the "ancient longhead" and sometimes called the Mediterranean Race. This latter name is somewhat incorrect, for though the people are to be found in the Mediterranean, they are centered in the area of the Indian Ocean. A better name for them would be the "Peoples of the Sea," for they are found upon every ancient shore-line.

211

monthly column, "Scientific Mysteries," was not eye-catching enough to draw in an audience, provocative subtitles such as "The White Race—Does It Exist?" and "Footprints of the Dragon" were sure to do so. Once she had her readers' attention, Hansen carefully led them through current debates over the issues at hand before adding her own field-based observations and hypotheses to the mix. Furthermore, she asserted her authority to speak about anthropological and geological issues through engagement with established scholarly traditions. Indeed, as Hansen's arguments grew more controversial, her scientific references grew more elaborate. Early articles such as "The White Race" rely on in-text citations and the occasional editorial note to connect Hansen's ideas with those of the greater scholarly community, while later ones such as "Footprints of the Dragon" include extensive reference lists and footnotes to do the same.

Finally, like SF science journalists Ellen Reed, Henrietta Brown, and Lynn Standish, Hansen strategically modified the conventions of science journalism to appeal to an audience that was eager to participate in scientific debate on its own terms. After carefully laying out her theories of human evolution in "The White Race—Does it Exist?" the author concludes by asking, "What do you think?" As the response from H. Malamud, I. Berkman, and H. Rogovin indicates, some readers did not think very much of Hansen's arguments at all, dismissing them as "harebrained" and "unbelievable." On first glance Hansen's tart reply—which promises that she will take "the keenest delight in crossing swords" with her detractors and then ruthlessly dismantles their arguments as "delightful fallacies"—seems to reassert the authority of the science writer over her audience. But the arch language employed by all the parties involved in this exchange is not, ultimately, that of scientific debate. Rather, it is the kind of lively if somewhat juvenile interaction common among first-generation SF fans. By responding in kind rather than retreating into the neutral academic language she employs elsewhere in "Scientific Mysteries," Hansen speaks to SF readers on their own terms, treating them as serious (if, in this particular case, seriously mistaken) partners in the construction of scientific knowledge.

··

L. Taylor Hansen, "Scientific Mysteries: The White Race—Does It Exist?"

Amazing Stories, July 1942

When we speak of the races of the Earth, is there really such a race as the white race? Is the color of a man's skin indicative of his origin?

There is no subject upon which more scientific nonsense, or rather let us say nonsense purporting to be science, has been written than upon the subject of race. The reason is not hard to find. Each man prefers his own type and considers his to be the highest. It is a subject that is more bound up with emotion than with reason, and the average man is still essentially an emotional animal.

Since the start of history, the question of a desirable racial type has run through as many fashions as women's clothes. The Germans, in preferring blonds, are not the first peoples to set a racial style. The Mayans admired slanting foreheads (and strangely enough, their ironed-out foreheads, done in infancy, did not affect their intelligence), the Incas admired large ears, certain African tribes large lips, the Turks once admired excess fat, and the Medieval artists thought excessively long necks were desirable.

The ideas of race that were popular during the days of our fathers are at a present giving place to other standards of differentiation. If the tendency continues to its inevitable conclusion, we are going to discover that there is no such thing as a white race. For the standards of color by which our parents learned to classify mankind are far too superficial for the most advanced anthropologists. Today the scientists are busy pointing out that skeletal differences are far more important than the shade of the subject's skin.

Modern science regards the white, yellow, black, red and brown, even when the latter is eliminated or classified with the red as a subgroup under the yellow, with profound distrust. Thus the deeper structural differences are leading the foremost thinkers to suspect the old classifications so strongly that they are going out of fashion in any scientific discussions worthy of the name.

For example, Huntington contends that skin color is now distributed over the Earth's surface according to the strength of the sun's rays, and is only man's reaction to his environment. Dixon of Harvard University argues that all men are to be divided by skeletal differences into round-heads with narrow noses, round-heads with broad noses, long-heads with narrow noses, etc., completely ignoring hair texture and the color of the skin. Both of these eminent scientists have agreed that the Negro is not a primitive, but a recently evolved tropical type. In other words, a group of the long heads, finding themselves in a tropical environment, evolved the spreading nostrils, thicker skull and blacker skin of the Negro. Thus the Negro is a late adaptation of Modern Man to a tropical environment.

Now it is interesting to note that mankind may be divided into two rather distinct types, which are called "harmonics." One is a long-headed, long-faced individual with long eye sockets. The hair in cross-section is inclined to be very oval, thus giving it a tendency to curl. The type is the Ancient Egyptian. Let us call him the "proto-Negroid" because in its extremity, the type becomes more Negroid—the hair becoming exaggeratedly curly, etc. The Negro is a late branch from the type. In its earlier form, the skin is a tan shade and the eyes are long and deep sunken, the nose delicate, the lips not too full. The stature is slight and slender. The hands and feet slender and delicate.

The "proto-Negroid" is sometimes called the "ancient longhead" and sometimes called the Mediterranean Race. This latter name is somewhat incorrect, for though the people are to be found in the Mediterranean, they are centered in the area of the Indian Ocean. A better name for them would be the "Peoples of the Sea," for they are found upon every ancient shoreline.

In London, for example, when dredging for a new building, in the lowest basement, while digging in the gravels in which are to be found the remains of the Great English Channel forest which once covered that submerged valley, the human skulls which are brought up are the true type of the ancient long-headed "People of the Sea."

Again in the Channel Islands of California, when the earliest skulls are unearthed, they are once more harmonic long-head. A map of the cephalic-index of living populations today would reveal that the long-heads would live along the seacoasts, with the exception of the western coast of the Americas, where round-heads have displaced the ancient long-headed population.

The other "harmonic" type is the round-headed, round-faced Asian with round eye sockets and straight hair that is in the cross-section completely round. In the extremity this type develops the mongoloid eye fold and becomes the typical Chinese.

These round-heads are concentrated most thickly in the region just north of the Himalayas. From here they pour in a thick stream from the Caspian into the Mediterranean and through Greece and Albania into Europe. Another arm runs northward through Russia into the Baltic while a third stream sweeps northeast across the Aleutian Islands and down the western coast of the Americas. Thus from the map of present distribution, it is easy to see that the round-head is an Asian and a landsman.

Now where does white man enter this picture? Is he a cross? We learn with surprise that his is not a true or a harmonic type. Between the poles of the long-headed proto-Negroid and the round-headed Asian, in head form, shape of the face, eye-sockets and cross-section of the hair, varies that section of Modern Man that we designate as the "White Race." The variation is so profound that not only do we see all combinations within the same nationality, but often within the same family group.

These facts force us to one of two conclusions. Either the white race is a very profound cross which has never remained in isolation long enough or inbred deeply enough to set its type, or it is the original stem from which the other two harmonics branched.

To meet these facts, some ingenious classifications have been offered. For example, there is Duckworth, who would make the round-heads the general type from which the long-heads, making their way into the Indian Ocean and spreading from this point, were an early branch. However, that of Wissler* seems to be the most logical. He would make White Man and perhaps also the Polynesian Race the original stem. As he points out, the White Man is the most hairy of all the races and this is certainly a primitive characteristic.

When studying the very ancient nations it is important for us to keep in mind the characteristic of facial hair. It is anthropological nonsense for us to classify the beardless Egyptians and Cretans as "White Men." It would be more honest for us of the white race to admit that the first civilizations were not founded by men of our race, but by the tan-skinned "People of the Sea," some of whom, nevertheless, have contributed to the blood of the modern European.

As for this matter of superiority, the honors for geniuses are so evenly divided between the two harmonics that one could not truthfully give the palm to either the one type or the other. It would be a controversial question, for example, whether the round-headed Beethoven and Socrates were any greater than the long-headed Wagner and Shakespeare. And I would venture to wager that the honors in the prisons are just as evenly divided! Apparently the only fair judge of potential intelligence is brain capacity in proportion to the frame, for much brain space is taken up in mere muscle control.

As for blondness, it is a stumbling block, for it is to be found in Northern Europe among both round- and long-heads. Dixon suggests that there may be something about the food grown in this soil or some other physical reason that might contribute to fair hair and pale skin. However, the blonds to be found among the San Blas Indians of Colombia are a denial to this theory of Dixon. The Indians have their own names for their whites. Significantly they are called "*yapisas*," or "hairy ones." Sometimes they are nicknamed "moon-children" in reference to the fact that white is the color sacred to the moon.

It is interesting to know that these blond Indians exist by the thousands. Some were taken to the Smithsonian Institute to be studied by the scientists. One of the most interesting facts to be discovered was that about one-third of their words come from the ancient Norse. After realizing that these Indians

* Wissler, Clark—Curator of Anthropology, Amer. Museum of Nat. Hist., New York City. —Ed.

did not have the white hair and pink eyes of the true albinos, but blue eyes and various shades of golden hair, the scientists decided that they were partial albinos. One sage expressed the opinion that the San Blas tribe was in the process of changing its racial type and that the proceeding would have gone much further if an abnormal hatred for the conquering Spaniard had not caused the blonds to be placed under a marriage taboo. (This fact was attested to by the Indians themselves.)

The designation that the blonds were partial albinos is an interesting one. The question that naturally arises is: if these people with their various shades of light hair and fair skin are to be scientifically classified as partial albinos, what are white Europeans? What is white man in general? Is he partial albino? Is white skin to be considered as various degrees of partial albinism? And if so, was this a general condition of the original stem along with a tendency to body hair, from which diverging types acquired a more hairless skin and a deeper color?

What do you think?

THE END

....

L. Taylor Hansen, "Scientific Mysteries: Footprints of the Dragon"

Amazing Stories, May 1944

The trail of the Dragon can be followed over all the Earth and through the legends of many isolated races of humankind.

We have seen how, in trying to track down to its lair the ancient colossus of the seas, the giant Dragon Totem, the weight of much evidence seems to point to two very important conclusions: (1) that the long-headed peoples of the Americas who occupy the refuge locations (thus indicating an early strata of population) also seem to carry the strongest suggestions of very ancient Dragon ritual, and (2) that the ceremonies and legends which these isolated tribes hold in common apparently center in the Antilles.

These facts certainly do not fit in with the centralization of the Dragon Totem in Asia, where it is at present carried largely by a round-headed population. Furthermore, if the Dragon entered Amerind ritual from Asia, then we would expect to find its traces through the Northwest of North America and down the Pacific Coast. This is not true. The Wolf Totem is the most powerful in the Northwest, with Coyote-Man the first figure in their pantheons. The

Great Bird is second, but even the Whale Totem is more powerful than the Reptile-gods. In fact, in no other part of the Americas, with the possible exception of the Southwest part of South America, are the Reptile-gods as weak as they are in the Pacific Northwest.

Yet certainly there is some meaning in the pattern which the distribution of Dragon-ritual presents, rippling outward as it does from the Antilles and resting most strongly in the *Aztecan* family of languages, which number most of their members from Mexican tribes. Just as there is most certainly a meaning behind the three main types of face painting and the distribution of each. The division of the face into two halves originally indicated the Totem of the Eagle, or the Great Bird. This is most strongly characteristic of the hawk-nosed disharmonic Old Red Race, which is largely crowded into the eastern part of North America. The painting or tattooing of the face into concentric whorls or circles is typical of the Spider Totem and is scattered through the South Seas and up some of the South American coasts. The horizontal banding of the face indicates the Serpent or the Great Dragon Totem. (The various colors stand for the four directions, which differ from tribe to tribe.)

For a moment, let us concentrate upon this horizontal banding, which some authorities have noted is so typical of the wild tribes islanded in refuge locations that they have suggested it may be typical of hunting tribes in general. The various Karib peoples of the Antilles, including the Aruaks, who speak a tongue akin to these Indians of the Caribbean, wore nosebands or in some manner indicated a horizontal line across the cheeks. The Itzaes* wore a hollow tube through the septum of the nose into which breathing holes had been punched. At the present time the Mayas wear a veil across their nose and mouth at night. When questioned about the matter, they insist that the night air is poisonous and they must protect their air passages (*The Ancient Mayas* by Stacy-Judd).

It was an old Indian sage who gave the present writer the needed hint that might serve to unravel this mystery. In remarking upon the continual connection between the horizontal banding of the face, in ritualistic dances of the Veiled-One (if not actually veiling the features) and the other characteristics of the Great Serpent or Great Dragon as compared to those of Egypt, he suddenly remarked: "Was the 'Veiled-One' of this Ancient Egypt always known as Ammon-Ra?"

"Why, no," I answered thoughtfully, "that was the joining of two sun gods into one. Ra came into Egypt from the east while Ammon or Amen came

---

* Itzaes, *"First Conquerors of Colkuas." They founded the Mayan Golden Age. In turn were conquered by Tutul-Xius.*

from the direction of the Atlantic . . ." But my mind was leaping ahead of my words. Was this Egyptian Amen the Zamna of the Mayas, the Tiaman of the Guatemala tribes—even the Tanama "Trembling-One" (Earthquake) of the Apaches?* Tanama had once walked among them, teaching them how to live. (Apparently this was a confusion with a later culture-hero, similar to the Quetzalcoatl legend.) Yet if this remark was thought provoking, the next observation by the old sage was almost startling.

"Of course, he does not always go by the same name. He is the god of breath or life. Therefore he sometimes goes by a name with a hissing sound."

"Osiris! The god of life and learning! The Egyptian son of Amen!" I gasped.

———

Other names were flashing to my mind. Some of the names of the ancient cities that history records once belonged to those mysterious veiled Tuaraks who rule the Libyan desert. Tafassaset! Khamissa! Essouk! And the mysterious secret society of the Sahara whose wasm* is the Serpent—the Senussi! Did the hissing sound of the serpent cause it to be early connected with breath and life? And the veil which the Tuaraks of today place upon a boy at puberty and which thereafter no one sees him without—they explain its presence by saying that they wish to protect their nasal passages from evil spirits! What connection did that have with the fact that Amen was known as "the Hidden One?"

There was another fact about Amen "the Two Horned" which kept pounding itself rhythmically to my attention. Amen had been known as the "Lord of the Two Lands." Sometimes he had been spoken of as being seated upon the "Throne of the Two Lands." What were these two lands? And what did the Tuaraks mean when they pointed to the Atlantic as their homeland?

Possibly all of this was mere coincidence. Yet there were the curious little three-sided stones found on both sides of the central section of the Southern Atlantic. Both Northern Africa and Central America had yielded them. On one side was a face, on the other side feet, and in the center the peak. They are distinct representations of a man buried under a mountain. What could they mean? What ritualistic significance did they have or what story were they trying to tell?

And then from both sides of the Atlantic at this point was the legend of the warrior-women—women who had removed the right breast in order to better handle their bows. Upon the American side there was the legend of the

* For Apache legend see E. L. Squier, "Children of the Twilight."
* Wasm, Arabic for trademark or signature. See De Prorok, "Mysterious Sahara."

women warriors who met the men of another tribe upon a certain designated night of each year and at that time returned all male infants born to them during the previous twelve months.

The Spanish did not find the legendary tribe. Yet they did find that the Karibs had fighting women. These women fought beside their men in battle, did no work and were very strong in all tribal councils. The work was all done by captive women from other tribes.

Strangely enough, the French priests traveling up the Mississippi River during the following century discovered that the Choctaws, who painted their faces with the sinuous horizontal of the Serpent and who boasted that they were immune from snakebite (evidently an ancient remedy, since all Serpent peoples the world over seem to share this knowledge), had a legendary woman chief who had been a particularly savage warrior. This is the most notable case of the Serpent Totem being found outside of the Uto-Aztecan block of languages with the exception of the Antillean group. As the relationship of the Antillean group is as yet very little understood, it is quite possible that they will be found to be connected, while the Choctaws, speaking a Muskhogean tongue related to the Creeks, shared with the Creeks their legend of a Mexican origin.

As yet so little is known of these various Indian tongues in their relation one with another that the investigator must be cautious and creep over the paths which, in another hundred years with the subsequent investigation of Central American and South American tongues and comparisons of them all, will, we hope, no longer be obscure and uncertain paths. Certain it is that here, in the Americas, there is more knowledge of the ancient figure of Ammon-Ra than the Old World has known since the burning of the great Egyptian and Alexandrian libraries. Yet that knowledge is in the form of fragmentary legends held in the memory of a priesthood that is gradually losing the fight against the encroachments of a much younger religion.

If this priesthood decides to die with their lips still sealed, then our scientists will write in blissful ignorance that the Red Man has childish notions of nature worship, and the last strands which connect the Americas to untold millenniums of forgotten history will fade away under the very spectacles of twentieth century science without that august body even suspecting its existence.

It is time for science to stop riding comfortably upon the theory of entire Asian migration. It is a theory that will no longer fit all of the facts. As more is learned about Amerind thought, it should become increasingly evident that *the Americas are culturally closer to ancient Egypt than they ever were to Asia!*

It is high time for some young scientist with vision to begin a lifetime pursuit of this figure of Amen from tribe to tribe. His names may vary but his characteristics are the same. He will spill over the barriers of the Uto-Aztecan tongues into the Athapascan Apaches of Arizona, where he is Tanama, or the Muskhogean Creeks and Choctaws of the lower Mississippi River, where he is the fire god and Master of Breath—Esskata-Emishe, or he will supervise the dancing ceremonies of the Matto Grosso, with his long whip and his banded face.

It is time for some young intellectual to raise the pertinent question—"If it is true that the god of a people is a deified culture-hero, and the oldest records we have from the archives of Ancient Egypt tell us that this Amen once sat upon the throne of *two lands*, are we any longer justified in accepting the long-held belief that these lands were Upper and Lower Egypt?" *What were those two lands*? Is it not possible that one of them was the land that today we so ironically call *the New World*?

REFERENCES

Daniel G. Brinton: "The Maya Chronicles," "The Annals of the Cakchiquels." (More recently discovered ancient Amerind books that had been rewritten with the Aryan alphabet.) Published in Philadelphia 1882 and 1885. Now out of print.

Brasseur de Bourbourg: "The Manuscript Tronano." Studies on the system of writing and the language of the Mayas, claiming to translate the original. Published in 2 vols., "Historical Researches," "Archeology and Languages of Mexico." Published in Paris 1869–1870. Now out of print.

Stacy Judd: "The Ancient Mayas." A Creek migration myth by Gatschet. Published in D. G. Brinton's "Library of Aboriginal Lit." (Now out of print but on ref. in many libraries.)

E. Squier (not the scientist): "Children of the Twilight." (A collection of legends.)

Clarke Wissler: "Indians of the U.S." (for Uto-Aztecan).

De Prorok: "B. Mysterious Sahara."

De Prorok: "Byron in Quest of Lost Worlds."

....

H. Malamud, I. Berkman, and H. Rogovin, "A Protest"
Amazing Stories, April 1943

Sirs:

This is a protest against that moronic, harebrained series of articles known as "Scientific Mysteries" which you have been so misguided as to publish. Such stupidity is remarkable—no, it is unbelievable. Without stopping to think, you take a few shreds of evidence, plus a goodly hunk of imagination, and draw fantastic conclusions, which, if true, would turn our everyday world into a science fictioneer's conception of Mars.

Take, for instance, your latest in this infamous series, "Totem of the Eagle." You take the fact that the eagle was used as an emblem in Imperial Russia, Greece, and Rome; that eagle feathers were used by two or three races; that feathers were used by the Polish knights and the Sioux and Aztecs; that winged beings other than birds were depicted by ancient peoples.

To these facts you add that the American Indians of the East trained their hair in what you call a "birdlike" crest. (Do you really think it is birdlike?)

With those facts, and nothing more, you retire to your fabrication room and produce a masterpiece about an "eagle-totem." Perhaps you have not heard of the swastika-totem. It was used by the Aztecs and other American Indians. At the present time it still survives among the primitive races, particularly near Milwaukee, although formerly it was most used on the coast. It may also be seen in Egyptian designs, ranging from textile designs to temple ornaments. The Eskimos of Greenland also used the swastika. Oddly enough, this totem still survives at the present time in a limited district surrounding Berchtesgaden.

From these facts I deduce that one of the following conclusions must be true: (1) That the ancient Egyptians, Aztecs, and Eskimos must have been Fascists. (2) That Germany is populated by Aztecs, Indians, Eskimos, and Egyptians. (3) It may have been a coincidence that all used the same design.

H. Malamud, I. Berkman, H. Rogovin
122 Eames Place
Bronx, N.Y.

Isn't it true that, when dealing with the past of which there are so few relics, theory enters into reconstruction to a great degree? And isn't it true that these articles serve to arouse discussion and thereby help attain the real truth of the past of mankind? We know that L. Taylor Hansen plans to publish these articles in book form, and such a contribution, however erroneous it may turn out to be, is of great value and interest to science, because of the collection and compilation of many related facts which can then be studied by other scientists and eventually may form a definite added link to the past.

As to the swastika, your editor could quote authorities who have dealt with this symbol at great length, and they do not arrive at your conclusions—although since your editor is a former Milwaukeean himself, we might agree that those primitive

peoples are no proof of anything even if they do use the swastika — and besides they
don't use it, but a reversed form, which is something quite different, we assure you.
    Perhaps we will run an article in the future on the swastika.
    —Ed. [Raymond A. Palmer]

....

L. Taylor Hansen, "L. Taylor Hansen Defends Himself"
Amazing Stories, June 1943

Sirs (Messrs. Malamud, Berkman, and Rogovin):
Although the editor of *Amazing Stories* defended my series of articles very
ably, yet I must answer in person because I enjoyed your letter so thoroughly.
You have a very real touch for satire, which is not a common ability. Therefore
I am taking the keenest delight in crossing swords with you.

It is true that the symbol of the Swastika was once as worldwide as that
of the Eagle. Furthermore, it was not only scattered over ancient Europe,
the Americas, and Egypt, but also the Mediterranean, the Indian Ocean, and
Northern Africa. Nuttall, the well-known Central American archaeologist,
who thought it a calendrical sign indicating a certain long epoch or passage
of time, wrote the best treatise upon the subject and published it long before
the word Nazi had been conceived.

Your conclusions therefore (1) "that the ancient Egyptians, Aztecs, and
Eskimos must have been fascists; (2) that Germany is populated by Aztecs,
Indians, Eskimos, and Egyptians; (3) it may have been a coincidence" were
delightfully refreshing.

However, may I point out: (1) that the only possible conclusion you have
offered, namely the last, is only true if the number of culture traits which
accompany a symbol do not exceed the law of averages; (2) that you forgot
another possibility—namely that the symbol under discussion with its accompanying culture traits might have migrated from a center, and therefore
could have been ancestral to them all even though the physical type carrying
it in that remote date has since been drowned in the subsequent migrations
of other ancestors which we must all claim a few millenniums ago?

As for Berchtesgaden and its emblem, it is not the Indian male, but rather
the female symbol. As one old Indian chuckled: "Him have a she-sign on
sleeve!"

In conclusion, may I add that I am only pursuing truth and could not, even
should I wish most fervently to do so, reach any hard and fast conclusions.
However, I must say that your delightful fallacies were so amusing that the

readers of the mag must be indebted to you if they were only partially as tickled as the author to whom you were tossing the brickbats.

L. Taylor Hansen

(address withheld)

Atta-boy, Hansen! They asked for it. And thanks for saying our own defense was "able."

We wish we could speak with your authority! — Ed. [Raymond A. Palmer]

4   EDITORS

The Anglophone periodical boom coincided with an influx of educated women into the labor force at the turn of the twentieth century; therefore, it is no surprise that such women sought careers in magazine editing of all sorts, including SF. Many of the women working in SF, such as Miriam Bourne at *Amazing Stories* and Catherine "Kay" Tarrant at *Astounding Science Fiction*, were employed in essential but largely behind-the-scenes support roles. A few, however, made their names as lead editors. Following the pattern established by their nineteenth-century predecessors in commercial women's magazine production, Dorothy McIlwraith of *Weird Tales* and Mary Gnaedinger of *Famous Fantastic Mysteries* guaranteed the success of their publications by adopting the role of the editor as facilitator. As such, they used written commentaries to suggest that the creation of SF as a popular genre was a joint endeavor between editors and readers, while quietly furthering their unique visions of SF through content selection. Meanwhile, Lilith Lorraine of *Different* chose a path similar to that of women editors from the early-twentieth-century modernist little-magazine movement, using her publication to speak directly about the relations of aesthetics and politics in both her editorials and her content choice.

Magazines dominated Anglophone literary culture from the mid-nineteenth to the mid-twentieth century. This was particularly true in the United States, where, as the feminist literary historian Ellen Gruber Garvey explains, "about 60% of Americans were regular magazine readers" by the opening decades of the twentieth century (xi). In an era when an increasing number of women sought paid work outside the home, editing seemed to be an ideal career because "many people believed editing was simply an extension of reading, and . . . women had long been associated with fiction reading" (xiv). In practice, however, editing required women to grow beyond conventional gender roles because it demanded a certain facility with "unwomanly" activities such as public speaking and business management (xix). Women accepted this challenge eagerly and found particular success as editors in two distinct areas: the commercial women's magazines that helped define the cult of domesticity and the rhetoric of separate spheres in the middle to late 1800s and the noncommercial literary magazines that shaped modernist politics and aesthetics in the early 1900s.

More than seven hundred women worked as editors at the wildly popular and profitable women's magazines that debuted in the Victorian Era. Such women often took on the editing persona of the facilitator to negotiate the gap between their publications' stated commitment to conservative gender ideals and their own, often more progressive social and political beliefs. Fionnuala Dillane explains that while men employed the "model of editor as impresario . . . authoritative, visionary, and entrepreneur-like," women gravitated to the model of editor as facilitator because while they were "aware that there would always be compromises on content" that exceeded their control, they could exert authority in terms of "how that content was delivered" (284). This is certainly true of Sarah Josepha Hale, who edited *Godey's Lady Book* from 1837 until 1877. On the one hand, Hale's editorial comments seemed to uphold "the notion that women, being innocent and fragile, are more suited to life in the home" (Darling 22). At the same time, she "subtly advocated a public role for women in the arts and letters" with story selections that encouraged a critical dialogue about traditional gender roles and editorials that linked education to the success of women's domestic labor—which, Hale suggested, might even be expanded to include teaching and writing (Darling 22). In a similar vein, Mary Louise Booth, who edited *Harper's Bazaar* from 1867 to 1889, "recognized the potential in the high-fashion magazine's position as trend-setter—its futuristic orientation—and exploited it from the start, using it as a cover for her advocacy of social . . . and gender reform" (Bennett 226).[1] By showing how the work of women as homemakers and consumers might coexist with and even facilitate their work in the realms of culture and politics, Hale and Booth ensured the ongoing success of their publications while disseminating progressive new ideas to large audiences.[2]

By way of contrast, the noncommercial modernist literary magazines that sprung up in the early twentieth century provided new opportunities for women editors to experiment more directly with creative expression. As the literary historian Jayne E. Marek explains, women working at these little magazines—many of which were owned and operated by the women who edited them—"refused to use editing as a passive facilitation of others' works and were instead visibly confrontational, juxtaposing editorials, reviews, and articles to highlight critical controversies" over everything from cubism and imagism to the ideas of Sigmund Freud and Emma Goldman (61). As they combined art and politics in their magazines, women often encountered resistance from male colleagues who advocated a strict separation between the two realms. This was particularly true of Dora Marsden and Harriet Shaw Weaver at the *New Freewoman* (later renamed the *Egoist*) and Margaret Anderson and Jane Heap at the *Little Review*, who, "to the perpetual frustration of men like [Ezra] Pound, John Quinn, William Carlos Williams and others . . . refused to separate art out into a special sphere of its own, somehow devoid of history, personality, and the micropolitics of everyday life" (Latham 408). In direct contrast to their counterparts in commercial magazine production, who often downplayed their innovative editing activities to ensure the continued success of their magazines, little-magazine editors proudly claimed such activities as their own.

Genre publications made their debut at the height of the commercial magazine boom in the 1920s, and their production was made possible by scores of women working in support roles. Many of these women were crucial to the success of their magazines. Miriam Bourne began her career at *Amazing Stories* in 1926 as a secretary, but quickly took on editorial work reading manuscripts and running interference between Hugo Gernsback and the many authors to whom he owed money. In 1928 Gernsback promoted Bourne to the position of associate editor, and in 1929 his successor, T. O'Conor Sloane, made her managing editor, in which position she handled the daily operations of the *Amazing* franchise.[3] In a similar vein, Catherine "Kay" Tarrant was hired at *Astounding Science Fiction* to perform secretarial work, but because her boss, John W. Campbell, preferred to do his own typing, she quickly assumed the role of manuscript editor. In this capacity, Tarrant ensured *Astounding's* reputation as a clean magazine suitable for readers of all ages by ruthlessly excising racy content from her authors' submissions.[4] What began as clerical jobs for both Bourne and Tarrant became editorial careers in which the two facilitated the success of their respective publications through a wide range of behind-the-scenes activities.

Women also adopted the persona of the facilitator in their work as lead editors. Like many of their nineteenth-century counterparts, both Mary Gnaedinger and Dorothy McIlwraith were seasoned professionals brought in from outside their respective magazines' generic communities to promote already established publishing agendas. For Gnaedinger, who was hired by the Munsey Company in 1939 to edit *Famous Fantastic Mysteries*, this meant ensuring the success of a magazine dedicated to reprinting SF and fantasy stories from the Munsey catalog. For McIlwraith, who became the editor of *Weird Tales* in 1940, this meant fulfilling her predecessor Farnsworth Wright's promise to print only "the cream of the weird scientific-fiction that is written today" (qtd. in Weinberg, "*Weird*" 120). Both women were also careful to follow the convention introduced by Hugo Gernsback in the first issue of *Amazing Stories* (and imitated by all other editors from this period) of building community with the promise that all editorial decisions would be guided by reader preferences. As Gnaedinger vowed in a brief March 1940 headnote,

"Each succeeding issue of *Famous Fantastic Mysteries* [will] conform further with the readers' requests" (41). Meanwhile, McIlwraith used *Weird Tales'* discussion forum, "The Eyrie," to solicit audience engagement by asking, "What do you readers think?" and encouraging fans to write in because "such letters are a great help to us in giving you the kinds of stories that you really want to see." Gnaedinger and McIlwraith may not have been familiar with speculative fiction prior to their work within the genre, but as experienced editors they quickly identified the conventions of their new communities and employed them to ensure a strong subscription base.

Neither Gnaedinger nor McIlwraith was prone to making extensive editorial pronouncements, but any such pronouncements were also designed to facilitate a sense of partnership between editor and readers. When All-Fiction Field bought *Famous Fantastic Mysteries* in 1943, Gnaedinger suddenly had the freedom to print both new and old stories of her own choosing. As she explained in her March 1943 editorial, "In our opinion, this change, far from diminishing the quality of the book, should improve it. . . . Now we have the fantastic lore of the world from which to choose" (113). While Gnaedinger goes on to preview a story that will appear in the next issue that is, "in our opinion, one of the most outstanding imaginative fantasies ever written," she concludes by assuring readers that she is also negotiating for the rights "to an English fantasy novel for which a lot of you have been clamoring for a long time" (113). Meanwhile, in her preface to the July 1941 readers' forum, McIlwraith uses a reader's comparison of *Weird Tales* to a kind of literary time machine as the occasion to explain why her magazine's multi-genre approach to fiction trumps the more narrow focus of the specialist genre magazines: employing genres such as "horror," "science fiction," and "fantasy of every kind" allows readers to explore the past, present, and future through stories "so varied that, no matter what your taste, you will be entertained" (122). The practice employed by Gnaedinger and McIlwraith of always emphasizing the positive and creative connections between editor and fan was a far cry from that of Hugo Gernsback, Farnsworth Wright, and Harry Bates of *Astounding*, all of whom courted readers when they needed money but testily corrected them when their ideas about SF departed from those of the editors themselves.[5]

Even as they worked to build a community among readers, Gnaedinger and McIlwraith expanded that community's understanding of speculative fiction through invisible editing activities, including art and story selection. Gnaedinger secured the early success of *Famous Fantastic Mysteries* by commissioning the much-loved *Weird Tales* artist Virgil Finlay to produce both interior and cover art. Moreover, in an era when editors such as John W. Campbell and Groff Conklin were loudly declaring that women could not write SF, Gnae-dinger preserved women's contributions to the genre by reprinting their stories and poems.[6] The fourth issue of *Famous Fantastic Mysteries* included Francis Stevens's 1918 tale "Behind the Curtain" as well as Lillian M. Ains-worth's 1917 horror story "An Astral Gentleman" (coauthored with Robert Wilbur Lull; see figure 4.1). Other issues of *Famous Fantastic Mysteries* fea-tured offerings by Laura Withrow, Minna Irving, and, once Gnaedinger was free to commission new works, C. L. Moore.

Similarly, when the death or departure of key *Weird Tales* contributors de-manded that McIlwraith rethink her predecessor's publishing agenda, she seized the opportunity to shift the magazine's focus away from the cosmic horror and sword and sorcery stories that appeared outdated to an Ameri-can audience increasingly interested in "atom bombs, space flight, and flying saucers" (Hanley). Accordingly, she introduced readers to new authors, includ-ing Fritz Leiber, Theodore Sturgeon, and Margaret St. Clair, all of whom would become central to the socially oriented SF that flourished at midcentury and paved the way for New Wave SF. For instance, in the November 1942 issue of *Weird Tales*, McIlwraith provides readers with offerings from longtime con-tributors H. P. Lovecraft, Robert Bloch, Stanton A. Coblentz, and David H. Keller alongside tales from Ray Bradbury, Fritz Leiber, and Hannes Bok, new-comers who were just a few years into their highly prolific, decades-spanning careers (see figure 4.2). She also introduced readers to new artists such as Frank Kelly Freas, whose fifty-year career in SF would earn him the title "the Dean of Science Fiction Artists" ("Presenting").[7] As such, Gnaedinger and Mc-Ilwraith can be seen as having facilitated the economic success of their maga-zines, the social cohesiveness of their audiences, and the literary development of SF itself.

While most women in the early SF community worked as editors for com-mercial magazines, Lilith Lorraine successfully edited her own noncommer-cial periodicals. An experienced genre professional who began publishing fiction with Gernsback in the late 1920s, Lorraine became alienated from commercial SF as it evolved away from the progressive political sensibilities that marked Gernsback's early magazines and toward what she perceived as a more juvenile, action-oriented format (for more details see the entry on Lorraine in chapter 1, "Authors," of this anthology). By the early 1940s, Lorraine had returned to her first love, poetry (see the entry on Lorraine in chapter 2, "Poets,") and was contemplating a move to editing. As she half-jokingly noted in a 1943 letter to the popular fanzine the *Acolyte*, "I may still return to science fiction one day, whenever the market ceases to be so stereo-typed and standardized. . . . [But I also] have a rather daring idea in mind of

Vol. 1   **JANUARY, 1940**   **No. 4**

THIS magazine is the answer to thousands of requests that we have received over a period of years, demanding a second look at the famous fantasies which, since their original publication, have become accepted classics.
—*The Editors.*

Coming in the February Issue

A Complete Novelet

The Man Who Saved the Earth

By Austin Hall

A compelling, exciting picture of what the last great world cataclysm might well be, given us through the eyes of a master of science fiction

By popular demand—

The Sky Woman

By Charles B. Stilson

Glamorous, fascinating, time-tested

And five more fine weird, science-fiction and space adventure stories.

STARTLING!
On the Brink of 2000.........Garret Smith   6
Supposing there was an invention that would enable you to see into the lives of others!

WEIRD!
Behind the Curtain........Francis Stevens   37
A story of exquisitely cruel revenge

ASTOUNDING!
The Radio Man........Ralph Milne Farley   43
In Three Parts—Part II

THRILLING!
The Red Germ of Courage......R. F. Starzl   65
Up to the stratosphere in space ships!

EERIE!
An Astral Gentleman....Robert Wilbur Lull
and Lillian M. Ainsworth   80
Any port in a storm—any body when you've none of your own

AMAZING!
The Conquest of the Moon Pool...A. Merritt   88
In Six Parts—Part III

STRANGE!
The "V" Force.............Fred C. Smale   120
What was the secret of its mysteriously destructive energy?

Weird Travel Tales..A Feature.....Bob Davis   78
The Readers' Viewpoint.....................   127

THE FRANK A. MUNSEY COMPANY, Publisher, 280 Broadway, New York, N. Y.
WILLIAM T. DEWART, *President*

THE CONTINENTAL PUBLISHERS & DISTRIBUTORS, LTD.
3 La Belle Sauvage, Ludgate Hill, London, E.C., 4
Paris: HACHETTE & CIE, 111 Rue Reaumur

Copyright, 1939, by The Frank A. Munsey Company
Published monthly. Single copy 15 cents. By the year, $1.50 in United States, its dependencies, Mexico and Cuba; Canada, $1.75. Other countries, $2.25. Currency should not be sent unless registered. Remittances should be made by check, express money order or postal money order. Copyrighted in Great Britain. Printed in U. S. A.
The February Issue Will Be On Sale January 3

4.1. Table of contents page for the January 1940 issue of *Famous Fantastic Mysteries*. From the holdings of the Eaton Collection of Science Fiction and Fantasy, Special Collections and University Archives, UCR Library, University of California, Riverside.

ALL STORIES NEW—NO REPRINTS

NOVEMBER, 1942   Cover by Richard Bennett

NOVELETTE

NURSEMAID TO NIGHTMARES . . . . Robert Bloch   6
Julius Margate collects horrors the way some people collect stamps

SHORT STORIES

THE HOUND . . . . Fritz Leiber   34
These monsters feed on our fears, they haunt us, terrorize us

THE CROOKED HOUSE . . . . Thorne Lee   45
A hunchbacked, brooding monster, this house with the twisted soul

THE VICTORY OF THE VITA-RAY . . . . Stanton A. Coblentz   60
Twenty bloodstained bigshots of history are recalled from eternity

THE GOLDEN BOUGH . . . . David H. Keller   67
*In the moonlight the laughing man would come, playing his Pan-like music
—and she knew she must dance or die*

THE GHOST OF THE MODEL T . . . . Betsy Emmons   78
This man was stalked by a phantom, the specter of his first car

THE CANDLE . . . . Ray Bradbury   83
The proprietor pronounced the candle an implement of destruction

THE LIPS OF CAYA WU . . . . Frank Owen   90
*There was no escape, for octopus-like, the Chinaman's schemes
spread out everywhere*

HERBERT WEST: REANIMATOR . . . . H. P. Lovecraft   96
*The scientist finds that the quest for the secret of life leads
surely through the grave*

THE POSSESSED . . . . Alice-Mary Schnirring   100
*Some macabre horror was here, changing this town and the people
in it in appearance as night drew near*

THE EVIL DOLL . . . . Hannes Bok   107
*Was it hypnotism or witchcraft—she must know for her sanity;
her very life depended on the answer*

VERSE

THE DEAD WORLD . . . . Clarence Edwin Flynn   77

INTO FANTASY . . . . Maria Moravsky   82

SUPERSTITIONS AND TABOOS . . . . Irwin J. Weill   58
THE EYRIE AND WEIRD TALES CLUB 120

*Except for personal experiences the contents of this magazine is fiction. Any use
of the name of any living person or reference to actual events is purely coincidental*

Published bi-monthly by Weird Tales, 9 Rockefeller Plaza, New York, N. Y. Reentered as second-class matter
January 26, 1940, at the Post Office at New York, N. Y., under the act of March 3, 1879. Single copies, 15 cents.
Subscription rates: One year in the United States and possessions, 90c. Foreign and Canadian postage extra.
English Office: Charles Lavell, Limited, 4 Clements Inn, Strand, London, W.C.2, England. The publishers are not
responsible for the loss of unsolicited manuscripts although every care will be taken of such material while in their
possession.   Copyright, 1942, by Weird Tales. Copyrighted in Great Britain.   173
Title registered in U. S. Patent Office.
PRINTED IN THE U. S. A.   Vol. 36, No. 8

D. McILWRAITH, *Editor.*   LAMONT BUCHANAN, *Associate Editor.*

4.2. Table of contents page for the November 1942 issue of *Weird Tales*. From the holdings of the Eaton Collection of Science Fiction and Fantasy, Special Collections and University Archives, UCR Library, University of California, Riverside.

starting a national magazine for the publication of rejected stories [to show what authors] can do if they are really turned loose" (n.p.). Lorraine did indeed go on to edit more than half a dozen amateur press publications dedicated to the project of turning authors loose. The most notable of these was *Different*, which Lorraine published from the mid-1940s to the mid-1950s and which, as the SF historian Mike Ashley notes, had a "freshness that attracted interest throughout the sf world and helped encourage a new generation of writers" (*History* 210).

The public persona that Lorraine developed in her little-magazine work was very much like that of her male counterparts in SF. Both Gernsback and Sloane at *Amazing* and, to a lesser extent, Harry Bates at *Astounding* and Farnsworth Wright at *Weird Tales* used their roles as impresarios to promote specific visions of their chosen genre and readers' roles within it.[8] Lorraine made similarly authoritative pronouncements about poetry, which she defines provocatively in "The Story of *Different*" not just as "the writing of verse," but as any "act of creative imagination, which is the atomic energy of poetry." These acts include both traditional literary production and lived activities such as "spanning a continent with a mighty railroad . . . tracking the foxes of disease and pestilence to their final lairs, [and] leading embattled peoples against their oppressors" (2). While Lorraine does not name SF as an act of creative imagination, she makes technoscientific activity central to her definition of poetry and employs science fictional language to describe poets as "star-illuminated legislators," "warriors of eternity," and "citizens of the galaxies" (2).[9] More prosaically, Lorraine also followed the example of her male counterparts in her complex attitude toward readers, assuring them that "an editor's duty is to ALL of his subscribers" while encouraging them to help her sell subscriptions because "unless the poets themselves support their last remaining mediums . . . [*Different*] will be forced to go down before the rising tide of postal rate increases" (6). Lorraine's inspirational vision for modern art and her practical approach to the economics of publishing reflect the sometimes contradictory forces that shaped early SF publishing agendas.

But Lorraine went beyond her male colleagues to insist on the political possibilities of her chosen art form as well. Like her counterparts at modernist periodicals such as the *New Freewoman* and the *Little Review*, Lorraine creatively juxtaposed poetry, fiction, artwork, and nonfiction essays to encourage dialogue about what she saw as the most pressing issues of her day: the commodification of art, the elision of education with vocational training, and the need to develop new models of global rather than national citizenship. She also treated these issues directly in her editorial writing. As she notes in "The Story of *Different*," Lorraine rejected offers to produce an "advertiser-controlled publication which must please everyone" because she believed that only independent magazines could "salvage some last remnants of American culture" and dismantle "the battlements of hate and terror" that threaten to become the hallmarks of modernity (6, 4, 4). Such matters are critical, she explains, in an era when liberal arts curricula designed to produce civically engaged citizens are being replaced by "specialized training" geared to produce workers who are "efficient cog[s] in the industrial machine" (3). Lorraine takes up this theme again in "Training for World Citizenship," where she argues passionately for a revised education system in which teachers are "paid fair and decent wages" to develop curricula grounded in the arts and the social sciences that will produce Americans who can "give to and receive from other nations that knowledge of world affairs that will enable us to fulfill our duties as citizens of the world" (3). While Gernsback and other male editors generally limited their comments about the social value of SF to the seemingly apolitical realms of science education and technological innovation, Lorraine insists that the creative imagination is essential to the fate of humanity as a whole.

Lorraine's insistence on the interconnected nature of art and politics was reflected in her choice of contributors. On the one hand, *Different*'s roster regularly featured such authors as fantastic poetry veterans August Derlith and Leah Bodine Drake (see chapter 2, "Poets," of this anthology), SF newcomers Marion Zimmer Bradley and Robert Silverberg, amateur press editors Manley Banister and Orma McCormick, and rocket expert R. L. Farnsworth. But Lorraine took care to juxtapose literary offerings with political and scientific ones as well. For instance, the second issue of *Different* included an editorial by Lorraine, fiction reviews by fantasy veteran Stanley A. Coblentz, an exposé of modern business practices by the sociology professor and editor of the liberal monthly the *Emancipator*, John C. Granbery, and one of the first treatises on lucid dreaming by the anthropologist Kilton Stewart (see figure 4.3). Like her counterparts in the modernist little-magazine movement, Lorraine quite literally refused to separate art from other aspects of life, weaving together articles on diverse topics in provocative ways.

The careers of Mary Gnaedinger, Dorothy McIlwraith, and Lilith Lorraine serve as a window into the history of women's work as magazine editors. As they adapted the practices of their counterparts in both commercial and noncommercial magazine production to the needs of the SF community, they ensured the success of their publications and paved the way for the scores of women working as SF editors today. Gnaedinger's commitment to publishing women in an era of feminist backlash anticipated the work of the midcentury editor Cele Goldsmith Lalli, who discovered Ursula K. Le Guin and Sonya

Different

The Voice of the Cultural Renaissance

VOLUME TWO	MAY-JUNE, 1946	NUMBER TWO

Dedicated to the finding and training of new writers, who, while not discarding the eternal values, are courageous enough to interpret them in the style and language of a changing world. Dedicated to the discovery and encouragement of genius in all its forms, that its gifts may not be lost to humanity or perverted by deprivation or misunderstanding. Dedicated to the fostering of a Cultural Renaissance in the United States, through forging closer cultural ties with other nations of the Western Hemisphere, that a unified culture may be developed. Dedicated to the discouragement of bewilderment, incoherence, cheap sophistication and defeatism in the arts, and to the fearless analysis of those forms of propaganda that menace the peace of the world through the corruption of culture. Dedicated to the belief, founded on the total collapse of the so-called "practical" but actually selfish values, that the golden rule is the only successful law of life and that "without vision, the people perish."

MANUSCRIPT REQUIREMENTS

PROSE: We want short stories of from 2,500 to 3,000 words, that are really "different" as to style and subject matter. We especially need distinctive love stories, fantasy stories and animal stories in which the author escapes from regimented plots and from imitative styles. We can use 400 to 800 word articles concerning children who are geniuses in any field, "behind-the-scenes" revelations on politics, practical ideas for the improvement of our educational system or for the strengthening of our cultural ties with other nations, and sound plans for an enduring world peace.

POETRY: Poems must be idealistic, technically sound, highly original in style and thought-content, dynamically simple and sincerely written, with no involved sentence structure, and of strong yet restrained emotional appeal. No escapism, pollyannism, preaching, atheism, or incoherent experimentalism. Limit 20 lines.

PAYMENT: Beginning with the March-April issue we shall pay $5.00 on acceptance for each story accepted, $1.00 for each article accepted, and $1.00 each for the best ten poems accepted. The payment for a large number of other poems may be effected through the contributions of our patrons at the same rate per poem. In lieu of more generous payments for both prose and poetry, which cannot be made until printing costs have returned to normal and our subscription list has been doubled, we shall give free criticism on each rejected story, poem or article, and marketing advice, should we believe the manuscript might find acceptance elsewhere.

IMPORTANT: As we are not responsible for any manuscript lost in the mail, authors are requested to keep copies of all material submitted to us. All manuscripts must be typewritten, double-spaced, with name and address of author in the upper left-hand corner of the page, as well as at the end of each poem, and be accompanied by a large-size, stamped, addressed envelope with sufficient postage for the return of the manuscript if not acceptable. Manuscripts which are not typewritten cannot be considered and those not accompanied by a stamped addressed envelope will be consigned to the wastebasket.

REPORTS ON MANUSCRIPTS ARE MADE IMMEDIATELY

OPINIONS expressed by our contributors and department heads are not necessarily those of the publisher and editors.

RATES: $2.00 per year, 35c per copy; same rate for foreign countries and for the armed forced overseas. No free samples. Make all checks and money orders payable to DIFFERENT,

ROGERS, ARKANSAS

CONTENTS

Cover Design .... Lucille S. Jackson

Cover Poem—

    Here on These Hills .... Lilith Lorraine

Greetings From Avalon in the Ozarks .... Lilith Lorraine 17

Ready For Her Hand .... Lewis Worthington Smith 14

Battle Across Time .... George C. Alborn 26

There Ought To Be A Law .... Josephine Prater 29

DEPARTMENTS

Editorial—

    Training for World Citizenship .... Lilith Lorraine 2

Now Department—Children of Freedom ... Lucille S. Jackson 4

The Raven Poetry Department .... Editor, Lilith Lorraine 5

Behind the Political Scene—

    Barons of Business .... John C. Granbery 13

Strange Experiences .... Editor, Dariell Dunay 15

Trails to Triumph .... Editor, Martha L. Hunter 19

Mightier Than The Sword—

    Prose .... Stanton A. Coblentz 21

    Poetry .... Lillian S. Holloway 21

Creative Dreaming .... Editor, Kilton Stewart 22

They Carry The Flame .... Editor, Lilith Lorraine 24

Prophets of Peace—

    The Dynamics of the Soul .... Powell Spring 25

Ask Me Anything—

    Women Who Make Me Sick .... Dariell Dunay 27

4.3. Table of contents page for the May–June 1946 issue of *Different*.

Dorman, as well as the work of the author-editor Marion Zimmer Bradley, whose *Fantasy Magazine* often featured short, humorous stories by women. It also anticipated the more overtly political recovery work of feminist SF anthologists, including Pamela Sargent and Justine Larbalestier. As the first female editor of *Weird Tales*, McIlwraith paved the way for contemporary women specializing in weird and horror fiction editing such as Ann Vander-Meer, the first woman to edit *Weird Tales* since McIlwraith's tenure, and Ellen Datlow, who has received more than thirty awards for editing, including the Bram Stoker Lifetime Achievement award for her contributions to the horror genre. Meanwhile Lilith Lorraine's commitment to small-press publishing is echoed in the careers of Bradley as well as Kelly Link and Cat Rambo, both of whom have been nominated for major awards multiple times on the basis of their noncommercial editing activities.

MARY GNAEDINGER (1897–1976) was an American editor noted for her work on *Famous Fantastic Mysteries*. She was born Mary Catherine Jacobson in Brooklyn, New York, where she lived for most of her life. In the late 1920s Mary Jacobson attended the Columbia University School of Journalism, where she met and married the news editor Louis Beverley Nichol Gnaedinger. After leaving Columbia, she embarked on a career as a "society reporter for the *Brooklyn Eagle*" and as an editor for E. P. Dutton & Company ("Mary Gnaedinger, Editor" 23). In 1939, Gnaedinger accepted the position of editor for the Frank A. Munsey Company's new magazine, *Famous Fantastic Mysteries*, a nostalgia-oriented publication that reprinted classic SF and fantasy stories from the Munsey catalog. The first issue of *Famous* was so successful that it was immediately moved from a bimonthly to a monthly publication schedule.[10]

Like many women in commercial magazine editing, Gnaedinger took on the role of community facilitator at *Famous Fantastic Mysteries*. In the debut issue, Gnaedinger introduced her magazine's mission as one grounded in the "thousands of requests" Munsey had received from readers to republish stories that "have become accepted classics" (2). Gnaedinger returned to this theme time and again throughout her tenure at *Famous*, insisting that the canon she was creating in the pages of her magazine was "dictated by *your* requests." Accordingly, her editorial comments praised fans for their knowledge of the genre and synthesized their observations about the excellent stories that she was only too happy to reprint. Additionally, Gnaedinger demonstrated her commitment to the SF community by attending meetings of the well-known New York fan group the Futurians and developing relationships with fellow SF editors such as Frederik Pohl. While she came to the genre as an outsider, then, Gnaedinger earned the trust (and subscriptions) of SF fans across the country by demonstrating sensitivity to their interests and needs.

As was also the case for many other women in commercial magazine publishing, Gnaedinger exerted her greatest influence in art and story selection. She commissioned the *Weird Tales* regular Virgil Finlay to create the first piece of interior art and the first illustrated magazine cover for *Famous Fantastic Mysteries*—all the while assuring readers that her decisions on this front were guided by the collective suggestion that "an illustrated cover would improve the appearance of the magazine" ("Editors' Page," 1940). Even more significantly, in an era when editors such as John W. Campbell and Groff Conklin publicly dismissed the notion that women could write SF, Gnaedinger republished poems and stories by classic women writers including Minna Irving, Francis Stevens (Gertrude Barrows Bennett), and Laura Withrow.[11] The immediate success of *Famous Fantastic Mysteries* attested to the wisdom of Gnaedinger's editorial choices, and in 1940 Munsey allowed the editor to branch out and develop a companion magazine entitled *Fantastic Novels*. While this second magazine did not enjoy the extensive success of its predecessor, Gnaedinger edited both until they folded in 1953.

Even when the Munsey Company sold *Famous* to All-Fiction Field in 1943 and she suddenly had the freedom to publish whatever she deemed fit, Gnaedinger maintained her public commitment to serving the needs of the SF community above all else. In a March 1943 editorial devoted to addressing reader concerns regarding what might happen to *Famous* in the wake of its sale, Gnaedinger explains that "where before we were restricted to an ever diminishing inventory of old Munsey classics, we now have the fantastic lore of the world from which to choose" (113). Moreover, while Gnaedinger offers her audience a personal take on a forthcoming story and—for the first time ever—signs her editorial with her own name, she concludes by pledging to readers "the same high quality of classics that [*Famous*] has given them in the past" (113). Gnaedinger edited *Famous* from its first issue in September 1939 to its final issue in June 1953, a rare instance of an editor holding such a position for the entire run of a magazine. This feat is even more impressive given that *Famous* saw three different publishers, outlasted many of its competitors, and survived many downturns in the SF magazine market. Though she never developed a flamboyant persona like many of her contemporaries, Gnaedinger was a respected and beloved editor of SF at the height of the pulp era whose magazine was both highly profitable and highly regarded.

....

"Editorial Note"
Famous Fantastic Mysteries, September–October 1939

This magazine is the answer to thousands of requests that we have received over a period of years, demanding a second look at famous fantasies that, since their original publication, have become accepted classics. Our choice has been dictated by your requests and our firm belief is that these are the aces of imagination.
—*The Editors*

....

"The Editor's Page"

Famous Fantastic Mysteries, March 1940

You will find that each succeeding issue of *Famous Fantastic Mysteries* conforms further with the readers' requests. Many readers have suggested that an illustrated cover would improve the appearance of the magazine. We hope you like the cover Virgil Finlay has done for you this month.

———

Next month will bring "The Devil of the Western Sea," the colorful classic that so many of you have been asking for. It is a complete novelette, and fantastic in the very best sense.

Letters have asked just when "Darkness and Dawn" will start. It is scheduled for the issue after next. That will be the May issue.

———

We have received hundreds of enthusiastic comments on the stories published in the first five numbers of *Famous Fantastic Mysteries*. There is no doubt about the standing of "The Radio Man" and "The Conquest of the Moon Pool" among the great fantastic stories of all time. The letters bear witness to their being "tops" and the only problem is to choose the order in which more of the same kind of classics are to be presented.

———

Your second installment of "The Blind Spot" will be on the newsstands March 6. The installment in this issue is the start-off of a real thriller that gets more exciting with every succeeding part. So get around to your news dealer before his supply is gone. If your news dealer is sold out, you can obtain back issues by sending 15¢ to *Famous Fantastic Mysteries*, 280 Broadway, New York.

———

Among the interesting suggestions in a letter to "The Readers' Viewpoint" from Norman Knudson of Ogden, Utah, was one that a list of past stories in order of merit should be printed. Below, you will find the published stories listed in the order of ratings given them in the readers' letters.

———

In Order of Popularity

Sept.–Oct.: The Girl in the Golden Atom; The Moon Pool; Karpen the Jew; The Whimpus; The Witch-Makers; Blind Man's Buff; Space Station No. 1.

November: The Conquest of the Moon Pool; Almost Immortal; The Moon Metal; The Radiant Enemies; Fruit of the Forbidden Tree; The World in the Balance; The Man with the Glass Heart.

December: The Radio Man; The Conquest of the Moon Pool; The Lord of

Death; The Diminishing Draft; Who Is Charles Avison?; Lights; The
Gravity Experiment.
January: On the Brink of 2000; The Conquest of the Moon Pool; The Radio
Man; An Astral Gentleman; The Red Germ of Courage; The "V" Force;
Behind the Curtain.
February: The Man Who Saved the Earth; The Conquest of the Moon Pool;
The Sky Woman; The Radio Man; Son of the Stars; The Plunge of the
"Knupfen"; The Kiss of Death.

The lists of stories sent in by readers who recall them as top-notch examples
of science fiction and weird yarns are very helpful. Let's have more from you!
—*The Editors*

....

"The Editor's Page"
Famous Fantastic Mysteries, March 1943

At this time it is only natural that there should be a lot of speculation as to
the present and future aims and policies of *Famous Fantastic Mysteries*. With
the sale of the Munsey publications to a house that has been a leader in a
fight against reprints in general, some modification of policy was, of course,
to be expected. The future running plan of this book may be stated briefly as
follows:

> *Famous Fantastic Mysteries* will publish only new stories of exceptional
> quality or stories that have never before appeared in magazine form.
> (Please see the footnote on page 114, regarding "Into the Infinite.")

In our opinion, this change, far from diminishing the quality of the book,
should infinitely improve it. Where before we were restricted to an ever diminishing inventory of old Munsey classics, we now have the fantastic lore of
the world from which to choose. The next issue, for example, will feature John
Taine's great classic "The Iron Star," in our opinion one of the most outstanding imaginative fantasies ever written. And while it is too early to go into details, we are negotiating for magazine rights to an English fantasy novel for
which a lot of you have been clamoring for a long time.

Famous Fantastic Mysteries pledges to its readers the same high quality of
classics that it has given them in the past, the same scrupulous fidelity in re-
producing them, the same outstanding artwork by the same craftsmen. If by
so doing we can make this magazine truly the golden book of fantasy, a book

to be kept and treasured with other great literature that has been written in this field, we will have considered our mission well worth the labor.

Our heartfelt thanks to our readers for their loyal and most cooperative support!

Mary Gnaedinger
EDITOR

DOROTHY STEVENS MCILWRAITH (1891–1976) was the Canadian editor based in New York who ran *Weird Tales* from 1940 to 1954. McIlwraith was born in Hamilton, Ontario, and graduated from McGill University in 1914. Her aunt, Jean McIlwraith, worked for almost two decades as an author, reader, and editor in New York during the early 1900s and McIlwraith followed in her trail. By the end of 1917 she had moved to the United States, settled in New York, and started working for the same company as her aunt: Doubleday, Page, and Company, which published books and magazines and was one of the most successful publishers in the country. In the 1920 census, McIlwraith listed her occupation as assistant editor of a magazine in New York, and by 1936 she had become editor of Doubleday's *Short Stories*. The magazine was sold to William J. Delaney's company, Short Stories, Inc., in 1937, and he kept McIlwraith on as the editor. When Delaney purchased *Weird Tales* in 1938, he moved the editorial offices to New York. Though he retained the longtime editor Farnsworth Wright, he made McIlwraith the associate editor of *Weird Tales* in 1939. Wright's health was in decline, however, and McIlwraith took over as the editor of *Weird Tales* just before Wright's death in 1940.[12]

Like most editors in commercial magazine production, McIlwraith often made editorial choices in response to external forces. When Delany hired McIlwraith to take over *Weird Tales*, he encouraged her to transform the financially struggling magazine into the "standard pulp mode" so it more closely resembled his classier and more successful publication, *Short Stories* (Ashley, *History* 140). McIlwraith had to confront other challenges as well. One such challenge came when the mayor of New York waged war on sex at the newsstands in 1939, which likely influenced McIlwraith's decision to stop commissioning the controversial nude covers of Margaret Brundage in favor of more standard—and well-clothed—scenes of weird action.[13] Another serious challenge came in the form of *Weird Tales*' reduced budget, which meant that McIlwraith had less money for stories and art and thus a more difficult time securing the best material for her magazine.

Nonetheless, McIlwraith managed to preserve key aspects of *Weird Tales* that had characterized the magazine since its inception. Most significantly, since *Short Stories* was also a multi-genre magazine, she was able to maintain *Weird Tales*' commitment to publishing horror, fantasy, and SF. McIlwraith also continued to acquire work from some of the most talented people in the field. Though the move to New York made it harder for Brundage to submit her artwork, McIlwraith continued to commission less risqué covers from the *Weird Tales* legend until 1945. McIlwraith also continued to publish fiction and poetry by the *Weird Tales* veterans August Derleth, Henry Kuttner, and Mary Counselman, while introducing readers to new talents, including Fritz Leiber and Ray Bradbury.

Where the editors of the SF specialist magazines often adopted flamboyant personas, McIlwraith took on the more subdued role of the editor as facilitator. Like Farnsworth Wright before her, McIlwraith used *Weird Tales'* discussion forum, "The Eyrie," to foster community, introducing stories in an upbeat manner and editing together letters from readers and authors to create a continuous dialogue with many voices. But while Wright was not above engaging in an occasional argument with readers, refuting all criticism of his editing practices and marshaling authors to his side to prove his point, McIlwraith defused criticism by deferring to the judgment of the *Weird Tales* community itself. For example, when a longtime fan wrote in to mourn the loss of "the old custom of voting for the best story in each issue," McIlwraith diplomatically responded by acknowledging that "it might be a good idea to restore this feature" and asking readers to "let us know what you think" ("Eyrie," November–December 1940). Thus McIlwraith went beyond her predecessor, publicly subsuming her own editorial preferences to maintain the sense of group identity she worked so hard to foster elsewhere in her editing practices.

When McIlwraith did exert her own voice, it was always in dialogue with her authors and readers. For instance, when Wright passed away, McIlwraith used the November–December 1940 "Eyrie" to briefly express her "profound regret" before introducing a much longer eulogy by the longtime *Weird Tales* author Seabury Quinn (123). In that same discussion forum, McIlwraith stitches together a reader's letter criticizing Frank Gruber's short story "The Chalice," Gruber's defensive response to the reader in question, and her own rather detailed explanation of the fantastic aspects of Arthurian legend. Indeed, while reader and author bicker over details such as whether or not the Holy Grail would have really been made of gold, McIlwraith works hard to defuse tension by noting that "the mystery of the Holy Grail remains one of the most fascinating unsolved riddles of all time," thereby reassuring reader and author alike that they may both be correct (126).

In the rare instances in which she wrote traditional editorials, McIlwraith also linked her ideas to those of the larger genre community. This is particularly evident in the July 1941 "Eyrie," where McIlwraith uses a reader's comparison of *Weird Tales* to a "Time-Machine" as the occasion for celebrating her magazine's unique mission to print "horror," "science fiction," and "fantasy of every kind" so readers might explore the past, present, and future from new perspectives (122). This broad publishing mandate, she argues, gives fans of each genre something to like about *Weird Tales* and stands in sharp contrast to single-genre magazines such as *Amazing Stories* and *Astounding Science Fiction*. Even as she outlined her vision of *Weird Tales* and its relation to the larger field of fantastic fiction,

McIlwraith maintained a positive, fan-oriented voice similar to that of her contemporary, Mary Gnaedinger, at *Famous Fantastic Mysteries*.

. . . .

"The Eyrie"
Weird Tales, May 1940

WEIRD TALES CLUB IDEAS
In the last "Eyrie," the idea of a *Weird Tales* club was discussed. A nation-wide club may or may not be possible, but certainly *Weird Tales* can help in the formation of local clubs and organizations. Then, wherever you may live, you, your friends—and, we hope, new friends found through *W.T.*—can provide each other with a congenial, "weird get-together." Below are printed some readers' letters concerning a *Weird Tales* club, and we hope that everyone who is interested in such a project will write in to us, so that in the next issue some definite plans can be formulated.

THE "IMAGI-NATION"
Louise F. Avery of 776 Ostrom Avenue, Syracuse, N.Y., writes: "Having read in your March issue of *W.T.* of the 'Outsiders' in Washington, D.C., and of the 'Insiders' in Los Angeles, and also having noted your suggestion of forming other *Weird Tales* clubs throughout the 'imagi-nation'; I should like to say that here in Syracuse, N.Y., where the population averages around two hundred and fifty thousand, would be an excellent place to have another such club. I know there are numerous *W.T.* fans in Syracuse who would doubtless like to start a *Weird Tales* club. I would like to try it, and if this department will co-operate with me and my *W.T.* enthusiasts, I'm sure we could have fun, and I suggest that if you could find a spot in your column for this note and state that those who are interested in forming a *Weird Tales* club call me at my home, No. 5-4796, or drop me a post card at my home address, 776 Ostrom Avenue, the ideas would meet with the approval of Syracuse's many *W.T.* admirers."

. . . .

"The Eyrie"
Weird Tales, November 1940

It is with profound regret that we announce the death of Farnsworth Wright, who was editor of *Weird Tales* for many years and was so largely responsible for the success of the magazine. It seems fitting that we should print here in the "Eyrie" a letter about Mr. Wright from a man who not only was one of his personal friends, but also a constant contributor to *Weird Tales*. The staff of *Weird Tales*, its contributors and countless of its readers, join with Seabury Quinn in his tribute to a great editor and scholar.

————

Farnsworth Wright
Like everyone who has long been a reader of or contributor to *Weird Tales*, I was greatly shocked and grieved at the news of Farnsworth Wright's passing. Anyone who has read *Weird Tales* must have been impressed by his thorough knowledge of weird literature, his complete understanding of the great background of folk lore, superstition, and comparative religions from which such literature is drawn, and his nice sense of discrimination in selecting the cream of such stories by modern authors to carry on the tradition of the Georgian and early Victorian masters of Gothic tales. Helped and encouraged by his expert criticism and kindly advice, a whole generation of writers was developed, and though many of these have "graduated" to other media of expression, none, I am sure, will ever forget the debt he owes to Farnsworth Wright. There is today hardly a writer of fantasy whose success does not date from the encouragement he received from Mr. Wright, and there is certainly no one engaged in creative work who ever dealt with Farnsworth Wright who does not think kindly of him.

To those of us who were privileged to know him personally the loss is even greater. We knew him as a cultured gentleman, a charming host, an incomparably congenial companion, and a true and loyal friend. His steadily failing health caused us all concern, but his courage and resolution were so great that none of us realized how near the great beyond he was. His cheerful letters lulled us into a sense of false optimism, and when news of his death came our surprise was almost equal to our grief.

As for his abilities, his work provides the finest monument possible. In the old files of *Weird Tales* can be read the biography of a man whose genius made possible a magazine that was and is truly unique. As to his epitaph: If it be true that in imitation lies the sincerest form of flattery, Farnsworth Wright has been eloquently acclaimed. When he assumed the editorial chair of *Weird Tales* almost twenty years ago he was a lone adventurer setting out to bring a highly specialized form of entertainment to the reading public. A recent issue of *Author & Journalist* lists twenty-two magazines devoted exclusively to fantasy or pseudo-scientific fiction. Could any greater or more sincere compliment be paid his vision or his work?
Seabury Quinn
[. . . .]

From Springfield, Missouri, Donald V. Allgeier writes:

"For ten years I have been a *W.T.* fan and during that time it has always been my favorite of all magazines. I still have nostalgic memories of some of the great stories in the magazine's past. I was afraid that bi-monthly publication might be necessary, but I was relieved to see that the high quality of the stories remained. Why not restore the old custom of voting for the best story each issue and printing the title of the winner? That used to spur me to write in at least once every two months.

"I like most of the illustrations. Bok is good, as is Ferman and, occasionally, del Campo. The best story in September was, by all odds, 'Sea Born.'"

[What do you readers think of Mr. Allgeier's "voting for the best story" suggestion? We feel it might be a good idea to restore this feature. Let us know what you think.]

Fact Articles

Blair Moffett writes from Springfield, Pennsylvania:

"Mr. Frank Bristol, several issues back, and Mr. Al MacDowell in the last, made a good suggestion: I'd like to second it. The suggestion was: why not publish short fact articles on occult, esoteric, mythological, and kindred subjects? This would add immensely to *W.T.*'s value, and give a sane and sound direction to the swiftly growing interest in this type of study that can be noticed all over the country. 'It Happened to Me' is, it seems, an absorbing step in this direction. Mr. MacDonald's article was excellent, and gives an interpretation esoterically, that explains one point of view. And 'The Black Art' finished the Eyrie off very nicely."

[We hope to continue printing more of "The Black Art" type of articles whenever there is sufficient space.]

Golden Chalice

From Dyersburg, Tenn., James G. Merriman writes:

"There is one point I'd like to raise. In the story 'The Golden Chalice' (July issue) there is nothing miraculous about the Cup itself—that is, it was excavated, not sent down from Heaven as in the legends—it was just a battered drinking vessel. How, then, does Mr. Gruber account for its being golden? Neither Jesus nor anyone personally connected with Him was rich, and He would not have used golden dishes, anyway."

In answer to the Holy Grail query raised by Mr. Merriman, the author of "The Golden Chalice" replies: "In the legends I've read about the Chalice, it has always been golden. Although the size and shape have varied according to the different legends, some even having it a shallow dish rather than a cup. But always it has been golden. The Holy Grail, which Sir Galahad sought so strenuously, was supposed to have been of gold.

"Religion must be taken on faith alone. Recorded history does not always bear out religion.

"If *He* could turn a few loaves into enough to feed a multitude, He could certainly change a dish made of baser material into gold—if He wanted to. Mr. Merriman must have skipped over his Bible a little hastily, if he says that everyone connected with Him was poor. At least one of the twelve apostles was a rich man. I leave the name for Mr. Merriman to discover.

"The particular cup in my story was based on the one shown at the Chicago World's Fair in 1933, which like the one in my story was excavated near Antioch. It was definitely golden.

"Why wouldn't He have used golden dishes?

"Frank Gruber."

———

The mystery of the Holy Grail remains one of the most fascinating unsolved riddles of all time. . . Certainly no other single object has collected about itself such a wealth of myth and legend—every Christian and semi-Christian land has its own especial version concerning this mystical vessel of thin and hammered gold (which, as you know, is reputed to have been used by Christ at the Last Supper).

In the Arthurian legends the Golden Chalice has the romantic name of the Holy Sangreal. Perhaps this—the quest by the knights of a legendary king for a legendary grail—is the most fascinating of all the chalice myths. Sir Launcelot, who captained the holy search party, traveled for many years through the dark forests of England's pre-mediaeval West—where in high towers wizards cast their spells and enchantment waited round every twist in the path.

In charming old English one legend relates: "So it befell on a night, at midnight, he arrived before a castle, which was rich and fair, and there was a postern opened towards the sea, and was open without any entry, save two lions kept the entry; and the moon shone clear." Sir Launcelot went into the castle, and after an encounter with a dwarf, who temporarily paralyzed his arm, came upon a chapel. Here he beheld the Holy Sangreal itself, covered with scarlet samite, and standing on an altar where one candle burned. But before he could approach it, he was suddenly struck with fire, and lay unconscious and near death for twenty-four days.

Men have searched in a thousand lands for the Holy Grail; no one, not even an archaeologist, has ever found it.

The *Weird Tales* Club is growing. During these last several weeks we have had the largest response since the Club first got under way, and, as you see, the list of members in this issue is three times as long as the list printed in the September number. This is all very encouraging, and we can all hope that in the not so distant future your Club will expand to proportions where it will be of real value to fans and readers.

You will be glad to hear that a membership card—carrying a design by Hannes Bok—is being prepared. This card will be sent to everyone enclosing a stamped addressed envelope.

Incidentally, a number of readers have suggested in their letters that we print members' ages. So perhaps all those desiring their ages published would tell us when writing in?

If you are not already a member, why not drop us a line, so that we can enroll you on the Club roster, and publish your name and address in the magazine?

We're looking to you to keep the *Weird Tales* Club rolling!

....

"The Eyrie"

Weird Tales, July 1941

Time Machine in Your Backyard!
One of our readers told us recently that he found *Weird Tales* as good as keeping a time machine in the backyard!

"I just sit back and relax in my favorite armchair," he said, "and *Weird Tales* does the rest—taking me back or forward in time—to other planets—or way outside this life."

"*Weird Tales* is really better than a time-machine," he added, "for it means no more effort than the turning of a page . . ."

We hope that all of you get equal pleasure from your magazine. We're doing all we can to see that your fireside adventuring into the occult is as weird and thrilling—as rich in variety—as it can be made.

Horror, ancient and modern—science fiction—fantasy of every kind—weird tragedy, weird humor, weird romance . . . ghosts, vampires, werewolves, monsters, and sorcerers—these and countless other kinds of stories make up *Weird Tales*.

One reader prefers one type of story; another goes for something completely different. One likes science fiction, another likes horror. Some enjoy both. You are agreed upon two things only: that each story be really interesting—and that each issue be so varied that, no matter what your taste, you will be entertained. We don't expect each story to please everyone. But we do hope that in every issue the majority of tales will thrill and delight you.

The lead story in this issue—Ray Cummings's "Robot God"—is a futuristic affair of rebellious machine men, space ships and barren asteroids, while its twin feature, the second part of the Lovecraft novel, is a horror tale in the traditional manner. And in between are stories, each different to the other, yet all blending into what we hope is a perfect reading whole.

We're hoping that as many of you as have the time will write to us and tell us what you feel about your magazine—for such letters are a great help to us in giving you the kind of stories that you really want to see in *Weird Tales*.

LILITH LORRAINE (1894–1967) was an American SF author, poet, and editor (for details about her life, see the entry on Lorraine in chapter 1, "Authors," of this anthology). She began her career in the 1920s as a fiction writer and poet, but in the early 1940s shifted her attention to editing. As she argued in a 1943 issue of the fanzine the *Acolyte*, the scientifically minded and politically daring editors who made SF a distinctive popular genre in the 1920s were all but gone from the field, replaced by a new generation of aesthetically and socially conservative ones whose "editorial fetishes" had contributed to what Lorraine perceived as the degraded state of modern SF ("Cracks" n.p.). As such, it was up to veterans such as Lorraine to revitalize the genre. Accordingly, she founded the Avalon World Arts Academy in the early 1940s to train poets and publish magazines based on her vision of SF. Lorraine willingly worked with genre and mainstream poets alike, featuring their verse alongside that of fiction writers, scientists, and other editors in the half-dozen amateur press publications she established between 1943 and her death in 1967.

As an editor, Lorraine is best remembered for her work on *Different*. Subtitled *The Voice of the Cultural Renaissance*, *Different* offered readers an independent vision of SF that stood in sharp contrast to that of the profit-driven SF magazines of the day. In "The Story of *Different*," an editorial in the March–April 1950 issue, Lorraine asserted that she received "no material remuneration" and made "considerable material sacrifice" for the sake of promoting and "training of the poetic temperament as it manifests in the various fields of creative art" (4). Lorraine derided those who were concerned about the "profits" and "monetary gain" of publishing, seeing them as warped by the "fetish of competition" that had narrowed human vision to short-term concerns (5).

By way of contrast, Lorraine saw her magazines as "encouraging poetic talent in others, seeking to raise poetic standards, and striving to make the world safe for the poetic temperament" ("Story" 2). As she defined it, the "poetic temperament" was "the next step in evolution" and manifested itself in all forms of "creative imagination," from literature and science to righteous revolution and divine sacrifice on the cross (2). As an experienced schoolteacher, Lorraine decried the deadening effects of a modern education system that deleted the classics and destroyed literacy, and dedicated her magazine to repairing that damage and contributing to the cultural renaissance announced on *Different*'s masthead.

Like editors working elsewhere in modernist little-magazine production, Lorraine put her discussions of aesthetics in explicitly political contexts. For instance, in her editorial for the May–June 1946 issue of *Different*, Lorraine proposes that America's cultural renaissance depends on a radically revised model of education designed to produce world citizens. Echoing the sentiments of scientists such as Albert Einstein, Lorraine writes that Americans must face the reality that "this is now one world" and the future of mankind depends on the ability of individuals from all nations to "love *all* humanity" (2). For this to happen, she argues, the United States must create a "Secretary or Minister of Education" who could supervise teachers trained to educate students in a critical understanding of government rather than blind obedience to authority (3). Unless we train our children for world citizenship, Lorraine argues, we might have another world war, which the atomic bomb would make fatal to the nation and the world. While commercial SF magazine editors such as Mary Gnaedinger and Dorothy McIlwraith limited their rare editorial comments to aesthetic issues raised first by readers, as an amateur press editor Lorraine was free to establish a politically progressive, independent voice and to produce magazines that were themselves socially conscious ventures.

....

"Cracks—Wise and Otherwise"
Acolyte, Spring 1943

Some years ago, I had several science-fiction stories published, among them: "Into the 28th Century," "The Isle of Madness," "The Jovian Jest," "The Brain of the Planet," "The Celestial Visitor," etc. I may still return to science fiction one day, whenever the market ceases to be so stereotyped and standardized that it kills out all new ideas and original manner of expressing them. I have a rather daring idea in mind of starting a national magazine for the publication of rejected stories and showing up just how fine some of the rejected stories of the really great science-fiction writers are; in other words, showing what people like Coblentz, Francis Flagg, Clark Ashton Smith, etc. can do if they are really turned loose, free from editorial fetishes.

....

"Training for World Citizenship"
Different, May–June 1946

As several great statesmen have remarked, whether we like it or not, this is now one world and we are all citizens of it. The policy of national indifference, fostered by spineless isolationism aided and abetted by the warmongers who fatten on conflict, has already plunged us into two world wars. If we permit ourselves to be hypnotized into a third one, we shall lose both national and world citizenship. We shall become citizens of a sphere whose location and mean temperature will, according to the best Christian teachings, be determined by the degree to which we have fulfilled our stewardship as our brother's keeper.

National citizenship, in its broader, saner and more reasonable basis, can be gauged only in terms of how good a citizen of the world one may be. For the way life is now constituted, he loves his country best who loves humanity more. He who does not love *all* humanity is a traitor to his country. He is giving aid and comfort to those forces that will turn the world into an armed camp against the nation that turns its back upon the common problems of the human race and pursues a selfish path of its own.

National patriotism in its narrower sense, in the sense of adopting an attitude of complacency founded on the moronic concept that we have, in its totality, the best government in the world, is a delusion and a snare. It is a tool in the hands of politicians and hypocrites. It is the fuel to the flame of war, the stirrer up of strife and the breeder of revolt.

We must never forget that though we have a fine *basis* for free government, embodied in the noblest instruments ever designed by the brain of man, the Constitution of the United States and the Declaration of Independence, there is a wide divergence between that foundation and the house of sand that weak and corrupt and clowning legislators have erected upon it. Yet in the last analysis it is our fault that we have sent clowns to Congress instead of statesmen, and clothed twelve-year-old mentalities with the garment of civic power. But this is no reflection on the few far-seeing statesmen that, by the grace of God, still sit in the halls of state.

We must remember that many other nations are far ahead of us in some respects while, at the same time, they lag far behind us in others. In our asinine refusal to believe that any good can come from beyond our own borders, we have refused to investigate the splendid laws and institutions that now exist in a great many countries, which because they have not indulged in a mad race for money and enthroned it as a God above human happiness and human rights, we have chosen to ignore. We have made Frigidaires synonymous of civilization, football analogous to brains and Frank Sinatra the symbol of the Muses.

How many Americans know, for instance, that the Republic of Mexico gave to the United States through Texas, which inherited many of the wisest measures in its constitution to that country, such laws as the homestead law, the community property law, and many laws for the protection of women and children? These laws and many others inherited from Mexico have since been channeled into the constitutions of other states and have greatly advanced the cause of human liberty.

Still fewer of us know that the Constitution of the United States owes its great principle of representative government, as we now know it, to its close conformity to the government of the Five Nations, or the five great Indian tribes who sent their tribal representatives to their Great Council.

How many of us realize that one of the first old age pension laws was passed in Germany during the reign of Kaiser Wilhelm? This was long before it even occurred to us that we owed any responsibility to the aged and infirm. Norway, it should be borne in mind, owed its prewar prosperity to the great cooperatives organized, not by any act of government, but by the people themselves. New Zealand and Australia have laws so far ahead of ours in many respects that it will take us a hundred years to catch up with them.

And now do we hear some moron rising out of the cesspools with the apely remark, "If you think our government is so bad why don't you go where there is a better one?" That is what the average American considers an answer to all arguments. No one denies that this is a fine government in many respects. It just isn't what it can be, when we throw off our complacency and our smarty smarty adolescence and attack the weak spots, preserve the strong foundations, and get it through our thick heads that just because some nation has to go half-starved is no reason why we should be satisfied to go one-fourth starved. Comparing our state of partial disintegration with some other country's total disintegration is only a coward's and a fool's way of bettering the situation. And just *because* I don't like a lot of things is why I'm staying right in here and pitching in and doing my part to make this the best nation on Earth, because it is *my* country and I have a right to do just that. And whoever doesn't like my efforts to make this the best country on Earth can do the getting out, because I'm staying right here in the land that some of my forefathers wrested from some of my other forefathers who were here when they came, but who still live in me and aren't afraid to live dangerously.

Therefore, though we may have the best *foundation* for government in the world, and I sincerely believe that we do, the structure that we have built on that foundation is decidedly shaky, wobbly, inadequate, and unable to weather the storms of the future. It is as though one had built a hut of straw upon the eternal rocks. But let us praise God that the foundation is there. The Founding Fathers took care of that. We need only another generation of men and women with their vision to build upon the rocks a temple worthy of its foundation.

Before we can do this, the youth of this nation must be trained for world citizenship. They must be taught, once and for all, that since we have one of the finest foundations for government on Earth, we could also have not only *one* of the best governments but *the* best government, once we get a few monkeys off our backs and some sense into our heads. But at present, the picture falls far short of the millennium that our children read about in the textbooks but of which they fail to discover any traces when they go forth in pursuit of the almighty dollar.

In literacy, for instance, we are running a losing race. We are so fast descending to the sublevels of the ten-year-old mind that the rising tide of ignorance and indifference has submerged the voices of the few educators who are attempting to call attention to the alarming implications of such a crisis.

What, however, can we expect when we consider the starvation wages that we pay those to whom we entrust the training of youth in this most perilous age of all history? What can we expect from a generation taught by the poor, cowed, frightened unfortunates who teach the lower grades during those years in which character is formed? Can a free, independent world citizenship be trained by the kind of teacher who permits a ward-heeling school board to tell her how long to wear her skirts, where she shall room and board, what church she shall attend, and who to vote for . . . or else?

Until teachers are paid fair and decent wages to enable them to live full and unintimidated lives, only a few great exceptions will have the inborn stamina that will enable them to rise above such a slavish environment and become leaders of the people. The profession that, next to the church, should be the greatest spiritual and moral influence in the land has been so deliberately prostituted to the uses of the materialistic powers that few who are qualified for any other profession that enables them to maintain a dignified station in life will ever enter it. If they do they will not remain in it very long after the noose begins to tighten around their freedom of thought and their democratic privileges.

But since the ward heelers know that qualified leadership in the teaching profession will sound the death knell of their own rottenness and corruption, unless the people finally take the matter into their own hands, they will certainly do nothing to stop the vicious circle.

For their very continuance in office depends directly on the suppression of academic freedom which creates an electorate taught obedience to tyranny and indoctrinated with fascist principles.

So before we can have an intelligent world citizenship, we must have teachers capable of training a generation fit for world citizenship. We must have teachers who will have a thorough knowledge of the social sciences and of the strong and weak points in all governments so that we may learn from all and may in turn give to all. We must forever discard the idea that we are the people and that wisdom shall perish with us.

We must learn to analyze propaganda and trace it to its source, especially the kind that fills us with lies about other nations in order to keep us in a state of constant suspicion and distrust that can readily be fanned into war whenever the money powers deem it most profitable.

We must have a truly free press, and I mean one that is free from pressure by big advertisers and who because of that pressure dares not print any facts that would endanger the profits of these advertisers. The only way to get a free press is to search diligently for the truth through many independent magazines and channels of information and let your big editors know that you have it, and then demand that it be published. In time these people will learn that no matter how many advertisers they may have, unless they also have readers and reader confidence they might as well go out of business. Remember, as I have told you so often, you are the real government of the country, the real arbiters of destiny. You have only to take the power into your hands, but quickly . . . for God's sake . . . quickly.

We must have a far-reaching system of cultural relations under the direction of a United States Secretary or Minister of Education. This Cabinet office will supervise a vast system of student and teacher exchanges so that we may give to and receive from other nations that knowledge of world affairs that will enable us to fulfill our duties as citizens of the world.

But before all this can take place, we must, of course, *have* a Minister of Education. Again and again, we are going to remind you that we are the only civilized nation that does not have one. We still believe that dollars can take the place of brains. We *did*, not so very long ago, have a representative of big business that we gave some sort of high-sounding title, as a cultural relations man. He was, we have been told, directly responsible for the recognition of fascist Argentina by the family of nations.

In closing, we quote from Miss Ellen Wilkinson, British Minister of Education who, as one of the British delegates to the General Assembly of the UNO, made some pertinent remarks concerning world citizenship. In answering a query on how world citizenship could be explained to students Miss Wilkinson said, "We want to show them that nationalism doesn't solve anything and that this particular country they belong to is not the best in the world in every respect. We have to work out how we can get the children to think in their school time of the whole world as a place they are living in and we must develop a practical point of view of explaining that concept. We have to get down into the class room in these things." Of course, if we *had* a Minister of Education, we might be able to quote from our own. Since we are deprived of that privilege, we shall just borrow from Britain. She borrows money and we borrow brains, but I fear poor Britain is going to get cheated on the deal.

"The Story of *Different*"

Different, March–April, 1950

There is nothing that your editor would like more on the threshold of *Different*'s sixth year of publication than to give you its complete and unexpurgated history. But the experience has been so unusual, the adventures into the labyrinths of the artistic temperament so fascinating, and the human contacts so intimate and revealing that all save the highlights had best be preserved in the Avalon Time-Casket for the entertainment of the post-atomic rock-slingers who, according to Einstein, will fight the Fourth World War.

Perhaps the question most often asked us during our lecture tours and in the course of our worldwide correspondence is, "How and why was this unusual publication started?" To avoid the repetition of our essential motivation in the entering upon this venture, we request you at this point to turn to our dedication paragraph on page one, read it carefully, and we'll go on from there.

Your editor, as you should understand, has had a varied experience as a high school teacher, efficiency expert, newspaper feature writer, columnist, and political reporter on two metropolitan dailies, small-town city editor, educational consultant and founder of her own academy of languages and commerce in old Mexico, lecturer on political science, personality building, and comparative religions, estate manager, poultry raiser, and occasional poet. Simultaneously with each separate occupation, she has managed a large home, cooked, washed, ironed, scrubbed floors, gone down in defeat before the "servant problem," and even made three shirts for her husband, the buttonholes of which unkind friends have compared to a certain crater in New Mexico after having been struck by an atom bomb.

During all this time, beginning with the reading of Shakespeare at the age of 10, Voltaire at the age of 11, studying comparative religions at 14, disavowing the Euclidian theory at 15, playing around with science, dancing, swimming, wild horses, psychology, philosophy, and boyfriends until 18, with periodical interruptions from then on as a result of 37 years of marriage to the same man, two world wars and a couple of Mexican revolutions, your editor has maintained a deep and abiding interest in poetry. This interest has not been essentially her own poetry, which she seldom feels inspired to write unless wars are raging, presses clanging, and planets disintegrating, but in encouraging poetic talent in others, seeking to raise poetic standards, and striving to make the world safe for the poetic temperament.

We sincerely believe that the poetic temperament as we define it constitutes the Divine Mutation of the human species, the next step in evolution, the man beyond humanity, the "mystical minority," the star-illuminated legislators for whom the ages wait. But please do not infer that we restrict the term "poetic temperament" only to those who devote themselves exclusively to the writing of verse, sitting out the housing shortage in assorted garrets and in ivory towers, reading little poems that "just came to them" at the women's club, or putting a bewildered world to shame by producing examples of planned paranoia as practiced by experts.

Actually the professor of the poetic temperament may never write a line of poetry. He may only live it. He may turn his creative imagination, which is the atomic energy of poetry, to spanning a continent with a mighty railroad, to harnessing an electric current that will transfigure the shadowed cities with the surge of radiant power, to tracking the foxes of disease and pestilence to their final lairs, to leading embattled peoples against their oppressors, to dying on crosses for the freedom of the soul, to lifting the broken sword that the warrior has let fall and wresting victory from defeat . . . these are the poets and this is the artistic temperament.

They are not earthbound for they are warriors of eternity, citizens of the galaxies by virtue of their fourth-dimensional vision that can see beyond time to eternity, beyond death to resurrection, beyond life to its meaning. Yes, all these are poets, while many who claim the poet's license because of some meager facility to box their prim souls within some metered cubicle or to parade their pale psychoses under the tattered banner of the "avant-garde" (actually as dated as Sodom and Gomorrah), these are not poets at all.

With these definitions in mind, which guided this editor in founding *Different* as an organ not completely devoted to poets in the narrow sense but more broadly to poetry in its universal sense, and to the encouragement of the poetic temperament wherever it might be found, striving to direct it into the most appropriate channels for its highest expression—we can go on with our story.

When the original Avalon Poetry Shrine, as the Avalon World Arts Academy was then known, was founded by this editor in 1940, to be followed a couple of years later by the publication of the *Raven* to provide a voice for its members, we did not realize the acuteness of the cultural starvation of the American people. To your editor, who, for several years after retirement from active business life, had been surrounded by a small but highly intellectual group of friends and co-workers who lived graciously, thought profoundly, and modeled their lives in accordance with the precepts of liberal educations received largely apart from the public school system—the knowledge came as a distinct shock.

We had failed to realize how quickly and thoroughly in these few years the Great Books and with them the heritage of the Great Minds who had inspired them, endowing their readers with the intellectual tools by which one may reason logically, calmly, and impersonally toward the solution of human problems, had been amputated from the body of modern education.

In the last days of our school teaching we had indeed heard the first faint rumblings of the program designed to reduce our people to the inglorious status which they have now attained, in which the comic strip is the *only* reading material in one home out of every five. In those days the spokesmen for powerful industrial concerns frequently invaded the schools as self-invited guests (flanked by substantial endowments) and orated at length on the necessity for "utilitarian education," or "training for one's job," so that the student leaving school might immediately become an "efficient cog in the industrial machine." Well, that wasn't so bad, or at least it didn't sound that way to the naïve educators. Why shouldn't the child learn a useful trade along with his general education?

What never entered our un-Machiavellian brains was that the end product of all this was designed to be not the addition of an adequate quota of training for an industrial age, but the substitution of specialized training for everything that had previously constituted the elements of a liberal education, which alone could have equipped these future citizens to meet the challenge of the democratic way of life.

Little by little, we the teachers, you the parents, and all of us, the voters, allowed this to be done to our country. Today, all save a few of our higher institutions of learning and most of our high schools, paying only the most supercilious lip service to the only kind of education that prepares for life as it should be lived, are turning out functionalized robots, unfit even for their specialized trades. For no man can be at his best in any trade or profession who lacks the broad general knowledge that would equip him to think and reason in an emergency, to exercise initiative in a crisis, to better his position, or to carry on harmonious human relations. No man can fulfill his family or civic responsibilities who lacks the ability to analyze and the courage to repudiate the propaganda devices that keep him chained to the machine, glued to the comic strip, wed to the soap opera, and eventually committed to the foxholes in wars declared by vicious old men of all nations and fought by idealistic young men believing in manufactured causes.

Not only do the schools turn out these zombies on their assembly lines, but the latest models are becoming unfit even for the purpose for which they were manufactured. The utter inefficiency that now runs rampant is so universal and we have grown so accustomed to shoddy products, broken contracts, sub-moronic service, plane crashes, and irresponsible management that our children will never believe that there was ever an age of smooth-running economy, ethical observances, guaranteed liberties, and water running from faucets in New York City.

For it has come about, slowly, subtly, and imperceptibly at first, but culminating finally in the open covenants of the "bread and butter" system of education, that the schools have finally donned the dunce cap of regimentation that has been designed for them. Teachers not in accord with this ideology are not encouraged in the profession, and salaries are at such a level that only those unfit for the keener competition of more remunerative jobs will accept them. Restrictions on freedom of thought and action have finally reached the point where save for a few candidates for martyrdom and helpless older teachers waiting for a pension, few others will sacrifice their human dignity for the dubious privilege of twisting the American mind into something foreign to the instincts of a free people.

This is all worked out according to plan and today our schools have reached a new low in that glorification of muscles over brains which has preceded the fall of every decadent civilization, and the mass production of conditioned reflexes now makes the mass mind ripe for whatever military, fascistic, or communistic regime succeeds in winning the battle of ideologies upon the grave of ideas.

The purpose back of all this should be plain to every citizen. Yet on the other hand, how can it be? For when the reasoning processes of a people must be carried on with a twelve-year-old vocabulary, how, since words are the tools of thought, can such a people match wits with the cunning men with the large vocabularies who possess exact knowledge of the meager equipment of the robot brains which they themselves have molded and conditioned?

How glibly have our people been lured down the poppied path of least resistance. How cleverly has the element of human laziness been glorified by the five-syllabled apostles of one-syllable English. How complacent are the self-confessed sweet, simple people whose masters have taught them the little serpent-slogans on which their lives are patterned. How often do we as editors have to listen to long lectures by these apostles of sweetness and simplicity and how deeply do we pity them. But we pity more ourselves and our kind, the reasoning minority, guarding the last books and probably thinking the last thoughts. For no one knows more surely than the thinkers what a howling mob sweet, simple people can become when the slogans change.

Among the student-poets the most asinine argument is that they "have been told" that to read the great poets or the great writers will make them imitative and destroy their originality. Meanwhile the poor unfortunates, whose originality is questionable in the first place, are imitating the jingler, the soap opera, and the gagman, while crude slang is so much a part of their vocabulary that they confuse it with correct English.

Vain it is to point out to them the fallacy of what they "have been told." Vain to remind them that if there is any logic in this idea they had better stop reading the Bible lest they be guilty of imitating Christ and thus lose their tendency to original sin. Vain to repeat that the imitation of greatness, granted one is not innately endowed with sufficient originality to maintain his individuality when it comes into contact with other ideas, is infinitely to be preferred to the imitation of gutterdom. Vain indeed for . . . they "have been told."

Despite the apparent hopelessness of the task, however, *Different* was founded as a sincere attempt to use whatever influence we might attain to salvage some last remnants of American culture and to restore within the limits of that influence some of the lost glory of the poetry of Earth. For poetry, as we have said before, is the atomic energy of the soul, which, exploded against the battlements of hate and terror, will level them in the dust of oblivion and leave the liberated soul free in an expanding universe.

For five exciting years your editor and publisher has given her time, her energy, her heart, and soul, with no material remuneration and considerable material sacrifice toward this end: the discovery, inspiration, promotion, and training of the poetic temperament as it manifests in the various fields of creative art. In that brief time *Different* and Avalon have invaded all the states and several foreign lands. They have secured the recognition and wide publication of hundreds of new authors and have encouraged many formerly timid but exceptionally competent members to fit themselves for places of leadership in their communities. We have deliberately moved our headquarters to various widely scattered locations that we might come to know personally the characteristics of the people of many regions and find the most effective method of training those who are to be the voices of these people.

And . . . we say it not to boast, but only to suggest that *it can be done*, that *Different* has never missed a deadline, never changed its subscription price, and never lowered the quality of its format. We have never failed to accept or reject a single manuscript, giving reasons in case of rejection, on the day it was received. We have never failed to fill an order, to answer a letter requiring an answer, or to return a corrected versification lesson on the day received. Sometimes while we were on a lecture trip, when mail could not be forwarded, we have had to wait until our return home before we answered correspondence, because save for a few months when *Different* first started, several months when we were assisted by Edsel Ford, and now when we have the deeply appreciated assistance of Evelyn Thorne, this has been a one-woman job. But we have always managed to travel by plane so as not to be more than four days away from the office, and though on returning we often found mail piled partway to the ceiling, we rarely rested until it had all been answered. Some of our esteemed fellow editors have even chided us for "spoiling the poets," but that's the way our parents taught us that human relations should be carried on, regardless of how the other fellow acted, and that's the way we do it.

We have trained about 400 poets each year in our elementary versification course, in which we gave the instruction at no cost for the instruction itself to those of our member-subscribers who desire this training and who avail themselves of the texts containing their assignments. This has been the heaviest task that we have imposed upon ourselves and the one that consumes the most of our time, but on the whole, it has been most rewarding. Naturally we have had a few students who do not realize the injustice they are doing other students entitled to an equal share of the instructor's time by repeatedly attempting to slip in poems not included in the assignments, but most of them scrupulously adhere to the requirements of the course.

During the eight years that we have rendered this service, we have received hundreds of letters revealing to us that almost 100% of those who actually completed the course have achieved publication in first-class magazines. But valued even more than this knowledge of our students' success is that, as they invariably word it, "a new world" has been opened to them. This is because they have been imbued with the spirit and mission of poetry in its highest sense, because beyond and apart from the teaching of the dry techniques and the more glamorous symbolic devices of their art, we have either returned them again, or turned them for the first time, to the study of great literature, to communion with great minds, and to the living of meaningful lives of civic service, as the only true sources of poetry which transcend the reportorial literalism of verse, the Undine soullessness of poesy, and the psychopathic existentialism of the pre-stone-age "moderns."

Naturally we work with dozens each year who fall by the wayside. Either through some fault of our own we are unable to make our full vision clear to them or they grasp the vision only too well, realize it means hard work and entirely too much self-revelation for comfort, and decline to meet the challenge. To all these we can utter only a friendly hail and farewell, for we are on our way. Nevertheless it is well that we met them, even though we may have passed like ships in the night, for there is an immutable law that nothing is ever lost, not even one iota of the energy expended in sincere service to one's fellow men. Those who cannot ascend to the mountaintops or who prefer to linger in the pleasant valleys rarely return to sea level once they have glimpsed the heights. For the ineffable vision is like a fever in the blood, a burning in the brain, an undying fire, and he who lights it, no matter how feeble the spark, can always rest assured that no power on Earth can quench it. Many of those who fall by the wayside belong to the types of mind who "have been told" that all this "crusading" is just silly because some bright morning, without any effort on the part of humanity, God is going to perform a miracle and "everything will be all right." So they are going to have a good time and "just not worry about it."

Of course, when the storm breaks it is they who will wail the loudest and wonder why it had to happen to them. Mournfully they will hang their little gold stars in the windows never realizing how much blood is on their own hands, never realizing that had they had the courage to "watch with *Him* for an hour" in the world's Gethsemane, to share the burden of the world's Thinkers, their only stars might be those that shine above us, over a world whose freedom that has been purchased with the coins of peace.

We have never considered ourselves a crusader, for actually those fellows never had much fun and we have plenty of it. Somehow we can't seem to shake off the illusion that all this milling around of the human species in a planetary crisis is an old play that we have seen a hundred times before, performed by new actors with new stage properties but always with the same words and music. But somehow we're never quite sure how the last act turns out, and somehow it seems like it might be partly up to us and partly up to the players to do a little ad-libbing and perhaps change the whole situation. And we get a tremendous thrill out of it, and we're awfully glad that we have forgotten how the play ended, because we might enjoy it so much. So we, too, just go on having our sort of good time, with this exception, that we have it with a clear conscience. For no matter what happens, we've never kept silent when there was the slightest chance to keep the hero from falling into the bear-trap. Of course, the darn thing might only be a movie, and then we couldn't help much, but in that case no one really gets hurt anyway. But we'll leave the philosophy to Dr. Grandbery.

Although we have traveled a path that, on the whole, has been star-strewn and rewarding, it has at times led through the slime of petty malice and the slough of vicious ignorance. Perhaps the most obnoxious types of mind we have encountered are those who are constantly concerned with the "enormity" of our profits. The fetish of competition (so ably treated by Bill Tullos in this same issue), and the belief that monetary gain is the only, or at least the primary, motive back of all human endeavors, has given rise to this. Vain to explain that practically every advertiser-free magazine and most certainly almost every poetry magazine is published either at a loss, through patronage, or at little or no profit. This happens because their editors are glorious lunatics (whose insanity is the sanity of God) who have at heart the love of poetry and the desire to give more of it to a dream-starved people as a patriotic service.

It is only necessary for such mice-souled individuals to secure these facts from any business consultant. In our case we started *Different* with fifty dollars and about 300 subscribers transferred from our *Raven* and from *Now*, our then coeditor's smaller publication. A printer who had dreams of millions in his grasp told me that for a mere investment of $20,000 he could guarantee to me overnight what it has actually taken me five years to achieve. But I told him I wasn't in any big hurry, and that besides I wasn't going to invest a penny of my personal capital, other than to make up any deficits that might occur by priming the pump with profits from sales of my own books. He asked me how much I intended to start on, and I told him fifty dollars, and he recommended a nice warm straightjacket. I never saw the man again. Men just can't seem to comprehend the capitalistic machinations of the American female, which might be why she possesses 80% of the national wealth.

At any rate, *Different* was launched with fifty dollars and a few ready-made subscribers on the perilous seas of the most fantastic era of all history. By the grace of God, substantially reinforced by my ancestral chromosomes, namely the good humor of the Irish, the diplomacy of the French (used only when needed), the stoicism of the Indian, and the muddle-through-somehow of the British, adding up to a chemical paradox known as an American, we have survived to this day.

Indispensable factors in that survival have been the wholehearted co-operation of about 90% of the nation's poetry editors, the goodwill of a large number of newspapers and many well-known columnists who have said nice things about us and reprinted from our poems and editorials, the inspiration received from many of the nation's finest poets and literary critics in sympathy with our aims and motives, the generosity of widely published and well-paid poets and authors who have contributed their work free, thus enhancing the prestige of our publication and setting a standard for our rising poets, the hard work, the many favors, and the understanding of our printers, the unprecedented cooperation of more than 100 radio stations, program directors, and broadcasters who have proven that they would use good poetry if they could get it by broadcasting widely and continuously from *Different*, the inspiring letters and the essential information on public affairs received by our many friends in the national Congress, the efficient service of our local postmistress and her staff in the mailing and distribution of our magazine, the dues of Avalon members, used to supplement deficits in our publication costs, the extra subscriptions secured by them in addition to their own, the cooperation of a number of progressive poetry organizations that have introduced both *Different* and its publisher to their members, and last, but most strangely stimulating, the weird and sometimes vicious epistolary attacks (frequently anonymous) to which we have on rare occasions been subjected. For he who never knows the kind of foe he faces is never utterly sure that he is on the right side, but if his foes expose themselves as small souled, evil, vicious, and ignorant, then he "marvels not that such despise him."

We are still, like most other poetry publications, under the continuous necessity of reminding our poet-subscribers that unless the poets themselves support their last remaining mediums by their own subscriptions and by telling their friends, their literary groups, and the general public about such magazines, unless the publisher owns his own press, we will be forced to go down before the rising tide of postal rate increases. Magazines like *Different*, in the general interest category and hence with a subscriptions list reaching into the prose field, may sometime get tired of priming the pump for unappreciative poets. For many could secure national newsstand distribution by the simple act of increasing their prose content, giving it a general appeal, keeping their long-established datelines, and cutting their poetry content to five or ten poems per issue. Naturally every editor with the interest of poetry at heart, and realizing that when a nation's poetry dies it is the beginning of the end, would hesitate a long time before taking such a step. But there are many who may not be able to afford *not* to take it, unless poets and poetry groups make an immediate, supreme, and concerted effort to do something about their own survival as poets.

Since this brief history of *Different* is written with utter frankness, it should be admitted that your editor has not been immune to deep spiritual shock when confronted by a certain cheapness of soul and smallness of mind that prevails among a few to whom we have given unstintingly of our time and services. We also admit another unfortunate human trait (why do editors have to be human beings?), that just two or three spiritually obscene revelations of the depths of cheapness and cunning to which human nature can descend tend temporarily to obscure the shining radiance of the goodness and nobility of the great majority of Earth's children.

Perhaps in our case such revelations of spiritual dwarfishness come as a shock because among poets it is least expected, for we certainly have had our share of beholding the subhuman characteristics in our newspaper experience. However, there is always the illuminating fact that during our entire time of publication not one single act of smallness, cheapness, deliberate distortion of editorial statements or motives, name-calling or outright lying has ever been indulged in by a poet or poet-editor whose own work exemplified what is universally acknowledged to be in the best tradition of poetry in its noblest sense. There is something about the consecrated poet that endows him with a wholeness of vision that enables him to understand motives, to cooperate with sincerity, to give and accept constructive comments, and to work harmoniously with his fellow men.

Like all others, we have had to face venom of certain authors whose work we have had to reject, than which Hell hath no comparable fury, the cheapness of the penny-pinchers who resort to the most unbelievable antics to make the world safe for a one-cent stamp, the spiritual pauperism of the "copy-panhandlers" who believe that their work is of such supreme importance to us that we should immediately send them free sample copies that they may "study our requirements," the petty arrogance of writers who, because for a few times in their lives they may have hit the top publications, believe that they should be exempted from sending us a stamped return envelope, and the intellectual vacuity of professional leftists, rightists, atheists, orthodox religionists, cultists, faddists, capitalists, labor unionists, and a lunatic fringe of readers who from time to time give us to understand that no poem, article, comment, or implication should ever appear in our pages which conflicts in the minutest detail with their particular "party line." This same "you-can't-change-me" contingency is also ready to obliterate from the memory of man at the drop of a hat the totality of the efforts, services, articles, poems, and productions of any person or publication if some one line or word departs from its specialized indoctrinations or is expressed in a manner that is either not understandable to it or in a way that it deliberately chooses to misinterpret for some purpose of its own.

It is useless to reason with one who indulges in these idiocies. It is useless to point out that an editor's duty is to *all* of his subscribers, so long as he can present all sides of their varying hopes, ideals, and ideas in a public forum which sincerely attempts to find the grain of truth in everything worth discussing, to discard the chaff of falsity, and through it all be true to his own conscience and to the responsibilities which he has assumed.

We are not, as an independent magazine, in the false position of the advertiser-controlled publication which must please everybody and hence end up by publishing nothing which will have other than dubious entertainment value to a people confronted with vast and terrible problems and who are desperately seeking for guidance in history's darkest hour. We have had the opportunity to become such an advertiser-controlled magazine. We have been taken to the mountaintop and been shown the kingdoms of this world and, confidentially, the odor wasn't good, or at least it didn't blend well with the rarefied atmosphere. In view of this, we shall continue to give you an all-round picture of life as we saw it from the mountaintop, where, thanks to the Tempter, we at least got a good fourth-dimensional view.

We are entering our sixth year in the same spirit with which we entered our first. Everything that we expected has happened, for we did not enter the field unprepared. Practically everything that we predicted editorially has happened in the world at large, and the worst is yet to come . . . unless . . . the Sleepers wake. The best is yet to come also, for we have the assurance that Peace on Earth is the exclusive heritage of all men of goodwill. Therefore with malice toward none, and with charity to all, with faith that in whatever darkness may descend upon the world, the poets will light a candle, and that in whatever Ark may be launched on the waters of the soul's final cataclysms, the poets will be the ultimate survivors, we invite you to voyage with us through the Phoenix Gate to a happy landing on the shore of Avalon.

5 ARTISTS

Visual art by women played an important role in both the aesthetics and economic viability of magazines that published SF. Visual art was also important to fans of the genre: from the 1920s to the 1940s, the letters pages of magazines that featured SF regularly included comments about the relative merits of the art in previous issues.[1] Most women artists who contributed to magazines that published SF were trained in commercial art and fashion illustration, which revolved around the figure of the modern, active woman. In the context of magazine SF, this training provided a way for female artists to literally paint women into stories. Fusing the Gothic traditions of art that emerged from the nineteenth century and her fashion illustration training, Margaret Brundage depicted women as actively engaged in terrifying and titillating activities that undermined the Enlightenment belief in a predictably clockwork universe. At the same time, women such as Dolly Donnell and Dorothy Les Tina contributed to an emerging technophilic tradition of SF art, depicting women as equal participants in the exploration and conquest of the universe. These artists emphasized female characters in a way that would be expanded upon by feminist authors working in the genre in the 1960s and 1970s, as well as by later fantasy and SF artists such as Rowena Morrill, Victoria Poyser-Lisi, and Julie Bell (Heller).[2]

One reason that fashion illustration had such an impact on women's magazine art in the early twentieth century was that many jobs in design, illustration, and fashion during this period were open to women because they "were considered within women's natural sphere" (Chalmers 238). Women came to dominate a number of lower-level jobs in the fashion industry by the 1920s, and even made an impact at the highest levels of the industry.[3] Early genre magazines such as the *Black Cat* hired women artists with training in fashion illustration to appeal to women readers, who were believed to be the primary purchasers of most magazines during this period.[4] The *Black Cat* emphasized stories of fantasy, weird mystery, and SF from its first publication in 1895 until its demise in 1922. Olivette Bourgeois contributed covers in the late 1910s that were attuned to changing images of women but had little to do with the contents of its stories. The covers she produced expanded the *Black Cat*'s aesthetic appeal by depicting scenes of sophisticated modern young women engaged in a variety of activities (see plate 5.1). During this period, much graphic design tended "to focus on the lives and leisure time of young women" (Eskilson 53), and these covers showed the influence of Bourgeois's training as a fashion illustrator and the impact of new fashion magazines for women on the design of seemingly unrelated publications.[5]

The work of Lucille Holling for *Oriental Stories* exemplifies how fashion illustration began to influence genre magazines in the 1930s. Holling, who began her career in the 1920s, was trained in fashion illustration and worked as a freelance artist. She also collaborated with her husband, with whom she wrote and illustrated a variety of works during a forty-year career. Her work often focused on Asian and Native American women wearing traditional textiles. Unlike the *Black Cat*, *Oriental Stories* covers generally depicted a scene from a story in the issue, and Holling's work on Asian fashion is likely what landed her the commission for the cover of the Autumn 1931 issue. That cover depicts a scene from the Warren Hastings Miller story "A Thrilling Tale of Burma," focusing on a partially nude Burmese woman in brightly colored clothing (see plate 5.2). The emphasis on textiles, fashion, and the graceful female form shows the kinship of Holling's cover with the fashion-oriented covers produced by Bourgeois. However, where Bourgeois's covers were designed to appeal to female readers, Holling's cover demonstrates the new orientation toward male readers that took place in magazine cover art with the success of the "adventure and action stories" of Edgar Rice Burroughs during the 1910s (Weinberg, *Biographical* 3–4). While Holling's piece for *Oriental Stories* reinforces the stereotype of the passive exotic beauty who puts her body on display for, but does not meet the gaze of, her (presumably male) audience, this cover departs from the usual *Oriental Stories* covers in that Holling emphasizes the patterned textiles and jewelry worn by her female subject as much as she emphasizes that subject's body, and she refuses all suggestion that this woman is in any way threatened by (racially other) men.

Margaret Brundage used her fashion illustration skills to transform the covers of *Weird Tales* in a similar manner. Brundage began her career in the 1920s doing fashion illustration for newspapers before taking on work at *Oriental Stories*. Her covers featuring scantily clad women became popular instantly, and the editor, Farnsworth Wright, quickly made her the main cover artist for his flagship publication, *Weird Tales*. Brundage's appeal stemmed from her unique fusion of fashion illustration with the American Gothic tradition of painting. American Gothic art of the nineteenth century was dominated by men such as Thomas Cole, whose work celebrated masculine rationality's conquest of unruly and horrifying nature and was characterized by "a dark vision of the American landscape as a place of mystery and terror" haunted by wild Indians (Mulvey-Roberts 9). Cole's work also made use of the damsel in distress to highlight this theme: his painting *The Death of Cora* (1927), which depicts a scene from James Fenimore Cooper's novel *The Last of the Mohicans* (1926), shows a dark-skinned "savage" ready to use his knife on a kneeling white women in a white gown. The cover art for *Weird Tales* initially fused this colonial American Gothic imagery with emerging twentieth-century fears of "yellow and black perils" (Franklin 133).[6] Instead of the wild "savages" of nineteenth-century Gothic painters, *Weird Tales* covers depicted stereotyped men from Asia, Africa, or the Middle East threatening white heroes and damsels in distress. Wright had also learned in the mid-1920s to make the damsels in distress scantily clad: issues with a partially clothed or nude woman on their covers sold better than those without one, showing the growing importance of the heterosexual male gaze in the magazine marketplace. This is also one reason Wright began to hire women with backgrounds in fashion illustration: they were much better at drawing women than were the male artists who worked for pulp magazines, men who tended to be trained "in the classical mode of representational painting" (Lesser 6).[7]

In Brundage's hands, the Gothic covers of *Weird Tales* began to focus even more on women's bodies in ways that pulled the art of the magazine in a different direction. In keeping with the magazine's American Gothic style, Brundage occasionally depicted women as helpless damsels threatened by non-white men. While these images sexualized women and catered to a male gaze, they also endowed their female subjects with personality, using their subjects' reactions to the situations at hand to critically assess masculine behavior. For example, the cover of the March 1937 issue depicts a scene from Dorothy Quick's "Strange Orchids" that shows the heroine in a revealing blue gown reeling from the shadow of an evil scientist (see plate 5.5).[8] Like Quick's story, Brundage's image evokes the tradition of the female Gothic, where "the male transgressor becomes the villain" and threatens the heroine with death or worse (Milbank 121).[9] Many of Brundage's women were powerful and mysterious, taking the stage by themselves. For instance, her cover for the October 1934 issue shows C. L. Moore's heroine, Jirel of Joiry, embracing a passive black statue with no men in the frame (see plate 5.3). Brundage's "ladies of the weird" challenged conventional, Enlightenment-based ideas about the rational nature of the universe and the good woman's place within it. At the same time, her commercial sensibility led her to create alluring women who appealed to the male gaze so successfully that she was largely responsible for pulling the magazine out of financial trouble.

In the early 1940s, women artists such as Dorothy Les Tina and Dolly Donnell began to produce interior artwork for SF specialist magazines that employed the technophilic style of art. The technophilic style was a branch of the American Gothic tradition that emerged in the late 1920s with the work of Frank R. Paul for Hugo Gernsback's magazines. The technophilic work of Paul, like the nineteenth-century Gothic paintings of Cole, represented men dwarfed by wild landscapes and menaced by the denizens of the wilderness. However, in the work of Paul, the landscapes were often extraterrestrial and populated by bug-eyed monsters, bizarre aliens, and "outrageous machines" (Aldiss 4–6). The technophilic style also celebrated scientific rationality's conquest of nature, emphasizing "colorful and imaginative" art that served a pedagogical purpose with its "painstakingly accurate and precisely designed" buildings, ships, and gadgets (Westfahl, "Artists" 22). In the late 1930s, SF specialist magazines began to include more images of women in their cover art. However, the women were usually depicted as helpless and hysterical, and thus the covers remained safely within the style of the traditional American Gothic.

Like Brundage, the women who contributed interior art in the technophilic style took the opportunity to portray women very differently from their male counterparts. The art of Les Tina and Donnell demonstrated that women could depict the Gothic dangers of alien landscapes as well as men. Les Tina contributed interior art to magazines such as *Science Fiction Quarterly* and *Future Fantasy and Science Fiction* in the early 1940s. Her art for the Carol Grey (a pseudonym of Robert A. W. Lowndes) story "The Leapers" (see plate 5.7) shows a group of humans who are being swept up in an extraterrestrial event. While the men look around blankly in awkward poses with negative expressions, the women gaze directly toward outer space, and the one in the lead is smiling. This motif of women confronting the future while men blanch in the face of progress is repeated in Les Tina's art for the John B. Michel story "Claggett's Folly" (see plate 5.8). In this image, the man is looking away from the technologies represented in the illustration, covering his ears in apparent pain, while the woman and the child—SF's unlikeliest subjects—look at them excitedly.

Donnell also placed women in active roles in her art. Donnell was a trained graphic artist whose work appeared in *Startling Stories* and *Thrilling Wonder Stories* from 1943 to 1945. In an illustration for the Summer 1944 issue of *Thrilling Wonder Stories*, Donnell's female character is posed so that she is facing danger with her male counterpart (see plate 5.9). The woman does not hold a gun like her companion, but neither is she the traditional victim cringing in distress. Moreover, her pose reflects Donnell's training in commercial illustration: it highlights the woman's body as active while allowing viewers to see her clothes. Both Les Tina and Donnell depicted women as active subjects

THE BLACK CAT

JAN. 1917

UNUSUAL SHORT STORIES

10 CENTS

Olivette Bourgeois

JACK LONDON'S FIRST STORY AND HOW THE BLACK CAT SAVED HIM IN THIS ISSUE

5.1. Cover of the *Black Cat* by Olivette Bourgeois for the January 1917 issue.

Oriental

S T O R I E S

FASCINATING TALES OF THE EAST

A Thrilling
Tale of Burma
by
WARREN HASTINGS
MILLER

S·B·H·HURST
ROBERT·E·HOWARD
BASSETT MORGAN
GEOFFREY VACE

5.2. Cover of *Oriental Stories* by Lucille Webster Holling for the Autumn 1931 issue.

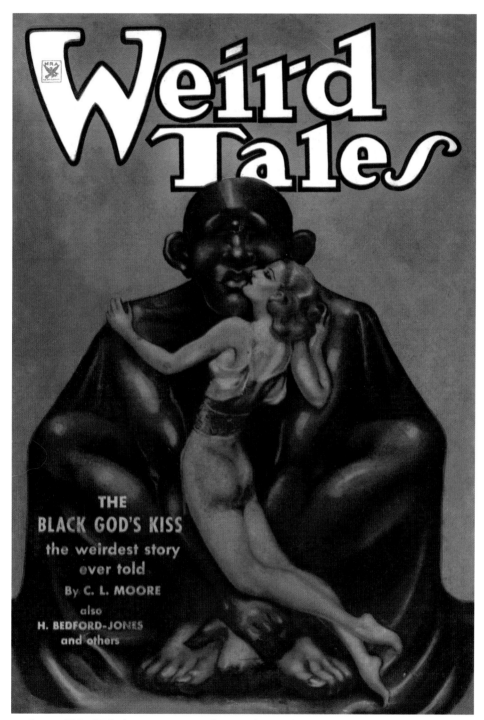

THE
BLACK GOD'S KISS
the weirdest story
ever told
By C. L. MOORE
also
H. BEDFORD-JONES
and others

5.3. Cover of *Weird Tales* by Margaret Brundage for the October 1934 issue. From the holdings of the Eaton Collection of Science Fiction and Fantasy, Special Collections and University Archives, UCR Library, University of California, Riverside.

5.4. Cover of *Weird Tales* by Margaret Brundage for the April 1935 issue. From the holdings of the Eaton Collection of Science Fiction and Fantasy, Special Collections and University Archives, UCR Library, University of California, Riverside.

All Stories Complete

Weird Tales

MARCH

The Unique Magazine

"STRANGE ORCHIDS"

a goose-flesh story
of weird happenings,
lovely girls, and
gorgeous flowers.
By DOROTHY QUICK

Eando Binder
G. G. Pendarves
Earl Peirce, Jr.
Robert Bloch
Henry Hasse

5.5. Cover of *Weird Tales* by Margaret Brundage for the March 1937 issue. From the holdings of the Eaton Collection of Science Fiction and Fantasy, Special Collections and University Archives, UCR Library, University of California, Riverside.

CHANGE FOR THE BITTER
By LEE FRANCIS

GOERING and Hirohito both dreamed—and each believed it meant he was the man of destiny

"You are destined to be Earth's true superman," the angel said

5.6. Interior art by Margaret Brundage for the April 1945 issue of *Fantastic Adventures*.

Illustration by Dorothy Les Tina

40

5.7. Interior art by Dorothy Les Tina for the December 1942 issue of *Future Fantasy and Science Fiction* depicting a scene from "The Leapers," by Carol Grey (pseudonym of Robert A. W. Lowndes).

Illustration by Dorothy Les Tina

5.8. Interior art by Dorothy Les Tina for the December 1942 issue of *Future Fantasy and Science Fiction* depicting a scene from the John B. Michel story "Claggett's Folly."

PRIESTESS of PAKMARI

By ALBERT DE PINA

With Civilization at Stake, Space Pilot Phillip Varon Crosses the Dread Jungles of Venus on a Mission of Many Perils!

CHAPTER I

Hazardous Venture

I T WAS over. Incredibly it was over, that humiliating trip to Mars where the malicious courtesy of a bitter people had added to his shame. For Dar Vaaijo, emperor of Mars, had never forgotten that Venus had put an end to his dreams of conquest. It was over—and it had ended in failure. Mars remained adamant. The Uranium embargo stood. And the precious isotope that powered Venus' complex civilization, a civilization opposed to Mars' predatory program, and Terra's domination, had dwindled to the danger point. Soon all atomic-powered machines would stop, spacers would be grounded, and hunger would

stalk the cities where multitudes already milled in growing fear. Then civilization would crash to ruins.

Phillip Varon's space-tanned features dripped perspiration as he stepped out of the airlock of his long, gleaming atomo-plane. To him Venus' Centralport was an Eden, riotous with fantastic blossoms, which stood out vividly against the purpling ramparts of the distant mountains. Above him, the cloud-cap was translucently blue, like a cosmic sheet of sapphirine glass lighted from behind.

"Excellency, the Council awaits your report. Your plane's ready."

The soft voice was deep and melodious, but slightly halting, as if unaccustomed to speech, for Venusians communicated largely by telepathy, unlike the millions of Terrans

5.9. Interior art by Dolly Donnell for the Summer 1944 issue of *Thrilling Wonder Stories*.

more frequently than their male counterparts, placing female characters at the center of the stories they illustrated.[10]

The aesthetic conventions forged by female artists during the 1930s and 1940s continue to serve as inspiration for women SF artists. Rowena Morrill, whose popular SF and fantasy art began to appear in the late 1970s, helped extend this sensibility to the covers of paperback books.[11] Morrill's art often focuses on women who are both powerful and sensual, a popular combination pioneered by Brundage.[12] Victoria Poyser-Lisi, winner of the 1986 Frank R. Paul Award for SF and fantasy art, also began working in the late 1970s. Mentored by Morrill, Poyser-Lisi creates art that bears the stamp of this same tradition: her work—which includes a number of novel covers for the legendary author and Science Fiction Writers of America Grand Master André Alice Norton—regularly put women at the center of the story's action. In the 1990s, the bodybuilder and artist Julie Bell extended this tradition. Bell's muscular amazons adorn magazine, book, and video game covers as well as comic book trading cards. Bell has also published several collections of her work, including *Hard Curves* (1995) and *Soft as Steel* (1999).[13] As these titles suggest, women artists have continued to illustrate women's bodies as infused with power. They are "neither lurid nor lewd": like Brundage's "Ladies of the Weird," they "stand or move with power" and have an interior strength that is undiminished by the threats posed by patriarchy (Guran 23, 26).

OLIVETTE BOURGEOIS (1892–1983) was an artist whose work appeared on sixteen covers of the *Black Cat* between 1916 and 1918. Bourgeois trained at the New School in Boston, where she received a scholarship for "first-year design" in 1915 ("New School" 13). The New School emphasized "practical training" in "fine or applied art" and offered classes in cartooning, commercial art, fashion illustration, and book design (*New School* 19). The fact that one of her "decorative design" pieces was featured on the back cover of the 1916–17 school catalog when she was just a second-year student indicates the strength of Bourgeois's work from an early age (*New School*). In addition to the *Black Cat*, her art appeared in Massachusetts-based children's magazines such as the *Youth's Companion* and *Little Folks Magazine*.

From its inception in 1895 until 1913, the *Black Cat* had covers consisting of either festively dressed anthropomorphic black cats or the face of a black cat surrounded by decorative designs. The *Black Cat* changed hands in 1913, but continued this style of cover until late 1916. The covers Bourgeois produced beginning in December 1916 reflected a clear shift of emphasis for the magazine. Referred to by one contemporary reviewer as "the aristocrat of artists," Bourgeois created covers featuring smiling, stylish people dressed for an outing or engaging in some kind of amusing activity ("Reviews" 4). In particular, the covers produced by Bourgeois emphasized happy, short-haired modern women engaged in such pursuits as exercising with dumbbells, reclining on swings, and, as in the illustration reprinted here, attending fancy-dress parties.

The fashion illustration training Bourgeois received at the New School was evident in covers like that of the *Black Cat*'s January 1917 issue, which depicts a couple out on New Year's Eve (see plate 5.1). This issue memorialized Jack London's death by reprinting "A Thousand Deaths," a *Frankenstein*-inspired tale of mad science originally published in 1899. The cover produced by Bourgeois had nothing to do with London's story or with any other SF story published in the issue. This was standard for the *Black Cat*: Bourgeois's covers were designed to hail the women readers who were the magazine's target audience, not to depict scenes from the fiction included therein. The outfits and hairstyles of her female subjects were consistent with changing images of women during the 1910s, when fashion magazines such as *Vogue* featured women in bright colors and everyday settings, and marketed a progressive and active lifestyle for modern women.[14] As such, Bourgeois infused the covers of the *Black Cat* with a sensibility characteristic of the New Woman. Moreover, the emphasis she placed on active female bodies anticipated that of later genre artists, including Margaret Brundage, Dorothy Les Tina, and Dolly Donnell.

LUCILLE WEBSTER HOLLING (1900–89) was an artist who contributed one cover to *Oriental Stories*, the sister magazine of *Weird Tales*. Holling was born on December 8, 1900, in Valparaiso, Indiana. Before she turned twenty she moved to Chicago to pursue her interest in art. She attended the Art Institute, where she met fellow student and artist Holling Clancy Holling. They married in 1925, and in 1926 they began teaching art and working with the drama department on costume design for New York University's first University World Cruise. Over the next few decades, Lucille Holling and her husband collaborated on more than fifteen illustrated children's books. Though her husband received most of the credit for these books, Holling was a major contributor to the research, writing, and art. The couple won many awards and made several appearances at universities and on radio and television. In 1980, their work was the subject of a special exhibition at the UCLA Library, where their papers now reside.

Like most of the other women who contributed art to magazines that published SF, Lucille Holling's training included fashion illustration. Her work extended far beyond her collaborations with her husband, as she produced art for a number of advertisements, magazines, and books. Her work included fashion drawings for Marshall Field department stores in the 1920s, three covers for *Child Life* magazine in the early 1930s, and the cover of a 1932 book entitled *Successful Farming*. Holling was particularly interested in ethnic fashion, and her portfolio included pictures created during her travels of Japanese dancers, Native American dancers, and traditional Russian costumes.

This emphasis on exotic fashion is likely what caught the eye of Farnsworth Wright, the editor of *Oriental Stories*. In 1931, Wright was struggling to help his Chicago-based magazines recover from financial disaster (Weinberg, *"Weird Tales"* 6). Wright began to offer more money to artists and found new talent to help elevate the sales of his magazines. Holling was hired to produce the cover for the Autumn 1931 issue of *Oriental Stories*. Her illustration emphasizes the body of a beautiful woman dressed stylishly (see plate 5.2). The cover is based on the Warren Hastings Miller story "The White Sawbwa of Möng Nam," and the woman's clothing and jewelry are, appropriately, based on Burmese designs. Keeping with Wright's established policy, the woman's clothing does not cover one of her breasts: Wright knew the importance of sex in increasing the sales of his magazines to male readers. Moreover, Holling's cover diverges from the previous *Oriental Stories* covers that invoked the colonial American Gothic imagination by depicting sinister non-white men threatening white heroes and white women. Holling's cover signaled a shift in emphasis for Wright's magazines, where female characters began to take center stage in a way that would affect SF magazine art for the next two decades.

MARGARET JOHNSON BRUNDAGE (1900–76) was one of the most popular, influential, and celebrated artists to ever work in magazines that published SF. She was born Margaret Hedda Johnson in Chicago, where she lived and worked for her entire life. Her art career started early, when the teenaged Johnson became involved with the *Voice* newspaper at McKinley High School, where she got to know her fellow student Walt Disney (Everts 25; Spurlock 129). Johnson later attended the Chicago Academy of Fine Arts, an institution that specialized in "commercial and applied art," including "fashion illustration" (Spurlock 133–134). She worked part time at a restaurant called the Dil Pickle, a hangout for members of the International Workers of the World. There, she met the union organizer and hobo activist Slim Brundage, whom she married in 1927. Though she shared her husband's political views, his low-paying work and freewheeling lifestyle did not suit Brundage, and the two divorced in 1939. Brundage had to support herself, her son, and her disabled mother with the income she made from her art. She did freelance fashion illustration during the 1920s, turning to magazine work when the Great Depression undermined the fashion industry. While working for *Weird Tales*, Brundage maintained her commitment to progressive politics by working with the African American arts movement centered in the south side of Chicago. Brundage helped found the South Side Community Art Center and served on its board in the 1940s and 1950s, thus playing a critical role in establishing an important center of African American culture that exists to this day.

During her career in SF, Brundage produced dozens of covers in a revamped Gothic style that emphasized beautiful and powerful women. Brundage's SF career began when she walked into the offices of *Weird Tales* in 1932 looking for magazine work, dropping off her portfolio with the "only magazine she had been able to find with offices in the city" (Weinberg, *"Weird Tales"* 65). Editor Farnsworth Wright was impressed with one of her pastel pieces and commissioned her to do similar work for the cover of his new magazine, *Oriental Stories*. The popularity of the cover led to more work with Wright, including many covers for *Weird Tales*. At the time, Wright's magazines were struggling because the "bank where much of the firm's money was kept" collapsed during the financial disasters of the Depression (Weinberg, *"Weird Tales"* 6). Brundage once said in an interview that she usually submitted "several sketches to Wright" and his business manager, William Sprenger, and "they always wanted the ones with the scantiest clad girls" (Weinberg, *"Weird Tales"* 68). Authors soon figured out the game and wrote stories with scenes in which a woman would become unclothed, thinking that Wright would deem it a more likely candidate for Brundage's cover art. This strategy paid off handsomely, and Brundage's art played a major role in pulling *Weird Tales* out of financial trouble.

Brundage used her fashion training to elevate *Weird Tales'* version of the American Gothic style, focusing her compositions on the female form in ways that were subtly subversive. The American Gothic style was originally developed by male artists in the nineteenth century and depicted strange colonial landscapes populated by hostile alien men. Brundage's pastel creations during her first two years at *Weird Tales* often followed this style, showing white women who were helpless, bound, and threatened by dark-skinned men. However, the longer she worked on the magazine, the more Brundage represented women characters by themselves, without any men in the frame. She often associated the women on her covers with supernatural powers, depicting them in ways that questioned Enlightenment notions of masculine order and rationality. Brundage's illustrations had little or no gore, and her women always had "a unique sense of dignity" even when frightened (Spurlock 148). When a female character was written as "more of a victim than a heroine," Brundage would still render her in such a way that there seemed "nothing powerless or weak about the woman" (Guran 21).

Responses to Brundage's art were mixed, but her work clearly struck a chord with *Weird Tales* readers. Each issue featuring a Brundage cover seemed to spark a new and entertaining controversy. Initially, Brundage used the gender-neutral name "M. Brundage" for the work commissioned by Wright. In the October 1934 issue, Wright attempted to settle the ongoing complaints about the nude women on the covers by revealing her gender. Brundage's cover for that October 1934 issue depicts a scene from the first Jirel of Joiry story entitled "Black God's Kiss" by another legendary woman of that period, C. L. Moore (see plate 5.3). Despite exchanging the heroine's chain mail, greaves, and sword for "clingy blue fabric," Brundage "tells the story . . . quite well" with her image (Guran 27). Brundage uses Moore's story to get away from the threatened-damsel motif, representing Jirel as active and independent: she freely embraces the passive male statue of a black god in a way that dramatizes both female desire and miscegenation. This subversive bent became more pronounced in Brundage's work as the 1930s progressed.

One notable exception to Brundage's standard style came with the April 1935 issue of *Weird Tales*, which is based on A. W. Bernal's SF story "The Man Who Was Two Men" (see plate 5.4). For that cover Brundage depicts a mad scientist, a complicated machine, two men in tubes, and no women at all. In this way, Brundage is consistent with the tradition of Gothic SF emphasizing the dangers of science and questioning the benefits of progress. However, the lack of any female characters on the cover sent up "the loudest howls" from readers and served as evidence that most fans liked Brundage's women (Weinberg, *"Weird Tales"* 71). Brundage quickly returned to her more standard covers with the compositions focused on alluring women. When Wright later gave her Dorothy Quick's mad scientist story "Strange Orchids" to illustrate for the March 1937 cover, she kept the mad scientist out of the picture (except for a menacing shadow) and centered her work on strong women in a weird situation (see plate 5.5). Just as in Quick's story (which is reprinted in chapter 1,"Authors," of this anthology), Brundage keeps the reader focused on the female protagonist's negative reaction to a misogynist mode of science that has dire consequences for women. This exemplified her approach to SF: carrying on Gothic traditions and catering to the heterosexual male gaze while depicting women as strong and fearless, even in harrowing situations.

By the early 1940s, the influence of Brundage on other SF magazines was widespread. For example, the art for *Startling Stories* and *Thrilling Wonder Stories* regularly featured a mixture of the technophilic and Gothic styles popularized by Frank R. Paul and Brundage. A typical cover included a scantily clad woman in the foreground who either was a powerful alien (like Brundage) or was being harassed by giant machines or monsters (like Paul). Brundage continued to produce covers for *Weird Tales* until 1945, long after the magazine had been sold and moved its operations to New York City. The new publishers stipulated that there be no more nudes on the covers, in part because of newsstand censorship in New York City. They also cut the amount of money they paid artists, which forced Brundage to begin looking for other work. Drawing clothed women posed no problem for the former fashion illustrator, but Brundage had to pick up interior art jobs from magazines such as *Fantastic Adventures* to make ends meet (see plate 5.6). Brundage's work inspired generations of women writers and artists, and her influence is still apparent in the art of well-known women such as Rowena Morill, Victoria Poyser-Lisi, and Julie Bell. Their strong and sexy amazons are modern versions of Brundage's alluring women, a legacy that has contributed to Brundage's status as the "queen" of pulp-era magazine art (Heller; Korshak 11; Roberts 43–45).

DOROTHY LOUISE LES TINA (1917–2003) worked in SF magazines as an author and artist in the 1940s and 1950s (for details about her personal life, see the entry on Les Tina in Chapter 1, "Authors," of this anthology). Les Tina worked as an assistant at Popular Publications in the early 1940s, where she met Frederik Pohl and other authors and editors associated with the Futurian fan group. During that period, she produced several pieces of artwork for Futurian Robert A. W. Lowndes's genre publications. After a decade of military service, she returned briefly to SF, contributing interior art to several issues of Hugo Gernsback's *Science Fiction Plus* in the 1950s before moving on to other, non-genre writing projects.

Like Margaret Brundage at *Weird Tales*, Les Tina combined the characteristics of her chosen genre's art traditions with images of strong women. Her illustrations included rockets, buildings, and planets in the background, which was consistent with the technophilic style of art favored by most SF specialist magazines of the day. This can be seen in her two pieces of interior art for the December 1942 issue of *Future Fantasy and Science Fiction*. For that issue, Les Tina illustrated editor Robert A. W. Lowndes's novelette "The Leapers" (published under the pseudonym Carol Grey) and John B. Michel's short story "Claggett's Folly." In "The Leapers" illustration, the most prominent figure is a woman who—in direct contrast to the awkward, fearful-looking men around her—is joyfully rising from a building toward the moon (see plate 5.7).

In "Claggett's Folly," Les Tina depicts a montage of a rocket, a record, a man, a child, and a woman. While the man seems to recoil from the rocket and the record and the child looks at them in with curiosity, the woman gazes upon them with a smile (see plate 5.8). Neither woman is a damsel in distress who needs rescuing by a man. Instead, both seem to lead the people around them with their eager curiosity in the face of technological marvels and adventure. As such, Les Tina adapted the technophilic style of SF art to suggest that women will lead humanity to truly new and different futures.

DOLLY RACKLEY DONNELL (1906–94) was a Missouri-born illustrator who contributed interior art to *Startling Stories* and *Thrilling Wonder Stories* from 1943 to 1945. Her illustrations proved immediately popular with readers, several of whom wrote letters that lavished praise on her work and recommended that she do cover art for future issues. Fans initially assumed Donnell was a man, but in the Summer 1944 issue of *Thrilling* the editor, Oscar J. Friend, explained, "She is a gal illustrator" (106). Friend mistakenly referred to Donnell as "A. J. Donnelly" but in the Fall 1944 issue printed a letter from Donnell in which she gave her name as "D. Donnell" and noted that Friend had confused her name with that of her husband, A.J., who was on active duty "in the Army Air Forces in England" (Donnell, "Abject," 99). After the war, A.J. followed in his wife's footsteps and contributed covers to a number of SF novels produced by Fantasy Press.

Dolly Donnell worked for magazines whose editors preferred artwork in the technophilic style of Frank R. Paul. Donnell contributed to this style by depicting women as active partners in the exploration of the universe rather than as damsels in distress. This is most apparent in the Summer 1944 issue of *Thrilling*, where her interior artwork directly contrasts with Earle Bergey's cover. The full-color Bergey cover portrays a scene from Albert De Pina's "The Priestess of Pakmari" with a woman swooning into the arms of a man who is firing a gun at a tentacled, bug-eyed monster. The woman's see-through outfit barely conceals her buttocks, which are facing the reader. Donnell's interior art for the story depicts the same scene, but in her version Nereida, the priestess of the title, is wearing the "beryllium-mesh suit" described in the story and is in an active pose beside the man (see plate 5.9). While she is not holding the "atomo-pistol," she is the guide of Phillip Varon, the action hero of the story, and is depicted by Donnell as standing up to the creature instead of swooning in fear. One fan seemed to be confused by her representation of the active woman, complaining that "Miss Donnell is a good artist, but she doesn't know how to draw humans correctly and she puts them into such peculiar positions" (Schick 99). However, Donnell's techniques were consistent with fashion magazines of the day, where active women were depicted in poses that highlighted their clothing. Donnell's approach seemed preferable to the many fans who cited her work as superior to that of men such as Bergey (Hamil, "That Screaming" 100; Harmon 100; Hesson 103). Donnell's vision of women who actively confront the Gothic horrors of space anticipated both the move toward stronger women on midcentury SF magazine covers and the proliferation of women as amazons popularized by modern SF artists such as Julie Bell.

CONCLUSION
CHALLENGING THE NARRATIVE, OR,
WOMEN TAKE BACK SCIENCE FICTION

....

KATHLEEN ANN GOONAN

[Science fiction and fantasy] are dedicated to the exploration of the future and myth and history. Dreams, if you want to frame it that way. Yet the enforced [single white male] dominance of these genres means that the dreams of whole groups of people have been obliterated from the Zeitgeist.
— N. K. Jemisin, Guest of honor speech at Wiscon 38

SF is a big tent. Clowns and preachers, warriors and pacifists, space-farers, life forms, philosophies, genders, scantily clothed gedankenexperiments, utopias and dystopias, politicos, thieves, adventurers, and mad American housewives crowd in. Thrilling, fantastic, incredibly serious fights continuously ensue as to what, exactly, this time-traveling circus is to be called, who will be allowed to be part of the show, who will be tossed beneath the elephant's parade once hired, who gets to keep the money box, and even who the audience (SF's real source of power) might be as marks mill outside eyeing, with delight or repugnance, lurid posters of the Astoundingly Buxom Chain-Mail-Bikini-Clad Woman and considering whether they want to pay to enter this flimsy construction alive with the outline of raised fists as it emits the eerie, alluring wail of the Unknown, the Different, the Amazing, and the Astounding brain-changing word potions of an infinite array of weird, dangerous, and thought-provoking wild worlds.

Or let's say that SF is a generation ship on which the pilots are always men—usually white men—because only they have the mental capacity to imagine, to plan, to lead, to build. Well, sometimes women hijack the ship and fly it to new, strange, unmanly galaxies where SF is uncomfortable—where, some say, SF can't even *exist*, so of course the men don't remember those weird time shifts even when they experience them firsthand.

But we now know the truth: many of those inside the tent, the starship—oh, heck, the *genre*—are women. And surprisingly enough to some (even to some women), from the very beginning women wrote, illustrated, poeticized, and edited SF. They weren't just in the tent or the generation ship—

they helped build it, and then they used their scientific and literary brilliance to steer it to new galaxies.

Yet, as often happens to the work of women, their accomplishments became invisible over the decades. Some even claimed, as Dogs said of Humans in Clifford Simak's *City* and as Joanna Russ pointed out in *How to Suppress Women's Writing*, that Humans—especially women—couldn't possibly have done such things because they were clearly incapable of building wonders—or, if they did, these wonders were certainly not of the caliber of wonders built by men and that, in fact, they were inevitably ineffective, ill-conceived, poorly executed wonders.

Now, at the same time as the truth of how women shaped SF, how they gained and wielded their power, has emerged and come into sharp focus as the result of painstaking research, women are, once again, claiming their place in SF. They declare, through their fiction, their blogs, their speeches, and their scholarship, that the edges of the ship are nowhere and everywhere, and that women of all colors, nationalities, and visions are qualified to design, build, and pilot the ship.

For some men—those who have learned to believe that only men have ever shaped and written SF, and that only men read it, and that men must join the battle to save it—this argument over Who Can Write SF is not pretty. But the struggle for equality has never been pretty. This battle has always been deeply necessary, as innate and inevitable as our envisioning, inventing, and eager using of technology.

This essay will discuss the history of women's naming and unnaming and how they are now—as always, for women in SF seem always to be disappearing and resurfacing—naming themselves again as thinkers, as artists, as writers, and as the rabble-rousers they were born to be. It will relate this issue to the larger culture from which SF emerges. It will show that some things are changing rapidly and that others are changing much too slowly. It will speculate as to why. It will conclude with a loud explosion. (Just kidding. Or maybe not.)

WOMEN AND SF: WRITERS, EDITORS, AND READERS

Girls and women are the ultimate outsiders, so it makes sense that they would understand the role of the alien and try to subvert—to change—the societal construct that tells them "girls can't" and "women aren't as (intelligent, strong, capable)" as men. After more than a century of activism, girls still get the message that they cannot *be*. They cannot be scientists, writers, engineers, architects, computer programmers, game designers, mathematicians, artists, CEOs, presidents—that is, they cannot be powerful. This narrative is shouted at girls by images, behaviors, admonitions, and models in the world and in stories, our most powerful form of communication, from birth. Often, the narrative is backed up by harassment, sometimes so subtle that even the perpetrators can successfully claim that it wasn't there, that the harassers were misunderstood, or that the alleged harassment has to do with innate biological differences between the sexes. If that doesn't work, harassment sometimes becomes overt, and ugly.

Women who publish science fiction are, therefore, doubly strong, admirably conditioned for the time when rumbling turns to out-and-out battle. These women have beaten the invidious "you can't" and almost always shape new narratives that women and men who read and dream would want their daughters and sons to read, books and stories that steer the ship of thought and action in new social directions, books that examine gender, history, power, culture, and technology and use them in new ways to speak from new viewpoints.

Because women have had to become so strong, this time they will not be silenced, erased, or forgotten.

They are very angry. Because of this, they are very loud.

————————

This loudness annoys some people, to the point that it provokes online sexual slurs, bullying, and even death threats. One would not think that this would be the case in a field whose works are widely supposed to be written by the most intelligent for the most intelligent; that men would not be so angered. One would think that everyone in science fiction and fantasy (SFF) would have been delighted when women won every Nebula Award for work published in 2013, because women had so long been in the minority when it came to winning awards.

This was true of both the Nebula and the Hugo Awards, which are two of SF's most prestigious prizes. The Hugos were established in 1953, but no woman received one until 1967, when Anne McCaffrey's novella "Weyr Search" and Kate Wilhelm's short story "Baby, You Were Great" garnered awards. In 1968, McCaffrey and Wilhelm became the first women to win Nebula Awards— McCaffrey for her novella "Dragonrider" and Wilhelm for her short story "The Planners." In 1970, Ursula K. Le Guin was the first woman to take home both a Hugo and a Nebula Award in the novel category for *The Left Hand of Darkness*, a spectacular win that some might have seen as indicative of the field's becoming increasingly inclusive of women. But in fact, the statistics remained dismal: "From 1968 to 2011 there were 46 awards to women in all the professional [SFF] fiction categories (just over 20%)" (http://www.sf-encyclopedia.com/entry/women_sf_writers#sthash.KlRiI11x.dpuf).

Despite this, there wasn't exactly an all-inclusive celebration when the all-woman winner's list was published in May 2014 (http://www.sfwa.org/2014/05/2013-nebula-awards-winners/). A few men characterizing themselves as "Sad Puppies 1" and "Sad Puppies 2" made it clear that they saw these wins as a loss of their own power to writers who might be characterized as feminist, non-white, of non-European descent, gay, transgendered, or any combination thereof—writers who, according to one of the Puppies, wrote SFF that might be about "racial prejudice and exploitation . . . sexism and the oppression of women . . . gay and transgender issues, [or the] evils of capitalism and the despotism of the wealthy" (Torgersen).

On the level playing field of the internet some of these feminist, activist, award-winning writers accused of causing genre-wrecking change voiced their history, their concerns, and their anger so articulately that the Sad Puppies, in their various iterations, have several times attempted to toss the board game in the air by bloc voting (entirely legal according to Hugo nomination rules) in order to return SF to its more traditional fare of manly men doing manly things with other manly men.

In 1991, in the speech in which she launched the Tiptree Award, Pat Murphy said, "A persistent rumbling that I have heard echoing through science fiction . . . says, in essence, that women don't write science fiction. Put a little more rudely, this rumbling says: 'Those damn women are ruining science fiction.' They are doing it by writing stuff that isn't 'real' science fiction; they are writing 'soft' science fiction and fantasy" (Murphy, "Illusion and Expectation").

This begs the question: what is SF? One can easily find fifty sturdy definitions online, some directly contradicting others and most, of course, formulated by men. How can SF be ruined or destroyed if there is little agreement on what it is? Why is it so fragile?

The field of SF did, in fact, change significantly when the Science Fiction Writers of America changed its name to the Science Fiction and Fantasy Writers of America in 1992 through a member vote (although it still uses the acronym SFWA). The long process leading up to the vote brought out the natural vitriol of SFWA members as they kicked the idea around in their usual way, with personal insults and resultant waves of side-taking outrage. At heart, the debate centered on the fact that some writers produced strange and estranging stories that, they claimed, were SF. Yet sometimes the stories seemed suspiciously like . . . fantasy! And if fantasy was admitted for Nebula consideration, hard SF would be forever crushed, because it is fragile and rare. The practical result, when the dust settled, was that more SFF written by women—much of it different from what men had been writing, much of it feminist, much of it, because it was "soft" SF (code for narratives that focus on anthropology, psychology, linguistics, relationships, or even out-and-out fantasy rather than on physics, chemistry, mathematics, etc.), not previously eligible to win a Nebula Award—were now included on ballots.

And winning.

This is what it looks like when women speak out and take action.

———

The scholarly research discussed in this book clearly shows that women took to what was called "scientifiction" in the early twentieth century as eagerly as did men. They edited, illustrated, and published fiction, science fact articles, editorials, poetry, and fan materials with great enthusiasm, shaping the field during the 1920s, 1930s, and 1940s.

American women of that period had reason to feel good about themselves. For the first time, they were full members of the society in which they lived. Women had fought to gain the right to vote. That fight united them. Women had agency, and with this agency they became increasingly dedicated to bringing about change through political means.

The 1920s were prosperous and optimistic. The United States had played a pivotal role in winning the Great War, which, it was thought, would end all war. Automobiles, washing machines, radio, enlightened awareness of birth control options, increased access to higher education, and the introduction of an equal rights amendment to the Constitution in the U.S. Congress were indicative of the sociocultural changes taking place at that time. In the arts, modernism and jazz reflected the technocultural changes taking place in the wake of the popularization of Darwin's theory of evolution, Einstein's theory of relativity, and Freud's theory of the unconscious. In general, the feeling that everything—from the world, matter, and time to what we knew about our own bodies and minds—was much different than anything we had previously believed or lived by blossomed, grew, and persists.

But we don't always remember this history or, especially, women's various roles within it. Consider the case of Lise Meitner, the second woman to earn a PhD in physics from the University of Vienna, who was a full participant in the gifted circle that included Niels Bohr, Albert Einstein, Werner Heisenberg, Erwin Schrödinger, Wolfgang Pauli, Paul Dirac, and others who delved into the curious secrets of matter. Her scientific brilliance, which she made evident in spite of barriers that women of that age were just beginning to surmount, earned her a physics lab at the Kaiser Wilhelm Institute in Berlin. However, her discovery of nuclear fission was written out of history when Otto Hahn claimed a postwar Nobel Prize for that accomplishment. Like many of the women involved in early SF, her important contributions to history are not well known. How many have heard of Mary Sherman Morgan, who formulated Hydyne, the fuel of the Redstone Rocket, when Von Braun's team failed (G. Morgan)? Rosalind Franklin, a Cambridge scientist with a PhD in chemistry who was pursuing the holy grail of modern genetics, lost the opportunity to win a Nobel Prize for her work when her images of X-ray diffraction confirming the helical structure of DNA were unethically shown (by another male scientist) to her rival, James Watson. As scholars increasingly recognize, "Had Watson, Crick, and Wilkins properly acknowledged Franklin's contribution, Rosalind Franklin would have shared the enormous public recognition that Watson and Crick received for discovering the helical structure of the DNA molecule" (Rapaport). The list of cases like these is long.

It is not news that many women engineers and inventors have been written out of history, but, in this context, it bears repeating—particularly because SF is informed by and has a strong relationship with science and technology. The writing out of women from the history of SF parallels this process, and the stark, well-documented landmarks that show the process are disturbing to anyone who cares about losing the contributions of half of the human race to prejudice.

But in the 1920s, these erasures were in the future, and women's optimism about and increasing involvement with the greater world were reflected in their SF. Far from being passive sex objects waiting for rescue, women in early female-authored SFF fiction and poetry drove cars and piloted rocket ships. They explored space, fought aliens and mad scientists, made peace with demons, toyed with gender identity, and ruled both planets and homes with scientific care. But women did more than just write stories about egalitarian futures. They helped shape those futures through the work they did in the SFF community writing editorials, reporting on groundbreaking scientific and technological phenomena, and producing cover art. They performed these activities in professional and amateur publications alike, some of which they even published themselves. In short, they did everything that men did in the field. Statistics presented in this anthology show that this involvement in SF never slowed—in fact, over the decades, it increased. Women were always a part of SF. Women have always written SF.

Editors, then, now, and in the decades between, publish stories that they believe will help sell a magazine—stories that will elicit interest in readers and help the magazine gain new readers. They comb slush piles to find stories that are not only publishable, but also good.

Editors also shape the field by buying stories from certain writers and rejecting stories by others. Hugo Gernsback, T. O'Conor Sloane, and David Lasser actively courted women to contribute stories to their magazines, including Leslie F. Stone, Claire Winger Harris, Lilith Lorraine, and L. Taylor Hansen. Farnsworth Wright and Dorothy McIlwraith of *Weird Tales* regularly featured women writers such as Dorothy Quick and C. L. Moore, as well as infamous cover artist Margaret Brundage. All of these women became regulars in early SFF magazines precisely because they wrote the kind of stories and produced the kind of artwork that editors sought. Some of these women left SFF when Groff Conklin and John W. Campbell began their editorial reigns in the late 1930s. But others—including Dorothy Les Tina and Leslie Perri, both of whom are featured in this anthology and whose work anticipates that of the midcentury luminaries Judith Merril, Carol Emshwiller, and Ann McCaffrey—took advantage of the new editorial landscape to make their voices heard. Despite evidence that Campbell did not publish stories by some of the pioneering women in SF, he was instrumental in launching the careers of new women writers and in nurturing the careers of others who were able to shape their stories to accord with his vision of what SF should be.

And yet—

A century after this bright beginning, in 2014, women publish only 28.1 percent of SF short fiction (Connolly). Women author a mere quarter of all SF novels (Heimbach). Most SF anthologies have abysmal ratios of women to men—hardly ever half or more, and too often, one, or none (C. Morgan).

If there is discrimination—which publishers and editors usually deny—where does such discrimination come from?

All arts emerge from the culture in which they are embedded. If SF is full of sexual stereotypes that repel female readers, it is because these stereotypes are also the face of our culture. Female scientists in media are usually amazing, exotic creatures, a striking, weird anomaly, because they are able to think in ways in which women are not supposed to be able to think. The online document "Are Boys and Girls Equally Prepared for Life?", published by the Organisation for Economic Co-operation and Development (OECD), uses academic testing statistics gathered in 2012 by the Programme for International Student Assessment (PISA) to show that girls in Iceland, Jordan, Thailand, Qatar, Malaysia, and Shanghai-China scored better than boys on the same mathematics tests. Yet when Larry Summers, former president of Harvard University, argued that biological differences in men and women account for the small number of women in mathematics and engineering, he was defended by the intellectual celebrity Steven Pinker. When he left his post because of the controversy, he was tapped by President Obama to be chairman of the Federal Reserve (Summers withdrew his name because of a vigorous campaign against his appointment).

These are still strange times.

Who reads SF?

SF has been a predominantly closed system since the 1920s. The writers, the literature, and the fans form a feedback loop upon which publishers depend. It is common to hear someone outside SF culture declare, "I don't read science fiction," without any qualifiers. SF rarely makes inroads in this demographic, and most people who say this are women. Markers warning of SF content splash book covers, and the literature is segregated in bookstores. Reviews are ghettoized—SF is not "literature," but reviewed in special "science fiction" sections—a practice that allows potential readers to avoid being caught by surprise when a review sounds intriguing.

Because fiction readers are not a large segment of the population and because SF is a very small slice of that demographic, the SF literature market is small. Moreover, many publishers, editors, and even writers claim that SF is a literature for males written by males and imply that women should stay out of the clubhouse, or enter at their peril. This attitude creates a dearth of realistically portrayed girls and women in the literature; instead, stories, books, and covers are overwhelmingly filled with sexual stereotypes of females, if there are any females at all. Most protagonists have been, and still are, grown-up white males—aliens, as far as young girls are concerned, and so these young girls avoid SF in droves. Somewhat ironically, however, in order to read much of anything at all, many learn early on to see through the eyes of a male protagonist anyway. After all, we are all "men," right?

That is, we are all men until some of us are reminded by the world that we are female and "can't"—can't understand mathematics, can't explore the Yucatan, can't earn a PhD in a scientific field or, thereafter, find a job that promises fair promotions, can't shoot wild animals, can't work for the CIA, or can't do much of anything that Alice Sheldon spoke of as having done in letters to colleagues including Ursula K. Le Guin, Robert Silverberg, and Joanna Russ when writing under the pseudonym and playing the part of James Tiptree, Jr. When Tiptree began winning Hugo and Nebula Awards, the SF community realized that no one had ever seen Tiptree, despite his voluminous correspondence, in which Sheldon described her alter ego as being a painfully shy recluse. Alice Sheldon, a PhD biochemist, big game hunter, explorer, and CIA agent, had easily infused her letters with male-seeming verisimilitude. Still, people speculated as to whether the mysterious James Tiptree, Jr., might be a woman. In response to this rumor, Robert Silverberg, in his introduction to Tiptree's first short story collection, *Warm Worlds and Otherwise*, famously wrote: "It has been suggested that Tiptree is female, a theory that I find absurd, for there is to me something ineluctably masculine about Tiptree's writing. I don't think the novels of Jane Austen could have been written by a man nor the stories of Earnest Hemingway by a woman, and in the same way I believe the author of the James Tiptree stories is male" (xii). And the world machine conspired to keep it that way. Although the reasons are personal and complicated, Alice Sheldon did not do nearly as well as a writer as did the multiple-award-winning author James Tiptree, Jr. once her secret identity was revealed.

Women are often described as being invisible in early SF because they used their initials, or took male pseudonyms, or wrote in partnership with a man. That is, "they didn't write it." However, writing under pseudonyms—even multiple pseudonyms—both was and is common for men and women alike. Because SF checks do not provide much food for the children, a writer might have several stories running in the same magazine under different by-lines. Sometimes, women—and men, for that matter—have pseudonyms thrust upon them. When Ursula K. Le Guin became the first woman to sell a short story ("Nine Lives") to *Playboy* magazine, the editors asked her to use only initials because "their readers would be frightened by a female byline on the story" (Le Guin 77). Le Guin complied—and used the *Playboy* check to buy a Volkswagen bus. When asked for a bio, she wrote, "It is commonly suspected that the writings of U. K. Le Guin are not actually written by U. K. Le Guin, but by another person of the same name" (77). Thus Le Guin—much like those early-twentieth-century SFF authors who used initials or androgynous names but provided editors with decidedly feminine portraits and biographies of themselves—both did and did not accept the identity thrust upon her by her chosen genre.

Are men really frightened of SF written by women? Or do male writers of SF grumble because women take up space in magazines, in bookstores, and on award ballots that used to be filled by men?

Or are editors and publishers just supplying the kinds of stories that the SF readership wants? Who *does* read SF? After conducting an extremely detailed statistical survey, hard SF author Mark Niemann-Ross came up with a number: 57 percent of those who read science fiction are men.

This means that 43 percent of all SF readers are women. This isn't a bad number, but it could be better. As Sheila Williams, the executive editor of *Asimov's*, says, "I'm frustrated by the gender imbalance among science fiction readers. Girls need to know from an early age that science and technology are cool. Advances in both will shape much of our future, and they should be encouraged to be fifty percent of these industries. Good science fiction with strong and exciting female protagonists can give teens a framework for their dreams and aspirations" (qtd. in Wilde).

So how might women writers bring about a situation in which girls and women are better represented in SF? Pat Murphy points to the challenge of changing the situation: "Consider a 2012 study, in which science faculty from a number of universities considered the application of a student for a laboratory manager position. The student was randomly assigned a male or female name. Otherwise, the application was identical. Yet men and women both judged John to be more competent than Jennifer—more valuable to the tune of $4000 a year in salary, more worthy of mentorship, and generally more likely to be hired." If it is this difficult for scientists—who are supposed to embrace value-free modes of analysis and decision making—to put aside their cultural biases when evaluating who should or should not be allowed into their community, then little wonder that similar difficulties persist in SF.

SF magazines may also have a difficult time increasing their female audiences because they publish much more SF written by men than by women. As Susan E. Connolly notes, "The actual, editorial market for science fiction written by women is small. Of five short-fiction markets that publish SF only, the gender gap is huge—71.9% of stories are written by men; 28.1%, by women." Why might this be the case? Apparently, women are not as motivated to write SF as are men. Magazines depend upon submissions; they cannot publish what they are not sent. Williams says that less than 30 percent of her submissions are from women and that 30 to 33 percent of *Asimov's* stories are written by women (Wilde).

Short-fiction editors who solicit stories from writers have more control over gender balance. One such editor is Ellen Datlow, who mainly publishes original and reprint anthologies as well as stories for Tor.com, but who, like Williams, reads for quality, not to achieve gender balance. As she explains, "I'm glad to see that more young female writers and writers of color are entering the fantastic field. . . . But when it comes down to what I or any editor buys it's always going to be the story itself, not who wrote it" (qtd. in Newitz).

Similarly, Julie Crisp, a novel editor at Tor UK, says, "I'm a woman. Yes, a female editor commissioning and actively looking for good genre—male AND female. . . . The sad fact is, we can't publish what we're not submitted." After analyzing 503 submissions between January and July 2013, she produced a graph showing that "when it comes to science fiction only 22% of the submissions we received were from female writers" (Crisp).

There is a strong correlation between statistics regarding women in SF and women in STEM professions (science, technology, engineering, and mathematics). As a paper recently released by the White House Office of Science and Technology Policy notes, only 24 percent of scientists and engineers in the United States are women ("Women and Girls"). Gender imbalance is a cultural phenomenon. Interestingly, Joanna Russ's bullet points in "How to Suppress Women's Writing" apply equally to women in science. Consider, for instance, this report on women in science written by Eileen Pollack for the *New York Times* (I insert Russ's laws in bracketed italics):

> As Nancy Hopkins, one of the professors who initiated the disparity between men and women study (a mid-1990's MIT investigation into marginality experienced by female scientists at MIT), put it in an online forum: "I have found that even when women win the Nobel Prize, someone is bound to tell me they did not deserve it or the discovery was really made by a man [*She didn't write it*] or the important result was made by a man [*She wrote it, but she had help*], or the woman really isn't that smart [*She wrote it, but she isn't really an artist, and it really isn't art*]. This is what discrimination looks like in 2011."

Similar attitudes that marginalize the perceived abilities of girls and women are mouthed by the former president of Harvard, one's grumpy uncle, and, often, by women themselves.

The previously cited Programme for International Student Assessment results suggest that excellence in STEM-related skills depends on that delicate dance each of us, male and female, does, from birth, with our environment in order to understand and become a member of the society into which we are born. When young and powerless, we must keenly absorb clues regarding how to act in order to please others and, thus, survive.

Ben Barres, a neuroscientist who underwent a female-to-male sex change operation, has firsthand experience with sexual discrimination in the sciences. As he wrote in a 2006 article for *Nature*:

> If innate intellectual abilities are not to blame for women's slow advance in science careers, then what is? The foremost factor, I believe, is the societal assumption that women are innately less able than men. Many studies, summarized in Virginia Valian's excellent book *Why So Slow?*, have demonstrated a substantial degree of bias against women—more than is sufficient to block women's advancement in many professions. Here are a few examples of bias from my own life as a young woman. As an undergrad at the Massachusetts Institute of Technology (MIT), I was the only person in a large class of nearly all men to solve a hard maths problem, only to be told by the professor that my boyfriend must have solved it for me. I was not given any credit. I am still disappointed about the prestigious fellowship competition I later lost to a male contemporary when I was a PhD student, even though the Harvard dean

who had read both applications assured me that my application was much stronger (I had published six high-impact papers whereas my male competitor had published only one). Shortly after I changed sex, a faculty member was heard to say, "Ben Barres gave a great seminar today, but then his work is much better than his sister's." (134)

Barres's experience backs up the claim of unconscious bias that Murphy notes in relation to SF, a bias that is prevalent in all spheres of our culture.

But the problem doesn't stop with science—it is part of our larger cultural fabric. Mitch McConnell, Senate minority leader, says, "We've come a long way in pay equity, and there are a ton of women CEOs now running major companies. . . . I don't grant the assumption that we need to sort of give preferential treatment to the majority of our population, which is, in my view, leading and performing." Joan Walsh, the author of the *Salon* piece that includes this quote, goes on to dryly remark: "McConnell is a little shaky on the facts, unless he considers 5 percent of Fortune 500 CEOs to be 'a ton of women.'"

When women participate in predominantly male cultures, they are accorded fewer resources than men. In February 2012, the American Institute of Physics published a survey of 15,000 male and female physicists in 130 countries. In almost all cultures, the female scientists received less financing, lab space, office support, and grants for equipment and travel, even after the researchers controlled for differences other than sex. "In fact," the researchers concluded, "women physicists could be the majority in some hypothetical future yet still find their careers experience problems that stem from often unconscious bias" (Ivie and Tesfaye).

I suggest that a parallel process of unconscious bias affects the success of female SF writers. There are processes in publishing that authors are usually not privileged to know or participate in. Consider the very visible issue of cover art. Cover art is perhaps the most powerful marketing tool that publishers have at their disposal. They commission cover art that they think will attract the target audience. Authors usually have no power over this process. As Kat Goodwin notes in her response to Julie Crisp's assertion that there is no gender bias in publishing:

> Women authors trying to break in, who would mostly love to be published by Tor or Tor UK, know it's not that simple. They have eyes. And what they see is SFFH publishers not publishing as many women, not promoting them as much as male authors, giving them feminized book covers or scantily clad ladies in leather, describing and marketing urban mysteries as paranormal romance, and so forth. . . . It's that

female authors tend to more often be given covers like Evans did, or the twisty, half-naked women, no matter what sort of story they are writing. They are marketed as women authors first, fantasy or science fiction or sometimes horror authors second, and their books are so frequently marketed as for women only. And that means that their ability to reach the widest possible audience is curtailed.

But cover art is just the beginning. The decisions of editors, marketers, and publicists regarding market placement strategies for any novel (which are, again, closely held ones usually available only in-house rather than for public statistical analysis) play a major part in how well a book sells. Books are marketed to different audiences by means of cover art, blurbs, book placement, budgets for author tours, advertisement, and publicity plans for media appearances. Often, in SF, books have a minuscule promotional budget. Even when there is a decent budget, if an editor or marketing team decides to market to only a small slice of potential readers, book sales suffer. As Nancy Kress put it in her 1993 guest of honor speech at the Michigan-based SF convention ConFuse:

> I'd like to read you a quote from a popular history of science fiction written by a respected editor in the field, in fact he was my editor, a man who's been involved in science fiction in myriad capacities for over thirty years. He says: "It matters little that most of the women writing science fiction command popularity with only a minority of the total science fiction community. The source of the power of these new women writers in the field at present is that within their own core audience of (for the most part) adolescent and young women, they are transcendently heroic." I don't know whom this editor thinks it "matters little" to if women science fiction writers have only a minority readership, but I can assure you that it doesn't matter only little to me. It matters a lot to me whether I have a minority readership or a large readership. It matters a lot to me, to my royalty checks, to my reputation. How many people are interested in reading me and how many people are not interested in reading me not because they think I am a lousy writer which is their choice but simply because they have decided that they don't want to read female science fiction. I think this editor has completely missed the boat and what is depressing is that if I told you he was, he is, one of the most respected and actually one of the most competent editors in the field.

Even as women gain power in our culture as a whole and SF in particular, they are faced with myriad challenges stemming from editors who continue—

consciously or not—to promote female writers to the general public differently than they promote male writers.

———

Then, there are events that we have seen, read about, or heard of. I personally saw this one. In 2000, Connie Willis (one of the four women who has been named a Grand Master of Science Fiction) was toastmaster at the Hugo Awards ceremony. Connie is delightful, witty, funny—a true professional when it comes to public speaking. At the podium, Harlan Ellison flanked her. As they engaged in the amusing repartee that characterizes award ceremonies, Harlan took it in his mind to grab Connie's breast. She did not appear to lose her professional pace, but in that split second, perhaps she wanted to haul off and punch him in the face. But . . . maybe it was an accident?

No. He did it again. You can watch it here: https://www.youtube.com/watch?v=Zxd1jFDXzsU.

This rude, sexist, demeaning, and insulting act of harassment was a tremendous surprise to everyone in the audience. It also seemed a surprise to Harlan that people were upset and that he was expected to apologize to Connie. When she did not answer his repeated calls, he accused her of being unsportsmanlike. What was the message? No one knows what Ellison was thinking, but the message I got from his behavior was "You think you're something, you woman writer on the stage. I'm a Grand Master too. In fact, I am grander than you because I can humiliate you sexually with this public grope, by using your gender against you."

My reaction, as a woman, was anger.

Perhaps it raised the question in the minds of women thinking about writing science fiction: Is this the true face of the genre? If one of the most lauded women in SF history can be publicly harassed in this manner, what might be taking place in less public venues? (In fact, sexual harassment at conventions is a constant problem.) Do I want to be a part of this community? Would it not be better to write something other than science fiction?

———

The *SFWA Bulletin*, SFWA's trade magazine and public face, is on newsstands and available to non-members. Since I joined the SFWA in 1990, the magazine has become slick and professional looking, and it usually features articles about writing and publishing useful to both beginning writers and the seasoned professionals who author the contents. But that doesn't mean its contributors don't occasionally still fall into bad old habits of bias—again, conscious or unconscious—against women.

The cover art of the January 2013 issue of the *SFWA Bulletin*—its 200th issue—painted by professional illustrator Jeff Easely, was an image of a powerful, chain-mail-bikini-clad woman straddling a giant she has just killed with her bloody, upraised sword. WorldCon art shows are chock-full of such images, as are the covers of old pulp magazines and current products such as *Dungeons and Dragons*. However, many members of SFWA were not pleased with this retro cover, which, perhaps, is a good example of why women who read general fiction cringe at the thought of reading SFF. It seems reasonable that cover art might refer specifically to book content, but in this field cover art is often just a marker. Rocket ships are sometimes on the covers of books with nothing of the sort inside.

SFWA members voiced complaints about what they thought of as an inappropriate and sexist cover on the grounds that it did not represent the organization's mission or aspirations. Moreover, it might cause writers to reconsider their present membership and cause those who had been considering joining to change their mind.

I identify with this image about as much as I identify with the grown white male protagonists in most 1960s SF paperbacks. Later, I learned that the image refers to the classic high-fantasy heroine Red Sonja, and I can definitely identify with her backstory—that of a barbarian seeking revenge for terrible crimes. But I can't help but wonder: would it be possible to be Red Sonja without taking steroids? Her body is as unbelievable as Barbie's—and that is a strange comparison to make in the world of SF.[1]

Having fun yet? This is just the beginning.

As if the cover of *SFWA Bulletin* 200 wasn't enough, in that same issue Mike Resnick and Barry Malzberg, two seasoned SF professionals, engage in their monthly chat, which, over the years, has covered writing craft, the business of writing, and such topics as "The State of the Field" (issue 157), "Agents" (issue 144), and "Pseudonyms" (issue 153). These conversations are usually quite informative. This particular chat, titled "Literary Ladies (part 2)," was something quite different.

I've always been interested in the history of women in SF so I began to read what they had to say. I read that Bea Mahaffey, a longtime SF fan and pioneering SF magazine editor from the 1950s, "was competent, unpretentious, and beauty pageant gorgeous . . . as photographs make quite clear. . . . She was a knockout as a young woman" and "according to [another fan], during its first few years of existence CFG [the Cincinnati Fantasy Group] was populated exclusively by men. Then Bea joined. Then the members' wives got a look at Bea in her swimsuit at the 1950 MidwestCon. Then the club's makeup changed to the 50% men and 50% women that has existed ever since." I didn't finish reading the column. I put it down, discouraged. But I also realized that Resnick and Malzberg were seeing, thinking, and writing from a male point of view. Furthermore, like other SF authors past and present, male and female, they wrote what might be called racy sex stories during lean times. Resnick, in particular, has historically anthologized women on the basis of the quality of their work; I have never found him to be sexist in person, and he has the reputation of being an honest and generous anthology editor. But in their male bubble, Resnick and Malzberg mused according to their own past (and presumably SF's past, since that is the column's slant) and their own attitudes, including that of giving equal or more weight to the way a woman looks when mentioning her skills and abilities. They were not taking their task, or the women mentioned, seriously enough for their audience. I was not surprised, just disappointed at how little things have changed, and at someone's bad editorial judgment in using my SFWA dues to put this in front of me. Perhaps I was not surprised because over the years I have become numb to this kind of thing. Which is not good.

Others, women and men alike, did get angry. Very angry. In a later *Bulletin* Resnick and Malzburg defended their conversation, seemingly blind to why it irritated so many. Instead of asking themselves why their dialogue might have offended some readers, they complained of censorship and the abridgement of First Amendment rights, and called those who had objected to their characterization of female editors in the column "liberal fascists" ("Talk Radio Redux" 50).

The kind of epic blowup for which SFWA is famous erupted. In the past, these fights had been semiprivate, contained within the organizational boundaries of long-ago member-only print or bulletin board online forums. This time, the firestorm engulfed the blogosphere. If you are interested in all the gruesome details, you can read about them here: http://www.slhuang .com/blog/2013/07/02/a-timeline-of-the-2013-sfwa-controversies/.

Heads rolled.

Things changed.

We actually should thank Resnick and Malzberg for bringing these galvanizing attitudes to our attention. These particular columns made many SF writers aware of iniquities and pervasive sexist attitudes in the field and encouraged them to participate in a process of change. The influence of activist women has increased tremendously in the past decade as younger women have entered the field, voiced their dismay, and used their strength and sense of community to raise awareness of subtle and overt sexism in all spheres of SF. These women responded swiftly to the SFWA blowup.

In September 2013, *Lightspeed* magazine announced its all-women-edited and -written "Women Destroy Science Fiction" project, which would include a double issue for online subscribers, a stand-alone e-book, and a print edition. On January 15, 2014, the magazine opened its Kickstarter campaign and by February 16 closed with 2,801 backers and $53,136.

In May 2014 SFWA announced the 2014 Nebula Award winners. For the first time in history, every winner was a woman. Jubilation ensued among female fans: http://www.themarysue.com/the-2014-nebula-awards/.

In June 2014 *Lightspeed* published *Women Destroy Science Fiction!* (issue 49), which highlights the history of women in SF and features marvelous essays, new and reprint SF, and illustrations by female artists. It has garnered a lot of attention. As Tempest Bradford notes in a review of this special issue for NPR, the authors and artists featured in it "are less focused on technological changes and more on the relations between people, or between people and society, or changing cultural and gender roles. That's true across the issue." This echoes the ways women have treated technoculture in SF since the inception of the genre in the 1920s.

There is a concerted call for writers to become more aware of how they portray women, as in Kameron Hurley's Hugo Award–winning essay "We Have Always Fought: Challenging the Women, Cattle, and Slaves Narrative." Hurley writes that "populating a world with men, with male heroes, male people, and their 'women, cattle, and slaves' is a political act. You are making a conscious choice to erase half the world. As storytellers, there are more interesting choices we can make."

Of course, young authors are not alone in their call for more interesting choices in SFF. Short fiction editors have considerable power in the field, and two experienced women editors are particularly influential today.

Ellen Datlow first became visible as the fiction editor of *Omni* from 1981 to 1998. *Omni* was conceived as a slick newsstand magazine "that explored all realms of science and the paranormal, that delved into all corners of the unknown and projected some of those discoveries into fiction" (Ashley, *Gateways* 367–68). While at *Omni*, Datlow showcased the early short fiction of William Gibson ("Burning Chrome," "The New Rose Hotel," and "Johnny Mnemonic") and published original SF by Connie Willis, Karen Joy Fowler, Ursula K. Le Guin, Elizabeth Hand, Suzy McKee Charnas, and many other women.

Datlow, presently an anthologist and an acquiring editor at Tor.com, has won a prodigious number of editing awards. She has structured her career so that she is able to invite writers to participate in her anthologies and in her online venues; thus, although she always looks for the best stories, she does not depend on submissions from the relatively small number of women who write SF but is able to invite and include a much larger percentage of women in her collections than do magazine editors. Daring in her wide-ranging publishing choices and deeply respected for her editorial acumen by writers and readers alike, Datlow showcases the writing of women in a vast range of fiction that includes SF, horror, fantasy, and mainstream stories. As such, she is very much the editorial heir to early SFF editors such as Mary Gnaedinger, Dorothy McIlwraith, and Lilith Lorraine, all of whom demanded the highest quality of work from writers and all of whom were eager to showcase the offerings of both men and women.

In a similar vein, Sheila Williams, the managing editor of *Asimov's* from 1982 to 2004, when she became executive editor, has since won two Hugo Awards for best professional editor and has, over the course of her career, enlarged upon the vision of editorial predecessors. Williams's informative, entertaining, and personally slanted editorial columns strengthen the links between science, technology, society, and SF readers, much as did earlier editorial columns of important women SF magazine editors. They encourage readers to think about space exploration, the history of science fiction, the excitement of new scientific discoveries, and how SF is related to and manifests in our daily lives with terrific range, verve, and insight. The Annual Reader's Award, begun under the editorship of Gardner Dozois, encourages readers' feedback, and Williams began the practice of including readers' comments in her editorial column. This is very much in the tradition of community-building characteristic of all early SF editors, but especially those women who wanted to capitalize on readers' passions and interests to improve the genre as a whole.

Like McIlwraith and Lorraine in particular, Williams also actively encourages young SF writers. In 1992, Williams and Rick Wilber, a professor of mass media at the University of South Florida, established the Dell Magazines Award for Undergraduate Excellence in Science Fiction and Fantasy Writing (http://www.dellaward.com/), which confers on the recipient a five-hundred-dollar prize and a paid trip to Orlando, Florida, to receive the first prize at the International Conference for the Fantastic in the Arts.

Of her editing style, Williams says:

> We still publish things that get us in trouble all the time. We don't know what's going to get us in trouble, or who with. That's the whole nature of magazine publishing. It's very exciting to be a magazine editor, because you know someone's going to get mad at you sometime. You don't know

when or who or whether it will be someone on the left or the right —
but someone's going to be mad. I find that kind of exhilarating, and a
little bit nerve-wracking. I don't set out to upset anyone, but we want to
break ground. The magazine is my magazine. It's stories I like. We're out
to explore new directions. I don't think that any editor at *Asimov's* was
afraid of publishing women or anyone from any particular background
that wasn't the traditional angle. But there's been a fantastic wonderful
explosion of talent from diverse backgrounds recently. Fiction in general
can only benefit from that." ("Sheila Williams")

"WE HAVE ALWAYS FOUGHT"

Since Mary Shelly published *Frankenstein* in 1818, there has probably never
been a time when women have not written about, edited, and envisioned
the future through art. *Sisters of Tomorrow* shows that women have indeed
always fought — and that, in the opening decades of the modern SF community, at least some women fought by dreaming of worlds where women were
not cattle or slaves but were, instead, creative and compassionate people who
used every scientific and social device available to build better futures for all.

In this endeavor, they were part of the community of women contributing to the work of becoming fully active members of society using their own
particular talents, whether those talents were political, educational, artistic, scientific, or completely idiosyncratic syntheses of ambitions and skills,
as they forged a new kind of literature. Women did not just participate in
the accelerated, exhilarating, mad rush of change that has marked the rise of
technosociety — women were the change. Women stormed barricades, rioted,
and starved themselves for the right to vote, and then ran for office. At the
same time, and using that same energy, women invented telescopes through
which they saw previously unknown stars and undertook the voyage to reach
them. Women imagined human-friendly societies that gave us ways to think
about how to build better futures. Women, knowing what it was to live as
aliens, created aliens with depth and uncanny powers. In early SF, women
went to space, used ray guns with alacrity, and explored wild planets. They
also applied their energies to their own planet, imagining alternative Earths
where women fought off evil scientists, perfected new modes of political
governance, and transformed both the home and the men with whom they
shared it in startling ways. Women invented, shaped, and inhabited this unruly, hard-to-define art form that now infuses and sometimes drives society
and invention. Women are quite fully this nova, this power, these shining,
strange new worlds that we call science fiction.

Women thrilled, astonished, and startled as they wrote, edited, and illustrated wondrous, marvelous, amazing, and astounding tales. They had fun. They made money. They were independent. They fought for that independence and fought to maintain it.

And women, it is clear, must and will continue to fight to define themselves, the world they live in, and the worlds that they invent.

But must we always fight? Science fiction writers, whose vocation and profession is to imagine the future, are perfectly situated to think of ways to better communicate, and to imagine how we will use our own potential and that of our planet and of infinite space not only to understand and mediate our problems, but also to become a wiser species, able to celebrate all visions of our shared future through the complex, deeply human art of nuanced, finely wrought science fictional storytelling. If publishers and the public do yet not realize the nobility and potential of this calling, it is only because we, as writers from backgrounds as diverse and myriad as the worlds we invent, whose tales tap and unfurl the strength of dreams, have not yet fully grasped our power. Welcoming all voices, understanding that we are all on the same side, is the first step toward using that strength to point our universe toward unlimited future.

NOTES

INTRODUCTION

1. Figures cited in this book regarding the number of women working in SF between 1926 and 1945 are derived from our count of those listed in Stephen T. Miller and William G. Contento, *The Locus Science Fiction, Fantasy, and Weird Magazine Index (1890–2001)*. We began by asking our research assistant, Amelia Shackleford, to compile lists of all known women and men who published or otherwise worked in SF during the period under question, including those who contributed to both professional and amateur SF publications as well as multi-genre magazines with substantial SF offerings. Lisa Yaszek then confirmed these numbers in an independent review of the *Index*, cross-referencing each author to make sure we were not double-counting known pen names or counting house pseudonyms. Our estimates are conservative in that we did not count authors with gender-neutral names whose sex we could not verify.

2. As Justine Larbalestier and Helen Merrick have shown elsewhere, a significant number of women fans helped shape SF as a modern popular genre through their letters to professional magazines. While we consider women's work as contributors to amateur SF publications throughout this anthology, we recommend that readers interested in women's work as fan correspondents see Larbalestier's *The Battle of the Sexes in Science Fiction* and Merrick's *The Secret Feminist Cabal*.

3. Indeed, as Jane Donawerth points out, by 1931 Gernsback also considered women regular contributors to SF, noting, in his introduction to Lilith Lorraine's 1930 short story, "Into the 28th Century," that "it speaks well of the times in which we are living when women authors such as Lilith Lorraine have the vision to take science fiction seriously" (qtd. in Donawerth, "Lilith Lorraine" 252).

4. For further discussion of Gernsback's positive reception of women contributors, see the introduction to Jean Stine, Janrae Frank, and Forrest J Ackerman's *New Eves*.

5. For an overview of David Lasser's role in supporting politically progressive SF and recommendations for further reading on this subject, see Eric Leif Davin's "Gernsback, His Editors, and Women Writers" and *Pioneers of Wonder*.

6. For a discussion of gender in the marketing of early magazines, see the introduction to Robert Weinberg's *Biographical Dictionary of Science Fiction and Fantasy Artists*. For a discussion of the early days of the *Black Cat*, see the first chapter of Mike Ashley's *The Time Machines*.

7. Of course, other scholars have noted that SF production occurs outside fiction writing as well. Both Robin Roberts's *A New Species* and Brian Attebery's *Decoding Gender in Science Fiction* briefly address representations of sex and gender in SF art and advertising, while Robin Anne Reid's *Women in Science Fiction and Fantasy* contains entries on women poets and editors. As such, we see *Sisters of Tomorrow* as extending the lines of inquiry begun by these fellow critics. Furthermore, it is important to note that Justine Larbalestier's *The Battle of the Sexes in Science Fiction* and Helen Merrick's *Secret Feminist*

Cabal both explore the one area of women's engagement with magazine SF that we do not address in this anthology: fan letters. Indeed, we decided not to include such writing precisely because Larbalestier and Merrick have done such thorough work on this subject that it seemed best to focus on other types of SF production that have not been addressed elsewhere in a sustained manner and to simply refer readers to those outstanding publications.

1. AUTHORS

1. For further discussion of Gernsback's vision for SF and its influence on other genre editors of the early twentieth century, see Gary Westfahl's *The Mechanics of Wonder*, the introduction to Michael Ashley's *The History of the Science Fiction Magazine*, Vol. 1: *1926–1935*, and Paul A. Carter's "Extravagant Fiction Today—Cold Fact Tomorrow."

2. Wright began using this exact language for framing and advertising the magazine on the first page of the February 1928 issue, and McIlwraith continued to use it in advertising copy into the 1940s. For further discussion of the editorial visions and story types associated with *Weird Tales*, see Michael Ashley's *The History of the Science Fiction Magazine*, Vol. 1: *1926–1935*. For an overview of the surprisingly close relations between science fiction and weird fiction in the first part of the twentieth century, see chapter 1 of David Hartwell's *Age of Wonders* and Roger Luckhurst's *Science Fiction*.

3. For further discussion of the thought-variant tale, especially as it anticipates the science fictional themes and techniques advocated by midcentury editor John W. Campbell, see Westfahl's *The Mechanics of Wonder*.

4. For in-depth discussion of the home in the domestic Gothic, see Donna Heiland's *Gothic and Gender*; Kate Ferguson Ellis's *The Contested Castle*; and Elizabeth A. Fay's *A Feminist Introduction to Romanticism*. Additionally, Nancy Armstrong's *Desire and Domestic Fiction* provides an excellent overview of the close relations between the female Gothic and domestic fiction. For an assessment of domestic reform in women's utopian SF, see chapter 1 of Jane Donawerth's *Frankenstein's Daughters* and for an overview of domestic science fiction as a distinct mode of SF unto itself, see Lisa Yaszek's "A Parabola of Her Own: Domestic Science Fiction."

5. For a detailed discussion of how women SF writers use male narrators, see chapter 1 of Robin Roberts's *A New Species* and chapter 3 of Jane Donawerth's *Frankenstein's Daughters*.

6. In 1886 Smith constructed "the nation's first building dedicated to women's scientific studies and experimentation," and in 1905 the college received funds from Andrew Carnegie to create a second such building (Hamlin 63–64). Harris therefore studied science in what were likely the best scientific facilities available for women in the country at the time.

7. Harris won 100 dollars for third prize, which worked out to "1.21 cents a word," quite a large payment from any early genre magazine editor (Ashley and Lowndes 130).

8. For further discussion of Stone's fiction as it engages the scientific and social debates of its time, see Batya Weinbaum's "Twentieth-Century American Women's Progress and the Lack Thereof in Leslie F. Stone's 'Out of the Void.'"

9. For further discussion of Hansen's gender masquerade as stemming from her desire

to follow new literary conventions, see Jane Donawerth's *Frankenstein's Daughters*. For further discussion of Hansen as an author who wished to keep her various professional identities distinct from one another, see Eric Leif Davin's *Partners in Wonder*.

10. It is also worth noting that Hansen was not entirely alone in her experiments with new representations of the alien other. Both Stanley G. Weinbaum's 1934 short story "A Martian Odyssey" and Leslie F. Stone's "Out of the Void" (reprinted in this anthology) depict aliens as potentially friendly and potentially wiser, in at least some respects, than their human counterparts.

11. For further reading on comic SF, see Andrew Butler's entry on comedy in *The Greenwood Encyclopedia of Science Fiction and Fantasy*.

12. For details regarding the ban on Futurians at the 1939 WorldCon, see Andrew Liptak's "The Futurians and the 1939 World Science Fiction Convention."

13. See Justine Larbalestier's *Battle of the Sexes in Science Fiction* for a full discussion of these debates among authors, editors, and fans.

2. POETS

1. For further discussion of nineteenth-century fantastic poetry, see Patrick D. Murphy's essay "The Fantastic Experience in Poetry: Or, the Monsters Are There, Where Are the Critics?", as well as the introduction to his edited collection, *The Poetic Fantastic*.

2. The one professional magazine that did not feature speculative verse was *Astounding* under John W. Campbell's editorship. Since he did buy poems for the fantasy magazine *Unknown*, it seems this decision was driven by Campbell's desire to create a new kind of "no-nonsense" SF publication (Green xv). Indeed, after World War II many other genre magazine editors decided to emulate the feel of *Astounding* and eliminated poetry from their pages as well (Green xv).

3. The poet who appeared most frequently in the *Amazing* franchise in its opening decades was amateur astronomer Leland S. Copeland, who created *Sky & Telescope* magazine's "Deep-Sky Wonders" column. Green ties for second place with SF author Bob Olsen.

4. The kind of light but thoughtful SF verse that Green wrote for the *Amazing* franchise in the opening decades of the twentieth century is very much with us today, appearing especially frequently in *Asimov's Science Fiction* magazine. For a short but incisive explanation of why seemingly old-fashioned light verse continues to appeal to SF readers, see Isaac Asimov's "Editorial: Poetry."

5. For further discussion of modern feminist SF poetry, see Diedre Bryne's "What Is Not Owned," as well as Patrick D. Murphy's foreword to *The Poetic Fantastic* (and his essay in that volume, "The Left Hand of Fabulation: The Poetry of Ursula K. Le Guin").

6. The Milford Writers Workshop originally took place in Milford, Pennsylvania, where Kidd and Blish were living at the time. After the couple divorced, Blish moved to England and took the workshop with him.

7. For further information about Drake's life and work, including facsimiles of her most famous poems, see Terence E. Hanley's biography on the *Teller of Weird Tales* blog.

8. When Eyde began to receive awards for her pioneering work in lesbian journalism, she was quick to note how the production of SF fanzines shaped the creation of her own publication and to credit her friend Forrest J Ackerman for his contributions. For further

discussion, see the ZineWiki entry "Eydthe Eyde" and Andy Mangels's "Why Is the Passing of Forrest J Ackerman of GLBT Importance?"

9. At that time, Eyde also returned to her musical roots, performing in local gay clubs and, in 1960, releasing an original single called "Cruisin' Down the Boulevard" (the flip side featured a lesbian version of "Frankie and Johnnie").

3. JOURNALISTS

1. While Wells was one of the first writers to argue that scientific information should be presented in an entertaining way, he was not alone in this belief. Many turn-of-the-century reporters had literary aspirations and so experimented with news writing that combined fact and story. For further discussion, see Karen Roggenkamp's *Narrating the News* and Derek John Dreidger's "Writing and Circulating Modern America."

2. Women who went to science demonstrations in the Enlightenment often wrote about their experiences for one another. By the end of the nineteenth century, that audience had expanded to include children and men, and the popularity of female science writers rivaled that of male scientists themselves. For further discussion, see Barbara T. Gates and Anne B. Shteir's introduction to *Natural Eloquence*.

3. For an excellent discussion of women reporters at the turn of the century, see Jean Marie Lutes's *Front Page Girls*.

4. The three most prolific male science writers for *Amazing* and *Fantastic Adventures* were A. Morris (with eighty-four articles published between 1942 and 1951); Pete Bogg (with seventy-three articles published between 1944 and 1947); and Carter T. Wainwright (with forty-eight articles published between 1942 and 1948). All numbers included here are based on our count of entries in the *Locus Science Fiction, Fantasy, and Weird Fiction Magazine Index*.

5. Evidence suggesting that the Laura Moore Wright who published the 1946 science essay "Sunlight" in *Amazing Stories* was indeed the Canadian Laura Moore Wright who wrote *Victory Verses* (1942), *The Song of Roland* (1960), and *Campaigns of Napoleon* (1963) is tentative at best. The University of Calgary's Canadian Literary and Art Archives includes a 1944 letter from one Laura Moore Wright to the *Western Producer* editor Violet McNaughton regarding the editor's possible interest in two of her poems ("Wright, Laura Moore"). Given the temporal proximity of this inquiry to the publication of "Sunlight," it is entirely possible that the two Laura Moore Wrights were one and the same. However, Canadian census records have two Laura M. Wrights on their midcentury registered voter lists, and U.S. Census data list dozens of Laura Moores and Laura M. Wrights whose birth dates suggest that any one of them could be the Laura Moore Wright under consideration here.

6. In the final few years of her column, Hansen expanded her argument to suggest that Indigenous Americans were also the last remnants of a great civilization based on the lost city of Atlantis. Significantly, her argument turned from debate over scientific theory to exploration of scientific mystery around the same time that editor Ray Palmer began publishing the wildly successful Shaver Mystery, a series of stories based on letters from Pennsylvania factory worker Richard Shaver, who claimed to have discovered an ancient, evil, and technologically advanced civilization in caverns under the Earth.

4. EDITORS

1. As Dillane explains, even those rare midcentury Victorian women who worked at literary periodicals—such as Marian Evans, better known to literary history as George Eliot—adopted the persona of the facilitator. For further discussion, see Dillane's "'The Character of Editress.'"

2. Women editors continued to adopt the role of the facilitator even as women's magazines diversified their content and attitudes toward sex and gender roles at the turn of the century. For further discussion, see Beth Palmer's "Ella Hepworth Dixon and Editorship."

3. See chapters 11 and 14 of Mike Ashley and Robert A. W. Lowndes's *The Gernsback Days* for a detailed discussion of the early days at *Amazing Stories* and excerpts from the letters Bourne wrote to authors during her time at the magazine.

4. For a discussion of Tarrant, see Frederik Pohl's "*Astounding*: The Campbell Years, Riding High."

5. For further discussion of Gernsback's, Sloane's, and Bates's relationship to readers, see Gary Westfahl's *The Mechanics of Wonder*. For further discussion of Wright's arguments about weird fiction, see Robert Weinberg's *The "Weird Tales" Story* and Michael Ashley's *The History of the Science Fiction Magazine*, Vol. 1: 1926–1935.

6. For further discussion of Gnaedinger's commitment to printing SF stories by women, see chapters 6 and 11 of Eric Leif Davin's *Partners in Wonder*.

7. Indeed, as a number of authors from this period recall, it was precisely McIlwraith's willingness to strike out in new directions that enabled *Weird Tales* to continue publishing until the mid-1950s, despite low pay for authors and an increasingly erratic publishing schedule. For further discussion, see Graeme Flanagan's *Robert Bloch* and Darrell Schweitzer's "What about Dorothy McIlwraith?"

8. For further discussion of Gernsback's, Sloane's, and Bates's pronouncements about SF, see Gary Westfahl's *The Mechanics of Wonder*. For further discussion of Wright's arguments about weird fiction, see Robert Weinberg's *The "Weird Tales" Story* and Michael Ashley's *The History of the Science Fiction Magazine*, Vol. 1: 1926–1935.

9. Elsewhere, Lorraine did indeed make bold pronouncements about the meaning and value of SF. See in particular her 1954 essay "Not an Escape but a Challenge," published in *Miscellaneous Man*.

10. See chapter 4 of Mike Ashley, *The Time Machines*.

11. For discussion of Gnaedinger's commitment to printing SF stories by women, see chapters 6 and 11 of Eric Leif Davin's *Partners in Wonder*.

12. See Robert Weinberg's history of *Weird Tales* in the first chapter of *The "Weird Tales" Story*.

13. See Robert Weinberg's discussion of the cover art of *Weird Tales* in chapter 6 of *The "Weird Tales" Story* (1977).

5. ARTISTS

1. See chapter 4 of Justine Larbalestier's *The Battle of the Sexes in Science Fiction* for a discussion of gender and art in the letters pages of SF magazines.

2. For an excellent discussion of how SF art from this period influenced later feminist SF authors, see chapter 2 of Robin Roberts's *A New Species*. See also Rowena Morrill's

homage to Brundage in the foreword to Stephen D. Korshak and J. David Spurlock's *The Alluring Art of Margaret Brundage, Queen of Pulp Pin-Up Art.*

3. For a detailed discussion of women in the fashion industry during this period, see Valerie Steele's *Women of Fashion* and Isabelle Anscombe's *A Woman's Touch.*

4. For a discussion of gender in the marketing of early magazines, see the introduction to Robert Weinberg's *Biographical Dictionary of Science Fiction and Fantasy Artists.* For a discussion of the early days of the *Black Cat*, see the first chapter of Mike Ashley's *The Time Machines.*

5. See Cally Blackman's *100 Years of Fashion Illustration* for a discussion of art in the early fashion magazines for women.

6. For a more detailed discussion of "yellow peril" and "black peril" stories, see H. Bruce Franklin's *War Stars* and Patrick B. Sharp's *Savage Perils.*

7. At least one male illustrator from the early SF community, Frank R. Paul, contested the assumption that women were better than men at figural representation. As he explained in a 1934 interview, he was often accused of mangling the human figure, but "the story usually mentions that the scientist is a humpback, or has a strongly developed forehead, so I draw them that way. . . . What do readers want, a gigolo?" (qtd. in Schwartz 72). For Paul, then, the issue was not that he could not draw scientists (or, presumably, other people including women), but that the stories he illustrated dictated that he take liberties with the conventional human form.

8. Quick's "Strange Orchids" is reprinted in chapter 1, "Authors," of this anthology.

9. The female Gothic also shows the transformation of the female protagonist from victim to heroine, a trajectory that is followed in Quick's story when the main character, Louise Howard, goes undercover for the authorities to unmask the story's predatory villain.

10. For an excellent discussion of how SF art from this period influenced later feminist SF authors, see chapter 2 of Robin Roberts's *A New Species.*

11. See the entry on Morrill in Jane Frank's *Science Fiction and Fantasy Artists of the Twentieth Century.*

12. See Morrill's homage to Brundage in the foreword to Stephen D. Korshak and J. David Spurlock's *The Alluring Art of Margaret Brundage.* Also see editor Paula Guran's article, "Our Queen, Our Mother, Our Margaret," from the Summer 2010 issue of *Weird Tales.*

13. See the entry on Bell in Jane Frank's *Science Fiction and Fantasy Artists of the Twentieth Century.*

14. See Cally Blackman's *100 Years of Fashion Illustration* for a discussion of art in the early fashion magazines for women.

CONCLUSION: CHALLENGING THE NARRATIVE

1. While it might seem strange to compare Red Sonja and Barbie, it is also appropriate, in that the iconic toy eventually did make her way into the SFWA debacle. *SFWA Bulletin* 201 features "Taxes and the Short Story Writer" by Tom Knowles, "Those Who Can, Teach" by Gregory A. Wilson, and an article titled "Reinventing the Wheelhouse" by C. J. Henderson, who has written seventy novels, hundreds of short stories, and thousands of

nonfiction pieces in his forty-year career. He discusses the ways in which he reinvented himself during those decades to take advantage of changes in publishing, technology, and the market—certainly a necessary mindset for a writer. Toward the end of his piece, Henderson takes what seems, in hindsight, a tack that he has not thoroughly thought out. Using the history of the Barbie doll as an analogy, he writes that though she was first marketed as a fashion queen, she changed with the times and became a teacher, nurse, superhero, doctor, and astronaut. He then claims that Barbie's success (characterizing her as a person rather than a toy) lies in the fact that she

> never abandoned her core values. Yes, Barbie has always been long-legged and tiny-waisted, perfectly proportioned in every way with dazzling blue eyes, terrific hair and, oh right, quite the pair of sweater-fillers as well. But that is not who she is inside.
>
> The reason for Barbie's unbelievable staying power, when every contemporary and wanna-be has fallen by the wayside[,] is, she's a nice girl. Let the Bratz girls dress like tramps and whores. Barbie never had any of that. Sure, there was a quick buck to be made going that route, but it wasn't for her. Barbie got her college degree, but she never acted as if it was something owed to her, or that Ken ever tried to deny her.
>
> She has always been a role model for young girls, and has remained popular with millions of them throughout their entire lives, because she maintained her quiet dignity the way a woman should. (42)

What conclusions might we draw from this analogy? That dolls are people and have core values? That good-looking women always ponder the option of becoming prostitutes? That when women demand education they lose their all-important "quiet dignity"? That the image of women in the 1950s is still strongly manifest in the lives of millions of women today? That giving Barbie to little girls who will never grow up to look like this, but who may consequently starve themselves or undergo surgery to more closely resemble the doll, is a good thing?

BIBLIOGRAPHY

Aldiss, Brian. *Science Fiction Art: The Fantasies of SF*. New York: Bounty, 1975.

Anscombe, Isabelle. *A Woman's Touch: Women in Design from 1860 to the Present Day*. New York: Penguin, 1985.

Armstrong, Nancy. *Desire and Domestic Fiction: A Political History of the Novel*. New York: Oxford University Press, 1990.

Ashley, Michael. *The History of the Science Fiction Magazine*, Vol. 1: *1926–1935* [1974]. Chicago: Henry Regnery, 1976.

Ashley, Mike. *Gateways to Forever: The Story of the Science-Fiction Magazines from 1970 to1980*. Liverpool: Liverpool University Press, 2007.

———. *The Time Machines: The Story of the Pulp Science Fiction Magazines from the Beginning to 1950*. Liverpool: Liverpool University Press, 2001.

Ashley, Mike, and Robert A. W. Lowndes. *The Gernsback Days: A Study of the Evolution of Modern Science Fiction from 1911 to 1936*. Holicong, PA: Wildside Press, 2004.

Asimov, Isaac, ed. *Before the Golden Age: A Science Fiction Anthology of the 1930s*. Garden City, NY: Doubleday, 1974.

———. "Editorial: Poetry" (2005). *Asimov's Science Fiction*. http://www.asimovs.com/_issue_0506/editorial.shtml. Accessed 20 Mar. 2014.

Attebery, Brian. "Cultural Negotiations of Science Fiction Literature and Film." *Journal of the Fantastic in the Arts* 11.4 (2001): 346–58.

———. *Decoding Gender in Science Fiction*. New York: Routledge, 2002.

Barres, Ben A. "Does Gender Matter?" *Nature* 442.13 (July 2006): 133–36.

Baym, Nina. *Woman's Fiction: A Guide to Novels by and about Women in America, 1820–1870*. Ithaca, NY: Cornell University Press, 1978.

Beams, David. "An Octogenarian Reader." Letter. *Weird Tales* 29.5 (May 1937): 638.

Bennett, Paula Bernat. "Subtle Subversion: Mary Louise Booth and *Harper's Bazaar* (1867–1889)." In *Blue Pencils and Hidden Hands: Women Editing Periodicals, 1830–1910*. Ed. Sharon M. Harris. Boston: Northeastern University Press, 2004. 225–43.

Blackman, Cally. *100 Years of Fashion Illustration*. London: Laurence King, 2007.

Bleiler, Everett Franklin, and Richard J. Bleiler. *Science-Fiction—The Gernsback Years: A Complete Coverage of the Genre Magazines "Amazing," "Astounding," "Wonder," and Others from 1926 through 1936*. Kent, OH: Kent State University Press, 1998.

Bloom, Harold. *Science Fiction Writers of the Golden Age*. New York: Chelsea House, 1994.

Bourgeois, Olivette. Cover illustration. *Black Cat* (Jan. 1917).

Bradford, K. Tempest. "Women Are Destroying Science Fiction! (That's OK; They Created It)." National Public Radio. 28 June 2014. http://www.npr.org/2014/06/28/322544552/women-are-destroying-science-fiction-thats-ok-they-created-it. Accessed 2 Nov. 2014.

Brown, Henrietta. "Marine Engineering in the Insect World." *Fantastic Adventures* 7.3 (July 1945): 141.

Brundage, Margaret. Cover illustration. *Weird Tales* 24.4 (Oct. 1934).

————. Cover illustration. *Weird Tales* 25.4 (Apr. 1935).

————. Cover illustration. *Weird Tales* 29.3 (Mar. 1937).

————. Illustration for "Change for the Bitter." *Fantastic Adventures* 7.2 (Apr. 1945): 101.

Burns, Sarah. *Painting the Dark Side: Art and the Gothic Imagination in Nineteenth-Century America*. Berkeley: University of California Press, 2004.

Butler, Andrew. "Comedy." *The Greenwood Encyclopedia of Science Fiction and Fantasy: Themes, Works, and Wonders*. Ed. Gary Westfahl. Westport, CT: Greenwood, 2005. 144–46.

Byrne, Diedre. "What Is Not Owned: Feminist Strategies in Ursula K. Le Guin's Poetry." *Foundation* 114 (Spring 2012–13): 10–30.

Carter, Paul A. "Extravagant Fiction Today—Cold Fact Tomorrow: A Rationale for the First American Science Fiction Magazines." *Journal of Popular Culture* 5.4 (Spring 1972): 842–57.

Chalmers, Graeme F. "The Early History of the Philadelphia School of Design for Women." *Journal of Design History* 9.4 (1996): 237–52. http://www.jstor.org/. Accessed 19 Sept. 2014.

Clute, John. "Quick, Dorothy." *The Encyclopedia of Science Fiction*. Eds. John Clute, David Langford, Peter Nicholls, and Graham Sleight. *Gollancz*, 23 Oct. 2014. http://www.sf-encyclopedia.com/entry/quick_dorothy. Accessed 28 Oct. 2014.

Combs, Virginia. Letter. *Future Combined with Science Fiction* 2.3 (Feb. 1942): 108.

"Comic Science Fiction." *Wikipedia, The Free Encyclopedia*. 20 Oct. 2014. http://en.wikipedia.org/wiki/Comic_science_fiction. Accessed 27 Oct. 2014.

Connolly, Susan E. "The Issue of Gender in Genre Fiction: A Detailed Analysis." *Clarkesworld Magazine* 93 (June 2014). http://clarkesworldmagazine.com/connolly_06_14/. Accessed 30 Oct. 2014.

Crisp, Julie. "Sexism in Genre Publishing: A Publisher's Perspective." *Tor Books Blog*. 10 July 2013. http://torbooks.co.uk/2013/07/10/sexism-in-genre-publishing-a-publishers-perspective/. Accessed 30 Oct. 2014.

Darling, Kristina. "'Such Happiness Will Smile No More for Me': Domesticity, Women's Writing, and Sarah J. Hale's Editorial Career." *MP: An Online Feminist Journal* 2.4 (2009): 14–29.

Davin, Eric Leif. "Gernsback, His Editors, and Women Writers." *Science Fiction Studies* 17 (1990): 418–20.

————. *Partners in Wonder: Women and the Birth of Science Fiction, 1926–1965*. New York: Lexington Books, 2006.

————. *Pioneers of Wonder: Conversations with the Founders of Science Fiction*. Amherst, NY: Prometheus, 1999.

Del Rey, Lester. "Forty Years of C. L. Moore." In *The Best of C. L. Moore*. Ed. Lester Del Rey. New York: Ballantine Books, 1975. ix–xv.

Dillane, Fionnuala. "'The Character of Editress': Marian Evans at the *Westminster Review*, 1851–54." *Tulsa Studies in Women's Literature* 30.2 (Fall 2011): 269–90.

Donawerth, Jane. *Frankenstein's Daughters: Women Writing Science Fiction*. Syracuse, NY: Syracuse University Press, 1997.

————. "Lilith Lorraine: Feminist Socialist Writer in the Pulps." *Science Fiction Studies* 17.2 (1990): 252–58. www.jstor.org. Accessed 16 April 2014.

———. "Science Fiction by Women in the Early Pulps." In *Utopian and Science Fiction by Women: Worlds of Difference*. Eds. Jane L. Donawerth and Carol Kolmerten. Liverpool: Liverpool University Press, 1994. 137–52.

Donnell, Dolly. "Abject Apologies." *Thrilling Wonder Stories* 26.2 (Fall 1944): 99.

———. Illustration for "Priestess of Pakmari." *Thrilling Wonder Stories* 26.1 (Summer 1944): 64–65.

Doore, Kathy. "Did He Walk the Americas?" *Labyrinthina*. http://www.labyrinthina.com /ltaylorhansen.htm. Accessed 1 July 2014.

Drake, Leah Bodine. "Sea-Shell." *Weird Tales* 37.1 (Sept. 1943): 87.

———. "They Run Again." *Weird Tales* 34.1 (June–July 1939): 36.

———. "The Wood-Wife." *Weird Tales* 36.4 (Mar. 1942): 59.

Dreidger, Derek John. "Writing and Circulating Modern America: Journalism and the American Novelist, 1872–1938." Diss., University of Nebraska–Lincoln, 2007. http:// digitalcommons.unl.edu/englishdiss/5. Accessed 19 May 2014.

"Edythe Eyde." *ZineWiki: The Independent Media Wikipedia*. 8 Apr. 2014. http://www .zinewiki.com/Eydthe_Eyde. Accessed 26 Apr. 2014.

Elgin, Suzette Haden. *The Science Fiction Poetry Handbook*. Cedar Rapids, IA: Sam's Dot Publishing, 2005.

Elliott, Jeffrey M. "C. L. Moore: Poet of Far-Distant Futures." *Pulp Voices; or, Science Fiction Voices*, #6. San Bernardino, CA: Borgo, 1983. 45–51.

Ellis, Kate Ferguson. *The Contested Castle: Gothic Novels and the Subversion of Domestic Ideology*. Champaign: University of Illinois Press, 1989.

Eskilson, Stephen J. *Graphic Design: A New History*. New Haven, CT: Yale University Press, 2007.

Everts, R. Alain. "Margaret Brundage." In *The Alluring Art of Margaret Brundage: Queen of Pulp Pinup Art*. Eds. Stephen D. Korshak and J. David Spurlock. Lakewood, NJ: Vanguard Productions, 2013. 25–32.

Fay, Elizabeth A. *A Feminist Introduction to Romanticism*. Hoboken, NJ: Wiley-Blackwell, 1991.

Flanagan, Graeme. *Robert Bloch: A Bio-Bibliography*. Canberra City: Graeme Flanagan, 1979.

Foust, James C. "E. W. Scripps and the Science Service." *Journalism History* 21.2 (Summer 1995): 58–64.

Frank, Jane. *Science Fiction and Fantasy Artists of the Twentieth Century: A Biographical Dictionary*. Jefferson, NC: McFarland, 2009.

Franklin, H. Bruce. *War Stars: The Superweapon and the American Imagination*. New York: Oxford University Press, 1988.

Franks, Suzanne. *Women and Journalism*. London: I. B. Tauris, 2013.

Friend, Oscar J. "The Reader Speaks." *Thrilling Wonder Stories* 26.1 (Summer 1944): 106.

Garvey, Ellen Gruber. "Forward." In *Blue Pencils and Hidden Hands: Women Editing Periodicals, 1830–1910*. Ed. Sharon M. Harris. Boston: Northeastern University Press, 2004. xi–xxiv.

Gates, Barbara T., and Ann B. Shteir. "Introduction: Charting the Tradition." *Natural Eloquence: Women Reinscribe Nature*. Eds. Barbara T. Gates and Ann B. Shteir. Madison: University of Wisconsin Press, 1997. 3–24.

Gernsback, Hugo. "A New Sort of Magazine." *Amazing Stories* 1.1 (Apr. 1926): 3. https://archive.org/details/AmazingStoriesVolume01Number01. Accessed October 6, 2014.

———. "Headnote to 'Into the 28th Century.'" *Science Wonder Quarterly* 1.2 (Winter 1930): 251.

———. Headnote to "The Evolutionary Monstrosity." *Amazing Stories Quarterly* 2.1 (Winter 1929): 70.

———. Headnote to "The Fate of the *Poseidonia*." *Amazing Stories* 2.3 (June 1927): 245.

Gnaedinger, Mary. "Editorial Note." *Famous Fantastic Mysteries* 1.1 (Sept.–Oct. 1939): 2.

———. "The Editor's Page." *Famous Fantastic Mysteries* 1.6 (Mar. 1940): 41.

———. "The Editor's Page." *Famous Fantastic Mysteries* 5.3 (Mar. 1943): 113.

Goodwin, Kat. "Reality and the Welcome Sign—Gender and SFFH." *Open Window.* 13 July 2013. http://katgoodwin.wordpress.com/tag/julie-crisp/. Accessed 30 Oct. 2014.

Green, Julia Boynton. "Evolution." *Amazing Stories* 6.5 (Aug. 1931): 401.

———. "Radio Revelations." *Amazing Stories Quarterly* 5.3 (Fall–Winter 1932): 38.

———. "The Night Express." *Amazing Stories* 6.4 (July 1931): 371.

Green, Scott. *Contemporary Science Fiction, Fantasy, and Horror Poetry: A Resource Guide and Biographical Directory.* Westport, CT: Greenwood Press, 1989.

Griffith, Nicola. "Introduction." *Bending the Landscape: Science Fiction.* New York: Overlook Press, 1999. 7–12.

Gubar, Susan. "C. L. Moore and the Conventions of Women's Science Fiction." *Science Fiction Studies* 7.1 (1980): 16–27. www.jstor.org. Accessed 7 Oct. 2014.

Guran, Paula. "Our Queen, Our Mother, Our Margaret: How One Artist's Magazine Covers Shaped the Vision of a Genre for a Gender." *Weird Tales* 65:2 (Summer 2010): 20–27.

Hamil, Austin. "Kinder Treatment." *Startling Stories* 11.3 (Winter 1945): 104.

———. "That Screaming Cover Girl." *Thrilling Wonder Stories* 26.2 (Fall 1944): 100.

Hamlin, Kimberly A. *From Eve to Evolution: Darwin, Science, and Women's Rights in Gilded Age America.* Chicago: University of Chicago Press, 2014.

Hanley, Terence E. "Dorothy McIlwraith (1891–76), Part I." *Tellers of Weird Tales: Artists and Writers in The Unique Magazine.* 14 Apr. 2012. http://tellersofweirdtales.blogspot.com/2012/04/dorothy-mcilwraith-1891–1976.html. Accessed 24 Sept. 2014.

Hansen, L. Taylor. "L. Taylor Hansen Defends Himself." *Amazing Stories* 17.6 (June 1943): 201–202.

———. "Scientific Mysteries: Footprints of the Dragon." *Amazing Stories* 18.3 (May 1944): 194–96, 210.

———. "Scientific Mysteries: The White Race: Does It Exist?" *Amazing Stories* 16.7 (July 1942): 210–13.

———. *The Ancient Atlantic.* Amherst, WI: Amherst, 1969.

———. "The Man from Space." *Amazing Stories* 4.11 (Feb. 1930): 1034–44.

Hanley, Terence E. "Leah Bodine Drake." *Tellers of Weird Tales: Writers & Artists of the Unique Magazine.* 28 Apr. 2011. http://tellersofweirdtales.blogspot.com/2011/04/leah-bodine-drake-1914–1964.html. Accessed 28 Apr. 2014.

Harmon, Ken. "Poor 'Mr. Donnel.'" *Startling Stories* 11.3 (Winter 1945): 100.

Harris, Clare Winger. *Away from the Here and Now: Stories in Pseudo-Science.* 1947. Vancleave, MS: Surinam Turtle Press, 2011.

————. "Possible Science Fiction Plots." *Wonder Stories* 3.3 (Aug. 1931): 426–27.

————. "The Evolutionary Monstrosity." *Amazing Stories Quarterly* 2.1 (Winter 1929): 70–77.

Hartwell, David. *Age of Wonders: Exploring the World of Science Fiction*. New York: Walker, 1984.

Heiland, Donna. *Gothic and Gender: An Introduction*. Malden, MA: Blackwell, 2004.

Heimbach, Alex. "Why Aren't There More Woman Sci-Fi Writers?" *Slate*. 25 Apr. 2013. http://www.slate.com/blogs/xx_factor/2013/04/25/strange_horizons_report_on _woman_authors_is_science_fiction_and_fantasy.html. Accessed 17 Mar. 2015.

Heller, Steven. "The Revenge of Margaret Brundage, 'The Queen of the Pulps.'" *Atlantic* 31 Jan. 2013. http://www.theatlantic.com/entertainment/archive/2013/01/the -revenge-of-margaret-brundage-the-queen-of-the-pulps/272715/. Accessed 18 Sept. 2014.

Henderson, C. J. "Reinventing the Wheelhouse." *SFWA Bulletin* 47.2 (Spring 2013): 36–43.

Hesson, Bill. "Heredity Fan." *Thrilling Wonder Stories* 26.2 (Fall 1944): 102–103.

History of Science Journalism. "Musée de la civilisation, 2013." http://journalisme -scientifique.podcastmcq.org/en/introduction2.php. Accessed 10 June 2014.

Holling, Lucille. Cover illustration. *Oriental Stories* (Autumn 1931).

Hollinger, Veronica. "'Something Like a Fiction': Speculative Intersections of Sexuality and Technology." In *Queer Universes: Sexualities in Science Fiction*. Ed. Wendy Gay Pearson, Veronica Hollinger, and Joan Gordon. Liverpool: University of Liverpool Press, 2008. 140–60.

Hurley, Kameron. "We Have Always Fought: Challenging the Women, Cattle, and Slaves Narrative." *A Dribble of Ink*. 20 May 2013. http://aidanmoher.com/blog/featured -article/2013/05/we-have-always-fought-challenging-the-women-cattle-and-slaves -narrative-by-kameron-hurley/. Accessed 30 Oct. 2014.

Ivie, Rachel, and Casey Langer Tesfaye. "Global Survey of Physicists: A Tale of Limits." American Institute of Physicists. Feb. 2012. http://www.aip.org/statistics/reports /global-survey-physicists. Accessed 30 Oct. 2014.

James, Edward. *Science Fiction in the 20th Century*. New York: Oxford University Press, 1994.

Jemisin, N. K. "Wiscon 38 Guest of Honor Speech." *N. K. Jemison*. 25 May 2014. http:// nkjemisin.com/2014/05/wiscon-38-guest-of-honor-speech/. Accessed 27 Oct. 2014.

Kidd, Virginia. "From a Kidd 13." Letter. *Wonder Stories* 6.5 (Oct. 1934): 628.

————. Untitled Poem. *Fantasy Fan* 1.4 (Dec. 1933): 55.

Killheffer, Robert K J, Brian M Stableford, and David Langford. "Aliens." In *The Encyclopedia of Science Fiction*. Eds. John Clute, David Langford, Peter Nicholls, and Graham Sleight. *Gollancz*, 25 Sept. 2014. http://www.sf-encyclopedia.com/entry /aliens. Accessed 24 Oct. 2014.

Knight, Damon. *The Futurians*. New York: John Day, 1977.

Korshak, Stephen D. "Introduction: Queen of the Pulps." In *The Alluring Art of Margaret Brundage, Queen of Pulp Pin-Up Art*. Eds. Stephen D. Korshak and J. David Spurlock. Coral Gables, FL: Vanguard, 2013. 11–12.

Korshak, Stephen D., and J. David Spurlock. Eds. *The Alluring Art of Margaret Brundage, Queen of Pulp Pin-Up Art*. Coral Gables, FL: Vanguard, 2013.

Kress, Nancy. "ConFuse Guest of Honor Speech, 1993." *Lysator*. http://www.lysator.liu.se
/lsff/mb-nr21/Speech_by_Nancy_Kress.html. Accessed 30 Oct. 2013.

Larbalestier, Justine. *The Battle of the Sexes in Science Fiction*. Middletown, CT: Wesleyan
University Press, 2002.

Langford, David. "Mad Scientist." In *The Encyclopedia of Science Fiction*. Eds. John Clute,
David Langford, Peter Nicholls, and Graham Sleight. *Gollancz*, 9 July 2014. http://
www.sf-encyclopedia.com/entry/mad_scientist. Accessed 25 Aug. 2014.

———. "Thought-Variant." In *The Encyclopedia of Science Fiction*. Eds. John Clute, David
Langford, Peter Nicholls, and Graham Sleight. *Gollancz*, 5 Apr. 2012. http://www.sf
-encyclopedia.com/entry/thought-variant. Accessed 27 Oct. 2014.

Latham, Sean. "The Mess and Muddle of Modernism: The Modernist Journals Project
and Modern Periodical Studies." *Tulsa Studies in Women's Literature* 30.2 (Fall 2011):
407–28.

Lazlo, Esther, Ayelet Baram-Tsabari, and Bruce V. Lewenstein. "A Growth Medium for
the Message: Online Science Journalism Affordances for Exploring Public Discourse
of Science and Ethics." *Journalism* 12 (2011): 847–70.

Le Guin, Ursula K. "The Golden Age." *New Yorker* 88.16 (2012): 77.

Lesser, Robert, ed. *Pulp Art*. New York: Sterling, 1997.

Les Tina, Dorothy. Illustration for "The Leapers." *Future Fantasy and Science Fiction* 3.2
(Dec. 1942): 40.

———. "When You Think That . . . Smile!" *Future Fantasy and Science Fiction* 3.3 (Feb.
1943): 55–59.

"Lilith Lorraine and the Avalon Arts Academy." *The Nekromantikon: The Amateur
Magazine of Weird and Fantasy* (Fall 1950): 55–58.

Liptak, Andrew. "The Clients of Agent Virginia Kidd." *Kirkus Reviews*. 27 Feb. 2014.
https://www.kirkusreviews.com/features/clients-agent-virginia-kidd/. Accessed 10
May 2014.

———. "The Futurians and the 1939 World Science Fiction Convention." *Kirkus Reviews*.
9 May 2013. https://www.kirkusreviews.com/features/futurians-and-1939-world
-science-fiction-conventio/. Accessed 24 Oct. 2014.

———. "The Many Names of Catherine Lucille Moore." *Kirkus Reviews*. 7 Feb. 2013.
https://www.kirkusreviews.com/features/many-names-catherine-lucille-moore/.
Accessed 24 Oct. 2014.

Long, Amelia Reynolds. "Reverse Phylogeny." *Astounding* 19.4 (June 1937): 72–79.

———. "Time Traveling." *Startling Stories* 1.2 (Mar. 1939): 122.

Lorraine, Lilith. "Cracks—Wise and Otherwise." *Acolyte* (Spring 1943): n.p.

———. "Earthlight on the Moon." *Stirring Science Stories* 1.3 (June 1941): 61.

———. "Into the 28th Century." *Science Wonder Quarterly* 1.2 (Winter 1930): 250–67.

———. "Men Keep Strange Trysts." 1946. Reprinted in Lilith Lorraine, *Let the Patterns
Break*. Rogers, AK: Avalon Press, 1947. 203.

———. "Not An Escape but a Challenge." *Miscellaneous Man* 1.3 (1954): 13–14.

———. "The Acolytes." *Acolyte* 14.4 (Spring 1946): 11.

———. "The Story of *Different*." *Different* 6.1 (Mar.–Apr. 1950): 2.

———. "Training for World Citizenship." *Different* 2.2 (May–June 1946): 2–3.

Lowndes, Robert A. W. "Station X." *Future Combined with Science Fiction* 2.4 (Apr. 1942): 102–103.

Luckhurst, Roger. *Science Fiction*. Cambridge: Polity Press, 2005.

Lutes, Jean Marie. *Front Page Girls: Women Journalists in American Culture and Fiction, 1880–1930*. Ithaca, NY: Cornell University Press, 2006.

Malamud, H., I. Berkman, and H. Rogovin, "A Protest." *Amazing Stories* 17.5 (Apr. 1943): 236–37.

Malzberg, Barry N., and Mike Resnick. "Talk Radio Redux." *SFWA Bulletin* 47.3 (Summer 2013): 45–50.

———. "The Resnick/Malzberg Dialogues LX—Literary Ladies, Part 2." *SFWA Bulletin* 47.1 (Winter 2013): 63–71.

Mangels, Andy. "Why Is the Passing of Forrest J Ackerman of GLBT Importance?" *Prism Comics*. http://prismcomics.org/display_print.php?id=1667. Accessed 9 May 2014.

Marek, Jayne E. *Women Editing Modernism: "Little" Magazines and Literary History*. Lexington: University of Kentucky Press, 1995.

"Mary Gnaedinger, Editor of Fantasy Magazines, 78." Obituary. *New York Times*, 3 Aug. 1976. *ProQuest Historical Newspapers*. http://www.proquest.com. Accessed 10 June 2014.

Mayper, Victor, Jr. Letter. *Future Combined with Science Fiction* 2.3 (Feb. 1942): 108.

Merrick, Helen. *The Secret Feminist Cabal: A Cultural History of Science Fiction Feminisms*. Seattle: Aqueduct Press, 2009.

McIlwraith, Dorothy. "The Eyrie." *Weird Tales* 35.3 (May–June 1940): 124.

———. "The Eyrie." *Weird Tales* 35.6 (Nov.–Dec. 1940): 123–26.

———. "The Eyrie." *Weird Tales* 35.10 (July–Aug. 1941): 2, 122.

Milbank, Alison. "Female Gothic." In *The Handbook of the Gothic*. 2d ed. Ed. Marie Mulvey. New York: New York University Press, 2009. 120–24.

Miles, Fran. "Oil for Bombing." *Fantastic Adventures* 6.4 (Oct. 1944): 198.

Miller, Stephen T., and William G. Contento. *The Locus Science Fiction, Fantasy, and Weird Magazine Index (1890–2001)*. Oakland, CA: Locus Press, 2002.

Moers, Ellen. *Literary Women: The Great Writers*. New York: Doubleday, 1976.

Moore, C. L. "Footnote to *Shambleau* . . . and Others." *The Best of C. L. Moore*. Ed. Lester Del Rey. New York: Ballantine Books, 1975. 365–68.

———. "Shambleau." *Weird Tales* 22.5 (Nov. 1933): 531–50.

Morgan, Cheryl. "Anthologies: Some Data." *Cheryl's Mewsings*. July 16 2011. http://www.cheryl-morgan.com/?p=11096. Accessed 17 Mar. 2015.

Morgan, George D. *Rocket Girl: The Story of Mary Sherman Morgan, America's First Female Rocket Scientist*. New York: Prometheus Books, 2013.

Morrill, Rowena. "Foreword." In *The Alluring Art of Margaret Brundage, Queen of Pulp Pin-Up Art*. Eds. Stephen D. Korshak and J. David Spurlock. Coral Gables, FL: Vanguard, 2013. 7–9.

"Mrs. John Adams Mayer Author of First Novel." *New York Post*, 24 Jan. 1938. http://www.findagrave.com/cgi-bin/fg.cgi?page=gr&GRid=96225916. Accessed 27 Oct. 2014.

Mulvey-Roberts, Marie, ed. *The Handbook of the Gothic*. 2d ed. New York: New York University Press, 2009.

Murphy, Pat. "Illusion and Expectation: Wiscon 15 March 2 1991." *Wiscon: The World's Leading Feminist Science Fiction Convention*. 1991. http://www.wiscon.info/downloads /patmurphy.pdf. Accessed Oct. 2014.

———. "Illusion, Expectation, and World Domination through Bake Sales." *Lightspeed*, Special Issue: "Women Destroy Science Fiction!" 49 (June 2014).

Murphy, Patrick D. "Foreword." *The Poetic Fantastic: Studies in an Evolving Genre*. Eds. Patrick D. Murphy and Vernon Hyles. Westport, CT: Greenwood Press, 1989. xi–xxv.

———. "The Fantastic Experience in Poetry: Or, the Monsters Are There, Where Are the Critics?" *Extrapolation* 28.1 (1987): 23–36.

———. "The Left Hand of Fabulation: The Poetry of Ursula K. Le Guin." In *The Poetic Fantastic: Studies in an Evolving Genre*. Eds. Patrick D. Murphy and Vernon Hyles. Westport, CT: Greenwood Press, 1989. 123–36.

Nadis, Fred. *The Man from Mars: Ray Palmer's Amazing Pulp Journey*. New York: Penguin, 2013.

Newitz, Annalee. "Hugo-Winner Ellen Datlow on the Art of Editing Short Fiction." *io9*. 13 Aug. 2009. http://io9.com/5336103/hugo-winner-ellen-datlow-on-the-art-of -editing-short-fiction. Accessed 30 Oct. 2014.

Niemann-Ross, Mark. "Who Reads Science Fiction?" *SFWA: Science Fiction and Fantasy Writers of America*. 2 Jan. 2014. https://www.sfwa.org/2014/01/reads-science -fiction/. Accessed 30 Oct. 2014.

Organisation for Economic Co-operation and Development. "Are Boys and Girls Equally Prepared for Life?" 2012. http://www.oecd.org/pisa/pisaproducts/PIF-2014-gender -international-version.pdf. Accessed 17 Mar. 2015.

Palmer, Beth. "Ella Hepworth Dixon and Editorship." *Women's Writing* 19.1 (Feb. 2012): 96–109.

Palmer, Raymond A. "Reply to H. Malamud et al." *Amazing Stories* 17.4 (Apr. 1943): 236–37.

———. "The Observatory." *Amazing Stories* 18.4 (Sept. 1944): 6.

Perri, Leslie. "Space Episode." *Future Combined with Science Fiction* 2.2 (Dec. 1941): 106–12.

Pfaelzer, Jean. *The Utopian Novel in America, 1886–1896*. Pittsburgh: University of Pittsburgh Press, 1989.

Pohl, Frederik. "*Astounding*: The Campbell Years, Riding High." http://www.thewaythe futureblogs.com/2009/12/astounding-campbell-years/. Accessed 1 Aug. 2014.

———. *The Way the Future Was: A Memoir*. New York: Del Rey, 1979.

Pollack, Eileen. "Why Are There Still So Few Women in Science?" *New York Times*, 3 Oct. 2011. http://www.nytimes.com/2013/10/06/magazine/why-are-there-still-so-few -women-in-science.html?pagewanted=all&_r=0. Accessed 30 Oct. 2014.

"Presenting the 2006 Hall of Fame Inductees." *Science Fiction Museum and Hall of Fame*. 15 Mar. 2006. https://web.archive.org/web/20060426115756/http://www .sfhomeworld.org/make_contact/article.asp?articleID=239. Accessed Oct. 2014.

Quick, Dorothy. "Strange Orchids." *Weird Tales* 29.3 (Mar. 1937): 258–73.

Rapaport, Sarah. "Rosalind Franklin: Unsung Hero of the DNA Revolution." *History Teacher* 36.1 (Nov. 2002): 116–27.

Reed, Ellen. "Natural Ink." *Fantastic Adventures* 4.6 (June 1942): 135.

Reid, Robin Anne, ed. *Women in Science Fiction and Fantasy*. Westport, CT: Greenwood
   Press, 2009.
Rensberger, Boyce. "Science Journalism: Too Close for Comfort." *Nature* 459 (25 June
   2009): 1055–56.
"Reviews for Readers." *Feilding Star* (2 Apr. 1917): 4. http://paperspast.natlib.govt.nz
   /cgi-bin/paperspast?a=d&d=FS19170402.2.48. Accessed 4 Apr. 2014.
Rhees, David J. "A New Voice for Science: Science Service under Edwin E. Slosson,
   1921–29." Master's thesis, University of North Carolina at Chapel Hill, 1979. http://
   scienceservice.si.edu/thesis/.Accessed 11 June 2014.
Rich, Mark. *C. M. Kornbluth: The Life and Works of a Science Fiction Visionary*. New York:
   McFarland, 2009.
Roberts, Robin. *A New Species: Gender and Science in Science Fiction*. Urbana: University
   of Illinois Press, 1993.
Roggenkamp, Karen. *Narrating the News: New Journalism and Literary Genre in
   Late Nineteenth-Century American Newspapers and Fiction*. Kent, OH: Kent State
   University Press, 2005.
Romubio, Kay. "Obit. Dorothy Louise (Les Tina) Johnson." *Ancestry.com*. 13 Jan. 2004.
   http://boards.ancestry.com/surnames.johnson/14149/mb.ashx?pnt=1. Accessed 24
   Oct. 2014.
Schick, Robert X. "A Pitiful Thing." *Thrilling Wonder Stories* 26.1 (Fall 1944): 99.
Schwartz, Julius. "An Interview with Frank R. Paul." *Fantasy Magazine* 4.3 (Dec. 1934–
   Jan. 1935): 71–72.
Schweitzer, Darrell. "What about Dorothy McIlwraith?" In *WT50: A Tribute to "Weird
   Tales."* Ed. Robert Weinberg. Oak Lawn, IL: Robert Weinberg, 1974. 94–96.
Sharp, Patrick B. *Savage Perils: Racial Frontiers and Nuclear Apocalypse in American
   Culture*. Norman: University of Oklahoma Press, 2007.
"Sheila Williams: New Directions." *Locus Online*. 7 Nov. 2013. http://www.locusmag.com
   /Perspectives/2013/11/sheila-williams-new-directions/. Accessed 1 Nov. 2014.
Silverberg, Robert. "Who Is Tiptree, What Is He?" *Warm Worlds and Otherwise*: 12
   Sparkling Stories by James Tiptree, Jr. New York: Ballantine Del Rey, 1975. ix–xviii.
Smith, Allan Lloyd. "American Gothic." In *The Handbook of the Gothic*. 2d ed. Ed. Marie
   Mulvey-Roberts. New York: New York University Press, 2009. 267–75.
Sneyd, Steve. *Elsewhen Unbound: Poetry in American SFanzines — The 1930s to 1960s*. West
   Yorkshire: Hiltop Press, 2004.
———. "Empress of the Stars: A Reassessment of Lilith Lorraine, Pioneering Fantasy
   Poet." *Fantasy Commentator* 7.3 (Spring 1992): 206–31.
———. *Fierce Far Suns: Proto-SF and SF Poetry in America, the 1750s to the 1960s*. West
   Yorkshire: Hiltop Press, 1997.
———. "Lilith Lorraine: A Postscript." *Fantasy Commentator* 9.3 (1998): 194–99.
Spivack, Charlotte. "'The Hidden World Below': Victorian Women Fantasy Poets." In *The
   Poetic Fantastic*. Eds. Patrick D. Murphy and Vernon Hyles. Westport, CT: Greenwood
   Press, 1989. 54–64.
Spurlock, David J. "The Secret Life of Margaret Brundage." In *The Alluring Art of
   Margaret Brundage: Queen of Pulp Pinup Art*. Eds. Stephen D. Korshak and J. David
   Spurlock. Lakewood, NJ: Vanguard Productions, 2013. 125–81.

Standish, Lynn. "Scientific Oddities." *Amazing Stories* 19.4 (Dec. 1945): 144–45.

———."The Battle of the Sexes." *Amazing Stories* 17.4 (Apr. 1943): 224.

Stansell, Christine. *American Moderns: Bohemian New York and the Creation of a New Century*. New York: Henry Holt, 2000.

Steele, Valerie. *Women of Fashion: Twentieth-Century Designers*. New York: Rizzoli, 1991.

Stefans, Brian Kim. "Three Women Los Angeles Poets." *Free Space Comix*. 28 July 2013. http://www.arras.net/fscIII/?cat=13. Accessed 27 Apr. 2014.

Stine, Jean, Janrae Frank, and Forrest J Ackerman. *New Eves: Science Fiction about the Extraordinary Women of Today and Tomorrow*. Stamford, CT: Longmeadow Press, 1994.

Stone, Leslie F. "Day of the Pulps." *Fantasy Commentator* (Fall 1997): 100–103, 152.

———. "Out of the Void: Part I." *Amazing Stories* 4.5 (Aug. 1929): 440–55.

———. "Out of the Void: Part II." *Amazing Stories* 4.6 (Sep. 1929): 544–65.

Streitmatter, Rodger. *Unspeakable: The Rise of the Gay and Lesbian Press in America*. London: Faber & Faber, 1995.

The New School: Illustration, Design, Painting. School catalog. Boston, 1916. https://archive.org/details/newschoolillustrooscho. Accessed 12 Apr. 2014.

"The New School: List of Scholarships and Awards Made by the Faculty of the Boylston Street Institution." *Boston Evening Transcript*, 8 June 1915: 13. http://news.google.com/newspapers?nid=2249&dat=19150608&id=DTknAAAAIBAJ&sjid=6QMGA AAAIBAJ&pg=3385,1524422. Accessed 4 Apr. 2014.

Tigrina. "Affinity." *Acolyte* 10.3 (Spring 1945): 17.

———. "Defiance." *Acolyte* 9.3 (Winter 1945): 17.

"T. O'Conor Sloane." *Wikipedia, The Free Encyclopedia*. 26 Apr. 2014. http://en.wikipedia.org/wiki/T._O'Conor_Sloane. Accessed 15 June 2014.

Torgersen, Brad R. "SAD PUPPIES 3, the unraveling of an unreliable field." 4 Feb. 2015. https://bradrtorgersen.wordpress.com/2015/02/04/sad-puppies-3-the-unraveling-of-an-unreliable-field/. Accessed 10 July 2015.

Tressider, Mary. "Women and Science at Science Service." *Smithsonian Institution Archives*, 2005. http://siarchives.si.edu/research/sciservwomen.html. Accessed 11 June 2014.

Wagner, Frank. "Wright, Mary Maude Dunn." *Handbook of Texas Online*. Texas State Historical Association, 15 June 2010. http://www.tshaonline.org/handbook/online/articles/fwr19. Accessed 4 May 2014.

Walsh, Joan. "Mitch McConnell's Female Surprise: Why He Really Thinks Sexism Is Dead." *Salon*. 16 July 2014. http://www.salon.com/2014/07/16/mitch_mcconnells_female_surprise_why_he_really_thinks_sexism_is_dead/. Accessed 30 Oct. 2014.

Weinbaum, Batya. "Twentieth-Century American Women's Progress and the Lack Thereof in Leslie F. Stone's 'Out of the Void.'" *Foundation* 36.101 (Winter 2007): 34–48.

Weinberg, Robert. Ed. *A Biographical Dictionary of Science Fiction and Fantasy Artists*. Westport, CT: Greenwood Press, 1988.

———. *The "Weird Tales" Story* [1977]. San Bernardino, CA: Borgo, 1999.

Westfahl, Gary. "Artists in Wonderland: Toward a True History of Science Fiction Art." In *Unearthly Visions: Approaches to Science Fiction and Fantasy Art*. Eds. Gary Westfahl,

George Slusser, and Kathleen Church Plummer. Westport, CT: Greenwood Press, 2002. 19–38.

———. *The Mechanics of Wonder: The Creation of the Idea of Science Fiction*. Liverpool: Liverpool University Press, 1998.

Wilde, Fran. "10 Questions with Award-Winning Science Fiction Editor Sheila Williams." *GeekMom*. 27 Feb. 2014. http://geekmom.com/2014/02/sheila-williams/. Accessed 30 Oct. 2014.

Willard, Frances Elizabeth, and Mary Ashton Rice Livermore. *American Women: Fifteen Hundred Biographies with Over 1,400 Portraits—A Comprehensive Encyclopedia of the Lives and Achievements of American Women in the Nineteenth Century*. Springfield, OH: Mast, Crowell & Kirkpatrick, 1897.

Williamson, Chet. "A Visit with Amelia Reynolds Long." *A Tribute to Amelia Reynolds Long*. 1976. http://amelialong.tripod.com/avisit.htm. Accessed 3 July 2014.

"Women and Girls in Science, Tech, Engineering and Math." White House Office of Science and Technology Policy. June 2013. http://www.whitehouse.gov/sites/default /files/microsites/ostp/stem_factsheet_2013_07232013.pdf. Accessed 30 Oct. 2014.

Wright, Farnsworth. "The Eyrie." *Weird Tales* 29.5 (May 1937): 634–35.

"Wright, Laura Moore." *University of Calgary Library Canadian Literary and Art Collection*. University of Calgary Library, 2003. http://www.ucalgary.ca/lib-old/SpecColl/wright .htm. Accessed 25 June 2014.

Wright, Laura Moore. "Sunlight." *Amazing Stories* 20.2 (May 1946): 111.

Yaszek, Lisa. "A Parabola of Her Own: Mapping the Domestic Science Fiction Story." In *Parabolas of Science Fiction*. Eds. Brian Attebery and Veronica Hollinger. Westport, CT: Wesleyan University Press, 2013. 106–24.

———. *Galactic Suburbia: Recovering Women's Science Fiction*. Columbus: Ohio State University Press, 2008.

INDEX

accentual verse, 237

Ackerman, Forrest J, xvi, 142, 223, 253, 365–66n8

Acolyte fanzine, xviii, 254–55, 257, 315

"The Acolytes" (Lorraine), 257–58

"Affinity" (Tigrina), 255

African American arts movement, xvi, 338

Ainsworth, Lillian M., 294

Alice in Wonderland (Carroll), 164

aliens: as antagonists, 27; as superwomen, 165; as teachers, 144; wiser than human, 365n10

All-Fiction Field publications, 293–94, 302

All-Story Weekly, xvii

Amazing Stories/Amazing magazine: "The Fate of the *Poseidonia*" (C. W. Harris) in, 8; Green's poems in, 242–44; journalistic articles in, 261–64; L. M. Wright's articles in, 273; Long's stories in, 212; Lorraine's stories in, 106; L. T. Hansen's journalistic articles in, 275, 278, 282, 286, 288; L. T. Hansen's stories in, 142–44, 212; Malamud and Rogovin's protest letter to, 286; M. Bourne as editor of, 290, 292; most prolific writers for, 366n4; poetry in, 365nn3–4; scientific explanations in, 1–2; scientific extrapolation in, xvii–xix; Standish's articles in, 265, 269, 271; Stone's stories in, 26–27; verse as filler in, 239; women authors in, xxi

Amazing Stories Quarterly, xvii, 8–9, 242, 244

American Gothic illustration, 332–34, 339

American Institute of Physics, 354

American Women (Willard and Livermore), 239

ancient mysteries, in science fiction, 142, 212

Anderson, Margaret, 291

Anglophone periodicals, 290. *See also* editors

Annual Reader's Award, 360

anthropology, in science fiction, 212

apocalyptic futures, in science fiction, 8

archaeology, in science fiction, 212

Argosy magazine, 26

"Argument" (Kidd), 247

art: in magazines, 291–92; politics connected to, xvi; by V. Finlay, 301; *Weird Tales* controversy over, 306

artists in science fiction: Bourgeois, 331–32, 336; Brundage, 338–40 (*see also* Brundage, Margaret); Donnell, xxiii, 331, 333–34, 342; Les Tina, xvi, xxiii, 3–4, 230–31, 331, 333–34, 336, 341; L. W. Holling, 332, 337; overview, 331–35; technophilic and Gothic, xxiii, 26

Ashley, Michael, xviii, 9, 12, 306, 359

Asimov, Isaac, xv, 239, 365n4

Asimov's Science Fiction magazine, 351, 360, 365n4

Astonishing Stories, 230

Astounding Science Fiction, 3, 212–13, 290, 292, 365n2

"An Astral Gentleman" (Ainsworth), 294

Atlantic Monthly, 249

Atlantis, lost city of, 366n6

Attebery, Brian, 275, 363n7

Atwood, Margaret, 243

authors: C. W. Harris, xvi, xviii–xix, 1, 3, 8–25, 364nn6–7; "The Evolutionary Monstrosity," 1, 3, 9–25; "Into the 28th Century," 1, 108–41, 363n3; introduction to, xxi, 1–7; Les Tina, xvi, 3–4, 230–31; Long, xvi, xx–xxi, 3, 212–13; Lorraine, 106–8 (*see also* Lorraine, Lilith); L. T. Hansen, 142–44 (*see also* Hansen, L. Taylor); "The Man from Space," 2, 144–63; Moore, 164–66 (*see*

also Moore, C. L.); "Out of the Void," 1, 4, 27–105, 365n10; Perri, 3, 5, 223–24; Quick, 191–92 (*see also* Quick, Dorothy Gertrude); "Reverse Phylogeny," 3, 213–22; "Shambleau," 2–3, 166–90; "Space Episode," 3, 5, 224–29; Stone, 26–27 (*see also* Stone, Leslie F.); "Strange Orchids," 2–3, 5, 192–211; "When You Think That . . . Smile!," 3–4, 231–36
Avalon World Arts Academy, 256, 314
Away from the Here and Now (C. W. Harris), 8–9

"Baby, You Were Great" (Wilhelm), 345
bacterial evolution, science fiction inspired by, 1, 8
Baird, Edwin, xvii, 239
Banister, Manley, 298
Barnes, Arthur K., 213
Barres, Ben, 353–54
Bates, Harry, 293, 297
"The Battle of the Sexes" (Standish), 269–71
The Battle of the Sexes in Science Fiction (Larbalestier), 363–64n7
Baudelaire, Charles, 237
Baumgardt, Doris Marie Claire "Doë" (Leslie Perri), xxi, 3, 4, 5, 6, 223–24, 230
Baym, Nina, 6, 106
Beams, Davie, 165
Before Stonewall (film), 253
"Behind the Curtain" (Stevens), 294
Bell, Julie, 331, 335, 340, 342
Ben, Lisa, 253. *See also* Tigrina (Edith Eyde)
Bennett, Gertrude Barrows (Francis Stevens), 294, 301. *See also* Stevens, Francis
Bergey, Earle, 342
Berkman, I., 278, 286
Bernal, A. W., 339
Black Cat magazine, xvii, 331, 336
"Black God's Kiss" (Moore), 339
"black peril" stories, 333
Blake, William, 237
Blish, James, 247, 365n6
Bloch, Robert, 164, 294

Bogg, Pete, 366n4
Bohr, Niels, 347
Bok, Hannes, 294
Booth, Mary Louise, 291
Boston Transcript, 242
Bourgeois, Olivette, 331–32, 336
Bourne, Miriam, 290, 292
Bourne, Randolph, xv
Brackett, Leigh, xxi
Bradbury, Ray, 294, 306
Bradford, Tempest, 359
Bradley, Marion Zimmer, 298, 300
"The Brain of the Planet" (Lorraine), 106
Brown, Henrietta, 262, 263, 265–69, 278
Brundage, Margaret, xvi, xviii, xx, xxiii, 191, 306, 331–33, 338–40, 341, 349
Brundage, Slim, 338
Burns, Robert, 237, 249
Burroughs, Edgar Rice, xix, 26, 164
Butler, Octavia E., 7
Byron, George Gordon (Lord Byron), 238

Campaigns of Napoleon (Wright), 366n5
Campbell, John W., 293, 301, 349, 365n2
Carnegie, Andrew, 364n6
Carroll, Lewis, 164
Carter, John, 164
CFG (Cincinnati Fantasy Group), 357
"The Chalice" (Gruber), 307
Challenge magazine, xviii, 106, 239, 256
Charnas, Suzy McKee, 359
Chicago Academy of Fine Arts, 338
Chicago African American arts movement, xvi, 338
Cincinnati Fantasy Group (CFG), 357
City (Simak), 344
"The City on the Cloud" (Hansen), 142
civil rights activism, xvi
"Claggett's Folly" (Michel), 334, 341
Clemens, Samuel, 191
Coblentz, Stanley A., 239, 256, 294, 298
Cole, Thomas, 332–33
Coleridge, Samuel, 237
Coleridge, Sara, 238, 241
Combs, Virginia, 224

comedy, in science fiction, 213

Comet fanzine, xviii

ConFuse SF convention (1993), 355

Conklin, Groff, 294, 301, 349

Connolly, Susan E., 352

Cooper, James Fenimore, 333

Copeland, Leland S., 365n3

Cosmic poetry movement, 239, 256

Counselman, Mary, 306

Cowdry, Albert E., 7

"Cracks — Wise and Otherwise" (Lorraine), 315

creative expression, in magazines, 291

Crisp, Julie, 352, 354

"Cruisin' Down the Boulevard" (Eyde), 366n9

cyberpunk, 242

dark fantasy poetry, 238

Dark of the Moon (Derlith), 249

Dark Side of the Moon (Derlith), 237

Datlow, Ellen, 300, 352, 359–60

Daughters of Earth (Larbalestier), xxi, 9

Davin, Eric Leif, 265

The Death of Cora (Cole), 333

de Camp, L. Sprague, 213

Decoding Gender in Science Fiction (Attebery), 363n7

"Defiance" (Tigrina), 254–55

Delaney, William J., 306

Dell Magazines Award for Undergraduate Excellence in Science Fiction and Fantasy Writing, 360

democratization of science, 260

De Pina, Albert, 342

Derlith, August, 237, 249, 256, 298, 306

dialect, in poetry, 237–38, 249

Different magazine: Avalon World Arts Academy and, 256; development of, 297–98; example table of contents (1946), 299; Lorraine as editor of, xxiii, 106, 290; "Men Keep Strange Trysts" (Lorraine), 258; purpose of, 314; "The Story of *Different*," 320–30; "Training for World Citizenship," 315–19

Dillane, Fionnuala, 291

Dirac, Paul, 347

Disney, Walt, 338

domestic fiction: gender ideals in, 27; in "Into the 28th Century," 106; patriarchal impulses of science from, xxi–xxii, 6–7; scientific adventure in, 9; in "Strange Orchids," 192

domestic technologies, 4, 231

Donawerth, Jane, 5, 363n3

Donnell, Dolly Rackley, xxiii, 331, 333–34, 342

Dorman, Sonya, 247, 300

Doubleday, Page, and Company, 306

Dozois, Gardner, 360

"Dragonrider" (McCaffrey), 345

Drake, Leah Bodine, xvi, xxii, 240–41, 249–50, 253–54, 298

The Dreaming Sex (Ashley), 9

dream visions, stories framed as, 143

"Earthlight on the Moon" (Lorraine), 257

Easely, Jeff, 356–57

Edges (Kidd and Le Guin), 247

"Editorial Note" in *Famous Fantastic Mysteries* (M. Gnaedinger), 302

editors: of All-Fiction Field publications, 293–94; of commercial magazines, 290–91; "Cracks — Wise and Otherwise" in *Acolyte*, 315; "Editorial Note" in *Famous Fantastic Mysteries*, 302; "Editor's Page" in *Famous Fantastic Mysteries*, 303–5; "The Eyrie" in *Weird Tales*, 293, 308–13; of genre publications, 292–93; Lorraine, xxiii, 106, 290, 300, 314–15 (*see also* Lorraine, Lilith); McIlwraith, 306–8 (*see also* McIlwraith, Dorothy); M. Gnaedinger, 301–2 (*see also* Gnaedinger, Mary); of noncommercial literary magazines, 291–92, 294–98; overview, xxii–xxiii; "The Story of *Different*" in *Different*, 320–30; "Training for World Citizenship" in *Different*, 315–19; women as, 298–300

"Editor's Page" in *Famous Fantastic Mysteries* (M. Gnaedinger), 303–5

education, reforms in, 314–15

egalitarian environment, of science fiction writing, xx

Egoist, 291

Elgin, Suzette Haden, 237

Eliot, George, 367n1

Ellison, Harlan, 356

Elwood, Roger, 247

Emshwiller, Carol, 349

engineering paradigm, dark side of, 165

Enlightenment rationality, 191

Evans, Marian, 367n1

"Evolution" (Green), 244

"The Evolutionary Monstrosity" (C. W. Harris), 1, 3, 9–25

E. W. Scripps' Science Service, xxii, 259–61

Eyde, Edith (Tigrina), xvi, xviii, xxii, 241, 253–54, 365–66nn8–9

"The Eyrie" in *Weird Tales* (D. McIlwraith), 293, 307–13

facilitators, editors as, 291, 301, 307, 367nn1–2

"Facts of the Future" column, in *Amazing Stories*, 262

family interdependence, in "When You Think That . . . Smile!" (Les Tina), 231

Famous Fantastic Mysteries: "Editorial Note" (M. Gnaedinger), 302; "Editor's Page" (M. Gnaedinger), 303–5; example table of contents (1940), 295; Gnaedinger as editor of, xviii, xxii, 290, 301; women writers in, 294

Fantastic Adventures, 261–62, 267–68, 340, 366n4

Fantastic Novels, 302

fantastic verse, 237–38

Fantasy Amateur Press Association, 223

Fantasy Fan magazine, xviii, 248

Fantasy magazine, 300

fantasy magazines, 2

Farnsworth, R. L., 298

fashion illustration, magazine art and, 331–32, 338–39

"The Fate of the *Poseidonia*" (C. W. Harris), 8

FBI (Federal Bureau of Investigation), xvi, 106, 256

feminist science fiction: anthologies of, xxi; contemporary, 1; Kidd and, 247; in "Out of the Void," 27; revival of, 7; in "Space Episode," 224; in "When You Think That . . . Smile!," 231

feminist-socialist utopian elements, 106

feminist speculative poetry, 237

feminist utopian beliefs, 27

Fiend without a Face (film), 212

Finlay, Virgil, 293, 301, 303

Fire and Sleet and Candelight (Derlith), 256

First Fandom, 247

Fowler, Karen Joy, 359

Frank, Janrae, 223

Frankenstein (Shelley), xv, 3, 5, 8, 143, 242, 336, 361

Franklin, Rosalind, 348

Freas, Frank Kelly, 294

free verse, 237, 242

Freud, Sigmund, 291

Friend, Oscar J., 342

Future Fantasy, 230

Future Fantasy and Science Fiction, 231, 334, 341

Future Fiction, 3

Future magazine, 223–24

Futurian Society, 223, 230, 239, 247

Garvey, Ellen Gruber, 290

gay news reporting, xvi, xviii, 253, 365–66n8

"Gee-Whiz" model of science writing, 262, 266

gender issues: bias in publishing, 354–55; controversies based on, xxiii; identity, 143; imbalance in, 351–53; in magazines, 290–91; representations of, in art and advertising, 363n7; in "Shambleau," 165; in Space Episode," 224; in "When You Think That . . . Smile!," 231

Gernsback, Hugo: and Gothic fiction, xvii; and Harris, 8; as innovative publisher, xv, 1; as inspiration to women magazine editors, 292–94; introduction of poetry, 239, 242; and Les Tina, 341; and Lorraine, 106; recruitment of women as writers, 348, 363nn3; reliance on scientists and engineers, 261; and Stone, 26; and utopian fiction, xvii; and women writers, xx, xxi, 1–2; on youth-driven technocultural progress, 248

Gibson, William, 359

Gilman, Charlotte Perkins, 4–5, 106

Gnaedinger, Louis Beverley Nichol, 301

Gnaedinger, Mary, xvi, xviii, xxii–xxiii, 292–93, 298, 301–2, 308, 315, 360

"Goblin Market" (Rossetti), 238

Godey's Lady Book, 291

Goldman, Emma, 291

Goodwin, Kat, 354

Goonan, Kathleen Ann, xxiii, 343–69

Gothic fiction: in "The Evolutionary Monstrosity," 8; female protagonist in, 368n9; Gernsback and, xvii; inspiration from, xxi, 3; in "Shambleau," 165–66; in "Space Episode," 224; in "Strange Orchids," 192

Gothic illustration, xxiii, 338

Grand Master of Fantasy, 164

Green, Julia Boynton, xvi–xvii, xxii, 239, 240, 242–43, 248, 365nn3–4

Griffith, Nicola, 253

Gruber, Frank, 307

Hahn, Otto, 347

Hale, Sarah Josepha, 291

Hansen, A. Fred, 142

Hansen, L. Taylor, xvi–xix, xxi–xxii, 2, 142–44, 262–65, 275–78, 282, 287–89, 364–65n10, 366n6

Hard Curves (Bell), 335

Harper's Bazaar, 291

Harris, Clare Winger, xvi, xviii–xix, xxi, 1, 3–4, 6, 8–25, 27, 191, 349, 364nn6–7

Harris, Frank C., 8

Heap, Jane, 291

Heiland, Donna, 3

Heisenberg, Werner, 347

Hemans, Felicia, 238, 243, 249

Henderson, C. J., 368–69n1

Hergenrader, Trent, 7

Herland (Gilman), 4, 106

He Walked the Americas (L. T. Hansen), 142

hierarchical model of reporting, xxii

Holling, Holling Clancy, 337

Holling, Lucille Webster, 332, 337

Hopkins, Nancy, 353

A Hornbook for Witches (Drake), 249

horror fiction, 300

horror magazines, 2

horror poetry, 238, 249

How to Suppress Women's Writing (Russ), 344, 353

Hugo Award, xviii, xxiii, 345, 350, 356, 360

"The Human Pets of Mars" (Stone), xv

human "super-race," 106–7

humor, in science fiction, 213

Hurley, Kameron, 359

Hymn to Satan (Tigrina), xviii, 253

hypnosis, in Long's "Reverse Phylogeny," 212

imagination, power of, 238

impresario, editor as, xxiii, 291, 297

informational model of science writing, 261–62

Ingelow, Jean, 238, 243

International Conference for the Fantastic in the Arts, 360

International Workers of the World, 338

interracial marriage, 106

"Into the 28th Century" (Lorraine), 1–2, 106, 108–41, 363n3

Irving, Minna, 294, 301

The Island of Dr. Moreau (Wells), 8

Jacobson, Mary Catherine. *See* Gnaedinger, Mary
Jemisin, N. K., 343
Johnson, Margaret Hedda. *See* Brundage, Margaret
Johnson, Raymond E., 230
Jones, Alice Eleanor, 6, 231
journalists: "The Battle of the Sexes," 269–71; Brown, 265–69; L. M. Wright, xxii, 263, 265–67, 273, 366n5; "L. Taylor Hansen Defends Himself," 288–89; L. T. Hansen, 275–78 (*see also* Hansen, L. Taylor); Malamud, 275, 278, 286–88; "Marine Engineering in the Insect World," 268–69; Miles, 263, 265–68; "Natural Link," 267; "Oil for Bombing," 267–68; overview, 259–64; "A Protest," 286–88; Reed, xxii, 263, 264, 265–67, 278; Rogovin, 278, 286–88; "Scientific Mysteries: Footprints of the Dragon," 282–86; "Scientific Mysteries: The White Race—Does It Exist?," 278–82; "Scientific Oddities," 271–73; Standish, xxii, 262–63, 265–67, 269, 271, 278; "Sunlight," 273–74, 366n5

Kaiser Wilhelm Institute (Berlin, Germany), 347
Keats, John, 238
Keller, David H., 294
Kidd, Virginia, xvi, xviii–xix, 6, 239, 240–41, 247–48, 365n6
Kinesis magazine, 247
Knight, Damon, 247
Kornbluth, Cyril, 223
Kress, Nancy, 355
Kuttner, Henry, 164, 213, 306

Ladder magazine, 253
Laing, Patrick (A. R. Long), xvi, xx–xxi, 3, 212–13
Lalli, Cele Goldsmith, 298
Landon, Laetitia Elizabeth, 238
Lane, Mary E. Bradley, 4, 106
Larbalestier, Justine, xxi, 9, 300, 363–64n7

Lasser, David, xvii, 106, 348
The Last of the Mohicans (Cooper), 333
"The Leapers" (Lowndes), 334, 341
The Left Hand of Darkness (Le Guin), 345
Le Guin, Ursula K., 243, 247, 298, 345, 350–51, 359
Leiber, Fritz, 294, 306
Lesbian Hall of Fame, xvi
lesbian issues, xvi, xviii, 241
lesbian journalism, 253, 365–66n8
Les Tina, Dorothy, xvi, xxi, xxiii, 3–4, 5–6, 223, 230–31, 331, 333–34, 336, 341, 349
letters, stories framed as, 143
Lightspeed magazine, 358–59
Lines and Interlines (Green), 242
Link, Kelly, 300
literary traditions in science fiction, xvii
"little-magazine" movement, xxiii, 290. See also *Different* magazine
Little Review, 291
Livermore, Mary Ashton Rice, 239, 242
London, Jack, 336
Long, Amelia Reynolds, xvi, xvii, xx–xxi, 3, 5, 212–13, 223
Lorraine, Lilith: "The Acolytes," 257–58; as author, 106–7; biographical sketch, 106–8; as Cosmic poet, 239; "Cracks—Wise and Otherwise," 315; "Earthlight on the Moon," 257; as editor, xxiii, 106, 290, 300, 314–15; escape from patriarchy theme, 250; "Into the 28th Century," 1–2, 106, 108–41, 363n3; as New Woman, xvi–xviii; "The Story of *Different*," 320–30; "Training for World Citizenship," 315–19; on value of SF, 367n9; *Wine of Wonder*, 237, 240, 256
"Los Angeles boosterism," 242
Los Angeles Manuscripters, 9
Los Angeles Science Fiction Society, 164, 253
"lost generation" of poets, 242
Lovecraft, H. P., 294
Lowndes, Robert A. W., 3, 223–24, 230, 247, 334, 341

"L. Taylor Hansen Defends Himself" (L. T. Hansen), 288–89
Lull, Robert Wilbur, 294

mad scientist characters: domestic heroism in, 6; in *The Island of Dr. Moreau*, 8–9; in isolated home locations, 4; in "Strange Orchids," 5, 191–92, 340; in "A Thousand Deaths," 336
magazines: commercial, 290–91; noncommercial literary, 291–92, 294–98; popularity of, 290. *See also* editors; *individual magazines and fanzines by name*
Mahaffey, Bea, 357
Malamud, H., 275, 278, 286–88
male narrators in stories, 5, 7, 27
Malzberg, Barry, 357–58
"The Man from Space" (Hansen), 2, 144–63
"The Man Who Was Two Men" (Bernal), 339
Marek, Jayne E., 291
"Marine Engineering in the Insect World" (Brown), 268–69
Mark Twain and Me (Quick), 191
marriage: interracial, 106; in utopian fiction, 4; in "When You Think That . . . Smile!," 231
Marsden, Dora, 291
"A Martian Odyssey" (Weinbaum), 365n10
mass audience for science information, 260
Mayer, Dorothy Gertrude Quick. *See* Quick, Dorothy Gertrude
Mayer, John Adams, 191
Mayper, Victor, Jr., 224
McCaffrey, Anne, 6, 247, 345, 349
McConnell, Mitch, 354
McCormick, Orma, 239, 298
McIlwraith, Dorothy, xvi–xviii, xxii–xxiii, 2, 239, 290, 292–93, 298, 300, 306–8, 315, 349, 360, 367n7
McIlwraith, Jean, 306
McNaughton, Violet, 366n5
Meitner, Lise, 347

"Men Keep Strange Trysts" (Lorraine), 258
Merrick, Helen, 363–64n7
Merril, Judith, 6, 231, 239, 247, 349
mesmerism, 3
Michel, John B., 334, 341
Miles, Fran, 263, 265–68
Milford Writers Workshop, 247, 365n6
Millennial Women (Kidd), 247
Miller, Warren Hastings, 332, 337
Mizora: A Prophecy (Lane), 4, 106
modernist little-magazine movement, 290
modernity, atmosphere of, 237
Moore, C. L., xvi, xix–xxi, xxii, 2–4, 143, 164–66, 294, 333, 339, 349
Morgan, Mary Sherman, 348
Morrill, Rowena, 331, 335, 340
Morris, A., 366n4
Movie Love Stories (Perri, ed.), 223
Munsey Company, 292, 301
Murphy, Pat, 346, 352
music, science fiction and fantasy, 253
Mutant fanzine, xviii, 253
mythic figures, modernization of, 240–41

National Institutes of Health, xvi, 26
Native American storytelling traditions, 142
"Natural Link" (Reed), 267
Nature, 259, 353
Nebula Award, 345–46, 350, 359
New Eves (Stine, Frank, and Ackerman), 223
New Freewoman, 291
New School (Boston, MA), 336
A New Species (Roberts), 363n7
New Wave experiments in science fiction, 247
New Yorker, 249
New York Post, 191
Niemann-Ross, Mark, 351
"The Night Express" (Green), 243–44
Niven, Larry, 164
Nobel Prize, 347–48
Norton, André Alice, 335
novels. *See* authors

Obama, Barack, 349
O'Donnell, Lawrence, 164
"Oil for Bombing" (Miles), 267–68
"Ok, O Che? by K." (Kidd), 247
Omni magazine, 359
ONE, Inc., 253
Ore, Rebecca, 7
Oriental Stories, 191, 332, 337–38
"Out of the Void" (Stone), 1, 4, 27–105,
    365n10
outsider characters, in speculative fiction,
    253
Owens, Thomas, 223

Padgett, Lewis, 164
Palmer, Raymond A., xvi–xvii, 142, 261–
    62, 264, 275, 366n6
Pantazos, Ione Athena, 142
Pantazos, Iwanne, 142
paranormal publications, 261
Patchwork Quilt sequence (Quick), 191
Paul, Frank R., 334, 340, 368n7
Pauli, Wolfgang, 347
Perri, Leslie, xxi, 3, 4, 5, 6, 223–24, 230
Persephone of Eleusis (C. W. Harris), 8
"Pictures in a Fire" (Proctor), 238
Piercy, Marge, 7
Pinckard, Tom and Terri, 164
Pinker, Steven, 349
PISA (Programme for International Stu-
    dent Assessment), 349, 353
"The Planners" (Wilhelm), 345
Playboy magazine, 351
Poe, Edgar Allen, 165, 237
poetry: "The Acolytes" (Lorraine), 257–
    58; "Affinity" (Tigrina), 255; *Challenge*
    magazine, xviii, 106, 239; "Defiance"
    (Tigrina), 254–55; Drake, xvi, xxii, 240–
    41, 249–50, 253–54, 298; "Earthlight
    on the Moon" (Lorraine), 257; "Evo-
    lution" (Green), 244; fantastic, xxii;
    Green, xvi–xvii, xxii, 239, 240, 242–43,
    248, 365nn3–4; Kidd, xvi, xviii–xix,
    6, 239, 240–41, 247–48, 365n6; Lilith

Lorraine, 237, 240, 256–58 (*see also*
    Lorraine, Lilith); "Men Keep Strange
    Trysts" (Lorraine), 258; "The Night Ex-
    press" (Green), 243–44; "Radio Reve-
    lations" (Green), 244–46; "Sea-Shell"
    (Drake), 252; seditious speculative, xvi,
    106; speculative, 237–43; "They Run
    Again" (Drake), 250–51; Tigrina (Edith
    Eyde), xvi, xviii, xxii, 241, 253–54, 365–
    66nn8–9; "Untitled" (Kidd), 248; "The
    Wood-Wife" (Drake), 251–52
Poetry Chapbook, 249
Poetry Society of America, 249
Pohl, Frederik, 223, 230, 239, 301, 341
political expression: art connected with,
    xvi; in magazines, 291–92, 300; science
    fiction as form of, xx
Popular Publications, 230, 341
post-singularity science fiction, 242
Pound, Ezra, 292
power relations, men and women in, 7
Poyser-Lisi, Victoria, 331, 335, 340
"The Priestess of Pakmari" (De Pina), 342
Proctor, Adelaide, 238, 243, 249
Programme for International Student As-
    sessment (PISA), 349, 353
"prophetic" poetry, 240
"prophet of doom," science fiction as, xx
"A Protest" (Malamud and Rogovin),
    286–88
pseudoscience, 5

"Quest of the Starstone" (Moore and Kutt-
    ner), 164
Quick, Dorothy Gertrude, xxi, 2–3, 5, 6,
    9, 191–92, 249, 253–54, 333, 340, 349,
    368n9
Quinn, John, 292
Quinn, Seabury, 307

racism, scientific, xvii, 263
Radcliffe, Anne, 3
"Radio Revelations" (Green), 244–46
Ralph 124C41+ (Gernsback), 2

Rambo, Cat, 300
Raven magazine, 256
reader preferences, editorial decisions based on, 292–93, 301
Reed, Ellen, xxii, 263, 264, 265–67, 278
Reid, Robin Anne, 363n7
"Reinventing the Wheelhouse" (Henderson), 368–69n1
reporting: gay news, xvi, xviii; hierarchical model of, xxii; lesbian journalism, 253, 365–66n8; on science, xxii. *See also* journalists
reproductive technologies, 7, 9
Resnick, Mike, 357–58
"Reverse Phylogeny" (Long), 3, 213–22
Reynolds, Adrian or Peter (A. R. Long), xvi, xx–xxi, 3, 212–13
Rhees, David J., 260
Ritter, William E., 259
Roberts, Robin, 363n7
Robinson, Kim Stanley, 7
rocket propulsion, description of, 26
Rogovin, H., 278, 286–88
romance, in science fiction, 2
Rose, Billy, 249
Rossetti, Christina, 238, 241, 243
"A Runaway World" (C. W. Harris), 8
Rupert, Margaret F., 106
Russ, Joanna, 7, 224, 344, 350, 353
Ryman, Geoff, 7

Sargent, Pamela, xxi, 300
Saturday Evening Post, 249
Saving Worlds (Kidd and Elwood), 247
Schrödinger, Werner, 347
science: journalism on, xxii; patriarchal impulses of, xxi; science fiction as extrapolation of, xvii, 9; women writers, 366n2; writers' interest in, xviii
science fiction: ancient mysteries in, 142; apocalyptic futures in, 8; conclusion overview, 343–45; meaning and value debate on, 1; nuclear weapons' impact on, 26; post-singularity, 242; socially

oriented, 294; "thought-variant," 212, 223, 230; women as artists of, 361–62; women as writers, editors, and readers of, 345–61
Science Fiction and Fantasy Writers of America, xxiii, 346
Science Fiction magazine, 230
Science Fiction Plus, 341
Science Fiction Poetry Association, 237
Science Fiction Quarterly, 230, 334
Science Wonder Quarterly, 106–7
Scientific American, 261
"Scientific Mysteries" column in *Amazing Stories*, 262, 275
"Scientific Mysteries: Footprints of the Dragon" (L. T. Hansen), 282–86
"Scientific Mysteries: The White Race—Does It Exist?" (L. T. Hansen), 278–82
"Scientific Oddities" (Standish), 271–73
"Scientific Oddities" column in *Amazing Stories*, 262, 266
scientific racism, xvii, 263
Scripps, Edward W., 259–60
"Sea-Shell" (Drake), 252
The Secret Feminist Cabal (Merrick), 363–64n7
seditious speculative poetry, xvi, 106
SFWA Bulletin, 356–58, 368–69n1
"Shambleau" (Moore), 2–3, 166–90
Shaver, Richard, 264, 366n6
Shaver Mystery stories, 264, 366n6
Sheldon, Alice, 7, 350–51
Shelley, Mary Wollstonecraft, xv, 3, 5, 8–9, 143, 191, 242
Short Stories, Inc., 306
Silberberg, Leslie Frances, xv. *See also* Stone, Leslie F.
Silverberg, Robert, 298, 350
Simak, Clifford, 344
Sky & Telescope magazine, 365n3
Sloane, T. O'Conor, xvii, xx, 2, 143, 261, 292, 348
Slosson, Edwin E., 260
Smith, Clark Ashton, 239, 256

Smith College, xviii, 8, 364n6

Sneyd, Steve, 106, 247, 249

social activism, xvi

socially oriented science fiction, 294

social sciences: in *Different* magazine, 298; in science fiction, 3; science fiction as extrapolation of, 9; in "When You Think That . . . Smile!," 230

Soft as Steel (Bell), 335

The Song of Roland (Wright), 366n5

South Side Community Art Center (Chicago), 338

"Space Episode" (Perri), 3, 5, 224–29

Space Fact and Fiction, 223

space flight, 3, 26

speculative ideas, as story drivers, 3

Spinrad, Norman, 164

Spivack, Charlotte, 238

Sprenger, William, 338

Stackpole Books, 212

Standish, Lynn, xxii, 262–63, 265–67, 269, 271, 278

Stardust magazine, 212

Starlanes magazine, 239

Startling Stories, 334, 340, 342

St. Clair, Margaret, 294

Stefans, Brian Kim, 242

Stellar poetry movement, 239, 256

STEM professions, 352–53

Sterling, Bruce, 7

Stevens, Francis, 294, 301

Stine, Jean, 223

Stirling, George, 239

Stirring Science Stories, 257

Stone, Leslie F., xv–xvii, xix–xxi, 1–2, 4, 5, 6, 26–27, 106, 143, 231, 248, 349, 365n10

"The Story of *Different*" (Lorraine), 320–30

Strange Awakenings (Quick), 191

"Strange Orchids" (Quick), 2–3, 5, 192–211, 333, 340

Streitmatter, Rodger, 253

Sturgeon, Theodore, 294

Summers, Larry, 349

"Sunlight" (Wright), 273–74, 366n5

"super-race" of humans, 106–7

symbolism, in poetry, 237

Taine, John, xix

Tarrant, Catherine "Kay," 290, 292

tastemakers, women as, 240

taxonomy of science fiction themes, 9

technocultural people, xxi

technophilic tradition in SF art, xxiii, 331, 333–34, 341–42

telepathy, 3, 106

The Testimony of the Suns (Stirling), 239

"They Run Again" (Drake), 250–51

This Enchanted Coast (Green), 242

Thomas, Reggie, 164

"The Thought Monster" (Long), 212

thought-variant science fiction, 3, 212, 223, 230

"A Thousand Deaths" (London), 336

"A Thrilling Tale of Burma" (Miller), 332

Thrilling Wonder Stories, 334, 340, 342

Tigrina (Edith Eyde), xvi, xviii, xxii, 241, 253–54, 365–66nn8–9

The Time Stream (Taine), xix

Tiptree, James, Jr., 7, 224, 250, 350–51

Tiptree Award, 346

Tor.com, 352, 359

"Training for World Citizenship" in *Different* (Lorraine), 315–19

Tremaine, F. Orlin, 3, 212, 223

trend-setting nature of magazines, 291

Twain, Mark, 191

University of Vienna, 347

Unknown magazine, 191, 365n2

"Untitled" (Kidd), 248

utopian fiction: feminist, 4–5; Gernsback and, xvii; as high-tech future, 2; inspiration from, xxi; in "Into the 28th Century," 106

Vagabond magazine (Indiana University), 164

Vandermeer, Ann, 300

Vanguard Amateur Press Association, xviii, 247

Van Vogt, A. E., 164

Varley, John, 7

Verne, Jules, xix, 8

Vice Versa magazine, xviii, 253

Victory Verses (Wright), 366n5

video game covers, art for, 335

Virginia Kidd Literary Agency, 247

visual art, in science fiction, xxiii. *See also* artists in science fiction

Vombiteur Littéraire, 223

Von Braun, Werner, 348

Wainwright Carter T., 366n4

Walsh, Joan, 354

Warm Worlds and Otherwise (Tiptree), 350

Warner, Susan, 6

Warner Brothers Studios, 164

Watson, James, 348

Weaver, Harriet Shaw, 291

"We Have Always Fought" (Hurley), 359

Weinbaum, Batya, xix

Weinbaum, Stanley G., 365n10

Weir, Mordred (A. R. Long), xvi, xx–xxi, 3, 212–13

Weird Tales: D. McIlwraith as editor of, 290, 300, 367n7; Drake's poetry in, 249–52; example table of contents (1942), 296; experimental poetry forms in, 239–40; "The Eyrie," 293, 308–13; Long's stories in, 212; "mad scientist" characters in, 5; M. Brundage as artist for, xx, 332; Quick's stories in, 191–92; "A Runaway World" (C. W. Harris), 8; science fiction in, 2; "Shambleau" (Moore), 164–66; Stone's stories in, 26; women as contributors to, xvii–xviii

Wells, H. G., xix, 8, 259, 366n1

Western Producer, 366n5

"Weyr Search" (McCaffrey), 345

"When You Think That . . . Smile!" (Les Tina), 3–4, 231–36

White House Office of Science and Technology Policy, 352

"The White Sawbwa of Möng Nam" (Miller), 337

Whitman, Walt, 237

The Wide, Wide World (Warner), 6

Wilber, Rick, 360

Wilhelm, Kate, 345

Willard, Frances Elizabeth, 239, 242

William Penn Museum (Harrisburg, PA), xvi, 212

Williams, Sheila, 351, 360–61

Williams, William Carlos, 292

Willis, Connie, 356, 359

Wilson, Richard, 223

Wine of Wonder (Lorraine), 237, 240, 256

Withrow, Laura, 294, 301

Wolfe, Gene, 247

Women Destroy Science Fiction! in *Lightspeed* magazine, 359

Women in Science Fiction and Fantasy (Reid), 363n7

Women of Wonder (Sargent), xxi

Wonder Stories, xvii, xix, 9, 26

"The Wood-Wife" (Drake), 251–52

World Science Fiction Convention of 1939, 223

Wright, Farnsworth, xvii, 2, 165, 191, 239, 292–93, 306, 332, 337–39

Wright, Laura Moore, xxii, 263, 265–67, 273, 366n5

Wright, Mary Maude, 106. *See also* Lorraine, Lilith

"yellow peril" stories, 333

Yolen, Jane, 243

Ziff-Davis, Inc., 261–62, 264

THE WESLEYAN EARLY CLASSICS OF SCIENCE FICTION SERIES

GENERAL EDITOR Arthur B. Evans

The Centenarian
    Honoré de Balzac
We Modern People: Science Fiction and the Making of Russian Modernity
    Anindita Banerjee
Cosmos Latinos: An Anthology of Science Fiction from Latin America and Spain
    Andrea L. Bell and Yolanda Molina-Gavilán, eds.
The Coming Race
    Edward Bulwer-Lytton
Imagining Mars: A Literary History
    Robert Crossley
Caesar's Column: A Story of the Twentieth Century
    Ignatius Donnelly
Vintage Visions: Essays on Early Science Fiction
    Arthur B. Evans, ed.
Subterranean Worlds: A Critical Anthology
    Peter Fitting, ed.
Lumen
    Camille Flammarion
The Time Ship: A Chrononautical Journey
    Enrique Gaspar
The Last Man
    Jean-Baptiste Cousin de Grainville

The Emergence of Latin American Science Fiction
    Rachel Haywood Ferreira
The Battle of the Sexes in Science Fiction
    Justine Larbalestier
The Yellow Wave: A Romance of the Asiatic Invasion of Australia
    Kenneth Mackay
The Moon Pool
    A. Merritt
Castaway Tales: From Robinson Crusoe to Life of Pi
    Christopher Palmer
Colonialism and the Emergence of Science Fiction
    John Rieder
The Twentieth Century
    Albert Robida
Three Science Fiction Novellas: From Prehistory to the End of Mankind
    J.-H. Rosny aîné
The Black Mirror and Other Stories: An Anthology of Science Fiction from Germany and Austria
    Franz Rottensteiner, ed., and Mike Mitchell, tr.
The Fire in the Stone: Prehistoric Fiction from Charles Darwin to Jean M. Auel
    Nicholas Ruddick
The World as It Shall Be
    Emile Souvestre
Star Maker
    Olaf Stapledon
The Begum's Millions
    Jules Verne
Five Weeks in a Balloon
    Jules Verne
Invasion of the Sea
    Jules Verne
The Kip Brothers
    Jules Verne

The Mighty Orinoco
  Jules Verne
The Mysterious Island
  Jules Verne
Travel Scholarships
  Jules Verne
H. G. Wells: Traversing Time
  W. Warren Wagar

Star Begotten
  H. G. Wells
Deluge
  Sydney Fowler Wright
Sisters of Tomorrow:
    The First Women of Science Fiction
    Lisa Yaszek and Patrick B. Sharp, eds.

ABOUT THE EDITORS

Lisa Yaszek is professor and associate chair in the School of Literature, Media, and Communication at Georgia Tech. Yaszek has been a recipient of the SFRA Pioneer Award for outstanding scholarship and recently received Georgia Tech's Ivan Allen Legacy Award for leadership in her chosen field of research. Her essays on science fiction as a global language crossing centuries, cultures and continents appear in journals such as *Foundation, NWSA Journal,* and *Rethinking History.* She is the author of *Galactic Suburbia: Recovering Women's Science Fiction* and the editor of the anthology *Practicing Science Fiction: Critical Essays on Writing, Reading and Teaching the Genre.* Her webpage is http://pwp.gatech.edu/lyaszek/.

Patrick Sharp is professor and chair of liberal studies at California State University, Los Angeles. He is the author of *Savage Pearls: Racial Frontiers and Nuclear Apocalypse in American Culture* and the editor of *Darwin in Atlantic Cultures: Evolutionary Visions of Race, Gender, and Sexuality.* He has also published articles on nuclear narratives, gender, and science fiction in journals such as *Twentieth Century Literature* and *Science Fiction Film and Television.*

Kathleen Ann Goonan, a Professor of the Practice at Georgia Institute of Technology, is the author of seven critically acclaimed novels, including her groundbreaking Nanotech Quartet: the *New York Times* Notable Book *Queen City Jazz*, the Darrell Award winner *Mississippi Blues*, and Nebula Award finalists *Crescent City Rhapsody* and *Light Music. In War Times* won the John W. Campbell Award for Best Science Fiction Novel of 2007 and was the American Library Association's Best SF Novel of 2007. Her most recent novel is *This Shared Dream.* She has published over fifty stories in such places as *Discover Magazine, Asimov's,* the *Magazine of Fantasy and Science Fiction*, and numerous Best of Year anthologies, some of which are collected in *Angels and You Dogs.* Her most recent academic work appeared in *SFRA Review* and in *Intelligence Unbound: The Future of Uploaded and Machine Minds*, edited by Russell Blackford and Damien Broderick. Her web site is www.goonan.com.